Dead Water

Black As He's Painted

Artists in Crime

Clutch of Constables
Colour Scheme
Death and the Dancing Footman
Death at the Bar
Death at the Dolphin
Death in Ecstasy
Death in a White Tie
Died in the Wool
Enter a Murderer
False Scent
Final Curtain
Grave Mistake
Hand in Glove
Last Ditch
Light Thickens
A Man Lay Dead
The Nursing Home Murder
Off with his Head
Opening Night
Overture to Death
Photo-Finish
Scales of Justice
Singing in the Shrouds
Spinsters in Jeopardy
Surfeit of Lampreys
Swing, Brother, Swing
Tied up in Tinsel
Vintage Murder
When in Rome

Dead Water

Black As He's Painted

Artists in Crime

Ngaio Marsh

Diamond Books
An Imprint of HarperCollins*Publishers*,
77–85 Fulham Palace Road
Hammersmith, London W6 8JB

This Diamond Books Omnibus edition first published 1994

Dead Water © Ngaio Marsh Limited 1964
Black As He's Painted © Ngaio Marsh Limited 1973, 1974
Artists in Crime © Ngaio Marsh Limited 1938

The Author asserts the moral right to be identified as the author of this work

ISBN 0 261 66270 8

Printed in Great Britain by
BPC Hazells Ltd

Dead Water

for Alister and Doris McIntosh with love

CONTENTS

CAST OF CHARACTERS

WALLY TREHERN of *Fisherman's Bay, Portcarrow Island*
JENNY WILLIAMS. *School-mistress*
MRS. TREHERN. *Wally's mother*
JAMES TREHERN. *Her husband*
DR. MAINE. *Of the Portcarrow Convalescent Home*
THE REV. MR. ADRIAN CARSTAIRS. *Rector of Portcarrow*
MRS. CARSTAIRS. *His wife*
MAJOR KEITH BARRIMORE. *Landlord of The Boy-and-Lobster*
MRS. BARRIMORE. *His wife*
PATRICK FERRIER. *Her son*
MISS ELSPETH COST. *A shopkeeper*
KENNETH JOYCE. *A journalist*
MRS. THORPE. *A patient*
MISS EMILY PRIDE. *Suzerain of the Island*
MR. IVES NANKIVELL. *Mayor of Portcarrow*
SUPERINTENDENT COOMBE. *Portcarrow Constabulary*
SERGEANT PENDER. *Portcarrow Constabulary*
P.C. CAREY. *Portcarrow Constabulary*
P.C. POMEROY. *Portcarrow Constabulary*
SUPERINTENDENT RODERICK ALLEYN. *C.I.D. Scotland Yard*
TROY ALLEYN. *His wife*
DETECTIVE-INSPECTOR FOX. *Scotland Yard*
DETECTIVE-SERGEANT BAILEY. *Scotland Yard*
DETECTIVE-SERGEANT THOMPSON. *Scotland Yard*
SIR JAMES CURTIS. *Home Office Pathologist*
CISSY POLLOCK. *Telephonist*
TRETHAWAY. *A father*

1. *Prelude*

A boy stumbled up the hillside, half-blinded by tears. He fell and, for a time, choked and sobbed as he lay in the sun but presently blundered on. A lark sang overhead. Farther up the hill he could hear the multiple chatter of running water. The children down by the jetty still chanted after him :

> *Warty-hog, warty-hog*
> *Put your puddies in the bog*
> *Warty Walter, Warty Walter*
> *Wash your warties in the water.*

The spring was near the top. It began as a bubbling pool, cascaded into a miniature waterfall, dived under pebbles, earth and bracken and at last, loquacious and preoccupied, swirled mysteriously underground and was lost. Above the pool stood a boulder, flanked by briars and fern, and above that the brow of the hill and the sun in a clear sky.

He squatted near the waterfall. His legs ached and a spasm jolted his chest. He gasped for breath, beat his hands on the ground and looked at them. Warty-hog. Warts clustered all over his fingers like those black things that covered the legs of the jetty. Two of them bled where he'd cut them. The other kids were told not to touch him.

He thrust his hands under the cold pressure of the cascade. It beat and stung and numbed them, but he screwed up his blubbered eyes and forced them to stay there. Water spurted icily up his arms and into his face.

9

" Don't cry."

He opened his eyes directly into the sun or would have done so if she hadn't stood between: tall and greenish, above the big stone and rimmed about with light like something on the telly so that he couldn't see her properly.

" Why are you crying ? "

He ducked his head, and stared like an animal that couldn't make up its mind to bolt. He gave a loud, detached sob and left his hands under the water.

" What's the matter ? Are you hurt ? Tell me."

" Me 'ands."

" Show me."

He shook his head and stared.

" Show me your hands."

" They'm mucky."

" The water will clean them."

" No, t'won't, then."

" Show me."

He withdrew them. Between clusters of warts his skin had puckered and turned the colour of dead fish. He broke into a loud wail. His nose and eyes ran salt into his open mouth.

From down below a voice, small and distant, half-heartedly chanted : " Warty Walter. Warty Walter. Stick your warties in the water." Somebody shouted: " Aw *come* on." They were going away.

He held out his desecrated hands towards her as if in explanation. Her voice floated down on the sound of the waterfall.

" Put them under again. If you believe: they will be clean."

" Uh ? "

" They will be clean. Say it. Say ' Please take away my

10

warts.' Shut your eyes and do as I tell you. Say it again when you go to bed. Remember. Do it."

He did as she told him. The sound of the cascade grew very loud in his ears. Blobs of light swam across his eyeballs. He heard his own voice very far away, and then nothing. Ice-cold water was bumping his face on drowned pebbles.

When he lifted his head up there was no one between him and the sun.

He sat there letting himself dry and thinking of nothing in particular until the sun went down behind the hill. Then, feeling cold, he returned to the waterfront and his home in the bay.

II

For about twenty-four hours after the event, the affair of Wally Trehern's warts made very little impression on the island. His parents were slugabeds: the father under the excuse that he was engaged in night-fishing and the mother without any excuse at all unless it could be found in the gin bottle. They were not a credit to the Island. Wally, who slept in his clothes, got up at his usual time, and went out to the pump for a wash. He did this because somehow or another his new teacher had fixed the idea in his head and he followed it out with the sort of behaviourism that can be established in a domestic animal. He was still little better than half-awake when he saw what had happened.

Nobody knows what goes on in the mind of a child: least of all in a mind like Wally Trehern's where the process of thought was so sluggish as to be no more than a reflex of simple emotions: pleasure, fear or pride.

He seemed to be feeling proud when he shambled up to his teacher and, before all the school, held out his hands.

11

" Why—! " she said. " Why—why—*Wally* ! " She took both his hands in hers and looked and pressed and looked again. " I can't believe it," she said. " It's not true."

" Be'ant mucky," he said. " All gone," and burst out laughing.

The school was on the mainland but the news about Wally Trehern's warts returned with him and his teacher to the Island. The Island was incorrectly named : it was merely a rocky blob of land at the end of an extremely brief, narrow and low-lying causeway which disappeared at full tide and whenever the seas along that coast ran high. The Island was thus no more than an extension of the tiny fishing village of Portcarrow and yet the handful of people who lived on it were accorded a separate identity as if centuries of tidal gestures had given them an indefinable status. In those parts they talked of " islanders " and " villagers " making a distinction where none really existed.

The Portcarrow school-mistress was Miss Jenny Williams, a young New Zealander who was doing post graduate research in England, and had taken this temporary job to enrich her experience and augment her bursary. She lodged on the Island at The Boy-and-Lobster, a small Jacobean pub, and wrote home enthusiastically about its inconveniences. She was a glowing, russet-coloured girl and looked her best that afternoon, striding across the causeway with the wind snapping at her hair and moulding her summer dress into the explicit simplicity of a shift. Behind her ran, stumbled and tacked poor Wally, who gave from time to time a squawking cry not unlike that of a seagull.

When they arrived on the Island she told him she would like to see his mother. They turned right at the jetty, round a point and into Fisherman's Bay. The Treherns lived in the least prepossessing of a group of cottages. Jenny could feel nothing but dismay at its smell and that of Mrs. Trehern who sat on the doorstep and made ambiguous sounds of greeting.

"She'm sozzled," said Wally, and indeed, it was so.

Jenny said : "Wally : would you be very kind and see if you can find me a shell to keep. A pink one." She had to repeat this carefully and was not helped by Mrs. Trehern suddenly roaring out that if he didn't do what his teacher said she'd have the hide off of him.

Wally sank his head between his shoulders, shuffled down to the foreshore and disappeared behind a boat.

"Mrs. Trehern," Jenny said, "I do hope you don't mind me coming : I just felt I must say how terribly glad I am about Wally's warts and—and—I did want to ask about how it's happened. I mean," she went on, growing flurried, "it's so extraordinary. Since yesterday. I mean—well—it's—— *Isn't* it ? "

Mrs. Trehern was smiling broadly. She jerked her head and asked Jenny if she would take a little something.

"No, thank you." She waited for a moment and then said: "Mrs. Trehern, haven't you noticed ? Wally's hands ? Haven't you seen ? "

"Takes fits," said Mrs. Trehern. "Our Wally ! " she added with an air of profundity. After several false starts she rose and turned into the house. "You come on in," she shouted bossily. "Come on."

Jenny was spared this ordeal by the arrival of Mr. Trehern who lumbered up from the foreshore where she fancied he had been sitting behind his boat. He was followed at a distance by Wally.

James Trehern was a dark, fat man with pale eyes, a slack mouth and a manner that was both suspicious and placatory. He hired out himself and his boat to visitors, fished and did odd jobs about the village and the Island.

He leered uncertainly at Jenny and said it was an uncommon brave afternoon and he hoped she was feeling pretty clever herself. Jenny at once embarked on the disappearance of the warts and found that Trehern had just become aware of it. Wally had shown him his hands.

" Isn't it amazing, Mr. Trehern ? "

" Proper flabbergasting," he agreed without enthusiasm.

" When did it happen exactly, do you know ? Was it yesterday, after school ? Or when ? Was it—sudden ? —I mean his hands were in such a state, weren't they ? I've asked him, of course, and he says—he says it's because of a lady. And something about washing his hands in the spring up there. I'm sorry to pester you like this but I felt I just *had* to know."

It was obvious that he thought she was making an unnecessary to-do about the whole affair, but he stared at her with a sort of covert intensity that was extremely disagreeable. A gust of wind snatched at her dress and she tried to pin it between her knees. Trehern's mouth widened. Mrs. Trehern advanced uncertainly from the interior.

Jenny said quickly : " Well, never mind, anyway. It's grand that they've gone, isn't it ? I mustn't keep you. Good evening."

Mrs. Trehern made an ambiguous sound and extended her clenched hand. " See yurr," she said. She opened her hand. A cascade of soft black shells dropped on the step.

" Them's our Wally's," she said. " In 'is bed."

" All gone," said Wally.

He had come up from the foreshore. When Jenny turned to him, he offered her a real shell. It was broken and discoloured but it was pink. Jenny knelt down to take it. " Thank you very much," she said. " That's just what I wanted."

It seemed awful to go away and leave him there. When she looked back he waved to her.

14

That evening in the private tap at The Boy-and-Lobster Wally Trehern's warts were the principal topic of conversation. It was a fine evening and low-tide fell at eight o'clock. In addition to the regular Islanders, there were patrons who had strolled across the causeway from the village : Dr. Maine of the Portcarrow Convalescent Home ; the rector, the Rev. Mr. Adrian Carstairs, who liked to show, as was no more than the case, that he was human ; and a visitor to the village, a large pale young man with a restless manner and a general air of being on the look-out for something. He was having a drink with Patrick Ferrier, the stepson of the landlord, down from Oxford for the long vacation. Patrick was an engaging fellow with a sensitive mouth, pleasant manners and a quick eye which dwelt pretty often upon Jenny Williams. There was only one other woman in the private beside Jenny. This was Miss Elspeth Cost, a lady with vague hair and a tentative smile who, like Jenny, was staying at The Boy-and-Lobster and was understood to have a shop somewhere and to be interested in handicrafts and the drama.

The landlord, Major Keith Barrimore, stationed between two bars, served both the public and the private taps : the former being used exclusively by local fishermen. Major Barrimore was well-set-up and of florid complexion. He shouted rather than spoke, had any amount of professional bonhomie and harmonised perfectly with his background of horse-brasses, bottles, glasses, tankards and sporting prints. He wore a check coat, a yellow waistcoat and a signet ring and kept his hair very smooth.

" Look at it whichever way you choose," Miss Cost said, " it's astounding. Poor little fellow ! To think ! "

" Very dramatic," said Patrick Ferrier, smiling at Jenny.

" Well it was," she said. " Just that."

" One hears of these cases," said the restless young man, " Gipsies and charms and so on."

" Yes, I know one does," Jenny said. " One *hears* of them but I've never met one before. And who, for heaven's sake, was the green lady ? "

There was a brief silence.

" Ah," said Miss Cost. " Now that *is* the really rather wonderful part. The green lady ! " She tipped her head to one side and looked at the rector. " M-m—? " she invited.

" Poor Wally ! " Mr. Carstairs rejoined. " All a fairytale, I daresay. It's a sad case."

" The cure isn't a fairytale," Jenny pointed out.

" No, no, no. Surely not. Surely not," he said in a hurry.

" A *fairy*tale. I wonder. Still pixies in these yurr parts, Rector, d'y'm reckon ? " asked Miss Cost essaying a roughish burr.

Everyone looked extremely uncomfortable.

" All in the poor kid's imagination, I should have thought," said Major Barrimore and poured himself a double Scotch. " Still : damn' good show, anyway."

" What's the medical opinion ? " Patrick asked.

" Don't ask me ! " Dr. Maine ejaculated, throwing up his beautifully kept hands. " There is no medical opinion as far as I know." But seeing perhaps that they all expected more than this from him, he went on half-impatiently. " You do, of course, hear of these cases. They're quite well-established. I've heard of an eminent skin-specialist who actually mugged up an incantation or spell or what have-you and used it on his patients with marked success."

" There ! You see ! " Miss Cost cried out, gently clapping her hands. She became mysterious. " You wait ! " she said. " You jolly well wait ! "

Dr. Maine glanced at her distastefully.

"The cause of warts is not known," he said. "Probably viral. The boy's an epileptic," he added. "*Petit mal.*"

"Would that predispose him to this sort of cure?" Patrick asked.

"Might," Dr. Maine said shortly. "Might predispose him to the right kind of suggestibility." Without looking at the rector, he added: "There's one feature that sticks out all through the literature of reputed cures by some allegedly supernatural agency. The authentic cases have emotional or nervous connotations."

"Not all, surely," the Rector suggested.

Dr. Maine shot a glance at him. "I shouldn't talk," he said. "I really know nothing about such matters. The other half, if you please."

Jenny thought: "The Rector feels he ought to nip in and speak up for miracles and he doesn't like to because he doesn't want to be parsonic. How tricky it is for them! Dr. Maine's the same, in his way. He doesn't like talking shop for fear of showing off. English reticence," thought Jenny, resolving to make the point in her next letter home. "Incorrigible amateurs."

The restless young man suddenly said: "The next round's on me," and astonished everybody.

"Handsome offer!" said Major Barrimore. "Thank you, sir."

"Tell me," said the young man expansively and at large. "Where is this spring or pool or whatever it is?"

Patrick explained. "Up the hill above the jetty."

"And the kid's story is that some lady in green told him to wash his hands in it? And the warts fell off in the night. Is that it?"

"As far as I could make out," Jenny agreed. "He's not at all eloquent, poor Wally."

"Wally Trehern, did you say? Local boy?"

17

" That's right."

" Were they bad ? The warts ? "

" Frightful."

" Mightn't have been just kind of ripe to fall off ? Co-incidence ? "

" Most unlikely, I'd have thought," said Jenny.

" I see," said the young man, weighing it up. " Well, what's everybody having ? Same again, all round ? "

Everybody murmured assent and Major Barrimore began to pour the drinks.

Jenny said : " I could show you a photograph."

" No ? Could you, though ? I'd very much like to see it. I'd be very interested, indeed. Would you ? "

She ran up to her room to get it : a colour-slide of the infant-class with Wally in the foreground, his hands dangling. She put it in the viewer and returned to the bar. The young man looked at it intently, whistling to himself. " Quite a thing," he said. " Quite something. Nice sharp picture, too."

Everybody wanted to look at it. While they were handing it about, the door from the house opened and Mrs. Barrimore came in.

She was a beautiful woman, very fine-drawn with an exquisite head of which the bone-structure was so delicate and the eyes so quiet in expression that the mouth seemed like a vivid accident. It was as if an artist, having started out to paint an ascetic, had changed his mind and laid down the lips of a voluptuary.

With a sort of awkward grace that suggested shyness, she moved into the bar, smiling tentatively at nobody in particular. Dr. Maine looked quickly at her and stood up. The Rector gave her good-evening and the restless young man offered her a drink. Her husband, without consulting her, poured a glass of lager.

18

"Hallo, Mum. We've all been talking about Wally's warts," Patrick said.

Mrs. Barrimore sat down by Miss Cost. "Have you ?" she said. "Isn't it strange ? I can't get over it." Her voice was charming : light and very clear. She had the faintest hesitation in her speech and a trick of winding her fingers together. Her son brought her drink to her and she thanked the restless young man rather awkwardly for it. Jenny, who liked her very much, wondered, not for the first time, if her position at The Boy-and-Lobster was distasteful to her and exactly why she seemed so alien to it.

Her entrance brought a little silence in its wake. Dr. Maine turned his glass round and round and stared at the contents. Presently Miss Cost broke out in fresh spate of enthusiasm.

". . . Now, you may all laugh as loud as you please," she cried with a reckless air. " *I* shan't mind. I daresay there's some clever answer explaining it all away or you can, if you choose, call it coincidence. But I don't care. I'm going to say my little say." She held up her glass of port in a dashing manner and gained their reluctant attention. " I'm an asthmatic ! " she declared vaingloriously. " Since I came here, I've had my usual go, regular as clockwork, every evening at half past eight. I daresay some of you have heard me sneezing and wheezing away in my corner. Very well. Now ! This evening, when I'd heard about Wally, I walked up to the spring and while I sat there, it came into my mind. Quite suddenly. ' *I wonder*.' And I dipped my fingers in the waterfall——" She shut her eyes, raised her brows and smiled. The port slopped over on her hand. She replaced the glass. " I wished my wee wish," she continued. " And I sat up there, feeling ever so light and unburdened, and then I came down." She pointed dramatically to the bar clock. " Look at the time ! " she exulted. " Five past ten ! " She

19

slapped her chest. "Clear as a bell! And I *know*, I just *know* it's happened. To ME."

There was a dead silence during which, Jenny thought, everyone listened nervously for asthmatic manifestations from Miss Cost's chest. There were none.

"Miss Cost," said Patrick Ferrier at last. "How perfectly splendid!" There were general ambiguous murmurs of congratulation. Major Barrimore, looking as if he would like to exchange a wink with somebody, added: "Long may it last!" They were all rather taken aback by the fervency with which she ejaculated. "Amen! Yes, indeed. Amen!" The Rector looked extremely uncomfortable. Dr. Maine asked Miss Cost if she'd seen any green ladies while she was about it.

"N-n-o!" she said and darted a very unfriendly glance at him.

"You sound as if you're not sure of that, Miss Cost."

"My eyes were closed," she said quickly.

"I see," said Dr. Maine.

The restless young man who had been biting at his nails said loudly: "Look!" and having engaged their general attention, declared himself. "Look!" he repeated, "I'd better come clean and explain at once that I take a—well, a professional interest in all this. On holiday: but a news-hound's job's never done, is it? It seems to me there's quite a story here. I'm sure my paper would want our readers to hear about it. *London Sun* and I'm Kenneth Joyce. 'K.J.'s Column.' You know? 'What's The Answer?' Now, what do you all say? Just a news item. Nothing spectacular."

"O, *no*!" Mrs. Barrimore ejaculated and then added: "I'm sorry. It's simply that I really do so dislike that sort of thing."

"Couldn't agree more," said Dr. Maine. For a second they looked at each other.

" I really think," the Rector said, " *not*. I'm afraid I dislike it too, Mr. Joyce."

" So do I," Jenny said.

" *Do* you ? " asked Mr. Joyce. " I'm sorry about that. I was going to ask if you'd lend me this picture. It'd blow up quite nicely. My paper would pay——"

" No," said Jenny.

" Golly, how fierce ! " said Mr. Joyce, pretending to shrink. He looked about him. " Now *why* not ? " he asked.

Major Barrimore said : " I don't know why not. I can't say I see anything wrong with it. The thing's happened, hasn't it, and it's damned interesting. Why shouldn't people hear about it ? "

" O, I *do* agree," cried Miss Cost. " I'm sorry but I *do* so agree with the Major. When the papers are full of such dreadful things *shouldn't* we welcome a lovely, lovely true story like Wally's. O, yes ! "

Patrick said to Mr. Joyce : " Well, at least you declared yourself," and grinned at him.

" He wanted Jenny's photograph," said Mrs. Barrimore quietly. " So he had to."

They looked at her with astonishment. " Well, honestly Mama ! " Patrick ejaculated. " What a very crisp remark ! "

" An extremely cogent remark," said Dr. Maine.

" I don't think so," Major Barrimore said loudly and Jenny was aware of an antagonism that had nothing to do with the matter under discussion.

" But, of course I had to," Mr. Joyce conceded with a wide gesture and an air of candour. " You're dead right. I *did* want the photograph. All the same, it's a matter of professional etiquette, you know. My paper doesn't believe in pulling fast ones. That's not *The Sun's* policy, at all. In proof of which I shall retire gracefully upon a divided house."

21

He carried his drink over to Miss Cost and sat beside her. Mrs. Barrimore got up and moved away. Dr. Maine took her empty glass and put it on the bar.

There was an uncomfortable silence, induced perhaps by the general recollection that they had all drunk at Mr. Joyce's expense and a suspicion that his hospitality had not been offered entirely without motive.

Mrs. Barrimore said : " Good night, everybody," and went out.

Patrick moved over to Jenny. " I'm going fishing in the morning if it's fine," he said. " Seeing it's a Saturday, would it amuse you to come ? It's a small, filthy boat and I don't expect to catch anything."

" What time ? "

" Dawn. Or soon after. Say half past four."

" Crikey ! Well, yes, I'd love to if I can wake myself up."

" I'll scratch on your door like one of the Sun King's courtiers. Which door is it ? Frightening, if I scratched on Miss Cost's ! "

Jenny told him. " Look at Miss Cost now," she said. " She's having a whale of a time with Mr. Joyce."

" He's getting a story from her."

" O, no ! "

" O, yes ! And to-morrow, betimes, he'll be hunting up Wally and his unspeakable parents. With a camera."

" He won't ! "

" Of course he will. If they're sober they'll be enchanted. Watch out for K.J.'s ' What's The Answer ' column in *The Sun*."

" I do think the gutter-press in this country's the rock bottom."

" Don't you have a gutter-press in New Zealand ? "

" Not as low."

" Well done, you. All the same, I don't see why K.J.'s

22

idea strikes you as being so very low. No sex. No drugs. No crime. It's as clean as a whistle, like Wally's hands." He was looking rather intently into Jenny's face. " Sorry," he said. " You didn't like that, either, did you ? "

" It's just—I don't know, or yes, I think I do. Wally's so vulnerable. I mean, he's been jeered at and cowed by the other children. He's been puzzled and lonely and now he's a comparatively happy little creature. Quite a hero, in a way. He's not attractive : his sort aren't, as a rule, but I've got an affection for him. Whatever's happened ought to be private to him."

" But he won't take it in, will he ? All the ballyhoo, if there *is* any ballyhoo ? He may even vaguely enjoy it."

" I don't want him to. All right," Jenny said crossly, " I'm being bloody-minded. Forget it. P'raps it won't happen."

" I think you may depend upon it," Patrick rejoined. " It will."

And, in the event, he turned out to be right.

IV

WHAT'S THE ANSWER?

Do You Believe in Fairies ?
Wally Trehern does. Small boy of Portcarrow Island had crop of warts that made life a misery.
Other Kids Shunned Him Because of his Disfigurement. So Wally washed his hands in the Pixie Falls and—you've guessed it.
This is what they looked like before.

And here they are now.

23

Wally, seen above with parents, by Pixie Falls, says
mysterious green lady " told me to wash them off."
Parents say no other treatment given.
Miss Elspeth Cost (inset) cured of chronic asthma?
Local doctor declines comment.
(Full story on Page 9.)

Dr. Maine read the full story, gave an ambiguous ejaculation and started on his morning round.

The Convalescent Home was a very small one : six single rooms for patients, and living quarters for two nurses and for Dr. Maine who was a widower. A veranda at the back of the house looked across a large garden and an adjacent field towards the sea and the Island.

At present he had four patients, all convalescent. One of them, an elderly lady, was already up and taking the air on the veranda. He noticed that she, like the others, had been reading *The Sun*.

" Well, Mrs. Thorpe," he said, bending over her, " this is a step forward, isn't it ? If you go on behaving nicely we'll soon have you taking that little drive."

Mrs. Thorpe wanly smiled and nodded. " So unspoiled," she said waving a hand at the prospect. " Not many places left like it. No horrid trippers."

He sat down beside her, laid his fingers on her pulse and looked at his watch. " This is becoming pure routine," he said cheerfully.

It was obvious that Mrs. Thorpe had a great deal more to say. She scarcely waited for him to snap his watch shut before she began.

" Dr. Maine, *have* you see *The Sun* ? "

" Very clearly. We're in for a lovely day."

She made a little dab at him. " Don't be provoking ! You know what I mean. The paper. *Our* news ! The *Island* ! "

24

" Oh that. Yes, I saw that."

" Now, *what* do you think ? Candidly. Do tell me."

He answered her as he had answered Patrick Ferrier.
One heard of such cases. Medically there could be no
comment.

" But you don't pooh-pooh ? "

No, no. He didn't altogether do that. And now he really
must——

As he moved away she said thoughtfully, " My little
nephew is dreadfully afflicted. They *are* such an eyesore,
aren't they ? And infectious, it's thought. One can't help
wondering——"

His other patients were full of the news. One of them had
a first cousin who suffered abominably from chronic asthma.

Miss Cost read it over and over again : especially the bit
on page nine where it said what a martyr she'd been and how
she had perfect faith in the waters. She didn't remember
calling them the Pixie Falls but now she came to think of it,
the name was pretty. She wished she'd had time to do her
hair before Mr. Joyce's friend had taken the snapshot and
it would have been nicer if her mouth had been quite shut.
But still. At low tide she strolled over to the newsagent's
shop in the village. All their copies of *The Sun*, unfortunately, had been sold. There had been quite a demand. Miss
Cost looked with a professional and disparaging eye at the
shop. Nothing really at all in the way of souvenirs and
the postcards were very limited. She bought three of the
Island and covered the available space with fine writing.
Her friend with arthritic hands would be interested.

Major Barrimore finished his coffee and replaced the cup
with a slightly unsteady hand. His immaculately shaven
jaws wore their morning purple tinge and his eyes were dull.

" Hasn't been long about it," he said, referring to his

25

copy of *The Sun*. "Don't waste much time, these paper wallahs. Only happened day-before-yesterday."

He looked at his wife. " Well. Haven't you read it ? " he asked.

" I looked at it."

" I don't know what's got into you. Why've you got your knife into this reporter chap ? Decent enough fellah of his type."

" Yes, I expect he is."

" It'll create a lot of interest. Enormous circulation. Bring people in, I wouldn't wonder. Quite a bit about The Boy-and-Lobster." She didn't answer and he suddenly shouted at her. " Damn it, Margaret, you're about as cheerful as a dead fish. You'd think there'd been a death on the Island instead of a cure. God knows we could do with some extra custom."

" I'm sorry, Keith. I know."

He turned his paper to the racing page. " Where's that son of yours ? " he said presently.

" He and Jenny Williams were going to row round as usual to South Bay."

" Getting very thick, aren't they ? "

" Not alarmingly so. She's a dear girl."

" If you can stomach the accent."

" Hers is not so very strong do you think ? "

" P'raps not. She's a fine strapping filly, I will say. Damn' good legs. Oughtn't he to be swotting ? "

" He's working quite hard, really."

" Of course *you'd* say so." He lit a cigarette and returned to the racing notes. The telephone rang.

" I will," said Mrs. Barrimore.

She picked up the receiver. " Boy-and-Lobster. Yes. Yes." There was a loud crackle and she said to her husband, " It's from London."

26

"If it's Mrs. Winterbottom," said her husband, referring to his suzerain. "I'm out."

After a moment or two the call came through. "Yes," she said. "Certainly. Yes, we can. A single room? May I have your name?"

There were two other long-distance calls during the day. By the end of the week the five rooms at The Boy-and-Lobster were all engaged.

A correspondence had got underway in *The Sun* on the subject of faith-healing and unexplained cures. On Friday there were inquiries from a regular television programme.

The school holidays had started and Jenny Williams had come to the end of her job at Portcarrow.

While the Barrimores were engaged in their breakfast discussion, the Rector and Mrs. Carstairs were occupied with the same topic. The tone of their conversation was, however, dissimilar.

"There!" Mr. Carstairs said, smacking *The Sun* as it lay by his plate. "There! Wretched creature! He's gone and done it!"

"'T, yes, so he has. I saw. Now for the butcher," said Mrs. Carstairs who was worrying through the monthly bills.

"No, Dulcie, but it's too much. I'm furious," said the Rector uncertainly. "I'm livid."

"Are you? Why? Because of the vulgarity or what? And *what*," Mrs. Carstairs continued, "does Nankivell mean by saying '2 lbs bst fil.' when we never order fillet let alone best? Stewing steak at the utmost. He must be mad."

"It's not only the vulgarity, Dulcie. It's the effect on the village."

"What effect? And threepence ha'penny is twelve, two, four. It doesn't even begin to make sense."

"It's not that I don't rejoice for the boy. I do. I rejoice like anything and remember it in my prayers."

"Of course you do," said his wife.

"That's my whole point. One should be grateful and not jump to conclusions."

"I shall speak to Nankivell. What conclusions?"

"Some ass," said the Rector, "has put it into the Treherns' heads that—O dear!—that there's been a—a——"

"Miracle?"

"Don't! One shouldn't. It's not a word to be bandied about. And they are bandying it about, those two."

"So much for Nankivell and his rawhide," she said, turning to the next bill. "No, dear, I'm sure it's not. All the same it *is* rather wonderful."

"So are all recoveries. Witnesses to God's mercy, my love."

"Were the Treherns drunk?"

"Yes," he said shortly. "As owls. The Romans know how to deal with these things. Much more talk and we'll be in need of a devil's advocate."

"Don't fuss," said Mrs. Carstairs, "I expect it'll all simmer down."

"I hae me doots," her husband darkly rejoined. "Yes, Dulcie. I hae me doots."

"How big is the Island?" Jenny asked, turning on her face to brown her back.

"Teeny. Not more than fourteen acres, I should think."

"Who does it belong to?"

"To an elderly lady called Mrs. Fanny Winterbottom who is the widow of a hairpin king. He changed over to

28

bobby-pins at the right moment and became a millionaire. The Island might be called his Folly."

" Pub and all ? "

" Pub and all. My mother," Patrick said, " has shares in the pub. She took it on when my stepfather was axed out of the Army."

" It's Heaven : the Island. Not too pretty. This bay might almost be at home. I'll be sorry to go."

" Do you get homesick, Jenny ? "

" A bit. Sometimes. I miss the mountains and the way people think. All the same, it's fun trying to get tuned-in. At first, I was all prickles and antipodean prejudice, belly-aching away about living-conditions like the Treherns' cottage and hidebound attitudes and so on. But now—" she squinted up at Patrick. " It's funny," she said, " but I resent that rotten thing in the paper much more than you do and it's not only because of Wally. It's a kind of insult to the Island."

" It made me quite cross too, you know."

" English understatement. Typical example of."

He gave her a light smack on the seat.

" When I think," Jenny continued, working herself into a rage, " of how that brute winkled the school group out of the Treherns and when I think how he had the damned impertinence to put a ring round *me*——"

" ' Red-headed Jennifer Williams says warts were frightful '," Patrick quoted.

" How he dared ! "

" It's not red, actually. In the sun it's copper. No, gold almost."

" Never you mind what it is. O Patrick——"

" Don't say ' Ow Pettruck '."

" Shut up."

" Well, you asked me to stop you. And it is my name."

29

" All right.   Ae-oh, Pe-ah-trick, then."

" What ? "

" Do you suppose it might lead to a ghastly invasion ?
People smothered in warts and whistling with asthma bearing down from all points of the compass ? "

" Charabancs."

" A Giffte Shoppe."

" Wire-netting round the spring."

" And a bob to get in."

" It's a daunting picture," Patrick said. He picked up a
stone and hurled it into the English Channel. " I suppose,"
he muttered, " it would be profitable."

" No doubt." Jenny turned to look at him and sat up.
" Oh, no doubt," she repeated. " If that's a consideration."

" My dear, virtuous Jenny, of course it's a consideration.
I don't know whether, in your idyllic antipodes, you've
come across the problem of constant hardupness. If you
haven't I can assure you it's not much cop."

" Well, but I have. And, Patrick, I'm sorry. I didn't
know."

" I'll forgive you. I'll go further and tell you that unless
things look up a bit at The Boy-and-Lobster or, alternatively,
unless my stepfather can be moved to close his account with
his bookmaker and keep his hands off the whisky bottle
you'll be outstaying us on the Island."

" Patrick ! "

" I'm afraid so. And the gentlemen of the Inns of Court
will be able to offer their dinners to some more worthy candidate. I shan't eat them. I shall come down from Oxford
and sell plastic combs from door to door. Will you buy one
for your red-gold hair ? " Patrick began to throw stones as
fast as he could pick them up. " It's not only that," he said
presently. " It's my Mama. She's in a pretty dim situation,
anyway, but here, at least, she's——" He stood up. " Well,

Jenny," he said. " There's a sample of the English reticence that strikes you as being so comical." He walked down to the boat and hauled it an unnecessary inch or two up the beach.

Jenny felt helpless. She watched him and thought that he made a pleasing figure against the sea as he tugged back in the classic posture of controlled energy.

" What am I to say to him ? " she wondered. " And does it matter what I say ? "

He took their luncheon basket out of the boat and returned to her.

" Sorry about all that," he said. " Shall we bathe before the tide changes and then eat ? Come on."

She followed him down to the sea and lost her sensation of inadequacy as she battled against the incoming tide. They swam, together and apart, until they were tired and then returned to the beach and had their luncheon. Patrick was well-mannered and attentive and asked her a great many questions about New Zealand and the job she hoped to get, teaching English in Paris. It was not until they had decided to row back to their own side of the Island and he had shipped his oars, that he returned to the subject that waited, Jenny felt sure, at the back of both their minds.

" There's the brow of the hill," he said. " Just above our beach. And below it on the far side, is the spring. Did you notice that Miss Cost, in her interview, talked about the Pixie Falls ? "

" I did. With nausea."

He rowed round the point into Fisherman's Bay.

" Sentiment and expediency," he said, " are uneasy bedfellows. But, of course, it doesn't arise. It's quite safe to strike an attitude and say you'd rather sell plastic combs than see the prostitution of the place you love. There won't be any upsurge of an affluent society on Portcarrow Island. It will stay like this—as we both admire it, Jenny. Only we shan't be here to see.   Two years from now and everybody will have forgotten about Wally Trehern's warts."

He could scarcely have been more at fault.   Before two years had passed everybody in Great Britain who could read a newspaper knew all about Wally Trehern's warts and because of them the Island had been transformed.

2. *Miss Emily*

" The trouble with my family," said Miss Emily Pride, speaking in exquisite French and transferring her gaze from Alleyn to some distant object, " is that they go too far."

Her voice was pitched on the high didactic note she liked to employ for sustained narrative. The sound of it carried Alleyn back through time on a wave of nostalgia. Here he had sat, in this very room that was so much less changed than he or Miss Emily. Here, a candidate for the Diplomatic Service, he had pounded away at French irregular verbs and listened to entrancing scandals of the days when Miss Emily's papa had been chaplain at our embassy in Paris. How old could she be now ? Eighty ? He pulled himself together and gave her his full attention.

" My sister, Fanny Winterbottom," Miss Emily announced, " was not free from this fault. I recall an informal entertainment at our Embassy in which she was invited to take part. It was a burlesque. Fanny was grotesquely attired and carried a vegetable bouquet. She was not without talent of a farouche sort and made something of a hit. *Verb. sap.:* as you shall hear. Inflamed by success she improvised a short equivocal speech at the end of which she flung her bouquet at H.E. It struck him in the diaphragm and might well have led to an incident."

Miss Emily recalled her distant gaze and focused it upon Alleyn. " We are none of us free from this wild strain," she said, " but in my sister Fanny its manifestations were extreme. I cannot help but think there is a connection."

" Miss Emily, I don't quite see what you mean."

" Then you are duller than your early promise led me to expect. Let me elaborate." This had always been an ominous threat with Miss Emily. She resumed her narrative style.

" My sister Fanny," she said, " married. A Mr. George Winterbottom who was profitably engaged in Trade. So much for him. He died, leaving her a childless widow with a more than respectable fortune. Included in her inheritance was the soi-disant island which I mentioned in my letter."

" Portcarrow ? "

" Precisely. You cannot be unaware of recent events on this otherwise characterless promontory."

" No, indeed."

" In that case I shall *not* elaborate. Suffice it to remind you that within the last two years there has arisen, fructified and flourished, a cult of which I entirely disapprove and which is the cause of my present concern and of my calling upon your advice."

She paused. " Anything I can do, of course——" Alleyn said.

" Thank you. Your accent has deteriorated. To continue. Fanny, intemperate as ever, encouraged her tenants in their wart-claims. She visited the Island, interviewed the child in question, and, having at the time an infected outbreak on her thumb, plunged it in the spring whose extreme coldness possibly caused it to burst. It was no doubt ripe to do so but Fanny darted about talking of miracles. There were other cases of an equally hysterical character. The thing had caught on and my sister exploited it. The inn was enlarged, the spring was enclosed, advertisements appeared in the papers. A shop was erected on the island. The residents, I understand, are making money hand-over-fist."

34

"I should imagine so."

"Very well. My sister Fanny (at the age of 87), has died. I have inherited her estates. I need hardly tell you that I refuse to countenance this unseemly charade, still less to profit by it."

"You propose to sell the place?"

"Certainly not. Do," said Miss Emily sharply, "pull yourself together, Roderique. This is not what I expect of you."

"I beg your pardon, Miss Emily."

She waved her hand. "To sell would be to profit by its spurious fame and allow this nonsense full play. No, I intend to restore the Island to its former state. I have instructed my solicitors to acquaint the persons concerned."

"I see," said Alleyn. He got up and stood looking down at his old tutoress. How completely Miss Emily had taken on the character of a certain type of elderly Frenchwoman. Her black clothes seemed to disclaim, clear-sightedly, all pretence to allure. Her complexion was grey: her jewellery of jet and gold. She wore a general air of disassociated fustiness. Her composure was absolute. The setting was perfectly consonant with the person: pieces of buhl; formal, upholstered, and therefore dingy, chairs; yellowing photographs, among which his own young, thin face stared back at him, and an unalterable arrangement of dyed pampas plumes in an elaborate vase. For Miss Emily, her room was absolutely *comme-il-faut*. Yes, after all, she must be——

"At the age of eighty-three," she said, with uncanny prescience, "I am not to be moved. If that is in your mind, Roderique."

"I'm much too frightened of you, Miss Emily, to attempt any such task."

35

"Ah, no ! " she said in English. " Don't say that ! I hope not."

He kissed her dry little hand as she had taught him to do. " Well," he said, " tell me more about it. What *is* your plan ? "

Miss Emily reverted to the French language. " In effect, as I have told you, to restore the *status quo*. Ultimately I shall remove the enclosure, shut the shop and issue a general announcement disclaiming and exposing the entire affair."

Alleyn said : " I've never been able to make up my mind about these matters. The cure of warts by apparently irrational means is too well-established to be questioned. And even when you admit the vast number of failures, there *is* a pretty substantial case to be made out for certain types of faith-healing. Or so I understand. I can't help wondering why you are so very fierce about it all, Miss Emily. If you are repelled by the inevitable vulgarities, of course——"

" As, of course, I am. Still more, by the exploitation of the spring as a business concern. But most of all by personal experience of a case that failed : a very dear friend who suffered from a malignancy and who was absolutely—but I assure you, *absolutely*—persuaded it would be cured by such means. The utter cruelty of her disillusionment, her incredulity, her agonised disappointment and her death : these made a bitter impression upon me. I would sooner die myself," Miss Emily said with the utmost vigour, " than profit in the smallest degree from such another tragedy."

There was a brief silence. " Yes," Alleyn said. " That does, indeed, explain your attitude."

" But not my reason for soliciting your help. I must tell you that I have written to Major Barrimore who is the incumbent of the inn, and informed him of my decision. I

36

have announced my intention of visiting the Island to see that this decision is carried out. And, since she will no doubt wish to provide for herself, I have also written to the proprietress of the shop, a Miss Elspeth Cost. I have given her three months' notice, unless she chooses to maintain the place as a normal establishment and refrain from exploiting the spring or mounting a preposterous anniversary festival which, I am informed, she has put in hand and which has been widely advertised in the Press."

" Major Barrimore and Miss Cost must have been startled by your letters."

" So much so, perhaps, that they have lost the power of communication. I wrote a week ago. There has been no *formal* acknowledgment."

She said this with such a meaning air that he felt he was expected to take it up. " Has there been an informal one ? " he ventured.

" Judge for yourself," said Miss Emily, crisply.

She went to her desk, and returned with several sheets of paper which she handed to him.

Alleyn glanced at the first, paused, and then laid them all in a row on an occasional table. There were five. " Hell ! " he thought, " this means a go with Miss Emily." They were in the familiar form of newsprint pasted on ruled paper which had been wrenched from an exercise book. The first presented an account of several cures effected by the springs and was headed with unintentional ambiguity, " Pixie Falls Again." It was, he recognised, from the London *Sun*. Underneath the cutting was an irregularly assembled sentence of separated words, all in newsprint.

" Do not Attempt THREAT to close you are WARNED." The second read, simply : " DANGER keep OUT," the third, " Desecration will be prevented all costs," the fourth : " Residents are prepared interference will prove FATAL,"

and the last, in one strip, " DEATH OF ELDERLY WOMAN "
with a piecemeal addendum " this could be you."

" Well," Alleyn said, " that's a pretty collection, I must
say. When did they come ? "

" One by one, over the last five days. The first must have
been posted immediately after the arrival of my letter."

" Have you kept the envelopes ? "

" Yes. The postmark is Portcarrow."

" May I see them ? "

She produced them : five cheap envelopes. The address
had been built up from newsprint.

" Will you let me keep these ? And the letters ? "

" Certainly."

" Any idea who sent them ? " he asked.

" None."

" Who has your address ? "

" The landlord. Major Barrimore."

" It's an easy one to assemble from any paper. Thirty-
seven Forecast Street. Wait a moment though. This one
wasn't built up piece-meal. It's all in one. I don't recognise
the type."

" Possibly a local paper. At the time of my inheritance."

" Yes. Almost certainly."

He asked her for a larger envelope and put the collection
into it.

" When do you plan to go to Portcarrow ? "

" On Monday," said Miss Emily composedly. " Without
fail."

Alleyn thought for a moment and then sat down and took
her hand in his. " Now, my dear Miss Emily," he said.
" Please do listen to what I'm going to say—in English, if
you don't mind."

" Naturally, I shall listen carefully since I have invited
your professional opinion. As to speaking in English—very

well, if you prefer it. *Enfin, en ce moment, on ne donne pas une leçon de français.*"

" No. One gives, if you'll forgive me, a lesson in sensible behaviour. Now, I don't suggest for a minute that these messages mean, literally, what they seem to threaten. Possibly they are simply intended to put you off and if they fail to do that, you may hear no more about it. On the other hand they do suggest that you have an enemy at Portcarrow. If you go there you will invite unpleasant reactions."

" I am perfectly well aware of that. Obviously. And," said Miss Emily on a rising note, " if this person imagines that I am to be frightened off——"

" Now, wait a bit. There's no real need for you to go, is there ? The whole thing can be done, and done efficiently, by your solicitors. It would be a—a dignified and reasonable way of settling."

" Until I have seen for myself what goes on in the Island I cannot give explicit instructions."

" But you can. You can get a report."

" That," said Miss Emily, " would not be satisfactory." He could have shaken her.

" Have you," he asked, " shown these things to your solicitors."

" I have not."

" I'm sure they would give you the same advice."

" I should not take it."

" Suppose this person means to do exactly what the messages threaten ? Offer violence ? It might well be, you know."

" That is precisely why I have sought your advice. I am aware that I should take steps to protect myself. What are they ? I am not," Miss Emily said, " proficient in the use of small-arms and I understand that, in any case, one requires a permit. No doubt in your position, you could obtain one and might possibly be so very kind as to give me a little instruction."

"I shall not fiddle a small-arms permit for you and nor shall I teach you to be quick on the draw. The suggestion is ridiculous."

"There are, perhaps, other precautions," she conceded, "such as walking down the centre of the road, remaining indoors after dark and making no assignations at unfrequented rendezvous."

Alleyn contemplated his old instructress. Was there or was there not a remote twinkle in that dead-pan eye ?

"I think," he said, "you are making a nonsense of me."

"Who's being ridiculous now ?" asked Miss Emily tartly.

He stood up. "All right," he said. "As a police officer it's my duty to tell you that I think it extremely unwise for you to go to Portcarrow. As a grateful, elderly, ex-pupil, I assure you that I shall be extremely fussed about you if you're obstinate enough to persist in your plan. Dear Miss Emily," said Alleyn, with a change of tone, "do, for the love of Mike, pipe down and stay where you are."

"You would have been successful," she said, "if you had continued in the Corps Diplomatique. I have never comprehended why you elected to change."

"Obviously, I've had no success in this instance."

"No. I shall go. But I am infinitely obliged to you, Roderique."

"I suppose this must be put down to the wild strain in your blood."

"Possibly." Indicating that the audience was concluded, she rose and reverted to French. "You will give my fondest salutations to your wife and son ?"

"Thank you. Troy sent all sorts of messages to you."

"You appear to be a little fatigued. When is your vacation?"

"When I can snatch it. I hope, quite soon," Alleyn said and was at once alarmed by a look of low cunning in Miss Emily. "Please *don't* go," he begged her.

She placed her hand in the correct position to be kissed. "*Au revoir*," she said, "*et mille remerciements*."

"*Mes hommages, madame*," said Alleyn crossly. With the profoundest misgivings he took his leave of Miss Emily.

<h2 style="text-align:center">II</h2>

It was nine o'clock in the evening when the London train reached Dunlowman where one changed for the Portcarrow bus. On alighting, Jenny was confronted by several posters depicting a fanciful Green Lady across whose image was superimposed a large notice advertising "The Festival of the Spring." She had not recovered from this shock when she received a second one in the person of Patrick Ferrier. There he was, looking much the same after nearly two years, edging his way through the crowd, quite a largish one, that moved towards the barrier. "Jenny!" he called. "Hi! I've come to meet you."

"But it's miles and miles!" Jenny cried, delighted to see him.

"A bagatelle. Hold on. Here I come."

He reached her and seized her suitcases. "This *is* fun," he said. "I'm so glad."

Outside the station a number of people had collected under a sign that read "Portcarrow Bus." Jenny watched them as she waited for Patrick to fetch his car. They looked, she thought, a singularly mixed bunch and yet there was something about them—what was it?—that gave them an exclusive air, as if they belonged to some rather outlandish

41

sect. The bus drew up and as these people began to climb in, she saw that among them there was a girl wearing a steel brace on her leg. Further along the queue a man with an emaciated face and terrible eyes quietly waited his turn. There was a plain, heavy youth with a bandaged ear and a woman who laughed repeatedly, it seemed without cause, and drew no response from her companion, an older woman, who kept her hand under the other's forearm and looked ahead. They filed into the bus and although there were no other outward signs of the element that united them, Jenny knew what it was.

Patrick drove up in a two-seater. He put her luggage into a boot that was about a quarter of the size of the bonnet and in a moment they had shot away down the street.

" This is very handsome of you, Patrick," Jenny said. " And what a car ! "

" Isn't she pleasant ? "

" New, I imagine."

" Yes. To celebrate. I'm eating my dinners, after all, Jenny. Do you remember ? "

" Of course. I do congratulate you."

" You may not be so polite when you see how it's been achieved, however. Your wildest fantasies could scarcely match the present reality of the Island."

" I did see the English papers in Paris and your letters were fairly explicit."

" Nevertheless you're in for a shock, I promise you."

" I expect I can take it."

" Actually, I rather wondered if we ought to ask you."

" It was sweet of your mama and I'm delighted to come. Patrick, it's wonderful to be back in England. When I saw the Battersea power-station, I cried. For sheer pleasure."

" You'll probably roar like a bull when you see Portcarrow and not for pleasure, either. You haven't lost your

42

susceptibility for places, I see. By the way," Patrick said after a pause, " you've arrived for a crisis."

" What sort of crisis ? "

" In the person of an old, old angry lady called Miss Emily Pride, who has inherited the Island from her sister (Winterbottom, deceased). She shares your views about exploiting the spring. You ought to get on like houses on fire."

" What's she going to do ? "

" Shut up shop unless the combined efforts of interested parties can steer her off. Everybody's in a frightful taking-on about it. She arrives on Monday, breathing restoration and fury."

" Like a wicked fairy godmother ? "

" Very like. Probably flourishing a black umbrella and emitting sparks. She's flying into a pretty solid wall of opposition. Of course," Patrick said abruptly, " the whole thing has been fantastic. For some reason the initial story caught on. It was the silly season and the papers, as you may remember, played it up. Wally's warts became big news. That led to the first lot of casual visitors. Mrs. Winterbottom's men of business began to make interested noises and the gold-rush, to coin a phrase, set in. Since then it's never looked back."

They had passed through the suburbs of Dunlowman and were driving along a road that ran out towards the coast.

" It was nice getting your occasional letters," Patrick said, presently. " Operative word ' occasional '."

" And yours."

" I'm glad you haven't succumbed to the urge for black satin and menacing jewellery that seems to overtake so many girls who get jobs in France. But there's a change, all the same."

43

"You're not going to suggest I've got a phoney foreign accent?"

"No, indeed. You've got no accent at all."

"And that, no doubt, makes the change. I expect having to speak French has cured it."

"You must converse with Miss Pride. She is, or was, before she succeeded to the Winterbottom riches, a terrifically high-powered coach for chaps entering the Foreign Service. She's got a network of little spokes all round her mouth from making those exacting noises that are required by the language."

"You've seen her, then?"

"Once. She visited with her sister about a year ago and left in a rage."

"I suppose," Jenny said after a pause, "this is really very serious, this crisis?"

"It's hell," he rejoined with surprising violence.

Jenny asked about Wally Trehern and was told that he had become a menace. "He doesn't know where he is but he knows he's the star-turn," Patrick said. "People make little pilgrimages to the cottage which has been tarted up in a sort of Peggotty-style *Kitsch*. Seaweed round the door almost, and a boat in a bottle. Mrs. Trehern keeps herself to herself and the gin bottle but Trehern is a new man. He exudes a kind of honest-tar sanctity and sells Wally to the pilgrims."

"You appal me."

"I thought you'd better know the worst. What's more, there's an Anniversary Festival next Saturday, organised by Miss Cost. A choral procession to the Spring and Wally, dressed up like a wee fisher lad, reciting doggerel if he can remember it, poor little devil."

"Don't!" Jenny exclaimed. "Not true!"

"True, I'm afraid."

44

" But Patrick—about the cures ? The people that come ?
What happens ? "

Patrick waited for a moment. He then said in a voice that
held no overtones of irony : " I suppose, you know, it's
what always happens in these cases. Failure after failure
until one thinks the whole thing is an infamous racket and is
bitterly ashamed of having any part of it. And then, for no
apparent reason, one, perhaps two, perhaps a few more,
people do exactly what the others have done but go away
without their warts or their migraine or their asthma or their
chronic diarrhoea. Their gratitude and sheer exuberance !
You can't think what it's like, Jenny. So then, of course, one
diddles oneself—or is it diddling ?—into imagining these
cases wipe out all the others and all the ballyhoo, and my
fees and this car, and Miss Cost's Giffte Shoppe. She really
has called it that, you know. She sold her former establishment and set up another on the Island. She sells tiny plastic
models of the Green Lady and pamphlets she's written
herself, as well as handwoven jerkins and other novelties
that I haven't the face to enumerate. Are you sorry you
came ? "

" I don't think so. And your mother ? What does she
think ? "

" Who knows ? " Patrick said, simply. " She has a gift
for detachment, my mama."

" And Dr. Maine ? "

" Why he ? " Patrick said sharply, and then : " Sorry :
Why not ? Bob Maine's nursing home is now quite large
and invariably full."

Feeling she had blundered, Jenny said : " And the Rector ? How on earth has he reacted ? "

" With doctrinal *léger de main*. No official recognition on
the one hand. Proper acknowledgments in the right
quarter on the other. Jolly sensible of him, in my view."

Presently they swept up the downs that lie behind the coastline, turned into a steep lane and were, suddenly, on the cliffs above Portcarrow.

The first thing that Jenny noticed was a red neon sign, glaring up through the dusk : " Boy-and-Lobster." The tide was almost full and the sign was shiftingly reflected in dark water. Next, she saw that a string of coloured lights connected the Island with the village and that the village itself must now extend along the foreshore for some distance. Lamps and windows, following the convolutions of bay and headland, suggested a necklace that had been carelessly thrown down on some night-blue material. She supposed that in a way the effect must be called pretty. There was a number of cars parked along the cliffs with people making love in them or merely staring out to sea. A large, prefabricated, multiple garage had been built at the roadside. There was also a café.

" There you have it," Patrick said. " We may as well take the plunge."

They did so literally, down a precipitous and narrow descent. That at least had not changed and nor at first sight had the village itself. There was the old post-office-shop and, farther along, the Portcarrow Arms with a new coat of paint. " This is now referred to as the Old Part," said Patrick. " Elsewhere there's a rash of boarding establishments and a multiple store. Trehern, by the way is Ye Ancient Ferryman. I'll put you down with your suitcase at the jetty, dig him out of the pub and park the car. O.K. ? "

There was nobody about down by the jetty. The high tide slapped quietly against wet pylons and whispered and dragged along the foreshore. The dank smell of it was pleasant and familiar. Jenny looked across the narrow gap to the Island. There was a lamp now, at the landing and a group of men stood by it. Their voices sounded clear and tranquil. She saw that the coloured lights were strung on metal poles mounted in concrete, round whose bases seawater eddied and slopped, only just covering the causeway.

Patrick returned and with him Trehern who was effusive in salutations and wore a peaked cap with " Boy-and-Lobster " on it.

" There's a motor launch," Patrick said, pointing to it. " For the peak hours. But we'll row over, shall we ? " He led the way down the jetty to where a smart dinghy was tied up. She was called, inevitably, *The Pixie*.

" There were lots of people in the bus," said Jenny.

" I expect so," he rejoined, helping her into the dinghy. " For the Festival, you know."

" Ar, the por souls ! " Trehern ejaculated. " May the Heavenly Powers bring them release from their afflictions."

" Cast off," said Patrick.

The gurgle of water and rhythmic clunk of oars in their rowlocks carried Jenny back to the days when she and Patrick used to visit their little bay.

" It's a warm, still night, isn't it ? " she said.

" Isn't it ? " Patrick agreed. He was beside her in the stern. He slipped his arm round her. " Do you know," he said in her ear, " it's extraordinarily pleasant to see you again."

Jenny could smell the Harris tweed of his coat. She glanced at him. He was staring straight ahead. It was very dark but she fancied he was smiling.

She felt that she must ask Trehern about Wally and did so.

" He be pretty clever, Miss, thank you. You'll see a powerful change in our little lad, no doubt, him having been the innocent means of joy and thanksgiving to them as seeked for it."

Jenny could find nothing better to say than :   " Yes, indeed."

"Not that he be puffed-up by his exclusive state, however," Trehern added. "Meek as a mouse but all-glorious within. That's our Wally."

Patrick gave Jenny a violent squeeze.

They pulled into the jetty and went ashore. Trehern begged Jenny to visit her late pupil at the cottage and wished them an unctuous good night.

Jenny looked about her. Within the sphere of light cast by the wharf lamp, appeared a shop-window which had been injected into an existing cottage front. It was crowded with small indistinguishable objects. "Yes," Patrick said. "That's Miss Cost. Don't dwell on it."

It was not until they had climbed the steps, which had been widened and re-graded and came face-to-face with The Boy-and-Lobster that the full extent of the alterations could be seen. The old pub had been smartened but not altered. At either end of it, however, there now projected large two-storied wings which completely dwarfed the original structure. There was a new and important entrance and a "lounge" into which undrawn curtains admitted a view of quite an assemblage of guests, some reading, others playing cards or writing letters. In the background was a ping-pong table and beyond that, a bar.

Patrick said, "There you have it."

They were about to turn away when someone came out of the main entrance and moved uncertainly towards them. He was dressed in a sort of Victorian smock over long trousers and there was a jellybag cap on his head. He had grown much taller. Jenny didn't recognise him at first but as he shambled into a patch of light she saw his face.

"Costume," Patrick said, "by Maison Cost."

"Wally!" she cried. "It's Wally."

He gave her a sly look and knuckled his forehead. "'Evening, 'evening," he said. His voice was still un-

48

broken. He held out his hands. "I'm Wally," he said.
"Look. All gone."

"Wally, do you remember me? Miss Williams? Do
you?"

His mouth widened in a grin. "No," he said.

"Your teacher."

"One lady gave me five bob, she done. One lady done."

"You mustn't ask for tips," Patrick said.

Wally laughed. "I never," he said and looked at Jenny.
"You come and see me. At Wally's place."

"Are you at school, still?"

"At school. I'm in the fustivell." He showed her his
hands again, gave one of his old squawks and suddenly ran
off.

"Never mind," Patrick said. "Come along. Never
mind, Jenny."

He took her in by the old door, now marked Private, and
here everything was familiar. "The visitors don't use this,"
he said. "There's an office and reception desk in the new
building. You're *en famille*, Jenny. We've put you in my
room. I hope you don't mind."

"But what about you?"

"I'm all right. There's an emergency bolt-hole."

"Jenny!" said Mrs. Barrimore, coming into the little
hall. "How lovely!"

She was much more smartly dressed than she used to be
and looked, Jenny thought, very beautiful. They kissed
warmly. "I'm so glad," Mrs. Barrimore said. "I'm so
very glad."

Her hand trembled on Jenny's arm and, inexplicably,
there was a blur of tears in her eyes. Jenny was astounded.

"Patrick will show you where you are and there's supper
in the old dining-room. I—I'm busy at the moment.
There's a sort of meeting. Patrick will explain," she said

hurriedly. " I hope I shan't be long. You can't think how pleased we are, can she, Patrick ? "

" She hasn't an inkling," he said. " I forgot about the emergency meeting, Jenny. It's to discuss strategy and Miss Pride. How's it going, Mama ? "

" I don't know. Not very well. I don't know."

She hesitated, winding her fingers together in the old way. Patrick gave her a kiss. " Don't give it a thought," he said. " What is it they say in Jenny's antipodes ? ' She'll be right ' ? She'll be right, Mama, never you fear."

But when his mother had left them, Jenny thought for a moment he looked very troubled.

III

In the old bar-parlour Major Barrimore with Miss Pride's letter in his hand and his double-Scotch on the chimney-piece, stood on the hearthrug and surveyed his meeting. It consisted of the Rector, Dr. Maine, Miss Cost and Mr. Ives Nankivell, who was the newly-created Mayor of Port-carrow, and also its leading butcher. He was an undersized man with a look of perpetual astonishment.

" No," Major Barrimore was saying, " apart from yourselves I haven't told anyone. Fewer people know about it, the better. Hope you all agree."

"From the tone of her letter," Dr. Maine said, " the whole village'll know by this time next week."

" Wicked ! " Miss Cost cried out in a trembling voice, " that's what she must be. A wicked woman. Or mad," she added, as an afterthought. " Both, I expect."

The men received this uneasily.

" How, may I inquire, Major, did you frame your reply ? " the Mayor asked.

"Took a few days to decide," said Major Barrimore,

50

" and sent a wire. Accommodation reserved will be glad to discuss matter outlined in your letter '."

" Very proper."

" Thing is, as I said when I told you about it : we ought to arrive at some sort of agreement among ourselves. She gives your names, as the people she wants to see. Well, we've all had a week to think it over. What's our line going to be ? Better be consistent, hadn't we ? "

" But can we be consistent ? " the Rector asked. " I think you all know my views. I've never attempted to disguise them. In the pulpit or anywhere else."

" But you don't," said Miss Cost, who alone had heard the Rector from the pulpit, " you *don't* deny the truth of the cures, now *do* you ? "

" No," he said. " I thank God for them but I deplore the—excessive publicity."

" Naow, naow, naow," said the Mayor excitedly. " Didn't we ought to take a wider view ? Didn't we ought to think of the community as a whole ? In my opinion, sir, the remarkable properties of our Spring has brought nothing but good to Portcarrow : nothing but good. And didn't the public at large ought to be made aware of the benefits we offer ? I say it did and it ought which is what it has and should continue to be."

" Jolly good, Mr. Mayor," said Barrimore. " Hear, hear ! "

" Hear ! " said Miss Cost.

" Would she sell ? " Dr. Maine asked suddenly.

" I don't think she would, Bob."

" Ah well, naow," said the Mayor, " Naow ! Suppose— and mind, gentlemen, I speak unofficially. Private—— But, suppose she would. There might be a possibility that the borough itself would be interested. As a spec——" He caught himself up and looked sideways at the Rector. " As

51

a civic duty. Or maybe a select group of right-minded residents——"

Dr. Maine said dryly : " They'd find themselves competing in pretty hot company, I fancy. If the Island came on the open market."

" Which it won't," said Major Barrimore. " If I'm any judge. She's hell-bent on wrecking the whole show."

Mr. Nankivell allowed himself a speculative grin. " Happen she don't know the value, however," he insinuated.

" Perhaps she's concerned with other values," the Rector murmured.

At this point Mrs. Barrimore returned.

" Don't move," she said and sat down in a chair near the door. " I don't know if I'm still——? "

Mr. Nankivell embarked on a gallantry but Barrimore cut across it. " You'd better listen, Margaret," he said, with a restless glance at his wife. " After all, she may talk to you."

" Surely, surely ! " the Mayor exclaimed. " The ladies understand each other in a fashion that's above the heads of us mere chaps, be'ant it, Miss Cost ? "

Miss Cost said : " I'm sure I don't know," and looked very fixedly at Mrs. Barrimore.

" We don't seem to be getting anywhere," Dr. Maine observed.

The Mayor cleared his throat. " This be'ant what you'd call a formal committee," he began, "but if it was and if I was in occupation of the chair, I'd move we took the temper of the meeting."

" Very good," Barrimore said. " Excellent suggestion. I propose His Worship be elected chairman. Those in favour ? " The others muttered a disjointed assent and the Mayor expanded. He suggested that what they really had to discover was how each of them proposed to respond to Miss Pride's onslaught. He invited them to speak in turn,

52

beginning with the Rector who repeated that they all knew his views and that he would abide by them.

"Does that mean," Major Barrimore demanded, "that if she says she's going to issue a public repudiation of the Spring, remove the enclosure and stop the festival, you'd come down on her side?"

"I shouldn't try to dissuade her."

The Mayor made an explosive ejaculation and turned on him: "If you'll pardon my frankness, Mr. Carstairs," he began, "I'd be obliged if you'd tell the company what you reckon would have happened to your Church Restoration Fund if Portcarrow hadn't benefited by the Spring to the extent it has done. Where'd you've got the money to repair your tower? You *wouldn't* have got it, no, nor anything like it."

Mr. Carstairs's normally sallow face reddened painfully. "No," he said, "I don't suppose we should."

"Hah!" said Miss Cost, "there you are!"

"I'm a Methodist myself," said the Mayor in triumph.

"Quite so," Mr. Carstairs agreed.

"Put it this way. Will you egg the woman on, sir, in her foolish notions. Will you do that?"

"No. It's a matter for her own conscience."

The Mayor, Major Barrimore and Miss Cost all began to expostulate. Dr. Maine said with repressed impatience: "I really don't think there's any future in pressing the point."

"Nor do I," said Mrs. Barrimore unexpectedly.

Miss Cost, acidly smiling, looked from her to Dr. Maine and then, fixedly, at Major Barrimore.

"Very good, Doctor," Mr. Nankivell said, "What about yourself, then?"

Dr. Maine stared distastefully at his own hands and said: "Paradoxically, I find myself in some sort of agreement with

53

the Rector. I, too, haven't disguised my views. I have an open mind about these cases. I have neither encouraged nor discouraged my patients to make use of the Spring. When there has been apparent benefit I have said nothing to undermine anyone's faith in its permanency. I am neutral."

" And from that impregnable position," Major Barrimore observed, " you've added a dozen rooms to your bloody nursing home. Beg pardon, Rector."

" Keith ! "

Major Barrimore turned on his wife. " Well, Margaret ? " he demanded. " What's *your* objection ? "

Miss Cost gave a shrill laugh.

Before Mrs. Barrimore could answer, Dr. Maine said very coolly, " You're perfectly right. I have benefited like all the rest of you. But as far as my practice is concerned, I believe Miss Pride's activities will make very little difference, in the long run. Either to it or to the popular appeal of the Spring. Sick people who are predisposed to the idea, will still think they know better. Or hope they know better," he added. " Which is, I suppose, much the same thing."

" That's all damn' fine but it won't be the same thing to the community at large," Barrimore angrily pointed out. " Tom, Dick and Harry and their friends and relations, swarming all over the place. The Island, a tripper's shambles, and the Press making a laughing-stock of the whole affair." He emptied his glass.

" And the Festival ! " Miss Cost wailed. " The Festival ! All our devotion ! The response ! The disappointment. The humiliation ! " She waved her hands. A thought struck her. " And Wally ! He has actually memorised ! After weeks of patient endeavour, he has memorised his little verses. Only this afternoon. One trivial slip. The choir is *utterly* committed."

" I'll be bound ! " said Mr. Nankivell heartily. " A credit

54

to all concerned and a great source of gratification to the borough if looked at in the proper spirit. We'm all waiting on the doctor, however," he added. " Now, Doctor, what is it to be ? What'll you say to the lady ? "

" Exactly what I said two minutes ago to you," Dr. Maine snapped. " I'll give my opinion if she wants it. I don't mind pointing out to her that the thing will probably go on after a fashion, whatever she does."

" I suppose that's something," said the Mayor gloomily. " Though not much, with an elderly female so deadly set on destruction."

" *I*," Miss Cost intervened hotly, " shall not mince my words. I shall tell her—— No," she amended with control. " I shall plead with her. I shall appeal to the nobler side. Let us hope that there is one. Let us hope so."

" I second that from the chair," said Mr. Nankivell. " Though with reservations prejudicial to an optimistic view. Major ? "

" What'll I do ? I'll try and reason with her. Give her a straight picture of the incontrovertible cures. If the man of science," Major Barrimore said with a furious look at Dr. Maine, " would come off his high horse and back me up, I might get her to listen. As it is——" he passed his palm over his hair and gave a half-smile, " I'll do what I can with the lady. I want another drink. Anyone join me ? "

The Mayor and, after a little persuasion, Miss Cost, joined him. He made towards the old private bar. As he opened the door, he admitted sounds of voices and of people crossing the flagstones to the main entrance.

Patrick looked in. " Sorry to interrupt," he said to his mother. " The bus load's arrived."

She got up quickly. " I must go," she said. " I'm sorry."

His stepfather said : " Damn ! All right." And to the others. " I won't be long. Pat, look after the drinks, here, will you ? Two double Scotches and a glass of the sweet port."

He went out followed by his wife and Patrick and could be heard welcoming his guests. " Good evening ! Good evening to you ! Now, come along in. You must all be exhausted. Awfully glad to see you——"

His voice faded.

There was a brief silence.

" Yes," said the Mayor. " Yes. Be-the-way, we didn't get round to axing the lady's view, did we? Mrs. Barrimore?"

For some reason they all looked extremely uncomfortable. Miss Cost gave a shrill laugh.

IV

" '——and I'd take it as a personal favour '," Alleyn dictated, " ' if you could spare a man to keep an eye on the Island when Miss Pride arrives there. Very likely nothing will come of these communications but, as we all know, they can lead to trouble. I ought to warn you that Miss Pride, though eighty-three, is in vigorous possession of all her faculties and if she drops to it that you've got her under observation, she may cut up rough. No doubt, like all the rest of us, you're under-staffed and won't thank me for putting you to this trouble. If your chap does notice anything out of the way, I would be very glad to hear of it. Unless a job blows up to stop me, I'm grabbing an overdue week's leave from tomorrow and will be at the above address.

" ' Again—sorry to be a nuisance,
Yours sincerely,'

" All right. Got the name ? Superintendent A. F. Coombe, Divisional H.Q. wherever it is—at Portcarrow itself, I fancy. Get it off straight away, will you ? "

When the letter had gone he looked at his watch. Five minutes past midnight. His desk was cleared and his files closed. The calendar showed Monday. He flipped it over. " I should have written before," he thought. " My letter will arrive with Miss Emily." He was ready to leave, but, for some reason, dawdled there, too tired, suddenly, to make a move. After a vague moment or two he lit his pipe, looked round his room and walked down the long corridor and the stairs, wishing the P.C. on duty at the doors good night.

It was his only superstition. " By the pricking of my thumbs."

As he drove away down the Embankment he thought : " Damned if I don't ring that Super up in the morning : be damned if I don't."

3. *Threats*

Miss Emily arrived at noon on Monday. She had stayed overnight in Dorset and was as fresh as paint. It was agreeable to be able to command a chauffeur-driven car and the man was not unintelligent.

When they drew up at Portcarrow jetty she gave him a well-considered tip, asked his name and told him she would desire, particularly, that he should be deputed for the return journey.

She then alighted, observed by a small gang of wharf loiterers.

A personable young man came forward to meet her.

" Miss Pride ? I'm Patrick Ferrier. I hope you had a good journey."

Miss Emily was well-disposed towards the young and, she had good reason to believe, a competent judge of them. She inspected Patrick and received him with composure. He introduced a tall, glowing girl who came forward, rather shyly, to shake hands. Miss Emily had less experience of girls but she liked the look of this one and was gracious.

" The causeway is negotiable," Patrick said, " but we thought you'd prefer the launch."

" It is immaterial," she rejoined. " The launch, let it be."

Patrick and the chauffeur handed her down the steps. Trehern stowed away her luggage and was profuse in cap-touching. They shoved-off from the jetty, still watched by idlers among whom, conspicuous in his uniform, was a police sergeant. " 'Morning, Pender!" Patrick called cheerfully as he caught sight of him.

In a motor launch, the trip across was ludicrously brief but even so Miss Emily, bolt upright in the stern, made it portentous. The sun shone and against it she displayed her open umbrella as if it were a piece of ceremonial plumage. Her black kid gloves gripped the handle centrally and her handbag, enormous and vice-like in its security, was placed between her feet. She looked, Patrick afterwards suggested, like some Burmese female deity. " We should have arranged to have had her carried, shoulder-high, over the causeway," he said.

Major Barrimore, with a porter in attendance, awaited her on the jetty. He resembled, Jenny thought, an illustration from an Edwardian sporting journal. " Well-tubbed " was the expression. His rather prominent eyes were a little bloodshot. He had to sustain the difficult interval that spanned approach and arrival and decide when to begin smiling and making appropriate gestures. Miss Emily gave him no help. Jenny and Patrick observed him with misgivings. " Good morning!" he shouted, gaily bowing, as they drew alongside. Miss Emily slightly raised and lowered her umbrella.

" That's right, Trehern. Easy does it. Careful, man," Major Barrimore chattered. " Heave me that line. Splendid!" He dropped the loop over a bollard and hovered, anxiously solicitous, with extended arm. " Welcome! Welcome!" he cried.

" Good morning, Major Barrimore," Miss Emily said. " Thank you. I can manage perfectly." Disregarding Trehern's outstretched hand, she looked fixedly at him. " Are you the father?" she asked.

Trehern removed his cap and grinned with all his might. " That I be, ma-am," he said. " If you be thinking of our

59

Wally, ma-am, that I be, and mortal proud to own up to him."

"I shall see you, if you please," said Miss Emily, "later."
For a second or two everyone was motionless.

She shook hands with her host.

"This *is* nice," he assured her. "And what a day we've produced for you! Now, about these steps of ours. Bit stiff, I'm afraid. May I——?"

"No, thank you. I shall be sustained in my ascent," said Miss Emily, fixing Miss Cost's shop and then the hotel façade in her gaze, "by the prospect."

She led the way up the steps.

"'Jove!'" the Major exclaimed when they arrived at the top. "You're too good for me, Miss Pride. Wonderful going! Wonderful!"

She looked briefly at him. "My habits," she said, "are abstemious. A little wine or cognac only. I have never been a smoker."

"Jolly good! Jolly good!" he applauded. Jenny began to feel acutely sorry for him.

Margaret Barrimore waited in the main entrance. She greeted Miss Emily with no marked increase in her usual diffidence. "I hope you had a pleasant journey," she said. "Would you like to have luncheon upstairs? There's a small sitting-room we've kept for you. Otherwise, the dining-room is here." Miss Emily settled for the dining-room but wished to see her apartment first. Mrs. Barrimore took her up. Her husband, Patrick and Jenny stood in the hall below and had nothing to say to each other. The Major, out of forgetfulness, it seemed, was still madly beaming. He caught his stepson's eye, uttered an expletive and without further comment, made for the bar.

Miss Emily, when she had lunched, took her customary siesta. She removed her dress and shoes, loosened her stays, put on a grey cotton peignoir and lay on the bed. There were several illustrated brochures to hand and she examined them. One contained a rather elaborate account of the original cure. It displayed a fanciful drawing of the Green Lady, photographs of the Spring, of Wally Trehern and a number of people passing through a sort of turnpike. A second gave a long list of subsequent healings with names and personal tributes. Miss Emily counted them up. Nine warts, five asthmas (including Miss Cost), three arthritics, two migraines and two chronic diarrhoeas (anonymous). "And many many more who have experienced relief and improvement," the brochure added. A folder advertised the coming Festival and, inset, Elspeth Cost's Giffte Shoppe. There was also a whimsical map of the Island with boats, fish, nets and pixies and, of course, a Green Lady.

Miss Emily studied the map and noted that it showed a direct route from The Boy-and-Lobster to the Spring.

A more business-like leaflet caught her attention.

THE TIDES AT PORTCARROW

The tides running between the village and the island show considerable variation in clock times. Roughly speaking, the water reaches its peak level twice in 24 hours and its lowest level at times which are about mid-way between those of high water. High and dead water times may vary from day to day with a lag of about 1-$1\frac{3}{4}$ hours in 24 hours. Thus if high water falls at noon on Sunday it may occur somewhere between 1 and 2.45 p.m. on Monday afternoon. About a fortnight may elapse before the cycle is completed and high water again falls between noon and 1.45 on Sunday.

Visitors will usually find the causeway is negotiable for 2 hours before and after low water. The hotel

61

launch and dinghies are always available and all the
jetties reach into deep water at low tide.

Expected times for high tide and dead water will be
posted up daily at the Reception Desk in the main
entrance.

Miss Emily studied this information for some minutes.
She then consulted the whimsical map.

At five o'clock she caused tea to be brought to her. Half
an hour later, she dressed and descended, umbrella in
hand, to the vestibule.

The hall-porter was on duty. When he saw Miss Emily he
pressed a bell-push on his desk and rose with a serviceable
smirk. " Can I help you, madam ? " he asked.

" In so far as I require admission to the enclosure, I
believe you may. I understand that entry is effected by
means of some plaque or token," said Miss Emily.

He opened a drawer and extracted a metal disc. " I shall
require," she said, " seven," and laid two half-crowns and a
florin on the desk. The hall-porter completed the number.

" No, no, no ! " Major Barrimore expostulated, bouncing
out from the interior. " We can't allow this. Nonsense ! "
He waved the hall-porter away. " See that a dozen of these
things are sent up to Miss Pride's suite," he said and bent
gallantly over his guest. " I'm so sorry ! Ridiculous ! "

" You are very good," she rejoined, " but I prefer to pay."
She opened her reticule, swept the discs into it and shut it
with a formidable snap. " Thank you," she said dismissing
the hall-porter. She prepared to leave.

" I don't approve," Major Barrimore began, " I—really,
it's very naughty of you. Now, may I—as it's your first
visit since—may I just show you the easiest way——? "

" I have, I think, discovered it from the literature
provided and need not trespass upon your time, Major

62

Barrimore. I am very much obliged to you." Something in her manner, or perhaps a covert glance from his employer, had caused the hall-porter to disappear. " In respect of my letter," Miss Emily said, with a direct look at the Major, " I would suggest that we postpone any discussion until I have made myself fully conversant with prevailing conditions on my property. I hope this arrangement is convenient ? "

" Anything ! " he cried. " Naturally. Anything ! But I do hope——"

" Thank you," said Miss Emily and left him.

The footpath from the hotel to the Spring followed, at an even level, the contour of an intervening slope. It was wide and well-surfaced and, as she had read in one of the brochures, amply provided for the passage of a wheeled chair. She walked along it at a steady pace, looking down as she did so at Fisherman's Bay, the cottages, the narrow strip of water and a not very distant prospect of the village. A mellow light lay across the hillside ; there was a prevailing scent of sea and of bracken. A lark sang overhead. It was very much the same sort of afternoon as that upon which, two years ago, Wally Trehern had blundered up the hillside to the Spring. Over the course he had so blindly taken there was now a well-defined, tar-sealed, and tactfully graded route which converged with Miss Emily's footpath at the entrance to the Spring.

The Spring itself, its pool, its modest waterfall and the bouldered slope above it, were now enclosed by a high wire-netting fence. There were one or two rustic benches outside this barricade. Entrance was effected through a turn-pike of tall netted flanges which could be operated by the insertion into a slot-machine of one of the discs with which Miss Emily was provided.

She did not immediately make use of it. There were

people at the Spring. An emaciated man whose tragic face had arrested Jenny Williams's attention at the bus stop and a young woman with a baby. The man knelt by the fall and seemed only by an effort to sustain his thin hands against the pressure of the water. His head was downbent. He rose, and, without looking at them, walked by the mother and child to a one-way exit from the enclosure. As he passed Miss Emily his gaze met hers and his mouth hesitated in a smile. Miss Emily inclined her head and they said " Good evening " simultaneously. " I have great hopes," the man said rather faintly. He lifted his hat and moved away downhill.

The young woman, in her turn, had knelt by the fall. She had bared the head of her baby and held her cupped hand above it. A trickle of water glittered briefly. Miss Emily sat down abruptly on a bench and shut her eyes.

When she opened them again, the young woman with the baby was coming towards her.

" Are you all right ? " she asked. " Can I help you ? Do you want to go in ? "

" I am not ill," Miss Emily said and added, " thank you, my dear."

" Oh, excuse me. I'm sorry. That's all right, then."

" Your baby. Has your baby——? "

" Well, yes. It's a sort of deficiency, the doctor says. He just doesn't seem to thrive. But there've been such wonderful reports—you can't get away from it, can you ? So I've got great hopes."

She lingered on for a moment and then smiled and nodded and went away.

" Great hopes ! " Miss Emily muttered. " *Ah, Mon Dieu!* Great hopes indeed."

She pulled herself together and extracted a nickel disc from her bag. There was a notice by the turnstile saying that arrangements could be made at the hotel for stretcher cases to be admitted. Miss Emily let herself in and inspected the terrain. The freshet gurgled in and out of its pool. The waterfall prattled. She looked towards the brow of the hill. The sun shone full in her eyes and dazzled them. She walked round to a ledge above the Spring and found a flat rock upon which she seated herself. Behind her was a bank, and, above that, the boulder and bracken where Wally's green lady was generally supposed to have appeared. Miss Emily opened her umbrella and composed herself.

She presented a curious figure, motionless, canopied and black and did indeed resemble, as Patrick had suggested, some outlandish presiding deity, whether benign or inimical must be a matter of conjecture. During her vigil seven persons visited the Spring and were evidently much taken aback by Miss Emily.

She remained on her perch until the sun went down behind the hill and, there being no more pilgrims to observe, descended and made her way downhill to Fisherman's Bay, and thence, round the point, to Miss Cost's shop. On her way she overtook the village police sergeant who seemed to be loitering. Miss Emily gave him good evening.

II

It was now a quarter to seven. The shop was open and, when Miss Emily went in, deserted. There was a bell on the counter but she did not ring it. She examined the welter of objects for sale. They were as Patrick had described them to Jenny: fanciful reconstructions in plastic of the Spring, the waterfall and " Wally's Cottage " ; badly printed rhymesheets ; booklets, calendars and postcards all of which covered much the same ground. Predominant amongst all these wares, cropping up everywhere, in print and in plastic, smirking, even, in the form of doll and cut-out, was the Green Lady. The treatment was consistent—a verdigris-coloured garment, long yellow hair, upraised hand and a star on the head. There was a kind of madness in the prolific insistence of this effigy. Jostling each other in a corner were the products of Miss Cost's handloom ; scarves, jerkins and cloaks of which the prevailing colours were sad blue and mauve. Miss Emily turned from them with a shudder of incredulity.

A door from the interior opened and Miss Cost entered on a wave of cottage-pie and wearing one of her own jerkins.

" I thought I heard—" she began and then she recognised her visitor. " Ae-oh ! " she said. " Good evening. Hem ! "

" Miss Cost, I believe. May I have a dozen threepenny stamps, if you please."

When these had been purchased Miss Emily said : " There is possibly no need for me to introduce myself. My name is Pride. I am your landlord."

" So I understand," said Miss Cost. " Quite."

" You are no doubt aware of my purpose in visiting the Island but I think perhaps I should make my position clear."

Miss Emily made her position very clear indeed. If Miss Cost wished to renew her lease of the shop in three months' time, it could only be on condition that any object which directly or indirectly advertised the Spring was withdrawn from sale.

Miss Cost listened to this with a fixed stare and a clasp-knife smile. When it was over she said that she hoped Miss Pride would not think it out of place if she, Miss Cost, mentioned that her little stock of fairings had been highly praised in discriminating quarters and had given pleasure to thousands. Especially, she added, to the kiddies.

66

Miss Emily said she could well believe it but that was not the point at issue.

Miss Cost said that each little novelty had been conceived in a spirit of reverence.

Miss Emily did not dispute the conception. The distribution, however, was a matter of commercial enterprise, was it not ?

At this juncture a customer came in and bought a plastic Green Lady.

When she had gone, Miss Cost said she hoped that Miss Pride entertained no doubts about the efficacy of the cures.

" If I do," said Miss Emily, " it is of no moment. It is the commercial exploitation that concerns us. That, I cannot tolerate." She examined Miss Cost for a second or two and her manner changed slightly. " I do not question your faith in the curative properties of the Spring," she said. " I do not suggest, I assure you, that in exploiting public credulity, you do so consciously and cynically."

" I should hope not ! " Miss Cost burst out. " I ! I ! My asthma——! I, who am a living witness ! Ae-oh ! "

" Quite so. Moreover, when the Island has been restored to its former condition, I shall not prevent access to the Spring any more than I shall allow extravagant claims to be canvassed. It will not be closed to the public. Quite on the contrary."

" They will ruin it ! The vandalism ! The outrages ! Even now with every precaution. The desecration ! "

" That can be attended to."

" Fairy ground," Miss Cost suddenly announced, " is holy ground."

" I am unable to determine whether you adopt a pagan or a Christian attitude," said Miss Emily. She indicated a rhyme-sheet which was clothes-pegged to a line above the counter.

Ye olde wayes, *it read*, were wise old wayes
(Iron and water, earthe and stone)
Ye Hidden Folke of antient dayes
Ye Greene Companions' Runic Layes
Wrought Magick with a Bone.

Ye plashing Falles ther Secrette holde.
(Iron and water, earthe and stone)
On us as on those menne of olde
Their mighte of healing is Bestowed
And wonders still are showne.

O, thruste your handes beneath the rille
(Iron and water, earthe and stone)
And itte will washe awaye your ille
With neweborn cheere your bodie fille
That antient Truth bee knowne.

"Who," asked Miss Emily, fixing her gaze upon Miss
Cost, "is the author of this doggerel?"

"It is unsigned," she said loudly. "These old rhymes—"

"The spelling is spurious and the paper contemporary.
Does it express your own views, Miss Cost?"

"Yes," said Miss Cost, shutting her eyes. "It does. A
thousand times, yes."

"So I imagined. Well, now," Miss Emily briskly continued, "you know mine. Take time to consider. There is
one other matter."

Her black kid forefinger indicated a leaflet advertising the
Festival. "This," she said.

A spate of passionate defiance broke from Miss Cost. Her
voice was pitched high and she stared at some object beyond
Miss Emily's left shoulder. "You can't stop us!" she cried.
"You can't! You can't prevent people walking up a hill.
You can't prevent them singing. I've made inquiries. We're

68

not causing a disturbance and it's all authorised by the Mayor. He's part of it. Ask him ! Ask the Mayor ! Ask the Mayor. We've got hundreds and hundreds of people coming and you can't stop them. You can't. *You can't!* "

Her voice cracked and she drew breath. Her hands moved to her chest.

Into the silence that followed there crept a very small and eerie sound : a faint, rhythmic squeak. It came from Miss Cost.

Miss Emily heard it. After a moment she said, with compassion : " I am sorry. I shall leave you. I shall not attempt to prevent your Festival. It must be the last but I shall not prevent it."

As she prepared to leave, Miss Cost, now struggling for breath, gasped after her.

" You wicked woman ! This is your doing." She beat her chest. " You'll suffer for it. More than I do. Mark my words ! You'll suffer."

Miss Emily turned to look at her. She sat on a stool behind the counter. Her head nodded backwards and forwards with her laboured breathing.

" Is there anything I can do ? " Miss Emily asked. " You have an attack———"

" I haven't ! *I haven't ! Go away.* Wicked woman ! Go away."

Miss Emily, greatly perturbed, left the shop. As she turned up from the jetty, a boy shambled out of the shadows, stared at her for a moment, gave a whooping cry and ran up the steps. It was Wally Trehern.

The encounter with Miss Cost had tired her. She was upset. It had, of course, been a long day and there were still those steps to be climbed. There was a bench half-way up and she decided to rest there for a few minutes before making the final ascent. Perhaps she would ask for an early dinner

in her room and go to bed afterwards. It would never do to
let herself get overdone. She took the steps slowly, using her
umbrella as a staff and was rather glad when she reached the
bench. It was a relief to sit there and observe the foreshore, the causeway and the village.

Down below, at the end of the jetty, a group of fishermen
stood talking. The police-sergeant, she noticed, had joined
them. They seemed to be looking up at her. " I daresay it's
got about," she thought, " who I am and all the rest of it.
Bah ! "

She stayed on until she was refreshed. The evening had
begun to close in and she was in the lee of the hill. There
was a slight coolness in the air. She prepared, after the
manner of old people, to rise.

At that moment she was struck between the shoulder
blades, on the back of her neck and head and on her arm.
Stones fell with a rattle at her feet. Above and behind her
there was a scuffling sound of retreat and of laughter.

She got up, scarcely knowing what she did. She supposed afterwards that she must have cried out. The next
thing that happened was that the sergeant was running
heavily uphill towards her.

" Hold hard, now, ma'am," he was saying. " Be you
hurt, then ? "

" No. Stones. From above. Go and look."

He peered at her for a moment and then scrambled up the
sharp rise behind the bench. He slithered and skidded,
sending down a cascade of earth. Miss Emily sank back on
the bench. She drew her glove off and touched her neck
with a trembling hand. It was wet.

The sergeant floundered about overhead. Unexpectedly
two of the fishermen had arrived and, more surprisingly still,
the tall bronze girl. What was her name ?

" Miss Pride," she was saying, " you're hurt. What

70

happened ? " She knelt down by Miss Emily and took her hands.

The men were talking excitedly and presently the sergeant was there again, swearing and breathing hard.

" Too late," he was saying. " Missed 'im."

Miss Emily's head began to clear a little.

" I am perfectly well," she said rather faintly and more to herself than to the others. " It is nothing."

" You've been hurt. Your neck ! " Jenny said, also in French. " Let me look."

" You are too kind," Miss Emily murmured. She suffered her neck to be examined. " Your accent," she added more firmly, " is passable though not entirely *d'une femme du monde*. Where did you learn ? "

" In Paris," said Jenny. " There's a cut in your neck, Miss Pride. It isn't very deep but I'm going to bind it up. Mr. Pender, could I borrow your handkerchief ? And I'll make a pad of mine. Clean, luckily."

While Miss Emily suffered these ministrations the men muttered together. There was a scrape of boots on the steps and a third fisherman came down from above. It was Trehern. He stopped short. " Hey ! " he ejaculated. " What's amiss, then ? "

" Lady's been hurt, poor dear," one of the men said.

" Hurt ! " Trehern exclaimed. " How ? Why, if it be'ant Miss Pride. Hurt ! What way ? "

" Where would you be from then, Jim ? " Sergeant Pender asked.

" Up to pub as usual, George," he said. " Where else ? " A characteristic parcel protruded from his overcoat pocket. " Happen she took a fall ? Them steps be treacherous going for females well-gone into the terrors of antiquity."

" Did you leave the pub this instant-moment ? "

" Surely. Why ? "

71

" Did you notice anybody up-along, off of the steps, like ? In the rough ? "

" Are you after them courting couples again, George Pender ? "

" No," said Mr. Pender shortly. " I be'ant."

" I did *not* fall," said Miss Emily loudly. She rose to her feet and confronted Trehern. " I was struck," she said.

" Lord forbid, ma'am ! Who'd take a fancy to do a crazy job like that ? "

Jenny said to Pender : " I think we ought to get Miss Pride home."

" So we should, then. Now, ma'am," said Pender with an air of authority, " you'm not going to walk up them steps, if you please, so if you've no objection us chaps'll manage you, same as if we was bringing you ashore in a rough sea."

" I assure you, officer——"

" Very likely, ma'am, and you with the heart of a lion as all can see, but there'd be no kind of sense in it. Now then, souls. Hup ! "

And before she knew what had happened, Miss Emily was sitting on a chair of woollen-clad arms with her own arms neatly disposed by Mr. Pender round a pair of slightly fishy shoulders and her face in close association with those of her bearers.

" Pretty as a picture," Pender said. " Heave away, chaps. Stand aside, if you please, Jim."

" My umbrella."

" I've got it," said Jenny. " And your bag."

When they reached the top Miss Emily said : " I am extremely obliged. If you will allow me, officer, I would greatly prefer it if I might enter in the normal manner. I am perfectly able to do so and it will be less conspicuous." And to Jenny : " Please ask them to put me down."

" I think she'll be all right," Jenny said.

" Very good, ma'am," said Pender. " Set 'er down, chaps.
That's clever. Gentle as a lamb."

They stood round Miss Emily, and grinned bashfully at
her.

" You have been very kind," she said. " I hope you will
be my guests though it will be wiser perhaps, if I do not give
myself the pleasure of joining you. I will leave instructions.
Thank you very much."

She took her umbrella and handbag from Jenny, bowed to
her escort and walked quite fast towards the entrance. Jenny
followed her. On the way they passed Wally Trehern.

Patrick was in the vestibule. Miss Emily inclined her head
to him and made for the stairs. Her handbag was bloody
and conspicuous. Jenny collected her room key from the
desk.

" What on earth——? " Patrick said coming up to her.

" Get Dr. Maine, could you ? Up to her room. And
Patrick—there are two fishermen and Mr. Pender outside.
She wants them to have drinks on her. Can you fix it ? I'll
explain later."

" Good lord ! Yes, all right."

Jenny overtook Miss Emily on the landing. She was
shaky and, without comment, accepted an arm. When they
had reached her room she sat on her bed and looked at Jenny
with an expression of triumph.

" I am not surprised," she said. " It was to be expected,
my dear," and fainted.

III

" Well," said Dr. Maine, smiling into Miss Emily's face,
" there's no great damage done. I think you'll recover."

" I have already done so."

73

" Yes, I daresay, but I suggest you go slow for a day or two, you know. You've had a bit of shock. How old are you ? "

" I'm eighty-three and four months."

" Good God ! "

" Ours is a robust family, Dr. Maine. My sister, Fanny Winterbottom, whom I daresay you have met, would be alive to-day if she had not, in one of her extravagant moods, taken an excursion in a speedboat."

" Did it capsize ? " Jenny was startled into asking.

" Not at all. But the excitement was too much and the consequent depression exposed her to an epidemic of Asiatic influenza. From which she died. It was quite unnecessary and the indirect cause of my present embarrassment."

There was a short silence. Jenny saw Dr. Maine's eyebrows go up.

" Really ? " he said. " Well, now, I don't think we should have any more conversation to-night. Some hot milk with a little whisky or brandy, if you like it, and a couple of aspirins. I'll look in to-morrow."

" You do not, I notice, suggest that I bathe my injuries in the Spring."

" No," he said, and they exchanged a smile.

" I had intended to call upon you to-morrow with reference to my proposals. Have you heard of them ? "

" I have. But I'm not going to discuss them with you to-night."

" Do you object ? To my proposals ? "

" No. Good night, Miss Pride. Please don't get up until I've seen you."

" And yet they would not, I imagine, be to your advantage."

There was a tap on the door and Mrs. Barrimore came in.

" Miss Pride," she said. " I'm so sorry. I've just heard. I've come to see if there's anything——" she looked at Dr. Maine.

" Miss Pride's quite comfortable," he said. " Jenny's going to settle her down. I think we'll leave her in charge, shall we ? "

He waited while Mrs. Barrimore said another word or two, and then followed her out of the room. He shut the door and they moved down the passage.

" Bob," she said, " what is it ? What happened ? Has she been attacked ? "

" Probably some lout from the village."

" You don't think——? "

" No." He looked at her. " Don't worry," he said. " Don't worry so, Margaret."

" I can't help it. Did you see Keith ? "

" Yes. He's overdone it to-night. Flat out in the old bar parlour. I'll get him up to bed."

" Does Patrick know ? "

" I've no idea."

" He wasn't flat out an hour ago. He was in the ugly stages. He—he—was talking so wildly. What he'd do to her—to Miss Pride. You know ? "

" My dear girl, he was plastered. Don't get silly ideas into your head, now, will you ? Promise ? "

" All right," she said. " Yes. All right."

" Good night," he said and left her there with her fingers against her lips.

IV

On the next day, Tuesday, Miss Emily kept to her room, where in the afternoon she received in turn, Mr. Nankivell (the Mayor of Portcarrow), Dr. Maine and the Rev. Mr.

75

Carstairs. On Wednesday she called at Wally's Cottage. On Thursday she revisited the Spring, mounted to her observation post and remained there, under her umbrella, for a considerable time, conscientiously observed by Sergeant Pender to whom she had taken a fancy, and by numerous visitors as well as several of the local characters, including Miss Cost, Wally Trehern and his father.

On Friday she followed the same routine, escaping a trip-wire which had been laid across her ascent to the ledge and removed by Mr. Pender two minutes before she appeared on the scene.

An hour later, this circumstance having been reported to him, Superintendent Alfred Coombe rang up Roderick Alleyn at his holiday address.

v

Alleyn was mowing his host's tennis court when his wife hailed him from the terrace. He switched the machine off.

" Telephone," she shouted. " Long distance."

" Damnation ! " he said and returned to the house.

" Where's it from, darling ? "

" Portcarrow. District Headquarters. That'll be Miss Emily, won't it ? "

" Inevitably, I fear."

" Might it only be to say there's nothing to report ? " Troy asked doubtfully.

" *Most* unlikely."

He answered the call, heard what Coombe had to say about the stone-throwing and turned his thumb down for Troy's information.

" Mind you," Coombe said, " it might have been some damned Ted larking about. Not that we've had trouble of that sort on the Island. But she's raised a lot of feeling locally. Seeing what you've told us, I thought I ought to let you know."

" Yes, of course. And you've talked to Miss Pride ? "

" I have," said Coombe with some emphasis. " She's a firm old lady, isn't she ? "

" Gibraltar is as butter compared to her."

" What say ? "

" I said : Yes, she is."

" I asked her to let me know what her plans might be for the rest of the day. I didn't get much change out of her. The doctor persuaded her to stay put on Tuesday but ever since she's been up and about, worse luck. She's taken to sitting on this shelf above the Spring and looking at the visitors. Some of them don't like it."

" I bet they don't."

" The thing is, with this Festival coming along to-morrow the place is filling up and we're going to be fully extended. I mean, keeping observation, as you know, takes one man all his time."

" Of course. Can you get reinforcements ? "

" Not easily. But I don't think it'll come to that. I don't reckon it's warranted. I reckon she'll watch her step after this. But she's tricky. You've got to face it : she is tricky."

" I'm sorry to have landed you with this, Coombe."

" Well, I'd rather know. I'm glad you did. After all she's in my district—and if anything did happen——"

" *Has* there been anything else ? "

" That's why I'm ringing. My chap, Pender, found a trip-wire stretched across the place where she climbs up to her perch. He was hanging about waiting for her to turn up and noticed it. Workman-like job. Couple of iron pegs and a length of fine clothes-line. Could have been nasty. There's a five foot drop to the pond. And rocks."

" Did you tell her ? "

77

" Yes. She said she'd have spotted it for herself."

" When was this ? "

" This morning. About an hour ago."

" Damn."

" Quite so."

" Does she suspect anyone ? "

" Well, yes. She reckons it's a certain lady. Yes, Mr. Mayor. Good morning, sir. I won't keep you a moment."

" Has your Mayor just walked in ? "

" That's right."

" Did you by any chance, mean the shop-keeper ? Miss Cost, is it ? "

" That's right."

" I'll ring up Miss Pride. I suppose she knocks off for lunch, does she ? Comes off her perch ? "

" That's right. Quite so."

" What's the number of the pub ? "

" Portcarrow 1212."

" You'll keep in touch ? "

" That'll be quite all right, sir. We'll do that for you."

" Thank you," Alleyn said. " No matter what they say I've got great faith in the police. Good-bye."

He heard Coombe give a chuckle and hung up.

" O, Rory ! " his wife said. " Not again ? Not this time ? It's been such fun, our holiday."

" I'm going to talk to her. Come here to me and keep your fingers crossed. She's hell when she's roused. Come here."

He kept his arm round her while he waited for the call to go through. When at last Miss Emily spoke from her room at the Boy-and-Lobster, Troy could hear her quite clearly though she had some difficulty in understanding since Miss Emily spoke in French. So did Alleyn.

" Miss Emily, how are you getting on ? "

" Perfectly well, I thank you, Roderique."

78

" Have there been unpleasantnesses of the sort that were threatened ? "

" Nothing of moment. Do not disarrange yourself on my account."

" You have been hurt."

" It was superficial."

" You might well have been hurt again."

" I think not."

" Miss Emily, I must ask you to leave the Island."

" In effect : you have spoken to the good Superintendent Coombe. It was kind but it was not necessary. I shall not leave the Island."

" Your behaviour is, I'm afraid, both foolish and inconsiderate."

" Indeed ? Explain yourself."

" You are giving a great deal of anxiety and trouble to other people. You are being silly, Miss Emily."

" That," said Miss Emily distinctly, " was an improper observation."

" Unfortunately not. If you persist I shall feel myself obliged to intervene."

" Do you mean, my friend," said Miss Emily with evident amusement, " that you will have me arrested ? "

" I wish I could. I wish I could put you under protective custody."

" I am already protected by the local officer who is, for example, a man of intelligence. His name is Pender."

" Miss Emily, if you persist you will force me to leave my wife."

" That is nonsense."

" Will you give me your word of honour that you will not leave the hotel unaccompanied ? "

" Very well," said Miss Emily after a pause. " Understood."

" And that you will not sit alone on a shelf ? Or anywhere? At any time ? "

" There is no room for a second occupant on the shelf."

" There must be room somewhere. Another shelf. Somewhere."

" It would not be convenient."

" Nor is it convenient for me to leave my wife and come traipsing down to your beastly Island."

" I beg that you will do no such thing. I assure you——" Her voice stopped short. He would have thought that the call had been cut off if he hadn't quite distinctly heard Miss Emily catch her breath in a sharp gasp. Something had fallen.

" Miss Emily ! " he said. " Hallo ! Hallo ! Miss Emily !"

" Very well," her voice said. " I can hear you. Perfectly."

" What happened ? "

" I was interrupted."

" Something's wrong. What is it ? "

" No, no. It is nothing. I knocked a book over. Roderique, I beg that you do not break your holiday. It would be rather ridiculous. It would displease me extremely, you understand. I assure you that I will do nothing foolish. Good-bye, my dear boy."

She replaced the receiver.

Alleyn sat with his arm still round his wife. " Something happened," he said. " She sounded frightened. I swear she was frightened. Damn and blast Miss Emily for a pigheaded old effigy. What the hell does she think she's up to ! "

" Darling : she promised to be sensible. She doesn't want you to go. Does she, now ? "

" She was frightened," he repeated. " And she wouldn't say why."

At the same moment Miss Emily with her hand pressed to

her heart was staring at the object she had exposed when she had knocked the telephone directory on its side.

This object was a crude plastic image of a Green Lady. A piece of ruled paper had been jammed down over the head and on it was pasted a single word of newsprint.

" Death."

Miss Emily surveyed the assembled company.

There were not enough chairs for them all in her sitting-room. Margaret Barrimore, the Rector and the Mayor were seated. Jenny and Patrick sat on the arms of Mrs. Barrimore's chair. Major Barrimore, Superintendent Coombe and Dr. Maine formed a rather ill-assorted group of standees.

" That then," said Miss Emily, " is the situation. I have declared my purpose. I have been threatened. Two attempts have been made upon me. Finally, this object—" she waved her hand in the direction of the Green Lady which, with its unlovely label still about its neck, simpered at the company "—this object has been placed in my room by someone who evidently obtained possession of the key."

" Now, my dear Miss Pride," Barrimore said. " I do assure you that I shall make the fullest possible investigation. Whoever perpetrated this ridiculous——" Miss Emily raised her hand. He goggled at her, brushed up his moustache and was silent.

" I have asked you to meet me here," she continued exactly as if she had not been interrupted, " in order to make it known, first, that I am not of course, to be diverted by threats of any sort. I shall take the action I have already outlined. I have particularly invited you, Mr. Mayor, and the Rector and Dr. Maine because you are persons of authority in Portcarrow and also because each of you will be affected in some measure by my decision. As perhaps more directly, will Major Barrimore and his family. I regret that Miss Cost finds she is unable to come. I have met each of you independently since I arrived and I hope you are all convinced that I am not to be shaken in my intention."

Mr. Nankivell made an unhappy noise.

"My second object in trespassing upon your time is this. I wish, with the assistance of Superintendent Coombe, to arrive at the identity of the person who left this figurine, with its offensive label, on my desk. It is presumably the person who is responsible for the two attempts to inflict injury. It was—I believe ' planted ' is the correct expression —while I was at luncheon. My apartment was locked. My key was on its hook on a board in the office. It is possible to remove it without troubling the attendant and without attracting attention. That is what must have been done, and done by a person who was aware of my room number. Unless, indeed, this outrage was performed by somebody who is in possession of, or has access to, a duplicate or master key." She turned with splendid complacency to Superintendent Coombe. "That is my contention," said Miss Emily. "Perhaps you, Mr. Coombe, will be good enough to continue the investigation."

An invitation of this sort rested well outside the range of Superintendent Coombe's experience. Under the circumstances, he met the challenge with good sense and discretion. He kept his head.

"Well, now," he said. "Miss Pride, Mr. Mayor and ladies and gentlemen, I'm sure we're all agreed that this state of affairs won't do. Look at it whatever way you like, it reflects no credit on the village or the Island."

"Yurr-yurr," said the Mayor who was clearly fretted by the minor role for which he seemed to be cast. "Speak your mind, Alfred. Go ahead."

" So I will, then. Now. As regards the stone-throwing and the trip-wire incidents. Inquiries have been put in hand. So far, from information received, I have nothing to report. As regards this latest incident : in the ordinary course of events, it having been reported to the police, routine inquiries would be undertaken. That would be the normal procedure."

" It has been reported," said Miss Emily. " And I have invited you to proceed."

" The method, if you will pardon me, Miss Pride, has *not* been normal. It is not usual to call a meeting on such an occasion."

" Evidently I have not made myself clear. I have called the meeting in order that the persons who could have effected an entry into this room by the means I have indicated, may be given an opportunity of clearing themselves."

This pronouncement had a marked but varied effect upon her audience. Patrick Ferrier's eyebrows shot up and he glanced at Jenny who made a startled grimace. Mrs. Barrimore leant forward in her chair and looked, apparently with fear, at her husband. He, in his turn, had become purple in the face. The Mayor's habitual expression of astonishment was a caricature of itself. Dr. Maine scrutinised Miss Emily as if she were a test case for something. The Rector ran his hands through his hair and said : " Oh, but surely ! "

Superintendent Coombe, with an air of abstraction, stared in front of him. He then produced his notebook and contemplated it as if he wondered where it had sprung from.

" Now, *just* a *minute* ! " he said.

" I must add," said Miss Emily, " that Miss Jenny Williams may at once be cleared. She very kindly called for me, assisted me downstairs and to my knowledge remained in the dining-room throughout luncheon, returning to my table to perform the same kind office. Do you wish to record this ? "

He opened his mouth, shut it again and actually made a note.

" It will perhaps assist the inquiry if I add that Major Barrimore did not come into the dining-room at all, that Mrs. Barrimore left it five minutes before I did and that Mr. Patrick Ferrier was late in arriving there. They will no doubt wish to elaborate."

" By God ! " Major Barrimore burst out. " I'll be damned if I do ! By God, I'll——"

" No, Keith ! Please ! " said his wife.

" You shut up, Margaret."

" I suggest," Patrick said, " that on the whole it might be better if *you* did."

" Patrick ! " said the Rector. " No, old boy."

Superintendent Coombe came to a decision.

" I'll ask you all for your attention, if you please," he said, and was successful in getting it. " I don't say this is the way I'd have dealt with the situation," he continued, " if it had been left to me. It hasn't. Miss Pride has set about the affair in her own style and has put me in the position where I haven't much choice but to take up the inquiry on her lines. I don't say it's a desirable way of going about the affair and I'd have been just as pleased if she'd have had a little chat with me first. She hasn't and that's that. I think it'll be better for all concerned if we get the whole thing settled and done with by taking routine statements from everybody. I hope you're agreeable."

Patrick said quickly : " Of course. Much the best way." He stood up. " I was late for lunch," he said, " because I was having a drink with George Pender in the bar. I went

84

direct from the bar to the dining-room. I didn't go near the office. What about you, Mama?"

Mrs. Barrimore twisted her fingers together and looked up at her son. She answered him as if it were a matter private to them both. "Do you mean, what did I do when I left the dining-room? Yes, I see. I—I went into the hall. There was a crowd of people from the bus. Some of them asked about—oh, the usual things. One of them seemed—very unwell—and I took her into the lounge to sit down. Then I went across to the old house. And——"

Dr. Maine said: "I met Mrs. Barrimore as she came in. I was in the old house. I'd called to have a word with her about Miss Pride. To learn if she was," he glanced at her, "if she was behaving herself," he said dryly. "I went into the old bar-parlour. Major Barrimore was there. I spoke to him for a minute or two and then had a snack lunch in the new bar. I then visited a patient who is staying in the hotel and at two-thirty I called on Miss Pride. I found her busy at the telephone summoning this meeting. At her request I have attended it."

He had spoken rapidly. Mr. Coombe said, "Just a minute if you please, Doctor," and they were all silent while he completed his notes. "Yes," he said at last. "Well, now. That leaves His Worship, doesn't it and——"

"I must say," Mr. Nankivell interrupted, "and say it I do and will, I did not anticipate when called upon at a busy and inconvenient time, to be axed to clear myself of participation in a damn' fool childish prank. Further, I take leave to put on record that I look upon the demand made upon me as one unbecoming to the office I have the honour to hold. Having said which, I'll thank you to make a note of it, Alf Coombe. I state further that during the first part of the period in question I was in the Mayoral Chambers at the execution of my duties from which I moved to the back office of my butchery attending to my own business which is more than can be said of persons who shall for purposes of this discussion, remain nameless."

Mr. Coombe made a short note : " In his Butchery," and turned to the Rector.

" I've been trying to think," said Mr. Carstairs. " I'm not at all good at times and places, I fear, and it's been a busy day. Let me see. O, yes. I visited the cottages this morning. Actually, the main object was to call on that wretched Mrs. Trehern. Things have been very much amiss, there. It's a sad case. And one or two other folk on the Island. I don't know when I walked back but I believe I was late for lunch. My wife, I daresay, could tell you."

" Did you come up to The Boy-and-Lobster, sir ? "

" Did I ? Yes, I did. As a matter of fact, Miss Pride, I intended to call on you to see if you were quite recovered, but the main entrance was crowded and I saw that luncheon had begun so—I didn't, you see."

" You went home, sir ? " asked the Superintendent.

" Yes. Late."

Mr. Coombe shut his notebook. " All right," he said, " so far as it goes. Now, in the normal course of procedure these statements would be followed up and follow them up I shall which takes time. So unless anyone has anything further to add—Yes, Miss Pride ? "

" I merely observe, Superintendent, that I shall be glad to support you in your investigations. And to that end," she added, in the absence of any sign of enthusiasm, " I shall announce at once, that I have arrived at my own conclusion. There is, I consider, only one individual to whom these outrages may be attribnted and that person, I firmly believe, is——"

The telephone rang.

It was at Miss Emily's elbow. She said " T'ch ! " and picked it up. " Yes ? Are you there ? " she asked.

A treble voice, audible to everybody in the room asked :

" Be that Miss Emily Pride ? "

" Speaking."

" You leave us be, Miss Emily Pride, or the Lady will get you. You'll be dead as a stone, Miss Emily Pride."

" Who is that ? "

The telephone clicked and began to give the dialling sound.

Patrick said : " That was a child's voice. It must have been——"

" No," said Miss Emily. " I think not. I have an acute ear for phonetics. It was an assumed accent. And it was not a child. It was the voice of Miss Elspeth Cost."

4. *Fiasco*

The persons taking part in the Festival celebrations assembled at four o'clock on Saturday at the foot of the hill in Fisherman's Bay. There was a company of little girls wearing green cheesecloth dresses and stars in their hair, about a dozen larger girls, similarly attired, and a few small boys in green cotton smocks. In the rear of this collection came Wally Trehern, also smocked, with his hair sleeked down and a bewildered expression on his face. His hands were noticeably clean. The Mayor and City Councillors and other local dignitaries were yet to come.

Miss Cost marshalled and re-marshalled her troupe. She wore a mop cap and a hand-woven cloak of the prevailing green over a full skirt and an emerald velveteen bodice. The afternoon was sultry and her nose and eyebrows glittered. She carried a camera and a sheaf of papers clipped to a board and exhibited signs of emotional stress.

Thunderous clouds were massed in the north-west and everybody eyed them with distrust. Not a breath of air stirred. An ominous, hot, stillness prevailed.

The enclosure was packed. An overflow of spectators had climbed the hill above the Spring and sat or lay in the blinding heat. The route from the foreshore to the Spring—" Wally's Way," in the programme—was lined with spectators. Seats in the enclosure were provided for the ailing and for the official party and other persons of importance. These included the Barrimores, Jenny, Dr. Maine and the Carstairs. The Rector, preserving his detachment, had declined any official part in the ceremony. " Though I must say," he confided to his wife, " it sounds innocuous enough, in a way, from what I've heard. I'm afraid Miss Cost's verse is really pretty dreadful, poor dear."

" Tell me the moment you see Miss Pride."

" I can't help hoping that in the event we shan't see her at all."

" I suppose that chair by Mrs. Barrimore is reserved for her."

" Let us hope she occupies it and doesn't return to her original plan. She would look *too* out of place on the ledge."

" It would put Wally off his poetry, I have no doubt," Mrs. Carstairs agreed.

" Not only that, but I understand they use it in their pageant or whatever it is."

" Then it would be very inconsiderate if she insisted."

" Mind you, Dulcie, I maintain that in principle she is right."

" Yes, dear, I'm sure you do," said Mrs. Carstairs. She gave a little sigh and may have been thinking that things had been a good deal easier over the last two years.

Patrick said to Jenny : " Did you see her before we left ? "

" Yes. She's agreed not to sit on the ledge."

" How did you do it, you clever girl ? "

" I told her I thought it would be unbecoming and that the children would giggle and the gentlemen look at her legs."

" Do you suppose she'll cut up rough at any stage ? "

" I've no idea. Listen."

" What ? "

" Wasn't that thunder ? "

" I wouldn't be surprised. Look, there's Coombe coming in now. Who's that with him, I wonder. The tall chap."

89

" Jolly good-looking," said Jenny.

" Jolly good tailor, anyway."

" P'raps it's one of Miss Pride's smart chums. She's got masses, it appears, nearly all diplomats of the first water, she told me."

" There's the band. It must have been the big drum you heard, not thunder."

" It was thunder," said Jenny.

The band debouched from the village towards the jetty. It was a small combination entirely dominated by the drum. Behind it walked Mr. Nankivell in full regalia, supported by his Council. They embarked in the large motor launch, manned by Trehern, who was got up as a sort of wherryman. The band filled a small fleet of attendant dinghies and continued to play with determination if a trifle wildly throughout the short passage. Miss Cost could be seen darting up and down the length of her procession, taking photographs.

A union of the two elements was achieved and soon they ascended the hill. The children sang. The band attempted a diminuendo.

" *Through the night of doubt and sorrow.*"

" Now, why *that* ! " the Rector exclaimed. " You see ? No, Dulcie, it's too much ! "

" Look, dear. Do look. There she is."

Miss Emily had approached by the path from the hotel. She inserted her disc, entered the enclosure and advanced to her seat just before the procession arrived. Major Barrimore stood up to welcome her, looking furious.

A double gate, normally locked and only used to admit stretcher cases, was now opened. The procession marched in and disposed itself in a predestined order.

It is doubtful if any of the official party paid much attention to the Mayor's inaugural address. They were all too busy furtively keeping an eye on Miss Emily. She sat bolt upright with her hands clasped over the handle of her furled umbrella and she stared at Mr. Nankivell.

"... and so, Ladies and Gentlemen, I have great pleasure in declaring the First—the *First* Festival of Portcarrow Island Springs, O—PEN."

He sat down to a patter of applause through which Miss Cost advanced to a position near the little waterfall. Wally stood behind her. A microphone had been set up but she neglected to use it consistently. When she did speak into it, it seized upon her words and loud-speakers savagely flung them upon the heavy air. When she turned aside she changed into a voiceless puppet that opened and shut its mouth, cast up its eyes and waved its arms. The Mayor, nodding and smiling, pointed repeatedly to the microphone but Miss Cost did not observe him.

"—One Wonderful Afternoon—little Boy—so Sorrowful—who can tell ?—Ancient Wisdom—Running Water—" Evidently she approached her climax but all was lost until she turned sharply and the loud speakers bellowed " All Gone."

The words reverberated about the hillside in a very desolate fashion—" all gone—all gone——" Miss Cost was bowing and ineffably smiling. She added something that was completely inaudible and, with an arch look at her audience, turned to Wally and found he had vanished. He was extricated from the rear of the choir where he had retired to sit down on some seepage from the Spring.

Miss Cost led him forward. The back of his smock was slimy and green. Unfortunately she did not place him before the microphone but for the first time herself directly confronted it.

" Now, Wally, *now*," roared the loud speakers. " ' *Once upon a Summer's day.*' Go *on*, dear."

At first, little of Wally's recitation was lost since he re-

91

quired constant prompting which Miss Cost, unwittingly, fed into the microphone. At the second stanza, however, the Mayor advanced upon her and in his turn was broadcast. " Shift over," the loudspeakers advised. " Come 'ere, you silly lad." The Mayor, quick to perceive his error, backed away.

" O *dear* ! " cried Miss Cost, publicly, and effected the change.

"Got it right this time ! " said Major Barrimore loudly and gave a snort of laughter. Miss Cost evidently heard him. She threw him a furious glance.

Wally's recitation continued.

" *Be not froightened sayed the Loidy . . .*"

" This is killing me," Jenny whispered.

" Shut up, for pity's sake. O, God ! " Patrick muttered.

" What now ? What's he saying now ? "

" Shut up."

Mrs. Carstairs turned and shook her head at them. They moaned together in agony.

Wally came to an unexpected stop and walked away.

The audience, relieved, burst into sustained applause.

Miss Emily remained immovable.

The choir, accompanied by tentative grunts from the band, began to sing. Wally, recaptured, squatted beside the waterfall, looked cheerfully about him, and pushed his hands under the stream.

" This will be the inexplicable dumb show," Patrick said.

" Look ! O, look ! "

From behind a boulder above the Spring emerged a large girl dressed in green cheesecloth. She was a blonde and the most had been made of her hair which was crowned by a tinsel star. From her left hand depended a long string of glittering beads, symbolic, clearly, of Water. Her right hand was raised. The gesture, inappropriately, was accompanied by a really formidable roll of thunder. The sun was now overcast and the heavens were black.

Wally looked up at the newcomer, gave one of his strange cries, pointed to her and laughed uproariously.

" *Thus*," sang the choir, " *the Magic Spell was wroughten Thus the little lad was healed*——"

The Green Lady executed some weaving movements with her left hand. A sudden clap of thunder startled her. The string of beads fell on the ledge below. She looked helplessly after it and continued her pantomime. The choir sang on and began a concerted movement. They flanked the Spring and formed up in set groups, kneeling and pointing out the green girl to the audience. Miss Cost propelled Wally towards the ledge. It was the dénouement.

The applause had scarcely died away when Miss Emily rose and approached the microphone.

" Mr. Mayor," she began, " ladies and gentlemen. I wish to protest——"

Major Barrimore had risen to his feet with an oath. At the same moment there was a blinding flash of lightning, followed immediately by a stentorian thunder-clap, a deluge of rain, and a shout of uncontrollable laughter from Dr. Maine.

II

The stampede was immediate. Crowds poured out of the enclosure and down to the foreshore. The launch filled. There were clamorous shouts for dinghies. The younger element ran round the point of the bay, made for the hotel causeway and splashed precariously across it. The Boy-and-Lobster contingent took to the path that led directly to the hotel. It was a holocaust. Miss Cost, wildly at large among her drenched and disorganised troupe, was heard to scream : "It's a judgment." Unmindful they swept past her. She was deserted. Her velvet bodice leaked green dye into her blouse. Green rivulets ran down her arms. Her hair was plastered like seaweed against her face. The text of the play fell from her hand, and lay, disregarded, in the mud.

Mrs. Barrimore held a brief exchange with Miss Emily who had opened her umbrella and from beneath it, steadily regarded Superintendent Coombe's late companion. She waved her hostess aside. Mrs. Barrimore took to her heels, followed by her husband and Dr. Maine. She outdistanced them, fled the enclosure, ran like a gazelle along the path to The Boy-and-Lobster and disappeared.

Major Barrimore and Dr. Maine, who was still laughing, made after her. They were confronted at the gate by Miss Cost.

It was an ugly and grotesque encounter. She pushed her wet face towards them and her jaw trembled as if she had a rigor. She looked from one to the other. " *You,*" she stuttered. " *You !* Both of you. Animals. Now wait ! Now, wait and see ! "

Major Barrimore said : " Look here, Elspeth," and Dr. Maine said : " My dear Miss Cost ! "

She broke into uncertain laughter and mouthed at them. " Oh, for God's sake ! " Barrimore said. She whispered something and he turned on his heel and left her. He was scarlet in the face.

" Miss Cost," Maine said, " you'd better go home. You're overwrought and I'm sorry if I——"

" You *will* be sorry," she said. " All of you. Mark my words."

He hesitated for a moment. She made an uncouth and ridiculous gesture and he, too, left her.

Miss Emily was motionless under her umbrella. Miss Cost

made for her, stumbling on the muddy slope. "Wicked, *wicked* woman," she said. "You will be punished."

"My poor creature——" Miss Emily began but Miss Cost screamed at her, turned aside and floundered down the path. She passed through the gates into Wally's Way and after a precipitant descent, was lost among those of her adherents who were clustered round the jetty.

Jenny and Patrick had set off after the others but, on looking back, saw Miss Emily alone in the downpour. At Jenny's suggestion they returned and she approached Miss Emily. "Miss Pride," she said. "Let's go back. Come with us. You'll be drenched."

"Thank you, dear child, I have my umbrella," said Miss Emily. She was still staring across the Spring at Superintendent Coombe's late companion who now advanced towards her. "Please don't wait for me," she said. "I have an escort."

Jenny hesitated. "I insist," said Miss Emily impatiently. Patrick took Jenny's arm. "Come on," he said. "We're not needed." They hunched their shoulders and ran like hares.

Alleyn crossed the enclosure. "Good evening, Miss Emily," he said. "Shall we go?"

On the way to The Boy-and-Lobster he held her umbrella over her. "I am sufficiently protected by my waterproof and overshoes," she said. "The forecast was for rain. Pray, let us share the umbrella." She took his arm. The path was now deserted.

They hardly spoke. Rain drummed down on the umbrella in a pentateuchal deluge. Earth and sea were loud with its onslaught and the hillside smelt of devouring grass and soil. Miss Emily, in her goloshes, was insecure. Alleyn closed his hand round her thin old arm and was filled with a sort of infuriated pity.

The entrance to the hotel was deserted except for the man

on duty who stared curiously at them. Miss Emily drew her key from her reticule. "I prefer," she said loudly, "to retain possession. Will you come up? I have a so-called suite."

She left Alleyn in her sitting-room with injunctions to turn on the heater and dry himself while she retired to change.

He looked about him. The plastic Green Lady, still wearing its infamous legend round its neck, had been placed defiantly in a glass fronted wall cupboard. He looked closely at it without touching it. A stack of London telephone directories stood near the instrument on the writing desk.

Miss Emily called from her bedroom. "You will find cognac and soda-water in the small cupboard. Help yourself, I beg you. And me. Cognac, *simplement*." She sounded quite gay. Alleyn poured two double brandies.

"Don't wait for me," Miss Emily shouted. "Drink at once. Remove and dry your shoes. Have you engaged the heater?"

He did everything she commanded and felt that he was putting himself at a disadvantage.

When Miss Emily reappeared, having changed her skirt, shoes and stockings, she looked both complacent and stimulated. It occurred to Alleyn that she got a sort of respectable kick out of entertaining him so dashingly in her suite. She sat in an armchair and jauntily accepted her brandy.

"First of all, you must understand that I am extremely angry with you," she said. She was almost coquettish. "Ah—ah-ah! And now you have the self-conscious air?" She shook her finger at him.

"I may look sheepish," he rejoined, "but I assure you I'm in a devil of a temper. You are outrageous, Miss Emily."

"When did you leave and how is your dear Troy?"

" At seven o'clock this morning and my dear Troy is furious."

" Ah, no ! " She leaned forward and tapped his hand. " You should not have come, my friend. I am perfectly able to look after myself. It was kind but it was not necessary."

" What were you going to say to that crowd if you hadn't been cut off by a cloud-burst ? No, don't tell me. I know. You must be mad, Miss Emily."

" On the contrary, I assure you. And why have you come, Roderique ? As you see, I have taken no harm."

" I want to know, among other matters, the full story of that object over there. The obscene woman with the label."

Miss Emily gave him a lively account of it.

" And where, precisely, was it planted ? "

" Behind one of the London telephone directories which had been placed on its edge, supported by the others."

" And you knocked the book over while you were speaking to me ? "

" That is correct. Revealing the figurine."

He was silent for some time. " And you were frightened," Alleyn said at last.

" It was a shock. I may have been disconcerted. It was too childish a trick to alarm me for more than a moment."

" Do you mind if I take possession of this object ? "

" Not at all."

" Has anybody but you touched it, do you know ? "

" I think not. Excepting of course the culprit."

He wrapped it carefully, first in a sheet of writing-paper from the desk and then in his handkerchief. He put it in his pocket.

" Well," he said. " Let's see what we can make of all this nonsense."

He took her through the events of the last five days and found her account tallied with Superintendent Coombe's. When she had finished he got up and stood over her.

" Now look," he said. " None of these events can be dismissed as childish. The stones might have caused a serious injury. The trip-wire almost certainly would have done so. The first threats that you got in London have been followed up. You've had two other warnings—the figurine and the telephone call. They will be followed up, too. Coombe tells me you suspect Miss Cost. Why ? "

" I recognised her voice. You know my ear for the speaking voice, I think."

" Yes."

" On Monday, I interviewed her in her shop. She was in an extremity of anger. This brought on an attack of asthma and that in its turn added to her chagrin."

Alleyn asked her if she thought Miss Cost had dogged her to the steps, swarmed up the hill and thrown stones at her, asthma notwithstanding.

" No," said Miss Emily coolly. " I think that unfortunate child threw the stones. I encountered him after I had left the shop and again outside the hotel. I have no doubt he did it : possibly at his father's instigation who was incited in the first instance, I daresay, by that ass Cost. The woman is a fool and a fanatic. She is also, I think, a little mad. You saw how she comported herself after that fiasco."

" Yes, I did. All right. Now, I want your solemn promise that on no condition will you leave your rooms again this evening. You are to dine and breakfast up here. I shall call for you at ten o'clock and I shall drive you back to London or, if you prefer it, put you on the train. There are no two ways about it, Miss Emily. That is what you will do."

" I *will not* be cowed by these threats. I *will not*."

" Then I shall be obliged to take you into protective

custody and you won't much fancy that, I promise you," Alleyn said and hoped it sounded convincing.

Miss Emily's eyes filled with angry tears.

" Roderique—to me ? To your old *institutrice* ? "

" Yes, Miss Emily." He bent down and gave her a kiss : the first he had ever ventured upon. "To my old *institutrice*," he said. " I shall set a great strapping policewoman over you and if that doesn't answer, I shall lock you up, Miss Emily."

Miss Emily dabbed her eyes.

" Very well," she said. " I don't believe you, of course, but very well."

Alleyn put on his shoes.

" Where are you staying ? " she asked.

" Coombe's giving me a bed. The pubs are full. I must go. It's seven o'clock."

" You will dine with me, perhaps ? "

"I don't think——" He stopped. "On second thoughts," he said, " I should be delighted. Thank you *very* much."

" Are you going to ' taste ' my wine ? " she asked, ironically.

" And I might do that, too," he said.

III

He left her at nine.

She had settled for the eleven o'clock train from Dunlowman in the morning. He had arranged to book a seat for her and drive her to the station. He had also telephoned her *bonne-à-tout-faire* as she called the pugnacious Cockney who, in spite of Miss Emily's newly acquired riches, served her still. He saw that the outside doors to her apartment could be locked and made certain that, on his departure, she would lock them. He bade her good night and went downstairs, wondering how big a fuss he might be making over nothing in particular.

Major Barrimore was in the office smelling very strongly of whisky, smoking a large cigar and poring uncertainly over a copy of *The Racing Supplement*. Alleyn approached him.

" Major Barrimore ? Miss Pride has asked me to tell you she will be leaving at ten in the morning and would like coffee and toast in her room at eight o'clock."

" Would she, by God ! " said the Major thickly and appeared to pull himself together. " Sorry," he said. " Yes, of course. I'll lay it on."

" Thank you."

Alleyn had turned away when the Major, slurring his words a little but evidently under a tight rein, said : "Afraid the lady hasn't altogether enjoyed her visit."

" No ? "

" No. Afraid not. But if she's been——" he swayed very slightly and leant on the desk. " Hope she hasn't been giving us a bad chit," he said. " Dunno who I'm talking to, acourse. Have the advantage of me, there."

" I'm a police officer," Alleyn said. " Superintendent Alleyn, C.I.D."

" Good God ! She's called in the Yard ! "

" No. I'm an old friend of Miss Pride's. The visit was unofficial."

Major Barrimore leant across the desk with an uncertain leer. " I say," he said, " what is all this ? You're no damned copper, old boy. You can't gemme t' b'lieve that. I know my drill. 'F y'ask me—more like a bloody guardee. What ? "

Patrick and Jenny came into the hall from the old house.

" I think I'll just run up, first, and see how Miss Pride is," Jenny was saying.

" Must you ? "

" She's all right," Major Barrimore said loudly. " She's

under police protection. Ask this man. M'—I—introduce Miss Jenny Williams and my step-son ? Superintendent, or so he tells me. . . . Sorry, I forget your name, sir."

"Alleyn."

They murmured at each other. Patrick said to his step-father : "I'll take the office if you'd like to knock off."

"The clerk fellah's on in ten minutes. What d'you mean ? I'm all right."

"Yes, of course."

Alleyn said to Jenny : "Miss Pride was thinking about a bath and bed when I left her."

"She's going. In the morning," said the Major, and laughed.

"Going !" Jenny and Patrick exclaimed together. "Miss Pride !"

"Yes," Alleyn said. "It seems a sensible move. I wonder if you can tell me whether the causeway's negotiable and if not, whether there'll be a ferryman on tap."

"It'll be negotiable," Patrick said, "but not very pleasant. Jenny and I are going down. We'll row you across, sir. It won't take ten minutes."

"That's very civil of you. Are you sure ?"

"Perfectly. We'd thought of taking the boat out anyway."

"Then in that case——" Alleyn turned to Major Barri-more. "Good night, sir."

"G'night," he said. When they had moved away he called after Alleyn. "If you put her up to it, you've done us a damn' good turn. Have a drink on it, won't you ?"

"Thank you very much but I really must be off. Good night."

They went out of doors. The sky had cleared and was alive with stars. The air was rain-washed and fresh.

As they walked down the steps Patrick said abruptly : "I'm afraid my step-father was not exactly in his best form."

101

" No doubt he's been rather highly tried."

" No doubt," said Patrick shortly.

" You were at the Festival, weren't you ? " Jenny asked.
" With Mr. Coombe ? "

" I was, yes."

" You don't have to be polite about it," Patrick said.
" The burning question is whether it was as funny as it was
embarrassing. I can't really make up my mind."

" I suppose it depends upon how far one's sympathies
were engaged."

They had reached the half-way bench. Alleyn halted for a
moment and glanced up the dark slope above it.

" Yes," Jenny said. " That was where she was."

" You arrived on the scene, I think, didn't you ? Miss
Emily said you were a great help. What *did* happen exactly?"

Jenny told him how she had come down the steps, heard
the patter of stones, Miss Emily's cry, and a high-pitched
laugh. She described how she found Miss Emily with the
cut on her neck. " Very much shaken," said Jenny, " but
full of fight."

" A high-pitched laugh ? " Alleyn repeated.

" Well, really more of a sort of squawk like——" Jenny
stopped short. " Just an odd sort of noise," she said.

" Like Wally Trehern, for instance ? "

" Why do you say that ? "

" He gave a sort of squawk this afternoon when that
regrettable green girl appeared."

" Did he ? "

" You taught him at school, didn't you ? "

" How very well informed you are, Mr. Alleyn," said
Patrick airily.

" Coombe happened to mention it."

" Look," Jenny said, " your visit isn't really unofficial,
is it ? "

" To tell you the truth," Alleyn said, " I'm damned if I know. Shall we move on ? "

On the way across, Jenny said she supposed Alleyn must be worried on Miss Pride's account and he rejoined cheerfully that he was worried to hell. After all, he said, one didn't exactly relish one's favourite old girl being used as a cockshy. Patrick, involuntarily, it seemed, said that she really had rather turned herself into one, hadn't she ? " Sitting on her ledge under that umbrella, you know, and admonishing the pilgrims. It made everyone feel so shy."

" *Did* she admonish them ? "

" Well, I understand she said she hoped they'd enjoy a recovery but they oughtn't to build on it. They found it very off-putting."

Jenny said : " Will an effort be made to discover who's behind all these tricks ? "

" That's entirely over to Superintendent Coombe."

" Matter of protocol ? " Patrick suggested.

" Exactly."

The dinghy slid into deep shadow and bumped softly against the jetty. " Well," Alleyn said. " I'm very much obliged to you both. Good night."

" I can't imagine why it should be so," Jenny said, " but Miss Pride's rather turned into my favourite old girl, too."

" Isn't it extraordinary ? She doesn't present any of the classic features. She is not faded or pretty nor as far as I've noticed does she smell of lavender. She's by no means gentle or sweet, and doesn't exude salty common-sense. She is, without a shadow of doubt, a pig-headed, arrogant old thing." He rose and steadied himself by the jetty steps. " Do you subscribe to the Wally-gingered-up-by-Miss Cost theory ? " he asked.

" It's as good as any other," Patrick said. " I suppose."

" There's only one thing against it," Jenny said. " I

don't believe Wally would ever deliberately hurt anyone. And he's a *very* bad shot."

Alleyn stepped ashore.

" I expect," said Patrick's voice quietly from the shadowed boat, " you'll be relieved to get her away."

" Yes," he said. " I shall. Good night."

As he walked down the jetty he heard the dip of Patrick's oars and the diminishing murmur of their voices.

He found Superintendent Coombe's cottage and his host waiting for him. They had a glass of beer and a talk and turned in. Alleyn thought he would telephone his wife in the morning and went fast to sleep.

IV

He was wakened at seven by a downpour of rain. He got up, bathed and found breakfast in preparation. Mr. Coombe, a widower, did for himself.

" Bit of a storm again," he said, " but it's clearing fast. You'll have a pleasant run."

He went into his kitchen from whence, presently, the splendid smell of panfrying bacon arose. Alleyn stood at the parlour window and looked down on a deserted front, gleaming mud-flats and the exposed spine of the causeway.

" Nobody about," he said.

" It's clearing," Coombe's voice said above the sizzle of bacon. " The local people think the weather's apt to change at low tide. Nothing in it."

" It's flat out, now."

" Yes," Coombe said. " Dead water."

And by the time breakfast was over, so was the rain. Alleyn rang up his wife and said he'd be back for dinner. He put his suitcase in his car and as it was still too early to collect Miss Emily, decided, it being low tide, to walk over the causeway up Wally's Way and thence by footpath to the hotel. He had an inclination to visit the Spring again. Coombe, who intended to fish, said he'd come as far as the jetty. Alleyn drove there and left him with the car. The return trip with Miss Emily and her luggage, would be by water.

When he reached the Island, the bell for nine o'clock service was ringing in Mr. Carstairs's church, back on the mainland.

Wally's Way was littered with evidence of yesterday's crowds: ice-cream wrappers, cigarette cartons and an occasional bottle. He wondered whose job it was to clear up.

It was a steep pull but he took it at a fair clip and the bell was still ringing when he reached the top.

He walked towards the enclosure and looked through the netting at the Spring.

On the shelf above it, open, and lying on its side was a large black umbrella.

It was one of those moments without time that strike at body and mind together with a single blow. He looked at the welling pool below the shelf. A black shape, half-inflated, pulsed and moved with the action of the spring. Its wet surface glittered in the sun.

The bell had stopped and a lark sang furiously overhead.

He had to get through the turnstile.

The slot machine was enclosed in a wire cage, with a padlock which was open. He had no disc.

For a second or two, he thought of using a rock, if he could find one, or hurling his weight against the netted door, but he looked at the slot mechanism and with fingers that might have been handling ice, searched his pockets. A half-crown? No. A florin? As he pushed it down, he saw a printed notice that had been tied to the netting: "Warning," it was headed, and was signed: "Emily Pride." The florin

jammed. He picked up a stone, hit it home and wrenched at
the handle. There was a click and he was through and running to the Spring.

She was lying face-down in the pool, only a few inches
below the water, her head almost at the lip of the water-fall.

Her sparse hair, swept forward, rippled and eddied in
the stream. The gash in her scalp had stopped bleeding and
gaped flaccidly.

Before he had moved the body over on its back he knew
whose face would be upturned towards his own. It was
Elspeth Cost's.

5. *Holiday Task*

When he had made certain, beyond all shadow of a doubt, that there was nothing to be done, he ran out of the enclosure and a few yards along the footpath. Down below, on the far side of the causeway he saw Coombe, in his shirt-sleeves, with his pipe in his mouth, fishing off the end of the jetty. He looked up, saw Alleyn, waved and then straightened. Alleyn beckoned urgently and signalled that they would meet at the top of the hotel steps. Coombe, seeing him run, himself broke into a lope, back down the jetty and across the causeway. He was breathing hard when he got to the top of the steps. When Alleyn had told him, he swore incredulously.

" I'll go into the hotel and get one of those bloody discs," Alleyn said. " I had to lock the gate, of course. And I'll have to get a message to Miss Pride. I'll catch you up. Who's your div. surgeon ? "

" Maine."

" Right."

There was no one in the office. He went in, tried the drawers, found the right one, and helped himself to half a dozen discs. He looked at the switchboard, plugged in the connection and lifted the receiver. He noticed with a kind of astonishment that his hand was unsteady. It seemed an eternity before Miss Emily answered.

He said : " Miss Emily ? Roderick. I'm terribly sorry but there's been an accident and I'm wanted here. It's serious. Will it be a great bore if we delay your leaving ? I'll come back later and explain."

" By all means," Miss Emily's voice said crisply. " I shall adjust. Don't disarrange yourself on my account ! "

" You admirable woman," he said and hung up.

He had just got back on the lawful side of the desk when the hall-porter appeared, wiping his mouth. Alleyn said : " Can you get Dr. Maine quickly ? There's been an accident. D'you know his number ? "

The porter consulted a list and, staring at Alleyn, dialled it.

" What is it, then ? " he asked. " Accident ? Dearrr, dearr ! "

While he waited for the call to come through, Alleyn saw that a notice, similar to the one that had been tied to the enclosure, was now displayed in the letter rack. " Warning." And signed " Emily Pride." He had started to read it when the telephone quacked. The porter established the connection and handed him the receiver.

Alleyn said : " Dr. Maine ? Speaking? This is a police call. I'm ringing for Superintendent Coombe. Superintendent Alleyn. There's been a serious accident at the Spring. Can you come at once ? "

" At the *Spring* ? "

" Yes. You'll need an ambulance."

" What is it ? "

" Asphyxia following cranial injury."

" Fatal ? "

" Yes."

" I'll be there."

" Thank you."

He hung up. The porter was agog. Alleyn produced a ten-shilling note. " Look here," he said. " can you keep

108

quiet about this ? I don't want people to collect. Be a good chap, will you, and get Sergeant Pender on the telephone. Ask him to come to the Spring. Say the message is from Mr. Coombe. Will you do that ? And don't talk."

He slid the note across the desk and left.

As he returned by the footpath, he saw a car drive along the foreshore to the causeway. A man with a black bag in his hand got out.

Coombe, waiting by the gate, was peering into the enclosure.

" I may have broken the slot-machine," Alleyn said. But it worked and they went through.

He had dragged the body on to the verge of the pool and masked it, as well as he could, by the open umbrella.

Coombe said : " Be damned, when I saw that brolly, if I didn't think I'd misheard you and it was the other old— Miss Pride."

" I know."

" How long ago, d'you reckon ? "

" I should have thought about an hour. We'll see what the doctor thinks. He's on his way. Look at this, Coombe."

The neck was rigid. He had to raise the body by the shoulders before exposing the back of the head.

" Well, well," said Coombe. " Just fancy that, now. Knocked out, fell forward into the pool and drowned. That the story ? "

" Looks like it, doesn't it ? And, see here."

Alleyn lifted a fold of the dripping skirt. He exposed Miss Cost's right hand, bleached and wrinkled. It was rigidly clenched about a long string of glittering beads.

" Cor ! " said Coombe.

" The place is one solid welter of footprints but I think you can pick hers : leading up to the shelf. The girl dropped the beads yesterday from above, I remember. They dangled over this ledge, half in the pool. In the stampede nobody rescued them."

" And she came back ? To fetch them ? "

" It's a possibility, wouldn't you think ? There's her handbag on the shelf."

Coombe opened it. " Prayer-book and purse," he said.

" When's the first service ? "

" Seven, I think."

" There's another at nine. She was either going to church or had been there. That puts it at somewhere before seven for the first service. Or round about eight-forty-five if she had attended it or was going to the later one. When did it stop raining ? About eight-thirty, I think. If those are her prints, they've been rained into and she'd got her umbrella open. Take a look at it."

There was a ragged split in the wet cover which was old and partly perished. Alleyn displayed the inside. It was stained round the split and not with rainwater. He pointed a long finger. " That's one of her hairs," he said. " There was a piece of rock in the pool. I fished it out and left it on the ledge. It looked as if it hadn't been there long and I think you'll find it fits."

He fetched it and put it down by the body. " Any visual traces have been washed away," he said. " You'll want to keep these exhibits intact, won't you ? "

" You bet I will," said Coombe.

There was a sound of footsteps and a metallic rattle. They turned and saw Dr. Maine letting himself in at the turnstile. Coombe went down to meet him.

" What's it all about ? " he asked. " 'Morning, Coombe."

" See for yourself, Doctor."

They joined Alleyn who was introduced. " Mr. Alleyn made the discovery," said Coombe and added : " Rather a coincidence."

110

Dr. Maine, looking startled, said : " Very much so."

Alleyn said : " I'm on a visit. Quite unofficial. Coombe's your man."

" I wondered if you'd been produced out of a hat," said Dr. Maine. He looked towards the Spring. The umbrella, still open, masked the upper part of the body. " Good God!" he ejaculated. " So it *has* happened after all ! "

Coombe caught Alleyn's eye and said nothing. He moved quickly to the body and exposed the face. Dr. Maine stood stock-still. " *Cost* ! " he said. " Old *Cost* ! Never ! "

" That's right, Doctor."

Dr. Maine wasted no more words. He made his examination. Miss Cost's eyes were half-open and so was her mouth. There were flecks of foam about the lips and the tongue was clenched between the teeth. Alleyn had never become completely accustomed to murder. This grotesque shell, seconds before its destruction, had been the proper and appropriate expression of a living woman. Whether here, singly, or multiplied to the monstrous litter of a battlefield, or strewn idiotically about the wake of a nuclear explosion, or dangling with a white cap over a cyanosed, tongue-protruding mask ; the destruction of one human being by another was the unique offence. It was the final outrage.

Dr. Maine lowered the stiffened body on its back. He looked up at Alleyn. " Where was she ? "

" Face down and half-submerged. I got her out in case there was a chance but obviously there was none."

" Any sign of rigor ? "

" Yes."

" It's well on its way now," said Dr. Maine.

" There's the back of the head, Doctor," said Coombe. " There's that too."

Dr. Maine turned the body and looked closely at the head. " Where's the instrument ? " he said. " Found it ? "

Alleyn said : " I think so."

Dr. Maine glanced at him. " May I see it ? "

Alleyn gave it to him. It was an irregular jagged piece of rock about the size of a pineapple. Dr. Maine turned it in his hands and stooped over the head. " Fits," he said.

" What's the verdict then, Doctor ? " Coombe asked.

" There'll have to be a p.m. of course. On the face of it : stunned and drowned." He looked at Alleyn. " Or, as you would say : ' asphyxia following cranial injury '."

" I was attempting to fox the hotel porter."

" I see. Good idea."

" And when would it have taken place ? " Coombe insisted.

" Again, you'll have to wait before you get a definite answer to that one. Not less than an hour ago, I'd have thought. Possibly much longer."

He stood up and wiped his hands on his handkerchief. " Do you know," he said, " I saw her. I saw her : it must have been about seven o'clock. Outside the church with Mrs. Carstairs. She was going in to early service. I'd got a confinement on the Island and was walking down to the foreshore. Good Lord ! " said Dr. Maine. " I saw her."

" That's a help, Doctor," said Coombe. " We were wondering about church. Now, that means she couldn't have got over here until eight at the earliest, wouldn't you say ? "

" I should say so. Certainly. Rather later if anything."

" And Mr. Alleyn found her at nine. I suppose you didn't notice anyone about the cottages or anything of the sort, Doctor ? "

" Not a soul. It was pouring heavens-hard. Wait a moment though."

" Yes ? "

He turned to Alleyn. " I've got my own launch and jetty,

and there's another jetty straight opposite on the foreshore by the cottages. I took the launch across. Well, the baby being duly delivered, I returned by the same means and I do remember that when I'd started up the engine and cast off, I saw that fantastic kid—Wally Trehern—dodging about on the road up to the Spring."

" Did you watch him ? " Coombe asked.

" Good lord, no. I turned the launch and had my back to the Island."

" When would that be, now, Doctor ? "

" The child was born at 7.30. Soon after that."

" Yes. Well. Thanks," said Coombe, glancing rather self-consciously at Alleyn. " Now : any ideas about *how* it happened ?"

" On what's before us, I'd say that if this bit of rock *is* the instrument, it struck the head from above. Wait a minute."

He climbed to the higher level above the shelf and Coombe followed him.

Alleyn was keeping a tight rein on himself. It was Coombe's case and Alleyn was a sort of accident on the scene. He thought of Patrick Ferrier's ironical remark : " Matter of protocol " and silently watched the two men as they scrambled up through bracken to the top level.

Dr. Maine said : " There are rocks lying about up here. And yes—— But this is your pigeon, Coombe. You'd better take a look."

Coombe joined him.

" There's where it came from," said Maine, " behind the boulder. You can see where it was prized up."

Coombe at last said, " We'd better keep off the area, Doctor." He looked down at Alleyn : " It's clear enough."

" Any prints ? "

" A real mess. People from above must have swarmed all over it when the rain came. Pity."

"Yes," Alleyn said. "Pity."

The other two men came down.

"Well," Dr. Maine said. "That's that. The ambulance should be here by now. Glad you suggested it. We'll have to get her across. How's the tide ?" He went through the exit gates and along the footpath to a point from where he could see the causeway.

Alleyn said to Coombe : "I asked the porter to get on to Pender and say you'd want him. I hope that was in order."

"Thanks very much."

"I suppose you'll need a statement from me, won't you ?"

Coombe scraped his jaw. "Sounds silly, doesn't it ?" he said. "Well, yes, I suppose I will." He had been looking sideways at Alleyn, off and on, for some time.

"Look," he said abruptly. "There's one thing that's pretty obvious about this affair, isn't there ? Here's a case where a Yard man with a top reputation is first on the scene and you might say, starts up the investigation. Look at it what way you like, it'd be pretty silly if I just said : ' thanks, chum ' and let it go at that. Wouldn't it now ? I don't mind admitting I felt it was silly, just now, with you standing by, tactful as you please and leaving it all to me."

"Absolute rot," Alleyn said. "Come off it."

"No, I mean it. And, anyway," Coombe added on a different note, "I haven't got the staff." It was a familiar plaint.

"My dear chap," Alleyn said, " I'm meant to be on what's laughingly called a holiday. Take a statement for pity's sake, and let me off. I'll remove Miss Pride and leave you with a fair field. You'll do well. ' Coombe's Big Case '." He knew, of course, that this would be no good.

"You'll remove Miss Pride, eh ?" said Coombe. "And what say Miss Pride's the key figure, still ? *You* know what

114

I'm driving at. It's sticking out a mile. Say I'm hiding up there behind that boulder. Say I hear someone directly below and take a look-see. Say I see the top of an open umbrella and a pair of female feet, which is what I've been waiting for. Who do I reckon's under that umbrella ? Not Miss Elspeth Cost. Not her. O, dear me no ! " said Coombe in a sort of gloomy triumph. " I say : ' That's the job,' and I bloody well let fly ! But I bring down the wrong bird. I get——"

" All right, all right," Alleyn said exasperated by the long build-up. " And you say : ' Absurd mistake. Silly old me ! *I* thought you were Miss Emily Pride '."

II

The upshot, as he very well knew it would be, was an understanding that Coombe would get in touch with his Chief Constable and then with the Yard.

Coombe insisted on telling Dr. Maine that he hoped Alleyn would take charge of the case. The ambulance men arrived with Pender and for the second time in twenty-four hours, Miss Cost went in procession along Wally's Way.

Alleyn and Coombe stayed behind to look over the territory again. Coombe had a spring-tape in his pocket and they took preliminary measurements and decided to get the areas covered in case of rain. He showed Alleyn where the trip-wire had been laid : through dense bracken on the way up to the shelf. Pender had caught a glint of it in the sunshine and had been sharp enough to investigate.

They completed their arrangements. The handbag, the string of beads and the umbrella were to be dropped at the police-station by Pender who was then to return with extra help if he could get it. The piece of rock would be sent with

the body to the nearest mortuary which was at Dunlowman.
When they were outside the gates, Alleyn drew Coombe's
attention to the new notice, tied securely to the wire-netting.
" Did you see this ? "
It had been printed by a London firm.

WARNING

*Notice is given that the owner of this property wishes to
disassociate herself from any claims that have been made,
in any manner whatsoever, for the curative properties of
the spring. She gives further notice that the present enclosure is to be removed. Any proceedings of any nature
whatsoever that are designed to publicise the above claims
will be discontinued. The property will be restored, as far
as possible, to conditions that obtained two years ago and
steps will be taken to maintain it in a decent and orderly
condition.*

(Signed) *Emily Pride*

" When the hell was this put up ? " Coombe ejaculated.
" It wasn't there yesterday. There'd have been no end of a
taking-on."
" Perhaps this morning. It's been rained on. More than
that. It's muddied. As if it had lain face-downwards on the
ground. Look. Glove marks. No finger-prints, though."
" P'raps she dropped it."
" Perhaps," Alleyn said. " There's another on display in
the hotel letter-rack. It wasn't there last night."
" Put them there herself ? Miss Pride ? "
" I'm afraid so."
" There you are ! " Coombe said excitedly. " She came
along the footpath. Somebody spotted her, streaked up
Wally's Way, got in ahead and hid behind the boulder.. She
hung up her notice and went back to the pub. Miss Cost

arrives by the other route, goes in, picks up her beads and Bob's your uncle."

" Is he, though ? " Alleyn muttered, more to himself than to Coombe. " She promised me she wouldn't leave the pub. I'll have to talk to Miss Emily." He looked at Coombe. " This is going to be tricky," he said. " If your theory's the right one, and at this stage it looks healthy enough, do we assume that the stone-chucker, wire-stretcher, composite letter-writer, dumper of green lady and telephonist are one and the same person and that this person is also the murderer of Miss Cost ? "

" That's what I reckon. I know you oughtn't to get stuck on a theory. I know that. But unless we find something that cuts dead across it——"

" You'll find that all right," Alleyn said. " Miss Pride, you may remember, is convinced that the ringer-up was Miss Cost."

Coombe thought this over and then said, well, all right, he knew that, but Miss Pride might be mistaken. Alleyn said Miss Pride had as sharp a perception for the human voice as was possible for the human ear. " She's an expert," he said. " If I wanted an expert witness in phonetics I'd put Miss Pride in the box."

" Well, all right, if you tell me so. So where does that get us ? Does she reckon Miss Cost was behind *all* the attacks ? "

" I think so."

" Conspiracy, like ? "

" Sort of."

Coombe stared ahead of him for a moment or two. " So where does *that* get us ? " he repeated.

" For my part," Alleyn said, " it gets me rather quicker than I fancy, to Wally Trehern and his papa."

Coombe said with some satisfaction that this, at any rate,

made sense. If Wally had been gingered up to make the attacks, who more likely than Wally to mistake Miss Cost for Miss Pride and drop the rock on the umbrella?

" Could Wally rig a trip-wire? You said it was a workman-like job."

" His old man could," said Coombe.

" Which certainly makes sense. What about this pad-locked cage over the slot-machine? Is it ever used? "

Coombe made an exasperated noise. " That was her do-ing." he said. " She used to make a great to-do about courting couples. Very hot, she used to get : always lodging complaints and saying we ought to do something about it. Disgusting. Desecration and all that. Well, what could I do? Put Pender on the job all day and half the night, dodging about the rocks? It couldn't be avoided and I told her so. We put this cage over to pacify her."

" Is it never locked? "

" It's supposed to be operated by the hotel at eight o'clock, morning and evening. In the summer that is. But a lot of their customers like to stroll along to the Spring of a sum-mer's evening. Accordingly, it is not kept up very con-sistently."

" We'd better get the key. I'll fix it now," Alleyn said and snapped the padlock. It was on a short length of chain : not long enough, he noticed, to admit a hand into the cage.

On the way back to the hotel they planned out the rest of the day. Coombe would ring the Yard from the station. Alleyn in the meantime would start inquiries at the hotel. They would meet in an hour's time. It was now half past ten.

They had rounded the first spur along the path and come up with an overhanging outcrop of rock, when Alleyn stopped.

118

" Half a minute," he said.

" What's up ? "

Alleyn moved to the edge of the path and stooped. He picked something up and walked gingerly round behind the rock. " Come over here," he called. " Keep wide of those prints, though."

Coombe looked down and then followed him.

" There's a bit of shelter here," Alleyn said. " Look."

The footprints were well defined on the soft ground, and, in the lee of the outcrop, fairly dry. " Good, well-made boots," he said. " And I don't think the owner was here so very long ago. Here's where he waited and there, a little gift for the industrious officer, Coombe, is his cigar ash." He opened his hand. A scarlet paper ring lay on the palm. " Very good make," he said. " The Major smokes them. Sells them, too, no doubt, so what have you ? Come on."

They continued on their way.

As soon as Alleyn went into The Boy-and-Lobster he realised that wind of the catastrophe was abroad. People stood about in groups with a covert, anxious air. The porter saw him and came forward.

" I'm very sorry, sir. It be'ant none of my doing. I kept it close as a trap. But the ambulance was seen and the stretcher party and there you are. I said I supposed it was somebody took ill at the cottages but there was Sergeant Pender, sir, and us—I mean, they—be all wondering why it's a police matter."

Alleyn said ambiguously that he understood. " It'd be a good idea," he suggested, " if you put up a notice that the Spring will be closed to-day."

" The Major'll have to be axed about that, sir."

" Very well. Where is he ? "

" He'll be in the old house, sir. He be'ant showed up round hereabouts."

119

" I'll find him. Would you ring Miss Pride's rooms and say I hope to call on her within the next half-hour ? Mr. Alleyn."

He went out and in again by the old pub door. There was nobody to be seen but he heard voices in what he thought was probably the ex-bar-parlour and tapped on the door. It was opened by Patrick Ferrier.

" Hallo. Good morning, sir," said Patrick and then : " Something's wrong, isn't it ? "

" Yes," Alleyn said. " Very wrong. May I see your step-father ? "

" Well—yes, of course. Will you come in ? "

They were all seated in the parlour—Mrs. Barrimore, Jenny Williams and the Major who looked very much the worse for wear but assumed a convincing enough air of authority, and asked Alleyn what he could do for him.

Alleyn told them in a few words what had happened. Margaret Barrimore turned white and said nothing. Jenny and Patrick exclaimed together : " *Miss Cost !* Not Miss Cost ! "

Major Barrimore said incredulously : " Hit on the head and drowned ? Hit with what ? "

" A piece of rock, we think. From above."

" You mean it was an accident ? Brought down by the rains, what ? "

" I think not."

" Mr. Alleyn means she was murdered, Keith," said his wife. It was the first time she had spoken.

" Be damned to that ! " said the Major furiously. " Murdered ! Old Cost ! Why ? "

Patrick gave a sharp ejaculation. " Well ! " his step-father barked at him, " what's the matter with you ? "

" Did you say, sir, that she was under an umbrella ? "

120

" Yes," Alleyn said and thought : " This is going to be everybody's big inspiration."

He listened to Patrick as he presented the theory of mistaken identity.

Jenny said : " Does Miss Pride know ? "

" Not yet."

" It'll be a shock for her," said Jenny. " When will you tell her ? "

" As soon as I've left you." He looked round at them. " As a matter of form," he said. " I must ask you all where you were between half past seven and nine this morning. You will understand, won't you——"

" That it's purely a matter of routine," Patrick said. " Sorry. I couldn't help it. Yes, we do understand."

Mrs. Barrimore, Jenny and Patrick had got up and bathed in turn, round about eight o'clock. Mrs. Barrimore did not breakfast in the public dining-room but had toast and coffee by herself in the old kitchen which had been converted into a kitchen-living-room. Jenny had breakfasted at about nine and Patrick a few minutes later. After breakfast they had gone out of doors for a few minutes, surveyed the weather and decided to stay in and do a crossword together. Major Barrimore, it appeared, slept in and didn't get up until half past nine. He had two cups of coffee but no breakfast.

All these movements would have to be checked but at the moment there was more immediate business. Alleyn asked Major Barrimore to put up a notice that the Spring was closed.

He at once objected. Did Alleyn realise that there were people from all over the country—from overseas, even— who had come with the express purpose of visiting the Spring ? Did he realise that it was out of the question coolly to send them about their business : some of them, he'd have Alleyn know, in damned bad shape ?

121

Alleyn said that the Spring could probably be reopened in two day's time.

" *Two days*, my dear fellah, *two days* ! You don't know what you're talking about. I've got one draft going out to-night and a new detachment coming in to-morrow. Where the hell d'you suppose I'm going to put them ? Hey ? "

Alleyn said it was no doubt extremely inconvenient.

" Inconvenient ! It's outrageous."

" So," Alleyn suggested, " is murder."

" I've no proof of where you get your authority and I'll have you know I won't act without it. I refuse point blank," shouted the Major. " And categorically," he added as if that clenched the matter.

" The authority," Alleyn said, " is Scotland Yard and I'm very sorry, but you really can't refuse, you know. Either you decide to frame an announcement in your own words and get it out at once or I shall be obliged to issue a police notice. In any case that will be done at the Spring itself. It would be better, as I'm sure you must agree, if intending visitors were stopped here rather than at the gates."

" Of course it would," said Patrick impatiently.

" Yes, Keith. Please," said Mrs. Barrimore.

" When I want your suggestions, Margaret, I'll ask for them."

Patrick looked at his step-father with disgust. He said to Alleyn : " With respect, sir, I suggest that my mother and Jenny leave us to settle this point."

Mrs. Barrimore at once rose.

" May we ? " she asked. Jenny said : " Yes, please, may we ? "

" Yes, of course," said Alleyn, and to Patrick, " Let the court be cleared of ladies, by all means, Mr. Ferrier."

Patrick gave him a look and turned pink. All the same, Alleyn thought, there was an air of authority about him. The

122

wig was beginning to sprout and would probably become this young man rather well.

" Here. Wait a bit," said the Major. He spread his hands. " All right. *All right*," he said. " Have it your own way." He turned on his wife. " You're supposed to be good at this sort of rot, Margaret. Get out a notice and make it tactful. Say that owing to an accident in the area—no, my God, that sounds bloody awful. Owing to unforeseen circumstances—I don't know. *I* don't know. Say what you like. Talk to them. But get it *done*." Alleyn could cheerfully have knocked him down.

Mrs. Barrimore and Jenny went out.

Patrick, who had turned very white, said : " I think it will be much better if we help Mr. Alleyn as far as we're able. He wants to get on with his work, I'm sure. The facts will have to become known sooner or later. We'll do no good by adopting delaying tactics."

Major Barrimore contemplated his step-son with an un-attractive smile. " Charming ! " he said. " Now, I know exactly how I should behave, don't I ? " He appeared to undergo a change of mood and illustrated it by executing a wide gesture and then burying his face in his hands. " I'm sorry," he said and his voice was muffled. " Give me a moment."

Patrick turned his back and walked over to the window. The Major looked up. His eyes were bloodshot and his expression dolorous. " Bad show," he said. " Apologise. Not myself. Truth of the matter is, I got a bit plastered last night and this has hit me rather hard." He stood up and made a great business of straightening his shoulders and blowing his nose. " As you were," he said bravely. " Take my orders from you. What's the drill ? "

" Really, there isn't any at the moment," Alleyn said cheerfully. " If you can persuade your guests not to collect

123

round the enclosure or use the path to it we'll be very grateful. As soon as possible we'll get the approaches cordoned off and that will settle the matter, won't it ? And now, if you'll excuse me——"

He was about to go when Major Barrimore said : " Quite so. Talk to the troops, what ? Well—sooner the better." He put his hand on Alleyn's arm. " Sorry, old boy," he said gruffly. " Sure you understand."

He frowned, came to attention and marched out.

" Not true," Patrick said to the window. " Just not true."

Alleyn said : " Never mind," and left him.

When he re-entered the main buildings he found Major Barrimore the centre of a group of guests who showed every sign of disgruntlement tempered with avid curiosity. He was in tremendous form. " Now, I know you're going to be perfectly splendid about this," he was saying. " It's an awful disappointment to all of us and it calls for that good old British spirit of tolerance and understanding. Take it on the chin and look as if you liked it, what ? And you can take it from me——" He was still in full cry as Alleyn walked up the stairs and went to call on Miss Emily.

III

She was of course dressed for travel. Her luggage, as he saw through the open door, was ready. She was wearing her toque.

He told her what had happened. Miss Emily's sallow complexion whitened. She looked very fixedly at him and did not interrupt.

" Roderique," she said when he had finished. " This is my doing. I am responsible."

" Now, my dearest Miss Emily——"

124

" No. Please. Let me look squarely at the catastrophe. This foolish woman has been mistaken for me. There is no doubt in my mind at all. It declares itself. If I had obeyed the intention and not the mere letter of the undertaking I gave you, this would not have occurred."

" You went to the Spring this morning with your notice ?"

" Yes. I had, if you recollect, promised you not to leave my apartment again last night and to breakfast in my apartment this morning. A loophole presented itself."

In spite of Miss Emily's distress there was more than a hint of low cunning in the sidelong glance she gave him. " I went out," she said. " I placed my manifesto. I returned. I took my *petit dejeuner* in my room."

" When did you go out ? "

" At half past seven."

" It was raining ? "

" Heavily."

" Did you meet anybody ? Or see anybody ? "

" I met nobody," said Miss Emily. " I *saw* that wretched child. Walter Trehern. He was on the roadway that leads from the cottages up to the Spring. It has, I believe, been called——" She closed her eyes. " Wally's Way. He was half-way up the hill."

" Did he see you ? "

" He did. He uttered some sort of gibberish, gave an uncouth cry and waved his arms."

" Did he see you leave ? "

" I think not. When I had affixed my manifesto and faced about, he had already disappeared. Possibly he was hiding."

" And you didn't, of course, see Miss Cost."

" No ! "

" You didn't see her umbrella on your ledge above the pool ? As you were tying up your notice ? "

" Certainly not. I looked in that direction. It was not there."

" And that would be at about twenty to eight. It wouldn't, I think, take you more than ten minutes to walk there, from the pub ? "

" No. It was five minutes to eight when I re-entered the hotel."

" Did you drop the notice, face down in the mud ? "

" Certainly not. Why ? "

" It's no matter. Miss Emily : please try to remember if you saw anybody at all on the village side of the causeway or indeed anywhere. Any activity round the jetty, for instance, or on the bay or in the cottages ? Then, or at any time during your expedition."

" Certainly not."

" And on your return journey ? "

" The rain was driving in from the direction of the village. My umbrella was therefore inclined to meet it."

" Yes. I see."

A silence fell between them. Alleyn walked over to the window. It looked down on a small garden at the back of the old pub. As he stood there, absently staring, someone came into the garden from below. It was Mrs. Barrimore. She had a shallow basket over her arm and carried a pair of secateurs. She walked over to a clump of Michaelmas daisies and began to cut them, and her movement was so unco-ordinated and wild that the flowers fell to the ground. She made as if to retrieve them, dropped her secateurs and then the basket. Her hands went to her face and for a time she crouched there, quite motionless. She then rose and walked aimlessly and hurriedly about the paths, turning and returning as if the garden were a prison yard. Her fingers twisted together. They might have been encumbered with rings of which she tried fruitlessly to rid them.

126

" That," said Miss Emily's voice, " is a very unhappy creature."

She had joined Alleyn without attracting his notice.

" Why ? " he asked. " What's the matter with her ? "

" No doubt her animal of a husband ill-treats her."

" She's a beautiful woman," Alleyn said. He found himself quoting from—surely ?—an inappropriate source. " ' What is it she does now? Look how she rubs her hands ' " and Miss Emily replied at once : " ' It is an accustomed action with her, to seem thus washing her hands '."

" Good heavens ! " Alleyn ejaculated. " What do we think we're talking about ! "

Margaret Barrimore raised her head and instinctively they both drew back. Alleyn walked away from the window and then, with a glance at Miss Emily, turned back to it.

" She has controlled herself," said Miss Emily. " She is gathering her flowers. She is a woman of character, that one."

In a short time Mrs. Barrimore had filled her basket and returned to the house.

" Was she very friendly," he asked, " with Miss Cost ? "

" No. I believe, on the contrary, that there was a certain animosity. On Cost's part. Not, as far as I could see, upon Mrs. Barrimore's. Cost," said Miss Emily, " was, I judged, a spiteful woman. It is a not unusual phenomenon among spinsters of Cost's years and class. I am glad to say I was not conscious, at her age, of any such emotion. My sister Fanny, in her extravagant fashion, used to say I was devoid of the mating instinct. It may have been so."

" Were you never in love, Miss Emily ? "

" That," said Miss Emily, " is an entirely different matter."

" Is it ? "

" In any case it is neither here nor there. What do you

127

wish me to do, Roderique ? Am I to remain in this place ? "
She examined him. " I think you are disturbed upon this
point," she said.

Alleyn thought : " She's sharp enough to see I'm worried
about her and yet she can't see why. Or can she ? "

He said : " It's a difficult decision. If you go back to
London I'm afraid I shall be obliged to keep in touch and
bother you with questions and you may have to return.
There will be an inquest, of course. I don't know if you will
be called. You may be."

" With whom does the decision rest ? "

" Primarily, with the police."

" With you, then ? "

" Yes. It rests upon our report. Usually the witnesses
called at an inquest are the persons who found the body ;
me, in this instance, together with the investigating officers,
the pathologist and anyone who saw or spoke to the deceased
shortly before the event. Or anyone else who the police
believe can throw light on the circumstances. Do you think,"
he asked, " you can do that ? "

Miss Emily looked disconcerted. It was the first time,
he thought, that he had ever seen her at a loss.

" No," she said. " I think not."

" Miss Emily, do you believe that Wally Trehern came
back after you had left the enclosure, saw Miss Cost under
her umbrella, crept up to the boulder by a roundabout way
(there's plenty of cover) and threw down the rock, thinking
he threw it on you ? "

" How could that be ? How could he get in ? The enclosure was locked."

" He may have had a disc, you know."

" What would be done to him ? "

" Nothing very dreadful. He would probably be sent to
an institution."

128

She moved about the room with an air of indecision that reminded him, disturbingly, of Mrs. Barrimore. "I can only repeat," she said at last, "what I know. I saw him. He cried out and then hid himself. That is all."

"I think we may ask you to speak of that at the inquest."

"And in the meantime?"

"In the meantime, perhaps we should compromise. There is, I'm told, a reasonably good hotel in the hills outside Dunlowman. If I can arrange for you to stay there, will you do so? The inquest may be held at Dunlowman. It would be less of a fuss for you than returning from London."

"It's inadvisable for me to remain here?"

"Very inadvisable."

"So be it," said Miss Emily. His relief was tempered by a great uneasiness. He had never known her so tractable before.

"I'll telephone the hotel," he said. "And Troy, if I may," he added with a sigh.

"Had I taken your advice and remained in London, this would not have happened."

He was hunting through the telephone book. "That," he said, "is a prime example of utterly fruitless speculation. I am surprised at you, Miss Emily." He dialled the number. The Manor Court Hotel would have a suite vacant at five o'clock the next day. There would also be a small single room. There had been cancellations. He booked the suite. "You can go over in the morning," he said, "and lunch there. It's the best we can do. Will you stay indoors to-day, please?"

"I have given up this room."

"I don't think there will be any difficulty."

"People are leaving?"

"I daresay some will do so."

"O," she said, "I am so troubled, my dear. I am so troubled."

This, more than anything else she had said, being completely out of character, moved and disturbed him. He sat her down and because she looked unsettled and alien in her travelling toque, carefully removed it. "There," he said, "and I haven't disturbed the coiffure. Now, you look more like my favourite old girl."

"That is no way to address me," said Miss Emily. "You forget yourself." He unbuttoned her gloves and drew them off. "Should I blow in them?" he asked. "Or would that be *du dernier bourgeois*?"

He saw with dismay that she was fighting back tears.

There was a tap at the door. Jenny Williams opened it and looked in. "Are you receiving?" she asked and then saw Alleyn. "Sorry," she said. "I'll come back later."

"Come in," Alleyn said. "She may, mayn't she, Miss Emily?"

"By all means. Come in, Jennifer."

Jenny gave Alleyn a look. He said: "We've been discussing appropriate action to be taken by Miss Emily," and told her what he had arranged.

Jenny said: "Can't the hotel take her to-day?" And then hurried on: "Wouldn't you like to be shot of the Island as soon as possible, Miss Pride? It's been a horrid business, hasn't it?"

"I'm afraid they've nothing until to-morrow," Alleyn said.

"Well then, wouldn't London be better, after all? It's so anti-climaxy to gird up one's loins and then ungird them. Miss Pride, if you'd at all like me to, I'd love to go with you for the train journey."

"You are extremely kind, dear child. Will you excuse me

for a moment. I have left my handkerchief in my bedroom, I think."

Jenny, about to fetch it, caught Alleyn's eye and stopped short. Alleyn opened the door for Miss Emily and shut it again.

He said quickly : " What's happened ? Talk ? "

" She mustn't go out. Can't we get her away ? Yes. Talk. Beastly, unheard-of, *filthy* talk. She mustn't know. God ! " said Jenny, " how I hate *people*."

" She's staying indoors all day."

" Has she any idea what they'll be saying ? "

" I don't know. She's upset. She's gone in there to blow her nose and pull herself together. Look. Would you go with her to Dunlowman ? It'll only be a few days. As a job?"

" Yes, of course. Job be blowed."

" Well, as her guest. She wouldn't hear of anything else."

" All right. If she wants me. She might easily not."

" Go out on a pretence message for me and come back in five minutes. I'll fix it."

" O.K."

" You're a darling, Miss Williams."

Jenny pulled a grimace and went out.

When Miss Emily returned she was in complete control of herself. Alleyn said Jenny had gone down to leave a note for him at the office. He said he'd had an idea. Jenny, he understood from Miss Emily, herself was hard up and had to take holiday jobs to enable her to stay in England. Why not offer her one as companion for as long as the stay in Dunlowman lasted ?

" She would not wish it. She is the guest of the Barrimores and the young man is greatly attached."

" I think she feels she'd like to get away," Alleyn lied. " She said as much to me."

131

"In that case," Miss Emily hesitated. "In that case I—I shall make the suggestion. Tactfully, of course. I confess it—it would be a comfort." And she added firmly : "I am feeling old."

It was the most devastating remark he had ever heard from Miss Emily.

6. Green Lady

When he arrived downstairs it was to find Major Barrimore and the office clerk dealing with a group of disgruntled visitors who were relinquishing their rooms. The Major appeared to hang on to his professional aplomb with some difficulty. Alleyn waited and had time to read a notice that was prominently displayed and announced the temporary closing of the Spring owing to unforeseen circumstances.

Major Barrimore made his final bow, stared balefully after the last guest and saw Alleyn. He spread his hands. " My God," he said.

" I'm very sorry."

" Bloody people ! " said the Major in unconscious agreement with Jenny. " God, how I hate bloody people."

" I'm sure you do."

" They'll all go ! The lot ! They'll cackle away among themselves and want their money back and change their minds and jibber and jabber and in the bloody upshot, they'll be off. The whole bloody boiling of them. And the next thing : a new draft ! Waltzing in and waltzing out again. What the——" His language grew more fanciful ; he sweated extremely. A lady with a cross face swept out of the lounge and up the stairs. He bowed to her distractedly. " That's right, madam," he whispered after her. " That's the drill. Talk to your husband and pack your bags and take your chronic eczema to hell out of it." He smiled dreadfully at Alleyn. " And what can I do for *you* ? " he demanded.

133

" I hardly dare ask you for a room."

" You can have the whole pub. Bring the whole Yard."

Alleyn offered what words of comfort he could muster. Major Barrimore received them with a moody sneer but presently became calmer. " I'm not blaming you," he said. " You're doing your duty. Fine service, the police. Always said so. Thought of it myself when I left my regiment. Took on this damned poodlefaking instead. Well, there you are."

He booked Alleyn in and even accepted, with gloomy resignation, the news that Miss Emily would like to delay her departure for another night.

As Alleyn was about to go he said : " Could you sell me a good cigar ? I've left mine behind and I can't make do with a pipe."

" Certainly. What do you smoke ? "

" Las Casas, if you have them."

" No can do. At least—well, as a matter of fact, I do get them in for myself, old boy. I'm a bit short. Look here— let you have three, if you like. Show there's no ill-feeling. But not a word to the troops. If you want more, these things are smokable."

Alleyn said : " Very nice of you but I'm not going to cut you short. Let me have one Las Casas and I'll take a box of these others."

He bought the cigars.

The Major had moved to the flap end of the counter. Alleyn dropped his change and picked it up. The boots, he thought, looked very much as if they'd fit. They were wet round the welts and flecked with mud.

He took his leave of the Major.

When he got outside the hotel he compared the cigar band with the one he had picked up and found them to be identical.

Coombe was waiting for him. Alleyn said : " We'd better get the path cordoned off as soon as possible. Where's Pender ? "

" At the Spring. Your chaps are on their way. Just made the one good train. They should be here by five. I've laid on cars at Dunlowman. And I've raised another couple of men. They're to report here. What's the idea, cordoning the path ? "

" It's that outcrop," Alleyn said and told him about the Major's cigars. " Of course," he said, " there may be a guest who smokes his own Las Casas and who went out in a down-pour at the crack of dawn to hide behind a rock, but it doesn't seem likely. We may have to take casts and get hold of his boots."

" The Major ! I *see* ! "

" It may well turn out to be just one of those damn' fool things. But *he* said he got up late."

" It'd fit. In a way, it'd fit."

" At this stage," Alleyn said. " Nothing fits. We collect. That's all."

" Well, I know that," Coombe said quickly. He had just been warned against the axiomatic sin of forming a theory too soon. " Here are these chaps now," he said.

Two policemen were walking over the causeway.

Alleyn said : " Look, Coombe. I think our next step had better be the boy. Dr. Maine saw him and so did Miss Pride. Could you set your men to patrol the path and then join me at Trehern's cottage ? "

" There may be a mob of visitors there. It's a big attrac-tion."

" Hell ! Hold on. Wait a bit, would you ? "

Alleyn had seen Jenny Williams coming out of the old pub. She wore an orange-coloured bathing dress and a short white coat and looked as if she had had twice her fair share of sunshine.

He joined her. " It's all fixed with Miss Emily," she said, " I'm a lady's companion as from to-morrow morning. In the meantime, Patrick and I are thinking of a bathe."

" I don't know what we'd have done without you. And loath as I am to put anything between you and the English Channel, I have got another favour to ask."

" Now, what is all this ? "

" You know young Trehern, don't you ? You taught him ? Do you get on well with him ? "

" He didn't remember me at first. I think he does now. They've done their best to turn him into a horror but—yes— I can't help having a—I suppose it's a sort of compassion," said Jenny.

" I expect it is," Alleyn agreed. He told her he was going to see Wally and that he'd heard she understood the boy and got more response from him than most people. Would she come down to the cottage and help with the interview ?

Jenny looked very straight at him and said : " Not if it means you want me to get Wally to say something that may harm him."

Alleyn said : " I don't know what he will say. I don't in the least know whether he is in any way involved in Miss Cost's death. Suppose he was. Suppose he killed her, believing her to be Miss Emily. Would you want him to be left alone to attack the next old lady who happened to annoy him ? Think."

She asked him, as Miss Emily had asked him, what would be done with Wally if he was found to be guilty. He gave her the same answer : nothing very dreadful. Wally might be sent to an appropriate institution. It would be a matter for authorised psychiatrists. " And they do have successes in these days, you know. On the other hand, Wally may have nothing whatever to do with the case. But I must find out. Murder," Alleyn said abruptly, " is always abominable. It's hideous and outlandish. Even when the impulse is understandable and the motive overpowering, it is still a terrible, unique offence. As the law stands, its method of dealing with homicide is, as I think, open to the gravest criticism. But for all that, the destruction of a human being remains what it is : the last outrage."

He was to wonder after the case had ended, why on earth he had spoken as he did.

Jenny stared out, looking at nothing. " You must be an unusual kind of cop," she said. And then : " O.K. I'll tell Patrick and put on a skirt. I won't be long."

The extra constables hàd arrived and were being briefed by Coombe. They were to patrol the path and stop people climbing about the hills above the enclosure. One of them would be stationed near the outcrop.

Jenny reappeared wearing a white skirt over her bathing dress.

" Patrick," she said, " is in a slight sulk. I asked him to pick me up at the cottage."

" My fault, of course. I'm sorry."

" He'll get over it," she said cheerfully.

They went down the hotel steps. Jenny moved ahead. She walked very quickly past Miss Cost's shop, not looking at it. A group of visitors stared in at the window. The door was open and there were customers inside.

Coombe said : " The girl that helps is carrying on."

" Yes. All right. Has she been told not to destroy anything—papers—rubbish—anything ? "

" Well, yes. I mean, I said : just serve the customers and attend to the telephone calls. It's a sub-station for the Island. One of the last in the country."

" I think the shop would be better shut, Coombe. We

can't assume anything at this stage. We'll have to go through her papers. I suppose the calls can't be operated through the central station ? "

" Not a chance."

" Who is this assistant ? "

" Cissy Pollock. She was that green girl affair in the show. Pretty dim type, is Cissy."

" Friendly with Miss Cost ? "

" Thick as thieves, both being hell-bent on the Festival."

" Look. Could you wait until the shop clears and then lock up ? We'll have to put somebody on the board or simply tell the subscribers that the Island service is out of order."

" The Major'll go mad. Couldn't we shut the shop and leave Cissy on the switchboard ? "

" I honestly don't think we should. It's probably a completely barren precaution but at this stage——"

" 'We must not '," Coombe said, " ' allow ourselves to form a hard-and-fast theory to the prejudice of routine investigation.' I know. But I wouldn't mind taking a bet on it that Miss Cost's got nothing to do with this case."

" Except in so far as she happens to be the body ? "

" You know what I mean. All right : she fixed the earlier jobs. All right : she may have got at that kid and set him on to Miss Pride. In a way, you might say she organised her own murder."

" Yes," Alleyn said. " You might indeed. It may well be that she did." He glanced at his colleague. " Look," he said. " Pender will be coming back this way any time now, won't he ? I suggest you put him in the shop just to see Miss Cissy Thing doesn't exceed her duty. He can keep observation in the background and leave you free to lend a hand in developments at Wally's joint or whatever it's called. I'll be damned glad of your company."

138

"All right," Coombe said. "If you say so."

This, Alleyn thought, is going to be tricky.

"Come on," he said and put his hand on Coombe's shoulder. "It's a hell of a bind but, as the gallant Major would say, it *is* the drill."

"That's right," said Superintendent Coombe. "I know that. See you later, then."

Alleyn left him at the shop.

Jenny was waiting down by the seafront. They turned left, walked round the arm of the bay, and arrived at the group of fishermen's dwellings. Boats pulled up on the foreshore, a ramshackle jetty and the cottages themselves, tucked into the hillside, all fell, predictably, into a conventional arrangement.

"In a moment," said Jenny, "you will be confronted by Wally's Cottage, but *not* as I remember it. It used to be squalid and dirty and it stank to high heaven. Mrs. Trehern is far gone in gin and Trehern, as you may know, is unspeakable. But somehow or another the exhibit has been evolved : very largely through the efforts of Miss Cost egged on— well——"

"By whom ? By Major Barrimore ?"

"Not entirely," Jenny said quickly. "By the Mayor, who is called Mr. Nankivell, and his councillors and anybody in Portcarrow who is meant to be civic-minded. And principally, I'm afraid, by Mrs. Fanny Winterbottom and her financial advisors. Or so Patrick says. So, of course, does your Miss Emily. It's all kept up by the estate. There's a guild or something that looks after the garden and supervises the interior. Miss Emily calls the whole thing ' *complètement en toc*.' There you are," said Jenny as they came face-to-face with their destination. "That's Wally's Cottage, that is."

It was, indeed, dauntingly pretty. Hollyhocks, daisies,

foxgloves and antirrhinums flanked a cobbled path: honey-suckle framed the door. Fishing-nets of astonishing cleanliness festooned the fence. Beside the gate, in gothic lettering, hung a legend: "Wally's Cottage. Admission 1/-. West-country Cream-Teas, Ices."

"There's an annex at the back," explained Jenny. "The teas are run by a neighbour, Mrs. Trehern not being up to it. The Golden Record's in the parlour with other exhibits."

"The Golden Record?"

"Of cures," said Jenny shortly.

"Will Wally be on tap?"

"I should think so. And his papa, unless he's ferrying. There are not nearly as many visitors as I'd expected. O!" exclaimed Jenny stopping short. "I suppose—will that be because of what's happened? Yes, of course it will."

"We'll go in," Alleyn said, producing the entrance money.

Trehern was at the receipt of custom.

He leered ingratiatingly at Jenny and gave Alleyn a glance in which truculence, subservience and fear were un-attractively mingled. Wally stood behind his father. When Alleyn looked at him he grinned and held out his hands.

Jenny said: "Good morning, Mr. Trehern. I've brought Mr. Alleyn to have a look round. Hallo, Wally."

Wally moved towards her: "You come and see me," he said. "You come to school. One day soon." He took her hand and nodded at her.

"Look at that, now!" Trehern ejaculated. "You was always the favourite, miss. Nobody to touch Miss Williams for our poor little chap, is there, then, Wal?"

There were three visitors in the parlour. They moved from one exhibit to another, listened, and looked furtively at Jenny.

140

Alleyn asked Wally if he ever went fishing. He shook his head contemptuously and, with that repetitive, so obviously conditioned, gesture, again exhibited his hands. A trained animal, Alleyn thought with distaste. He moved away and opened the Golden Record which was everything that might be expected of it: like a visitors' book at a restaurant in which satisfied clients are invited to record their approval. He noted the dates where cures were said to have been effected and moved on.

The tourists left with an air of having had their money's-worth by a narrow margin.

Alleyn said: " Mr. Trehern, I am a police officer and have been asked to take charge of investigations into the death of Miss Elspeth Cost. I'd like to have a few words with Wally, if I may. Nothing to upset him. We just wondered if he could help us."

Trehern opened and shut his hands as if he felt for some object to hold on by. " I don't rightly know about that," he said. " My little lad be ant like other little lads, mister. He'm powerful easy put out. Lives in a world of his own, and not to be looked to if it's straight-out facts that's required. No hand at facts, be you, Wal ? Tell you the truth, I doubt he's took in this terrible business of Miss Cost."

" She'm dead," Wally shouted. " She'm stoned dead." And he gave one of his odd cries. Trehern looked very put out.

" Poor Miss Cost," Jenny said gently.

" Poor Miss Cost," Wally repeated cheerfully. Struck by some association of ideas he suddenly recited: " *Be not froightened sayed the loidy Ended now is all your woe,*" and stopped as incontinently as he had begun.

Alleyn said : " Ah ! That's your piece you said yesterday, isn't it ? " He clapped Wally on the shoulders. " Hallo, young fellow, you've been out in the rain ! You're as wet as a shag. That's the way to get rheumatism."

Trehern glowered upon his son. " Where you been ? " he asked.

" Nowheres."

" You been mucking round they boats. Can't keep him away from they boats," he said ingratiatingly. " Real fisherman's lad, our Wal. Be'ant you, Wal ? "

" I dunno," Wally said nervously.

" Come and show me these things," Alleyn suggested. Wally at once began to escort him round the room. It was difficult to determine how far below normal he was. He had something to say about each regrettable exhibit and what he said was always, however uncouth, applicable. Even if it was parrot-talk, Alleyn thought, it at least proved that Wally could connect the appropriate remark with the appointed object.

Jenny stayed for a minute or two, talking to Trehern who presently said something of which Alleyn only caught the tone of the voice. This was unmistakable. He turned quickly, saw that she was disconcerted and angry and called out : " How do you feel about tea and a bun ? Wally : do you like ice-cream ? "

Wally at once took Jenny's hand and began to drag her to a door marked Teas at the end of the room.

There was nobody else in the tea-room. An elderly woman, whom Jenny addressed by name, took their order.

" Was he being offensive, that type in there ? " Alleyn asked in French.

" Yes."

" I'm sorry."

" It doesn't matter in the least," Jenny said. " What sort of tea do you like ? Strong ? "

142

"Weak and no milk." Alleyn contemplated Wally whose face was already daubed with ice-cream. He ate with passionate, almost trembling, concentration.

"It was raining this morning, wasn't it, Wally?"

He nodded slightly.

"Were you out in the rain?"

Wally laughed and blew ice-cream across the table.

"Wally, don't," Jenny said. "Eat it properly, old boy. You were out in the rain, weren't you? Your shoes are muddy."

"So I wor, then. I don't mind the rain, do I?"

"No," Jenny said and added rather sadly: "You're a big boy now."

"I don't suppose," Alleyn suggested, "there was anybody else out in that storm was there? I bet there wasn't."

"Was there, Wally? Out in the rain?"

"There wur! *There wur!*" he shouted and banged the table.

"All right. All right. Who was it?"

Wally thrust his tongue into the cornet. "There wur," he said.

"This is heavy work," Alleyn observed mildly.

Jenny asked the same question and Wally at once said: "I seen 'er. I seen the old b . . . *Yah!*"

"Who do you mean? Who did you see?"

He flourished his right arm: the gesture was as uncoordinated and wild as a puppet's, but it was not to be mistaken. He made as if to throw something. Jenny caught back an exclamation.

"Who did you see? Was it—" Jenny looked at Alleyn who nodded. "Was it Miss Pride?"

"*Pridey-Pridey bang on the bell
Smash and bash 'er and send 'er to hell.*"

"*Wally!* who taught you that?"

143

"The kids," he said promptly, and began again : " *Prid Pridey*——"

"Stop. Don't do that, Wally. Be quiet." She said to Alleyn : " It's true, I heard them, yesterday evening."

Wally pushed the last of the cornet into his mouth. " I want another," he said indistinctly.

Coombe had come in from the parlour. Wally's back was towards him. Alleyn gave a warning signal and Coombe stayed where he was. Trehern loomed up behind him, smirking and curious. Coombe turned and jerked his thumb. Trehern hesitated and Coombe shut the door in his face.

"More," said Wally.

"You may have another," Alleyn said, before Jenny could protest. " Tell me what happened when you were out in the rain this morning."

He lowered his head and glowered. "Another one. More," he said.

"Where was Miss Pride ? "

"Up along."

"By the gate ? "

"By the gate," he repeated like an echo.

"Did you see her go away ? "

"She come back."

Jenny's hand went to her lips.

Alleyn said : " Did Miss Pride come back ? "

He nodded.

"Along the path ? When ? "

"She came back," Wally shouted irritably. " Back ! "

"A long time afterwards ? "

"Long time."

"And went into the Spring ? She went through the gate and into the Spring ? Is that right ? "

"It's *my* Spring. She be'ant allowed up to my Spring."

144

He again made his wild throwing gesture. " Get out ! " he bawled.

" Did you throw a rock at Miss Pride ? Like that ? "

Wally turned his head from side to side. " You dunno what I done," he said. " I ain't telling."

" Tell Miss Williams."

" No, I won't, then."

" Did you throw stones, Wally ? " Jenny asked. " One evening ? Did you ? "

He looked doubtfully at her and then said : " Where's my dad ? "

" In there. Wally, tell me."

He leant his smeared face towards her and she stooped her head. Alleyn heard him whisper : " It's a secret."

" What is ? "

" They stones. Like my dad said."

" Is the rock a secret, too ? "

He pulled back from her. " I dunno nothing about no rock," he said vacantly. " I want another."

" Was Miss Cost at the Spring ? " Alleyn asked.

Wally scowled at him.

" Wally," Jenny said, taking his hand, " did you see Miss Cost ? In the rain ? This morning ? Was Miss Cost at the Spring ? "

" At the fustyvell."

" Yes, at the festival. Was she at the Spring this morning too ? In the rain ? "

" This is getting positively fugal," Alleyn muttered.

" This morning," Jenny repeated.

" Not this morning. At the fustyvell," said Wally. " I want another one."

" In a minute," Alleyn said. " Soon. Did you see a man this morning in a motor-boat ? " And, by a sort of compulsion, he added : " In the rain ? "

145

" My dad's got the biggest launch."

" Not your dad's launch. Another man in another launch.
Dr. Maine. Do you know Dr. Maine ? "

" Doctor," said Wally vacantly.

" Yes. Did you see him ? "

" I dunno."

Alleyn said to Jenny : " Maine noticed him at about half
past seven." He waited for a moment and then pressed on :
" Wally : where were you when you saw the lady at the
Spring ? Where were you ? "

Wally pushed his forefinger round and round the table,
leaving a greasy trail on the plastic surface. He did this with
exaggerated violence and apparently no interest.

" You couldn't get in, could you ? " Alleyn suggested.
" You couldn't get through the gates."

With his left hand, Wally groped under his smock. He
produced a number of entrance discs, let them fall on the
table and shoved them about with violent jabs from his forefinger. They clattered to the floor.

" Did you go into the Spring this morning ? "

He began to make a high whimpering sound.

" It's no good," Jenny said. " When he starts that it's no
good. He'll get violent. He may have an attack. Really,
you mustn't. *Really*. I promise, you mustn't."

" Very well," Alleyn said. " I'll get him his ice-cream."

" Never mind, Wally, it's all right," Jenny said. " It's
all right now. Isn't it ? "

He looked at her doubtfully and then, with that too
familiar gesture, reached his hands out towards her.

" O don't ! " Jenny whispered. " O Wally, *don't* show me
your hands."

When Wally had absorbed his second ice-cream they left the tea-room by a door that, as it turned out, led into the back garden.

Coombe said : " We've come the wrong way," but Alleyn was looking at a display of greyish undergarments hung out to dry. A woman of unkempt appearance was in the yard. She stared at them with bleared disfavour.

" Private," she said and pointed to a dividing fence. " You'm trespassing."

" I'm sorry, Mrs. Trehern," Jenny said. " We made a mistake."

Trehern had come out through a back door. " Get in, woman," he said. " Get in." He took his wife by her arm and shoved her back into the house. " There's the gate," he said to Alleyn. " Over yon."

Alleyn had wandered to the clothes-line. A surplus length dangled from the pole. It had been recently cut.

" I wonder," he said, " if you could spare me a yard of this. The bumper-bar on my car's loose."

" Be'ant none to spare. Us needs it. Rotten anyways and no good to you. There's the gate."

" Thank you," Alleyn said and they went out.

" Was it the same as the trip-wire ? " he asked Coombe.

" Certainly was : but I reckon they all use it."

" It's old but it's been newly cut. Have you kept the trip-wire ? "

" Yes."

" How was it fastened ? "

" With iron pegs. They use them when they dry out their nets."

" Well, let's move on, shall we ? "

147

Patrick was sitting in a dinghy alongside the jetty, looking aloof and disinterested. Wally made up to a new pair of sight-seers.

" That was very nice of you," Alleyn said to Jenny. " And I'm more than obliged."

" I hated it. Mr. Alleyn, he really isn't responsible. You can see what he's like."

" Do you think he threw the stones at Miss Emily the other night ? "

She said, very unhappily : " Yes."

" So do I."

" But nothing else. I'm sure : nothing more than that."

" You may be right. I'd be very grateful, by the way, if you'd keep the whole affair under your hat. Will you do that ? "

" Yes," she said slowly. " All right. Yes, of course, if you say so."

" Thank you *very* much. One other thing. Have you any idea who the Green Lady could have been ? "

Jenny looked startled. " No, I haven't. Somehow or another I've sort of forgotten to wonder. She may not have been real at all."

" What did he say about her ? "

" Only that she was very pretty and her hair shone in the sun. And that she said his warts would be all gone."

" Nothing else ? "

" No—nothing."

" Has he got that sort of imagination—to invent her ? "

Jenny said slowly : " I don't think he has."

" I don't think so either."

" Not only that," Jenny said. " He's an extraordinarily truthful little boy. He never tells lies—never."

" That's an extremely valuable piece of information," Alleyn said. " Now go and placate your young man."

"I'll be blowed if I do. He can jolly well come off it," she rejoined but Alleyn thought she was not altogether displeased with Patrick. He watched her climb down into the dinghy. It ducked and bobbed towards the far point of the bay. She looked up and waved to him. Her tawny hair shone in the bright sunshine.

"That's a pleasing young lady," said Coombe. "What did you make of the lad?"

"We're not much further on, are we?"

"Aren't we, though? He as good as said he threw the stones that evening and what's more he has good as let on his dad had told him to keep his mouth shut."

"Yes. Yes, it looked like that, didn't it?"

"Well, then?"

"He wouldn't say anything about the rock. He says he saw Miss Pride leave and return. The figure that returned may have been Miss Cost."

"Ah!" said Coombe with satisfaction.

"Dr. Maine, you remember, noticed Wally dodging about the road up to the Spring soon after half past seven. Miss Pride saw him at much the same time. Miss Pride got back to the pub at five to eight. She didn't encounter Miss Cost. Say the seven o'clock service ended about ten to eight —we'll have to find out about that—it would mean that Miss Cost would get to the causeway—when?"

"About eight."

"Just after Miss Pride had gone indoors. And to the Spring?"

"Say a quarter past."

"And I found her body at ten past nine."

Coombe said: "The kid would have had time between seven-thirty and eight-fifteen, to let himself into the enclosure and take cover behind that boulder. Before she came."

" Why should he do that ? He thought Miss Pride had gone. He saw her go. Why should he anticipate her return ? "

" Just one of his silly notions."

" Yes," Alleyn said. " One of his silly notions. Put that boy in the witness-box and we'd look as silly as he does. If he's at the end of this case, Coombe, we'll only get a conviction on factual evidence, not on anything the poor little devil says. Unmistakable prints of his boots behind the boulder, for instance."

" You saw the ground. A mess." Coombe reddened. " I suppose I slipped up there. We were *on* the place before I thought."

" It's so easy," Alleyn said, saving his face for him. " Happens to the best of us."

" It was all churned up, wasn't it ? Almost as if——? "

" Yes ? "

" Now I come to think of it, almost as if, before the doctor and I went up, someone had kind of scuffled it."

" Yes. Behind the boulder and the trace of the rock. There was a flat bit of stone, did you notice, lying near the bank. Muddy edge. It might have been used to obliterate prints."

" I suppose," Coombe said, " in a quiet type of division like this, you get a bit rusty. I could kick myself. At my time of life ! "

" It may not amount to much. After all, we can isolate your prints and Dr. Maine's from the rest."

" Well, yes. Yes, you can do that, all right. But still ! "

Alleyn looked at his watch. It was just on noon. He suggested that they return to the mainland and call on the rectory. The tide was coming in and they crossed the channel by dinghy. There was Alleyn's car by the jetty with his

luggage in it. If things had gone according to plan, he would
have been half-way to Troy by now.

They left it where it stood. The rectory was a five minutes' walk along the front. It stood between a small and
charming Norman church and Dr. Maine's Convalescent
Home: a pleasant late-Georgian house with the look,
common to parsonages, of being exposed to more than its
fair share of hard usage.

" It was a poorish parish, this," Coombe said, " but with
the turn things have taken over the last two years, it's in
better shape. The stipend's gone up for one thing. A lot of
people that reckon they've benefited by the Spring, make
donations. It'd surprise you to know the amounts that are
put into the restoration-fund boxes. I'm people's warden,"
he added, " should have been there myself at ten-thirty for
the family service. The Rector'll be back home by now. It's
his busy day, of course."

They found Mrs. Carstairs briskly weeding. She wore a
green linen dress and her hair, faded yellow, made an
energetic sort of halo round her head. Her church-going
hat, plastic raincoat, gloves and prayer-book were scattered
in a surrealistic arrangement along the border. When
Alleyn was introduced she shook hands briskly and said she
supposed he'd come about this dreadful business and wanted
to see her husband who was, of course, appalled.

" He's in the study," she said to Coombe. " Those
accounts from the dry-rot people are *all* wrong again, Mr.
Coombe, and the Mayor suggests a combined memorial
service but we don't *quite* think—however."

" I'd really like a word with *you*, if I may," Alleyn said.
" We're trying to trace Miss Cost's movements early this
morning."

" O *dear*! Yes. Well, of *course*."

She confirmed Dr. Maine's account. Miss Cost had

attended the first celebration at seven o'clock and they had met at the gate. " She was in a great fuss, poor thing, because of my necklace."

" Your necklace ? "

" Yes. It's really rather a nice old one. Pinchbeck and paste but long and quite good. I lent with reluctance but she was so keen to have it because of the glitter and then, of course, what must her great Cissy do but drop it at the first thunder-clap and in the stampede, nobody remembered. I said we'd retrieve it after church or why not let Cissy go ? But no : she made a great to-do, *poor* Miss Cost (when one *thinks*) and insisted that she would go herself. She was rather an *on-goer* : conversationally, if you know what I mean : on and on and I wanted to go into church and say my prayers and it was pouring. So then she saw Dr. Maine and she was curious to know if it was Mrs. Trethaway's twins, though of course in the event it *wasn't* twins, (that was all nonsense) so I'm afraid I left her to tackle him as she clearly died to do. And after church I saw her streak off through the rain before anyone could offer. Isn't it *dreadful* ? " Mrs. Carstairs asked energetically. " Well, *isn't* it ? Adrian ! Can you spare a moment, dear ? "

" Coming."

The Rector, wearing his cassock, emerged through french windows. He said how extraordinary it was that Alleyn should have been at Portcarrow, added that they were lucky to have him and then became doubtful and solemn. " One finds it hard to believe," he said. " One is appalled."

Alleyn asked him when the first service ended and he said at about a quarter to eight. " I'd expected a large congregation. There are so many visitors. But the downpour, no doubt, kept a lot of folk away and there were only six communicants. The nine o'clock was crowded."

Alleyn wondered absently why clergymen were so prone

152

to call people " folk " and asked Mr. Carstairs if he knew
Miss Cost very well. He seemed disturbed and said : well,
yes, in so far as she was a member of his congregation. He
glanced at his wife and added : " Our friendship with Miss
Cost was perhaps rather limited by our views on the Spring.
I could not sympathise or, indeed, approve of her, as I
thought, rather extravagant claims. I thought them woolly,"
said the Rector. " Woolly and vulgar." He expounded, carefully, his own attitude which, in its anxious compromise,
declared, Alleyn thought, its orthodoxy.

" And you saw her," he asked, " after the service ? "
They said simultaneously that they did.

" I'm one of those parsons who come out to the porch
and see folk off," the Rector explained. " But Miss Cost
was on her way when I got there. Going down the path.
Something about my wife's necklace. Wasn't it, Dulcie ? "

" Yes, dear. I told Mr. Alleyn."
Coombe said : " The necklace has been recovered and will
be returned in due course, Mrs. Carstairs."

" O, dear ! " she said. " Will it ? I—I don't think——"
" Never mind, dear," said her husband.
Alleyn asked if anybody from the Island had been at the
first service. Nobody, it appeared. There were several at
the nine o'clock.

" The Barrimores, for instance ? "
No, not the Barrimores.
There was a silence through which the non-attendance of
the Barrimores was somehow established as a normal state-
of-affairs.

" Although," Mrs. Carstairs said, in extenuation of a
criticism that no one had voiced, " Margaret used to come
quite regularly at one time, Adrian. Before Wally's Warts,
you remember ? "

" Not that there's any connection, Dulcie."

153

" Of course not, dear. And Patrick and *nice* Jenny Williams have been to evensong, we must remember."

" So we must," her husband agreed.

" Poor things. They'll all be terribly upset no doubt," Mrs. Carstairs said to Alleyn. " Such a shock for everyone."

Alleyn said carefully : " Appalling. And apart from everything else a great worry for Barrimore, one imagines. After all, it won't do his business any good, this sort of catastrophe."

They looked uncomfortable and faintly shocked. " Well——" they both said and stopped short.

" At least," Alleyn said casually, " I suppose The Boy-and-Lobster *is* his affair, isn't it ? "

" It's the property of the estate," Coombe said. " Miss Pride's the landlord. But I have heard they put everything they'd got into it."

" *She* did," Mrs. Carstairs said firmly. " It was Margaret Barrimore's money, wasn't it, Adrian ? "

" My dear, I don't know. In any case——"

" Yes, dear. Of course," said Mrs. Carstairs, turning pink. She glanced distractedly at the knees of her linen dress. " O, look ! " she said. " Now, I shall have to change. It was that henbane that did it. What a disgrace I am. Sunday and everything."

" You melt into your background, my dear," the Rector observed. " Like a wood-nymph," he added, with an air of recklessness.

" Adrian, you are awful," said Mrs. Carstairs automatically. It was clear that he was in love with her.

Alleyn said : " So there would be a gap of about an hour and a quarter between the first and second services ? "

" This morning, yes," said the Rector. " Because of the rain, you see, and the small attendance at seven."

" How do you manage ? " Alleyn asked Mrs. Carstairs.
" Breakfast must be quite a problem."

" Oh, there's usually time to boil an egg before nine. This
morning, as you see, we had over an hour. At least," she
corrected herself. " *You* didn't, did you, dear ? Adrian had
to make a visit : poor old Mr. Thomas," she said to Coombe.
" Going, I'm afraid."

" So you were alone after all. When did you hear of the
tragedy, Mrs. Carstairs ? "

" Before matins. Half past ten. Several people had seen
the—well, the ambulance and the stretcher, you know. And
Adrian met Sergeant Pender and—and there it was."

" Is it true ? " the Rector asked abruptly. " Was it—
deliberate ? Pender said—I mean ? "

" I'm afraid so."

" How very dreadful," he said. " How appallingly dreadful."

" I know," Alleyn agreed. " A woman, it appears, with no
enemies. It's incomprehensible."

Coombe cleared his throat. The Carstairses glanced at each
other quickly and as quickly looked away.

" Unless, I suppose," Alleyn said, " you count Miss
Pride ? "

" There, I'm afraid," the Rector said, and Alleyn
wondered if he'd caught an overtone of relief, " there, it was
all on Miss Cost's side, poor soul."

" You might say," his wife added, " that Miss Pride had
the whip-hand."

" Dulcie ! "

" Well, Adrian, you know what I mean."

" It's quite beside the point," said the Rector with
authority.

A telephone rang in the house. He excused himself and
went indoors.

155

" There was nothing, I suppose, in her day-to-day life to make people dislike her," Alleyn said. " She seems, as far as I can make out, to have been a perfectly harmless obsessive."

Mrs. Carstairs began to pick up her scattered belongings, rather as if she was giving herself time to consider. When she straightened up, with her arms full, she was quite red in the face.

" She wasn't always perfectly kind," she said.

" Ah ! Which of us is ? "

" Yes, I know. You're quite right. Of course," she agreed in a hurry.

" Did she make mischief ? " he asked lightly.

" She tried. My husband—— Naturally, we paid no attention. My husband feels very strongly about that sort of thing. He calls it a cardinal sin. He preaches *very* strongly against. *Always*," Mrs. Carstairs looked squarely at Alleyn. " I'm offending, myself, to tell you this. I can't think what came over me. You must have a—have a talent for catching people off guard."

He said wryly : " You make my job sound very unappetising. Mrs. Carstairs, I won't bother you much longer. One more question and we're off. Have you any idea who played those ugly tricks on Miss Pride ? If you have, I do hope you will tell me."

She seemed, he thought, to be relieved. She said at once : " I've always considered she was behind them. Miss Cost."

" Behind them ? You thought she encouraged someone else to take the active part ? "

" Yes."

" Wally Trehern ? "

" Perhaps."

" And was that what you were thinking of when you said Miss Cost was not always kind ? "

"O no!" she ejaculated and stopped short. "Please don't ask me any more questions, Mr. Alleyn. I shall not answer them, if you do."

"Very well," he said. He thanked her and went away, followed, uncomfortably, by Coombe.

They lunched at the village pub. The whole place was alive with trippers. The sun glared down, the air was degraded by transistors and the ground by litter. Groups of sightseers in holiday garments crowded the foreshore, eating, drinking and pointing out the Island to each other. The tide was full. The hotel launch and a number of dinghies plied to and fro and their occupants stared up at the enclosure. It was obvious that the murder of Miss Cost was now common knowledge.

The enclosure itself was not fully visible from the village, being masked by an arm of Fisherman's Bay, but two constables could be seen on the upper pathway. Visitors returning from the Island told each other and anybody that cared to listen, that you couldn't get anywhere near the Spring. "There's nothing to see," they said. "The coppers have got it locked up. You wouldn't know."

When they had eaten a flaccid lunch they called on the nearest J.P. and picked up a search-warrant for Wally's Cottage. They went on to the station where Alleyn collected a short piece of the trip-wire. It was agreed that he would return to The Boy-and-Lobster. Coombe was to remain at the station, relieving his one spare constable, until the Yard men arrived. He would then telephone Alleyn at The Boy-and-Lobster. Pender would remain on duty at Miss Cost's shop.

Coombe said : " It's an unusual business, this. You finding the body and then this gap before your chaps come in."

"I hope you'll still be on tap, but I do realise it's taking more time than you can spare."

"Well, you know how it is." He waited for a moment and then said: "I appreciate your reluctance to form a theory too soon. I mean, it's what we all know. You can't. But as I'm pulling out I can't help saying it looks a sure thing to me. Here's this dopey kid as good as letting on he pitched in with the stones. There's more than a hint that his old man was behind it and a damn' good indication that he set the trip-wire. The kid says Miss Pride came back and there's every likelihood he mistook Miss Cost for her. I reckon he'd let himself into the enclosure and was up by the boulder. He looked down and saw the umbrella below and let fly at it. I mean: well, it hangs together, doesn't it?"

"Who do you think planted the figurine in Miss Pride's sitting-room and sent her the anonymous message and rang her up?"

"Well, *she* reckons Miss Cost."

"So Miss Cost's death was the end product of the whole series? Laid on, you might say, by herself?"

"In a sense. Yes."

"Has it struck you at all," Alleyn asked, "that there's one feature of the whole story about which nobody seems to show the slightest curiosity?"

"I can't say it has."

Alleyn took from his pocket the figurine that he had wrapped in paper and in his handkerchief. He opened it up and, holding it very gingerly, stood it on Coombe's desk. The single word, Death, gummed to a sheet of paper, was still fixed in position.

"Nobody," Alleyn said, "as far as I can gather, has ever asked themselves who was the original Green Lady."

" That piece of paper," Alleyn said, " is not the kind used
for the original messages. It's the same make as this other
piece which is a bit of The Boy-and-Lobster letter paper.
The word ' Death ' is not in a type that is used in your local
rag. I can't be sure but I think it's from a London sporting
paper called *The Racing Supplement*. The printer's ink, as
you see, is a bluish black and the type's distinctive. Was
Miss Cost a racing fan ? "

" Her ? " Coombe said. " Don't be funny."

" The Major is. He takes *The Racing Supplement*."

" Does he, by gum ! "

" Yes. Have you got a dabs-kit handy ? "

" Nothing very flash, but, yes : we've got the doings."

Alleyn produced his box of cigars. " He opened this up.
There ought to be good impressions inside the lid. Bailey
can give it the full works, if necessary, but we'll take a fly at
it, shall we ? "

Coombe got out his insufflator and a lens. They developed
a good set of prints on the lid and turned to the paper impaled over the figurine's head.

After a minute or two Alleyn gave a satisfied grunt.

" Fair enough," he said. " The index and thumb prints
are as good as you'd ask. I think I'll call on the gallant
Major."

He left Coombe still poring lovingly over the exhibits,
walked down to his car, collected his suitcases and crossed by
the hotel launch to the Island. Trehern was in charge. His
manner unattractively combined truculence with servility.

It was now two o'clock.

The Major, it presently transpired, was in the habit of
taking a siesta.

"He got used to it in India," Mrs. Barrimore said. " People do."

Alleyn had run into her at the door of the old pub. She was perfectly composed and remote in her manner: a beautiful woman who could not, he thought, ever be completely unaware of the effect she made. It was inescapable. She must, over and over again, have seen it reflected in the eyes of men who looked at, and at once recognised, her. She was immensely attractive.

He said : " Perhaps, in the meantime, I may have a word with you ? "

" Very well. In the parlour, if you like. The children are out, just now."

" The children ? "

" Jenny and Patrick. I should have said ' the young ' I expect. Will you come in."

He could hardly recognise the woman he had seen in her garden, veering this way and that like a rudderless ship and unable to control her hands. She sat perfectly still and allowed him to look at her while she kept her own gaze on her quietly, interlaced fingers.

He supposed she must have had a hand in the transformation of the old bar-parlour into a private living-room : if so she could have taken little interest in the process. Apart from the introduction of a few unexceptionable easy-chairs, one or two photographs, a non-committal assembly of books and a vase of the flowers she had so mishandled in the garden, it must be much as it was two years ago : an impersonal room.

Alleyn began by following the beaten paths of routine investigation. He tried to establish some corroboration of her alibi, though he did not give it this name, for the period covered by Miss Emily's visit to the enclosure up to the probable time of Miss Cost's death. There was none to be had. Nobody had visited the kitchen-dining-room while she drank her coffee and ate her toast. The servants were all busy in the main building. Jenny and Patrick had breakfasted in the public dining-room, her husband was presumably asleep. Alleyn gathered that they occupied separate rooms. She had no idea how long this solitary meal had lasted. When it was over she had attended to one or two jobs, interviewed the kitchen staff and then gone up to her room and changed from a housecoat to a day dress. When she came downstairs again she had found the young people in the parlour. Alleyn had arrived soon afterwards.

" And for the rest of the morning," he asked casually, " did you go out at all ? "

" No farther than the garden," she said after a fractional pause. " I went into the garden for a time."

" To cut flowers ? " he suggested, looking at those in the room.

She lifted her eyes to his for a moment. " Yes," she said, " to cut flowers. I do the flowers on Sunday as a rule : it takes quite a time. Jenny helped me," she added as an afterthought

" In the garden ? "

Again the brief look at him, this time perhaps, fractionally less controlled. " No. Not in the garden. In the house. Afterwards."

" So you were alone in the garden ? "

She said quickly with the slight hesitation he had noticed before in her speech : " Yes. Alone. Why d-do you keep on about the garden ? What interest can it have for you ? It was after—afterwards. Long afterwards."

" Yes, of course. Did the news distress you very much, Mrs. Barrimore ? "

The full, unbridled mouth so much at variance with the rest of her face, moved as if to speak, but, as in a badly-

161

synchronised sound-film, her voice failed. Then she said :
" Naturally. It's a terrible thing to have happened, isn't
it ? "

" You were fond of Miss Cost ? "

Something in her look reminded him, fantastically, of the
strange veiling of a bird's eyes. Hers were heavy-lidded and
she had closed them for a second. " Not particularly," she
said. " We had nothing——" She stopped, unaccountably.

" Nothing in common ? "

She nodded. Her hands moved but she looked at them
and refolded them in her lap.

" Had she made enemies ? "

" I don't know of any," she said at once as if she had
anticipated the question. " I know very little about her."

Alleyn asked her if she subscribed to the theory of mistaken identity and she said that she did. She was emphatic
about this and seemed relieved when he spoke of it. She was,
she said, forced to think that it might have been Wally.

" Excited, originally, by Miss Cost herself ? "

" I think it's possible. She was—— It doesn't matter."

" Inclined to be vindictive ? "

She didn't answer.

" I'm afraid," Alleyn said, " that in these cases one can't
always avoid speaking ill of the dead. I did rather gather
from something in Mrs. Carstairs' manner——"

" Dulcie Carstairs ! " she exclaimed, spontaneously and
with animation. " She never says anything unkind about
anybody."

" I'm sure she doesn't. It was just that—well, I thought
she was rather desperately determined not to do so in this
case."

She gave him a faint smile. It transfigured her face.

" Dear Dulcie," she murmured.

" She and the Rector are horrified, of course. They

162

struck me as being such a completely unworldly pair, those two."

" Did they ? You were right. They are."

" I mean—not only about Miss Cost but about the whole business of the Spring being more or less discredited by the present owner. The events of the last two years must have made a great difference to them, I suppose."

" Yes," she said. " Enormous."

" Were they very hard up before ? "

" O yes. It was a dreadfully poor parish. The stipend was the least that's given, I believe, and they'd no private means. We were all so sorry about it. Their clothes ! She's nice-looking but she needs careful dressing," said Mrs. Barrimore with all the unconscious arrogance of a woman who would look lovely in a sack. " Of course everyone did what they could. I don't think she ever bought anything for herself."

" She looked quite nice this morning, I thought."

" Did she ? " For the first time, Margaret Barrimore spoke as if there was some kind of rapprochement between them. " I thought men never noticed women's clothes," she said.

" Do you bet me I can't tell you what you wore yesterday at the Spring ? "

" Well ? "

" A white linen dress with a square neck and a leather belt. Brown Italian shoes with large buckles. Brown suede gloves. A wide string-coloured straw hat with a brown velvet ribbon. A brown leather bag. No jewellery."

" You win," said Mrs. Barrimore. " You don't look like the sort of man who notices but I suppose it's part of your training and I shouldn't feel flattered. Or should I ? "

" I would like you to feel flattered. And now I'm going to ruin my success by telling you that Mrs. Carstairs, too,

163

wore a linen dress, this morning." He described it. She listened to this talk about clothes as if it was a serious matter.

" White ? " she asked.

" No. Green."

" O yes. That one."

" Was it originally yours ? "

" If it's the one I think it is, yes."

" When did you give it to her ? "

" I don't in the least remember."

" Well: as long as two years ago ? "

" Really, I've no idea."

" Try."

" But I *don't* remember. One doesn't remember. I've given her odd things from time to time. You make me feel as if I'm parading—as if I'm making a lot of it. As if it was charity. Or patronage. It was nothing. Women do those sorts of things."

" I wouldn't press it if I didn't think it might be relevant."

" How can it be of the slightest interest ? "

" A green dress ? If she had it two years ago ? Think." She was on her feet with a quick controlled movement.

" But that's nonsense ! You mean—Wally ? "

" Yes. I do. The Green Lady."

" But—most people have always thought he imagined her. And even if he didn't—there are lots of green dresses in the summer-time."

" Of course. What I'm trying to find out is whether this was one of them. Is there nothing that would call to mind when you gave it to her ? "

She waited for a moment, looking down at her hands.

" Nothing. It was over a year ago, I'm sure." She turned aside. " Even if I could remember, which I can't, I don't think I would want to tell you. It can't have any bearing on this ghastly business—how could it?—and suppose you're right, it's private to Dulcie Carstairs."

" Perhaps she'd remember."

" I don't believe it. I don't for a moment believe she would think of playing a—a fantastic trick like that. It's not like her. She was never the Green Lady."

" I haven't suggested she was, you know." Alleyn walked over to her. She lifted her head and looked at him. Her face was ashen.

" Come," he said, " don't let us fence any more. You were the Green Lady, weren't you ? "

7. *The Yard*

He wondered if she would deny it and what he could say if she did. Very little. His assumption had been based largely on a hunch and he liked to tell himself that he didn't believe in hunches. He knew that she was deeply shocked. Her white face and the movement of her hands gave her away completely but she was, as Miss Emily had remarked, a woman of character.

She said : " I have been very stupid. You may, I suppose, congratulate yourself. What gave you the idea ? "

" I happened to notice your expression when that monstrous girl walked out from behind the boulder. You looked angry. But, more than that, I've been told Wally sticks to it that his Green Lady was tall and very beautiful. Naturally, I thought of you."

A door slammed upstairs. Someone, a man, cleared his throat raucously.

She twisted her hands into his. Her face was a mask of terror. " Mr. Alleyn, promise me, for God's sake, promise me you won't speak about this to my husband. It won't help you to discuss it with him. I swear it won't. You don't know what would happen if you did."

" Does he not know ? "

She tried to speak but only looked at him in terror.

" He *does* know ? "

" It makes no difference. He would be—he would be angry. That you knew."

" Why should he mind so much ? You said what you said,

166

I expect, impulsively. And it worked. Next morning the boy's hands were clean. You couldn't undo your little miracle."

" No, no, no, you don't understand. It's not that. It's— O God, he's coming down. O God, how can I make you ? What shall I do ! Please, please."

" If it's possible I shall say nothing." He held her hands firmly for a moment until they stopped writhing in his. " Don't be frightened," he said and let her go. " He'd better not see you like this. Where does that door lead to ? The kitchen ? " He opened it. " There you are. Quickly."

In a moment she was gone.

Major Barrimore came heavily downstairs. He yawned, crossed the little hall and went into the old private bar. The slide between it and the parlour was still there. Alleyn heard the clink of glass. A mid-afternoon drinker; he thought and wondered if the habit was long-established. He picked up his suitcase, went quietly into the hall and out at the front door. He then noisily returned.

" Anyone at home ? " he called.

After an interval, the door of the private opened and Barrimore came out, dabbing at his mouth with a freshly-laundered handkerchief and an unsteady hand. He was, as usual, impeccably turned-out. His face was puffy and em-purpled and his manner sombre.

" Hallo," he said. " You."

" I'm on my way to sign in," Alleyn said cheerfully. " Can you spare me a few minutes ? Routine, as usual. One's never done with it."

Barrimore stared dully at him and then opened the door of the parlour. " In here," he said.

Margaret Barrimore had left the faintest recollection of her scent behind her but this was soon lost in the Major's blended aura of Scotch-cigar-and-hair-lotion.

167

"Well," he said. "What's it, this time? Made any arrests?"

"Not yet."

"Everybody nattering about the boy, I s'ppose. You'd think they'd all got their knife into the poor kid."

"You don't agree?"

"I don't. He's too damn' simple, f'one thing. No harm in him, f'r'nother. You get to know 'bout chap's character in a regiment. Always pick the bad 'uns. He's not."

"Have you any theories yourself?"

The Major predictably said: "No names, no pack drill."

"Quite. But I'd be glad of your opinion."

"You wouldn't, old boy. You'd hate it."

Now, Alleyn thought, this is it. I know what this is going to be. "I?" he said, "why?"

"Heard what they're saying in the village?"

"No. What are they saying?"

"I don't necessarily agree, you know. Still: they hated each other's guts, those two. Face it."

"Which two?"

"The females. Beg pardon: the ladies. Miss P. and Miss C. And she was *there*, old boy. Can't get away from it. She was on the spot. Hanging up her bloody notice."

"*How do you know?*" Alleyn said and was delighted to speak savagely.

"Here! Steady! Steady, the Buffs!"

"The path has been closed. No one has been allowed near the enclosure. How do you know Miss Pride was there? How do you know she hung up her notice?"

"By God, sir——"

"I'll tell you. You were there yourself."

The blood had run into patches in the Major's jowls. "You must be mad," he said.

"You were on the path. You took shelter behind an outcrop of stone by the last bend. After Miss Pride had left and returned to the hotel, you came out and went to the enclosure."

He was taking chances again, but, looking at that outfaced blinking man, he knew he was justified.

" You read the notice, lost your temper and threw it into the mud. The important thing is that you were there. If you want to deny it you are, of course, at perfect liberty to do so."

Barrimore drew his brows together and went through a parody of brushing his moustache. He then said : " Mind if I get a drink ? "

" You'd better not, but I can't stop you."

" You're perfectly right," said the Major. He went out. Alleyn heard him go into the private and pushed back the slide. The Major was pouring himself a Scotch. He saw Alleyn and said : " Can I persuade you ? No. S'pose not. Not the drill."

" Come back," Alleyn said.

He swallowed his whisky neat and returned.

" Better," he said. " Needed it." He sat down. " There's a reasonable explanation," he said.

" Good. Let's have it."

" I followed her."

" Who ? Miss Pride ? "

" That's right. Now, look at it this way. I wake. Boiled owl. Want a drink of water. Very well. I get up. Raining cassandogs. All v'y fine. Look outer th'window. Cassandogs. And there *she* is with her bloody great brolly, falling herself in, down below. Left wheel and into the path. What's a man going to do ? Coupler aspirins and into some togs. Trench coat. Hat. Boots. See what I mean ? You can't trust her an inch. Where was I ? "

" Following Miss Pride along the path to the enclosure."

169

" Certainly. She'd gained on me. All right. Strategy of indirect approach. Keep under cover. Which I did. Just like you said, old boy. Perfectly correct. Don't fire till you see the whites of their eyes." He leered at Alleyn.

" Do you mean that you confronted her ? "

" Me ! No, thank you ! "

" You mean you kept under cover until she'd gone past you on her way back to the hotel."

" What I said. Or did I ? "

" Then you went to the enclosure ? "

" Nasherally."

" You read the notice and threw it aside ? "

" 'Course."

" And then ? What did you do ? "

" Came back."

" Did you see Wally Trehern ? "

The Major stared. " I did not."

" Did you meet anyone ? "

A vein started out on Barrimore's forehead. Suddenly, he looked venomous.

" Not a soul," he said loudly.

" Did you see anyone ? "

" No ? "

" You met Miss Cost. You must have done so. She was on the path a few minutes after Miss Pride got back. You either met her at the enclosure itself or on the path. Which was it ? "

" I didn't see her. I didn't meet her."

" Will you sign a statement to that effect ? "

" I'll be damned if I do." Whether through shock or by an astonishing effort of will, he had apparently got himself under control. " I'll see you in hell first," he said.

" And that's your last word ? "

" Not quite." He got up and confronted Alleyn, staring

170

into his face. " If there's any more of this," he said. " I'll ring up the Yard and tell your O.C. you're a prejudiced and therefore an untrustworthy officer. I'll have you court-martialled, by God ! Or whatever they do in your show."

" I really think you'd better not," Alleyn said mildly.

" No ? I'll tell them what's no more than the case : you're suppressing evidence against an old woman who seems to be a very particular friend. No accounting for taste."

" Major Barrimore," Alleyn said. " You will not persuade me to knock your tongue down your throat but you'd do yourself less harm if you bit it off."

" I know what I'm talking about; You can't get away from it. Ever since she came here she's had her knife into poor old Cost. Accusing her of writing letters. Chucking stones. Telephone messages. Planting ornaments."

" Yes," Alleyn said. " Miss Pride was wrong there, wasn't she ? Miss Cost didn't put the Green Lady in Miss Pride's room. You did."

Barrimore's jaw dropped.

" Well," Alleyn said. " Do you deny it ? I shouldn't if I were you. It's smothered in your finger-prints and so's the paper round its neck."

" You're lying. You're bluffiing."

" If you prefer to think so. There's been a conspiracy between you, against Miss Pride, hasn't there ? You and Miss Cost, with the Treherns in the background ? You were trying to scare her off. Miss Cost started it with threatening messages pieced together from the local paper. You liked the idea and carried on with the word ' Death ' cut out of your *Racing Supplement* and stuck round the neck of the image. You didn't have to ask Miss Cost for one. They're for sale in your pub."

" Get to hell out of here. *Get out.*"

Alleyn picked up his suitcase. " That's all for the present.

171

I shall ask you to repeat this conversation before a witness. In the meantime, I suggest that you keep off the whisky and think about the amount of damage you've done to yourself. If you change your mind about any of your statements I'm prepared to listen to you. You will see to it, if you please, that Miss Pride is treated with perfect civility during the few hours she is most unfortunately obliged to remain here as your guest."

He had got as far as the door when the Major said : " Hold on. Wait a bit."

" Well ? "

" Daresay I went too far. Not myself. Fellah shouldn't lose his temper, should he ? What ! "

" On the contrary," said Alleyn, " the exhibition was remarkably instructive." And went out.

II

" And after all that," he thought, " I suppose I should grandly cancel my room and throw myself on Coombe's hospitality again. I won't though. It's too damned easy and it's probably exactly what Barrimore hopes I'll do."

He collected his key at the office and went up to his room. It was now a quarter past three. Miss Emily would still be having her siesta. In an hour and forty-five minutes, Detective-Inspector Fox, Detective-Sergeant Bailey and Detective-Sergeant Thompson would arrive. Curtis, the pathologist, would be driving to Dunlowman under his own steam. Coombe had arranged for Dr. Maine to meet him there. The nearest mortuary was at Dunlowman. Alleyn would be damned glad to see them all.

He unpacked his suitcase and began to write his notes on hotel paper. It was the first time he'd ever embarked on a case without his regulation kit and he felt uncomfortable and amateurish. He began to wonder if, after all, he should hand over to Fox or somebody else. Triumph for the gallant Major, he thought.

For a minute or two he indulged in what he knew to be fantasy. Was it, in the smallest degree, remotely possible that Miss Emily, inflamed by Miss Cost's activities, could have seen her approaching, bolted into the enclosure, hidden behind the boulder and under a sudden access of exasperation, hurled a rock at Miss Cost's umbrella ? It was not. But supposing for a moment that it was ? What would Miss Emily then have done ? Watched Miss Cost as she drowned in the pool; as her hair streamed out over the fall; as her dress inflated and deflated in the eddying stream ? Taken another bit of rock, and scraped out her own footprints and walked back to The Boy-and-Lobster ? And, where, all that time, was the Major ? What became of his admission that he tore down the notice and threw it away ? Suppose there was an arrest and a trial and defending council used Miss Emily as a counterblast ? Could her innocence be established ? Only, as things stood, by the careful presentation of the Major's evidence and the Major thought, or pretended to think, she was guilty. And, in any case, the Major was a chronic alcoholic.

He got up and moved restlessly about the room. A silly, innocuous print of anemones in a mug, had been hung above the bed. He could have wrenched it down and chucked it, with as much fury as had presumably inspired the Major, into the wastepaper basket.

There must have been an encounter between Barrimore and Miss Cost. He had seen Emily pass and repass, had come out of concealment and gone to the enclosure. By that time Miss Cost was approaching. Why, when he saw her, should he again take cover, and where ? No : they must have met. What, then, did they say to each other in the pour-

173

ing rain ? Did she tell him she was going to retrieve the
necklace ? Or did he, having seen her approaching, let himself into the enclosure and hide behind the boulder ? But
why ? And where, all this time, was Wally ? Dr. Maine and
Miss Emily had both seen him, soon after half past seven.
He had shouted at Miss Emily and then ducked out of sight.
The whole damned case seemed to be littered with people
that continually dodged in and out of concealment. What
about Trehern ? Out and about in the landscape with the
rest of them ? Inciting his son to throw rocks at a supposed
Miss Emily ? Dr. Maine had not noticed him but that
proved nothing.

Next, and he faced this conundrum with distaste, what
about Mrs. Barrimore alias the Green Lady ? Did she fit in
anywhere or had he merely stumbled down an odd, irrelevant
by-way ? But why was she so frightened at the thought of
her husband being told of her masquerade ? The Green
Lady episode had brought Barrimore nothing but material
gain. Wouldn't he simply have ordered her to shut up about
it and if anything, relished the whole story ? She had seemed
to suggest that the fact of Alleyn himself being aware of it
would be the infuriating factor. And why had she been
so distressed when she was alone in the garden ? At that
stage there was no question of her identity with the Green
Lady being discovered.

Finally, of course, was Miss Cost murdered, as it were, in
her own person, or because she was mistaken for Miss
Emily ?

The answer to that one must depend largely upon motive
and motive is one of the secondary elements in police
investigation. The old tag jog-trotted through his mind.
" *Quis ? Quid ? Ubi ? Quibus auxilis ? Cur ? Quomodo ?
Quando ?* " Which might be rendered : " Who did the

174

deed ? What was it ? Where was it done ? With what ? Why was it done ? And how done ? When was it done ? " The lot !

He completed his notes and read them through. The times were pretty well established. The weapon. The method. The state of the body. The place—no measurements yet, beyond the rough ones he and Coombe had made on the spot. Bailey would attend to all that. The place ? He had described it in detail. The boulder ?—between the boulder and the hill behind it, was a little depression, screened by bracken and soft with grass. A " good spot for courting couples," as Coombes had remarked, " when it wasn't raining." The ledge——

He was still poring over his notes when the telephone rang. Mr. Nankivell, the Mayor of Portcarrow, would like to see him.

" Ask him to come up," Alleyn said and put his notes in the drawer of the desk.

Mr. Nankivell was in a fine taking-on. His manner suggested a bothering confusion of civic dignity, awareness of Alleyn's reputation and furtive curiosity. There was another element, too. As the interview developed, so did his air of being someone who has information to impart and can't quite make up his mind to divulge it. Mr. Nankivell, for all his *opéra bouffe* façade, struck Alleyn as being a pretty shrewd fellow.

" This horrible affair," he said, " has taken place at a very regrettable juncture, Superintendent Alleyn. This, sir, is the height of our season. Portcarrow is in the public eye. It has become a desirable resort. We'll have the Press down upon us and the type of information they'll put out will not conduce to the general benefit of our community. A lot of damaging clap-trap is what we may expect from those chaps and we may as well face up to it."

175

" When does the local paper come out ? "

" Tuesday," said the Mayor gloomily. " But they've got their system. Thick as thieves with London—agents, as you might say. They'll have handed it on."

" Yes," Alleyn said. " I expect they will."

" Well, there now ! " Mr. Nankivell said waving his arm. " There yarr ! A terrible misfortunate thing to overtake us."

Alleyn said : " Have you formed any opinion yourself, Mr. Mayor ? "

" So I have, then. Dozens. And each more objectionable than the last. The stuff that's being circulated already by parties that ought to know better ! Now, I understand, sir, and I hope you'll overlook my mentioning it, that Miss Pride is personally known to you."

With a sick feeling of weariness Alleyn said : " Yes. She's an old friend." And before Mr. Nankivell could go any further he added : " I'm aware of the sort of thing that is being said about Miss Pride. I can assure you that, as the case has developed, it is clearly impossible that she could have been involved."

" Is that so ? Is that the case ? " said Mr. Nankivell. " Glad to hear it, I'm sure." He did not seem profoundly relieved, however. " And then," he said, " there's another view. There's a notion that the one lady was took for the other ! Now, there's a very upsetting kind of a fancy to get hold of. When you think of the feeling there's been and them that's subscribed to it."

" Yourself among them ? " Alleyn said lightly. " Ridiculous, when you put it like that, isn't it ? "

" I should danged well hope it is ridiculous," he said violently and at once produced his own alibi. " Little though I ever thought to be put in the way of making such a demeaning statement," he added angrily. " However. Being a Sunday, Mrs. Nankivell and I did not raise up until nine o'clock and was brought our cup of tea at eight by the girl that does for us. The first I hear of this ghastly affair is at ten-thirty when Mrs. Nankivell and I attended chapel and then it was no more than a lot of chatter about an accident and George Pender, looking very big, by all accounts, and saying he'd nothing to add to the information. When we come out it's all over the village. I should of been informed at the outset but I wasn't. Very bad."

Alleyn did his best to calm him.

"I'm very grateful to you for calling," he said. "I was going to ring up and ask if you could spare me a moment this afternoon but I wouldn't have dreamt of suggesting you took the trouble to come over. I really must apologise."

"No need, I'm sure," said Mr. Nankivell, mollified.

"Now, I wonder, if, in confidence, Mr. Mayor, you can help me at all. You see, I know nothing about Miss Cost and it's always a great help to get some sort of background. For instance, what was she like? She was, I take it, about forty to forty-five years old and, of course, unmarried. Can you add anything to that? A man in your position is usually a very sound judge of character, I've always found."

"Ah!" said the Mayor, smoothing the back of his head. "It's an advantage, of course. Something that grows on you with experience, you might say."

"Exactly. Handling people and getting to know them. Now, between two mere males, how would you sum up Miss Elspeth Cost?"

Mr. Nankivell raised his brows and stared upon vacancy. A slow, knowing smile developed. He wiped it away with his fingers but it crept back.

"A proper old maiden, to be sure," he said.

"Really?"

"Not that she was what you'd call ancient: forty-five, as

177

you rightly judged and a tricksy time of life for females, which is a well-established phenomenon, I believe."

" Yes, indeed. You don't know," Alleyn said cautiously, " what may turn up."

" God's truth, if you never utter another word," said Mr. Nankivell with surprising fervour. He eased back in his chair, caught Alleyn's eye and chuckled. " The trouble I've had along of that lady's crankiness," he confided, " you'd never credit."

Alleyn said " Tch ! "

" Ah ! With some it takes the form of religious activities. Others go all out for dumb animals. Mrs. Nankivell herself, although a very level-headed lady, worked it off in cats which have in the course of nature simmered down to two. Neuters, both. But with Miss Cost, not to put too fine a point on it, with Miss Cost, it was a matter of her female urges."

" Sex ? "

" She spotted it everywhere," Mr. Nankivell exclaimed. " Up hill and down dell, particularly the latter. Did I know what went on in the bay of an evening ? Was I aware of the opportunities afforded by open dinghies ? Didn't we ought to install more lights along the front ? And when it came to the hills round about the Spring she was a tiger. Alf Coombe got it. The Rector got it, the doctor got it and I came in for it, hot and strong, continuous. She was a masterpiece."

Alleyn ventured a sympathetic laugh.

" You may say so, but beyond a joke nevertheless. And that's not the whole story. The truth of the matter is, and I tell you this, sir, in the strictest confidence, the silly female was—dear me, how can I put it ?—she was chewed-up by the very fury she come down so hard upon. Now, that's a fact and well-known to all and sundry. She was a man-hunter, was poor Elspeth Cost. In her quiet, mousy sort of fashion, she raged to and fro seeking whom she might devour. Which was not many."

" Any success ? "

The Mayor, to Alleyn's infinite regret, pulled himself up. " Well, now," he said. " That'd be talking. That'd be exceeding, sir."

" I can assure you that if it has no bearing on the case, I shall forget it. I'm sure, Mr. Mayor, you would prefer me to discuss these, quite possibly irrelevant matters with you, rather than make widespread inquiries through the village. We both know, don't we, that local gossip can be disastrously unreliable ? "

Mr. Nankivell thought this over. " True as fate," he said at last. " Though I'm in no position myself to speak as to facts and don't fancy giving an impression that may mislead you. I don't fancy that, at all."

This seemed to Alleyn to be an honest scruple and he said warmly : " I think I can promise you that I shan't jump to conclusions."

The Mayor looked at him. " Very good," he said. He appeared to be struck with a sudden thought. " I can tell you this much," he continued with a short laugh. " The Rector handled her with ease, being well-versed in middle-aged maidens. And she had no luck with me and the doctor. Hot after him, she was, and drawing attention and scorn upon herself right and left. But we kept her at bay, poor wretch, and in the end she whipped round against us with as mighty a fury as she'd let loose on the pursuit. Very spiteful. Same with the Major."

" What ! " Alleyn ejaculated. " Major Barrimore ! "

Mr. Nankivell looked extremely embarrassed. " That remark," he said, " slipped out. All gossip, I daresay, and better forgotten, the whole lot of it. Put about by the

Ladies' Guild upon which Mrs. Nankivell sits, *ex officio*, and, as she herself remarked, not to be depended upon."

" But what is it that the Ladies' Guild alleges ? That Miss Cost set her bonnet at Major Barrimore and he repelled her advances ? "

" Not azackly," said the Mayor. His manner strangely suggested a proper reticence undermined by an urge to communicate something that would startle his hearer.

" Come on, Mr. Mayor," Alleyn said. " Let's have it, whatever it is. Otherwise you'll get me jumping to a most improper conclusion."

" Go on, then," invited Mr. Nankivell, with hardihood, " Jump ! "

" You're not going to tell me that Miss Cost is supposed to have had an affair with Major Barrimore ? "

" Aren't I ? I am, then. And a proper, high-powered, blazing set to at that. While it lasted," said Mr. Nankivell.

III

Having taken his final hurdle, Mr. Nankivell galloped freely down the straight. The informant, it appeared, was Miss Cissy Pollock, yesterday's Green Lady and Miss Cost's assistant and confidante. To her, Miss Cost was supposed to have opened her heart. Miss Pollock, in her turn, had retailed the story, under a vow of strictest secrecy, to the girl-friend of her bosom whose mother, a close associate of Mrs. Nankivell, was an unbridled gossip. You might as well, the Mayor said, have handed the whole lot over to the Town Crier and have done with it. The affair was reputed to have been of short duration and to have taken place at the time of Miss Cost's first visit to the Island. There was dark talk of an equivocal nature about visits paid by Major Barrimore,

180

to an unspecified rival in Dunlowman. He was, Mr. Nankivell remarked, a full-blooded man.

With the memory of Miss Cost's face, as Alleyn had seen
it that morning made hideous by death, this unlovely story
took on a grotesque and appalling character. Mr. Nankivell
himself seemed to sense something of this reaction : he
became uneasy and Alleyn had to assure him, all over again,
that it was most unlikely that the matter would turn out to be
relevant and that supposing it was, Mr. Nankivell's name
would not appear as everything he had said came under the
heading of hearsay and would be inadmissible as evidence.
This comforted him and he took his leave with the air of a
man who, however, distasteful the task, has done his duty.

When he had gone, Alleyn got his notes out again and
added a fairly lengthy paragraph. He then lit his pipe and
walked over to the window.

It looked down on the causeway, the landing jetty and the
roof of Miss Cost's shop. Across the channel, in the village,
trippers still dappled the foreshore. There were several
boats out in the calm waters and among them, pulling towards
the Island, he saw Patrick's dinghy with Jenny Williams in
the stern. She sat bolt upright and seemed to be looking
anywhere but at her companion. He was rowing with
exaggerated vigour, head down and shoulders hunched.
Even at that distance, he looked as if he was in a temper.
As they approached the jetty, Jenny turned towards him
and evidently spoke. He lifted his head, seemed to stare at
her and then back-paddled into a clear patch of water and
half-shipped his oars. The tide was going out and carried
them very slowly towards the point of Fisherman's Bay.
They were talking now. Jenny made a quick repressed
gesture and shook her head.

" Lovers' quarrel," Alleyn thought. " Damned awkward
in a boat. He won't get anywhere, I daresay."

"You won't get anywhere," Jenny was saying in a grand voice, "by sulking."

"I am *not* sulking."

"Then you're giving a superb imitation of it. As the day's been such a failure why don't we pull in and bring it to an inglorious conclusion?"

"All right," he said but made no effort to do so.

"Patrick."

"What?"

"Couldn't you just mention what's upset your applecart? It'd be better than huffing and puffing behind a thundercloud."

"You're not so marvellously forthcoming yourself."

"Well, what am I meant to do? Crash down on my knees in the bilge water and apologise for I don't know what?"

"You do know what."

"O Lord!" Jenny pushed her fingers through her dazzling hair, looked at him and began to giggle. "Isn't this *silly*?" she said.

The shadow of a grin lurked about Patrick's mouth and was suppressed. "Extremely silly," he said. "I apologise for being a figure of fun."

"Look," Jenny said. "Which is it? Me going off with Mr. Alleyn to see Wally? Me being late for our date? Or me going to Dunlowman with Miss Emily to-morrow? Or the lot? Come on."

"You're at perfect liberty to take stewed tea and filthy cream buns with anybody you like for as long as you like. It was evidently all very private and confidential and far be me from it—I mean it from me—to muscle in where I'm not wanted."

"But I *told* you. He asked me not to talk about it."

Patrick inclined, huffily. "So I understand," he said.

"Patrick! I'm sorry, but I do find that I respect Mr.

Alleyn. I'm *anti* a lot of things that I suppose you might say he seems to stand for, although I'm not so sure, even, of that. He strikes me as being—well—far from reactionary," said young Jenny.

" I'm sure he's a paragon of enlightenment."

She wondered how it would go if she said : " Let's face it, you're jealous," and very wisely decided against any such gambit. She looked at Patrick : at his shock of black hair, at his arms and the split in his open shirt where the sunburn stopped and at his intelligent, pig-headed face. She thought : " He's a stranger and yet he's so very familiar." She leant forward and put her hand on his bony knee.

" Don't be unhappy," she said. " What is it ? "

" Good God !" he said. " Can you put it out of your mind so easily ! It's Miss Cost, with her skull cracked. It's Miss Cost, face down in our wonderful Spring. It's your pin-up detective, inching his way into our lives. Do you suppose I enjoy the prospect of——" He stopped short. " I happen," he said, " to be rather attached to my mother."

Jenny said quickly : " Patrick—yes, of course you are. But——"

" You must know damned well what I mean."

" All right. But surely it's beside the point. Mr. Alleyn can't think——"

" Can't he ? " His eyes slid away from her. " She was a poisonous woman," he said.

A silence fell between them and suddenly Jenny shivered : unexpectedly as if some invisible hand had shaken her.

" What's the matter ? " he said irritably. " Are you cold ?"

He looked at her miserably and doubtfully.

Jenny thought : " I don't know him. I'm lost." And at once was caught up in a wave of compassion.

" Don't let's go on snarling," she said. " Let's go home

183

and sort ourselves out. It's clouded over and I'm getting rather cold."

He said : "I don't blame you for wanting to get away from this mess. What a party to have let you in for ! It's better you should go to Dunlowman."

"Now *that*," said Jenny, "is really unfair and you know it, darling."

He glowered at her. "You don't say that as a rule. Everyone says 'darling' but you don't."

"That's right. I'm saying it now for a change. Darling."

He covered her hand with his. "I'm sorry," he said. "I am really sorry. Darling Jenny."

From his bedroom window Alleyn watched and thought : "He'll lose his oar."

It slipped through the rowlock. Patrick became active with the other oar. The dinghy bobbed and turned about. They both reached dangerously overboard. Through the open window Alleyn faintly caught the sound of their laughter.

"That's done the trick," he thought. The telephone rang and he answered it.

"Fox here, sir," said a familiar placid voice. "Speaking from Portcarrow station."

"You sound like the breath of spring."

"I didn't quite catch what you said."

"It doesn't matter. Have you brought my homicide kit ? "

"Yes."

"Then come, Birdie, come."

Mr. Fox replaced the receiver and said to Superintendent Coombe and the Yard party : "We're to go over. He's worried."

"He sounded as if he was acting the goat or something," said Coombe.

184

" That's right," said Fox. " Worried. Come on, you chaps."

Detective-Sergeants Bailey and Thompson, carrying their kit, accompanied him to the Island. Coombe showed them the way, saw them off and returned to his office.

They walked in single file over the causeway. Alleyn saw them from his window, picked up his raincoat and went down the steps to meet them. They had attracted a considerable amount of attention.

" Quite a picturesque spot," said Mr. Fox. " Popular, too, by the looks of it. What's the story, Mr. Alleyn ? "

" I'll tell you on the way, Br'er Fox."

They had their suitcases with them. Alleyn gave a likely-looking boy five shillings to take them up to the hotel. Numbers of small boys had collected and were shaping up to accompany them. " Move along," said Mr. Fox majestically. " Shove along, now. Right away. Clear out of it."

They backed off.

" You'm Yard men, be'ant you, mister ? " said the largest of the boys.

" That's right," Alleyn said. " Push off or we'll be after you."

They broke into peals of derisive but gratified laughter and scattered. One of them started a sort of chant but the others told him to shut up.

Alleyn took his own kit from Fox and suggested that they all walked round the arm of Fisherman's Bay and up by Wally's route to the enclosure. On the way he gave them a résumé of the case.

" Complicated," Mr. Fox remarked when Alleyn had finished. " Quite a puzzle."

" And that's throwing roses at it."

" Which do you favour, Mr. Alleyn ? Mistaken identity or dead on the target ? "

" I don't want to influence you—not that I flatter myself I can—at the outset. The popular theory with Coombe is the first. To support it this wretched boy says he saw Miss Pride arrive, leave and return. She herself saw *him*. Down on the road we're coming to in a minute. So did Dr. Maine. Now the second figure, of course, must have been Miss Cost not Miss Pride. But between the departure of Miss Pride and the arrival of Miss Cost, Barrimore went to the gates and chucked away the notice. Who replaced it ? The murderer ? Presumably. And when did Wally let himself into the enclosure ? If he did ? It must have been before Miss Cost appeared or she would have seen him. So we've got to suppose that for some reason Wally *did* go in and *did* hide behind the boulder, after Miss Pride had left, and avoiding Barrimore who didn't see him. I don't like it. It may be remotely possible but I don't like it. And I'm certain he wouldn't replace the notice. He hasn't got the gumption. Anyway the time-table barely allows all this."

" He'd hardly mistake the deceased for Miss Pride, silly and all as he may be, if he got anything like a fair look at her."

" Exactly, Br'er Fox. As for the galloping Major : he swims round in an alcoholic trance. Never completely drunk. Hardly ever sober. And reputed, incredibly enough, to have had a brief fling with Miss Cost at about the same time as Wally's warts vanished. He is thought to have proved fickle and to have aroused her classic fury. She also set her bonnet, unsuccessfully, it seems, at the doctor, the Rector and the Mayor. Barrimore's got a most beautiful and alluring wife who is said to be bullied by him. She showed signs of acute distress after she heard the news. She's the original Green Lady. It's all in the notes : you can have a nice cosy read any time you fancy."

" Thanks."

" That's Wally's Cottage. We are about to climb Wally's

Way and that is Wally's mama, another alcoholic, by the by, leering over the back fence. His father is ferryman at high-tide and general showman in between. The whole boiling of them, the Barrimores, the parson, the doctor, the Major, the Treherns, Miss Cost herself, with pretty well everybody else in the community, stood to lose by Miss Pride's operations. Apart from arousing the cornered fury of a hunted male, it's difficult to discover a motive for Miss Cost's murder. Good evening, Mrs. Trehern," Alleyn shouted and lifted his hat.

" Yoo-hoo ! " Mrs. Trehern wildly returned, clinging to her back fence. " Lock 'er up. Bloody murderess."

" Who's she mean ? " asked Fox.

" Miss Pride."

" Bless my soul ! *Quelle galère !* " Fox added, cautiously.

" You must meet Miss Pride, Br'er Fox, she's a top authority on French as she should be spoke."

" Ah ! " said Fox, " To be properly taught from the word go ! That's the thing. What does she think of the gramophone method ? "

" Not much."

" That's what I was afraid of," said Fox with a heavy sigh.

Mrs. Trehern gave a screech, not unlike one of her son's and tacked into the cottage. Alleyn went over to the fence and looked into the back garden. The clothes-line had been removed.

They climbed up Wally's Way to the enclosure. One of Coombe's men was standing a little way along the hotel path.

Alleyn said to Bailey : " The whole area was trampled over when the rain came down. From below, up to the boulder, it's thick broken bracken and you won't get results, I'm afraid. On the shelf above the pool where the deceased was crouched, leaning forward, you'll find her prints superimposed over others. Above that, behind the boulder, is the area where our man, woman or child is thought to have hidden. There's a clear indication of the place where the rock was prised up and signs that some effort was made to scrape out the footprints. All this, on top of the mess left by the crowd. And to add to your joy, Superintendent Coombe and Dr. Maine were up there this morning. Their prints ought to be fairly easy to cut out. The Super was wearing his regulation issue and the doctor's are ripple-soled. Thompson, give us a complete coverage, will you? And we'll need casts, Bailey. Better take them as soon as possible." He looked up at the sky. Heavy clouds were rolling in from the north-west and a fresh wind had sprung up. The sea was no longer calm. " Anyone notice the forecast?"

" Yes," said Fox. " Gales and heavy rain before morning."

" Damn."

He produced Coombe's key for the wire cage which had been locked over the slot machine.

" Notice this, Br'er Fox, would you? It was installed at Miss Cost's insistence to baffle courting couples after dark, and not often used. I think it might be instructive. Only Coombe and The Boy-and-Lobster had keys. You can get out of the enclosure by the other gate, which is on a spring and is self-locking on the inside. You could go in by this turnstile and, if you used a length of string, pull the padlock, on the slack of its chain, round to the netting and lock yourself in."

" Any reason to think it's been done?"

" Only this : there's a fragment of frayed string, caught in the groove of the wire. Get a shot of it, Thompson, will you, before we take possession."

Thompson set up his camera. Alleyn unlocked the cage. He gave each of the others a disc and, in turn, they let themselves in. The shelf and the area above it, round the boulder, had been covered with tarpaulins. " Laid on by Coombe's chaps," Alleyn said. " He's done a good job, never mind his great boots." He stood there for a moment and watched the movement of the welling pool, the sliding lip of water, its glassy fall and perpetual disappearance. Its voices, consulting together, filled the air with their colloquy.

" Well," Alleyn said. " Here you are, Bailey. We'll leave you to it. I'd better have a word with the local P.C.'s. Here are my notes, Fox. Have a look at them for what they're worth."

Mr. Fox drew out his spectacle case and seated himself in the lee of the hillside. Bailey, a man of few words, at once began work and in a minute or two, Thompson joined him. Alleyn returned to the gates and let himself out. He stood with his back to the enclosure where Miss Emily had hung her notice. He looked down Wally's Way to the spot where Wally himself had waved and shouted at her and, beyond that, to the back of the Treherns' cottage and the jetty in Fisherman's Bay. He was very still for a moment. Then he called to Fox who joined him.

" Do you see what I see ? " he asked.

Fox placidly related what he saw.

" Thank you," Alleyn said. " Bear it in mind, Br'er Fox, when you digest those notes. I'm going along to that blasted outcrop." He did so and was met by the constable on duty. The wind was now very strong and much colder. Clouds, inky dark and blown ragged at their edges, drove swiftly in from the sea which had turned steely and was whipped into broken corrugations. The pleasure boats, all heading inshore, danced and bucketed as they came. Portcarrow front was deserted and a procession of cars crawled up the road to the downlands. The hotel launch was discharging a load of people for whom a bus waited by the village jetty. " There goes the Major's drink-cheque," thought Alleyn.

189

" 'Evening," he said to the constable. " This doesn't look too promising, does it ? What are we in for ? "

" A dirty spell, sir, by all tokens. When she bears in sudden and hard like this from the nor'west there's only one way of it. Rain, high seas and a gale."

" Keep the trippers off, at least. Have you had much trouble ? "

" A lot of foolish inquiries, sir, and swarms of they nippers from down along."

" Where's your mate ? Round the point there ? "

" Yes, sir. Nobody's come past the point, though there was plenty that tried. Sick ones and all."

" Anyone you knew ? "

" Two of the maids from The Boy-and-Lobster, sir, giggling and screeching after their silly fashion. The Major came. One of his visitors had dropped a ring, they reckoned, behind that rock, and he wanted to search for it. Us two chaps took a look but it warn't thereabouts. We kept off the ground, sir. So did he, though not best pleased to be said by us."

" Good for you. Sergeant Bailey will deal with it in a minute and we'll get some pictures. Did Major Barrimore leave any prints, did you notice ? "

" So he did, then, and us reckons they'm the dead spit-identicals for the ones that's there already."

" You use your eyes, I see, in this division. What's your name ? "

" Carey, sir."

" I'll come along with you."

They went to the outcrop where Carey's mate, P.C. Pomeroy, kept a chilly watch. Alleyn was shown the Major's footprints where he had pushed forward to the soft verge. He measured them and made a detailed comparison with those behind the outcrop.

190

"Good as gold," he said. "We'll get casts. You've done well, both of you."

They said : "Thank you, sir," in unison and glanced at each other. Alleyn asked if they could raise another tarpaulin for the area and Pomeroy said he'd go down to Fisherman's Bay and borrow one.

They returned with him to the enclosure and found Fox in argument with James Trehern who was wearing an oilskin coat and looked like a lifeboat hero who had run off the rails. His face was scarlet and his manner both cringing and truculent.

"I left my launch in charge of my mate," he was saying, "to come up yurr and get a fair answer to a fair question which is what the hell's going on in these parts ? I got my good name to stand by, mister, and my good name's being called in question. Now."

Fox, who had his notebook in his palm said : "We'll just get this good name and your address, if you please, and then find out what seems to be the trouble."

"Well, Mr. Trehern," Alleyn said, "what *is* the trouble?"

Pomeroy gave Trehern a disfavouring look and set off down the road. Trehern pulled at the peak of his cap and adopted a whining tone. "Not to say, sir," he said to Alleyn, "as how I'm out to interfere with the deadly powers of the law. Us be lawful chaps in this locality and never a breath of anything to the contrary has blowed in our direction. Deny that if you've got the face to, Bill Carey ! " he added turning on that officer.

"Address yourself," Carey said stuffily, "to them that's axing you. Shall I return to my point, sir ? "

"Yes, do, thank you, Carey," Alleyn said and received a salute followed by a smart turn. Carey tramped off along the path.

"Now," Alleyn said to Trehern. "Give Inspector Fox

191

your name and address and we'll hear what you've got to say."

He complied with an ill grace. " I've no call to be took down in writing," he said.

" I thought you were lodging a complaint. Didn't you, Mr. Fox ? "

" So I understood, sir. *Are* you ? " Fox asked Trehern, and looked placidly at him over the top of his spectacles. " We may as well know, one way or the other, while we're about it."

" Just for the record," Alleyn agreed.

" Not to say a complaint," Trehern temporised. " Don't put words into my mouth, souls. No call for that."

" We wouldn't dream of it," Fox rejoined. " Take your time."

After an uneasy silence, Trehern broke into a long, dis-jointed plaint. People, he said, were talking. Wally, he inferred, had been taken aside and seduced with ice-cream. Anybody would tell them that what the poor little lad said was not to be relied upon since he was as innocent as a babe unborn and was only out to please all and sundry, such being his guileless nature. They let him ramble on disconsolately until he ran out of material. Fox took notes throughout.

Alleyn said : " Mr. Trehern, we meant to call on you this evening but you've anticipated us. We want to search your house and have a warrant to do so. If it suits you we'll come down with you, now."

Trehern ran the tip of his tongue round his mouth and looked frightened. " What's that for ? " he demanded. " What's wrong with my property ? I be'ant got nothing but what's lawful and right and free for all to see."

" In that case you can have no objection."

" It's a matter of principle, see ? "

" Quite so."

192

Trehern was staring through the wire enclosure at the Spring where Bailey and Thompson had begun to pack up their gear. " Yurr ! " he said. " What's that ! What be they chaps doing up there ? Be they looking fur footprints ? "

" Yes."

" They won't find our Wal's then ! They won't find his'n. Doan't 'ee tell me they will, mister. I know better."

" He was there yesterday."

" Not up to thicky shelf, he warn't. Not up to the top neither."

" How do you know it matters where he may have been ? Do you know how Miss Cost was killed ? "

Trehern gaped at him.

" Well," Alleyn said, " do you feel inclined to tell us, Mr. Trehern ? "

He said confusedly that everyone was talking about stones being thrown.

" Ah," Alleyn said. " You're thinking of the night you encouraged Wally to throw stones at Miss Pride, aren't you?"

Trehern actually ducked his head as if he himself was some sort of target. " What's the lad been telling you ? " he demanded. " He's silly. He'll say anything."

Alleyn said : " We'll leave it for the moment and go down to the house."

He called through the gate for Bailey and Thompson to follow and led the way down. Trehern looked at his back and opened and shut his hands.

" Will you move along, Mr. Trehern ? " Fox invited him. " After you."

Trehern walked between them down to his cottage.

There were no visitors. The nets were half blown off the fence. The hollyhocks along the front path bent and sprang back in the wind, and the sign rattled.

Trehern stopped inside the gate. " I want to see thick. I want to see the writing."

Alleyn showed him the warrant. He examined it with a great show of caution and then turned to the door.

Alleyn said : " One moment."

" Well ? What then ? "

" It will save a great deal of time and trouble if you will let us see the thing we're most interested in. Where have you put the clothes-line ? "

" I don't have to do nothing," he said, showing the whites of his eyes. " You can't force me."

" Certainly not. It's your choice." He looked at Fox. " Will you take the outhouses ? We can go round this way."

He led the way round to the backyard.

Fox said pleasantly : " This'll be the shed where you keep all your gear, won't it ? I'll just take a look round, if you please."

It was crammed with a litter of old nets, broken oars, sacking, boxes, tools and a stack of empty gin bottles. Alleyn glanced in and then left it to Fox. There was a hen coop at the far end of the yard with a rubbish heap near-by that looked as if it had been recently disturbed.

" Give me that fork, would you, Fox ? " he said and walked down the path with it. Trehern started to follow him and then stood motionless. The first of the rain drove hard on their backs.

The clothes-line had been neatly coiled and buried under the rubbish. Alleyn uncovered it in a matter of seconds.

" Shall we get under shelter ? " he said and walked back past Trehern to the shed. He wondered, for a moment, if Trehern would strike out at him but he fumbled with his oilskin coat and stayed where he was.

" All right, Fox," Alleyn said. " First time lucky. Here we are."

194

He gave Fox the coil and took from his pocket the piece of trip-wire from Coombe's office. They held the ends together. "That's it," said Fox.

Alleyn looked at Trehern. "Will you come here for a moment ?" he asked.

He thought Trehern was going to refuse. He stood there with his head lowered and gave no sign. Then he came slowly forward, lashed now, by the rain ; a black shining figure.

"I am not going to arrest you at this juncture," Alleyn said, "but I think it right to warn you that you are in a serious position. It is quite certain that the wire which, two days ago, was stretched across the way up to the shelf above the Spring, has been cut from this line. Photography and accurate measurements of the strands will prove it. Is there anything you want to say ?"

Trehern's jaw worked convulsively as if he were chewing gum. He made a hoarse indeterminate sound in his throat : like a nervous dog, Alleyn thought. At last he said : "Whosumdever done them tricks was having no more than a bit of fun. Boy-fashion. No harm in it."

"You think not ?"

"If it was my Wal, I'll have the hide off of him."

"I shouldn't go in for any more violence if I were you, Mr. Trehern. And Wally didn't rig the trip-wire. It was done by a man who knows how to use his hands and it was done with a length of your clothes-line which you've tried to conceal. Will you make a statement about that ? You are not compelled to do so. You must use your own judgment."

"A statement ! And be took down in writing ? Not such a damned fool. Lookie-yurr ! What's these silly larks to do with Elspeth Cost ? It's her that's laying cold, be'ant it ? Not t'other old besom."

"Of course," Alleyn said, swallowing the epithet. After

all, he'd thrown one or two himself, at Miss Emily. " So you don't think," he said, " that Miss Cost was mistaken for Miss Pride ? "

" I do not, mister. Contrariwise. I reckon one female done it on t'other."

" What were *you* doing at half past seven this morning ? "

" Asleep in my bed."

" When did you wake ? "

" How do I know when I woke ? Hold on, though."

" Yes ? "

" Yes, b'God ! " Trehern said slowly. " Give a chap time to think, will you ? I disremembered but it's come back, like. I heered the lad, banging and hooting about the place. Woke me up, did young Wal, and I hollered out to him to shut his noise. He takes them fits of screeching. Por lil' chap." Trehern added with a belated show of parental concern. " Gawd knows why, but he does. I look at the clock and it's five past eight. I rouse up my old woman which is a masterpiece of a job she being a mortal heavy slumberer, and tell 'er to wet a pot of tea. Nothing come of it. She sunk back in her beastly oblivyan. So I uprose myself and put the kettle on and took a look at the weather which were mucky."

" Was Wally still in the house ? "

" So 'e were, then, singing to hisself after his simple fashion and setting in a corner."

" Did you see anybody about when you looked out of doors ? "

Trehern peered sidelong at him. He waited for a moment and then said : " I seed the doctor, in 'is launch. Putting out across the gap to go home, he was, having seen Bessy Trethaway, over the way, yurr, come to light with another in this sinful vale of tears."

" Is your clock right ? "

" Good as gold," he said quickly. " Can't go wrong."

" Can I see it ? "

He looked as if he might refuse but in the end, lurched into the house, followed by Fox, and returned with a battered alarm clock. Alleyn checked it by his watch.

" Six minutes slow," he said.

Trehern burst out angrily : " I don't have no call for clocks ! I'm a seafaring chap and read the time of day off of the face of nature. Sky and tides is good enough for me and my mates in the bay'll bear me out. Six minutes fast or six minutes slow by thicky clock's no matter to me. I looked outer my winder and it wur dead water and dead water come when I said it come and if that there por female was sent to make the best of 'erself before 'er Maker when I looked outer my winder she died at dead water and that's an end of it."

" Trehern," Alleyn said, " what are you going to make of this ? Mrs. Trethaway's baby was born at seven-thirty and Dr. Maine left in his launch about ten minutes later. You're a full half hour out in your times."

There was a long silence.

" Well ? " Alleyn said. " Any comment ? "

He broke into a stream of oaths and disjointed expostulations. Did they call him a liar ? Nobody called Jim Trehern a liar and got away with it. If they weren't going to believe him why did they ask ? There was talk against him in the bay. Jealousy seemed to be implied. His anger modulated through resentfulness and fear into his familiar occupational whine. Finally he said that a man could make mistakes, couldn't he ? When Alleyn asked if he meant that he'd mistaken the time, Trehern said he didn't want his words taken out of his mouth and used against him. He could scarcely have made a more dubious showing. He was joined briefly by his spouse who emerged from the interior,

197

stood blinking in the back doorway, and was peremptorily ordered back by her husband. Inside the cottage, actors could be heard, galloping about on horses and shouting " C'm' on. Let's go," to each other. Wally, Alleyn supposed, was enjoying television.

Trehern suddenly bawled out : " You boy ! Wal ! Come yurr ! Come out of it when you're bid ! "

Wally shambled into the back porch, saw Alleyn and smiled widely.

" Come on ! " his father said and took him by the arm. Wally began to whimper.

" Now then. Tell truth and shame the devil. You been chucking rocks ? "

" No. No, I be'ant."

" No, and better not. Speak up and tell these yurr gents. Swear if you hope you won't get half-skinned for a liar as you never chucked no rocks at nobody."

" I never chucked no rocks only stones," Wally said, trembling. " Like you said to."

" That'll do ! " his father said ferociously. " Get in." Wally bolted.

Alleyn said : " You'd better watch your step with that boy. Do you thrash him ? "

" Never raise a hand to him, mister. Just a manner of speaking. He don't understand nothing different. Never had no mother-love, poor kid : I have to pour out sufficient for both and a heavy job it is."

" You may find yourself describing it to the welfare officer, one of these days."

" Them bastards ! "

" Now, look here, Trehern, you heard what the boy said. ' No rocks only stones, like you said to.' Hadn't you better make the best of that statement and admit he threw stones at Miss Pride and you knew it. Think it out."

198

Trehern made a half-turn, knocked his boot against an old tin and kicked it savagely to the far end of the yard. This, apparently, made up his mind for him.

" If I say he done it in one of his foolish turns meaning no harm and acting the goat—all right—I don't deny it and I don't axcuse it. But I do deny and will, and you won't shift me an inch, he never heaved no rock at Elspeth Cost. I'll take my Bible oath on it and may I be struck dead if I lie."

" How can you be so sure ? Miss Pride saw the boy in the lane at about twenty to eight. So did Dr. Maine. You weren't there. Or were you ? "

" I was not. *By God I was not*, and I'll lay anyone cold that says different. And how can I be so sure ? " He advanced upon Alleyn and thrust his face towards him. His unshaven jowls glittered with raindrops. " I'll tell you flat how I can be so sure. That boy never told a lie in his life, mister. He'm too simple. Ax anybody. Ax his teacher. Ax parson. Ax his mates. He'm a truth-speaking lad, por little sod, and for better or worse, the truth's all you'll ever get out of our Wal."

Alleyn heard Jenny Williams's voice: " He's an extraordinarily truthful little boy. He never tells lies—never." He looked at Trehern and said: " All right. We'll let it go at that, for the moment. Good evening to you."

As they walked round the side of the house Trehern shouted after them: " What about the female of the speeches ? Pride ? Pride has to take a fall, don't she ? "

There was a wild scream of laughter from Mrs. Trehern and a door banged.

" That will do to go on with," Alleyn said to Fox, and aped Wally's serial: " C'm. Let's go."

8. The Shop

They found Bailey and Thompson outside, locked in their mackintoshes with an air of customary usage and with their gear stowed inside waterproof covers. Rain cascaded from their hat brims.

" We'll go back to the pub," Alleyn said. " In a minute."

The Trethaways' cottage was across the lane from the Treherns'. Alleyn knocked at the back door and was invited in by the proud father : an enormous grinning fellow. The latest addition was screaming very lustily in the bedroom. Her father apologised for this drawback to conversation.

" 'Er be a lil' maid, 'er be," he said, " and letting fly with 'er vocal powers according."

They stood by the kitchen window which looked up the lane towards the Spring. Seeing this, Alleyn asked him if he'd happened to notice Wally in the lane at about the time the baby was born or soon after and was given the reasonable answer that Mr. Trethaway's attention was on other matters. The baby had indeed been born at seven-thirty and Dr. Maine had in fact left very soon afterwards.

Alleyn congratulated Trethaway, shook his hand, rejoined his colleagues and told them what he'd gleaned.

" So why does Trehern say he saw the doctor leave at about five past eight ? " Fox asked. " There's usually only one reason for that sort of lie, isn't there ? Trying to rig the time, so that you look as if you couldn't have been on the spot. That's the normal caper."

200

" So it is then," Alleyn agreed with a reasonable imitation of the local voice. " But there are loose ends here. Or are there ? "

" Well yes," Fox said. " In a way."

" Bailey : what did you get ? Any fisherman's boots superimposed on the general mess ? Or boy's boots ? I couldn't find any."

" Nothing like that, Mr. Alleyn. But as you said yourself, this flat slice of stone's been used to cut out recent prints. We've picked up enough to settle that point," Bailey said grudgingly, " not much else. The only nice jobs are the ones left after this morning's rain by a set of regulation tens and another of brogues or gentleman's country shoes, size nine-and-a-half ripple soles and in good repair."

" I know. The Super and the doctor."

" That's right, sir, from what you've mentioned."

" What about the stuff near the outcrop and behind it ? "

" What you thought, Mr. Alleyn. They match. Hand-sewn, officer's type. Ten-and-a-half but custom-made. Worn but well-kept."

" In a sense you might be describing the owner. Did you tell Carey he could go off duty ? "

" Yes, sir. There seemed no call for him to stay. We've got all the casts and photographs we want. I used salt in the plaster, seeing how the weather was shaping. It was O.K. Nice results."

" Good. It's getting rougher. Look at that sea."

In the channel between Island and village, the tide now rolled and broke in a confusion of foam and jetting spray. Out at sea there were white horses everywhere. The horizon was dark and broken. The causeway was lashed by breakers that struck, rose, fell across it and withdrew, leaving it momentarily exposed and blackly glinting in what remained of the daylight. The hotel launch bucketed and rolled at the jetty. A man in oilskins was mounting extra fenders. Above the general roar of sea and rain, the thud of the launch's starboard side against the legs of the jetty could be clearly heard.

Light shone dimly behind the windows of Miss Cost's Giffte Shoppe.

" P.C. Pender's locked up in there with Miss Cissy Pollock on the switchboard," Alleyn muttered. " I'll just have a word with him." He tapped on the door. After a moment, it was opened a crack and Mr. Pender said : " Be'ant no manner of use pestering—" and then saw Alleyn. " Beg pardon, sir, I'm sure," he said. " Thought you was one of they damned kids come back." He flung open the door. Alleyn called to Fox and the others and they went in.

The shop smelt fustily of cardboard, wool and gum. In the postal section, Miss Cissy Pollock bulged at a switchboard : all eyes and teeth when she saw the visitors.

Pender said that a call had come through for Alleyn from Dunlowman. " Sir James Curtis, it were, sir," he said with reverence. Curtis was the Home Office pathologist. " Wishful to speak with you. I intercepted the call, sir, and informed the station and The Boy-and-Lobster."

" Where was he ? "

" Dunlowman mortuary, sir, along with the body and the doctor. I've got the number."

" Aw, dear ! " Miss Pollock exclaimed. " Be'ant it shocking though ! " She had removed her headphones.

Alleyn asked if she could put him through. She engaged to do so and directed him to an instrument in a cubbyhole.

The mortuary attendant answered and said Sir James was just leaving but he'd try to catch him. He could be heard pounding off down a concrete passage. In a minute or two the great man spoke.

" Hullo, Rory, where the devil have you been ? I've done this job for you. Want the report ? "

" Please."

It was straightforward enough. Death by drowning following insensibility caused by a blow on the head. The piece of rock was undoubtedly the instrument. Contents of stomach, Sir James briskly continued, showed that she'd had a cup of tea and a biscuit about an hour and three-quarters before she died. On Dr. Maine's evidence he would agree that she had probably been dead about an hour when Alleyn found her. Sir James had another case more or less on the way back to London and would like to get off before he himself was drowned. Would Alleyn let him know about the inquest ? Dr. Maine would tell him anything else he wanted to hear and was now on his way back to Portcarrow. " I'm told you're on an island," said Sir James, merrily. " You'll be likely to stay there if the weather report's to be trusted. What book will you choose if you can only have one ? "

" *The Gentle Art of Making Enemies*," said Alleyn and hung up.

He told Pender that he and Fox would return after dinner and asked him what he himself would do for a meal. Pender said that there was a cut loaf and some butter and ham in Miss Cost's refrigerator and would it be going too far if he and Cissy made sandwiches ? There was also some cheese and pickle. They could, he said, be replaced.

" You can't beat a cheese and pickle sandwich," Fox observed, " if the cheese is tasty."

Alleyn said that under the circumstances he felt Pender might proceed on the lines indicated and left him looking relieved.

They climbed the hotel steps, staggering against the gale, and entered The Boy-and-Lobster. It was now five minutes to eight.

Alleyn asked the reception clerk if he could find rooms for

his three colleagues and learnt that the guests had dwindled to thirty. All incoming trains and buses had been met at Dunlowman and intending visitors told about the situation. Accommodation had been organised with various establishments over a distance of fifteen miles and, in view of the weather forecast and the closure of the Spring, most of the travellers had elected, as the clerk put it, to stay away. " We can be cut off," he said, " if it's really bad. It doesn't often happen but if this goes on, it might." The guests in residence had all come by car and were now at dinner.

Alleyn left the others to collect their suitcases and arranged to meet them in the dining-room. He went to his own room, effected a quick change and called on Miss Emily who was four doors away.

She was finishing her dinner. She sat bolt upright, peeling grapes. A flask of red wine was before her and a book was at her elbow with a knife laid across to keep it open. She was perfectly composed.

" I've only looked in for a moment," he said. " We're running late. How are you, Miss Emily ? Bored to sobs, I'm afraid."

" Good evening, Roderique. No, I am not unduly bored, though I have missed taking my walk."

" It's no weather for walking, I assure you. How are they treating you ? "

" This morning the chambermaid's manner was equivocal and at luncheon I found the waiter impertinent. To-night, however, there is a marked change. It appears that I am, or was, suspected of murder," said Miss Emily.

" What makes you think so ? "

" Before taking my siesta I ventured out on the balcony. There was a group of children on the steps leading to the hotel. When they saw me they began to chant. I will not trouble you with the words. The intention was inescapable."

" Little animals."

" Oh, perfectly. It was of no moment."

There was a tap on the door and a waiter came in.

" Thank you," said Miss Emily. " You may clear."

Alleyn watched the man for a moment and then said :
" I'd like a word with you, if you please."

" With me, sir ? "

" Yes. I am a Superintendent of Scotland Yard, in charge
of investigations into the death of Miss Elspeth Cost. I
think perhaps the staff of the hotel should be informed that
this lady is associated with me in the case and may be regarded as an expert. Do you understand ? "

" Yes, sir. Certainly, sir. I'm sure I hope madam has no
complaints, sir."

" I hope so, too. She hasn't made any but I shall do so if
any more idiotic nonsense is circulated. You may say so to
anybody that is interested."

" Thank you, sir," said the waiter and withdrew.

" *Chose remarquable !* " said Miss Emily. " So now, it
appears I am a detectrice."

" It'll be all over the hotel in five minutes and Portcarrow will have it by morning. About your transport to
Dunlowman——"

" Do not trouble yourself. The young man—Patrick—has
offered to drive us," Miss Emily said with an air of amusement.

" I see. It may be pretty rough going across to the village,
if this weather persists."

" No matter."

" Before I go, would you mind very much if we went over
one incident : the few minutes, round about twenty to eight,
when you hung your notice by the Spring ? "

" Certainly," Miss Emily said. She repeated her story.
She had seen Wally down on the road. He had whooped,

205

chanted, waved his arms and afterwards disappeared. She had seen nobody else and had returned to the hotel with her umbrella between herself and the prospect.

" Yes," he said. " I know. I just wanted to hear it again. Thank you, Miss Emily. You don't ask me how the case progresses, I notice."

" You would tell me, no doubt, if you wished to do so."

" Well," he said. " I always think it's unlucky to talk at this stage : but it does progress."

" Good. Go and have your dinner. If you are not too fatigued I should be glad if you would call upon me later in the evening."

" When do you retire ? "

" Not early. I find I am restless," said Miss Emily.

They fell silent. The wind made a sudden onslaught on her windows. " Perhaps it is the storm," she said.

" I'll see if there's a light under your door. *Au revoir*, then, Miss Emily."

" *Au revoir*, my dear Roderique. Enjoy, if that is not too extravagant a word, your dinner. The dressed crab is not bad. The *filet mignon*, on the other hand, is contemptible."

She waved her hand and he left her.

Fox, Bailey and Thompson were already in the dining-room. Alleyn had been given a table to himself. As there was not room at theirs, he took it, but joined them for a minute or two before he did so.

Everyone else had gone except Jenny and Patrick who sat at the family table, nursing balloon glasses. They had an air of subdued celebration and as often as they looked at each other, broke into smiles. When Jenny saw Alleyn, she waggled her fingers at him.

Alleyn said : " Afraid it's a case of pressing on, chaps. We'll meet in the hall, afterwards, and go down to the shop. Have you ordered drinks ? "

" Not so far, Mr. Alleyn."

" Well, have them with me. What shall it be ? Waiter ! "

They settled for beer. Alleyn went to his own table and was fawned upon by Miss Emily's waiter. Jenny and Patrick passed by and Jenny paused to say : " We're going to try and whip up a bit of *joie de vivre* in the lounge, like they do in ships. Patrick's thought up a guessing game. Come and help."

" I'd love to," Alleyn said, "but I'm on a guessing game of my own, bad luck to it." He looked at Patrick. " I hear you've offered to do the driving to-morrow. Very civil of you. Miss Emily's looking forward to it."

" It's going to be a rough crossing if this keeps up."

" I know."

" Will she mind ? "

" Not she. At the age of sixty, she was a queen-pin in the *Résistance* and hasn't noticed the passage of time. Get her to tell you how she dressed up a couple of kiwis as nuns."

" Honestly ! " Jenny exclaimed.

" It's quite a story."

The waiter came up to say that Dr. Maine had arrived and was asking for him.

" Right," Alleyn said. " I'll come."

" In the writing-room, sir."

It was a small deserted place off the entrance hall. Dr. Maine had removed his mackintosh and hung it over the back of a chair. He was shaking the rain off his hat when Alleyn came in. " What a night ! " he said. " I thought I wouldn't make it."

" How did you cross ? "

" In my launch. Damned if I know how she'll take it going back. The causeway's impossible. Sir James thought you'd like to see me and I had to come over, anyway, to a patient."

Alleyn said : " I'm glad to see you. Not so much about the p.m. ! Curtis made that clear enough. I wanted to check up one or two points. Have a drink, won't you ? "

" I certainly will. Thank you."

Alleyn found a bell-push. " I hope you won't mind if I don't join you," he said. " I've had my allowance and I've got a night's work ahead of me."

" I suppose you get used to it—like a G.P."

" Very much so, I imagine. What'll you have ? "

Dr. Maine had a whisky and soda. " I thought I'd take a look at Miss Pride while I'm here," he said. " She's recovered, of course, but she had quite a nasty cut in her neck. I suppose I mustn't ask about the police view of that episode. Or doesn't it arise ? "

" I don't see why you shouldn't. It arises in a sort of secondary way, if only to be dismissed. What do you think?"

" On the face of it, Wally Trehern. Inspired by his father, I daresay. It's Miss Pride's contention and I think she may well be right."

" I think so, too. Does it tie up with the general pattern of behaviour—from your point of view ? "

" Oh yes. Very characteristic. He gets over-excited and wildish. Sometimes this sort of behaviour is followed up by an attack of *petit mal*. Not always, but it's quite often the pattern."

" Can't anything be done for the boy ? "

" Not much, I'm afraid. When they start these attacks in early childhood. it's a poorish prospect. He should lead a quiet, regular life. It may well be that his home background and all the nonsense of producing him as a showpiece, is bad for him. I'm not at all sure," Dr. Maine said, " that I shouldn't have taken his case up with the child-welfare people but there's been no marked deterioration and I've hesitated. Now, well—now, one wonders."

" One wonders—*what* exactly ? "

" A, if he shouldn't, in any case, be removed to a suitable institution and B, whether he's responsible for heaving that rock at Miss Cost."

" If he did heave it, it must have been about half an hour after you saw him doing his stuff on Wally's Way."

" I know. Sir James puts the death at about eight o'clock, give and take twenty minutes. I wish I'd watched the boy more closely but of course there was no reason to do so. I was swinging the launch round."

" And it *was* about seven-forty, wasn't it ? "

" About that, yes. Within a couple of minutes, I should say."

" You didn't happen to notice Miss Pride ? She was in the offing too, and saw Wally."

" *Was* she, by George ! No, I didn't see her. The top of the wheel-house would cut off my view, I fancy."

" What *exactly* was Wally doing ? Sorry to nag on about it, but Miss Pride may have missed some little pointer. We need one badly enough, Lord knows."

" He was jumping about with his back towards me. He waved his arms and did a sort of throwing gesture. Now that you tell me Miss Pride *was* up by the gates, I should think his antics were directed at her. I seem to remember that the last thing I saw him do was to take a run uphill. But it was all quite momentary, you know."

" His father says Wally was in the house at five past eight."

Dr. Maine considered this. " It would still be possible," he said. " There's time, isn't there ? "

" On the face of it—yes. Trehern also says that at five past eight or soon afterwards, he saw you leave in your launch."

" Does he, indeed ! He lies like a flat-fish," said Dr. Maine. He looked thoughtfully at Alleyn. " Now, I wonder just why," he said thoughtfully. " I wonder."

"So do I, I assure you." They stared meditatively at each other. Alleyn said : " Who do you think was the original Green Lady ? "

Dr. Maine was normally of a sallow complexion but now a painful red blotted his lean face and transfigured it. " I have never considered the matter," he said. " I have no idea. It's always been supposed that he imagined the whole thing."

" It was Mrs. Barrimore."

" You can have no imaginable reason for thinking so," he said angrily.

" I've the best possible reason," said Alleyn. " Believe me. Every possible reason."

" Do you mean that Mrs. Barrimore herself told you this?"

" Virtually, yes. I am not," Alleyn said, " trying to equivocate. I asked her and she said she supposed she must congratulate me."

Dr. Maine put his glass down and walked about the room with his hands in his pockets. Alleyn thought he was giving himself time. Presently he said : " I can't for the life of me, make out why you concern yourself with this. Surely it's quite beside the point."

" I do so because I don't understand it. Or am not sure that I understand it. If it turns out to be irrelevant I shall make no more of it. What I don't understand, to be precise, is why Mrs. Barrimore should be so distressed at the discovery."

" But, good God, man, of course she's distressed ! Look here. Suppose—I admit nothing—but suppose she came across that wretched kid, blubbing his eyes out because he'd been baited about his warts. Suppose she saw him trying to wash them off and on the spur of the moment, remembering the history of wart-cures, she made him believe they would clear up if he thought they would. Very well. The boy goes home and they do. Before we know—she knows—where

210

she is, the whole thing blows up into a highly publicised nine-days-wonder. She can't make up her mind to disabuse the boy or disillusion the people that follow him. It gets out of hand. The longer she hesitates, the harder it gets."

" Yes," Alleyn said. " I know. That all makes sense and is perfectly understandable."

" Very well, then ! " he said impatiently.

" She was overwhelmingly anxious that I shouldn't tell her husband."

" I daresay," Dr. Maine said shortly. " He's not a suitable subject for confidences."

" Did she tell you ? All right," Alleyn said answering the extremely dark look Dr. Maine gave him. " I know I'm being impertinent. I've got to be."

" I am her doctor. She consulted me about it. I advised her to say nothing."

" Yes ? "

" The thing was working. Off and on, as always happens in these emotional—these faith-cures, if you like—there are authentic cases. With people whose troubles had a nervous connotation, the publicising of this perfectly innocent deception would have been harmful."

" Asthma, for one ? "

" Possibly."

" Miss Cost, for instance ? "

" If you like."

" Was Miss Cost a patient of yours ? "

" She was. She had moles that needed attention ; she came into my nursing home and I removed them. About a year ago, it would be."

" I wish you'd tell me what she was like."

" Look here, Alleyn, I really do not see that the accident of my being called out to examine the body requires me to

211

disregard my professional obligations. I do *not* discuss my patients alive or dead, with any layman."

Alleyn said mildly : " His Worship the Mayor seems to think she was a near-nymphomaniac."

Dr. Maine snorted.

" Well, was she ? "

' All right. All right. She was a bloody nuisance, like many another frustrated spinster. Will that do ? "

" Nicely, thank you. Do you imagine she ever suspected the truth about the Green Lady ? "

" I have not the remotest idea but I should think it most unlikely. She, of all people ! Look at that damn' farce of a show yesterday. Look at her shop ! Green Ladies by the gross. If you want my opinion on the case which I don't suppose you do——"

" On the contrary I was going to ask for it."

" Then, I think the boy did it, and I hope that, for his sake, it will go no further than finding that he's irresponsible and chucked the rock aimlessly or at least with no idea of the actual damage it would do. He can then be removed from his parents, who are no good to him anyway, and given proper care and attention. If I'm asked for an opinion at the inquest that will be it."

" Tidy. Straightforward. Obvious."

" And you don't believe it ? "

" I would like to believe it," said Alleyn.

" I need hardly say I'd be interested to know your objections."

" You may say they're more or less mechanical. No," Alleyn said correcting himself. " That's not quite it, either. We'll just have to press on and see how we go. And press on I must, by the same token. My chaps'll be waiting for me."

" You're going out ? "

" Yes. Routine, you know. Routine."

212

" You'll be half-drowned."

" It's not far. Only to the shop. By the way, did you know we're moving Miss Pride in the morning ? She's going to the Manor Park Hotel outside Dunlowman."

" But why ? Isn't she comfortable here ? "

" It's not particularly comfortable to be suspected of homicide."

" But—oh, good *Lord* ! " he exclaimed disgustedly.

" The village louts shout doggerel at her and the servants have been unpleasant. I don't want her to be subjected to any more Portcarrow humour in the form of practical jokes."

" There's no chance of that, surely. Or don't you think Miss Cost inspired that lot ? "

" I think she inspired them, all right, but they might be continued in her permanent absence ; the habit having been formed and Miss Pride's unpopularity having increased."

" Absolute idiocy ! " he said angrily.

" I think, as a matter of fact, I've probably stopped the rot but it's better for her to get away from the place."

" You know, I very much doubt if the channel will be negotiable in the morning. This looks like being the worst storm we've had for years. In any case it'll be devilishly awkward getting her aboard the launch. We don't want a broken leg."

" Of course not. We'll simply have to wait and see what the day brings forth. If you're going to visit her, you might warn her about the possibility, will you ? "

" Yes, certainly."

They were silent for a moment. A sudden onslaught of the gale beat against The Boy-and-Lobster and screamed in the chimney. " Well, good night," Alleyn said.

He had got as far as the door when Dr. Maine said : " There *is* one thing you perhaps ought to know about Elspeth Cost."

" Yes ? "

" She lived in a world of fantasy. Again, with women of her temperament, condition and age, it's a not unusual state of affairs, but with her its manifestations were extreme."

" Was she in consequence a liar ? "

" Oh yes," he said. " It follows on the condition. You may say she couldn't help it."

" Thank you for telling me," Alleyn said.

" It may not arise."

" You never know. Good night, then, Maine."

II

When they were outside and the hotel doors had shut behind them, they were engulfed in a world of turbulence : a complex uproar into which they moved, leaning forward, with their heads down. They slipped on concrete steps, bumped into each other and then hung on by an iron rail and moved down crabwise towards the sea. Below them, riding-lights on the hotel launch tipped, rose, sank and shuddered. A single street lamp near the jetty was struck across by continuous diagonals of rain. On the far side, black masses heaved and broke against the front, obscured and revealed dimly-lit windows and flung their crests high above the glittering terrace. As the three men came to the foot of the steps they were stung and lashed by driven spume.

Miss Cost's shop window glowed faintly beyond the rain. When they reached it they had to bang on the door and yell at Pender before he heard them above the general clamour. It opened a crack. " Easy on, souls," Pender shouted, " or she'll blow in." He admitted them, one by one, with his shoulder to the door.

The interior fug had become enriched by a paraffin heater that reeked in Miss Cissy Pollock's corner and by Pender who breathed out pickled onions. Miss Pollock, herself a little bleary-eyed now, but ever-smiling, still presided at the switchboard.

" Wicked night," Pender observed bolting the door.

" You must be pretty well fed up, both of you," Alleyn said.

" No, sir, no. We be tolerably clever, thank you. Cissy showed me how her switchboard works. A simple enough matter to the male intelligence, it turned out to be, and I took a turn at it while she had a nap. She come back like a lion refreshed and I followed her example. Matter of fact, sir, I was still dozing when you hammered at the door, wasn't I, Ciss ? She can't hear with they contraptions on her head. A simple pattern of a female, she is, sir, as you'll find out for yourself, if you see fit to interrogate her, but rather pleased than otherwise to remain." He beamed upon Miss Pollock who giggled.

Fox gravely contemplated Sergeant Pender. He was a stickler for procedure.

Alleyn introduced Pender to his colleagues. They took off their coats and hats and he laid down a plan of action. They were to make a systematic examination of the premises.

" We're not looking for anything specific," he said. "I'd like to find out how she stood, financially. Correspondence, if any. It would be lovely if she kept a diary and if there's a dump of old newspapers, they'll have to be gone over carefully. Look for any cuts. Bailey, you'd better pick up a decent set of prints if you can find them. Cashbox—toothglass—she had false teeth—take your pick. Thompson, will you handle the shelves in here ? You might work the back premises and the bedroom, Fox. I'll start on the parlour."

He approached Cissy Pollock who removed her headphones and simpered.

" You must have known Miss Cost very well," he began. " How long have you been here with her, Miss Pollock ? "

A matter of a year and up, it appeared. Ever since the shop was made a post office. Miss Cost had sold her former establishment at Dunlowman and had converted a cottage into the premises as they now stood. She had arranged for a wholesale firm to provide the Green Ladies, which she herself painted, and for a regional printer to reproduce the rhyme-sheets. Cissy talked quite readily of these activities and Miss Cost emerged from her narrative as an experienced business-woman. " She were proper sharp," Cissy said appreciatively. When Alleyn spoke of yesterday's Festival she relapsed briefly into giggles but this seemed to be a token mani-festation, obligatory upon the star-performer. Miss Cost had inaugurated a Drama Circle of which the Festival had been the first-fruit and Cissy herself, the leading light. He edged cautiously towards the less public aspects of Miss Cost's life and character. Had she many close friends ? None that Cissy knew of though she did send Christmas cards. She hardly got any herself, outside local ones.

" So you were her best friend, then ? "

" Aw well," said Cissy and shuffled her feet.

" What about gentlemen friends ? "

This produced a renewed attack of giggles. After a great deal of trouble he elicited the now familiar story of advance and frustration. Miss Cost had warned Cissy repeatedly of the gentlemen and had evidently dropped a good many dark hints about improper overtures made to herself. Cissy was not pretty and was no longer very young. He thought that, between them, they had probably indulged in continuous fantasy and the idea rather appalled him. On Major Barri-more's name being introduced in a roundabout fashion, she became uncomfortable and said, under pressure, that Miss Cost was proper set against him, and that he'd treated her bad. She would say nothing more under this heading. She remembered Miss Cost's visit to the hospital. It appeared that she had tried the Spring for her moles but without success. Alleyn ventured to ask if Miss Cost liked Dr. Maine. Cissy, with a sudden burst of candour, said she fair worshipped him.

" Ah ! " said Sergeant Pender who had listened to all this with the liveliest attention. " So, she did then, and hunted the poor chap merciless, didn't she, Ciss ? "

" Aw, you do be awful, George Pender," said Cissy, with spirit.

" Couldn't help herself, no doubt, and not to be blamed for it," he conceded.

Alleyn again asked Cissy if Miss Cost had any close women friends. Mrs. Carstairs ? Or Mrs. Barrimore, for instance ?

Cissy made a prim face that was also, in some indefinable way, furtive. " She weren't terrible struck on Mrs. Barrimore," she said. " She didn't hold with her."

" Oh ? Why was that, do you suppose ? "

" She reckoned she were sly," said Cissy and was not to be drawn any further.

" Did Miss Cost keep a diary, do you know ? " Alleyn asked, and as Cissy looked blank, he added : " A book. A record of day-to-day happenings ? "

Cissy said Miss Cost was always writing in a book of an evening but kept it away careful-like, she didn't know where. Asked if she had noticed any change in Miss Cost's behaviour over the last three weeks, Cissy gaped at Alleyn for a second or two and then said Miss Cost had been kind of funny.

" In what way, funny ? "

" Laughing," said Cissy. " She took fits to laugh, sudden-like. I never see nothing to make her."

" As if she was—what ? Amused ? Excited ? "

" Axcited. Powerful pleased too. Sly-like."

" Did you happen to notice if she sent any letters to London ? "

Miss Cost had on several occasions put her own letters in the mailbag but Cissy hadn't got a look at them. Evidently, Alleyn decided, Miss Cost's manner had intrigued her assistant. It was on these occasions that Miss Cost laughed.

At this juncture, Cissy was required at the switchboard. Alleyn asked Pender to follow him into the back room. He shut the door and said he thought the time had come for Miss Pollock to return to her home. She lived on the Island, it appeared, in one of the Fisherman's Bay cottages. Alleyn suggested that Pender had better see her to her door as the storm was so bad. They could be shown how to work the switchboard during his absence.

When they had gone, Alleyn retired to the parlour and began operations upon Miss Cost's desk which, on first inspection, appeared to be a monument to the dimmest kind of disorder. Bills, dockets, trade-leaflets and business communications were jumbled together in ill-running drawers and overcrowded pigeon-holes. He sorted them into heaps and secured them with rubber bands.

He called out to Fox, who was in the kitchen : " As far as I can make out she was doing very nicely indeed, thank you. There's a crack-pot sort of day-book. No out-standing debts and an extremely healthy bank statement. We'll get at her financial position through the income-tax people, of course. What've you got ? "

" Nothing to rave about," Fox said.

" Newspapers ? "

" Not yet. It's a coal range, though."

" Damn."

They worked on in silence. Bailey reported a good set of impressions from a tumbler by the bed and Thompson, relieved of the switchboard, photographed them. Fox put on his mackintosh and retired with a torch to an outhouse, admitting, briefly, the cold and uproar of the storm. After an interval he returned, bland with success, and bearing a coal-grimed, wet, crumpled and scorched fragment of newsprint.

"This might be something," he said and laid it out for Alleyn's inspection.

It was part of a sheet from the local paper from which a narrow strip had been cleanly excised. The remainder of a headline read : "—— to Well-known Beauty Spot" and underneath : "The Natural Amenities Association. At a meeting held at Dunlowman on Wednesday it was resolved to lodge a protest at the threat to Hatcherds Common where it is proposed to build——" "That's it, I'm sure," Alleyn said. "Same type. The original messages are in my desk, blast it, but one of them reads 'Threat' (in these capitals) 'to close You are warned' : a good enough indication that she was responsible. Any more ?"

"No. This was in the ash-bin. Fallen into the grate, most likely, when she burnt the lot. I don't think there's anything else but I'll take another look by daylight. She's got a bit of a darkroom rigged up out there. Quite well-equipped, too, by the look of it."

"Has she now ? Like to take a slant at it, Thompson ?"

Thompson went out and presently returned to say it was indeed a handy little job of a place and he wouldn't mind using it. "I've got that stuff we shot up at the Spring," he said. "How about it, sir ?"

"I don't see why not. Away you go. Good. Fox, you might penetrate to the bedchamber. I can't find her blasted diary anywhere."

Fox retired to the bedroom. Pender came back and said it was rougher than ever out of doors and he didn't see himself getting back to the village. Would it be all right if he

219

spent the rest of the night on Miss Cost's bed ? "When vacant, in a manner of speaking," he added, being aware of Fox's activities. He emerged from a pitchpine wardrobe, obviously scandalised by Sergeant Pender's unconventional approach, but Alleyn said he saw nothing against the suggestion and set Pender to tend the switchboard and help Thompson.

He returned to his own job. The parlour was a sort of unfinished echo of the front shop. Rows of plastic ladies, awaiting coats of green, yellow and pink paint, smirked blankly from the shelves. There were stacks of rhyme-sheets and stationery and piles of jerkins, still to be sewn up the sides. Through the open door he could see the kitchen table with a jug and sugar-basin and a dirty cup with a sodden crust in its saucer. Miss Cost would have washed them up, no doubt, if she had returned from early service and not gone walking through the rain to her death.

In a large envelope he came across a number of photographs. A group of village maidens, Cissy prominent among them, with their arms upraised in what was clearly intended for corybantic ecstasy. Wally, showing his hands. Wally with his mouth open. Miss Cost herself, in a looking-glass with her thumb on the camera trigger and smiling dreadfully. Several snapshots, obviously taken in the grounds of the nursing home, with Dr. Maine caught in moments of reluctance shading into irritation. Views of the Spring and one of a dark foreign-looking lady with an intense expression.

He heard Fox pull a heavy piece of furniture across the wooden floor and then give an ejaculation.

" Anything ? " Alleyn asked.

" Might be. Behind the bed-head. A locked cupboard. Solid, mortise job. Now, where'd she have stowed the key ? "

" Not in her bag. Where do spinsters hide keys ? "

" I'll try the chest of drawers for a start," said Fox.

" You jolly well do. A favourite cache. Association of ideas. Freud would have something to say about it."

Drawers were wrenched open, one after another.

" By gum ! " Fox presently exclaimed. " You're right, Mr. Alleyn. Two keys. Here we are."

" Where ? "

" Wrapped up in her combs."

" In the absence of a chastity belt, no doubt."

" What's that, Mr. Alleyn ? "

" No matter. Either of them fit ? "

" Hold on. The thing's down by the skirting board. Yes. Yes, I do believe—here we are."

A lock clicked.

" Well ? "

" Two cash boxes, so far," Fox said, his voice strangely muffled.

Alleyn walked into the bedroom and was confronted by his colleague's stern, up-ended beneath an illuminated legend which read :

> " Jog on, jog on the footpath way
> And merrily hent the stile-a."

This was supported by a bookshelf on which the works of Algernon Blackwood and Dennis Wheatley predominated.

Fox was on his knees with his head to the floor and his arm in a cupboard. He extracted two japanned boxes and put them on the unmade bed, across which lay a rumpled nightgown embroidered with lazy daisies.

" The small key's the job for both," he said. " There you are, sir."

The first box contained rolled bundles of bank notes and a well-filled cashbag ; the second, a number of papers. Alleyn began to examine them. The top sheet was a carbon

221

copy with a perforated edge. It showed, in type, a list of dates and times covering the past twelve months.

The Spring.	15th August	8.15 p.m.
	21st ,,	8.20 ,,
	29th ,,	8.30 ,,

There were twenty entries. Two, placed apart from the others, and dated the preceding year, were heavily underlined. " 22nd July, 5 p.m." and " 30th September, 8.45."

" From a duplicating book in her desk," Alleyn said, " a page has been cut out. It'll be the top copy of this one."

" Typewritten," Fox commented.

" There's a decrepit machine in the parlour. We'll check but I think this'll be it."

" Do the dates mean anything to you, Mr. Alleyn ? "

" The underlined item does. Year before last. July 22nd 5 p.m. That's the date and time of the Wally's Warts affair. Yesterday was the second anniversary."

" Would the others be notes of later cures ? Was any record kept ? "

" Not to begin with. There is now. The book's on view at Wally's Cottage. We can check, but I don't think that's the answer. The dates are too closely bunched. They give—let's see ; they give three entries for August of last year, one for September, and then nothing until 27th April of this year. Then a regular sequence over the last three months up to—yes, by George !—up to a fortnight ago. What do you make of it, Br'er Fox ? Any ideas ? "

" Only that they're all within licensing hours. Very nice bitter, they serve up at The Boy-and-Lobster. It wouldn't go down too badly. Warm in here, isn't it ? "

Alleyn looked thoughtfully at him. " You're perfectly right," he said. He went into the shop. " Pender," he called

222

out, " who's the bar-tender in the evenings at The Boy-and-Lobster ? "

" In the old days, sir, it were always the Major hisself. Since these yurr princely extensions, however, there be a barmaid in the main premises and the Major serves in a little wee fancy kind of a place behind the lounge."

" Always ? "

" When he'm capable," said Pender dryly, " which is pretty well always. He'm a masterpiece for holding his liquor."

Pender returned to the shop. " There's one other thing," Alleyn said to Fox. " The actual times she's got here grow later as the days grow longer."

" So they do," Fox said. " That's right. So they do."

" Well : let it simmer. What's next ? Exhibit two."

It was an envelope containing an exposed piece of film and a single print. Alleyn was about to lay the print on Miss Cost's pillow. This bore the impress of her head and a single grey hair. He looked at it briefly, turned aside, and dropped the print on her dressing-table. Fox joined him.

It was a dull, indifferent snapshot : a tangle of bracken, a downward slope of broken ground and the top of a large boulder. In the foreground out of focus was the image of wire-netting.

" Above the Spring," Alleyn said. " Taken from the hillside. Look here, Fox."

Fox adjusted his spectacles. " Feet," he said. " Two pairs. Courting couple."

" Very much so. Miss Cost's anathema. I'm afraid Miss Cost begins to emerge as a progressively unattractive character."

" Shutter-peeping," said Fox. " You don't get it so often among women."

Alleyn turned it over. Neatly written across the back was the current year and " 17th June. 7.30 p.m."

" Last month," Alleyn said. " Bailey ! " he called out. " Here, a minute, would you ? " Bailey came in. " Take a look at this. Use a lens. I want you to tell me if you think the man's shoes in this shot might tally with anything you saw at the Spring. It's a tall order, I know."

Bailey put the snapshot under a lamp and bent over it. Presently he said : " Can I have a word with Thompson, sir ? " Sergeant Thompson was summoned from outer darkness. " How would this blow up ? " Bailey asked him. " Here's the neg."

" It's a shocking neg," Thompson said, and added grudgingly, " she's got an enlarger."

Alleyn said : " On the face of it, do you think there's any hope of a correspondence, Bailey ? "

Bailey, still using his lens said : " Can't really say, sir. The casts are in my room at the pub."

" What about you, Thompson ? Got your shots of the prints ? "

" They're in the dish now."

" Well, take this out and see what you make of it. Have you found her camera ? "

" Yes. Lovely job," Thompson said. " You wouldn't have expected it. Very fast." He named the make with reverence.

" Pender," Alleyn said, re-entering the shop. " Do you know anything about Miss Cost's camera ? "

Pender shook his head and then did what actors call a double-take. " Yes, I do, though," he said. " It was give her in gratitude by a foreign lady that was cured of a terrible bad rash. She was a patient up to hospital and Miss Cost talked her into the Spring."

224

" I see. Thompson, would it get results round about seven-thirty on a summer evening ? "

" Certainly would. Better than this affair, if properly handled."

" All right. See what you can do."

Bailey and Thompson went away and Alleyn rejoined Fox in the bedroom.

" Fox," Alleyn said distastefully, " I don't know whose feet the male pair may prove to be but I'm damn' sure I've recognised the female's."

" Really, Mr. Alleyn ? "

" Yes. Very good buckskin shoes with very good buckles. She wore them to the Festival. I'm afraid it's Mrs. Barrimore."

" Fancy ! " said Fox, after a pause, and he added with his air of simplicity : " Well, then, it's to be hoped the others turn out to be the Major's."

III

There were no other papers and no diary in either of the boxes.

" Did you reach to the end of the cupboard ? " Alleyn asked Fox.

" No, I didn't. It's uncommonly deep. Extends through the wall and under the counter in the shop," Fox grumbled.

" Let me try."

Alleyn lay on the bedroom floor and reached his long arm into the cupboard. His fingers touched something—a book. " She must have used her brolly to fish it out," he grunted. " Hold on. There are two of them—no, three. Here they come : I think—yes. Yes. Br'er Fox. This is *it*."

They were large commercial diaries and were held together with a rubber band. He took them into the parlour and laid

225

them out on Miss Cost's desk. When he opened the first he found page after page covered in Miss Cost's small skeleton handwriting. He read an entry at random :

". . . sweet spot, so quaint and *unspoilt*. Sure I shall like it. One feels the *tug* of earth and sea. The ' pub ' (!) is *really* genuine and goes back to smuggling days. Kept by a *gentleman*. Major B. I take my noggin ' of an evening ' in the taproom and listen to the wonderful ' burr ' in the talk of the fisherfolk. All v. friendly . . . Major B. kept looking at me. I know your sort, sez I. Nothing to object to, *really*. Just an awareness. The wife is rather peculiar : I am not altogether taken. A *man's* woman in every sense of the word, I'm afraid. He doesn't pay her v. much attention."

Alleyn read on for a minute or two. " It would take a day to get through it," he said. " This is her first visit to the Island. Two years ago."

" Interesting ? "

" Excruciating. Where's that list of dates ? "

Fox put it on the desk.

Alleyn turned the pages of the diary. References to Major B., later K., though veiled in unbelievable euphemisms, became more and more explicit. In this respect alone, Alleyn thought, the gallant Major had a lot to answer for. He turned back to the entry for the day after Wally's cure. It was ecstatic.

" I have always," wrote Miss Cost, " believed in fairies. The old magic of water and the spoken rune ! The Green Lady ! He *saw* her, this little lad *saw* her and obeyed her behest. Something *led* me to this Island." She ran on in this vein for the whole of the entry. Alleyn read it with a sensation of exasperated compassion. The entry itself was nothing to his purpose. But across it, heavily inked, Miss

226

Cost on some later occasion had put down an enormous mark of interrogation and, beside this, had added a note: " 30th Sept. 8.45."

This was the second of the two underlined dates on the paper. He turned it up in the diary.

" I am shocked and horrified and *sickened* by what I have seen this evening. My hand shakes. I can hardly bring myself to write it down. I *knew*, from the moment I first set eyes on her, that she was unworthy of him. One *always* knows. Shall not tell K. It would serve him right if I did. All these months and he never guessed. But I won't tell him. Not yet. Not unless—— But I must *write* it. Only so can I rid myself of the horror. I was sitting on the hill below the Spring, thinking so happily of all my plans and so glad I have settled for the shop and ordered my lovely Green Ladies. I was *feeling* the magic of the water. (Blessed, blessed water. *No* asthma, now, for *four* weeks.) And then I heard them. Behind the boulder, laughing. I shrank down in the bracken. And then *she* came out from behind the boulder in her green dress and stood above the pool. She raised her arms. I could hear the man laughing still but I couldn't see him. I *knew*. I *knew*. The wicked desecration of it! But I won't believe it. I'll put it out of my mind forever. She was mocking—pretending. I *won't* think anything else. She went back to him. I waited. And then, suddenly, I couldn't bear it any longer. I came back here. . . ."

Alleyn, looking increasingly grim, went over the entries for the whole list; throughout two summers, Miss Cost had hunted her evening quarry with obsessive devotion and had recorded the fruits of the chase as if in some antic game-book —time, place and circumstances. On each occasion that she spied upon her victims, she had found the enclosure padlocked and had taken up a point of vantage on the hillside. At no stage did she give the names of the lovers but their

227

identity was inescapable. "Mrs. Barrimore and Dr. Maine," Alleyn said. "To hell with this case!"

"Awkward," observed Fox.

"My dear old Fox, it's dynamite. And it fits," Alleyn said, staring disconsolately at his colleague. "The devil of it is, it fits."

He began to read the entries for the past month. Dr. Maine, Miss Cost weirdly concluded, was not to blame. He was a victim, caught in the toils, unable to free himself and therefore unable to follow his nobler inclination towards Miss Cost herself. Interlarded with furious attacks upon Miss Emily and covert allusions to the anonymous messages, were notes on the Festival, a savage comment on Miss Emily's visit to the shop and a distracted reference to the attack of asthma that followed it. "The dark forces of evil that emanate from this woman" were held responsible. There followed a number of cryptic asides :—

("Trehern agrees. It's *right*. I *know* it's right.")

"'It is the Cause, it is the Cause, my soul'," Alleyn muttered, disconsolately. "The old, phoney argument."

Fox, who had been reading over his shoulder, said : "It'd be a peculiar thing if she'd worked Trehern up to doing the job and then got herself mistaken for the intended victim."

"It sounds very neat, Br'er Fox, but in point of fact, it's lousy with loose ends. I can't take it. Just let's go through the other statements now."

They did this and Fox sighed over the result. "I suppose so," he said and added, "I like things to be neat and they so seldom are."

"You're a concealed classicist," Alleyn said. "We'd better go back to this ghastly diary. Read on."

They had arrived at the final week. Rehearsals for the Festival. Animadversions upon Miss Emily. The incident

228

of the Green Lady on Miss Emily's desk. "He did it. K. I'm certain. And I'm *glad*, glad. *She* no doubt, suspects *me*. I refused to go. She finds she can't order *me* about. To sit in that room with *her* and the two she has ruined ! *Never*."

Alleyn turned a page and there, facing them, was the last entry Miss Cost was to make in her journal.

"Yesterday evening," Alleyn said. "After the debacle at the Spring."

The thunderstorm, he was not surprised to find, was treated as a judgment. Nemesis, in the person of one of Miss Cost's ambiguous deities, had decided to touch-up the unbelievers with six of the cosmic best. Among these offenders Miss Emily was clearly included but it emerged that she was not the principal object of Miss Cost's spleen. "Laugh at your peril," she ominously wrote, "at the Great Ones." And, as if stung by this observation she continued, in a splutter of disjointed venom, to threaten some un-named persons. "At last," she wrote. "After the agony of months, the cruelty and now, the final insult, *at last* I shall speak. I shall face both of them with the facts. I shall tell *her* what was between us. And I shall show that other one how I know. He—both—all of them shall suffer. I'll drag their names through the papers. Now. To-night. I am determined. It is the end."

"And so it was," Fox said, looking up over his spectacles. "Poor thing. Very sad, really, these cases. Do you see your way through all this, Mr. Alleyn ? "

"I think I do, Br'er Fox. I'm afraid I do. And I'll tell you why."

He had scarcely begun, when Bailey, moving rather more quickly than he was wont, came through from the shop.

"Someone for you, sir. A Miss Williams. She says it's urgent."

Alleyn went to the telephone.

229

Jenny sounded as if it was very urgent indeed.

" Mr. Alleyn ? Thank God ! Please come up here, quickly. Please do. Miss Emily's rooms. I can't say anything else." Alleyn heard a muffled ejaculation. A man shouted distantly and a woman screamed. There was faint but unmistakable crash of broken glass. . . . " Please come," said Jenny.

" At once," Alleyn said. And to Fox : " Leave Pender on the board and you others follow as quick as you can. Room 35 to the right of the stairhead on the first floor."

Before they had time to answer he was out of the shop and had plunged, head down, into the storm outside.

9. *Storm*

It was not raining now but the night was filled with so vast
an uproar that there was no room for any perception but that
of noise : the clamour of wind and irregular thud and crash
of a monstrous tide. It broke over the foreshore and made
hissing assaults on the foot of the steps. Alleyn went up
them at a sort of shambling run, bent double and feeling his
way with his hands. When he reached the last flight and
came into range of the hotel windows, his heart pounded like
a ram and his throat was dry. He beat across the platform
and went in by the main entrance. The night porter was
reading behind his desk. He looked up in astonishment at
Alleyn who had not waited to put on his mackintosh.

" Did you get caught, sir ? "

" I took shelter," Alleyn said. " Good night."

He made for the stairs and when he was out of sight,
waited for a moment or two to recover his wind. Then he
went up to the first floor.

The passage had the vacant look of all hotel corridors at
night. A wireless blared invisibly. When he moved forward
he realised the noise was coming from Miss Emily's room. A
brass band was playing " Colonel Bogey."

He knocked on the door and was not answered. He
opened it and went in.

It was as if a tableau had been organised for his benefit ;
as if he had been sent out of the room while the figures
arranged themselves to their best effect. Miss Emily stood

on the hearthrug very pale and grand, with Jenny in support. Margaret Barrimore, with her hands to her mouth, was inside the door on his left. He had narrowly missed striking her with it when he came in. The three men had pride of place. Major Barrimore stood centre with his legs straddled and blood running from his nose into his gaping mouth. Dr. Maine faced him and frowned at a cut across the knuckles of his own well-kept doctor's hand. Patrick, dishevelled, stood between them, like a referee who had just stopped a fight. The wireless bellowed remorselessly. There was a scatter of broken glass in the fireplace.

They all turned their heads and looked at Alleyn. They might have been asking him to guess the word of their charade.

" Can we switch that thing off ? " he asked.

Jenny did so. The silence was deafening.

" I did it to drown the shouting," she said.

" Miss Emily," Alleyn said. " Will you sit down ? " She did so.

" It might be as well," he suggested, " if everyone did."

Dr. Maine made an impatient noise and walked over to the window. Barrimore sucked his moustache, tasted blood and got out his handkerchief. He was swaying on his feet. Alleyn pushed a chair under him and he collapsed on it. His eyes were out of focus and he reeked of whisky. Mrs. Barrimore moved towards Dr. Maine. Jenny sat on an arm of Miss Emily's chair and Patrick on the edge of the table.

" And now," Alleyn said, " what has happened ? "

For a second or two nobody spoke and then Jenny said : " I asked you to come so I suppose I'd better explain."

" You better hold your tongue," Barrimore mumbled through his bloodied handkerchief.

" That'll do," said Patrick dangerously.

Alleyn said to Jenny, " Will you, then ? "

232

"If I can. All right. I'd come in to say good night to Miss Emily. Patrick was waiting for me downstairs, I think. Weren't you?"

He nodded.

"Miss Emily and I were talking. I was just going to say good night when—when Mrs. Barrimore came in."

"Jenny—no! No!" Margaret Barrimore whispered.

"Don't stop her," Miss Emily said quietly, "it's better not to. I am sure of it."

"Patrick?" Jenny appealed to him.

He hesitated, stared at his mother and then said, "You'd better go on, I think. Just the facts, Jenny."

"Very well. Mrs. Barrimore was distressed and—I think—frightened. She didn't say why. She looked ill. She asked if she could stay with us for a little while and Miss Emily said yes. We didn't talk very much. Nothing that could matter."

Margaret Barrimore said rapidly: "Miss Pride was extremely kind. I wasn't feeling well. I haven't been well lately. I had a giddy turn: I was near her room. That's why I went in."

Dr. Maine said: "As Mrs. Barrimore's doctor I must insist that she's not troubled by any questioning. It's true that she is unwell." He jerked a chair forward and touched her arm. "Sit down, Margaret," he said gently and she obeyed him.

"'As Mrs. Barrimore's doctor'," her husband quoted and gave a whinnying laugh. "That's wonderful! That's a superb remark."

"Will you go on, please?"

"O.K. Yes. Well, that lasted quite a long time—just the three of us here. And then Dr. Maine came in to see Miss Pride. He examined the cut on her neck and he told us it would probably be too rough for us to cross the channel tomorrow. He and Mrs. Barrimore were saying good night when Major Barrimore came in."

So far Jenny had spoken very steadily but she faltered now, and looked at Miss Emily. " It's—it's then that—that things began to happen. I——"

Miss Emily with perfect composure, said : " In effect, my dear Roderique, there was a scene. Major Barrimore made certain accusations. Dr. Maine intervened. A climax was reached and blows were exchanged. I suggested, aside to Jenny, that she solicit your aid. The fracas continued. A glass was broken. Mrs. Barrimore screamed and Mr. Patrick arrived upon the scene. He was unsuccessful and, after a renewal of belligerency, Major Barrimore fell to the floor. The actual fighting came to a stop but the noise was considerable. It was at this juncture that the wireless was introduced. You entered shortly afterwards."

" Does everybody agree to this ? "

There was no answer.

" I take it that you do."

Dr. Maine said : " Will you also take it that whatever happened has not the remotest shade of bearing upon your case ? It was an entirely private matter and should remain so." He looked at Patrick and, with disgust, at Major Barrimore. " I imagine you agree," he said.

" Certainly," Patrick said shortly.

Alleyn produced his stock comment on this argument. " If it turns out that there's no connection, I assure you I shall be glad to forget it. In the meantime, I'm afraid I must make certain."

There was a tap at the door. He answered it. Fox, Bailey and Thompson had arrived. Alleyn asked Fox to come in and the others to wait.

" Inspector Fox," he said, " is with me on this case."

" Good evening, ladies and gentlemen," Fox said.

234

They observed him warily. Miss Emily said : " Good evening, Mr. Fox. I have heard a great deal about you."

" Have you, ma'am ? " he rejoined. " Nothing to my discredit, I hope." And to Alleyn : " Sorry to interrupt, sir."

Alleyn gave him a brief summary of the situation and returned to the matter in hand.

` " I'm afraid I must ask you to tell me what it was that triggered off this business," he said. " What were Major Barrimore's accusations ? "

Nobody answered. " Will you tell me, Miss Emily ? "

Miss Emily said : " I cannot. I am sorry. I—I find myself unable to elaborate upon what I have already said." She looked at Alleyn in distress. " You must not ask me," she said.

" Never mind." He glanced at the others. " Am I to know ? " he asked and, after a moment, " Very well. Let us make a different approach. I shall tell you instead, what we have been doing. We have, as some of you know, been at Miss Cost's shop. We have searched the shop and the living quarters behind it. I think I should tell you that we have found Miss Cost's diary. It is a long, exhaustive, and in many places, relevant document. It may be put in evidence."

Margaret Barrimore gave a low cry.

" The final entry was made last night. In it she suggests that as a result of some undefined insult she is going to make public certain matters which are not specifically set out in that part of the diary but will not, I think, be difficult to arrive at when the whole document is reviewed. It may be that after she made this last entry, she wrote a letter to the Press. If so, it will be in the mailbag."

" Has it gone out yet ? " Patrick asked sharply.

" I haven't inquired," Alleyn said coolly.

" It must be stopped."

235

" We don't usually intercept Her Majesty's mail."

Barrimore said thickly : " You can bloody well intercept this one."

" Nonsense," said Dr. Maine crisply.

" By God, sir, I won't take that from you. By God ! " Barrimore began, trying to get to his feet.

" Sit down," Alleyn said. " Do you want to be taken in charge for assault ? Pull yourself together."

Barrimore sank back. He looked at his handkerchief, now drenched with blood. His face was bedabbled and his nose still ran with it. " Gimme 'nother," he muttered.

" A towel, perhaps," Miss Emily suggested. Jenny fetched one from the bathroom.

" He'd better lie down," Dr. Maine said impatiently.

" I'll be damned if I do," said the Major.

" To continue," Alleyn said, " the facts that emerge from the diary and from the investigations are these. We now know the identity of the Green Lady. Miss Cost found it out for herself on 30th September of last year. She saw the impersonator repeating her initial performance for a concealed audience of one. She afterwards discovered who this other was. You will stay where you are, if you please, Major Barrimore. Miss Cost was unwilling to believe this evidence. She began, however, to spy upon the two persons involved. On 17th June of this year she took a photograph at the Spring."

Dr. Maine said : " I can't allow this," and Patrick said : " No, for God's sake ! "

" I would avoid it if I could," Alleyn said. " Mrs. Barrimore, would you rather wait in the next room ? Miss Williams will go with you, I'm sure."

" Yes, darling," Jenny said quickly. " Do."

" O no," she said. " Not now. Not now."

" It would be better," Patrick said.

" It would be better, Margaret," Dr. Maine repeated.

" No."

There was a brief silence. An emphatic gust of wind battered at the window. The lights flickered, dimmed and came up again. Alleyn's hearers were momentarily united in a new uneasiness. When he spoke again, they shifted their attention back to him with an air of confusion.

" Miss Cost," he was saying, " kept her secret to herself. It became, I think, an obsession. It's clear from other passages in her diary that some time before this discovery, she had conceived an antagonism for Major Barrimore. The phrases she uses suggest that it arose from the reaction commonly attributed to a woman scorned."

Margaret Barrimore turned her head and for the first time looked at her husband. Her expression, one of profound astonishment, was reflected in her son's face and Dr. Maine's.

" There is no doubt, I think," Alleyn said. " That during her first visit to the Island their relationship, however brief, had been of the sort to give rise to the later reaction."

" Is this true ? " Dr. Maine demanded of Barrimore.

He had the towel clapped to his face. Over the top of it his eyes, prominent and dazed, narrowed as if he were smiling. He said nothing.

" Miss Cost, as I said just now, kept her knowledge to herself. Later, it appears, she transferred her attention to Doctor Maine and was unsuccessful. It's a painful and distressing story and I shan't dwell on it except to say that up to yesterday's tragedy we have the picture of a neurotic who has discovered that the man upon whom her fantasy is now concentrated, is deeply attached to the wife of the man with whom she herself had a brief affair that ended in humiliation. She also knows that this wife impersonated the Green Lady in the original episode. These elements are so bound up together, that if she makes mischief, as her demon urges her to do, she will be obliged to expose the truth about the Green Lady and that would be disastrous. Add to this, the proposal to end all publicity and official recognition of the Spring and you get some idea, perhaps, of the emotional turmoil that she suffered and that declares itself in this unhappy diary."

"You do, indeed," said Miss Emily abruptly and added: "One has much to answer for, I perceive. I have much to answer for. Go on."

"In opposing the new plans for the Spring, Miss Cost may have let off a head of emotional steam. She sent anonymous messages to Miss Pride. She was drawn into the companionship of the general front made against Miss Pride's intentions. I think there is little doubt that she conspired with Trehern and egged-on ill feeling in the village. She had received attention. She had her Festival in hand. She was somebody. It was, I daresay, all rather exciting and gratifying. Wouldn't you think so ? " he asked Dr. Maine.

"I'm not a psychiatrist," he said. "But, yes. You may be right."

"Now this was the picture," Alleyn went on, " up to the time of the Festival. But when she came to write the final entry in her diary, which was last night, something had happened : something that revived all her sense of injury and spite, something that led her to write : ' Both—all of them—shall suffer. I'll drag their names through the papers. Now. To-night. I am determined. It is the end '."

Another formidable onslaught roared down upon The Boy-and-Lobster and again the lights wavered and recovered.

"She doesn't say, and we can't tell, positively, what inflamed her. I am inclined to think that it might be put down to aesthetic humiliation."

"What ! " Patrick ejaculated.

238

" Yes. One has to remember that all the first-night agonies that beset a professional director are also visited upon the most ludicrously inefficient amateur. Miss Cost had produced a show and exposed it to an audience. However bad the show, she still had to undergo the classic ordeal. The reaction among some of the onlookers didn't escape her notice."

" O dear ! " Jenny said. " O *dear* ! "

" But this is all speculation and a policeman is not allowed to speculate," Alleyn said. " Let us get back to hard facts, if we can. Here are some of them. Miss Cost attended early service this morning and afterwards walked to the Spring to collect a necklace. It was in her hand when we found her. We know, positively, that she encountered and spoke to three people : Mrs. Carstairs and Dr. Maine before church ; Major Barrimore afterwards."

" Suppose I deny that ? " Barrimore said thickly.

" I can't, of course, make any threats or offer any persuasion. You might, on consideration, think it wiser, after all, to agree that you met and tell me what passed between you. Major Barrimore," Alleyn explained generally, " has already admitted that he was spying upon Miss Pride who had gone to the enclosure to put up a notice which he afterwards removed."

Miss Emily gave a sharp ejaculation.

" It was later replaced." Alleyn turned to Barrimore and stood over him. " Shall I tell you what I think happened ? I think hard words passed between you and Miss Cost and that she was stung into telling you her secret. I think you parted from her in a rage and that when you came back to the hotel this morning, you bullied your wife. You had better understand at once, that your wife has not told me this. Finally, I believe that Miss Cost may even have threatened to reveal your former relationship with herself. She suggests

239

in her diary that she has some such intention. Now. Have you anything to say to all this ? "

Patrick said : " You had better say nothing." He walked over to his mother and put his arm about her shoulders.

" I didn't do it," Barrimore said. " I didn't kill her."

" Is that all ? "

" Yes."

" Very well. I shall move on," Alleyn said and spoke generally. " Among her papers we have found a type-written list of dates. It is a carbon copy. The top copy is missing. Miss Cost had fallen into the habit of sending anonymous letters. As we know only too well, this habit grows by indulgence. It is possible, having regard for the dates in question, that this document has been brought to the notice of the person most likely to be disturbed by it. Possibly with a print of the photograph. Now, this individual has, in one crucial respect, given a false statement as to time and circumstance and because of that——"

There was a tap at the door. Fox opened it. A voice in the passage shouted : " I can't wait quiet-like, mister. I got to see 'im." It was Trehern.

Fox said : " Now then, what's all this ? " And began to move out. Trehern plunged at him, head down and was taken in a half-nelson. Bailey appeared in the doorway. " You lay your hands off of me," Trehern whined. " You got nothing against me."

" Outside," said Fox.

Trehern struggling, looked wildly round the assembled company and fixed on Alleyn. " I got something to tell you, mister," he said. " I got something to put before all of you. I got to speak out."

" All right, Fox," Alleyn said and nodded to Bailey, who went out and shut the door. Fox relaxed his hold. " Well, Trehern, what is it ? "

Trehern wiped the back of his hand across his mouth and blinked. " I been thinking," he said.

" Yes ? "

" I been thinking things over. Ever since you come at me up to my house and acted like you done and made out what you made out which is not the case. I be'ant a quick-brained chap, mister, but the light has broke and I see me way clear. I got to speak and speak public."

" Very well. What do you want to say ? "

" Don't you rush me now, mister. What I got to say is a mortal serious matter and I need to take my time."

" Nobody's rushing you."

" No, nor they better not," he said. His manner was half truculent, half cringing. " It concerns this yurr half-hour in time what was the matter which you flung in my teeth. So fur so good. Now. This yurr lady," he ducked his head at Miss Emily, " tells you she seen my lil' chap in the road round about twenty to eight on this yurr fatal morning. Right ? "

" Certainly," said Miss Pride.

" Much obliged. And I says, so she might of then, for all I know to the contrariwise me being asleep in my bed. And I says I uprose at five past eight. Correct ? "

" That's what you said, yes."

" And God's truth if I never speak another word. And my lil' chap was then to home in my house. Right. Now then. Furthermore to that, you says the doctor saw him at that same blessed time, twenty to eight, which statement agrees with the lady."

" Yes."

" Yes. And you says, don't rush me, you says the doctor was in his launch at that mortal moment."

Alleyn glanced at Maine : " Agreed ? " he asked.

" Yes. I saw Wally from the launch."

Trehern moved over to Dr. Maine. " That's a bloody lie, Doctor," he said. " Axcusing the expression. I face you out with it, man to man. I seen you, doctor, clear as I see you now, moving out in thicky launch of yourn at five to ten bloody minutes past eight and by God, I reckon you'm not telling lies for the fun of it. I reckon as how you got half an hour on your conscience, Doctor Maine, and if the law doesn't face you out with it I'm the chap to do the law's job for it."

" I have already discussed the point with Superintendent Alleyn," Maine said, looking at Trehern with profound distaste. " Your story is quite unsupported."

" Is it ? " Trehern said. " Is it, then ? That's where you're dead wrong. You mind me. And you t'other ladies and gents and you, mister." He turned back to Alleyn. " After you shifted off this evening, I took to thinking. And I remembered. I remembered our young Wal come up when I was looking out of my winder and I remembered he said in his por simple fashion : ' Thick's doctor's launch, be'ant she ? ' You ax him, mister. You face him up with it and he'll tell you."

" No doubt ! " said Maine. He looked at Alleyn. " I imagine you accept my statement," he said.

" I haven't said so," Alleyn replied. " I didn't say so at the time, if you remember."

" By God, Alleyn ! " he said angrily and controlled himself. " This fellow's as shifty as they come. You must see it. And the boy ! Of what value is the boy's statement if you get one from him. He's probably been thrashed into learning what he's got to say."

" I never raised a hand——" Trehern began but Alleyn stopped him.

" I was coming to this point," he said, " when we were interrupted. It may as well be brought out by this means as any other. There are factors, apart from those I've already

242

discussed, of which Trehern knows nothing. They may be said to support his story." He glanced at Miss Emily. " I shall put them to you presently but I assure you they are cogent. In the meantime, Dr. Maine, if you have any independent support for your own version of your movements, you might like to say what it is. I must warn you——"

" *Stop.*"

Margaret Barrimore had moved out into the room. Her hands writhed together, as they had done when he saw her in the garden, but she had an air of authority and was, he thought, in command of herself.

She said : " Please don't go on, Mr. Alleyn. There's something that I see I must tell you."

" Margaret ! " Dr. Maine said sharply.

" No," she said. " No. Don't try to stop me. If you do I shall insist on seeing Mr. Alleyn alone. But I'd rather say it here. In front of you all. After all, everybody knows now, don't they ? We needn't pretend any more. Let me go on."

" Go on, Mrs. Barrimore," Alleyn said.

" It's true," she said. " He didn't leave the bay in his launch at half past seven or whenever it was. He came to the hotel to see me. I said I had breakfast alone. I wasn't alone. He was there. Miss Cost had told him she was going to expose—everything. She told him when they met outside the church so he came to see me and ask me to go away with him. He wanted us to make a clean break before it all came out. He asked me to meet him in the village to-night. We were to go to London and then abroad. It was all very hurried. Only a few minutes. We heard somebody coming. I asked him to let me think, to give me a breathing space. So he went away. I suppose he went back to the bay."

She walked over to Maine and put her hand on his arm. " I couldn't let you go on," she said. " It's all the same now.

243

It doesn't matter, Bob. It doesn't matter. We'll be together."

" Margaret, my dear," said Dr. Maine.

There was a long silence. Fox cleared his throat.

Alleyn turned to Trehern.

" And what have you to say to that ? " he asked.

Trehern was gaping at Mrs. Barrimore. He seemed to be lost in some kind of trance.

" I'll be going," he said at last. " I'll be getting back along." He turned and made for the door. Fox stepped in front of it.

Barrimore had got to his feet. His face, bedabbled with blood, was an appalling sight.

" Then it's true," he said very quietly. " She told me. She stood there, grinning and jibbering. She said she'd make me a public laughing stock. And when I said she could go to hell she—d'you know what she did ?—she spat at me. And I—I——"

His voice was obliterated by a renewed onslaught of the gale : heavier than any that had preceded it. A confused rumpus broke out. Some metal object, a dustbin perhaps, racketed past the house and vanished in a diminishing series of irregular clashes, as if it bumped down the steps. There was a second monstrous buffet. Somebody, Margaret Barrimore, Alleyn thought, cried out, and at the same moment the lights failed altogether.

The dark was absolute and the noise intense. Alleyn was struck violently on the shoulder and cannoned into something solid and damp : Fox. As he recovered, he was hit again and putting out his hand, felt the edge of the door.

He yelled to Fox : " Come on ! " and snatching at the door, dived into the passage. There, too, it was completely dark. But less noisy. He thought he could make out the thud

244

of running feet on carpet. Fox was behind him. A flash-light danced on a wall. "Give it me," Alleyn said. He grabbed it and it displayed for an instant the face of Sergeant Bailey. "Out of my way," he said. "Come on, you two. Fox—get Coombe."

He ran to the stairhead and flashed his torch downwards. For a split second it caught the top of a head. He went downstairs in a controlled plunge, using the torch, and arrived in the entrance hall as the front door crashed. His flashlight discovered, momentarily, the startled face of the night porter who said : "Here, what's the matter ?" and disappeared, open-mouthed.

The door was still swinging. He caught it and was once more engulfed in the storm.

It was raining again, heavily. The force of the gale was such that he leant against it and drove his way towards the steps in combat with it. Two other lights, Bailey's and Thompson's, he supposed, dodged eccentrically across the slanting downpour. He lost them when he reached the steps and found the iron rail. But there was yet another lancet of broken light beneath him. As Alleyn went down after it, he was conscious only of noise and idiot violence. He slipped, fell and recovered. At one moment, he was hurled against the rail.

"These bloody steps," he thought. "These bloody steps." When he reached the bottom flight he saw his quarry, a dark, foreshortened, anonymous figure, veer through the dull light from Miss Cost's shop window. "Pender's got a candle or a torch," Alleyn thought.

The other's torch was still going : a thin erratic blade. "Towards the jetty," Alleyn thought. "He's making for the jetty." And down there were the riding lights of the hotel launch, jauncing in the dark.

Here at last, the end of the steps. Now he was in seawater, sometimes over his feet. The roar of the channel was all-obliterating. The gale flattened his lips and filled his eyes with tears. When he made the jetty, he had to double-up and grope with his left hand, keeping the right, with Fox's torch still alive, held out in front : he was whipped by the sea.

He had gained ground. The other was moving on again, doubled up, like Alleyn himself, and still using a torch. There were no more than thirty feet between them. The riding-lights danced near at hand and shuddered when the launch banged against the jetty.

The figure was poised : it waited for the right moment. A torchlight swung through the rain and Alleyn found himself squinting into the direct beam. He ducked and moved on, half-dazzled but aware that the launch rose and the figure leapt to meet it. Alleyn struggled forward, took his chance, and jumped.

He had landed aft, among the passengers' benches ; had fallen across one of them and struck his head on another. He hung there, while the launch bucketed under him and then he fell between the benches and lay on the heaving deck, fighting for breath and helpless. His torch had gone and he was in the dark. There must have been a brief rent in the night sky because a company of stars careened across his vision, wheeled and returned. The deck tilted again and he saw the hotel windows, glowing. They curtsied and tipped. " The power's on," he thought, and a sudden deadly sinking blotted everything out. When he opened his eyes he thought with astonishment : " I was out." Then he heard the engine and felt the judder of a propeller racing above water. He laid hold of a bench and dragged himself to his knees. He could see his opponent, faintly haloed by light from the wheelhouse, back towards him, wrestling with the wheel itself. A great sea broke over them. The windows

246

along Portcarrow front lurched up and dived out of sight again.

Alleyn began to crawl down the gangway between rows of fixed seats, clinging to them as he went. His feet slithered. He fell sideways and propping himself up, managed to drag off his shoes and socks. His head cleared and ached excruciatingly. The launch was now in mid-channel, taking the seas full on her beam and rolling monstrously. He thought " she'll never make it," and tried to remember where the lifebelts should be.

Did that other, fighting there with the wheel, know he was aboard ? How had the launch been cast off ? Were the mooring-lines freed from their cleats and was she now without them ? Or had they been loosed from the bollards while he was unconscious ? What should he do ? " Keep observation ! " he thought sourly. An exquisite jab of pain shot through his eyeballs.

The launch keeled over and took in a solid weight of sea. He thought : " Well, this is it," and was engulfed. The iron legs of the bench bit into his hands. He hung on, almost vertical, and felt the water drag at him like an octopus. It was disgusting. The deck kicked. They wallowed for a suspended moment and then, shuddering, recovered and rose. The first thing he saw was the back of the helmsman. Something rolled against his chest : he unclenched his left hand and felt for it. The torch.

Street lamps along the front came alive and seemed dramatically near at hand. At the same time the engine was cut. He struggled to his feet and moved forward. He was close now, to the figure at the wheel. There was the jetty. Their course had shifted and the launch pitched violently. His left hand knocked against the back of a seat and a beam of light shot out from the torch and found the figure at the wheel. It turned.

247

Maine and Alleyn looked into each other's faces.

Maine lurched out of the wheelhouse. The launch lifted prodigiously, tilted, and dived, nose down. Alleyn was blinded by a deluge of salt water. When he could see again, Maine was on the port gunwale. For a fraction of time he was poised, a gigantic figure against the shore lights. Then he flexed his knees and leapt overboard.

The launch went about and crashed into the jetty. The last thing he heard was somebody yelling high above him.

He was climbing down innumerable flights of stairs. They were impossibly steep—perpendicular—but he had to go down. They tipped and he fell outwards and looked into an abyss laced with flashlights. He lost his hold, dropped into nothing, and was on the stairs again, climbing, climbing. Somebody was making comfortable noises. He looked into a face.

" Fox," he said, with immense satisfaction.

" There now ! " said Inspector Fox.

Alleyn went to sleep.

When he woke, it was to find Troy nearby. Her hand was against his face. " So there you are," he said.

" Hallo," said Troy and kissed him.

The wall beyond her was dappled with sunshine and looked familiar. He puzzled over it for a time and because he wanted to lay his face closer to her hand, turned his head and was stabbed through the temples.

" Don't move," Troy said. " You've taken an awful bash."

" I see."

" You've been concussed and all."

" How long ? "

" About thirty-four hours."

" This is Coombe's cottage."

" That's right, but you're meant not to talk."

" Ridiculous," he said and dozed off again.

Troy slid her hand carefully from under his bristled jaw and crept out of the room.

Superintendent Coombe was in his parlour with Sir James Curtis and Fox. " He woke again," Troy said to Curtis, " just for a moment."

" Say anything ? "

" Yes. He's—" her voice trembled. " He's all right."

" Of course he's all right. I'll take a look at him."

She returned with him to the bedroom and stood by the window while Curtis stooped over his patient. It was a brilliant morning. The channel was dappled with sequins. The tide was low and three people walked over the causeway: an elderly woman, a young man and a girl. Five boats ducked and bobbed in Fisherman's Bay. The hotel launch was still jammed in the understructure of the jetty and looked inconsequent and unreal, suspended above its natural element. A complete write-off, it was thought.

" You're doing fine," Curtis said.

" Where's Troy ? "

" Here, darling."

" Good. What happened ? "

" You were knocked out," Curtis said. " Coombe and two other chaps managed to fish you up."

" Coombe ? "

" Fox rang him from the hotel as soon as you'd set off on your wild goose chase. They were on the jetty."

" Oh yes. Yelling. Where's Fox ? "

" You'd better keep quiet for a bit, Rory. Everything's all right. Plenty of time."

" I want to see Fox, Curtis."

" Very well, but only for one moment."

Troy fetched him.

" This is more like it now," Fox said.

" Have you found him ? "

" We have, yes. Yesterday evening, at low tide."

" Where ? "

" About four miles along the coast."

" It was deliberate, Fox."

" So I understand. Coombe saw it."

" Yes, well now, that's quite enough," said Curtis.

Fox stepped back.

" Wait a minute," Alleyn said. " Anything on him ? Fox ? Anything on him ? "

" All right. Tell him."

" Yes, Mr. Alleyn, there was. Very sodden. Pulp almost, but you can make it out. The top copy of that list and the photograph."

" Ah ! " Alleyn said. " She gave them to him. I thought as much."

He caught his breath and then closed his eyes.

" That's right," Curtis said. " You go to sleep again."

III

" My sister, Fanny Winterbottom," said Miss Emily, two days later, " once remarked with characteristic extravagance (nay, on occasion, vulgarity), that, wherever I went, I kicked up as much dust as a dancing dervish. The observation was inspired more by fortuitous alliteration than by any degree of accuracy. If, however, she were alive to-day, she would doubtless consider herself justified. I have made disastrous mischief in Portcarrow."

" My dear Miss Emily, aren't you, yourself, falling into Mrs. Winterbottom's weakness for exaggeration ? Miss

250

Cost's murder had nothing to do with your decision on the future of the Spring."

" But it *had*," said Miss Emily, smacking her gloved hand on the arm of Superintendent Coombe's rustic seat. " Let us have logic. If I had not persisted with my decision, her nervous system, to say nothing of her emotions (at all times unstable), would not have been exacerbated to such a degree that she would have behaved as she did."

" How do you know ? " Alleyn asked. " She might have cut up rough on some other provocation. She had her evidence. The possession of a dangerous instrument is, in itself, a danger. Even if you had never visited the Island, Miss Emily, Barrimore and Maine would still have laughed at the Festival."

" She would have been less disturbed by their laughter," said Miss Emily. She looked fixedly at Alleyn. " I am tiring you, no doubt," she said. " I must go. Those kind children are waiting in the motor. I merely called to say *au revoir*, my dear Roderique."

" You are not tiring me in the least and your escort can wait. I imagine they are very happy to do so. It's no good, Miss Emily. I know you're eaten up with curiosity."

" Not curiosity. A natural dislike of unexplained detail."

" I couldn't sympathise more. Which details ? "

" No doubt you are always asked when you first began to suspect the criminal. When did you first begin to suspect Dr. Maine ? "

" When you told me that, at about twenty to eight, you saw nobody but Wally on the road down to Fisherman's Bay."

" And I should have seen Dr. Maine ? "

" You should have seen him pulling out from the bay jetty in his launch. And then Trehern, quite readily, said he saw the doctor leaving in his launch about five past eight.

251

Why should he lie about the time he left ? And what, as Trehern pointed out, did he do in the half-hour that elapsed ? "

" Did you not believe that poor woman when she accounted for the half-hour ? "

" Not for a second. If he had been with her she would have said so when I first interviewed her. He has a patient in the hotel and she could have quite easily given that as a reason and would have wanted to provide him with an alibi. Did you notice his look of astonishment when she cut in ? Did you notice how she stopped him before he could say anything ? No, I didn't believe her and I think he knew I didn't."

" And that, you consider, was why he ran away ? "

" Partly that, perhaps. He may have felt," Alleyn said, " quite suddenly, that he couldn't take it. He may have had his moment of truth. Imagine it, Miss Emily. The blinding realisation that must come to a killer : the thing that forces so many of them to give themselves up or to bolt or to commit suicide. Suppose we had believed her and they had gone away together. For the rest of his life he would have been tied to the woman he loved by the most appalling obligation it's possible to imagine."

" Yes," she said. " He was a proud man, I think. You are right. Pray go on."

" Maine had spoken to Miss Cost outside the church. She was telling Mrs. Carstairs she would go to the Spring after the service and collect the necklace that had been left on the shelf. She ran after Maine and Mrs. Carstairs went into church. We don't know what passed between them but I think she may, poor creature, have made some final advance and been rebuffed. She must have armed herself with her horrid little snapshot and list of dates and been carrying them about in her bag, planning to call on him, precipitate a

252

final scene and then confront him with her evidence. In any case she forced them on him and very likely told him she was going to give the whole story to the Press."

" Did she——? "

" Yes. It was in the mailbag."

" You said, I think, that you did not normally intercept Her Majesty's mail."

" I believe I did," said Alleyn blandly. " Nor do we. Normally."

" Go on."

" He knew she was going to the Spring. He was no doubt on the lookout as he washed his hands at the sink in the Trethaways' cottage. He saw Wally. He probably saw you pin up your notice. He saw Barrimore tear it down and go away. He went up and let himself in. He had admittance discs and used one when we sent for him. He hid behind the boulder and waited for Miss Cost. He knew of course that there were loose rocks up there. He was extremely familiar with the terrain."

" Ah, yes."

" When it was over he scraped away his footprints. Later on, when we were there, he was very quick to get up to the higher level and walk over it. Any prints that might be left would thus appear to be innocuous. Then he went back in his launch at ten minutes past eight and waited to be sent for to examine the body."

" It gives me an unpleasant *frisson* when I remember that he also examined mine," said Miss Emily. " A cool, resourceful man. I rather liked him."

" So did I," Alleyn said. " I liked him. He intended us, of course, to follow up the idea of mistaken identity but he was too clever to push it overmuch. If we hadn't discovered that you visited the Spring, he would have said he'd seen you. As it was he let us find out for ourselves. He hoped

253

Wally would be thought to have done it and would have given evidence of his irresponsibility and seen him bestowed in a suitable institution, which, as he very truly observed, might be the best thing for him, after all."

"I shall do something about that boy," said Miss Emily. "There must be special schools. I shall attend to it." She looked curiously at Alleyn. "What would you have done if the lights had not failed, or if you had caught up with him?"

"Routine procedure, Miss Emily. Asked him to come to Coombe's office and make a statement. I doubt if we had a case against him. Too much conjecture. I hoped, by laying so much of the case open, to induce a confession. Once the Wally theory was dismissed, I think Maine would have not allowed Barrimore or anyone else, to be arrested. But I'm glad it turned out as it did."

Fox came through the gate into Coombe's garden.

"*Bon jour, Mademoiselle*," he said laboriously. "*J'espère que vous êtes en bonne santé ce matin.*"

Miss Emily winced. "Mr. Fox," she said in slow but exquisite French. "You are, I am sure, a very busy man, but if you can spare an hour twice a week, I think I might be able to give you some assistance with your conversation. I should be delighted to do so."

Fox asked her if she would be good enough to repeat her statement and as she did so, blushed to the roots of his hair.

"*Mademoiselle*," he said, "*c'est bonne*, no blast—*pardon—bien aimable de vous*—I mean—*de votre part*. Would you really? I can't think of anything I'd like better."

"*Alors, c'est entendu*," said Miss Emily.

IV

Patrick and Jenny sat in his car down by the waterfront. Miss Emily's luggage and Jenny's and Patrick's suitcases

254

were roped into the open boot. Miss Emily had settled to spend a few days at the Manor Park Hotel and had invited them both to be her guests. Patrick felt he should stay with his mother but she was urgent for him to go.

" It made me feel terribly inadequate," he said. " As if somehow I must have failed her. And yet, you know, I thought we got on awfully well together, always. I'm fond of my mama."

" Of course you are. And she adores you. I expect it's just that she wants to be by herself until—well, until the first ghastly shock's over."

" By herself ? With him there ? "

" He's not behaving badly, Patrick. Is he ? "

" No. Oddly enough, no." He looked thoughtfully at Jenny. " I knew about Bob Maine," he said. " Of course I did. I've never been able to make out why I didn't like it. Not for conventional reasons. If you say Œdipus Complex I shall be furious."

" I won't say it then."

" The thing is, I suppose, one doesn't like one's mama being a *femme fatale*. And she is, a bit, you know. I'm so sorry for her," he said violently, " that it makes me angry. Why should that be ? I really don't understand it at all."

" Do you know, I think it's impossible for us to take the idea of older people being in love. It's all wrong, I expect, and I daresay it's the arrogance of youth or something."

" You may be right. Jenny, I do love you with all my heart. Could we get married, do you think ? "

" I don't see anything against it," said Jenny.

After a longish interval, Jenny said : " Miss Emily's taking her time, isn't she ? Shall we walk up to the cottage and say good-bye to that remarkable man ? "

" Well—if you like."

" Come on."

They strolled along the seafront, holding hands. A boy was sitting on the edge of the terrace, idly throwing pebbles into the channel.

It was Wally.

As they came up he turned and, when he saw them, held out his hands.

" All gone," he said.

Black As He's Painted

For Roses and Mike
with Love

The author's warmest thanks are due to
Sir Alister McIntosh, KCMG and
P. J. Humphries, Esq., for their very kind advice
on matters ambassadorial and linguistic.

CONTENTS

Cast of Characters

Mr Samuel Whipplestone	*Foreign Office (retired)*
Lucy Lockett	*A cat*
The Ambassador in London for Ng'ombwana	
A Lady	*Of Messrs Able &*
A Young Gentleman	*Virtue, Land & Estate*
A Youth	*Agents*
Chubb	*House Servant*
Mrs Chubb	*His wife*
A Veterinary Surgeon	
Mr Sheridan	*No. 1a Capricorn Walk (basement flat)*
His Excellency Bartholomew Opala, CBE	*The Boomer, President of Ng'ombwana*
An ADC	
Mr and Mrs Pirelli	*Of the Napoli, shop-keepers*
Colonel Cockburn-Montfort	*Late of the Ng'ombwanan Army (retired)*
Mrs Cockburn-Montfort	*His wife*
Kenneth Sanskrit	*Late of Ng'ombwana. Merchant*
Xenoclea Sanskrit	*His sister. Of the Piggie Pottery, Capricorn Mews, SW3*
A *mlinzi*	*Spear Carrier to The Boomer*
Sir George Alleyn. KCMG, etc. etc.	
Superintendent Roderick Alleyn	*CID*
Troy Alleyn	*Painter. His wife*

Inspector Fox	CID
Superintendent Gibson	Special Branch, CID
Jacks	A talented sergeant
Detective-Sergeant Bailey	A finger-print expert
Detective-Sergeant Thompson	A photographer
Sundry police, Ng'ombwanan servants and frequenters of the Capricorns, SW3	

1

Mr Whipplestone

The year was at the spring and the day at the morn and God may have been in his Heaven but as far as Mr Samuel Whipplestone was concerned the evidence was negligible. He was, in a dull, muddled sort of way, miserable. He had become possessed, with valedictory accompaniments, of two solid silver Georgian gravy-boats. He had taken his leave of Her Majesty's Foreign Service in the manner to which his colleagues were accustomed. He had even prepared himself for the non-necessity of getting up at 7.30, bathing, shaving, breakfasting at 8.00 – but there is no need to prolong the Podsnappian recital. In a word he had fancied himself tuned in to retirement and now realized that he was in no such condition. He was a man without propulsion. He had no object in life. He was finished.

By ten o'clock he found himself unable to endure the complacent familiarity of his 'service' flat. It was in fact at that hour being 'serviced', a ritual which normally he avoided and now hindered by his presence.

He was astounded to find that for twenty years he had inhabited dull, oppressive, dark and uncomely premises. Deeply shaken by this abrupt discovery, he went out into the London spring.

A ten-minute walk across the Park hardly raised his spirits. He avoided the great water-shed of traffic under the quadriga, saw some inappropriately attired equestrians, passed a concourse of scarlet and yellow tulips, left the Park under the expanded nostrils of Epstein's liberated elementals and made his way into Baronsgate.

As he entered that flowing cacophony of changing gears and revving engines, it occurred to him that he himself must now get into bottom gear and stay there, until he was

263

parked in some subfuse lay-by to await – and here the simile became insufferable – a final towing-off. His predicament was none the better for being commonplace. He walked for a quarter of an hour.

From Baronsgate the western entry into the Capricorns is by an arched passage too low overhead to admit any but pedestrian traffic. It leads into Capricorn Mews and, further along at right angles to the Mews, Capricorn Place. He had passed by it over and over again and would have done so now if it hadn't been for a small, thin cat.

This animal flashed out from under the traffic and shot past him into the passageway. It disappeared at the far end. He heard a scream of tyres and of a living creature.

This sort of thing upset Mr Whipplestone. He disliked this sort of thing intensely. He would have greatly preferred to remove himself as quickly as possible from the scene and put it out of his mind. What he did, however, was to hurry through the passageway into Capricorn Mews.

The vehicle, a delivery van of sorts, was disappearing into Capricorn Place. A group of three youths outside a garage stared at the cat which lay like a blot of ink on the pavement.

One of them walked over to it.

'Had it,' he said.

'Poor pussy!' said one of the others and they laughed objectionably.

The first youth moved his foot as if to turn the cat over. Astonishingly and dreadfully it scrabbled with its hind legs. He exclaimed, stooped down and extended his hand.

It was on its feet. It staggered and then bolted. Towards Mr Whipplestone who had come to a halt. He supposed it to be concussed, or driven frantic by pain or fear. In a flash it gave a great spring and was on Mr Whipplestone's chest, clinging with it small claws and – incredibly – purring. He had been told that a dying cat will sometimes purr. It had blue eyes. The tip of its tail for about two inches was snow white but the rest of its person was perfectly black. He had no particular antipathy to cats.

He carried an umbrella in his right hand but with his left arm he performed a startled reflex gesture. He sheltered the cat. It was shockingly thin, but warm and tremulous.

'One of 'er nine lives gawn for a burton,' said the youth. He and his friends guffawed themselves into the garage.

'Drat,' said Mr Whipplestone, who long ago had thought it amusing to use spinsterish expletives.

With some difficulty he hooked his umbrella over his left arm and with his right hand inserted his eyeglass and then explord the cat's person. It increased its purrs, interrupting them with a faint mew when he touched its shoulder. What was to be done with it?

Obviously, nothing in particular. It was not badly injured, presumably it lived in the neighbourhood and one had always understood its species to have a phenomenal homing instinct. It thrust its nut-like head under Mr Whipplestone's jacket and into his waistcoat. It palpated his chest with its paws. He had quite a business detaching it.

He set it down on the pavement. 'Go home,' he said. It stared up at him and went through the motion of mewing, opening its mouth and showing its pink tongue but giving no sound. 'No,' he said, 'go home!' It was making little preparatory movements of its haunches as if it was about to spring again.

He turned his back on it and walked quickly down Capricorn Mews. He almost ran.

It is a quiet little street, cobbled and very secluded. It accommodates three garages, a packing agency, two dozen or so small mid-Victorian houses, a minute bistro and four shops. As he approached one of these, a flower shop, he could see reflected in its side windows Capricorn Mews with himself walking towards him. And behind him, trotting in a determined manner, the little cat. It was mewing.

He was extremely put out and had begun to entertain a confused notion of telephoning the RSPCA when a van erupted from a garage immediately behind him. It passed him and when it had gone the cat had disappeared: frightened, Mr Whipplestone supposed, by the noise.

Beyond the flower shop and on the opposite side of the Mews was the corner of Capricorn Place, leading off to the left. Mr Whipplestone, deeply ruffled, turned into it.

A pleasing street: narrow, orderly, sunny, with a view, to the left, of tree-tops and the dome of the Baronsgate Basilica. Iron railings and behind them small well-kept Georgian and Victorian houses. Spring flowers in window-boxes. From somewhere or another the smell of freshly brewed coffee.

Cleaning ladies attacked steps and door-knockers. Household ladies were abroad with shopping baskets. A man of Mr Whipplestone's own age who reeked of the army and was of an empurpled complexion emerged from one of the houses. A perambulator with a self-important baby and an escort of a pedestrian six-year-old, a female propellant and a large dog, headed with a purposeful air towards the Park. The postman was going his rounds.

In London there are still, however precarious their state, many little streets of the character of the Capricorns. They are upper-middle-class streets and therefore, Mr Whipple-stone had been given to understand, despicable. Being of that class himself, he did not take this view. He found the Capricorns uneventful, certainly, but neither tiresomely quaint nor picturesque nor smug: pleasing rather, and possessed of a quality which he could only think of as 'sparkling'. Ahead of him was a pub, the Sun in Splendour. It had an honest untarted-look about it and stood at the point where the Place leads into Capricorn Square: the usual railed enclosure of plane trees, grass and a bench or two, well-kept. He turned to the right down one side of it, making for Capricorn Walk.

Moving towards him at a stately pace came a stout, superbly dressed coal-black gentleman leading a white Afghan hound with a scarlet collar and leash.

'My dear Ambassador!' Mr Whipplestone exclaimed. 'How very pleasant!'

'Mr Whipplestone!' resonated the Ambassador for Ng'ombwana. 'I am delighted to see you. You live in these parts?'

'No, no: a morning stroll. I'm – I'm a free man now, your Excellency.'

'Of course. I had heard. You will be greatly missed.'

'I doubt it. Your Embassy – I had forgotten for the moment – is quite close by, isn't it?'

'In Palace Park Gardens. I too enjoy a morning stroll with Ahman. We are not, alas, unattended.' He waved his gold-mounted stick in the direction of a large person looking anonymously at a plane tree.

'Alas!' Mr Whipplestone agreed. 'The penalty of distinction,' he added neatly, and patted the Afghan.

'You are kind enough to say so.'

Mr Whipplestone's highly specialized work in the Foreign Service had been advanced by a happy manner with Foreign, and particularly with African, plenipotentiaries. 'I hope I may congratulate your Excellency,' he said and broke into his professional style of verbless exclamation. 'The increased rapprochement! The new Treaty! Masterly achievements!'

'Achievements – entirely – of our great President, Mr Whipplestone.'

'Indeed, yes. Everyone is delighted about the forthcoming visit. An auspicious occasion.'

'As you say. Immensely significant.' The Ambassador waited for a moment and then slightly reduced the volume of his superb voice. 'Not,' he said, 'without its anxieties, however. As you know, our great President does not welcome –' he again waved his stick at his bodyguard – 'that sort of attention.' A sigh escaped him. 'He is to stay with us,' he said.

'Quite.'

'The responsibility!' sighed the Ambassador. He broke off and offered his hand. 'You will be at the reception, of course,' he said. 'We must meet more often! I shall see that something is arranged. Au revoir, Mr Whipple-stone.'

They parted. Mr Whipplestone walked on, passing and tactfully ignoring the escort.

Facing him at the point where the Walk becomes the north-east border of the Square was a small house between two large ones. It was painted white with a glossy black front door and consisted of an attic, two floors and a basement. The first-floor windows opened on a pair of miniature balconies, the ground-floor ones were bowed. He was struck by the arrangement of the window-boxes. Instead of the predictable daffodil one saw formal green swags that might have enriched a della Robbia relief. They were growing vines of some sort which swung between the pots where they rooted and were cunningly trimmed so that they swelled at the lowest point of the arc and symmetrically tapered to either end.

Some workmen with ladders were putting up a sign.

He had begun to feel less depressed. Persons who do not live there will talk about 'the London feeling'. They will tell you that as they walk down a London street they can be abruptly made happy, uplifted in spirit, exhilarated. Mr Whipplestone had always taken a somewhat incredulous view of these transports but he had to admit that on this occasion he was undoubtedly visited by a liberated sensation. He had a singular notion that the little house had induced this reaction. No. 1, as he now saw, Capricorn Walk.

He approached the house. It was touched on its chimneys and the eastern slope of its roof by sunshine. 'Facing the right way,' thought Mr Whipplestone. 'In the winter it'll get all the sun there is, I dare say.' His own flat faced north.

A postman came whistling down the Walk as Mr Whipplestone crossed it. He mounted the steps of No. 1, clapped something through the brass flap and came down so briskly that they nearly collided.

'Whoops-a-daisy,' said the postman. 'Too eager, that's my trouble. Lovely morning, though, innit?'

'Yes,' said Mr Whipplestone, judiciously conceding the point. 'It is. Are the present occupants – ' he hesitated.

'Gawn. Out last week,' said the postman. 'But I'm not to know, am I? People ought to make arrangements, din' they, sir?' He went off, whistling.

The workmen came down their ladders and prepared to make off. They had erected a sign.

FOR SALE
All enquiries to
Able, Virtue & Sons
17 Capricorn Street, SW7

II

The Street is the most 'important' of the Capricorns. It is wider and busier than the rest. It runs parallel to the Walk and in fact Messrs Able and Virtue's premises lie exactly back to back with the little house at No. 1.

'*Good* morning,' said the roundabout lady at the desk on the left-hand side. '*Can* I help you?' she pleaded brightly.

Mr Whipplestone pulled out the most non-committal stop in his FO organ and tempered its chill with a touch of whimsy.

'You may satisfy my idle curiosity if you will be so good,' he said. 'Ah – concerning No. 1, Capricorn Walk.'

'No. 1, the Walk?' repeated the lady. 'Yes. Our notice, ackshally, has only just gone up. For Sale with stipulations regarding the basement. I'm not quite sure – ' she looked across at the young man with a pre-Raphaelite hair-do behind the right-hand desk. He was contemplating his fingernails and listening to his telephone. 'What *is* it about the basement, of No. 1,' he rattled into it, 'is at present occupied as a pied – '

He clapped a languid hand over the receiver: 'Ay'm coping,' he said and unstopped the receiver. 'The basement of No. 1,' he rattled into it, 'is at present occupied as a pied-à-terre by the owner. He wishes to retain occupancy. The Suggested Arrangement is that total ownership pass to the purchaser and that he, the vendor, become the tenant of the basement at an agreed rent for a specified period.' He listened for a considerable interval. 'No,' he said, 'ay'm afraid it's a firm stipulation. Quate. Quate. Theng you, madam. Good morning.'

'That,' said the lady, offering it to Mr Whipplestone, 'is the situation.'

Mr Whipplestone, conscious of a lightness in his head, said: 'And the price?' He used the voice in which he had been wont to say: 'This should have been dealt with at a lower level.'

'Was it thirty-nine?' the lady asked her colleague.

'Thirty-eight.'

'Thirty-eight thousand,' she relayed to Mr Whipplestone, who caught back his breath in a civilized little hiss.

'Indeed?' he said. 'You amaze me.'

'It's a Desirable District,' she replied indifferently. 'Properties are at a premium in the Capricorns.' She picked up a document and glanced at it. Mr Whipplestone was nettled.

'And the rooms?' he asked sharply. 'How many? Excluding, for the moment, the basement.'

The lady and the pre-Raphaelite young gentleman became more attentive. They began to speak in unison and begged each other's pardon.

'Six,' gabbled the lady, 'in all. Excluding kitchen and Usual Offices. Floor-to-floor carpets and drapes included in purchase price. *And* the Usual Fitments: fridge, range, etcetera. Large recep' with adjacent dining-room, ground floor. Master bedroom and bathroom with toilet, first floor. Two rooms with shower and toilet, second floor. Late tenant used these as flat for married couple.'

'Oh?' said Mr Whipplestone, concealing the emotional disturbance that seemed to be lodged under his diaphragm. 'A married couple? You mean?'

'Did for him,' said the lady.

'I beg your pardon?'

'Serviced him. Cook and houseman. There was an Arrangement by which they also cleaned the basement flat.'

The young man threw in: 'Which it is hoped will continue. They are Strongly Recommended to purchaser with Arrangement to be arrived at for continued weekly servicing of basement. No obligation, of course.'

'Of course not.' Mr Whipplestone gave a small dry cough. 'I should like to see it,' he said.

'Certainly,' said the lady crisply. 'When would you – ?'

'Now, if you please.'

'I *think* that would suit. If you'll just wait while I – '

She used her telephone. Mr Whipplestone bumped into a sudden qualm of near-panic. 'I am beside myself,' he thought. 'It's that wretched cat.' He pulled himself together. After all he was committed to nothing. An impulse, a mere whim induced, he dared say, by unaccustomed idleness. What of it?'

The lady was looking at him. Perhaps she had spoken to him.

'I beg your pardon,' said Mr Whipplestone.

She decided he was hard-of-hearing. 'The house,' she articulated pedantically, 'is open to view. The late tenants have vacated the premises. The married couple leave at the end of the week. The owner is at home in the basement flat. Mr Sheridan,' she shouted. 'That's the vendor's name: Sheridan.'

'Thank you.'

'Mervyn!' cried the lady, summoning up a wan and uncertain youth from the back office. 'No. 1, the Walk. Gentleman to view.' She produced keys and smiled definitively upon Mr Whipplestone. 'It's a Quality Residence,' she said. 'I'm sure you'll think so.'

The youth attended him with a defeated air round the corner to No. 1, Capricorn Walk.

'Thirty-eight thousand pounds!' Mr Whipplestone inwardly expostulated. 'Good God, it's outrageous!'

The Walk had turned further into the sun, which now sparkled on No. 1's brass door-knocker and letter-box. Mr

Whipplestone, waiting on the recently scrubbed steps, looked down into the area. It had been really very ingeniously converted, he was obliged to concede, into a ridiculous little garden with everything on a modest scale.

'Pseudo-Japanese,' he thought in a panic-stricken attempt to discredit it.

'Who looks after *that*?' he tossed at the youth. 'The basement?'

'Yar,' said the youth.

('He hadn't the faintest idea,' thought Mr Whipplestone.)

The youth had opened the front door and now stood back for Mr Whipplestone to enter.

The little hall and stairway were carpeted in cherry red, the glossy walls were an agreeable oyster-white. This scheme was continued in a quite sizeable drawing-room. The two bow windows curtained in red and white stripes were large and the whole interior remarkably light for a London room. For some twenty years he had vaguely regretted the murkiness of his service flat.

Without warning he was overtaken by an experience that a less sophisticated man might have been tempted to call hallucinatory. He saw, with the utmost clarity, his own possessions occupying this light-hearted room. The Chippendale wall-desk, the crimson sofa with its companion table, the big red glass goblet, the Agatha Troy landscape, the late Georgian bookcase: all were harmoniously accommodated. When the youth opened double-doors into a small dining-room, Mr Whipplestone saw at a glance that his chairs were of precisely the right size and character.

He dismissed these visions. 'The partition folds back,' he said with a brave show of indifference, 'to form one room, I suppose?'

'Yar,' said the youth and folded it back. He opened red and white striped curtains in the rear wall and revealed a courtyard and tub-garden.

'Lose the sun,' Mr Whipplestone sneered, keeping his head. 'Get none in the winter.'

It was, however, receiving its full quota now.

'Damp,' persisted Mr Whipplestone defiantly. 'Extra expense. Have to be kept up.' And he thought: 'I'd do better to hold my tongue.'

The kitchen was on the left of the dining-room. It was a modernized affair with a service hatch. 'Cramped!' Mr Whipplestone thought of saying but his heart was not in it.

The stairs were steep which ought to have been a comfort. Awkward for trays and luggage and suppose one died how would they get one out of it? He said nothing.

The view from the master-bedroom through the french windows embraced in its middle distance the Square with the Sun in Splendour on the left and – more distantly on the right – the dome of the Basilica. In the foreground was the Walk with foreshortened views of pedestrians, parked cars and an intermittent passage of traffic. He opened a french window. They were ringing the bells in the Basilica. Twelve o'clock. Some service or another, he supposed. But you couldn't say the house was noisy.

The bells stopped. Somewhere, out of sight, a voice was raised in a reiterated, rhythmical shout. He couldn't distinguish the sense of it but it came nearer. He went out on one of the two little balconies.

'Air-eye-awf,' shouted the voice, and round the far corner of the Square came a horse-drawn cart, nodding with tulips and led by a red-faced man. He passed No. 1 and looked up.

'Any time. All fresh,' he bawled directly at Mr Whipplestone who hastily withdrew.

(His big red glass goblet in the bow window, filled with tulips.)

Mr Whipplestone was a man who did not indulge in histrionics but under the lash of whatever madness now possessed him he did, as he made to leave the window, flap the air with two dismissive palms. The gesture brought him face to face with a couple, man and woman.

'I beg your pardon,' they all said and the small man added. 'Sorry, sir. We just heard the window open and

273

thought we'd better see.' He glanced at the youth. 'Order to view?' he asked.

'Yar.'

'You,' said Mr Whipplestone, dead against his will, 'must be the – the upstairs – ah – the –'

'That's right, sir,' said the man. His wife smiled and made a slight bob. They were rather alike, being round-faced, apple-cheeked and blue-eyed and were aged, he thought, about forty-five.

'You are – I understand – ah – still – ah –'

'We've stayed on to set things to rights, sir. Mr Sheridan's kindly letting us remain until the end of the week. Gives us a chance to find another place, sir, if we're not wanted here.'

'I understand you would be – ah –'

'Available, sir?' they both said quickly and the man added, 'We'd be glad to stay on if the conditions suited. We've been here with the outgoing tenant six years, sir, and very happy with it. Name of Chubb, sir, references on request and the owner, Mr Sheridan, below, would speak for us.'

'Quite, quite quite!' said Mr Whipplestone in a tearing hurry. 'I – ah – I've come to no conclusion. On the contrary. Idle curiosity, really. However. In the event – the remote event of my – be very glad – but so far – nothing decided.'

'Yes, sir, of course. If you'd care to see upstairs, sir?'

'What!' shouted Mr Whipplestone as if they'd fired a gun at him. 'Oh. Thank you. Might as well, perhaps. Yes.'

'Excuse me, sir. I'll just close the window.'

Mr Whipplestone stood aside. The man laid his hand on the french window. It was a brisk movement but it stopped as abruptly as if a moving film had turned into a still. The hand was motionless, the gaze was fixed, the mouth shut like a trap.

Mr Whipplestone was startled. He looked down into the street and there, returning from his constitutional and attended by his dog and his bodyguard, was the Ambassador for Ng'ombwana. It was at him that the man, Chubb, stared. Something impelled Mr Whipplestone to look at the woman. She had come close and she too, over her husband's shoulder, stared at the Ambassador.

The next moment the figures animated. The window was shut and fastened and Chubb turned to Mr Whipplestone with a serviceable smile.

'Shall I show the way, sir?' asked Chubb.

The upstairs flat was neat, clean and decent. The little parlour was a perfectly respectable and rather colourless room, except perhaps for an enlarged photograph of a round-faced girl of about sixteen which attracted attention on account of its being festooned in black ribbon and flanked on the table beneath it by two vases of dyed *immortelles*. Some kind of china medallion hung from the bottom edge of the frame. Another enlarged photograph of Chubb in uniform and Mrs Chubb in bridal array, hung on the wall.

All the appointments on this floor, it transpired, were the property of the Chubbs. Mr Whipplestone was conscious that they watched him anxiously. Mrs Chubb said: 'It's home to us. We're settled like. It's such a nice part, the Capricorns.' For an unnerving moment he thought she was going to cry.

He left the Chubbs precipitately, followed by the youth. It was a struggle not to re-enter the drawing-room but he triumphed and shot out of the front door to be immediately involved in another confrontation.

'Good morning,' said a man on the area steps. 'You've been looking at my house, I think? My name is Sheridan.'

There was nothing remarkable about him at first sight, unless it was his almost total baldness and his extreme pallor. He was of middle height, unexceptionally dressed and well-spoken. His hair, when he had had it, must have been dark since his eyes and brows and the wires on the backs of his pale hands were black. Mr Whipplestone had a faint, fleeting and oddly uneasy impression of having seen him before. He came up the area steps and through the gate and faced Mr Whipplestone who, in politeness, couldn't do anything but stop where he was.

'Good morning,' Mr Whipplestone said. 'I just happened to be passing. An impulse.'

'One gets them,' said Mr Sheridan, 'in the spring.' He spoke with a slight lisp.

'So I understand,' said Mr Whipplestone, not stuffily but in a definitive tone. He made a slight move.

'Did you approve?' asked Mr Sheridan casually.

'Oh, charming, charming,' Mr Whipplestone said, lightly dismissing it.

'Good. So glad. Good morning, Chubb, can I have a word with you?' said Sheridan.

Mr Whipplestone escaped. The wan youth followed him to the corner. Mr Whipplestone was about to dismiss him and continue alone towards Baronsgate. He turned back to thank the youth and there was the house, in full sunlight now, with its evergreen swags and its absurd garden. Without a word he wheeled left and left again and reached Able, Virtue & Sons three yards in advance of his escort. He walked straight in and laid his card before the plump lady.

'I should like the first refusal,' he said.

From that moment it was a foregone conclusion. He didn't lose his head. He made sensible enquiries and took proper steps about the lease and the plumbing and the state of repair. He consulted his man of business, his bank manager and his solicitor. It is questionable whether, if any of these experts had advised against the move, he would have paid the smallest attention but they did not and, to his own continuing astonishment, at the end of a fortnight Mr Whipplestone moved in.

He wrote cosily to his married sister in Devonshire: ' – you may be surprised to hear of the change. Don't expect anything spectacular, it's a quiet little backwater full of old fogies like me. Nothing in the way of excitement or 'happenings' or violence or beastly demonstrations. It suits me. At my age one prefers the uneventful life and that,' he ended, 'is what I expect to enjoy at No. 1, Capricorn Walk.'

Prophecy was not Mr Whipplestone's strong point.

III

'That's all jolly fine,' said Superintendent Alleyn. 'What's the Special Branch think it's doing? Sitting on its fat bottom waving Ng'ombwanan flags?'

'What did he *say*, exactly?' asked Mr Fox. He referred to their Assistant Commissioner.

'Oh, *you* know!' said Alleyn. 'Charm and sweet reason were the wastewords of his ween.'

'What's a ween, Mr Alleyn?'

'I've not the remotest idea. It's a quotation. And don't ask me from where.'

'I only wondered,' said Mr Fox mildly.

'I don't even know,' Alleyn continued moodily, 'how it's spelt. Or what it means, if it comes to that.'

'If it's Scotch it'll be with an h, won't it? Meaning: "few". Wheen.'

'Which doesn't make sense. Or does it? Perhaps it should be 'weird' but that's something one drees. Now *you're* upsetting me, Br'er Fox.'

'To get back to the AC, then?'

'However reluctantly: to get back to him. It's all about this visit, of course.'

'The Ng'ombwanan President?'

'He. The thing is, Br'er Fox, I know him. And the AC knows I know him. We were at school together in the same house: Davidson's. Same study, for a year. Nice creature, he was. Not everybody's cup of tea but I liked him. We got on like houses on fire.'

'Don't tell me,' said Fox. 'The AC wants you to recall old times?'

'I do tell you precisely that. He's dreamed up the idea of a meeting – casual-cum-official. He wants me to put it to the President that unless he conforms to whatever procedure the Special Branch sees fit to lay on, he may very well get himself bumped off and in any case will cause acute anxiety, embarrassment and trouble at all levels from the Monarch down. And I'm to put this, if you please, tactfully. They don't want umbrage to be taken, followed by a highly

277

publicized flounce-out. He's as touchy as a sea-anemone.'

'Is he jibbing, then? About routine precautions?'

'He was always a pig-headed ass. We used to say that if you wanted the old Boomer to do anything you only had to tell him not to. And he's one of those sickening people without fear. And hellish haughty with it. Yes, he's jibbing. He doesn't want protection. He wants to do a Haroun el Raschid and bum round London on his own looking as inconspicuous as a coal box in paradise.'

'Well,' said Mr Fox judiciously, 'that's a very silly way to go on. He's a number one assassination risk, that gentleman.'

'He's a bloody nuisance. You're right, of course. Ever since he pushed his new industrial legislation through he's been a sitting target for the lunatic fringe. Damn it all, Br'er Fox, only the other day, when he elected to make a highly publicized call at Martinique, somebody took a pot shot at him. Missed and shot himself. No arrest. And off goes the Boomer on his merry way, six foot five of him, standing on the seat of his car, all eyes and teeth, with his escort having kittens every inch of the route.'

'He sounds a right daisy.'

'I believe you.'

'I get muddled,' Mr Fox confessed, 'over these emergent nations.'

'You're not alone, there.'

'I mean to say – this Ng'ombwana. What is it? A republic, obviously, but is it a member of the Commonwealth and if it is, why does it have an Ambassador instead of a High Commissioner?'

'You may well ask. Largely through the manoeuvrings of my old chum, The Boomer. They're still a Commonwealth country. More or less. They're having it both ways. All the trappings and complete independence. All the ha'pence and none of the kicks. That's why they insist on calling their man in London an Ambassador and setting him up in premises that wouldn't disgrace one of the great powers. Basically it's The Boomer's doing.'

'What about his own people? Here? At this Embassy? His Ambassador and all?'

'They're as worried as hell but say that what the President lays down is *it*: the general idea being that they might as well speak to the wind. He's got this notion in his head – it derives from his schooldays and his practising as a barrister in London – that because Great Britain, relatively, has had a non-history of political assassination there won't be any in the present or future. In its maddening way it's rather touching.'

'He can't stop the SB doing its stuff, though. Not outside the Embassy.'

'He can make it hellish awkward for them.'

'What's the procedure, then? Do you wait till he comes, Mr Alleyn, and plead with him at the airport?'

'I do not. I fly to his blasted republic at the crack of dawn tomorrow and you carry on with the Dagenham job on your own.'

'Thanks very much. What a treat,' said Fox.

'So I'd better go and pack.'

'Don't forget the old school tie.'

'I do not deign,' said Alleyn, 'to reply to that silly crack.'

He got as far as the door and stopped.

'I meant to ask you,' he said. 'Did you ever come across a man called Samuel Whipplestone? At the FO?'

'I don't move in those circles. Why?'

'He was a bit of a specialist on Ng'ombwana. I see he's lately retired. Nice chap. When I get back I might ask him to dinner.'

'Are you wondering if he'd have any influence?'

'We can hardly expect him to crash down on his knees and plead with the old Boomer to use his loaf if he wants to keep it. But I did vaguely wonder. 'Bye, Br'er Fox.'

Forty-eight hours later Alleyn, in a tropical suit, got out of a Presidential Rolls that had met him at the main Ng'ombwana airport. He passed in a sweltering heat up a grandiose flight of steps through a Ruritanian guard turned black, and into the air-conditioned reception hall of the Presidential Palace.

Communication at the top level had taken place and he got the full, instant VIP treatment.

'Mr Alleyn?' said a young Ng'ombwanan wearing an ADC's gold knot and tassel. 'The President is so happy at your visit. He will see you at once. You had a pleasant flight?'

Alleyn followed the sky-blue tunic down a splendid corridor that gave on an exotic garden.

'Tell me,' he asked on the way, 'what form of address is the correct one for the President?'

'His Excellency, the President,' the ADC rolled out, 'prefers that form of address.'

'Thank you,' said Alleyn, and followed his guide into an anteroom of impressive proportions. An extremely personable and widely smiling secretary said something in Ng'ombwanan. The ADC translated: 'We are to go straight in, if you please.' Two dashingly uniformed guards opened double-doors and Alleyn was ushered into an enormous room at the far end of which, behind a vast desk, sat his old school chum: Bartholomew Opala.

'Superintendent Alleyn, your Excellency, Mr President, sir,' said the ADC redundantly and withdrew.

The enormous presence was already on its feet and coming, light-footed as a prizefighter, at Alleyn. The huge voice was bellowing: 'Rory Alleyn, but all that's glorious!' Alleyn's hand was engulfed and his shoulder-blade rhythmically beaten. It was impossible to stand to attention and bow from the neck in what he had supposed to be the required form.

'Mr President – ' he began.

'What? Oh, nonsense, nonsense, nonsense! Balls, my dear man (as we used to say in Davidson's).' Davidson's had been their house at the illustrious school they both attended. The Boomer was being too establishment for words. Alleyn noticed that he wore the old school tie and that behind him on the wall hung a framed photograph of Davidson's with The Boomer and himself standing together in the back row. He found this oddly, even painfully, touching.

'Come and sit down,' The Boomer fussed. 'Where, now? Over here! Sit! Sit! I couldn't be more delighted.'

The steel-wool mat of hair was grey now and stood up

high on his head like a toque. The huge frame was richly endowed with flesh and the eyes were very slightly bloodshot but, as if in double-exposure, Alleyn saw beyond this figure that of an ebony youth eating anchovy toast by a coal fire and saying: 'You are my friend: I have had none, here, until now.'

'How well you look,' the President was saying. 'And how little you have changed! You smoke? No? A cigar? A pipe? Yes? Presently, then. You are lunching with us of course. They have told you?'

'This is overwhelming,' Alleyn said when he could get a word in. 'In a minute I shall be forgetting my protocol.'

'Now! Forget it now. We are alone. There is no need.'

'My dear –'

'"Boomer." Say it. How many years since I heard it!'

'I'm afraid I very nearly said it when I came in. My dear Boomer.'

The sudden brilliance of a prodigal smile made its old impression. 'That's nice,' said the President quietly and after rather a long silence: 'I suppose I must ask you if this is a visit with an object. They were very non-committal at your end, you know. Just a message that you were arriving and would like to see me. Of course I was overjoyed.'

Alleyn thought: this is going to be tricky. One word in the wrong place and I not only boob my mission but very likely destroy a friendship and even set up a politically damaging mistrust. He said –

'I've come to ask you for something and I wish I hadn't got to bother you with it. I won't pretend that my chief didn't know of our past friendship – to me a most valued one. I won't pretend that he didn't imagine this friendship might have some influence. Of course he did. But it's because I think his request is reasonable and because I am very greatly concerned for your safety, that I didn't jib at coming.'

He had to wait a long time for the reaction. It was as if a blind had been pulled down. For the first time, seeing the slackened jaw and now the hooded, lacklustre eyes he thought, specifically: 'I am speaking to a Negro.'

281

'Ah!' said the President at last, 'I had forgotten. You are a policeman.'

'They say, don't they, if you want to keep a friend, never lend him money. I don't believe a word of it, but if you change the last four words into 'never use your friendship to further your business' I wouldn't quarrel with it. But I'm not doing exactly that. This is more complicated. My end object, believe it or not, sir, is the preservation of your most valuable life.'

Another hazardous wait. Alleyn thought: 'Yes, and that's exactly how you used to look when you thought somebody had been rude to you. Glazed.'

But the glaze melted and The Boomer's nicest look – one of quiet amusement – supervened.

'Now, I understand,' he said. 'It is your watch-dogs, your Special Branch. "Please make him see reason, this black man. Please ask him to let us disguise ourselves as waiters and pressmen and men-in-the-street and unimportant guests and be indistinguishable all over the shop." I am right? That is the big request?'

'I'm afraid, you know, they'll do their thing in that respect, as well as they can, however difficult it's made for them.'

'Then why all this fuss-pottery? How stupid!'

'They would all be much happier if you didn't do what you did, for instance, in Martinique.'

'And what did I do in Martinique?'

'With the deepest respect: insisted on an extensive reduction of the safety precautions and escaped assassination by the skin of your teeth.'

'I am a fatalist,' The Boomer suddenly announced, and when Alleyn didn't answer: 'My dear Rory, I see I must make myself understood. Myself. What I am. My philosophy. My code. You will listen?'

'Here we go,' Alleyn thought. 'He's changed less than one would have thought possible.' And with profound misgivings he said: 'But of course, sir. With all my ears.'

As the exposition got under way it turned out to be an extension of The Boomer's schoolboy bloody-mindedness seasoned with, and in part justified by, his undoubted genius for winning the trust and understanding of his own people. He enlarged, with intermittent gusts of Homeric laughter, upon the machinations of the Ng'ombwanan extreme right and left who had upon several occasions made determined efforts to secure his death and were, through some mysterious process of reason, thwarted by The Boomer's practice of exposing himself as an easy target. 'They see,' he explained, 'that I am not (as we used to say at Davidson's) standing for their tedious codswallop.'

'*Did* we say that at Davidson's?'

'Of course. You must remember. Constantly.'

'So be it.'

'It was a favourite expression of your own. *Yes*,' shouted The Boomer as Alleyn seemed inclined to demur, 'always. We all picked it up from you.'

'To return, if we may, to the matter in hand.'

'*All* of us,' The Boomer continued nostalgically. 'You set the tone (at Davidson's),' and noticing perhaps a fleeting expression of horror on Alleyn's face, he leant forward and patted his knees. 'But I digress,' he said accurately, 'Shall we return to our muttons?'

'Yes,' Alleyn agreed with heartfelt relief. 'Yes. Let's.'

'Your turn,' The Boomer generously conceded. 'You were saying?'

'Have you thought – but of course you have – what would follow if you *were* knocked off?'

'As you say: of course I have. To quote your favourite dramatist (you see, I remember), "the filthy clouds of heady murder, spoil and villainy" would follow,' said The Boomer with relish. 'To say the least of it,' he added.

'Yes. Well now: the threat doesn't lie, as the Martinique show must have told you, solely within the boundaries of Ng'ombwana. In the Special Branch they know, and I mean they really *do* know, that there are lunatic fringes in London ready to go to all lengths. Some of them are composed of hangovers from certain disreputable backwaters of colonialism, others have a devouring hatred of your colour. Occasionally they are peope with a real and bitter grievance that has grown monstrous in stagnation. You name it. But they're there, in considerable numbers, organized and ready to go.'

'I am not alarmed,' said The Boomer with maddening complacency. 'No, but I mean it. In all truth I do not experience the least sensation of physical fear.'

'I don't share your sense of immunity,' Alleyn said. 'In your boots I'd be in a muck sweat.' It occurred to him that he had indeed abandoned the slightest nod in the direction of protocol. 'But, all right. Accepting your fearlessness, may we return to the disastrous effect your death would have upon your country? "The filthy clouds of heady murder" bit. Doesn't that thought at all predispose you to precaution?'

'But, my dear fellow, you don't understand. I shall not be killed. I know it. Within myself, I know it. Assassination is not my destiny: it is as simple as that.'

Alleyn opened his mouth and shut it again.

'As simple as that,' The Boomer repeated. He opened his arms. 'You see!' he cried triumphantly.

'Do you mean,' Alleyn said very carefully, 'that the bullet in Martinique and the spear in a remote village in Ng'ombwana and the one or two other pot-shots that have been loosed off at you from time to time were all predestined to miss?'

'Not only do I believe it but my people – *my people* – know it in their souls. It is one of the reasons why I am re-elected unanimously to lead my country.'

Alleyn did not ask if it was also one of his reasons why nobody, so far, had had the temerity to oppose him.

The Boomer reached out his great shapely hand and laid it on Alleyn's knee. 'You were and you are my good friend,' he said. 'We were close at Davidson's. We remained close while I read my law and ate my dinners at the Temple. And we are close still. But this thing we discuss now belongs to my colour and my race. My blackness. Please, do not try to understand: try only, my dear Rory, to accept.'

To this large demand Alleyn could only reply: 'It's *not* as simple as that.'

'No? But why?'

'If I talk about my personal anxiety for you I'll be saying in effect that I *don't* understand and *can't* accept, which is precisely what you do not want me to say. So I must fall back on my argument as an unwilling policeman with a difficult job. I'm not a member of the Special Branch but my colleagues in that Department have asked me to do what I can, which looks a bit like damn-all. I do put it to you that their job, a highly specialized and immensely difficult one, is going to be a hundred per cent more tricky if you decline to co-operate. If, for instance, on an impulse you change your route to some reception or walk out of your embassy without telling anybody and take a constitutional in Kensington Gardens all by yourself. To put it badly and brutally, if you are killed somebody in the Special Branch is going to be axed, the Department's going to fall into general disrepute at the highest and lowest levels, and a centuries-old reputation of immunity from political assassination in England is gone for good. You see, I'm speaking not only for the police.'

'The police, as servants of the people,' The Boomer began and then, Alleyn thought, very probably blushed.

'Were you going to say we ought to be kept in our place?' he mildly asked.

The Boomer began to walk about the room. Alleyn stood up.

'You have a talent,' The Boomer suddenly complained, 'for putting one in the wrong. I remember it of old at Davidson's.'

'What an insufferable boy I must have been,' Alleyn remarked. He was getting very bored with Davidson's and really there seemed to be nothing more to say. 'I have taken up too much of your Excellency's time,' he said. 'Forgive me,' and waited to be dismissed.

The Boomer looked mournfully upon him. 'But you are lunching,' he said. 'We have agreed. It is arranged that you shall lunch.'

'That's very kind, your Excellency, but it's only eleven o'clock. Should I make myself scarce in the meantime?'

To his intense dismay he saw that the bloodshot eyes had

filled with tears. The Boomer said, with immense dignity: 'You have distressed me.'

'I'm sorry.'

'I was overjoyed at your coming. And now it is all spoilt and you call me Excellency.'

Alleyn felt the corners of his mouth twitch and at the same time was moved by a contradictory sense of compassion. This emotion, he realized, was entirely inappropriate. He reminded himself that the President of Ng'ombwana was far from being a sort of inspired innocent. He was an astute, devoted and at times ruthless dictator with, it had to be added, a warm capacity for friendship. He was also extremely observant. 'And funny,' Alleyn thought, controlling himself. 'It's quite maddening of him to be funny as well.'

'Ah!' the President suddenly roared out, 'you are laughing! My dear Rory, you are laughing,' and himself broke into that Homeric gale of mirth. 'No, it is too much! Admit! It is too ridiculous! What is it all about? Nothing! Listen, I will be a good boy. I will behave. Tell your solemn friends in your Special Branch that I will not run away when they hide themselves behind inadequate floral decorations and dress themselves up as nonentities with enormous boots. There now! You are pleased? Yes?'

'I'm enchanted,' Alleyn said, 'if you really mean it.'

'But I do. I do. You shall see. I will be decorum itself. Within,' he added, 'the field of their naïve responsibilities. Within the UK in fact. OK? Yes?'

'Yes.'

'And no more Excellencies. No? Not,' The Boomer added without turning a hair, 'when we are *tête-à-tête*. As at present.'

'As at present,' Alleyn agreed and was instantly re-involved in an exuberance of hand-shaking.

It was arranged that he would be driven round the city for an hour before joining the President for luncheon. The elegant ADC reappeared. When they walked back along the corridor, Alleyn looked through its french windows into the acid-green garden. It was daubed superbly with

286

flamboyants and veiled by a concourse of fountains. Through the iridescent rise and fall of water there could be perceived, at intervals, motionless figures in uniform.

Alleyn paused. 'What a lovely garden,' he said.

'Oh yes?' said the ADC, smiling. Reflected colour and reflected lights from the garden glanced across his polished charcoal jaw and cheekbones. 'You like it? The President likes it very much.'

He made as if to move. 'Shall we?' he suggested.

A file of soldiers, armed, and splendidly uniformed, crossed the garden left, right, left, right, on the far side of the fountains. Distorted by prismatic cascades, they could dimly be seen to perform a correct routine with the men they had come to replace.

'The changing of the guard,' Alleyn said lightly.

'Exactly. They are purely ceremonial troops.'

'Yes?'

'As at your Buckingham Palace,' explained the ADC.

'Quite,' said Alleyn.

They passed through the grandiloquent hall and the picturesque guard at the entrance.

'Again,' Alleyn ventured, 'purely ceremonial?'

'Of course,' said the ADC.

They were armed, Alleyn noticed, if not to the teeth, at least to the hips, with a useful-looking issue of sophisticated weapons. 'Very smartly turned out,' he said politely.

'The President will be pleased to know you think so,' said the ADC and they walked into a standing bath of heat and dazzlement.

The Presidential Rolls heavily garnished with the Ng'ombwanan arms and flying, incorrectly since he was not using it, the Presidential standard, waited at the foot of the steps. Alleyn was ushered into the back seat while the ADC sat in front. The car was air-conditioned and the windows shut and, thought Alleyn, 'If ever I rode in a bullet-proof job – and today wouldn't be the first time – this is it.' He wondered if, somewhere in Ng'ombwana security circles there was an influence a great deal more potent than that engendered by the industrious evocation of Davidson's.

287

They drove under the escort of two ultra-smart, lavishly accoutred motor-cyclists. 'Skinheads, bikies, traffic cops, armed escorts,' he speculated, 'wherever they belch and rev and bound, what gives the species its peculiar air of menacing vulgarity?'

The car swept through crowded, mercilessly glaring streets. Alleyn found something to say about huge white monstrosities – a Palace of Culture, a Palace of Justice, a Hall of Civic Authority, a Free Library. The ADC received his civilities with perfect complacency.

'Yes,' he agreed. 'They are very fine. All new. All since The Presidency. It is very remarkable.'

The traffic was heavy but it was noticeable that it opened before their escort as the Red Sea before Moses. They were stared at, but from a distance. Once, as they made a right hand turn and were momentarily checked by an oncoming car, their chauffeur, without turning his head, said something to the driver that made him wince.

When Alleyn, who was married to a painter, looked at the current scene, wherever it might be, he did so with double vision. As a stringently trained policeman he watched, automatically, for idiosyncrasies. As a man very sensitively tuned to his wife's way of seeing, he searched for consonancies. Now, when confronted by a concourse of round, black heads that bobbed, shifted, clustered and dispersed against that inexorable glare, he saw this scene as his wife might like to paint it. He noticed that, in common with many of the older buildings, one in particular was in process of being newly painted. The ghost of a former legend showed faintly through the mask – SANS RIT IMPO T NG TR DI G CO. He saw a shifting, colourful group on the steps of this building and thought how, with simplification, re-arrangement and selection Troy would endow them with rhythmic significance. She would find, he thought, a focal point, some figure to which the others were subservient, a figure of the first importance.

And then, even as this notion visited him, the arrangement occurred. The figures reformed like fragments in a kaleidoscope and there was the focal point, a solitary man, inescapable because quite still, a grotesquely fat man, with long blond hair, wearing white clothes. A white man.

The white man stared into the car. He was at least fifty yards away but for Alleyn it might have been so many feet. They looked into each other's faces and the policeman said to himself: 'That chap's worth watching. That chap's a villain.'

Click, went the kaleidoscope. The fragments slid apart and together. A stream of figures erupted from the interior, poured down the steps and dispersed. When the gap was uncovered the white man had gone.

IV

'It's like this, sir,' Chubb had said rapidly. 'Seeing that No. 1 isn't a full-time place being there's two of us, we been in the habit of helping out on a part-time basis elsewhere in the vicinity. Like, Mrs Chubb does an hour every other day for Mr Sheridan in the basement and I go to the Colonel's — that's Colonel and Mrs Cockburn-Montfort in the Place — for two hours of a Friday afternoon, and every other Sunday evening we baby-sit at 17 The Walk. And — '

'Yes. I see,' said Mr Whipplestone, stemming the tide.

'You won't find anything scamped or overlooked, sir,' Mrs Chubb intervened. 'We give satisfaction, sir, in all quarters, really we do. It's just An Arrangement, like.'

'And naturally, sir, the wages are adjusted. We wouldn't expect anything else, sir, would we?'

They had stood side by side with round anxious faces, wide-open eyes and gabbling mouths. Mr Whipplestone had listened with his built-in air of attentive detachment and had finally agreed to the proposal that the Chubbs were all his for six mornings, breakfast, luncheon and dinner: that provided the house was well kept up they might attend upon Mr Sheridan or anybody else at their own and his convenience, that on Fridays Mr Whipplestone would lunch and dine at his club or elsewhere and that, as the Chubbs put it, the wages 'was adjusted accordingly'.

'Most of the residents,' explained Chubb when they had completed these arrangements and got down to details, 'has accounts at the Napoli, sir. You may prefer to deal elsewhere.'

'And for the butchery,' said Mrs Chubb, 'there's – '

They expounded upon the amenities in the Capricorns.

Mr Whipplestone said: 'That all sounds quite satisfactory. Do you know, I think I'll make a tour of inspection.' And he did so.

The Napoli is one of the four little shops in Capricorn Mews. It is 'shop' reduced to its absolute minimum; a slit of a place where the customers stand in single file and then only eight at a squeeze. The proprietors are an Italian couple, he dark and anxious, she dark and buxom and jolly. Their assistant is a large and facetious cockney.

It is a nice shop. They cure their own bacon and hams. Mr Pirelli makes his own pâté and a particularly good terrine. The cheeses are excellent. Bottles of dry Orvieto are slung overhead and other Italian wines crowd together inside the door. There are numerous exotics in line on the shelves. The Capricornians like to tell each other that the Napoli is 'a pocket Fortnum's'. Dogs are not allowed but a row of hooks has been thoughtfully provided in the outside wall and on most mornings there is a convocation of mixed dogs attached to them.

Mr Whipplestone skirted the dogs, entered the shop and bought a promising piece of Camembert. The empurpled army man, always immaculately dressed and gloved, whom he had seen in the street was in the shop and was addressed by Mr Pirelli as 'Colonel'. (Montfort? wondered Mr Whipplestone.) The Colonel's lady was with him. An alarming lady, the fastidious Mr Whipplestone thought, with the face of a dissolute clown and wildly overdressed. They both wore an air of overdone circumspection that Mr Whipplestone associated with the hazards of a formidable hangover. The lady stood stock still and bolt-upright behind her husband but as Mr Whipplestone approached the counter, she side-stepped and barged into him, driving her pin heel into his instep.

'I beg your pardon,' he cried in pain and lifted his hat.

'Not a bit,' she said thickly and gave him what could only be described as a half-awakened leer.

Her husband turned and seemed to sense a need for conversation. 'Not much room for manoeuvrin',' he shouted. 'What?'

'Quite,' said Mr Whipplestone.

He opened an account, left the shop and continued his explorations.

He arrived at the scene of his encounter with the little black cat. A large van was backing into the garage. Out of the tail of his eye he thought he saw briefly a darting shadow and when the van stopped he could have fancied, almost, that he heard a faint, plaintive cry. But there was nothing to support these impressions and he hurried on, oddly perturbed.

At the far end of the Mews, by the entrance to the passageway is a strange little cavern, once a stable, which has been converted into a shop. Here, at this period, a baleful fat lady made images of pigs either as doorstops or with roses and daises on their sides and a hole in their backs for cream or flowers as the fancy might take you. They varied in size but never in design. The kiln was at the back of the cavern and as Mr Whipplestone looked in the fat lady stared at him out of her shadows. Above the entrance was a notice: 'X. & K. Sanskrit. Pigs.'

'Commercial candour!' thought Mr Whipplestone, cracking a little joke for himself. To what nationality he wondered could someone called Sanskrit possibly belong? Indian, he supposed, And 'X'? Xavier perhaps. 'To make a living,' he wondered, 'out of the endless reduplication of pottery pigs? And why on earth does this extraordinary name seem to ring a bell?'

Conscious that the fat lady in the shadows still looked at him, he moved on into Capricorn Place and made his way to a rosy brick wall at the far end. Through an opening in this wall one leaves the Capricorns and arrives at a narrow lane passing behind the Basilica precincts and an alleyway ending in the full grandeur of Palace Park Gardens.

Here the Ng'ombwana Embassy rears its important front.

Mr Whipplestone contemplated the pink flag with its insignia of green spear and sun and mentally apostrophized it. 'Yes,' he thought, 'there you are and for my part, long may you stay there.' And he remembered that at some as yet unspecified time but, unless something awful intervened, in the near future, the Ambassador and all his minions would be in no end of a tig getting ready for the state visit of their dynamic President and spotting assassins behind every plane tree. The Special Branch would be raising their punctual plaint and at the FO, he thought, they'll be dusting down their imperturbability. 'I'm out of it all and (I'd better make up my mind to it) delighted to be so. I suppose,' he added. Conscious of a slight pang, he made his way home.

2

Lucy Lockett

Mr Whipplestone had been in residence for over a month. He was thoroughly settled, comfortable and contented and yet by no means lethargically so. On the contrary, he had been stimulated by his change of scene and felt lively. Already he was tuned in to life in the Capricorns. 'Really,' he wrote in his diary, 'it's like a little village set down in the middle of London. One runs repeatedly into the same people in the shops. On warm evenings the inhabitants stroll about the streets. One may drop in at the Sun and Splendour where one finds, I'm happy to say, a very respectable, nay, quite a distinguished, white port.'

He had been in the habit of keeping a diary for some years. Until now it had confined itself to the dry relation of facts with occasionally a touch of the irony for which he had been slightly famous at the FO. Now, under the stimulus of his new environment, the journal expanded and became, at times, almost skittish.

The evening was very warm. His window was open and the curtains, too. An afterglow had suffused the plane trees and kindled the dome of the Basilica but now was faded. There was a smell of freshly-watered gardens in the air and the pleasant sound of footfalls mingling with quiet voices drifted in at the open window. The muted roar of Baronsgate seemed distant, a mere background to quietude.

After a time he laid down his pen, let fall his eyeglass and looked with pleasure at his room. Everything had fitted to a miracle. Under the care of the Chubbs his nice old bits and pieces positively sparkled. The crimson goblet glowed in the window and his Agatha Troy seemed to generate a light of its own.

'How nice everything is,' thought Mr Whipplestone.

It was very quiet in his house. The Chubbs, he fancied,

were out for the evening but they were habitually so unobtrusive in their comings and goings that one was unaware of them. While he was writing, Mr Whipplestone had been aware of visitors descending the iron steps into the area. Mr Sheridan was at home and receiving in the basement flat.

He switched off his desk lamp, got up to stretch his legs and moved over to the bow window. The only people who were about were a man and a woman coming towards him in the darkening Square. They moved into a pool of light from the open doorway of the Sun in Splendour and momentarily he got a clearer look at them. They were both fat and there was something about the woman that was familiar.

They came on towards him into and out from the shadow of the plane trees. On a ridiculous impulse, as if he had been caught spying, Mr Whipplestone backed away from his window. The woman seemed to stare into his eyes: an absurd notion since she couldn't possibly see him.

Now he knew who she was: Mrs or Miss X. Sanskrit. And her companion? Brother or spouse? Brother, almost certainly. The pig-potters.

Now they were out of the shadow and crossed the Walk in full light straight at him. And he saw they were truly awful.

It wasn't that they were lard-fat, both of them, so fat that they might have sat to each other as models for their wares, or that they were outrageously got up. No clothes, it might be argued in these permissive days, could achieve outrageousness. It wasn't that the man wore a bracelet and an anklet and a necklace and earrings or that what hair he had fell like pond-weed from an embroidered headband. It wasn't even that she (fifty if a day, thought Mr Whipplestone) wore vast black leather hotpants, a black fringed tunic and black boots. Monstrous though these grotesqueries undoubtedly were, they were as nothing compared with the eyes and mouths of the Sanskrits which were, Mr Whipplestone now saw with something like panic, equally heavily made-up.

'They shouldn't be here,' he thought, confusedly protecting the normality of the Capricorns. 'People like that. They ought to be in Chelsea. Or somewhere.'

They had crossed the Walk. They had approached his house. He backed further away. The area gate clicked and clanged, they descended the iron steps. He heard the basement flat bell. He heard Mr Sheridan's voice. They had been admitted.

'No, really!' Mr Whipplestone thought in the language of his youth. 'Too much! And he seemed perfectly respectable.' He was thinking of his brief encounter with Mr Sheridan.

He settled down to a book. At least it was not a noisy party down there. One could hear little or nothing. Perhaps, he speculated, the Sanskrits were mediums. Perhaps Mr Sheridan dabbled in spiritism and belonged to a 'circle'. They looked like that. Or worse. He dismissed the whole thing and returned to the autobiography of a former chief of his Department. It was not absorbing. The blurb made a great fuss about a ten-year interval imposed between the author's death and publication. Why, God knew, thought Mr Whipplestone, since the crashing old bore could have nothing to disclose that would unsettle the composure of the most susceptible of vestal virgins.

His attention wandered. He became conscious of an uneasiness at the back of his mind: an uneasiness occasioned by sound, by something he would rather not hear, by something that was connected with anxiety and perturbation. By a cat mewing in the street.

Pah! he thought, as far as one can think 'pah'. Cats abounded in London streets. He had seen any number of them in the Capricorns: pampered pet cats. There was an enormous tortoiseshell at the Sun in Splendour and a supercilious white affair at the Napoli. Cats.

It had come a great deal nearer. It was now very close indeed. Just outside, one would suppose, and not moving on. Sitting on the pavement, he dared say, and staring at his house. At him, even. And mewing. Persistently. He made a determined effort to ignore it. He returned to his book. He thought of turning on his radio, loudly, to drown it. The cries intensified. From being distant and intermittent they were now immediate and persistent.

'I shall not look out of the window,' he decided in a fluster. 'It would only see me.'

'Damnation!' he cried three minutes later. 'How dare people lock out their cats! I'll complain to someone.'

Another three minutes and he did, against every fibre of disinclination in his body, look out of the window. He saw nothing. The feline lamentations were close enough to drive him dotty. On the steps: that's where they were. On the flight of steps leading up to his front door. 'No!' he thought. 'No, really this is not good enough. This must be stopped. Before we know where we are –'

Before he knew where he was, he was in his little hall and manipulating his double lock. The chain was disconnected on account of the Chubbs but he opened the door a mere crack and no sooner had he done so than something – a shadow, a meagre atomy – darted across his instep.

Mr Whipplestone became dramatic. He slammed his door to, leant against it and faced his intruder.

He had known it all along. History, if you could call an incident of not much more than a month ago history, was repeating itself. In the wretched shape of a small black cat: the same cat but now quite dreadfully emaciated, its eyes clouded, its fur staring. It sat before him and again opened its pink mouth in now soundless mews. Mr Whipplestone could only gaze at it in horror. Its haunches quivered and, as it had done when they last met, it leapt up to his chest.

As his hand closed round it he wondered that it had had the strength to jump. It purred and its heart knocked at his fingers.

'This is too much,' he repeated and carried it into his drawing-room. 'It will die, I dare say,' he said, 'and how perfectly beastly that will be.'

After some agitated thought he carried it into the kitchen and, still holding it, took milk from the refrigerator, poured some into a saucer, added hot water from the tap and set it on the floor and the little cat sat beside it. At first he thought she would pay no attention – he was persuaded the creature

296

was a female — her eyes being half-closed and her chin on the floor. He edged the saucer nearer. Her whiskers trembled. So suddenly that he quite jumped, she was lapping, avidly, frantically as if driven by some desperate little engine. Once she looked up at him.

Twice he replenished the saucer. The second time she did not finish the offering. She raised her milky chin, stared at him, made one or two shaky attempts to wash her face and suddenly collapsed on his foot and went to sleep.

Some time later there were sounds of departure from the basement flat. Soon after this, the Chubbs affected their usual discreet entry. Mr Whipplestone heard them put up the chain on the front door. The notion came to him that perhaps they had been 'doing for' Mr Sheridan at his party.

'Er — is that you, Chubb?' he called out.

Chubb opened the door and presented himself, apple-cheeked, on the threshold with his wife behind him. It struck Mr Whipplestone that they seemed uncomfortable.

'Look,' he invited, 'at this.'

Chubb had done so, already. The cat lay like a shadow across Mr Whipplestone's knees.

'A cat, sir,' said Chubb tentatively.

'A stray. I've seen it before.'

From behind her husband, Mrs Chubb said: 'Nothing of it, sir, is there? It don't look healthy, do it?'

'It was starving.'

Mrs Chubb clicked her tongue.

Chubb said: 'Very quiet, sir, isn't it? It hasn't passed away, has it?'

'It's asleep. It's had half a bottle of milk.'

'Well, excuse me, sir,' Mrs Chubb said, 'but I don't think you ought to handle it. You don't know where it's been, do you, sir?'

'No,' said Mr Whipplestone, and added with a curious inflection in his voice. 'I only know where it is.'

'Would you like Chubb to dispose of it, sir?'

This suggestion he found perfectly hateful but he threw out as airily as he could: 'Oh, I don't think so. I'll do something about it myself in the morning. Ring up the RSPCA.'

297

'I dare say if you was to put it out, sir, it'd wander off where it come from.'

'Or,' suggested Chubb. 'I could put it in the garden at the back, sir. For the night, like.'

'Yes,' Mr Whipplestone gabbled, 'thank you. Never mind. I'll think of something. Thank you.'

'Thank you, sir,' they said, meaninglessly.

Because they didn't immediately make a move and because he was in a tizzy, Mr Whipplestone, to his own surprise said, 'Pleasant evening?'

They didn't answer. He glanced up and found they stared at him.

'Yes, thank you, sir,' they said.

'Good!' he cried with a phoney heartiness that horrified him. 'Good! Good night, Chubb. Good night, Mrs Chubb.'

When they had gone into the kitchen. He felt sure they opened the refrigerator and he distinctly heard them turn on a tap. Washing the saucer, he thought guiltily.

He waited until they had retired upstairs and then himself sneaked into the kitchen with the cat. He had remembered that he had not eaten all the poached scallop Mrs Chubb gave him for dinner.

The cat woke up and ate quite a lot of scallop.

Entry into his back garden was effected by a door at the end of the passage and down a precipitous flight of steps. It was difficult, holding the cat, and he made rather a noisy descent but was aided by a glow of light from behind the blinds that masked Mr Sheridan's basement windows. This enabled him to find a patch of unplanted earth against the brick wall at the rear of the garden. He placed the cat upon it.

He had thought she might bolt into the shadows and somehow escape, but no: after a considerable wait she became industrious. Mr Whipplestone tactfully turned his back.

He was being watched from the basement through an opening between the blind and the window frame.

The shadowy form was almost certainly that of Mr Sheridan and almost certainly he had hooked himself a peephole and had released it as Mr Whipplestone turned. The shadowy form retreated.

At the same time a slight noise above his head caused Mr Whipplestone to look up to the top storey of his house. He was just in time to see the Chubbs' bedroom window being closed.

There was, of course, no reason to suppose they, also, had been watching him.

'I must be getting fanciful,' he thought.

A faint rhythmic scuffling redirected his attention to the cat. With her ears laid back and with a zealous concentration that spoke volumes for her recuperative powers, she was tidying up. This exercise was followed by a scrupulous personal toilette, which done, she blinked at Mr Whipplestone and pushed her nut-like head against his ankle.

He picked her up and returned indoors.

II

The fashionable and grossly expensive pet-shop round the corner in Baronsgate had a consulting-room, visited on Wednesday mornings by a veterinary surgeon. Mr Whipplestone had observed their notice to this effect and the next morning, being a Wednesday, he took the cat to be vetted. His manner of conveying his intention to the Chubbs was as guarded and non-committal as forty years' experience in diplomacy could make it. Indeed, in a less rarefied atmosphere it might almost have been described as furtive.

He gave it out that he was 'taking that animal to be attended to'. When the Chubbs jumped to the conclusion that this was a euphemism for 'put down' he did not correct them. Nor did he think it necessary to mention that the animal had spent the night on his bed. She had roused him at daybreak by touching his face with her paw. When he opened his eyes she had flirted with him, rolling on her side and looking at him from under her arm. And when Chubb came in with his early morning tray, Mr Whipplestone had contrived to throw his eiderdown over her and later on had treated her to a saucer of milk. He came downstairs with her under *The Times*, chose his moment to let her out by the back door into the garden, and presently called Mrs Chubb's attention to her. She was demanding vigorously to be let in.

So now he sat on a padded bench in a minute waiting-room, cheek by jowl with several Baronsgate ladies, each of whom had a dog in tow. One of them, the one next to Mr Whipplestone, was the lady who trod on his foot in the Napoli, Mrs Montfort as he subsequently discovered, the Colonel's lady. They said good morning to each other when they encountered, and did so now. By and large Mr Whipplestone thought her pretty awful, though not as awful as the pig-pottery lady of last night. Mrs Montfort carried on her over-dressed lap a Pekinese, which, after a single contemptuous look, turned its back on Mr Whipplestone's cat who stared through it.

He was acutely conscious that he presented a farcical appearance. The only container that could be found by the Chubbs was a disused birdcage, the home of their parrot, lately deceased. The little cat looked outraged sitting in it, and Mr Whipplestone looked silly nursing it and wearing his eye-glass. Several of the ladies exchanged amused glances.

'What,' asked the ultra-smart surgery attendant, note-book in hand, 'is pussy's name?'

He felt that if he said 'I don't know,' or 'It hasn't got one,' he would put himself at a disadvantage with these women. '*Lucy*,' he said loudly and added as an afterthought: 'Lockett.'

'I see!' she said brightly and noted it down. 'You haven't an appointment, have you?'

'I'm afraid not.'

'Lucy won't have long to wait,' she smiled, and passed on.

A woman with a huge, angry, short-haired tabby in her arms came through from the surgery.

The newly-named Lucy's fur rose. She made a noise that suggested she had come to the boil. The tabby suddenly let out a yell. Dogs made ambiguous comments in their throats.

'Oh lor!' said the newcomer. She grinned at Mr Whipplestone. 'Better make ourselves scarce,' she said, and to her indignant cat: 'Shut up, Bardolph, don't be an ass.'

When they had gone Lucy went to sleep and Mrs Montfort said: 'Is your cat very ill?'

'No!' Mr Whipplestone quite shouted and then explained that Lucy was a stray starveling.

'Sweet of you,' she said, 'to care. People are so awful about animals. It makes me quite ill. I'm like that.' She turned her gaze upon him. 'Kitty Montfort. My husband's the warrior with the purple face. He's called Colonel Montfort.'

Cornered, Mr Whipplestone murmured his own name.

Mrs Montfort smelt of very heavy scent and gin.

'I know,' she said archly, 'you're our new boy, aren't you? At No. 1, The Walk? We have a piece of your Chubb on Fridays.'

Mr Whipplestone, whose manners were impeccable, bowed as far as the birdcage would permit.

Mrs Montfort was smiling into his face. She had laid her gloved hand on the cage. The door behind him had opened. Her smiled became fixed as if pinned up at the corners. She withdrew her hand, and looked straight in front of her.

From the street there had entered a totally black man in livery with a white Afghan hound on a scarlet leash. The man paused and glanced round. There was an empty place on the other side of Mrs Montfort. Still looking straight in front of her, she moved far enough along the seat to leave insufficient room on either side of her. Mr Whipplestone instantly widened the distance between them and with a gesture, invited the man to sit down. The man said, 'Thank you, sir,' and remained where he was, not looking at Mrs Montfort. The hound advanced his nose towards the cage. Lucy did not wake.

'I wouldn't come too close if I were you, old boy,' Mr Whipplestone said. The Afghan wagged his tail and Mr Whipplestone patted him. 'I know you,' he said, 'you're the Embassy dog, aren't you? You're Ahman.' He gave the man a pleasant look and the man made a slight bow.

'Lucy Lockett?' said the attendant, brightly emerging. 'We're all ready for her.'

The consultation was brief but conclusive. Lucy Lockett was about seven months old and her temperature was normal, she was innocent of mange, ringworm or parasites, she was extremely undernourished and therefore in shocking condition. Here the vet hesitated. 'There are scars,' he said, 'and there's been a fractured rib that has looked after itself. She's been badly neglected – I think she may have been actively ill-treated.' And catching sight of Mr Whipplestone's horrified face he added cheerfully: 'Nothing that pills and good food won't put right.' He said she had been spayed. She was half-Siamese and half God knew what, the vet said, turning back her fur and handling her this way and that. He laughed at the white end to her tail and gave her an injection.

She submitted to these indignities with utter detachment, but when at liberty, leapt into her protector's embrace and performed her now familiar act of jamming her head under his jacket and lying next his heart.

'Taken to you,' said the vet. 'They've got a sense of gratitude, cats have. Especially the females.'

'I don't know anything about them,' said Mr Whipplestone in a hurry.

Motivated by sales-talk and embarrassment, he bought on his way out a cat bed-basket, a china dish labelled 'Kitbits', a comb and brush and a collar for which he ordered a metal tab with a legend: 'Lucy Lockett. 1 Capricorn Walk' and his telephone number. The shop assistant showed him a little red cat-harness for walking out and told him that with patience, cats could be induced to co-operate. She put Lucy into it and the result was fetching enough for Mr Whipplestone to keep it.

He left the parrot cage behind to be called for and heavily laden, with Lucy again in retreat under his coat, walked quickly home to deploy his diplomatic resources upon the Chubbs, little knowing that he carried his destiny under his jacket.

III

'This is perfectly delightful,' said Mr Whipplestone, turning from his host to his hostess with the slight inclinations of his head and shoulders that had long been occupational mannerisms. 'I *am* so enjoying myself.'

'Fill up your glass,' Alleyn said. 'I did warn you that it was an invitation with an ulterior motive, didn't I?'

'I am fully prepared: charmingly so. A superb port.'

'I'll leave you with it,' Troy suggested.

'No, don't,' Alleyn said. 'We'll send you packing if anything v.s. and c. crops up. Otherwise it's nice to have you. Isn't it, Whipplestone?'

Mr Whipplestone embarked upon a speech about his good fortune in being able to contemplate a 'Troy' above his fireplace every evening and now having the pleasure of contemplating the artist herself at her own fireside. He got a little bogged down but fetched up bravely.

'And when,' he asked, coming to his own rescue, 'are we to embark upon the ulterior motive?'

Alleyn said, 'Let's make a move. This is liable to take time.'

At Troy's suggestion they carried their port from the house into her detached studio and settled themselves in front of long windows overlooking a twilit London garden.

'I want,' Alleyn said, 'to pick your brains a little. Aren't you by way of being an expert on Ng'ombwana?'

'Ng'ombwana? I! That's putting it much too high, my dear man. I was there for three years in my youth.'

'I thought that quite recently when it was getting its independence – ?'

'They sent me out there, yes. During the exploratory period: mainly because I speak the language, I suppose. Having rather made it my thing in a mild way.'

'And you have kept it up?'

'Again, in a mild way: oh, yes. Yes.' He looked across the top of his glass at Alleyn. 'You haven't gone over to the Special Branch, surely?'

'That's a very crisp bit of instant deduction. No, I haven't.

But you may say they've unofficially roped me in for the occasion.'

'Of the forthcoming visit?'

'Yes, blast them. Security.'

'I see. Difficult. By the way, you must have been the President's contemporary at – ' Mr Whipplestone stopped short. 'Is it hoped that you may introduce the personal note?'

'You are quick!' Troy said and he gave a gratified little cackle.

Alleyn said: 'I saw him three weeks ago.'

'In Ng'ombwana?'

'Yes. Coming the old-boy network like nobody's business.'

'Get anywhere?'

'Not so that you'd notice: no, that's not fair. He did undertake not to cut up rough about our precautions but exactly what he meant by that is his secret. I dare say that in the upshot he'll be a bloody nuisance.'

'Well?' asked Mr Whipplestone, leaning back and swinging his eyeglass in what Alleyn felt had been his cross-diplomatic-desk gesture for half a lifetime. 'Well, my dear Roderick?'

'Where do you come in?'

'Quite.'

'I'd be grateful if you'd – what's the current jargon? – fill me in on the general Ng'ombwana background. From your own point of view. For instance, how many people would you say have cause to wish The Boomer dead?'

'The Boomer?'

'As he incessantly reminded me, that was His Excellency's schoolboy nickname.'

'An appropriate one. In general terms, I should say some two hundred thousand persons, at least.'

'Good Lord!' Troy exclaimed.

'Could you,' asked her husband, 'do a bit of name-dropping?'

'Not really. Not specifically. But again in general terms – well, it's the usual pattern throughout the new African independencies. First of all there are those Ng'ombwanan political opponents whom the President succeeded in breaking, the survivors of whom are either in prison or in this country waiting for his overthrow or assassination.'

'The Special Branch flatters itself it's got a pretty comprehensive list in that category.'

'I dare say,' said Mr Whipplestone drily. 'So did we, until one fine day in Martinique a hitherto completely unknown person with a phoney British passport fired a revolver at the President, missed, and was more successful with a second shot at himself. He had no record and his true identity was never established.'

'I reminded The Boomer of that incident.'

Mr Whipplestone said archly to Troy: 'You know, he's much more fully informed than I am. What's he up to?'

'I can't imagine, but do go on. I, at least, know nothing.'

'Well. Among these African enemies, of course, are the extremists who disliked his early moderation and especially his refusal at the outset to sack all his European advisers and officials in one fell swoop. So you get pockets of anti-white terrorists who campaigned for independence but are now prepared to face about and destroy the government they helped to create. Their followers are an unknown quantity but undoubtedly numerous. But you know all this, my dear fellow.'

'He's sacking more and more whites now, though, isn't he? However unwillingly?'

'He's been forced to do so by the extreme elements.'

'So,' Alleyn said, 'the familiar, perhaps the inevitable, pattern emerges. The nationalization of all foreign enterprise and the appropriation of properties held by European and Asian colonists. Among whom we find the bitterest possible resentment.'

'Indeed. And with some reason. Many of them have been ruined. Among the older groups the effect has been completely disastrous. Their entire way of life has disintegrated and they are totally unfitted for any other.' Mr Whipplestone rubbed his nose. 'I must say,' he added, 'however improperly, that some of them are *not* likeable individuals.'

Troy asked: 'Why's he coming here? The Boomer, I mean?'

'Ostensibly, to discuss with Whitehall his country's needs for development.'

'And Whitehall,' Alleyn said, 'professes its high delight while the Special Branch turns green with forebodings.'

"Mr Whipplestone, you said "ostensibly",' Troy pointed out.

'Did I, Mrs Rory? — Yes. Yes, well it has been rumoured through tolerably reliable sources that the President hopes to negotiate with rival groups to take over the oil and copper resources from the dispossessed who have, of course, developed them at enormous cost.'

'Here we go again!' said Alleyn.

'I don't suggest,' Mr Whipplestone mildly added, 'that Lord Karnley or Sir Julian Raphael or any of their associates are likely to instigate a lethal assault upon the President.'

'Good!'

'But of course behind those august personages is a host of embittered shareholders, executives and employees.'

'Among whom might be found the odd cloak-and-dagger merchant. And apart from all these more or less motivated persons,' Alleyn said, 'there are the ones policemen like least: the fanatics. The haters of black pigmentation, the lonely woman who dreams about a black rapist, the man who builds Anti-Christ in a black image or who reads a threat to his livelihood in every black neighbour. Or for whom the commonplace phrases — 'black outlook, black record, as black as it's painted, black villainy, the black man will get you' and all the rest of them, have an absolute reference. Black is bad. Finish.'

'And the Black Power lot,' Troy said, 'are doing as much for "white", aren't they? The war of the images.'

Mr Whipplestone made a not too uncomfortable little groaning noise and returned to his port.

'I wonder,' Alleyn said, 'I do wonder, how much of that absolute antagonism the old Boomer nurses in his sooty bosom.'

'None for you, anyway,' Troy said, and when he didn't answer, 'surely?'

'My dear Alleyn, I understood he professes the utmost *camaraderie*.'

'Oh, yes! Yes, he does. He lays it on with a trowel. Do you know, I'd be awfully sorry to think the trowel-work overlaid an inimical understructure. Silly, isn't it?'

'It is the greatest mistake,' Mr Whipplestone pronounced, 'to make assumptions about relationships that are not clearly defined.'

'And what relationship is ever that?'

'Well! Perhaps not. We do what we can with treaties and agreements, but perhaps not.'

'He did try,' Alleyn said. 'He did in the first instance try to set up some kind of multi-racial community. He thought it would work.'

'Did you discuss that?' Troy asked.

'Not a word. It wouldn't have done. My job was too tricky. Do you know, I got the impression that at least part of his exuberant welcome was inspired by a — well, by a wish to compensate for the ongoings of the new regime.'

'It might be so,' Mr Whipplestone conceded. 'Who can say?'

Alleyn took a folded paper from his breast pocket.

'The Special Branch has given me a list of commercial and professional firms and individuals to be kicked out of Ng'ombwana, with notes on anything in their history that might look at all suspicious.' He glanced at the paper.

'Does the same Sanskrit mean anything at all to you?' he asked. 'X. and K. Sanskrit to be exact. My dear man, what *is* the matter?'

Mr Whipplestone had shouted inarticulately, laid down his glass, clapped his hands and slapped his forehead.

'Eureka!' he cried stylishly. 'I have it! At last. At last!'

'Jolly for you,' said Alleyn, 'I'm delighted to hear it. What had escaped you?'

'"*Sanskrit, Importing and Trading Company, Ng'ombwana*".'

'That's it. Or was it.'

'In Edward VIIth Avenue.'

'Certainly, I saw it there: only they call it something else

307

now. And Sanskrit has been kicked out. Why are you so excited?'

'Because I saw him last night.'

'You *did!*'

'Well, it must have been. They are as alike as two disgusting pins.'

'They?' Alleyn repeated, gazing at his wife who briefly crossed her eyes at him.

'How could I have forgotten!' exclaimed Mr Whipplestone rhetorically. 'I passed those premises every day of my time in Ng'ombwana.'

'I clearly see that I mustn't interrupt you.'

'My dear Mrs Roderick, my dear Roderick, do please forgive me,' begged Mr Whipplestone, turning pink. 'I must explain myself: too gauche and peculiar. But you see – '

And explain himself he did, pig-pottery and all, with the precision that had eluded him at the first disclosure. 'Admit,' he cried when he had finished, 'it *is* a singular coincidence, now isn't it?'

'It's all of that,' Alleyn said. 'Would you like to hear what the Special Branch have got to say about the man – K. Sanskrit?'

'Indeed I would.'

'Here goes, then. This information, by the way, is a digest one of Fred Gibson's chaps got from the Criminal Record Office. "Sanskrit. Kenneth, for Heaven's sake. Age – approx 58. Height 5 foot 10. Weight: 16 stone 4. Very obese. Blond. Long hair. Dress: eccentric: Ultra modern. Bracelets. Anklet. Necklace. Wears make-up. Probably homosexual. One ring through pierced lobe. Origin: uncertain. Said to be Dutch. Name possibly assumed or corruption of a foreign name. Convicted of fraudulent practices involving the occult, London 1940. Served three months' sentence. Sus. connection with drug traffic, 1942. Since 1950 importer of ceramics, jewellery and fancy goods into Ng'ombwana. Large, profitable concern. Owned blocks of flats and offices now possessed by Ng'ombwanan interests. Strong supporter of apartheid. Known to associate with Anti-Black and African extremists. Only traceable relative: Sister, with whom he is now in partnership, pottery business 'The Piggery', Capricorn Mews, SW3."'

'There you are!' said Mr Whipplestone, spreading out his hands.

'Yes. There we are and not very far on. There's no specific reason to suppose Sanskrit constitutes a threat to the safety of the President. And that goes for any of the other names on the list. Have a look at it. Does it ring any more bells? Any more coincidences?'

Mr Whipplestone screwed in his eyeglass and had a look.

'Yes, yes, yes,' he said drily. 'One recognizes the disillusioned African element. *And* the dispossessed. I can add nothing. I'm afraid, my dear fellow, that apart from the odd circumstance of one of your remote possibilities being a neighbour of mine, I am of no use to you. And none in that respect, either, if one comes to think of it. A broken reed,' sighed Mr Whipplestone, 'I fear, a broken reed.'

'Oh,' Alleyn said lightly, 'you never know, do you? By the way, the Ng'ombwanan Embassy is in your part of the world, isn't it?'

'Yes, indeed. I run into old Karumba sometimes. Their Ambassador. We take our constitutional at the same hour. Nice old boy.'

'Worried?'

'Hideously, I should have thought.'

'You'd have been right. He's in a flat spin and treating the SB to a hell of a work-out. And what's more he's switched over to me. Never mind about security not being my proper pigeon. He should worry! I know The Boomer and that's enough. He wants me to teach the SB its own business. Imagine! If he had his wish there'd be total alarm devices in every ornamental urn and a security man under The Boomer's bed. I must say I don't blame him. He's giving a reception. I suppose you've been invited?'

'I have, yes. And you?'

'In my reluctant role as The Boomer's old school chum. And Troy, of course,' Alleyn said, putting his hand briefly on hers.

Then followed rather a long pause.

'Of course,' Mr Whipplestone said, at last, 'these things don't happen in England. At receptions and so on. Madmen at large in kitchens or wherever it was.'

'Or at upstairs windows in warehouses?'

'Quite.'

The telephone rang and Troy went out of the room to answer it.

'I ought to forbear,' Alleyn said, 'from offering the maddening observation that there's always a first time.'

'Oh, nonsense!' flustered Mr Whipplestone. 'Nonsense, my dear fellow! Really! Nonsense! Well,' he added uneasily, 'one *says* that.'

'Let's hope one's right.'

Troy came back. 'The Ng'ombwanan Ambassador,' she said, 'would like a word with you, darling.'

'God bless his woolly grey head,' Alleyn muttered and cast up his eyes. He went to the door but checked. 'Another Sanskrit coincidence for you, Sam. I rather think I saw him, too, three weeks ago in Ng'ombwana, outside his erstwhile emporium, complete with anklet and earring. The one and only Sanskrit, or I'm a displaced Dutchman with beads and blond curls.'

IV

The Chubbs raised no particular objection to Lucy: 'So long as it's not unhealthy, sir,' Mrs Chubb said, 'I don't mind. Keep the mice out, I dare say.'

In a week's time Lucy improved enormously. Her coat became glossy, her eyes bright and her person plumpish. Her attachment to Mr Whipplestone grew more marked and he, as he confided in his diary, was in some danger of making an old fool of himself over her. 'She is a beguiling little animal,' he wrote, 'I confess I find myself flattered by her attentions. She has nice ways.' The nice ways consisted of keeping a close watch on him, of greeting him on his reappearance after an hour's absence as if he had returned from the North Pole, of tearing about the house with her tail

310

up, affecting astonishment when she encountered him and of sudden onsets of attachment when she would grip his arm in her forelegs, kick it with her hind legs, pretend to bite him and then fall into a little frenzy of purrs and licks.

She refused utterly to accommodate to her red harness but when Mr Whipplestone took his evening stroll, she accompanied him: at first to his consternation. But although she darted ahead and pranced out of hiding places at him, she kept off the street and their joint expeditions became a habit.

Only one circumstance upset them and that was a curious one. Lucy would trot contentedly down Capricorn Mews until they had passed the garage and were within thirty yards of the pottery-pigs establishment. At that point she would go no further. She either bolted home under her own steam or performed her familiar trick of leaping into Mr Whipplestone's arms. On these occasions he was distressed to feel her trembling. He concluded that she remembered her accident and yet he was not altogether satisfied with this explanation.

She fought shy of the Napoli because of the dogs tied up outside but on one visit when there happened to be no customers and no dogs she walked in. Mr Whipplestone apologized and picked her up. He had become quite friendly with Mr and Mrs Pirelli and told them about her. Their response was a little strange. There were ejaculations of '*poverina*' and the sorts of noises Italians make to cats. Mrs Pirelli advanced a finger and crooned. She then noticed the white tip of Lucy's tail and looked very hard at her. She spoke in Italian to her husband, who nodded portentously and said '*Sì*' some ten times in succession.

'Have you recognized the cat?' asked Mr Whipplestone in alarm. They said they thought they had. Mrs Pirelli had very little English. She was a very large lady and she now made herself a great deal larger in eloquent mime, curving both arms in front of her and blowing out her cheeks. She also jerked her head in the direction of Capricorn Passage. 'You mean the pottery person,' cried Mr Whipplestone. 'You mean she was that person's cat!'

He realized bemusedly that Mrs Pirelli had made another gesture, an ancient one. She had crossed herself. She laid her hand on Mr Whipplestone's arm. 'No, no, no. Do not give back. No. *Cattivo. Cattivo,*' said Mrs Pirelli.

'Cat?'

'No, signor,' said Mr Pirelli. 'My wife is saying "bad". They are bad, cruel people. Do not return to them your little cat.'

'No,' said Mr Whipplestone confusedly. 'No, I won't. Thank you. I won't.'

And from that day he never took Lucy into the Mews.

Mrs Chubb, Lucy accepted as a source of food and accordingly performed the obligatory ritual of brushing round her ankles. Chubb, she completely ignored.

She spent a good deal of time in the tub garden at the back of the house making wild balletic passes at imaginary butterflies.

At 9.30 one morning, a week after his dinner with the Alleyns, Mr Whipplestone sat in his drawing-room doing *The Times* crossword. Chubb was out shopping and Mrs Chubb, having finished her housework, was 'doing for' Mr Sheridan in the basement. Mr Sheridan, who was something in the City, Mr Whipplestone gathered, was never at home on weekday mornings. At 11 o'clock Mrs Chubb would return to see about Mr Whipplestone's luncheon. The arrangement worked admirably.

Held up over a particularly cryptic clue, Mr Whipplestone's attention was caught by a singular noise, a kind of stifled complaint as if Lucy was mewing with her mouth full. This proved to be the case. She entered the room backwards with sunken head, approached crab-wise and dropped something heavy on his foot. She then sat back and gazed at him with her head on one side and made the inquiring trill that he found particularly fetching.

'What on earth have you got there?' he asked.

He picked it up. It was a ceramic no bigger than a medallion but it was heavy and must have grievously taxed her delicate little jaws. A pottery fish, painted white on one side and biting its own tail. It was pierced by a hole at the top.

'Where did you get this?' he asked severely.

Lucy lifted a paw, lay down, looked archly at him from under her arm and then incontinently jumped up and left the room.

'Extraordinary little creature,' he muttered. 'It must belong to the Chubbs.'

And when Mrs Chubb returned from below he called her in and showed it to her. 'Is this yours, Mrs Chubb?' he asked.

She had a technique of not replying immediately to anything that was said to her and she used it now. He held the thing out to her but she didn't take it.

'The cat brought it in,' explained Mr Whipplestone, who always introduced a tone of indifference in mentioning Lucy Lockett to the Chubbs. 'Do you know where it came from?'

'I think – it must be – I think it's Mr Sheridan's, sir,' Mrs Chubb said at last. 'One of his ornaments, like. The cat gets through his back window, sir, when it's open for airing. Like when I done it just now. But I never noticed.'

'Does she? Dear me! Most reprehensible! You might put it back, Mrs Chubb, could you? Too awkward if he should miss it!'

Mrs Chubb's fingers closed over it. Mr Whipplestone looking up at her, saw with surprise that her apple-pink cheeks had blanched. He thought of asking her if she was unwell but her colour began to reappear unevenly.

'All right, Mrs Chubb?' he asked.

She seemed to hover on the brink of some reply. Her lips moved and she brushed them with her fingers. At last she said: 'I haven't liked to ask, sir, but I hope we give satisfaction, Chubb and me.'

'Indeed you do,' he said warmly. 'Everything goes very smoothly.'

'Thank you, sir,' she said and went out. He thought: 'That wasn't what she was about to say.'

He heard her go upstairs and thought: 'I wish she'd return that damn'd object.' But almost immediately she came back.

He went through to the dining-room window and watched her descend the outside steps into the back garden

313

and disappear into Mr Sheridan's flat. Within seconds he heard the door slam and saw her return.

A white pottery fish. Like a medallion. He really must not get into the habit of thinking things had happened before or been heard of or seen before. There were scientific explanations, he believed, for such experiences. One lobe of one's brain working a billionth of a second before the other or something to do with Time Spirals. He wouldn't know. But of course, in the case of the Sanskrit person it was all perfectly straightforward: he *had* in the past seen the name written up. He had merely forgotten.

Lucy made one of her excitable entrances. She tore into the room as if the devil was after her, stopped short with her ears laid back and affected to see Mr Whipplestone for the first time: 'Heavens! You!'

'Come here,' he said sharply.

She pretended not to hear him, strolled absently nearer and suddenly leapt into his lap and began to knead.

'You are *not*,' he said, checking this painful exercise, 'to sneak into other people's flats and steal pottery fish.'

And there for the moment the matter rested.

Until five days later when, on a very warm evening, she once more stole the medallion and dumped it at her owner's feet.

Mr Whipplestone scarcely knew whether he was exasperated or diverted by this repeated misdemeanour. He admonished his cat, who seemed merely to be thinking of something else. He wondered if he could again leave it to Mrs Chubb to restore the object to its rightful place in the morning and then told himself that really this wouldn't do.

He turned the medallion over in his hand. There was some sort of inscription fired on the reverse side: a wavy X. There was a hole at the top through which, no doubt, a cord could be passed. It was a common little object, entirely without distinction. A keepsake of some sort, he supposed.

Mr Sheridan was at home. Light from his open kitchen window illuminated the back regions and streaked through gaps in his sitting-room curtains.

'You're an unconscionable nuisance,' Mr Whipplestone said to Lucy Lockett.

He put the medallion in his jacket pocket, let himself out at his front door, took some six paces along the pavement and passed through the iron gate and down the short flight of steps to Mr Sheridan's door. Lucy, anticipating an evening stroll, was too quick for him. She shot over his feet, and down the steps and hid behind a dwarfed yew tree.

He rang the door bell.

It was answered by Mr Sheridan. The light in his little entrance lobby was behind him so that his face was in shadow. He had left the door into his sitting-room open and Mr Whipplestone saw that he had company. Two armchairs in view had their backs towards him but the tops of their occupants' heads showed above them.

'I do apologize,' said Mr Whipplestone, 'not only for disturbing you but for –' he dipped into his pocket and then held out the medallion – 'this,' he said.

Mr Sheridan's behaviour oddly repeated that of Mrs Chubb. He stook stock still. Perhaps no more than a couple of seconds passed in absolute silence but it seemed much longer before he said:

'I don't understand. Are you – ?'

'I must explain,' Mr Whipplestone said: and did.

While he was explaining the occupant of one of the chairs turned and looked over the back. He could see only the top of the head, the forehead and the eyes but there was no mistaking Mrs Montfort. Their eyes met and she ducked out of sight.

Sheridan remained perfectly silent until the end of the recital and even then said nothing. He had made no move to recover his property but on Mr Whipplestone again offering it, extended his hand.

'I'm afraid the wretched little beast has taken to following Mrs Chubb into your flat. Through your kitchen window, I imagine. I am so very sorry,' said Mr Whipplestone.

Sheridan suddenly became effusive. 'Not another syllable,' he lisped. 'Don't give it another thought. It's of no value, as you can see. I shall put it out of reach. Thank you so much. Yes.'

'Good night,' said Mr Whipplestone.

'Good night, good night. Warm for the time of year, isn't it? Good night. Yes.'

Certainly, the door was not shut in his face but the moment he turned his back it was shut very quickly.

As he reached the top of the iron steps he was treated to yet another repetitive occurrence. The Sanskrits, brother and sister, were crossing the street towards him. At the same moment his cat who had come out of hiding barged against his leg and bolted like black lightning down the street.

The second or two that elapsed while he let himself out by the area gate brought the Sanskrits quite close. Obviously they were again visiting down below. They waited for him to come out. He smelt them and was instantly back in Ng'ombwana. What was it? Sandarac? They made incense of it and burnt it in the markets. The man was as outlandish as ever. Even fatter. And painted. Bedizened. And as Mr Whipplestone turned quickly away, what *had* he seen, dangling from that unspeakable neck? A medallion? A white fish? He was further disturbed by the disappearance so precipitately of Lucy, and greatly dismayed by the notion that she might get lost. He was in two minds whether to go after her to call to her and make a fool of himself in so doing.

While he still hesitated he saw a small shadow moving towards him. He did call and suddenly she came tearing back and, in her familiar fashion, launched herself at him. He carried her up his own steps.

'That's right,' he said. 'You come indoors. Come straight indoors. Where we both belong.'

But when they had reached their haven, Mr Whipplestone gave himself a drink. He had been disturbed by too many almost simultaneous occurrences, the most troublesome of which was his brief exchange with Mr Sheridan. 'I've seen him before,' he said to himself, 'and I don't mean here, when I took the house. I mean in the past. Somewhere. Somewhere. And the impression is not agreeable.'

But his memory was disobliging and after teasing himself with unprofitable speculation, he finished his drink and in a state of well-disciplined excitement, telephoned his friend Superintendent Alleyn.

Catastrophe

The Ng'ombwanan Embassy had been built for a Georgian merchant prince and was really far too grand, Alleyn saw, for an emergent African republic. It had come upon the market at the expiration of a long lease and had been snatched up by The Boomer's representatives in London. It would not have ill-become a major power.

He saw a splendid house, beautifully proportioned and conveying, by its very moderation, a sense of calm and spaciousness. The reception rooms, covering almost the whole of the ground floor, gave at the rear on to an extensive garden with, among other felicities, a small lake. The garden had fallen into disrepair but had been most elegantly restored by Vistas of Baronsgate. Their associated firm, Decor and Design, also of Baronsgate, had been responsible for the interior.

'They must have got more than they bargained for,' Alleyn said, 'when the occupants brought in their bits and pieces.'

He was casing the premises in the company, and at the invitation, of his opposite number in the Special Branch, Superintendent Fred Gibson, a vast, pale, muted man who was careful to point out that they were there at the express invitation of the Ng'ombwanan Ambassador and were, virtually, on Ng'ombwanan soil.

'We're here on sufferance if you like,' Gibson said in his paddy voice. 'Of course they're still a Commonwealth nation, of sorts, but I reckon they could say "thanks a lot, goodbye for now" any time they fancied.'

'I believe they could, Fred.'

'Not that I want the job. Gawd, no! But as soon as His Nibs pokes his nose out of doors he's our bit of trouble and no mistake.'

'Tricky for you,' said Alleyn. He and Gibson had been associates in their early days and knew each other pretty well.

They were at one end of a reception saloon or ballroom to which they had been shown by an enormous African flunkey, who had then withdrawn to the opposite end where he waited, motionless.

Alleyn was looking at a shallow recess which occupied almost the whole of their end. It was lined with a crimson and gold paper on which had been hung Ng'ombwanan artifacts – shields, masks, cloaks, spears – so assembled as to form a sort of giant African Trophy flanked with Heraldic Achievements. At the base of this display was a ceremonial drum. A spotlight had been set to cover the area. It was an impressive arrangement and in effect harked back to the days when the house was built and Nubian statues and little black turbaned pages were the rage in London. The Boomer, Alleyn thought, would not be displeased.

A minstrels' gallery ran round three sides of the saloon and Gibson explained that four of his men as well as the orchestra would be stationed up there.

Six pairs of french windows opened on the garden. Vistas had achieved a false perspective by planting on either side of the long pond yew trees – tall in the foreground, diminishing in size until they ended in miniatures. The pond itself had been correspondingly shaped. It was wide where the trees were tall and narrowed throughout its length. The *trompe l'oeil* was startling. Alleyn had read somewhere or another of Henry Irving's production of *The Corsican Brothers* with six-foot guardsmen nearest the audience and midgets in the background. The effect here, he thought, would be the reverse of Irving's, for at the far end of the little lake a pavilion had been set up where The Boomer, the Ambassador and a small assortment of distinguished guests would assemble for an *al fresco* entertainment. From the saloon, they would look like Gullivers in Lilliput. Which again, Alleyn reflected, would not displease The Boomer.

He and Gibson spoke in undertones on account of the flunkey.

318

'You see how the land lies,' said Gibson. 'I'll show you the plan in a sec. The whole show – this evening party – takes place on the ground floor. And later in the bloody garden. Nobody goes upstairs except the regular house-staff and we look after that one. Someone at every stairhead, don't you worry. Now. As you see, the entrance hall's behind us at a lower level and the garden through the windows in front. On your left are the other reception rooms: a smaller drawing-room, the dining-room – you could call it a banqueting hall without going too far – and the kitchens and offices. On our right, opening off the entrance hall behind us, is a sort of ladies' sitting-room and off that, on the other side of the alcove with all the hardware,' said Gibson indicating the Ng'ombwanan trophies, 'is the ladies cloakroom. Very choice. You know. Ankle-deep carpets. Armchairs, dressing-tables. Face-stuff provided and two attendants. The WCs themselves, four of them, have louvre windows opening on the garden. You could barely get a fair shot at the pavilion through any of them because of intervening trees. Still. We're putting in a reliable female sergeant.'

'Tarted up as an attendant?'

'Naturally.'

'Fair enough. Where's the men's cloakroom?'

'On the other side of the entrance hall. It opens off a sort of smoking-room or what-have-you that's going to be set up with a bar. The lavatory windows in their case would give a better line on the pavilion and we're making arrangements accordingly.'

'What about the grounds?'

'The grounds are one hell of a problem. Greenery all over the shop,' grumbled Mr Gibson.

'High brick wall, though?'

'Oh, yes. And iron spikes, but what of that? We'll do a complete final search – number one job – at the last moment. House, garden, the lot. And a complete muster of personnel. The catering's being handled by Costard et Cie of Mayfair. Very high class. Hand-picked staff. All their people are what they call maximum-trusted, long-service employees.'

'They take on extra labour for these sort of jobs though, don't they?'

'I know, but they say nobody they can't vouch for.'

'What about – ' Alleyn moved his head very slightly in the direction of the man in livery who was gazing out of the window.

'The Ng'ombwanan lot? Well. The household's run by one of them. Educated in England and trained at a first-class hotel in Paris. Top credentials. The Embassy staff was hand-picked in Ng'ombwana, they tell me. I don't know what that's worth, the way things are in those countries. All told, there are thirty of them but some of the President's household are coming over for the event. The Ng'ombwanans, far as I can make out, will more or less stand round looking pretty. That chap, there,' Mr Gibson continued, slurring his words and talking out of the corner of his mouth, 'is sort of special: you might say a ceremonial bodyguard to the President. He hangs round on formal occasions dressed up like a cannibal and carrying a dirty big symbolic spear. Like a mace-bearer, sort of, or a sword-of-state. You name it. He came in advance with several of the President's personal staff. The Presidential plane, as you probably know, touches down at eleven tomorrow morning.'

'How's the Ambassador shaping up?'

'Having kittens.'

'Poor man.'

'One moment all worked up about the party and the next in a muck sweat over security. It was at his urgent invitation we came in.'

'He rings me up incessantly on the strength of my knowing the great panjandrum.'

'Well,' Gibson said, 'that's why *I've* roped you in, isn't it? And seeing you're going to be here as a guest – excuse me if my manner's too familiar – the situation becomes what you might call provocative. Don't misunderstand me.'

'What do you want me to do, for pity's sake? Fling myself in a protective frenzy on The Boomer's bosom every time down in the shrubbery something stirs?'

'Not,' said Gibson, pursuing his own line of thought, 'that

I think we're going to have real trouble. Not really. Not at this reception affair. It's his comings and goings that are the real headache. D'you reckon he's going to co-operate? You know. Keep to his undertaking with you and not go drifting off on unscheduled jaunts?'

'One can but hope. What's the order of events? At the reception?'

'For a kick-off, he stands in the entrance hall on the short flight of steps leading up to his room, with this spear-carrying character behind him and the Ambassador on his right. His aides will be back a few paces on his left. His personal bodyguard will form a lane from the entrance right up to him. They carry sidearms as part of their full-dress issue. I've got eight chaps outside, covering the walk from the cars to the entrance and a dozen more in and about the hall. They're in livery. Good men. I've fixed it with the Costard people that they'll give them enough to do, handing champagne round and that, to keep them in the picture.'

'What's the drill, then?'

'As the guests arrive from 9.30 onwards, they get their names bawled out by the major-domo at the entrance. They walk up the lane between the guards, the Ambassador presents them to the President and they shake hands and pass in here. There's a band (Louis Francini's lot. I've checked them) up in the minstrels' gallery and chairs for the official party on the dais in front of the hardware. Other chairs round the walls.'

'And we all mill about in here for a spell, do we?'

'That's right. Quaffing your bubbly,' said Gibson tone-lessly. 'Until 10 o'clock when the french windows will all be opened and the staff, including my lot, will set about asking you to move into the garden.'

'And that's when your headache really sets in, is it, Fred?'

'My oath! Well, take a look at it.'

They moved out through the french windows into the garden. A narrow terrace separated the house from the wide end of the pond which was flanked on each converging side by paved walks. And there, at the narrow end, was the pavilion: an elegant affair of striped material caught up by giant spears topped with plumes. Chairs for the guests were set out on each side of that end of the lake and the whole assembly was backed by Mr Gibson's hated trees.

'Of course,' he said gloomily, 'there will be all these perishing fairy-lights. You notice even they get smaller as they go back. To carry out the effect, like. You've got to hand it to them, they've been thorough.'

'At least they'll shed a bit of light on the scene.'

'Not for long, don't you worry. There are going to be musical items and a film. Screen wheeled out against the house, here, and the projector on a perch at the far end. And while that's on, out go the lights except in the pavilion, if you please, where they're putting an ornamental god-almighty lamp which will show His Nibs up like a sitting duck.'

'How long does that last?'

'Twenty minutes all told. There's some kind of dance. Followed by a native turn-out with drums and one or two other items including a singer. The whole thing covers about an hour. At the expiration of which you all come back for supper in the banqueting room. And then, please God, you all go home.'

'You couldn't persuade them to modify their plans at all?'

'Not a chance. It's been laid on by headquarters.'

'Do you mean in Ng'ombwana, Fred?'

'That's right. Two chaps from Vistas and Decor and Design were flown out with plans and photographs of this pad at which the President took a long hard look and then dreamt up the whole treatment. He sent one of his henchmen over to see it was laid on according to specification. I reckon it's as much as the Ambassador's job's worth to change it. And how do you like this?' Gibson asked with a poignant note of outrage in his normally colourless voice. 'The Ambassador's given us definite instructions to keep well away from this bloody pavilion. President's orders and no excuse-me's about it.'

'He's a darling man is The Boomer.'

'He's making a monkey out of us. I set up a security measure only to be told the President won't stand for it.

322

Look – I'd turn the whole exercise in if I could get someone to listen to me. Pavilion and all.'

'What if it rains?'

'The whole shooting-match moves indoors and why the hell do I say 'shooting-match'?' asked Mr Gibson moodily.

'So we pray for a wet night?'

'Say that again.'

'Let's take a look indoors.'

They explored the magnificence of the upper floors, still attended by the Ng'ombwanan spear-carrier who always removed himself to the greatest possible distance, but never left them completely alone. Alleyn tried a remark or two but the man seemed to have little or no English. His manner was stately and utterly inexpressive.

Gibson re-rehearsed his plan of action for the morrow and Alleyn could find no fault in it. The Special Branch is a bit of a loner in the Service. It does not gossip about its proceedings and except when they overlap those of another arm, nobody asks it anything. Alleyn, however, was on such terms with Gibson and the circumstances were so unusual as to allow them to relax these austerities. They retired to their car and lit their pipes. Gibson began to talk about subversive elements from emergent independencies, known to be based on London and with what he called 'violence in their CRO'.

'Some are all on their own,' he said, 'and some kind of coagulate like blood. Small-time secret societies. Mostly they don't get anywhere but there are what you might call malignant areas. And of course you can't discount the pro.'

'The professional gun?'

'They're still available. There's Hinny Packmann. He's out after doing bird in a Swedish stir. He'd be available if the money was right. He doesn't operate under three thousand.'

'Hinny's in Denmark.'

'That's right, according to Interpol. But he could be imported. I don't know anything about the political angle,' Gibson said. 'Not my scene. Who'd take over if this man was knocked off?'

'I'm told there'd be a revolution of sorts, that mercenaries would be sent in, a puppet government set up and that in the upshot the big interests would return and take over.'

'Yes, well, there's that aspect and then again you might get the solitary fanatic. He's the type I really do *not* like,' Gibson said, indignantly drawing a nice distinction between potential assassins. 'No record, as likely as not. You don't know where to look for him.'

'You've got the guest list of course.'

'Of course. I'll show it to you. Wait a sec.'

He fished it out of an inner pocket and they conned it over. Gibson had put a tick beside some five dozen names.

'They've all been on the Ng'ombwanan scene in one capacity or another,' he said. 'From the oil barons at the top to ex-businessmen at the bottom and nearly all of them have been, or are in the process of being, kicked out. The big idea behind this reception seems to be a sort of "nothing personal intended" slant. "Everybody loves everybody" and please come to my party!'

'It hurts me more than it does you?'

'That's right. And they've all accepted, what's more.'

'Hullo!' Alleyn exclaimed, pointing to the list. 'They've asked *him*!'

'Which is that? Ah. Yes. Him. Now, he *has* got a record.'

'See the list your people kindly supplied to me,' Alleyn said and produced it.

'That's right. Not for violence, of course, but a murky background and no error. Nasty bit of work. I don't much fancy *him*.'

'His sister makes pottery pigs about one minute away from the Embassy,' said Alleyn.

'I know that. Very umpty little dump. You'd wonder why, wouldn't you, with all the money he must have made in Ng'ombwana.'

'Has he still got it, though? Mightn't he be broke?'

'Hard to say. Question of whether he laid off his bets before the troubles began.'

'Do you know about this one?' Alleyn asked, pointing to the name Whipplestone on the guest list.

Gibson instantly reeled off a thumbnail sketch of Mr Whipplestone.

'That's the man,' Alleyn said. 'Well now, Fred, this may be a matter of no importance but you may as well lay back your ears and listen.' And he related Mr Whipplestone's story of his cat and the pottery fish. 'Whipplestone's a bit perturbed about it,' he said in the end, 'but it may be entirely beside the point as far as we're concerned. This man in the basement, Sheridan, and the odious Sanskrit may simply meet to play bridge. Or they might belong to some potty little esoteric circle: fortune-telling or spiritism or what have you.'

'That's the type of thing Sanskrit first got borrowed for. Fortune-telling and false pretences. He's a sus for drugs. It was after he came out of stir that he set himself up as a merchant in Ng'ombwana. He's one of the dispossessed,' said Gibson.

'I know.'

'You do?'

'I think I saw him outside his erstwhile premises when I was there three weeks ago.'

'Fancy that.'

'About the ones that get together to bellyache in exile: you don't, I suppose, know of a fish medallion lot?'

'Hah!' said Gibson disgustedly.

'And Mr Sheridan doesn't appear on the guest list. What about a Colonel and Mrs Montfort? They were in Sheridan's flat that evening.'

'Here. Let's see.'

'No,' Alleyn said, consulting the list. 'No Montforts under the M's.'

'Wait a sec. I knew there was something. Look here. Under C "Lt-Col. Cockburn-Montfort, Barset Light Infantry (retd)." What a name. Cockburn.'

'Isn't it usually pronounced Coburn?' Alleyn mildly suggested. 'Anything about him?'

'Info. Here we are. "Organized Ng'ombwanan army. Stationed there from 1960 until Independence in 1971 when present government assumed complete control!"'

'Well,' Alleyn said after a longish pause, 'it still doesn't have to amount to anything. No doubt ex-Ng'ombwanan colonials tend to flock together like ex-Anglo-Indians. There may be a little clutch of them in the Capricorns all belly-aching cosily together. What about the staff? The non-Ng'ombwanans, I mean.'

'We're nothing if not thorough. Every last one's been accounted for. Want to look?'

He produced a second list. 'It shows the Costard employees together. Regulars first, extras afterwards. Clean as whistles, the lot of them.'

'This one?'

Gibson followed Alleyn's long index finger and read under his breath, '"Employed by Costards as extra waiter over period of ten years. In regular employment as domestic servant. Recent position: eight years. Excellent references. Present employment –" Hullo, 'ullo.'

'Yes?'

'"Present employment at 1 Capricorn Walk, SW3."'

'We seem,' Alleyn said, 'to be amassing quite a little clutch of coincidences, don't we?'

II

'It's not often,' Alleyn said to his wife, 'that we set ourselves up in this rig, is it?'

'You look as if you did it as a matter of course every night. Like the jokes about Empire builders in the jungle. When there was an Empire. Orders and decorations to boot.'

'What does one mean exactly, by "to boot"?'

'You tell me, darling, you're the purist.'

'I was when I courted my wife.'

Troy, in her green gown, sat on her bed and pulled on her long gloves. 'It's worked out all right,' she said. 'Us. Wouldn't you say?'

'I would say.'

'What a bit of luck for us.'

'All of that.'

He buttoned up her gloves for her. 'You look lovely,' he said. 'Shall we go?'

'Is our svelte hired limousine at the door?'

'It is.'

'Whoops, then, hark chivvy away.'

Palace Park Gardens had been closed to general traffic by the police so the usual crowd of onlookers was not outside the Ng'ombwanan Embassy. The steps were red-carpeted, a flood of light and strains of blameless and dated melodies, streamed through the great open doorway. A galaxy of liveried men, black and white, opened car doors and slammed them again.

'Oh, Lord. I've forgotten the damn card!' Troy exclaimed.

'I've got it. Here we go.'

The cards, Alleyn saw, were being given a pretty hard look by the men who received them and were handed on to other men seated unobtrusively at tables. He was amused to see, hovering in the background, Superintendent Gibson in tails and a white tie, looking a little as if he might be an Old Dominion Plenipotentiary.

Those guests wishing for the cloakrooms turned off to the right and left and on re-entering the hall were martialled back to the end of the double file of Ng'ombwanan guards where they gave their names to a superb black major-domo who roared them out with all the resonant assurance of a war drum.

Troy and Alleyn had no trappings to shed and passed directly into the channel of approach.

And there, at the far end of the flight of steps leading to the great saloon, was The Boomer himself, in great state, backed by his spear-carrier and wearing a uniform that might have been inspired by the Napoleonic Old Guard upon whom had been lightly laid the restraining hand of Sandhurst.

Troy muttered: 'He's wonderful. Gosh, he's glorious!'

She'd like to paint him, thought Alleyn.

The patiently anxious Ambassador, similarly if less gorgeously uniformed, was stationed on The Boomer's right. Their personal staff stood about in magnificent attitudes behind them.

'Mis-tar and Mrs Roderick Alleyn.'

That huge and beguiling smile opened and illuminated The Boomer's face. He said loudly: 'No need for an introduction here,' and took Alleyn's hands in both his gloved paws.

'And this is the famous wife!' he resonantly proclaimed. 'I am so glad. We meet later. I have a favour to ask. Yes?'

The Alleyns moved on, conscious of being the object of a certain amount of covert attention.

'Rory?'

'Yes, I know. Extra special, isn't he?'

'Whew!'

'What?'

'"Whew." Incredulous whistle.'

'Difficult, in competition with Gilbert and Sullivan.'

They had passed into the great saloon. In the minstrels' gallery instrumentalists, inconspicuously augmented by a clutch of Gibson's silent henchmen, were discussing *The Gondoliers*.

'When everyone is somebodee
Then no one's anybody,'

they brightly and almost inaudibly chirped.

Trays with champagne were circulated. Jokes about constabular boots and ill-fitting liveries were not appropriate. Among the white servants it was impossible to single out Fred Gibson's men.

How to diagnose the smell of a grand assembly? Beyond the luxurious complexity of cosmetics, scent, flowers, hairdressers' lotions, remote foods and alcohol, was there something else, something peculiar to this particular occasion? Somewhere in these rooms were they burning that stuff – what was it? – sandarac? That was it. Alleyn had last smelt it in the Presidential palace in Ng'ombwana. That and the indefinably alien scent of persons of a different colour. The curtains were drawn across the french windows but the great room was not overheated as yet. People moved about it like well-directed extras in the central scene of some feature film.

They encountered acquaintances: the subject of a portrait Troy had painted some years ago for the Royal Commonwealth Society; Alleyn's great white chief and his wife; someone he knew in the Foreign Office and, unexpectedly, his brother, Sir George Alleyn: tall, handsome, ambassadorial and entirely predictable. Troy didn't really mind her brother-in-law but Alleyn always found him a bit of an ass.

'Good Lord!' said Sir George. 'Rory!'

'George.'

'And Troy, my dear. Looking too lovely. Charming! Charming! And what, may one ask, are you doing, Rory, in this *galère*?'

'They got me in to watch the teaspoons, George.'

'Jolly good, ha-ha. Matter of fact,' said Sir George, bending archly down to Troy, 'between you and me and the gatepost I've no idea why I'm here myself. Except that we've all been asked.'

'Do you mean your entire family, George?' inquired his brother. 'Twins and all?'

'So amusing. I mean,' he told Troy, 'the *corps diplomatique* or at least those of us who've had the honour to represent Her Majesty's Government in "furrin parts",' said Sir George, again becoming playful. 'Here we all are!' *Why*, we don't quite know!' he gaily concluded.

'To raise the general tone, I expect,' said Alleyn gravely. 'Look, Troy, there's Sam Whipplestone. Shall we have a word with him?'

'Do let's.'

'See you later, perhaps, George.'

'I understand there's to be some sort of *fête champêtre*.'

'That's right. Mind you don't fall in the pond.'

Troy said when they were at a safe remove, 'If I were George I'd thump you.'

Mr Whipplestone was standing near the dais in front of the Ng'ombwanan display of arms. His faded hair was beautifully groomed and his rather withdrawn face wore a gently attentive air. His eyeglass was at the alert. When he caught sight of the Alleyns he smiled delightedly, made a little bow, and edged towards them.

'What a *very* grand party,' he said.

'Disproportionate, would you say?' Alleyn hinted.

'Well, coming it rather strong, perhaps. I keep thinking of Martin Chuzzlewit.'

'"Todgers were going it"?'

'Yes.' Mr Whipplestone looked very directly at Alleyn. 'All going well in your part of the picture?' he asked.

'Not *mine*, you know.'

'But you've been consulted.'

'Oh,' said Alleyn, 'that! Vaguely. Quite unofficial. I was invited to view. Brother Gibson's laid on a maximum job.'

'Good.'

'By the way, did you know your man was on the strength tonight? Chubb?'

'Oh, yes. He and Mrs Chubb have been on the caterer's supplementary list for many years, he tells me. They're often called upon.'

'Yes.'

'Another of our coincidences, did you think?'

'Well – hardly that, perhaps.'

'How's Lucy Lockett?' Troy asked.

Mr Whipplestone made the little grimace that allowed his glass to dangle. 'Behaving herself with decorum,' he said primly.

'No more thieving stories?'

'Thank God, no,' he said with some fervour. 'You must meet her, both of you,' he added, 'and try Mrs Chubb's cooking. Do say you will.'

'We'd like that very much,' said Troy warmly.

'I'll telephone tomorrow and we'll arrange a time.'

'By the way,' Alleyn said, 'talking of Lucy Lockett reminds me of your Mr Sheridan. Have you any idea what he does?'

'Something in the City, I think. Why?'

'It's just that the link with the Sanskrit couple gives him a certain interest. There's no connection with Ng'ombwana?'

'Not that I know.'

'He's not here tonight,' Alleyn said.

One of the ADCs was making his way through the thickening crowd. Alleyn recognized him as his escort in

330

Ng'ombwana. He saw Alleyn and came straight to him, all eyes and teeth.

'Mr Alleyn, His Excellency the Ambassador wishes me to say that the President will be very pleased if you and Mrs Alleyn will join the official party for the entertainment in the garden. I will escort you when the time comes. Perhaps we could meet here.'

'That's very kind,' Alleyn said. 'We shall be honoured.'

'Dear me,' said Mr Whipplestone when the ADC had gone, 'Todgers *are* going it an' no mistake.'

'It's The Boomer at it again. I wish he wouldn't.'

Troy said: 'What do you suppose he meant when he said he had a favour to ask?'

'He said it to you, darling. Not me.'

'I've got one I'd like to ask him, all right.'

'No prize offered for guessing the answer. She wants,' Alleyn explained to Mr Whipplestone, 'to paint him.'

'Surely,' he rejoined with his little bow, 'that wish has only to be made known – Good God!'

He had broken off to stare at the entrance into the saloon where the last arrivals were coming in. Among them, larger, taller, immeasurably more conspicuous than anyone else in their neighbourhood, were Mr Whipplestone's bugbears: the Sanskrits, brother and sister.

They were, by and large, appropriately attired. That is to say, they wore full evening dress. The man's shirt, to Mr Whipplestone's utterly conventional taste, was unspeakable, being heavily frilled and lacy, with a sequin or two winking in its depths. He wore many rings on his dimpled fingers. His fair hair was cut in a fringe and concealed his ears. He was skilfully but unmistakably *en maquillage*, as Mr Whipplestone shudderingly put it to himself. The sister, vast in green, fringed satin, also wore her hair, which was purple, in a fringe and side-pieces. These in effect squared her enormous face. They moved slowly like two huge vessels, shoved from behind by tugs.

'I thought you'd be surprised,' Alleyn said. He bent his head and shoulders, being so tall, in order that he and Mr Whipplestone could converse without shouting. The

331

conglomerate roar of voices now almost drowned the orchestra which, pursuing its course through the century, had now reached the heyday of Cochran's Revues.

'You knew they were invited?' Mr Whipplestone said, referring to the Sanskrits. 'Well, *really*!'

'Not very delicious, I agree. By the way, somewhere here there's another brace of birds from your Capricorn preserves.'

'Not –'

'The Montforts.'

'That is less upsetting.'

'The Colonel had a big hand, it appears, in setting up their army.'

Mr Whipplestone looked steadily at him. 'Are you talking about Cockburn-Montfort?' he said at last.

'That's right.'

'Then why the devil couldn't his wife say so,' he crossly exclaimed. 'Silly creature! Why leave out the Cockburn? Too tiresome. Yes, well, naturally, *he'd* be asked. I never met him. He hadn't appeared on the scene in my early days and he'd gone when I returned.' He thought for a moment. 'Sadly run to seed,' he said. 'And his wife, too, I'm afraid.'

'The bottle?'

'I should imagine, the bottle. I did tell you, didn't I, that they were in Sheridan's basement, that evening when I called? And that she dodged down?'

'You did, indeed.'

'And that she had – um –?'

'Accosted you in the pet-shop? Yes.'

'Quite so.'

'Well, I dare say she'll have another fling if she spots you tonight. You might introduce us, if she does.'

'Really?'

'Yes, really.'

After about ten minutes, Mr Whipplestone said that there the Cockburn-Montforts, in fact, were, some thirty feet away and drifting in their direction. Alleyn suggested that they move casually towards them.

'Well, my dear fellow, if you insist.'

332

So it was done. Mrs Cockburn-Montfort spotted Mr Whipplestone and bowed. They saw her speak to her husband, obviously suggesting they should effect an encounter.

'Good evening!' she cried as they approached. 'What odd places we meet in, don't we? Animal shops and Embassies.' And when they were actually face to face: 'I've told my husband about you and your piteous little pusscat. Darling, this is Mr Whipplestone, our new boy at No. 1, The Walk. Remember?'

'Hiyar,' said Colonel Cockburn-Montfort.

Mr Whipplestone, following what he conceived to be Alleyn's wishes, modestly deployed his social expertise. 'How do you do,' he said, and to the lady: 'Do you know, I feel quite ashamed of myself. I didn't realize, when we encountered, that your husband was *the* Cockburn-Montfort. Of Ng'ombwana,' he added, seeing that she looked nonplussed.

'Oh. Didn't you? We rather tend to let people forget the Cockburn half. So often and so shy-makingly mispronounced,' said Mrs Cockburn-Montfort, gazing up first at Alleyn and then at Mr Whipplestone, who thought: At least they both seem to be sober; and he reflected that very likely they were never entirely drunk. He introduced Alleyn and at once she switched all her attention to him, occasionally throwing a haggard, comradely glance at Troy upon whom, after a long, glazed look, the Colonel settled his attention.

In comparison with the Sanskrits they were, Mr Whipplestone thought, really not so awful or perhaps, more accurately, they were awful in a more acceptable way. The Colonel, whose voice was hoarse, told Troy that he and his wife had been hard on the Alleyns' heels when they were greeted by the President. He was evidently curious about the cordiality of their reception and began, without much subtlety, to fish. Had she been to Ng'ombwana? If so, why had they never met? He would certainly not have forgotten if they had, he added, and performed the gesture of brushing up his moustache at the corners while allowing his eyes to goggle slightly. He became quite persistent in his gallantries and Troy thought the best way to cut them short was to say that her husband had been at school with the President.

'Ah!' said the Colonel. 'Really? That explains it.' It would have been hard to say why she found the remark offensive.

A hush fell on the assembly and the band in the gallery became audible. It had approached the contemporary period and was discussing *My Fair Lady* when the President and his entourage entered the salon. They made a scarcely less than royal progress to the dais under the trophies. At the same time, Alleyn noticed, Fred Gibson turned up in the darkest part of the gallery and stood, looking down at the crowd. 'With a Little Bit of Luck,' played the band, and really, Alleyn thought, it might have been Fred's signature-tune. The players faded out obsequiously as The Boomer reached the dais.

The ceremonial spear-carrier had arrived and stood, motionless and magnificent, in a panoply of feathers, armlets, anklets, necklets and lion-skins against the central barbaric trophy. The Boomer seated himself. The Ambassador advanced to the edge of the dais. The conductor drew an admonitory flourish from his players.

'Your Excellency, Mr President, Sir. My Lords, Ladies and Gentlemen,' said the Ambassador and went on to welcome his President, his guests and, in general terms, the excellent rapprochement that obtained between his government and that of the United Kingdom, a rapprochement that encouraged the promotion of an ever-developing – his theme became a little foggy round the edges but he brought it to a sonorous conclusion and evoked a round of discreet applause.

The Boomer then rose. Troy thought to herself: I'm going to remember this. Sharply. Accurately. Everything. That great hussar's busby of grey hair. Those reflected lights in the hollows of temple and cheek. The swelling blue tunic, white paws and glittering hardware. And the background, for Heaven's sake! No, but I've got to. I've got to.

She looked at her husband who raised one eyebrow and muttered: 'I'll ask.'

She squeezed his hand violently.

The Boomer spoke briefly. Such was the magnificence of his voice that the effect was less than that of a human instrument than of some enormous double-bass. He spoke predictably of enduring bonds of fellowship in the Commonwealth and less formally of the joys of revisiting the haunts of his youth. Pursuing this theme, to Alleyn's deep misgiving, he dwelt on his schooldays and of strongly cemented, never to be broken, friendships. At which point, having obviously searched the audience and spotted his quarry, he flashed one of his startling grins straight at the Alleyns. A general murmur was induced and Mr Whipplestone, highly diverted, muttered something about 'the cynosure of all eyes'. A few sonorous generalities rounded off the little speech. When the applause had subsided, the Ambassador announced a removal to the gardens and simultaneously the curtains were drawn back and the six pairs of french windows flung open. An enchanting prospect was revealed. Golden lights, star-shaped and diminishing in size, receded into the distance and were reflected in the small lake, itself subscribing to the false perspective that culminated, at the far end, in the brilliantly lit scarlet and white pavilion. Vistas of Baronsgate had done themselves proud.

'The stage-management, as one feels inclined to call it,' said Mr Whipplestone, 'is superb. I look forward excitedly to seeing you both in the pavilion.'

'You've had too much champagne,' Alleyn said and Mr Whipplestone made a little crowing noise.

The official party passed into the garden and the guests followed in their wake. Alleyn and Troy were duly collected by the ADC and led to the pavilion. Here, they were enthusiastically greeted by The Boomer and introduced to ten distinguished guests, among whom Alleyn was amused to find his brother George, whose progress as a career-diplomat had hoisted him into more than one Ambassadorial post. The other guests consisted of the last of the British governors in Ng'ombwana and representatives of associated African independencies.

It would be incorrect to say that The Boomer was

enthroned in his pavilion. His chair was not raised above the others but it was isolated and behind it stood the ceremonial spear-bearer. The guests in arrow formation flanked the President. From the house and to the guests seated on their side of the lake they must present, Alleyn thought, a remarkable picture.

The musicians had descended from their gallery into the garden and were grouped, modestly, near the house among trees that partly concealed the lavatorial louvre windows Gibson had pointed out to Alleyn.

When the company was settled, a large screen was wheeled in front of the french windows, facing down the lake towards the pavilion. A scene in the Ng'ombwanan wild-lands was now projected on this screen. A group of live Ng'ombwanan drummers then appeared before it, the garden lights were dimmed and the drummer performed. The drums throbbed and swelled, pulsed and thudded, disturbing in their monotony, unseemly in their context: a most unsettling noise. It grew to a climax. A company of warriors, painted and armed, erupted from the dark and danced. Their feet thumped down on the mown turf. From the shadow, people, Ng'ombwanans presumably, began to clap the rhythm. More and more of the guests, encouraged perhaps by champagne and the anonymity of the shadows, joined in this somewhat inelegant response. The performance crashed to a formidable conclusion.

The Boomer threw out a few explanatory observations. Champagne was again in circulation.

Apart from the President himself, Ng'ombwana had produced one other celebrity: a singer, by definition a bass but with the astonishing vocal range of just over four octaves, an attribute that he exploited without the least suggestion of break or transition. His native name, being unpronounceable by Europeans, had been simplified as Karbo and he was world-famous.

He was now to appear.

He came from the darkened ballroom and was picked up in front of the screen by a strong spotlight: a black man in conventional evening dress, with a quite extraordinary air of distinction.

All the golden stars and all the lights in the house were out. The orchestra lamps were masked. Only the single lamp by the President, complained of by Gibson, remained alight, so that he – the President – and the singer, at opposite ends of the lake, were the only persons to be seen in the benighted garden.

The orchestra played an introductory phrase.

A single deep sustained note of extraordinary strength and beauty floated from the singer.

While it still hung on the air a sound like that of a whiplash cracked out and somewhere in the house a woman screamed and screamed and screamed.

The light in the pavilion went out.

What followed was like the outbreak of a violent storm: a confusion of voices, of isolated screams, less insistent than the continuous one, of shouted orders, of chairs overturned, of something or someone falling into water. Of Alleyn's hand on Troy's shoulder. Then of his voice: 'Don't move, Troy. Stay there.' And then, unmistakably, The Boomer's great voice roaring out something in his own tongue and Alleyn saying: 'No, you don't. No!' Of a short guttural cry near at hand and a thud. And then from many voices like the king and courtiers in the play: 'Lights! Lights! Lights!'

They came up, first in the ballroom and then overhead in the garden. They revealed some of the guests still seated on either side of the lake but many on their feet talking confusedly. They revealed also the great singer, motionless, still in his spotlight and a number of men who emerged purposefully from several directions, some striding up to the pavilion and some into the house.

And in the pavilion itself men with their backs to Troy shutting her in, crowding together and hiding her husband from her. Women making intermittent exclamations in the background.

She heard her brother-in-law's voice raised in conventional admonition: 'Don't panic, anybody. Keep calm. No need to panic,' and even in her confusion thought that

337

however admirable the advice, he did unfortunately sound ridiculous.

His instructions were in effect repeated, not at all ridiculously, by a large powerful man who appeared beside the singer.

'Keep quiet, and stay where you are, ladies and gentlemen, if you please,' said this person, and Troy at once recognized The Yard manner.

The screaming woman had moved away somewhere inside the house. Her cries had broken down into hysterical and incomprehensible speech. They became more distant and were finally subdued.

And now, the large purposeful man came into the pavilion. The men who had blocked Troy's view backed away and she saw that they had all been looking at it.

A prone figure, face down, arms spread, dressed in a flamboyant uniform, split down the back by a plumed spear. The sky blue tunic had a glistening patch round the place of entry. The plume, where it touched the split, was red.

Alleyn was kneeling by the figure.

The large purposeful man moved in front of her and shut off this picture. She heard Alleyn's voice: 'Better clear the place.' After a moment he was beside her, holding her arm and turning her away. 'All right?' he said. 'Yes,' she nodded and found herself being shepherded out of the pavilion with the other guests.

When they had gone Alleyn returned to the spiked figure and again knelt beside it.

He looked up at his colleague and slightly shook his head. Superintendent Gibson muttered, 'They've done it!'

'Not precisely,' Alleyn said. He stood up and at once the group of men moved further back. And there was The Boomer, bolt upright in the chair that was not quite a throne, breathing deeply and looking straight before him.

'It's the Ambassador,' Alleyn said.

Aftermath

The handling of the affair at the Ng'ombwanan Embassy was to become a classic in the annals of police procedure. Gibson, under the hard drive of a muffled fury, and with Alleyn's co-operation, had, within minutes, transformed the scene into one that resembled a sort of high-toned drafting-yard. The speed with which this was accomplished was remarkable.

The guests, marshalled into the ballroom, were, as Gibson afterwards put it, 'processed' through the dining-room. There they were shepherded up to a trestle table upon which the elaborate confections of Costard et Cie had been shoved aside to make room for six officers, summoned from Scotland Yard. These men sat with copies of the guest-list before them and with regulation tact checked off names and addresses.

Most of the guests were then encouraged to leave by a side door, a general signal having been sent out for their transport. A small group were asked, very civilly, to remain.

As Troy approached the table she saw that among the Yard officers Inspector Fox, Alleyn's constant associate, sat at the end of the row, his left ear intermittently tickled by the tail of an elaborately presented cold pheasant. When he looked over the top of his elderly spectacles and saw her, he was momentarily transfixed. She leant down. 'Yes, Br'er Fox, me,' she murmured, 'Mrs R. Alleyn, 48 Regency Close, SW3.'

'Fancy!' said Mr Fox to his list. 'What about getting home?' he mumbled. 'All right?'

'Perfectly. Hired car. Someone's ringing them. Rory's fixed it.'

Mr Fox ticked off the name, 'Thank you, madam,' he

said aloud. 'We won't keep you,' and so Troy went home, and not until she got there was she to realize how very churned up she had become.

The curtained pavilion had been closed and police constables posted outside. It was lit inside and glowed like some scarlet and white striped bauble in the dark garden. Distorted shadows moved, swelled and vanished across its walls. Specialists were busy within.

In a small room normally used by the controller of the household as an office, Alleyn and Gibson attempted to get some sort of sense out of Mrs Cockburn-Montfort.

She had left off screaming but had the air of being liable to start up again at the least provocation. Her face was streaked with mascara, her mouth hung open and she pulled incessantly at her lower lip. Beside her stood her husband, the Colonel, holding, incongruously, a bottle of smelling salts.

Three women in lavender dresses with caps and stylish aprons sat in a row against the wall as if waiting to make an entrance in unison for some soubrettish turn. The largest of them was a police sergeant.

Behind the desk a male uniformed sergeant took notes and upon it sat Alleyn, facing Mrs Cockburn-Montfort. Gibson stood to one side, holding on to the lower half of his face as if it was his temper and had to be stifled.

Alleyn said: 'Mrs Cockburn-Montfort, we are all very sorry indeed to badger you like this but it really is a most urgent matter. Now. I'm going to repeat, as well as I can, what I *think* you have been telling us and if I go wrong please, *please* stop me and say so. Will you?'

'Come on, Chrissy old girl,' urged her husband. 'Stiff upper lip. It's all over now. Here!' He offered the smelling salts but was flapped away.

'You,' Alleyn said, 'were in the ladies' cloakroom. You had gone there during the general exodus of the guests from the ballroom and were to rejoin your husband for the concert in the garden. There were no other guests in the cloakroom but these ladies, the cloakroom attendants, were there? Right? Good. Now. You had had occasion to use one

340

of the four lavatories, the second from the left. You were still there when the lights went out. So far, then, have we got it right?'

She nodded rolling her gaze from Alleyn to her husband.

'Now the next bit. As clearly as you can, won't you? What happened immediately after the lights went out?'

'I couldn't think what had happened. I mean *why*? I've told you. I really do think,' said Mrs Cockburn-Montfort squeezing out her voice like toothpaste, 'that I might be let off. I've been *hideously* shocked, I thought I was going to be killed. Truly. Hughie —?'

'Pull yourself together, Chrissy, for God's sake. Nobody's killed you. Get on with it. Sooner said, sooner we'll be shot of it.'

'You're so *hard*,' she whimpered. And to Alleyn: 'Isn't he? Isn't he *hard*?'

But after a little further persuasion she did get on with it.

'I was still *there*,' she said. 'In the loo. Honestly! — Too awkward. And all the lights had gone out but there was a kind of glow outside those slatted sort of windows. And I suppose it was something to do with the performance. You know. That drumming and some sort of dance. I knew you'd be cross, Hughie, waiting for me out there and the concert started and all that but one can't help these things, can one?'

'All right. We all know something had upset you.'

'Yes, well, they finished — the dancing and drums had finished — and — and so had I and I was nearly going when the door burst open and hit me. Hard. On — on the back. And he took hold of me. By the arm. Brutally. And threw me out. I'm bruised and shaken and suffering from shock and you keep me here. He threw me so violently that I fell. In the cloakroom. It was much darker there than in the loo. Almost pitch dark. And I lay there. And outside, I could hear clapping and after that there was music and a voice. I suppose it was wonderful but to me, lying there, hurt and shocked, it was like a lost soul.'

'Go on, please.'

'And then there was that ghastly shot. Close. Shattering,

in the loo. And the next thing – straight after that – he burst out and kicked me.'

'Kicked you! You mean deliberately – ?'

'He fell over me,' said Mrs Cockburn-Montfort. 'Almost fell, and in so doing kicked me. And I thought now he's going to shoot me. So of course I screamed. And screamed.'

'Yes?'

'And he bolted.'

'And then?'

'Well, then there were those three.' She indicated the attendants. 'Milling about in the dark and kicking me too. By accident, of course.'

The three ladies stirred in their seats.

'Where had they come from?'

'How should I know! Well, anyway, I *do* know because I heard the doors bang. They'd been in the other three loos.'

'All of them?'

Alleyn looked at his sergeant. She stood up. 'Well?' he asked.

'To try and see Karbo, sir,' she said, scarlet-faced. 'He was just outside. Singing.'

'Standing on the seats, I suppose, the lot of you.'

'Sir.'

'I'll see you later. Sit down.'

'Sir.'

'Now, Mrs Cockburn-Montfort, what happened next?'

Someone, it appeared, had had a torch, and by its light they had hauled Mrs Cockburn-Montfort to her feet.

'Was this you?' Alleyn asked the sergeant, who said it was. Mrs Cockburn-Montfort had continued to yell. There was a great commotion going on in the garden and other parts of the house. And then all the lights went on. 'And that girl,' she said, pointing at the sergeant, 'that one. There. *Do you know what she did?*'

'Slapped your face, perhaps, to stop you screaming?'

'How she *dared*! After all that. And shouting questions at me. And then she had the impertinence to say she couldn't hang round there and left me to the other two. I must say, they had the decency to give me aspirins.'

342

'I'm so glad,' said Alleyn politely. 'Now, will you please answer the next one very carefully. Did you get an impression at all of what this man was like? There was a certain amount of reflected light from the louvres. Did you get anything like a look at him, however momentary?'

'Oh, yes,' she said quite calmly. 'Yes, indeed I did. He was black.'

An appreciable silence followed this statement. Gibson cleared his throat.

'Are you sure of that? Really sure?' Alleyn asked.

'Oh perfectly. I saw his head against the window.'

'It couldn't, for instance, have been a white person with a black stocking over his head?'

'Oh, no. I think he *had* a stocking over his head but I could tell.' She glanced at her husband and lowered her voice. 'Besides,' she said, 'I smelt him. If you've lived out there as we did, you can't mistake it.'

Her husband made a sort of corroborative noise.

'Yes?' Alleyn said, 'I understand they notice the same phenomenon in us. An African friend of mine told me that it took him almost a year before he left off feeling faint in lifts during the London rush hours.'

And before anyone could remark upon this, he said: 'Well, and then one of our people took over and I think from this point we can depend upon his report.' He looked at Gibson. 'Unless you —?'

'No,' Gibson said, 'Thanks. Nothing. We'll have a type-written transcript of this little chat, madam, and we'll ask you to look over it and sign it if it seems OK. Sorry to have troubled you.' And he added the predictable coda. 'You've been very helpful,' he said. Alleyn wondered how much these routine civilities cost him.

The Colonel, ignoring Mr Gibson, barked at Alleyn. 'I take it I may remove my wife? She ought to see her doctor.'

'Of course. Do. Who is your doctor, Mrs Cockburn-Montfort? Can we ring him up and ask him to meet you at your house?'

She opened her mouth and shut it again when the

343

Colonel said: 'We won't trouble you, thank you. Good evening to you.'

They had got as far as the door before Alleyn said: 'Oh, by the way! Did you by any chance get the impression that the man was in some kind of uniform? Or livery?'

There was a long pause before Mrs Cockburn-Montfort said: 'I'm afraid not. No. I've no idea.'

'No? By the way, Colonel, are those your smelling-salts?'

The Colonel stared at him as if he was mad and then, vacantly, at the bottle in his hand.

'Mine!' he said. 'Why the devil should they be mine?'

'They are mine,' said his wife grandly. 'Anyone would suppose we'd been shop-lifting. Honestly!'

She put her arm in her husband's and, clinging to him, gazed resentfully at Alleyn.

'When that peculiar little Whipples-whatever-it-is introduced you, he might have told us you were a policeman. Come on, Hughie darling,' said Mrs Cockburn-Montfort and achieved quite a magnificent exit.

II

It had taken all of Alleyn's tact, patience and sheer authority to get The Boomer stowed away in the library, a smallish room on the first floor. When he had recovered from the effects of shock which must surely, Alleyn thought, have been more severe than he permitted himself to show, he developed a strong inclination to conduct inquiries on his own account.

This was extremely trickly. At the Embassy they were, technically, on Ng'ombwanan soil. Gibson and his Special Branch were there specifically at the invitation of the Ng'ombwanan Ambassador, and how far their authority extended in the somewhat rococo circumstances of that Ambassador having been murdered on the premises was a bit of a poser.

So, in a different key, Alleyn felt, was his own presence on the scene. The Special Branch very much likes to keep itself to itself. Fred Gibson's frame of mind, at the moment, was one of rigidly suppressed professional chagrin and personal mortification. His initial approach would never have been made under ordinary circumstances and now, Alleyn's presence on, as it were, the SB's pitch, gave an almost grotesque twist to an already extremely delicate situation. Particularly since, with the occurrence of a homicide, the focus of responsibility might now be said to have shifted to Alleyn in whose division the crime had taken place.

Gibson had cut through this dilemma by ringing up his principals and getting authority for himself and Alleyn with the consent of the Embassy to handle the case together. But Alleyn knew the situation could well become a very tricky one.

'Apparently,' Gibson said, 'we carry on until somebody stops us. Those are my instructions, anyway. Yours too, on three counts: your AC, your division, and the personal request of the President.'

'Who at the moment wants to summon the entire household including the spear-carrier and harangue them in their own language.'

'Bloody farce,' Gibson mumbled.

'Yes, but if he insists — Look,' Alleyn said, 'it mightn't be such a bad idea for them to go ahead if we could understand what they were talking about.'

'Well — '

'Fred, suppose we put out a personal call for Mr Samuel Whipplestone to come at once — you know: 'be kind enough' and all that. Not sound as if we're breathing down his neck.'

'What about it — ?' asked Gibson unenthusiastically.

'He speaks Ng'ombwanan. He lives five minutes away and will be at home by now. No. 1, Capricorn Walk. We can ring up. Not in the book yet, I dare say, but get through,' said Alleyn to an attendant sergeant, and as he went to the telephone, 'Samuel Whipplestone. Send a car round. I'll speak to him.'

'The idea being?' Mr Gibson asked woodenly.

'We let the President address the troops – indeed, come to that, we can't stop him, but at least we'll know what's being said.'

'Where is he, for God's sake? *You* put him somewhere,' Mr Gibson said as if the President was a mislaid household utensil.

'In the library. He's undertaken to stay there until I go back. We've got coppers keeping obbo in the passage.'

'I should hope so. If this was a case of the wrong victim, chummy may well be gunning for the right one.'

The sergeant was speaking on the telephone.

'Superintendent Alleyn would like a word with you, sir.'

Alleyn detected in Mr Whipplestone's voice an overtone of occupational cool. 'My dear Alleyn,' he said, 'this is a most disturbing occurrence. I understand the Ambassador has been – assassinated.'

'Yes.'

'How very dreadful. Nothing could have been worse.'

'Except the intended target taking the knock.'

'Oh . . . I see. The President.'

'Listen,' Alleyn said and made his request.

'Dear me,' said Mr Whipplestone.

'I know it's asking a lot. Damn cheek in fact. But it would take us some time to raise a neutral interpreter. It wouldn't do for one of the Ng'ombwanans . . . '

'No, no, no, no, quite. Be quiet, cat. Yes. Very well, I'll come.'

'I'm uncommonly grateful. You'll find a car at your door 'Bye.'

'Coming?' Gibson said.

'Yes. Sergeant, go and ask Mr Fox to meet him and bring him here, will you? Pale. About sixty. Eyeglass. VIP treatment.'

'Sir.'

And in a few minutes Mr Whipplestone, stepping discreetly and having exchanged his tailcoat for a well-used smoking jacket, was shown into the room by Inspector Fox, whom Alleyn motioned to stay.

Gibson made a morose fuss of Mr Whipplestone.

'You'll appreciate how it is, sir. The President insists on addressing his household staff and – '

'Yes, yes, I quite understand, Mr Gibson. Difficult for you. I wonder, could I know what happened? It doesn't really affect the interpreter's role, of course, but – briefly?'

'Of course you could,' Alleyn said. 'Briefly then: Somebody fired a shot that you must have heard, apparently taking aim from the ladies' loo. It hit nobody but when the lights went up the Ambassador was lying dead in the Pavilion, spitted by the ceremonial Ng'ombwanan spear that was borne behind the President. The spear-carrier was crouched a few paces back and as far as we can make out – he speaks no English – maintains that in the dark, when everybody was milling about in a hell of a stink over the shot, he was given a chop on the neck and his spear snatched from him.'

'Do you believe this?'

'I don't know. I was there, in the pavilion, with Troy. She was sitting next to the President and I was beside her. When the shot rang out I told her to stay put and at the same time saw the shape of The Boomer half rise and make as if to go. His figure was momentarily silhouetted against Karbo's spotlight on the screen at the other end of the lake. I shoved him back in his chair, told him to pipe down and moved in front of him. A split second later something crashed down at my feet. Some ass called out that the President had been shot. The Boomer and a number of others yelled for lights. They came up and – there was the Ambassador – literally pinned to the ground.'

'A mistake then?'

'That seems to be the general idea – a mistake. They were of almost equal height and similar build. Their uniforms, in silhouette, would look alike. He was speared from behind and, from behind, would show up against the spotlit screen. There's one other point. My colleage here tells me he had two security men posted near the rear entrance to the pavilion. After the shot they say the black waiter came plunging out. They grabbed him but say he

347

appeared to be just plain scared. That's right, isn't it, Fred?'

'That's the case,' Gibson said. 'The point being that while they were finding out what they'd caught, you've got to admit that it's just possible in that bloody blackout, if you'll excuse me, sir, somebody might have slipped into the pavilion.'

'Somebody?' said Mr Whipplestone.

'Well, anybody,' Alleyn said. 'Guest, waiter, what have you. It's unlikely but it's just possible.'

'And got away again? After the – event?'

'Again – just remotely possible. And now, Whipplestone, if you don't mind – '

'Of course.'

'Where do they hold this tribal gathering, Fred? The President said the ballroom. OK?'

'OK.'

'Could you check with him and lay that on, I'll see how things are going in the pavilion and then join you. All right? Would that suit you?'

'Fair enough.'

'Fox, will you come with me?'

On the way he gave Fox a succinct account of Mrs Cockburn-Montfort's story and of the pistol shot, if pistol shot it was, in its relation to the climactic scene in the garden.

'Quite a little puzzle,' said Fox cosily.

In the pavilion they found two uniformed policemen, a photographic and fingerprint expert – Detective-Sergeants Bailey and Thompson – together with Sir James Curtis, never mentioned by the press without the additional gloss of 'the celebrated pathologist'. Sir James had completed his superficial examination. The spear, horridly incongruous, still stuck up at an angle from its quarry and was being photographed in close-up by Thompson. Not far from the body lay an over-turned chair.

'This is a pretty kettle of fish you've got here, Rory,' said Sir James.

'Is it through the heart?'

'Plumb through and well into the turf underneath, I think we'll find. Otherwise it wouldn't be so rigid. It looks as though the assailant followed through the initial thrust and, with a forward lunge, literally pinned him down.'

'Ferocious.'

'Very.'

'Finished?' Alleyn asked Thompson as he straightened up. 'Complete coverage? All angles? the lot?'

'Yes, Mr Alleyn.'

'Bailey? What about dabs?'

Bailey, a mulishly inclined officer, said he'd gone over the spear and could find evidence of only one set of prints and that they were smeared. He added that the camera might bring up something latent but he didn't hold out many hopes. The angle of the spear to the body had been measured. Sir James said it had been a downward thrust. 'Which would indicate a tall man,' he said.

'Or a middle-sized man on a chair?' Alleyn suggested.

'Yes. A possibility.'

'All right,' Alleyn said. 'We'd better withdraw that thing.'

'You'll have a job,' Sir James offered.

They did have a job and the process was unpleasant. In the end the body had to be held down and the spear extracted by a violent jerk, producing a sickening noise and an extrusion of blood.

'Turn him over,' Alleyn said.

The eyes were open and the jaw collapsed, turning the Ambassador's face into a grotesque mask of astonishment. The wound of entry was larger than that of exit. The closely cropped turf was wet.

'Horrible,' Alleyn said shortly.

'I suppose we can take him away?' Sir James suggested. 'I'll do the PM at once.'

'I'm not so sure about that. We're on Ng'ombwanan ground. We're on sufferance. The mortuary van's outside all right but I don't think we can do anything about the body unless they say so.'

'Good Lord!'

'There may be all sorts of taboos, observances and what have you.'

'Well,' said Sir James, not best pleased, 'in that case I'll take myself off. You might let me know if I'm wanted.'

'Of course. We're all walking about like a gaggle of Agags, it's so tricky. Here's Fred Gibson.'

He had come to say that the President wished the body to be conveyed to the ballroom.

'What for?' Alleyn demanded.

'This assembly or what-have-you. Then it's to be put upstairs. He wants it flown back to Ng'ombwana.'

'Good evening to you,' said Sir James and left.

Alleyn nodded to one of the constables, who fetched two men, a stretcher and a canvas. And so his country's representative re-entered his Embassy, finally relieved of the responsibility that had lain so heavily on his mind.

Alleyn said to the constables: 'We'll keep this tent exactly as it is. One of you remains on guard.' And to Fox. 'D'you get the picture, Br'er Fox? Here we all were, a round dozen of us including, you'll be surprised to hear, my brother.'

'Is that so, Mr Alleyn? Quite a coincidence.'

'If you don't mind, Br'er Fox, we won't use that word. It's cropped up with monotonous regularity ever since I took my jaunt to Ng'ombwana.'

'Sorry, I'm sure.'

'Not at all. To continue. Here we were, in arrowhead formation with the President's chair at the apex. There's his chair and that's Troy's beside it. On his other side was the Ambassador. The spear-carrier, who is at present under surveillance in the gents' cloaks, stood behind his master's chair. At the rear are those trestle tables used for drinks and a bit further forward an overturned, pretty solid wooden chair, the purpose of which escapes me. The entrance into the tent at the back was used by the servants. There were two of them, the larger being one of the household henchmen and the other a fresh-faced, chunky specimen in Costard's livery. Both of them were in evidence when the lights went out.'

'And so,' said Fox, who liked to sort things out, 'as soon as this Karbo artist appears, his spotlight picks him up and makes a splash on the screen behind him. And from the back of the tent where this spear expert is stationed anybody who stands up between him and light shows up like somebody coming in late at the cinema.'

'That's it.'

'And after the shot was fired you stopped the President from standing up but the Ambassador *did* stand up and Bob, in a manner of speaking, was your uncle.'

'In a manner of speaking, he was.'

'Now then,' Fox continued in his stately manner. 'Yes. This shot. Fired, we're told by the lady you mentioned, from the window of the female conveniences. No weapon's been recoverd, I take it?'

'Give us a chance.'

'And nobody's corroborated the lady's story about this dirty big black man who kicked her?'

'No.'

'And this chap hasn't been picked up?'

'He's like an insubstantial pageant faded.'

'Just so. And do we assume, then, that having fired his shot and missed his man, an accomplice, spear-carrier or what have you, did the job for him?'

'That may be what we're supposed to think. To my mind it stinks. Not to high Heaven, but slightly.'

'Then what — ?'

'Don't ask me, Br'er Fox. But designedly or not, the shot created a diversion.'

'And when the lights came on?'

'The President was in his chair where I'd shoved him and Troy was in hers. The other two ladies were in theirs. The body was three feet to the President's left. The guests were milling about all over the shop. My big brother was ordering them in a shaky voice not to panic. The spear-carrier was on his knees nursing his carotid artery. The chair was over-turned. No servants.'

'I get the picture.'

'Good, come on, then. The corroboree, pow-wow,

conventicle or coven, call it what you will, is now in congress and we are stayed for.' He turned to Bailey and Thompson. 'Not much joy for you chaps at present but if you can pick up something that looks too big for a female print in the second on the left of the ladies' loo it will be as balm in Gilead. Away we go, Fox.'

But as they approached the house they were met by Gibson looking perturbed, with Mr Whipplestone in polite attendance.

'What's up, Fred?' Alleyn asked. 'Have your race relations fractured?'

'You could put it like that,' Mr Gibson conceded, 'He's making things difficult.'

'The President?'

'That's right. He won't collaborate with anyone but you.'

'Silly old chump.'

'He won't come out of his library until you've gone in.'

'What's bitten him, for the love of Mike?'

'I doubt if he knows.'

'Perhaps,' Mr Whipplestone ventured, 'he doesn't like the introduction of me into the proceedings?'

'I wouldn't say that, sir,' said Gibson unhappily.

'What a nuisance he contrives to be,' Alleyn said, 'I'll talk to him. Are the hosts of Ng'ombwana mustered in the ballroom?'

'Yes. Waiting for Master,' said Gibson.

'Any developments, Fred?'

'Nothing to rave about. I've had a piece of that sergeant in the cloakroom. It seems she acted promptly enough after she left her grandstand seat and attended to Mrs C-M. She located the nearest of my men and gave him the info. A search for chummy was set up with no results and I was informed. The men on duty outside the house say nobody left it. If they say so, nobody did,' said Gibson sticking his jaw out. 'We've begun to search for the gun or whatever it was.'

'It sounded to me like a pistol,' said Alleyn. 'I'd better

352

beard the lion in his library, I suppose. We'll meet here. I'm damned sorry to victimize you like this, Sam.'

'My dear fellow, you needn't be. I'm afraid I'm rather enjoying myself,' said Mr Whipplestone.

III

Alleyn scarcely knew what sort of reception he expected to get from The Boomer or what sort of tactics he himself should deploy to meet it.

In the event, The Boomer behaved pretty much according to pattern. He strode down upon Alleyn and seized his hands.

'Ah!' he roared. 'You are here at last. I am glad. Now we shall get this affair settled.'

'I'm afraid it's far from being settled at the moment.'

'Because of all these pettifogging coppers. And believe me, I do not include you in that category, my dear Rory.'

'Very good of you, sir.'

'"Sir, Sir. Sir" – what tommy-rot! Never mind. We shall not waste time over details. I have come to a decision and you shall be the first to hear what it is.'

'Thank you, I'll be glad to know.'

'Good. Then listen. I understand perfectly that your funny colleague: what is his name?'

'Gibson?' Alleyn ventured.

'Gibson, Gibson. I understand perfectly that the well-meaning Gibson and his band of bodyguards and so on were here at the invitation of my Ambassador. I am correct?'

'Yes.'

'Again, good. But my Ambassador has, as we used to say at Davidson's, kicked over the bucket and in any case the supreme authority is mine. Yes?'

'Of course it is.'

'Of course it is,' the Boomer repeated with immense satisfaction. 'It is mine and I propose to exercise it. An attempt has been made upon my life. It has failed as all such attempts are bound to fail. That I made clear to you on the happy occasion of your visit.'

'So you did.'

'Nevertheless, an attempt has been made.' The Boomer repeated. 'My Ambassador has been killed and the matter must be cleared up.'

'I couldn't agree more.'

'I therefore have called together the people of his household and will question them in accordance with our historically established democratic practice. In Ng'ombwana.'

As Alleyn was by no means certain what this practice might turn out to be, he said cautiously, 'Do you feel that somebody in the household may be responsible?'

'One may find that this is not so. In which case – ' The great voice rumbled into silence.

'In which case?' Alleyn hinted.

'My dear man, in which case I hope for your and the well-meaning Gibson's collaboration.'

So he'd got it all tidied up, Alleyn thought. The Boomer would handle the black elements and he and the CID could make what they liked of the white. Really it began to look like a sort of inverted form of apartheid.

'I don't have to tell you,' he said, 'that authorities at every level will be most deeply concerned that this should have happened. The Special Branch, in particular, is in a great taking-on about it.'

'Hah! So much,' said The Boomer with relish, 'for all the large men in the shrubberies. What?'

'All right. *Touché.*'

'All the same, my dear Rory, if it was true that I was the intended victim, it might well be said that I owe my life to you.'

'Rot.'

'Not rot. It would follow logically. You pushed me down in my chair and there was this unhappy Ambassador waving his arms about and looking like me. So – blam! Yes, yes, yes. In that case, I would owe you my life. It is a debt I would not willingly incur with anyone but you – with you I would willingly acknowledge it.'

'Not a bit,' Alleyn said, in acute embarrassment. 'It may turn out that my intervention was merely a piece of unnecessary bloody cheek.' He hesitated and was inspired to add, 'as we used to say at Davidson's.' And since this did the trick, he hurried on:

'Following that line of thought,' he said, 'you might equally say that I was responsible for the Ambassador's death.'

'That,' said The Boomer grandly, 'is another pair of boots.'

'Tell me,' Alleyn asked, 'have you any theories about the pistol shot?'

'Ah!' he said quickly. 'Pistol! So you have found the weapon?'

'No. I call it a pistol-shot, provisionally. Gun. Revolver. Automatic. What you will. With your permission we'll search.'

'Where?'

'Well – in the garden. And the pond, for instance.'

'The pond?'

Alleyn gave him a digest of Mrs Cockburn-Montfort's narrative. The Boomer, it appeared, knew the Cockburn-Montforts quite well and indeed had actually been associated with the Colonel during the period when he helped organize the modern Ng'ombwanan army. 'He was efficient,' said The Boomer, 'but unfortunately he took to the bottle. His wife is, as we used to say, hairy round the hocks.'

'She says the man in the lavatory was black.'

There followed a longish pause. 'If that is correct, I shall find him.' he said at last.

'He certainly didn't leave these premises. All the exits have been closely watched.'

If The Boomer was tempted to be rude once more about Mr Gibson's methods he restrained himself.

'What is the truth,' he asked, 'about this marksman? Did he in fact fire at me and miss me? Is that proved?'

355

'Nothing is proved. Tell me, do you trust – absolutely – the spear-carrier?'

'Absolutely. But I shall question him as if I do not.'

'Will you – and I'm diffident about asking this – will you allow me to be there? At the assembly?'

For a moment he fancied he saw signs of withdrawal but if so they vanished at once. The Boomer waved his paw.

'Of course. Of course. But, my dear Rory, you will not understand a word of it.'

'Do you know Sam Whipplestone? Of the FO and lately retired?'

'I know *of* him. Of course. He has had many connections with my country. We have not met until tonight. He was a guest. And he is present now with your Gibson. I couldn't understand why.'

'I asked him to come. He speaks your language fluently and he's my personal friend. Would you allow him to sit in with me? I'd be very grateful.'

And now, Alleyn thought, he really was in for a rebuff – but no, after a disconcerting interval The Boomer said: 'This is a little difficult. An enquiry of this nature is never open to persons who have no official standing. Our proceedings are never made public.'

'I give you my firm undertaking that they wouldn't be in this instance. Whipplestone is the soul of discretion, I can vouch for him.'

'You can?'

'I can and I do.'

'Very well,' said The Boomer. 'But no Gibsons.'

'All right. But why have you taken against poor Gibson?'

'Why? I cannot say why. Perhaps because he is too large.' The enormous Boomer pondered for a moment. 'And so pale,' he finally brought out. 'He is very, very pale.'

Alleyn said he believed the entire household was now assembled in the ballroom and The Boomer said that he would go there. Something in his manner made Alleyn think of a star actor preparing for his entrance.

'It is perhaps a little awkward,' The Boomer reflected. 'On such an occasion I should be attended by my

Ambassador and my personal *mlinzi* – my guard. But since the one is dead and the other possibly his murderer, it is not feasible.'

'Tiresome for you.'

'Shall we go?'

They left, passing one of Gibson's men in Costard's livery. In the hall they found Mr Whipplestone, patient in a high-backed chair. The Boomer, evidently minded to do his thing properly, was extremely gracious. Mr Whipplestone offered perfectly phrased regrets for the Ambassador's demise and The Boomer told him that the Ambassador had spoken warmly of him and had talked of asking him to tea.

Gibson was nowhere to be seen but another of his men quietly passed Alleyn a folded paper. While Mr Whipplestone and The Boomer were still exchanging compliments, he had a quick look at it.

'Found the gun,' it read. 'See you after.'

IV

The ballroom was shut up. Heavy curtains were drawn across the french windows. The chandeliers sparkled, the flowers were brilliant. Only a faint reek of champagne, sandarac and cigarette smoke suggested the aftermath of festivities.

The ballroom had become Ng'ombwana.

A crowd of Ng'ombwanans waited at the end of the great saloon where the red alcove displayed its warlike trophies.

It was a larger assembly than Alleyn had expected: men in full evening dress whom he supposed to be authoritative persons in the household, a controller, a secretary, undersecretaries. There were some dozen men in livery and as many women with white head-scarves and dresses, and there was a knot of under-servants in white jackets clustered at the rear of the assembly. Clearly they were all grouped in conformance with the domestic hierarchy. The President's aides-de-camp waited at the back of the dais.

357

And ranked on each side of it, armed and immovable, was his guard in full ceremonial kit: scarlet tunics, white kilts, immaculate leggings, glistening accoutrements.

And on the floor in front of the dais, was a massive table bearing under a lion's hide the unmistakable shape of the shrouded dead.

Alleyn and Mr Whipplestone entered in the wake of The Boomer. The guard came to attention, the crowd became very still. The Boomer walked slowly and superbly to his dais. He gave an order and two chairs were placed on the floor not far from the bier. He motioned Alleyn and Mr Whipplestone to take them. Alleyn would have greatly preferred an inconspicuous stand at the rear but there was no help for it and they took their places.

'I daren't write, dare I?' Mr Whipplestone muttered. 'And nor dare I talk.'

'You'll have to remember.'

'All jolly fine.'

The Boomer, seated in his great chair, his hands on the arms, his body upright, his chin raised, his knees and feet planted together, looked like an effigy of himself. His eyes, as always a little bloodshot, rolled and flashed, his teeth gleamed and he spoke in a language which seemed to be composed entirely of vowels, gutturals and clicks. His voice was so huge that Mr Whipplestone, trying to speak like a ventriloquist, ventured two words.

'Describing incident,' he said.

The speech seemed to grow in urgency. He brought both palms down sharply on the arms of his chair. Alleyn wondered if he only imagined that a heightened tension invested the audience. A pause and then, unmistakably, an order.

'Spear chap,' ventriloquized Mr Whipplestone. 'Fetch.'

Two of the guards came smartly to attention, marched to meet each other, faced front, saluted, about-turned and marched out. Absolute stillness followed this proceeding. Sounds from outside could be heard. Gibson's men in the garden, no doubt, and once, almost certainly, Gibson's voice.

When the silence had become very trying indeed, the soldiers returned with the spear-carrier between them.

He was still dressed in his ceremonial garments. His anklets and armbands shone in the lamplight and so did his burnished body and limbs. But he's not really *black*, Alleyn thought, 'If Troy painted him he would be anything but black – blue, mole, purple, even red where his body reflects the carpet and walls.' He was glossy. His close-cropped head sat above its tier of throat-rings like a huge ebony marble. He wore his lion's skin like a lion. Alleyn noticed that his right arm was hooked under it as if in a sling.

He walked between his guards to the bier. They left him there, isolated before his late Ambassador and his President and close enough to Alleyn and Mr Whipplestone for them to smell the sweet oil with which he had polished himself.

The examination began. It was impossible most of the time for Alleyn to guess what was being said. Both men kept very still. Their teeth and eyes flashed from time to time but their big voices were level and they used no gesture until suddenly the spearman slapped the base of his own neck.

'Chop,' breathed Mr Whipplestone. 'Karate. Sort of.'

Soon after this there was a break and neither man spoke for perhaps eight seconds and then, to Alleyn's surprise and discomfiture, The Boomer began to talk, still in the Ng'ombwanan tongue, to him. It was a shortish observation. At the end of it, The Boomer nodded to Mr Whipplestone who cleared his throat.

'The President,' he said, 'directs me to ask you if you will give an account of what you yourself witnessed in the pavilion. He also directs me to translate what you say as he wishes the proceedings to be conducted throughout in the Ng'ombwanan language.'

They stood up. Alleyn gave his account, to which The Boomer reacted as if he hadn't understood a word of it. Mr Whipplestone translated.

Maintaining this laborious procedure, Alleyn was asked if, after the death had been discovered, he had formed any opinions as to whether the spearman was, in fact, injured.

Looking at the superb being standing there like a rock, it was difficult to imagine that a blow on the carotid nerve or anywhere else for that matter could cause him the smallest discomfiture. Alleyn said: 'He was kneeling with his right hand in the position he has just shown. His head was bent, his left hand clenched and his shoulders hunched. He appeared to be in pain.'

'And then,' translated Mr Whipplestone, 'what happened?'

Alleyn repressed an insane desire to remind The Boomer that he was there at the time and invite him to come off it and talk English.

He said: 'There was a certain amount of confusion. This was checked by – ' he looked straight at The Boomer – 'the President, who spoke in Ng'ombwanan to the spearsman who appeared to offer some kind of statement or denial. Subsequently five men on duty from the Special Branch of the CID arrived with two of the President's guard who had been stationed outside the pavilion. The spearsman was removed to the house.'

Away went Mr Whipplestone again.

The Boomer next wished to know if the police had obtained any evidence from the spear itself. Alleyn replied that no report had been released under that heading.

This, apparently, ended his examination, if such it could be called. He sat down.

After a further silence, and it occurred to Alleyn that the Ng'ombwanans were adepts in non-communication, The Boomer rose.

It would have been impossible to say why the atmosphere, already far from relaxed, now became taut to twanging point. What happened was that the President pointed, with enormous authority, at the improvised bier and unmistakably pronounced a command.

The spearsman, giving no sign of agitation, at once extended his left hand – the right was still concealed in his bosom – and drew down the covering. And here was the

Ambassador, open-mouthed, goggle-eyed, making some sort of indecipherable declaration.

The spearsman, laying his hand upon the body, spoke boldly and briefly. The President replied even more briefly. The lionskin mantle was replaced, and the ceremony – assembly – trial – whatever it might be, was at an end. At no time during the final proceedings had The Boomer so much as glanced at Alleyn.

He now briefly harangued his hearers. Mr Whipplestone muttered that he ordered any of them who had any information, however trivial, bearing however slightly on the case, to speak immediately. This met with an absolute silence. His peroration was to the effect that he himself was in command of affairs at the Embassy. He then left. His ADCs followed and the one with whom Alleyn was acquainted paused by him to say the President requested his presence in the library.

'I will come,' Alleyn said, 'in ten minutes. My compliments to the President, if you please.'

The ADC rolled his eyes, said, 'But – ', changed his mind and followed his Master.

'That,' said Mr Whipplestone, 'was remarkably crisp.'

'If he doesn't like it he can lump it. I want a word with Gibson. Come on.'

Gibson, looking sulky, and Fox, were waiting for them at their temporary quarters in the controller's office. On the desk, lying on a damp unfolded handkerchief, was a gun. Thompson and Bailey stood near by with their tools of trade.

'Where?' said Alleyn.

'In the pond. We picked it up with a search lamp. Lying on the blue tiled bottom at the corner opposite the conveniences and three feet in from the margin.'

'Easy chucking distance from the loo window.'

'That's correct.'

'Anything?' Alleyn asked Bailey.

'No joy, Mr Alleyn. Gloves, I reckon.'

'It's a Luger,' Alleyn said.

'They are not hard to come by,' Mr Whipplestone said, 'in Ng'ombwana.'

361

'You know,' Alleyn said, 'almost immediately after the shot, I heard something fall into the pond. It was in the split second before the rumpus broke out.'

'Well, well,' said Fox. 'Not,' he reasoned, 'a very sensible way for him to carry on. However you look at it. Still,' he said heavily, 'that's how they do tend to behave.'

'Who do, Br'er Fox?'

'Political assassins, the non-professionals. They're a funny mob, by all accounts.'

'You're dead rght there, Teddy,' said Mr Gibson. 'I suppose,' he added, appealing to Alleyn, 'we retain possession of this Luger, do we?'

'Under the circumstances we'll be lucky if we retain possession of our wits. I'm damned if I know. The whole thing gets more and more like a revival of the Goon Show.'

'The AC, your department, rang.'

'What's *he* want?'

'To say the Deputy Commissioner will be calling in to offer condolences or what have you to the President. And no doubt,' said Gibson savagely, 'to offer me his advice and congratulations on a successful operation. *Christ!*' he said and turned his back on his colleagues.

Alleyn and Fox exchanged a look.

'You couldn't have done more,' Alleyn said after a moment. 'Take the whole lay-out, you couldn't have given any better coverage.'

'That bloody sergeant in the bog.'

'All right. But if Mrs Cockburn-Montfort's got it straight the sergeant wouldn't have stopped him in the dark, wherever she was.'

'I told them. I told these bastards they shouldn't have the blackout.'

'But,' said Fox, in his reasonable way, 'the gun-man didn't do the job anyway. There's that aspect, Mr Gibson, isn't there?'

Gibson didn't answer this. He turned round and said to Alleyn: 'We've to find out if the President's available to see the DC.'

'When?'

'He's on his way in from Kent. Within the hour.'

'I'll find out.' Alleyn turned to Mr Whipplestone. 'I can't tell you, Sam, how much obliged to you I am,' he said. 'If it's not asking too much, could you bear to write out an account of that black – in both senses – charade in there, while it's still fresh in your mind? I'm having another go at the great panjandrum in the library.'

'Yes, of course,' said Mr Whipplestone. 'I'd like to.'

So he was settled down with writing materials and immediately took on the air of being at his own desk in his own rather rarefied office with a secretary in deferential attendance.

'What's horrible for us, Fred?' Alleyn asked. It was a regulation inquiry for which he was known at the Yard.

'We've got that lot from the tent party still waiting. Except the ones who obviously hadn't a clue about anything. And,' Gibson added a little awkwardly, 'Mrs Alleyn. She's gone, of course.'

'I can always put her through the hoops at home.'

'And – er, and er,' said Gibson still more awkwardly, 'there is – er – your brother.'

'*What!*' Alleyn shouted, 'George! You don't tell me you've got George sitting on his fat bottom waiting for the brutal police bit?'

'Well – '

'Mrs Alleyn *and* Sir George,' said Fox demurely. 'And we're not allowed to mention coincidence.'

'Old George,' Alleyn pondered, 'what a lark! Fox, you might press on with statements from that little lot. Including George. While I have another go at The Boomer. What about you, Fred?'

'Get on with the bloody routine, I suppose. Could you lend me these two – ' he indicated Bailey and Thompson – 'for the ladies' conveniences? Not that there's much chance of anything turning up there. Still, we've got this Luger-merchant roaming round somewhere in the establishment. We're searching for the bullet, of course, and that's no piece of cake. Seeing you,' he said morosely and walked out.

'You'd better get on with the loo,' Alleyn said to Bailey and Thompson and himself returned to the library.

V

'Look,' Alleyn said, 'it's this way. You — Your Excellency — can, as of course you know, order us off whenever you feel like it. As far as inquiries inside the Embassy are concerned, we can become *persona non grata* at the drop of a hat and as such would have to limit our activities, of which you've no doubt formed an extremely poor opinion, to looking after your security whenever you leave these premises. We will also follow up any lines of enquiry that present themselves outside the Embassy. Quite simply, it's a matter of whether or not you wish us to carry on as we are or make ourselves scarce. Colonel Sinclaire, the Deputy Commissioner of the Metropolitan Police, is on his way. He hopes he may be allowed to wait upon you. No doubt he will express his deep regrets and put the situation before you in more or less the same terms as I have used.'

For the first time since they had renewed their acquaintance Alleyn found a kind of hesitancy in The Boomer's manner. He made as if to speak, checked himself, looked hard at Alleyn for a moment and then began to pace up and down the library with the magnificent action that really did recall clichés about caged panthers.

At last he stopped in front of Alleyn and abruptly took him by the arms. 'What,' he demanded, 'did you think of our enquiry? Tell me?'

'It was immensely impressive,' Alleyn said at once.

'Yes? You found it so? But you think it strange, don't you, that I who have eaten my dinners and practised my profession as a barrister, should subscribe to such a performance. After all, it was not much like the proceedings of the British Coroner's Inquest?'

'Not conspicuously like. No.'

'No. And yet, my dear Rory, it told me a great deal more

364

than would have been elicited by that highly respectable court.'

'Yes?' Alleyn said politely. And with a half-smile: 'Am I to know what it told Your Excellency?'

'It told My Excellency that my *nkuki mtu mwenye* – my *mlinzi* – my man with the spear, spoke the truth.'

'I see.'

'You are non-committal. You want to know how I know?'

'If it suits you to tell me.'

'I am,' announced The Boomer, 'the son of a paramount chief. My father and his and his, back into the dawn, were paramount chiefs. If this man, under oath to protect me, had been guilty of murdering an innocent and loyal servant he could not have uncovered the body before me and declared his innocence. Which is what he did. It would not be possible.'

'I see.'

'And you would reply that such evidence is not admissible in a British court-of-law.'

'It would be *admissible*, I dare say. It could be eloquently pleaded by able counsel. It wouldn't be accepted, *ipso facto*, as proof of innocence. But you know that as well as I do.'

'Tell me this. It is important for me. Do you believe what I have said?'

'I think I do,' Alleyn said slowly. 'You know your people. You tell me it is so. Yes. I'm not sure, but I am inclined to believe you are right.'

'Ah!' said The Boomer. 'So now we are upon our old footing. That is good.'

'But I must make it clear to you. Whatever I may or may not think has no bearing on the way I'll conduct this investigation: either inside the Embassy, if you'll have us here, or outside it. If there turns out to be cogent evidence, in our book, against this man, we'll follow it up.'

'In any case, the event having taken place in this Embassy, on his own soil, he could not be tried in England,' said The Boomer.'

'No. Whatever we find, in that sense, is academic. He would be repatriated.'

'And this person who fires off German weapons in ladies' lavatories. You say he also is black.'

'Mrs Cockburn-Montfort says so.'

'A stupid woman.'

'Tolerably so, I'd have thought.'

'It would be better if her husband beat her occasionally and left her at home,' said The Boomer with one of his gusts of laughter.

'I should like to know, if it isn't too distressing for you to speak of him, something of the Ambassador himself. Did you like him very much? Was he close to you? Those sorts of questions?'

The Boomer dragged his great hand across his mouth, made a long rumbling sound in his chest and sat down.

'I find it difficult,' he said at last, 'to answer your question. What sort of man was he? A fuddy-duddy, as we used to say. He has come up, in the English sense, through the ranks. The peasant class. At one time he was a nuisance. He saw himself staging some kind of *coup*. It was all rather ridiculous. He had certain administrative abilities but no real authority. That sort of person.'

Disregarding this example of Ng'ombwanan snob-thinking, Alleyn remarked that the Ambassador must have been possessed of considerable ability to have got where he did. The Boomer waved a concessionary hand and said that the trend of development had favoured his advancement.

'Had he enemies?'

'My dear Rory, in an emergent nation like my own every man of authority has or has had enemies. I know of no specific persons.'

'He was in a considerable taking-on about security during your visit,' Alleyn ventured, to which The Boomer vaguely replied: 'Oh. Did you think so?'

'He telephoned Gibson and me on an average twice a day.'

'Boring for you,' said The Boomer in his best public school manner.

'He was particularly agitated about the concert in the garden and the blackout. So were we for that matter.'

'He was a fuss-pot,' said The Boomer.

'Well, damn it all, he had some cause, as it turns out.'

The Boomer pursed his generous mouth into a double mulberry and raised his brows. 'If you put it like that.'

'After all, he is dead.'

'True,' The Boomer admitted.

Nobody can look quite so eloquently bored as a Negro. The eyes are almost closed, showing a lower rim of white, the mouth droops, the head tilts. The whole man suddenly seems to wilt. The Boomer now exhibited all these signals of ennui and Alleyn, remembering them of old, said: 'Never mind. I mustn't keep you any longer. Could we, do you think, just settle these two points: First, will you receive the Deputy Commissioner when he comes?'

'Of course,' drawled The Boomer without opening his eyes.

'Second. Do you now wish the CID to carry on inside the Embassy or would you prefer us to clear out? The decision is your Excellency's, of course, but we would be grateful for a definite ruling.'

The Boomer opened his slightly bloodshot eyes. He looked full at Alleyn. 'Stay,' he said.

There was a tap at the door and Gibson, large, pale and apologetic, came in.

'I'm sure I beg your pardon, sir,' he said to the President. 'Colonel Sinclaire, the Deputy Commissioner, has arrived and hopes to see you.'

The Boomer, without looking at Gibson, said: 'Ask my equerry to bring him in.'

Alleyn walked to the door. He had caught a signal of urgency from his colleague.

'Don't you go, Rory,' said The Boomer.

'I'm afraid I must,' said Alleyn.

Outside, in the passage, he found Mr Whipplestone

fingering his tie and looking deeply perturbed. Alleyn said: 'What's up?'

'It may not be anything,' Gibson answered. 'It's just that we've been talking to the Costard man who was detailed to serve in the tent.'

'Stocky, well-set up, fair-haired?'

'That's him. Name of Chubb,' said Gibson.

'Alas,' said Mr Whipplestone.

5

Small Hours

Chubb stood more-or-less to attention, looking straight before him with his arms to his sides. He cut quite a pleasing figure in Costard et Cie's discreet livery: midnight blue shell-jacket and trousers with gold endorsements. His faded blond hair was short and well-brushed, his fresh West Country complexion and blue eyes deceptively gave him the air of an outdoor man. He still wore his white gloves.

Alleyn had agreed with Mr Whipplestone that it would be best if the latter were not present at the interview. 'Though,' Alleyn said, 'there's no reason at all to suppose that Chubb, any more than my silly old brother George, had anything to do with the event.'

'I know, I know,' Mr Whipplestone had returned. 'Of course. It's just that, however illogically and stupidly, I would prefer Chubb *not* to have been on duty in that wretched pavilion. Just as I would prefer him *not* to have odd-time jobs with Sheridan and those beastly Montforts. And it *would* be rather odd for me to be there, wouldn't it? Very foolish of me no doubt. Let it go at that.'

So Alleyn and an anonymous sergeant had Chubb to themselves in the Controller's office.

Alleyn said: 'I want to be quite sure I've got this right. You were in and out of the pavilion with champagne which you fetched from an ice box that had been set up outside the pavilion. You did this in conjunction with one of the Embassy servants. He waited on the President and the people immediately surrounding him, didn't he? I remember that he came to my wife and me soon after we had settled there.'

'Sir,' said Chubb.

'And you looked after the rest of the party.'

369

'Sir.'

'Yes. Well now, Chubb, we've kept you hanging about all this time in the hope that you can give us some help about what happened in the pavilion.'

'Not much chance of that, sir. I never noticed anything, sir.'

'That makes two of us, I'm afraid,' Alleyn said. 'It happened like a bolt from the blue, didn't it? Were you actually in the pavilion? When the lights went out?'

Yes, it appeared. At the back. He had put his tray down on a trestle table, in preparation for the near blackout about which the servants had all been warned. He had remained there through the first item.

'And were you still there when the singer, Karbo, appeared?' Yes, he said. Still there. He had had an uninterrupted view of Karbo, standing in his spotlight with his shadow thrown up behind him on the white screen.

'Did you notice where the guard with the spear was standing?' Yes. At the rear. Behind the President's chair.

'On your left, would that be?'

'Yes, sir.'

'And your fellow-waiter?'

'The nigger?' said Chubb, and after a glance at Alleyn, 'Beg pardon, sir. The native.'

'The African, yes.'

'He was somewhere there. At the rear, I never took no notice,' said Chubb stonily.

'You didn't speak to either of them, at all?'

'No, thanks. I wouldn't think they knew how.'

'You don't like black people?' Alleyn said lightly.

'No, sir.'

'Well. To come to the moment when the shot was fired. I'm getting as many accounts as possible from the people who were in the pavilion and I'd like yours too, if you will. You remember that the performer had given out one note, if that's the way to put it. A long-drawn-out sound. And then – as you recall it – what?'

'The shot, sir.'

370

'Did you get an impression about where the sound came from?'

'The house, sir.'

'Yes. Well, now, Chubb. Could you just, as best as you are able, tell me your own impression of what followed the shot. In the pavilion, I mean.'

Nothing clear-cut emerged. People had stood up. A lady had screamed. A gentleman had shouted out not to panic. (George, Alleyn thought.)

'Yes. But as to what you actually *saw* from where you were, at the back of the pavilion?'

Hard to say, exactly Chubb said in his wooden voice. People moving about a bit but not much. Alleyn said that they had appeared, hadn't they? 'Like black silhouettes against the spotlight screen.' Chubb agreed.

'The guard – the man with the spear? He was on your left. Quite close to you. Wasn't he?'

'At the start, sir, he was. Before the pavilion lights went out.'

'And afterwards?'

There was a considerable pause: 'I couldn't say, exactly, sir. Not straight away, like.'

'How do you mean?'

Chubb suddenly erupted. 'I was grabbed,' he said. 'He sprung on me. *Me!* From behind. *Me!*'

'Grabbed? Do you mean by the spearsman?'

'Not him. The other black bastard.'

'The waiter?'

'Yes. Sprung it on me. From behind. *Me!*'

'What did he spring on you? A half-Nelson?'

'Head-lock! I couldn't speak. *And* he put in the knee.'

'How did you know it was the waiter?'

'I knew all right. I knew and no error.'

'But *how?*'

'Bare arm for one thing. And the smell: like salad oil or something. I knew.'

'How long did this last?'

'Long enough,' said Chubb, fingering his neck. 'Long enough for his mate to put in the spear, I reckon.'

'Did he hold you until the lights went up?'

'No, sir. Only while it was being done. So I couldn't see it. The stabbing. I was doubled up. *Me!*' Chubb reiterated with, if possible, an access of venom. 'But I heard. The sound. You can't miss it. And the fall.'

The sergeant cleared his throat.

Alleyn said: 'This is enormously important, Chubb. I'm sure you realize that, don't you? You're saying that the Ng'ombwanan waiter attacked and restrained you while the guard speared the Ambassador.'

'Sir.'

'All right. Why, do you suppose? I mean, why you, in particular?'

'I was nearest, sir, wasn't I? I might of got in the way or done something quick, mightn't I?'

'Was the small, hard chair overturned during this attack?'

'It might of been,' Chubb said after a pause.

'How old are you, Chubb?'

'Me, sir? Fifty-two, sir.'

'What did you do in World War II?'

'Commando, sir.'

'Ah!' Alleyn said, quietly, 'I see.'

'They wouldn't of sprung it across me in those days, sir.'

'I'm sure they wouldn't. One more thing. After the shot and before you were attacked and doubled up, you saw the Ambassador, did you, on his feet? Silhouetted against the screen?'

'Sir.'

'Did you recognize him?'

Chubb was silent.

'Well – did you?'

'I – can't say I did. Not exactly.'

'How do you mean – not exactly?'

'It all happened so quick, didn't it? I – I reckon I thought he was the other one. The President.'

'Why?'

'Well. Because. Well, because, you know, he was near where the President sat, like. He must of moved away from

372

his own chair, sir, mustn't he? And standing up like he was in command, as you might say. And the President had roared out something in their lingo, hadn't he?'

'So, you'd say, would you, Chubb, that the Ambassador was killed in mistake for the President?'

'I couldn't say that, sir, could I? Not for certain. But I'd say he might of been. He might easy of been.'

'You didn't see anybody attack the spearsman?'

'*Him!* He couldn't of been attacked, could he? I was the one that got clobbered, sir, wasn't I? Not him: he did the big job, didn't he?'

'He maintains that he was given a chop and his spear was snatched out of his grasp by the man who attacked him. He says that he didn't see who this man was. You may remember that when the lights came up and the Ambassador's body was seen, the spearsman was crouched on the ground up near the back of the pavilion.'

Through this speech of Alleyn's such animation as Chubb had displayed, deserted him. He reverted to his former manner, staring straight in front of him with such a wooden air that the ebb of colour from his face and its dark, uneven return, seemed to bear no relation to any emotional experience.

When he spoke it was to revert to his favourite observation.

'I wouldn't know about any of that,' he said, 'I never took any notice of that.'

'Didn't you? But you were quite close to the spearsman. You were standing by him. I happen to remember seeing you there.'

'I was a bit shook up. After what the other one done to me.'

'So it would seem. When the lights came on, was the waiter who attacked you, as you maintain, still there?'

'Him? He'd scarpered.'

'Have you seen him since then?'

Chubb said he hadn't but added that he couldn't tell one of the black bastards from another. The conventional mannerisms of the servant together with his careful grammar had almost disappeared. He sounded venomous. Alleyn then asked him why he hadn't reported the attack on himself immediately to the police and Chubb became injured and exasperated. What chance had there been for that, he complained, with them all being shoved about into queues and drafted into groups and told to behave quiet and act cooperative and stay put and questions and statements would come later.

He began to sweat and put his hands behind his back. He said he didn't feel too good. Alleyn told him that the sergeant would make a typescript of his statement and he would be asked to read and sign it if he found it correct.

'In the meantime,' he said, 'we'll let you go home to Mr Whipplestone.'

Chubb reverting to his earlier style said anxiously: 'Beg pardon, sir, but I didn't know you knew – '

'I know Mr Whipplestone very well. He told me about you.'

'Yes, sir. Will that be all, then, sir?'

'I think so, for the present. Good night to you, Chubb.'

'Thank you, sir. Good night, sir.'

He left the room with his hands clenched.

'Commando, eh?' said the sergeant to his notes.

II

Mr Fox was doing his competent best with the group of five persons who sat wearily about the apartment that had been used as a sort of bar-cum-smoking-room for male guests at the party. It smelt of stale smoke, the dregs of alcohol, heavy upholstery and, persistently, of the all-pervading sandarac. It wore an air of exhausted raffishness.

The party of five being interviewed by Mr Fox and noted down by a sergeant consisted of a black plenipotentiary and his wife, the last of the governors of British Ng'ombwana and *his* wife, and Sir George Alleyn, Bart. They were the only members of the original party of twelve

374

guests who had remembered anything that might conceivably have a bearing upon events in the pavilion and they remained after a painstaking winnowing had disposed of their companions.

The ex-governor, who was called Sir John Smythe, remembered that immediately after the shot was fired, everybody moved to the front of the pavilion. He was contradicted by Lady Smythe who said that for her part she had remained riveted in her chair. The plenipotentiary's wife, whose understanding of English appeared to be rudimentary, conveyed through her husband that she, also, had remained seated. Mr Fox reminded himself that Mrs Alleyn, instructed by her husband, had not risen. The plenipotentiary recalled that the chairs had been set out in an inverted V shape with the President and his Ambassador at the apex and the guests forming the two wide-angled wings.

'Is that the case, sir?' said Fox comfortably. 'I see. So that when you gentlemen stood up you'd all automatically be forward of the President? Nearer to the opening of the pavilion than he was? Would that be correct?'

'Quite right, Mr Fox. Quite right,' said Sir George, who had adopted a sort of uneasy reciprocal attitude towards Fox and had, at the outset, assured him jovially that he'd heard a great deal about him to which Fox replied: 'Is that the case, sir? If I might just have your name?'

It was Sir George who remembered the actual order in which the guests had sat and although Fox had already obtained this information from Alleyn, he gravely noted it down. On the President's left had been the Ambassador, Sir John and Lady Smythe, the plenipotentiary's wife, the plenipotentiary, a guest who had now gone home and Sir George himself. 'In starvation corner, what?' said Sir George lightly to the Smythes, who made little deprecatory noises.

'Yes, I see, thank you, sir,' said Fox. 'And on the President's right hand, sir?'

'Oh!' said Sir George waving his hand. 'My brother. My brother and his wife. Yes. 'Strordinary coincidence.'

Apparently feeling the need for some sort of endorsement he turned to his fellow guests. 'My brother, the bobby,' he explained. 'Ridiculous, what?'

'A very distinguished bobby,' Sir John Smythe murmured, to which Sir George returned: 'Oh, quite! Quite! Not for me to say but – he'll do.' He laughed and made a jovial little grimace.

'Yes,' said Fox to his notes. 'And four other guests who have now left. Thank you, sir.' He looked over the top of his spectacles at his hearers. 'We come to the incident itself. There's this report: pistol shot or whatever it was. The lights in the pavilion are out. Everybody except the ladies and the President gets to his feet. Doing what?'

'How d'you mean, doing what?' Sir John Smythe asked.

'Well, sir, did everybody face out into the garden, trying to see what was going on – apart from the concert item which, I understand, stopped short when the report was heard.'

'Speaking for myself,' said Sir George. 'I stayed where I was. There were signs of – ah – agitation and – ah – movement. Sort of thing that needs to be nipped in the bud if you don't want a panic on your hands.'

'And you nipped it, sir?' Fox asked.

'Well – I wouldn't go so far – one does one's best. I mean to say – I said something. Quietly.'

'If there had been any signs of panic,' said Sir John Smythe drily, 'they did not develop.'

' – "did not develop",' Mr Fox repeated. 'And in issuing your warning, sir, did you face inwards? With your back to the garden?'

'Yes. Yes, I did,' said Sir George.

'And did you notice anything at all out of the way, sir?'

'I couldn't see anything, my dear man. One was blinded by having looked at the brilliant light on the screen and the performer.'

'There wasn't any reflected light in the pavilion?'

'No,' said Sir George crossly. 'There wasn't. Nothing of the kind. It was too far away.'

'I see, sir,' said Fox placidly.

Lady Smythe suddenly remarked that the light on the screen was reflected in the lake. 'The whole thing,' she said, 'was dazzling and rather confusing.' There was a general murmur of agreement.

Mr Fox asked if during the dark interval anybody else had turned his or her back on the garden and peered into the interior. This produced a confused and doubtful response from which it emerged that the piercing screams of Mrs Cockburn-Montfort within the house had had a more marked effect than the actual report. The Smythes had both heard Alleyn telling the President to sit down. After the report everybody had heard the President shout out something in his own language. The plenipotentiary said it was an order. He shouted for lights. And immediately before or after that, Sir John Smythe said, he had been aware of something falling at his feet.

And then the light had gone up.

'And I can only add, Inspector,' said Sir John, 'that I really have nothing else to say that can have the slightest bearing on this tragic business. The ladies have been greatly shocked and I must beg you to release them from any further ordeal.'

There was a general and heartfelt chorus of agreement. Sir George said, 'Hear, hear,' very loudly.

Fox said this request was very reasonable he was sure, and he was sorry to have put them all to so much trouble and he could assure the ladies that he wouldn't be keeping them much longer. There were no two ways about it, he added, this was quite a serious affair, wasn't it?

'Well, then – ' said Sir John and there was a general stir.

At this juncture Alleyn came in.

In some curious and indefinable fashion he brought a feeling of refreshment with him rather like that achieved by a star whose delayed entry, however quietly executed, lifts the scene and quickens the attention of his audience.

'We are so sorry,' he said, 'to have kept you waiting like this. I'm sure Mr Fox will have explained. This is a very muddling, tragic and strange affair and it isn't made any

377

simpler for me, at any rate, by finding myself an unsatis-
factory witness and an investigating copper at one and the
same time.'

He gave Lady Smythe an apologetic grin and she said –
and may have been astonished to hear herself – 'You poor
man.'

'Well, there it is and I can only hope one of you has come
up with something more useful than anything I've been
able to produce.'

His brother said: 'Done our best. What!'

'Good for you,' Alleyn said. He was reading the
sergeant's notes.

'We're hoping,' said Sir John, 'to be released. The
ladies – '

'Yes, of course. It's been a beastly experience and you
must all be exhausted.

'What about yourself?' asked Lady Smythe. She
appeared to be a lady of spirit.

Alleyn looked up from the notes. 'Oh,' he said, 'you
can't slap me back. These notes seem splendidly exhaustive
and there's only one question I'd like to put to you. I
know the whole incident was extremely confused, but I
would like to learn if you all, for whatever reason
or for no reason, are persuaded of the identity of the
killer?'

'Good God!' Sir George shouted. 'Really, my dear Rory!
Who else could it be but the man your fellows marched off.
And I must compliment you on their promptitude, by the
way.'

'You mean – ?'

'Good God, I mean the great hulking brute with the
spear. I beg your pardon,' he said to the black plenipotentiary and himself turned scarlet. 'Afraid I spoke out
of turn. Sure you understand.'

'George,' said his brother with exquisite courtesy,
'would you like to go home?'

'I? We all would. Mustn't desert the post, though. No
preferential treatment.'

'Not a morsel, I assure you. I take it, then,' Alleyn said,

turning to the others, 'that you all believe the spear-carrier was the assailant?'

'Well – yes,' said Sir John Smythe. 'I mean – there he was. Who else? And, my God, there was the spear!'

The black plenipotentiary's wife said something rather loudly in their native tongue.

Alleyn looked a question at her husband, who cleared his throat, 'My wife,' he said, 'has made an observation.'

'Yes?'

'My wife has said that because the body was lying beside her, she heard.'

'Yes? She heard?'

'The sound of the strike and the death noise.' He held a brief consultation with his wife. 'Also a word. In Ng'ombwanan. Spoken very low by a man. By the Ambassador himself, she thinks.'

'And the word – in English?'

'"*Traitor*",' said the plenipotentiary. After a brief pause he added: 'My wife would like to go now. There is blood on her dress.'

III

The Boomer had changed into a dressing-gown and looked like Othello in the last act. It was a black and gold gown and underneath it crimson pyjamas could be detected. He had left orders that if Alleyn wished to see him he was to be roused and he now received Alleyn, Fox and an attenuated but still alert Mr Whipplestone, in the library. For a moment or two Alleyn thought he was going to jib at Mr Whipplestone's presence. He fetched up short when he saw him, seemed about to say something but instead decided to be gracious. Mr Whipplestone, after all, managed well with The Boomer. His diplomacy was of an acceptable tinge: deferential without being fulsome, composed but not consequential.

When Alleyn said he would like to talk to the Ng'ombwanan servant who waited on them in the pavilion The Boomer made no comment but spoke briefly on the house telephone.

'I wouldn't have troubled you with this,' Alleyn said, 'but I couldn't find anybody who was prepared to accept the responsibility of producing the man without your authority.'

'They are all in a silly state,' generalized The Boomer. 'Why do you want this fellow?'

'The English waiter in the pavilion will have it that the man attacked him.'

The Boomer lowered his eyelids. 'How very rococo,' he said and there was no need for him to add: 'as we used to say at Davidson's.' It had been a catch phrase in their last term and worn to death in the usage. With startling precision, it again returned Alleyn to that dark room smelling of anchovy toast and a coal-fire and to the group mannerisms of his and The Boomer's circle so many years ago.

When the man appeared he cut an unimpressive figure, being attired in white trousers, a singlet and a wrongly buttoned tunic. He appeared to be in a state of perturbation and in deep awe of his President.

'I will speak to him,' The Boomer announced.

He did so, and judging by the tone of his voice, pretty sharply. The man, fixing his white-eyeballed gaze on the far wall of the library, answered with, or so it seemed to Alleyn, the clockwork precision of a soldier on parade.

'He says no,' said The Boomer.

'Could you press a little?'

'It will make no difference. But I will press.'

This time the reply was lengthier. 'He says he ran into someone in the dark and stumbled and for a moment clung to this person. It is ridiculous, he says, to speak of it as an attack. He had forgotten the incident. Perhaps it was this servant.'

'Where did he go after this encounter?'

Out of the pavilion, it appeared, finding himself near the rear door, and frightened by the general rumpus. He had been rounded up by security men and drafted with the rest of the household staff to one end of the ballroom.

'Do you believe him?'

'He would not dare to lie,' said The Boomer calmly.

'In that case I suppose we let him go back to bed, don't we?'

This move having been effected, The Boomer rose and so, of course, did Alleyn, Mr Whipplestone and Fox.

'My dear Rory,' said The Boomer, 'there is a matter which should be settled at once. The body. It will be returned to our country and buried according to our custom.'

'I can promise you that every assistance will be offered. Perhaps the Deputy Commissioner has already given you that assurance.'

'Oh, yes. He was very forthcoming. A nice chap. I hear your pathologist spoke of an autopsy. There can be no autopsy.'

'I see.'

'A thorough enquiry will be held in Ng'ombwana.'

'Good.'

'And I think, since you have completed your investigations, have you not, it would be as well to find out if the good Gibson is in a similar case. If so I would suggest that the police, after leaving and at their convenience, kindly let me have a comprehensive report of their findings. In the meantime, I shall set my house in order.'

As this was in effect an order to quit, Alleyn gave his assurance that there would be a complete withdrawal of the Yard forces. The Boomer expressed his appreciation of the trouble that had been taken and said, very blandly, that if the guilty person was discovered to be a member of his own household, Alleyn, as a matter of courtesy, would be informed. On the other hand the police would no doubt pursue their security precautions outside the Embassy. These pronouncements made such sweeping assumptions that there was nothing more to be said. Alleyn had begun to take his leave when The Boomer interrupted him.

He said: 'There is one other matter I would like to settle.'

'Yes?'

'About the remainder of my stay in England. It is a little difficult to decide.'

Does he, Alleyn asked himself, does The Boomer, by any blissful chance, consider taking himself back to Ng'ombwana? Almost at once? With the corpse, perhaps? What paeans of thanksgiving would spring from Gibson's lips if it were so.

' – the Buck House dinner party, of course, stands,' The Boomer continued. 'Perhaps a quieter affair will be envisaged. It is not for me to say,' he conceded.

'When is that?'

'Tomorrow night. No. Tonight. Dear me, it is almost two in the morning!'

'Your other engagements?' Alleyn hinted.

'I shall cancel the tree-planting affair and of course I shall not attend the race-meeting. That would not look at all the thing,' he said rather wistfully, 'would it?'

'Certainly not.'

'And then there's the Chequers visit. I hardly know what to say.' And with his very best top-drawer manner to the fore The Boomer turned graciously to Mr Whipplestone. 'So difficult,' he said, 'isn't it? Now, tell me. What would you advise?'

This, Alleyn felt, was a question to try Mr Whipplestone's diplomatic resources to their limit. He rose splendidly to his ordeal.

'I'm quite sure,' he said, 'that the Prime Minister and, indeed, all the organizations and hosts who had hoped to entertain your Excellency will perfectly understand that this appalling affair puts anything of the sort out of the question.'

'Oh,' said The Boomer.

'Your Excellency need have no misgiving under that heading, at least,' Mr Whipplestone gracefully concluded.

'Good,' said The Boomer, a trifle dismally Alleyn thought.

'We mustn't keep you up any longer,' Alleyn said, 'but before we take ourselves off, I would like, if I may, to ask one final rather unorthodox question.'

'What is that?'

'You are, I know, persuaded that neither the Ng'ombwanan waiter nor the guard – the *mlinzi*, is it? – is a guilty man.'

'I am sure of it.'

'And you believe, don't you, that Mrs Cockburn-Montfort was mistaken in thinking her assailant was an African?'

'She is a very stupid, hysterical woman. I place no value on anything she says.'

'Have they – the Cockburn-Montforts – any reason to harbour resentment against you or the Ambassador?'

'Oh, yes,' he said promptly. 'They had reason and I've no doubt they still do. It is well known that the Colonel, having had a hand in the formation of our armed forces, expected to be retained and promoted. I believe he actually saw himself in a very exalted role. But, as you know, my policy has been to place my own people in all key positions. I believe the Colonel went into unwilling retirement, breathing fire. In any case,' The Boomer added as an afterthought, 'he had become alcoholic and no longer responsible.'

'But they were asked to the reception?'

'Oh yes! It was a suitable gesture. One could not ignore him. And now – what is this unorthodox question, my dear Rory?'

'Simply this. Do you suspect anyone – specifically – of the murder of your Ambassador?'

Again that well-remembered, hooded look with the half-closed eyes. After a very long pause The Boomer said: 'I have no idea, beyond my absolute certainty of the innocence of the *mlinzi*.'

'One of your guests in the pavilion?'

'Certainly not.'

'I'm glad about that, at least,' said Alleyn drily.

'My dear boy!' For a moment Alleyn thought they were to be treated to one of those bursts of Homeric laughter, but instead his friend touched him gently on the shoulder and gave him a look of such anxiety and affection that he found himself oddly moved.

'Of course it was not a guest. Beyond that,' The Boomer said, 'I have nothing to say.'

'Well, then –' Alleyn glanced at Fox and Mr Whipplestone who once more made appropriate motions for departure.

'I too have a question,' said The Boomer and they checked. 'My government wishes for a portrait to be hung in our Assembly. I would like, formally, to ask if your wife will accept this commission.'

'I'll deliver the message,' said Alleyn, concealing his astonishment.

At the door he muttered to the others: 'I'll join you in a moment,' and when they had gone he said: 'I've got to say this. You will look after yourself, won't you?'

'Of course,'

'After all –'

'You need have no qualms. I shall sleep very soundly with my *mlinzi* outside my door.'

'You don't mean – ?'

'Certainly. It is his treasured privilege.'

'For God's sake!'

'I shall also lock my door.'

Alleyn left on a gale of laughter.

They went in silence to their extemporized office. When they got there Mr Whipplestone passed his thin hand over his thinner hair, dropped into a chair and said, 'He was lying.'

'The President, sir?' asked Fox in his best scandalized voice. 'About the spearsman?'

'No, no, no, no! It was when he said he didn't suspect anybody – specifically – of the crime.'

'Come on,' Alleyn said. 'Tell us. Why?'

'For a reason that you will find perfectly inadmissible. His manner. I did, at one time, know these people as well, perhaps, as a white person can. I like them. They are not ready liars. But, my dear Alleyn, you yourself know the President very well indeed. Did you have the same reaction?'

Alleyn said: 'He is an honourable person and a very

384

loyal friend. I believe it'd go deeply against the grain for him to lie to me. Yes, I did think he was uncomfortable. I think he may suspect somebody. I think he is withholding something.'

'Have you any idea what?'

Alleyn shoved his hands down in his trouser pockets and walked about the room. In his white tie and tails with miniatures on his coat and with his general air of uncontrived elegance he presented an odd contrast to Mr Fox in his workaday suit, to the sergeant in uniform and even to Mr Whipplestone in his elderly smoking-jacket and scarf.

'I've nothing,' he said at last, 'that will bear the light of day. Let's leave it for the moment and stick to facts, shall we? Sam, could you, before we go, give us a résumé of what was said at that showdown in the ballroom? I know you've written a report and I'm damn grateful and will go over every word of it very carefully indeed. But just to go on with? And also exactly what the waiter said, which sounds like a sequel to what the butler saw, doesn't it? When he came into the library?'

'I'll try,' said Mr Whipplestone. 'Very well. The waiter. At the outset the President told him to give an account of himself during the crucial minutes before and after the murder took place. His reply as far as I can translate it literally was, "I will say what I must say."'

'Meaning, in effect, "I must speak the truth"?'

'Precisely, but he could equally have meant: "I will say what I am forced to say."'

'Suggesting that he had been intimidated?'

'Perhaps. I don't know. He then said that he'd collided with the other waiter in the dark.'

'Chubb?'

'Quite so,' said Mr Whipplestone uneasily.

'And Chubb says the man attacked him.'

'Exactly. So you have told me.'

'Do you think the man was lying?'

'I think he might have merely left out mention of the attack.'

'Yes, I see. And the man himself: the spearsman – *mlinzi* or whatever? Was he at all equivocal?'

Mr Whipplestone hesitated. 'No,' he said at last. 'No, with him it was different. He said – and I think I remember it exactly – that he had taken a terrible – in the sense of awe-inspiring – terrifying, if you like – oath of loyalty to the President and therefore could never, if he were guilty, declare his innocence to the President on the body of his victim.'

'That's almost exactly how the President translated him to me.'

'Yes. And I think it is a true statement. But – well, my dear Alleyn, I hope you won't think I've got an awful cheek if I suggest to you that the President is on the whole a naïve person and that he is not going to heed, not even perhaps notice, any vague ambiguities that might cast doubt upon his men. But of course you know him very well and I don't.'

'Do I?' said Alleyn. 'Perhaps. There are times when I wonder. It's not a simple story: I can assure you of that.'

'There's something very likeable about him. You were quite close friends, I think you said, at school.'

'He's always roaring out that I was his best friend. He was certainly one of mine. He's got a very good brain, you know. He sailed through his law like nobody's business. But you're right,' Alleyn said thoughtfully, 'he cuts dead anything he doesn't want to believe.'

'And of course he doesn't want to believe that one of his own people committed a crime?' Mr Whipplestone urged.

Fox made a noise of agreement.

Alleyn said: 'No. Perhaps he doesn't – *want* to,' and vexedly rubbed his nose. 'All the same,' he said, 'I think we may be fishing in the wrong pond. In very muddy waters, at all events.'

'Do you mind,' Mr Whipplestone asked, 'if I put a very direct question to you?'

'How can I tell, till I hear it?'

'Quite. Here goes then. Do you think an attempt was made upon the President?'

'Yes.'

'And do you think it will be repeated?'

'I think it's only too likely that something else may be tried. Only too likely,' said Alleyn.

There was a long silence.

'What happens now, Mr Alleyn?' asked Fox at last.

'I'm damned if I know. Call it a night, I suppose. We've been given our marching orders and no mistake. Come on. We'd better tell Fred Gibson, hadn't we?'

Mr Gibson was not sorry to get the sack from the Embassy. It relieved him of an untenable and undefinable task and left him free to supervise the orthodox business of mounting security measures outside the premises and wherever the President might take it into his head to go during the remainder of his visit. He expressed muffled but profound satisfaction when Alleyn pointed out that the public appearances would probably be curtailed when not cancelled.

'You could say,' he mumbled presently, 'that after a fashion we've picked up a bit of joy in this show.' And he divulged that they had found the shell of the shot fired from the Luger. It was on the ground outside the lavatory window. They'd had no luck with a bullet.

'But,' said Gibson with a kind of huffy satisfaction, 'I don't reckon we need to shed tears over that one. Take a look at this.'

He opened his large pale hand. Alleyn and Fox bent over it.

'Wad?' Fox said. 'Here! Wait a sec. I wonder now.'

'Yes,' Alleyn said, 'Fred. I wonder if you've drawn a blank.'

They left the Embassy.

Troy was awake when Alleyn got home. She called out to him to save him the trouble of trying not to disturb her. When he came in she was sitting up in bed with her arms round her knees.

'Not a nice party, after all,' he said. 'I'm sorry, my darling.'

'Have you – ?'

'No. Troy. I had to let you go off without a word. I couldn't look after you. Were you very much shocked?'

'I didn't really see. Well – yes – I did see but in a funny sort of way it didn't look – real. And it was only for a flash – not more than a second or two. In a way, I didn't believe it.'

'Good.'

'Everybody sort of milling round.'

'That's right.'

'And you got us all out of the way so very expeditiously.'

'Did I?'

'Yes. But –' she bit her lip and said very quickly – 'it was the spear, wasn't it? He was speared?'

He nodded and put her irregular dark locks of hair out of her eyes.

'Then,' Troy said, 'haven't you arrested that superb-looking being?'

'The Boomer says the superb-looking being didn't do it. And anyway we haven't the authority inside the Embassy. It's a rum go and no mistake. Do you want to hear?'

'Not now. You'd better get some sleep.'

'Same to you. I shall have a bath. Good morning, my love. Oh – I forgot. I have a present for you from The Boomer!'

'For me? What can you mean?'

'He wants you to paint him. His suggestion, not mine.'

Troy was immovable for several seconds. She then gave Alleyn a quick exultant look and suddenly burrowed into her pillow.

He stared down at her and reflected on things one was supposed to remember about the artistic temperament. He touched her hair and went off to his bath with the dawn light paling the window.

6

Afternoon in the Capricorns

When, in response to a telephone call taken by Troy, Alleyn called on the following afternoon at No. 1, Capricorn Walk, he was received on the front steps by Lucy Lockett, the cat.

She sat, with a proprietory air on the top step and had a good look at him.

'I know who *you* are,' said Alleyn. 'Good afternoon, my dear.' He extended his forefinger. Lucy rose, stretched elaborately, yawned and advanced her whiskers to within an inch of the fingertip. Mr Whipplestone looked out of his open bow window.

'There you are,' he said. 'I won't be a second.'

Lucy sprang adroitly from the steps to the window-sill and thence into the bosom of her master, who presently opened the front door, still carrying her.

'Come in, do, do,' he said. 'We've been expecting you.'

'What a nice house you've got.'

'Do you think so? I must say I like it.'

'You hadn't far to walk last night – or this morning.'

'No. Do you know, Alleyn, when I was coming home at whatever eldritch hour, I caught myself wondering – well, *almost* wondering – if the whole affair could have been some sort of hallucination. Rather like that dodging-about-in-time nonsense they do in science fiction plays: as if it had happened off the normal temporal plane. The whole thing – so very – ah – off beat. Wasn't it?'

'Was and is,' Alleyn agreed.

He found Mr Whipplestone himself rather off-beat as he sat primly on his desk chair in his perfectly tailored suit, with his Trumper-style hair-cut, his discreet necktie, his elegant cuff-links, his eyeglass and, pounding away at his impeccable waistcoat, his little black cat.

'About Chubb,' he said anxiously. 'I'm awfully *bothered* about Chubb. You see, I don't know – and he hasn't said anything – and I must say Mrs Chubb looks too ghastly for words.'

'He hasn't told you the black waiter attacked him?'

'He hasn't told me anything. I felt it was not advisable for me to make any approach.'

'What's your opinion of Chubb? What sort of impression have you formed, by and large, since the Chubbs have been looking after you?'

Mr Whipplestone had some difficulty in expressing himself but it emerged that from his point of view the Chubbs were as near perfection as made no difference. In fact, Mr Whipplestone said wistfully, one had thought they no longer existed except perhaps in the employment of millionaires.

'I've sometime wondered if they were too good to be true. Ominous foreboding!' he said.

'Didn't you say Chubb seemed to have taken a scunner on blacks.'

'Well, yes. I rather fancied so. It was when I looked over this house. We were in the room upstairs and – Oh, Lord, it was the poor old boy himself – the Ambassador – walked down the street. The Chubbs were near the window and saw him. It was nothing, really. They stared. My dear Alleyn, you won't take from this any grotesque suggestion that Chubb – well, no, of course you won't.'

'I only thought a prejudice of that sort might colour any statement he offered. He certainly made no bones about his dislike when we talked to him.'

'Not surprising when you tell me one of them had half-strangled him!'

'*He* told me that.'

'Don't you believe him?'

'I don't know,' Alleyn said with an odd twist in his voice. 'Perhaps. But with misgivings.'

'Surely,' Mr Whipplestone said, 'it can be a very straight-forward affair, after all. For whatever motive, the Ng'ombwanan guard and the waiter conspire to murder either the Ambassador or the President. At the crucial moment, the servant finds Chubb in the way and doubles him up, leaving the guard free to commit the crime. The guard kills the Ambassador. To the President he confesses himself to be what my poor Chubb calls clobbered.'

'Yes,' Alleyn said. 'As neat as a new pin – almost.'

'So you see – you see!' cried Mr Whipplestone, stroking the cat.

'And the pistol shot?'

'Part of the conspiracy – I don't know – yes. That awful lady says it was a black person, doesn't she? Well, then!'

'Whoever it was probably fired a blank.'

'Indeed? There you are, then. A diversion. A red-herring calculated to attract the attention of all of you away from the pavilion and to bring the President to his feet.'

'As I said,' Alleyn conceded. 'New pins aren't in it.'

'Then – *why* – ?'

'My dear man, I don't know. I promise you, I don't know. It's by the pricking of my thumbs or some other intimation not admissible in the police manuals. It just all seems to me to be a bit too much of a good thing. Like those fish in aspic that ocean-going cruisers display in the tropics and never serve.'

'Oh, come!'

'Still, there are more tenable queries to be raised. Item. Mrs C-M's black thug with a stocking over his head. Seen dimly against the loo window, unseen during the assault in the dressing-room. Rushed out of the "Ladies" into the entrance hall – there's no other exit – where there were four of Gibson's men, one of them hard by the door. They all had torches. None of them got any impression of anybody emerging precipitately into the hall. Incidentally there was another SB man near the master-switch in the rear passage, who killed the blackout about ten seconds after he heard the pistol shot. In those ten seconds the murder was done.'

'Well?'

'Well, our girl-friend has it that after the shot her assailant, having chucked her out of the loo, emerged still in the blackout, kicked her about a bit and then bolted, leaving her prone and still in the dark. And then, she says, the loo-ladies, including our blushing sergeant, emerged and fell about all over her. Still in the dark. The loo-ladies, on the other hand, maintain they erupted into the anteroom immediately after the shot.'

'They were confused, no doubt.'

'The sergeant wasn't.'

'Drat!' said Mr Whipplestone. 'What's all this got to do with my wretched Chubb?'

'I've not the remotest idea. But it tempts me to suspect that when it comes to equivocation your black candidates have nothing on Mrs Cockburn-Montfort.'

Mr Whipplestone thought this over. Lucy tapped his chin with her paw and then fell asleep.

'Do I take it,' he asked at last, 'that you think Mrs C-M lied extensively about the black man with the stocking over his head?'

'I think she invented him.'

'Then who the devil fired the shot?'

'Oh,' Alleyn said. 'No difficulty with that one, I fancy. She did.

II

Mr Whipplestone was much taken aback by this pronouncement. He gave himself time to digest its implications. He detached his cat and placed her on the floor where, with an affronted and ostentatious air, she set about cleaning herself. He brushed his waistcoat, crossed his legs, joined his finger-tips and finally said: 'How very intriguing.' After a further pause he asked Alleyn if he had any more specific material to support his startling view of Mrs Cockburn-Montfort's activities.

Not specific, perhaps, Alleyn conceded. But he pointed

out that a black male person planning to fire the pistol, whether or not it was loaded with a blank, would have been much better advised to do so from the men's lavatory, where his presence would not be noticed, than from the women's where it extravagantly would. In the men's he would be taken for an attendant if he was in livery and for a guest if he was not.

'Really,' Alleyn said, 'it would be the height of dottiness for him to muscle-in to the female offices where he might — as indeed according to Mrs C-M he *did* — disturb a lady already *in situ*.'

'True,' said Mr Whipplestone moodily. 'True. True. True.'

'Moreover,' Alleyn continued, 'the sergeant, who, however naughty her lapse, displayed a certain expertise in the sequel, is persuaded that no rumpus, beyond the shot and subsequent screams of Mrs C-M, disturbed the seclusion of those premises.'

'I see.'

'As for the weapon, an examination of the barrel, made by an expert this morning, confirms that the solitary round was probably a blank. There are no finger-prints. This is negative evidence except that the sergeant, supported by the two orthodox attendants, says that Mrs C-M was wearing shoulder length gloves. The normal practice under these circumstances is for such gloves to be peeled off the hand from the wrist. The glove is then tucked back into the arm-piece which remains undisturbed. But the lady was fully gloved and buttoned and according to her own account certainly had no chance to effect this readjustment. She would hardly sit on the floor putting on gloves and yelling pen and ink.'

'All very plausible,' said Mr Whipplestone. Alleyn thought that he was hurriedly re-arranging his thoughts to accommodate this new development.

'I fancy,' Alleyn said, 'it's better than that. I can't for the life of me think of any other explanation that will accommodate all the discrepancies in the lady's tarra-diddle. And what's more she was taking dirty great sniffs at

393

her own smelling-salts to make herself cry. At any rate I'm going to call upon her.

'When!' quite shouted Mr Whipplestone.

'When I leave you. Why? What's up?'

'Nothing.' he said in a hurry, 'nothing really. Except that you'll probably be admitted by Chubb.'

'By *Chubb*!'

'He, ah, he "does for" the Cockburn-Montforts on Friday afternoons. There's nothing in that, you know, Alleyn. The Chubbs have one or two, as it were, casual jobs about the neighbourhood. They baby-sit every other Sunday at No. 17 for instance. It's an arrangement.'

'And Mrs Chubb obliges your tenant in the basement, doesn't she?'

'An hour, every other day. She will give us tea, by the way.' He glanced at the clock. 'Any second now. I asked for it very early, hoping you would join me. Mrs Alleyn said something about you not having had time for luncheon.'

'How very kind, I shall enjoy it.'

Lucy, after some preparatory clawing at the foot of the door, succeeded in opening it widely enough to make an exit which she effected with her tail up and an ambiguous remark.

'Sometimes,' said Mr Whipplestone, 'I've felt almost inclined to pump the Chubbs.'

'About Sheridan and the Cockburn-Montforts?'

'Discreetly. Yes. But of course, one doesn't do that sort of thing. Or,' Mr Whipplestone said with a self-deprecatory lift of his hand, 'I don't.'

'No,' Alleyn said, 'I don't suppose you do. Do you mind, though, if I have a word with Mrs Chubb?'

'Here? Now?' he said, evidently dismayed by the suggestion.

'Well – later if you'd rather.'

'She's awfully upset. About Chubb being man-handled by that black waiter and interviewed afterwards.'

'I'll try not to add to her woes. It really is just routine, Sam as far as I know.'

394

'Well, I do hope it doesn't turn out to be – anything else. Sh!'

He held up his finger. From somewhere outside the room came a series of intermittent bumps or taps. They grew louder.

Alleyn went to the door into the hall, left ajar by Lucy Lockett, and looked out.

To see Lucy herself backing down the stairs crab-wise and dragging some small object by a chain. It bumped from step to wooden step. When she arrived at the bottom she contrived with some difficulty to take the object up in her mouth. Giving out distorted mews she passed Alleyn, re-entered the drawing-room and dropped her trophy at Mr Whipplestone's feet.

'Oh no, oh no!' he cried out. 'Not again. For pity's sake, not again!'

But it was, in fact, a white pottery fish.

While he still gazed at it with the liveliest dismay a clink of china sounded in the passage. With extraordinary swiftness Alleyn scooped up the fish and dropped it in his pocket.

'Not a word,' he said.

Mrs Chubb came in with a tea-tray.

Alleyn gave her good afternoon and brought forward a small table to Mr Whipplestone's chair. 'Is this the right drill?' he asked and she thanked him nervously and set down her tray. When she had left and he had heard her go upstairs he said: 'It's not Sheridan's fish. She brought it from above.'

Mr Whipplestone's jaw dropped. He stared at Alleyn as if he had never seen him before. 'Show me,' he said at last.

Alleyn produced the object and dangled it by its chain in front of Mr Whipplestone who said: 'Yes. It is. I've remembered.'

'What have you remembered?'

'I think I told you. The first time she stole it. Or rather one like it. From down below. I had the curious feeling I'd seen it before. And then again, that evening when I returned it to Sheridan. Round that ghastly fellow Sanskrit's fat neck. The same feeling. Now I've remembered: it was on the day I inspected the premises. The fish was in the Chubbs' room upstairs. Hanging from a photograph of a girl with black ribbon attached to the frame. Rather morbid. And this,' said Mr Whipplestone, ramming home his point, 'is it.' He actually covered his face with his hands. 'And that,' he said, 'is *very* uncomfortable news.'

'It may turn out to be of no great matter, after all. I wouldn't get too up-tight about it, if I were you. This may simply be the outward and visible sign of some harmlessly potty little cult they all belong to.'

'Yes, but *Chubb?* And those dubious – those more than dubious Cockburn-Montforts and those frankly appalling Sanskrits. No, I don't like it,' said Mr Whipplestone. 'I don't like it at all.' His distracted gaze fell upon Lucy who was posed tidily *couchant* with her paws tucked under her chest. 'And the cat!' he remembered. 'The cat, of whose reprehensible habits I say nothing, took fright at the very sight of that ghastly pair. She bolted. And the Pirellis at the Napoli think she belonged to the Sanskrit woman. And they seem to think she was ill-treated.'

'I don't quite see . . .'

'Very well. Very well. Let it pass. Have some tea.' Mr Whipplestone distractedly invited, 'and tell me what you propose to do about that thing: that medallion, that – fish.'

Alleyn took it from his pocket and turned it over in his hand. A trade-mark like a wavy X had been fired into the reverse side.

'Roughish little job,' he said. 'Lucky she didn't break it. If you don't mind, I think I'll go upstairs and return it to its owner. It gives me the entrée, doesn't it?'

'I suppose so. Yes. Well. If you must.'

'It'll save you a rather tricky confrontation, Sam.'

'Yes. Thank you. Very good. Yes.'

'I'll nip up before she has time to return to her kitchen. Which is their sitting-room?'

'First door on the landing.'

'Right.'

He left Mr Whipplestone moodily pouring tea, climbed the stairs and tapped at the door.

After a pause it was opened by Mrs Chubb who stared at him with something like terror in her eyes. He asked her if he might come in for a moment and for a split second wondered if she was going to say no and shut the door in his face. But she stood aside with her fingers at her lips and he went in.

He saw, at once, the photograph on the wall. A girl of about sixteen with a nice, round, fresh-looking face very like Mrs Chubb's. The black ribbons had been made into rosettes and fastened to the top corners of the frame. On the photograph itself, neatly written, was a legend: 'April 4, 1953–May 1st, 1969.'

Alleyn took the medallion from his pocket. Mrs Chubb made a strange little falsetto noise in her throat.

He said: 'I'm afraid Lucy has been up to her tricks again. Mr Whipplestone tells me she's done this sort of thing before. Extraordinary animals, cats, aren't they? Once they get a notion into their heads, there's no stopping them. It belongs here, doesn't it?'

She made no move to take it. A drawing-pin lay on the table under the photograph. Alleyn pushed it back into its hole and looped the chain over it. 'The cat must have pulled it out,' he said: and then: 'Mrs Chubb, you're feeling poorly, aren't you? I'm so sorry. Sit down, won't you, and let me see if I can do something about it? Would you like a drink of water? No. Then, do sit down.'

He put his hand under her arm. She was standing in front of a chair and dropped into it as if she couldn't help herself. She was as white as a sheet and trembling.

Alleyn drew up another chair for himself.

'Mr Whipplestone told me you'd been very much upset by what happened last night and now I'm afraid I've gone and made matters worse,' he said.

397

Still she didn't speak and he went on: 'I don't expect you know who I am. It was I who interviewed your husband last night. I'm an old friend of Mr Whipplestone's and I know how greatly he values your service.'

Mrs Chubb whispered: 'The police?'

'Yes, but there's no need to worry about that. Really.'

'He set on 'im,' she said. 'That — ' she shut her eyes for a second — '*black* man. Set on 'im.'

'I know. He told me.'

'It's the truth.' And with a startling force she repeated this, loudly. 'It's the truth. Sir. Do you believe that, sir? Do you believe it's the truth?'

Alleyn waited for a moment.

He thought: 'Do I believe this, do I believe the other thing? Everybody asking what one believes. The word becomes meaningless. It's what one knows that matters in this muddle.' He waited for a moment and then said: 'A policeman may only believe what he finds out for himself, without any possible doubt, to be true. If your husband was attacked, as he says he was, we shall find out.'

'Thank Gawd,' she whispered. And then: 'I'm sorry, I'm sure, to give way like this. I can't think what's come over me.'

'Never mind.'

He got up and moved towards the photograph. Mrs Chubb blew her nose.

'That's an attractive face,' Alleyn said. 'Is it your daughter?'

'That's right,' she said. 'Was.'

'I'm sorry. Long ago?'

'Six years.'

'An illness?'

'An accident.' She made as if to speak, pressed her lips together and then shot out, as if defiantly: 'She was the only one, our Glenys was.'

'I can see the likeness.'

'That's right.'

'Was the medallion special to her, perhaps?'

She didn't answer. He turned round and found her

staring at the photograph and wetting her lips. Her hands were clasped.

'If it was,' he said, 'of course you'd be very upset when you thought you'd lost it.'

'It wasn't hers.'

'No?'

'I hadn't noticed it wasn't there. It gave me a turn, like. When you – you held it out.'

'I'm sorry,' Alleyn repeated.

'It doesn't matter.'

'Was it in London – the accident?'

'Yes,' she said and shut her mouth like a trap.

Alleyn said lightly: 'It's a rather unusual-looking medallion, isn't it? An order or a badge or something of that sort, perhaps?'

She pulled her hands apart as if the gesture needed force to accomplish it.

'It's my husband's,' she said. 'It's Chubb's.'

'A club badge, perhaps?'

'You could call it that, I suppose.'

She had her back to the door. It opened and her husband stood on the threshold.

'I don't know anything about it,' she said loudly. 'It's got nothing to do with anything. Nothing.'

Chubb said: 'You're wanted downstairs.'

She got up and left the room without a glance at Alleyn or at her husband.

'Were you wanting to see me, sir?' Chubb asked woodenly. 'I've just come in.'

Alleyn explained about the cat and the medallion. Chubb listened impassively. 'I was curious,' Alleyn ended, 'about the medallion itself and wondered if it was a badge.'

Chubb said at once and without hesitation, 'That's correct, sir. It's a little social circle with an interest in ESP and so forth. Survival and that.'

'Mr and Miss Sanskrit are members, aren't they?'

'That's correct, sir.'

'And Mr Sheridan?'

'Yes, sir.'

'And you?' Alleyn said lightly.

'They was kind enough to make me an honorary member, like. Seeing I go in and do the servicing for some of their meetings, sir. And seeing I was interested.'

'In survival after death, do you mean?'

'That kind of thing.'

'Your wife doesn't share your interest?'

He said flatly: 'She doesn't come into it, does she? It's kind of complementary to my services, isn't it? Like wearing a livery button used to be.'

'I see. You must find a different place for it, mustn't you?' Alleyn said easily. 'Out of reach of Lucy Lockett. Good afternoon to you, Chubb.'

Chubb mouthed rather than sounded his response to this and Alleyn left him, almost as bleached as his wife had been five minutes earlier.

Mr Whipplestone was still sipping tea. Lucy was discussing a saucer of milk on the hearthrug.

'You must have some tea *at once*,' Mr Whipplestone said, pouring it out. 'And some anchovy toast. I hope you like anchovy toast. It's still quite eatable, I think.' He tipped back the lid of the hot-server and up floated the smell that of all others recalled Alleyn to his boyhood days with The Boomer. He took a piece of toast and his tea.

'I can't stay long,' he said. 'I oughtn't to stay at all, in fact, but here goes.'

'About the Chubbs?' Mr Whipplestone ventured. Alleyn gave him a concise account of his visit upstairs. On the whole it seemed to comfort him. 'As you suggested,' he said, 'the emblem of some insignificant little coterie and Chubb has been made a sort of non-commissioned officer in recognition of his serving them sandwiches and drinks. Perhaps they think he's psychic. That makes perfectly good sense. Well, doesn't it?'

'Yes, of course. It's not without interest, do you agree,' Alleyn asked, 'that Sanskrit is on the police records for fraudulent practice as a fortune-teller and a phoney

400

medium? *And* he's suspected of the odd spot of drug trafficking.'

'I am not in the least surprised,' Mr Whipplestone energetically declared. 'In the realms of criminal deception he is, I feel sure, *capable de tout*. From that point of view, if from no other, I do of course deplore the Chubb connection.'

'And there's Mrs Cockburn-Montfort, who seems to be a likely candidate for the attempt-on-the-President stakes. Not a nice influence either, would you say?'

'Oh *drat*!' said Mr Whipplestone. 'Very well, my dear fellow. I'm a selfish, square old bachelor and I don't want anything beastly to happen to my Chubbs because they make life pleasant for me.' His exasperated gaze fell upon his cat. 'As for *you*,' he scolded. 'If you'd be good enough to keep your paws to yourself this sort of thing wouldn't happen. Mind that!'

Alleyn finished his tea and toast and stood up.

'Are you going, my dear chap?' Mr Whipplestone asked rather wistfully.

'Needs must. Thank you for my lovely cuppa. Goodbye, my dear,' he said to Lucy Lockett. 'Unlike your boss, I'm much obliged to you. I'm off.'

'To see Mrs C-M?'

'On the contrary. To see Miss Sanskrit. She now takes precedence over the C-M.'

III

Alleyn had not come face to face with the Sanskrits at the Embassy. Like all the guests who had not been in or near the pavilion, they had been asked for their names and addresses by Inspector Fox, ticked off on the guest list and allowed to go home. He didn't think, therefore, that Miss Sanskrit would recall his face or, if she did, would attach more importance to it than to any that she had seen among a hundred others at the reception.

He walked down Capricorn Mews, past the Napoli

grocery shop, the flower shop and the garages. The late afternoon was warm, scents of coffee, provender, carnations and red roses drifted on the air and, for some reason, the bells in the Basilica were ringing.

At the far end of the Mews, at its junction with the passageway into Baronsgate, was the converted stable now devoted to the sale of pottery pigs. It faced up the Mews and was, therefore, in full view for their entire length. Alleyn, advancing towards it, entertained somewhere in the back of his thoughts a prospect of stamping and sweating horses, industrious stablemen, ammoniacal fumes and the rumble of Dickensian wheels. Pigeons, wheeling overhead, and intermittently flapping down to the cobbled passage, lent a kind authenticity to his fancies.

But there, as he approached, was the nonedescript signboard 'K. & X. Sanskrit. Pigs.' And there, deep in the interior and in a sort of alcove at the far end, was a faint red glow indicating the presence of a kiln and, looming over it, the dim bulk of Miss Sanskrit.

He made as if to turn off into the passageway, checked, and stopped to peer through the window at the exhibits ranked on shelves nearest to it. A particularly malevolent pig with forget-me-nots on its flanks glowered at him rather in the manner of Miss Sanskrit herself, who had turned her head in the shadows and seemed to stare at him. He opened the door and walked in.

'Good afternoon,' he said.

She rose heavily and lumbered towards him, emerging from the alcove, he thought, like some dinosaur from its lair.

'I wonder,' Alleyn said, as if suddenly inspired, 'if you can help me by any chance. I'm looking for someone who could make castings of a small ceramic emblem. It's to be the badge for a newly-formed club.'

'We don't,' rumbled an astonishingly deep voice inside Miss Sanskrit, 'accept commissions.'

'Oh. Pity. In that case,' Alleyn said, 'I shall do what I came to do and buy one of your pigs. The doorstop kind.

You don't have pottery cats, I suppose? With or without flowers?'

'There's one doorstop cat. Bottom shelf. I've discontinued the line.'

It was indeed the only cat: a baleful, lean, black, upright cat with blue eyes and buttercups on its haunches. Alleyn bought it. It was very heavy and cost five pounds.

'This is perfectly splendid!' he prattled while Miss Sanskrit busied her fat, pale hands in making a clumsy parcel. 'Actually it's a present for a cat. She lives at No. 1, Capricorn Walk and is positively the double of this one. Except that she's got a white tip to her tail. I wonder what she'll make of it.'

Miss Sanskrit had paused for a second in her wrapping. She said nothing.

He rambled chattily on. 'She's quite a character, this cat. behaves more like a dog, really. Retrieves things. Not above indulging in the odd theft, either.'

She turned her back on him. The paper crackled. Alleyn waited. Presently she faced round with the parcel in her hands. Her embedded eyes beneath the preposterous beetroot-coloured fringe were fixed on him.

'Thank you,' she growled and he took the parcel.

'I suppose,' he said apologetically, 'you couldn't recommend anybody for this casting job? It's quite small. Just a white fish with its tail in its mouth. About that size.'

There was something in the way she looked at him that recalled, however grotesquely, the interview with Mrs Chubb. It was a feral look: that of a creature suddenly alarmed and on guard and he was very familiar with it. It would scarcely be too fanciful to imagine she had given out a self-defensive smell.

'I'm afraid,' she said, 'I can't help you. Good afternoon.' She had turned her back and begun to waddle away when he said:

'Miss Sanskrit.'

She stopped.

'I believe we were both at the same party last night. At the Ng'ombwana Embassy.'

'Oh,' she said, without turning.

'You were with your brother, I think. And I believe I saw your brother a few weeks ago when I was in Ng'ombwana.'

No reply.

'Quite a coincidence,' said Alleyn. 'Good afternoon.'

As he walked away and turned the corner into Capricorn Place he thought: Now, I wonder if that *was* a good idea. She's undoubtedly rattled, as far as one can think of blubber rattling. She'll tell Big Brother and what will they cook up between them? That I'm fishing after membership? In which case, will they get in touch with the other fish to see what *they* know? Or will she suspect the worst of me and start at once, on her own account, ringing round the circle to warn them all? In which case she'll hear I'm a cop in as short a time as it takes Mrs Cockburn-Montfort to throw a temperament. And in *that* case we'll have to take damn good care she and Big Brother don't shoot the moon. I don't mind betting, he thought as he approached No. 19, The Place, that those dubious premises accommodate more than pottery pigs. Has Brother *quite* given up the drug connection? A nice point. Here we go again.

No. 19, Capricorn Place, although larger, was built in much the same style as Mr Whipplestone's little house. The window-boxes, however, were more commonplace, being given over to geraniums. As Alleyn crossed the street he saw, behind the geraniums, Mrs Cockburn-Montfort's bizarre face looking much the worse for wear and regarding him with an expression of horror. It dodged away.

He had to ring three times before the Colonel opened the door on a wave of gin. For a moment Alleyn thought, as he had with Chubb, that it might be slammed in his face. Inside the house someone was speaking on the telephone.

The Colonel said: 'Yes?'

'If it's not inconvenient I'd like to have two words with Mrs Cockburn-Montfort,' Alleyn said.

'Out of the question I'm 'fraid. She's unwell. She's in bed.'

'I'm sorry. In that case, with you, if you'll be so good as to put up with me.'

'It doesn't suit at the moment. I'm sorry. Any case we've nothing to add to what we said last night.'

'Perhaps, Colonel, you'd rather come down to the Yard. We won't keep you long.'

He glared, red-eyed, at nothing in particular and then said. 'Damn! All right. You'd better come in.'

'Thank you so much,' said Alleyn and did so, pretty smartly, passing the Colonel into a hall with a flight of stairs and two doors, the first of which stood ajar.

Inside the room a voice, hushed but unmistakably Mrs Cockburn-Montfort's was speaking. 'Xenny,' she was saying. 'It's true. Here! Now! I'm ringing off.'

'Not that door. The next,' shouted the Colonel, but Alleyn had already gone in.

She was dressed in a contemporary version of a garment that Alleyn had heard his mother refer to as a tea-gown: an elaborate confection worn, he rather thought, over pyjamas and held together by ribbons. Her hair had been arranged but insecurely so that it almost looked more dishevelled than it would have done if it had been left to itself. The same appraisement might have been made of her face. She was smoking.

When she saw Alleyn she gestured with both hands rather as if something fluttered near her nose. She took a step backwards and saw her husband in the doorway.

'Why've you come down, Chrissie?' he said. 'You're meant to stay in bed.'

'I — I'd run out of cigarettes.' She pointed a shaky finger at Alleyn. 'You again!' she said with a pretty awful attempt at playfulness.

'Me again, I'm afraid,' he said. 'I'm sorry to pounce like this but one or two things have cropped up.'

Her hands were at her hair. 'I'm in no state — Too shaming!' she cried. 'What *will* you think!'

'You'd better go back to bed,' her husband said brutally. 'Here! I'll take you.'

She's signalled, Alleyn thought. I can't prevent this.

'I'll just tidy up a bit,' she said. 'That's what I'll do.'

They went out, he holding her arm above the elbow.

And now, Alleyn thought, she'll tell him she's telephoned the Sanskrit. If it was the Sanskrit and I'll lay my shirt on it. They're cooking up what they're going to say to me.

He heard a door slam upstairs.

He looked round the drawing-room. Half conventional, half 'contemporary'. Different coloured walls, 'with-it' ornaments and one or two collages and a mobile mingled disconsolately with pouffes, simpering water-colours and martial photographs of the Colonel, one of which showed him in shorts and helmet with a Ng'ombwanan regiment forming a background. A ladylike desk upon which the telephone now gave out a click.

Alleyn was beside it. He lifted the receiver and heard someone dialling. The ringing sound set in. After a longish pause a muffled voice said 'Yes?'

'That you, Zenoclea?' The Colonel said, 'Chrissie rang you a moment ago, didn't she? All right. He's *here.*'

'Be careful.' (The Sanskrit, sure enough.)

'Of course. This is only to warn you.'

'Have you been drinking?'

'My dear Xenny! Look! He may call on you.'

'Why?'

'God knows. I'll come round later, or ring. 'Bye.'

A click and then the dialling tone.

Alleyn hung up and walked over to the window.

He was gazing at the distant prospect of the Basilica when the Colonel re-entered the room. Alleyn saw at once that he had decided on a change of manner. He came in jauntily.

'Ah!' he said. 'There we are! Chrissie's insisting on making herself presentable. She'll be down in a moment. Says she feels quite equal to it. Come and take a pew. I think a drink while we wait is indicated, don't you? What shall it be?'

'Very civil of you,' Alleyn said, speaking the language, 'but it's not on for me, I'm afraid. Please don't let me stop you, though.'

'Not when you're on guard duty, what? Bad luck! Well, just to show there's no ill-feeling,' said the Colonel, 'I think I will.'

He opened a door at the far end of the room and went into what evidently was his study. Alleyn saw a martial collection of sword, service automatic and a massive hunting rifle hung on the wall. The Colonel returned with a bottle in one hand and a very large gin in the other.

'Your very good health,' he said and drank half of it.

Fortified and refreshed, it seemed, he talked away easily about the assassination. He took it for granted, or appeared to do so, that the spearsman had killed the Ambassador in mistake for the President. He said that you never could tell with blacks, that he knew them, that he'd had more experience of them, he ventured to claim, than most. 'Bloody good fighting men, mind you, but you can't trust them beyond a certain point.' He thought you could depend upon it that when the President and his entourage had got back to Ng'ombwana the whole thing would be dealt with in their way and very little would be heard of it. 'There'll be a new *mlinzi* on duty and no questions asked, I wouldn't wonder. On the other hand, he may decide to make a public example.'

'By that do you mean a public execution?'

'Don't take me up on that, old man,' said the Colonel, who was helping himself to another double gin. 'He hasn't gone in for that particular exercise, so far. Not like the late lamented, f'instance.'

'The Ambassador?'

'That's right. He had a pretty lurid past in that respect. Between you and me and the gatepost.'

'Really?'

'As a young man. Ran a sort of guerrilla group. When

407

we were still there. Never brought to book but it's common knowledge. He's turned respectable of late years.'

His wife made her entrance: fully clothed, coiffured and regrettably made-up.

'Time for dinkies?' she asked. 'Super! Give me one, darling: kick-sticks.'

Alleyn thought: She's already given herself one or more. This is excessively distasteful.

'In a minute,' said her husband, 'sit down, Chris.'

She did, with an insecure suggestion of gaiety.

'What have you two been gossiping about?' she asked.

'I'm sorry,' Alleyn said, 'to bother you at an inopportune time and when you're not feeling well, but there is one question I'd like to ask you, Mrs Cockburn-Montfort.'

'Me? Is there? What?'

'Why did you fire off that Luger and then throw it in the pond?'

She gaped at him, emitted a strange whining sound that, incongruously enough, reminded him of Mrs Chubb. Before she could speak her husband said: 'Shut up, Chris. I'll handle it. I mean that. Shut up.'

He turned on Alleyn. The glass in his hand was unsteady but, Alleyn thought, he was in pretty good command of himself. One of those heavy drinkers who are seldom really drunk. He'd had a shock but he was equal to it.

He said: 'My wife will not answer any questions until we have consulted our solicitor. What you suggest is obviously unwarranted and quite ridiculous. And 'stremely 'fensive. You haven't heard the last of this, whatever-your-rank-is Alleyn.'

'I'm afraid you're right, there,' Alleyn said. 'And nor have you, perhaps. Good evening to you. I'll show myself out.'

IV

'And the odd thing about that little episode, Br'er Fox, is this: my bit of personal bugging on the Cockburn-

Montfort telephone exchange copped Miss Xenoclea Sanskrit – Xenny for short – in an apparently motiveless lie. The gallant Colonel said: "He – " meaning me – "may call on you" and instead of saying: "He *has* called on me," she merely growled "Why?" Uncandid behaviour from a comrade, don't you think?'

'If,' said Fox carefully, 'this little lot, meaning the Colonel and his lady, the Sanskrit combination, the Sheridan gentleman and this chap Chubb, are all tied up in some hate-the-blacks club and *if,* as seems possible, seeing most of them were at the party, and seeing the way the lady carried on, they're mixed up in the fatality – ' He drew breath.

'I can't wait,' Alleyn said.

'I was only going to say it wouldn't, given all these circumstances, be anything out of the way if they got round to looking sideways at each other,' He sighed heavily. 'On the other hand,' he said, 'and I must say on the face of it this is the view I'm inclined to favour, we may have a perfectly straightforward job. The man with the spear used the spear and what else took place round about in the dark has little or no bearing on the matter.'

'How about Mrs C-M and her Luger in the ladies' loo?'

'Blast!' said Fox.

'The whole thing's so bloody untidy,' Alleyn grumbled.

'I wouldn't mind going over the headings,' Fox confessed.

'Plough ahead and much good may it do you.'

'*A.*' said Fox, massively checking it off with finger and thumb. '*A.* The occurrence. Ambassador killed by spear. Spearsman stationed at rear in handy position. Says he was clobbered and his spear taken off him. Says he's innocent. *B.* Chubb. Ex-commando. Also at rear. Member of this secret society or whatever it is. Suggestion that he's a black-hater. Says *he* was clobbered by black waiter. *C.* Mrs C-M. Fires shot, probably blank, from ladies' conveniences. Why? To draw attention? To get the President on his feet, so's he could be speared? By whom? This is the nitty-gritty one.' said Fox. 'If the club's an anti-black show would they collaborate with the spearsman or the waiter? The answer is: unlikely. Very unlikely. Where does this take us?'

'Hold on to your hats, boys.'

'To Chubb,' said Fox. 'It takes us to Chubb. Well, doesn't it? Chubb, set up by the club, clobbers the spearsman, and does the job on the Ambassador and afterwards says the waiter clobbered *him* and held him down.'

'But the waiter maintains that he stumbled in the dark and accidentally grabbed Chubb. If Chubb was the spearsman, what are we to make of this?'

'Mightn't it be the case, though? Mightn't he have stumbled and momentarily clung to Chubb?'

'Before or after Chubb clobbered the spearsman and grabbed the spear?'

Fox began to look disconcerted. 'I don't like it much,' he confessed. 'Still, after a fashion it fits. After a fashion it does.'

'It's a brave show, Br'er Fox, and does you credit. Carry on.'

'I don't know that I've all that much more to offer. This Sanskrit couple, now. At least there's a CRO on *him*. Fraud, fortune-telling and hard drugs, I think you mentioned. Big importer into Ng'ombwana until the present government turned him out. They're members of this club, if Mr Whipplestone's right when he says he saw them wearing the medallion.'

'Not only that,' Alleyn said. He opened a drawer in his desk and produced his black pottery cat. 'Take a look at this,' he said and exhibited the base. It bore, as a trademark, a wavy X. 'That's on the reverse of the medallions, too,' he said. 'X for Xenoclea, I suppose. Xenny not only wears a medallion, she makes 'em in her little kiln, fat witch that she is.'

'You're building up quite a case, Mr Alleyn, aren't you? But against whom? And for what?'

'You tell me. But whatever turns up in the ambassadorial department, I'll kick myself all round the Capricorns if I

410

don't get something on the Sanskrits. What rot they talk when they teach us we should never get involved. Of course we get involved: we merely learn not to show it.'

'Oh, come now! *You* never do, Mr Alleyn.'

'Don't I? All right, Foxkin, I'm talking through my hat. But I've taken a scunner on la belle Xenny and Big Brother and I'll have to watch it. Look, let's get the CRO file and have a look for ourselves. Fred Gibson wasn't all that interested at that stage. One of his henchmen looked it up for him. There was nothing there that directly concerned security and he may not have given me all the details.'

So they called on the Criminal Records Office for the entry under Sanskrit.

Alleyn said, 'Just as Fred quoted it. Fraudulent practices. Fortune-telling. Suspected drug peddling. All in the past before he made his pile as an importer of fancy goods in Ng'ombwana. And he did, apparently, make a tidy pile before he was forced to sell out to a Ng'ombwanan interest.'

'That was recently?'

'Quite recently. I actually happened to catch sight of him standing outside the erstwhile premises when I was over there. He doesn't seem to have lost face – and God knows he's got plenty to lose – or he wouldn't have been asked to the party.'

'Wouldn't you say it was a bit funny their being invited, anyway?'

'Yes,' Alleyn agreed thoughtfully. 'Yes. I think I would.'

'Would you reckon this pottery business of the sister's was a money-spinner?'

'Not on a big scale.'

'Was she involved in any of the former charges?'

'She hasn't got a CRO. Wait a bit thought. There's a cross reference. 'See McGuigan, O.' Fetch us down the Macs.' The sergeant on duty obliged.

'Here you are,' said Mr Fox presently. 'Take a look,' and without waiting for Alleyn to do so he continued in the slightly catarrhal voice he kept for reading aloud: '"McGuigan, Olive, supposed widow of Sean McGuigan of whom nothing known. Sister of Kenneth Sanskrit q.v. Later assumed as first name, Xenoclea. Sus. drug traffic with brother. Charged with fortune-telling for which, fined, June 1953. Reported to RSPCA cruelty to cat, 1967. Charged and convicted. Fined with costs." Fred Gibson's henchmen left this out. He'll be getting some "advice" on this one,' said Fox.

'Ah. And Sam Whipplestone thinks she ill-treated his cat. Pretty little picture we're building up, aren't we? I must say I thought the "Xenoclea" bit was too good to be true,' Alleyn grunted.

'Is it a made-up job, then, that name?'

'Not by her, at least. Xenoclea was a mythical prophetess who wouldn't do her stuff for Hercules because he hadn't had a bath. After his Augean stables job, perhaps. I bet la belle Xenny re-christened herself and reverted to her maiden name when she took to her fortune-telling lay.'

'Where do they live?'

'Above the pottery pigs. There seems to be a flat up there: quite a sizeable one, by the look of it.'

'Does the brother live there with her — wait a bit,' said Fox interrupting himself. 'Where's the guest list we made last night?'

'In my office but you needn't worry. I looked it up. That's their joint address. While we're at it, Br'er Fox, let's see, for the hell of it, whether there's anything on Sheridan, A. R. G., 1a, Capricorn Walk.'

But Mr Sheridan had no criminal record.

'All the same,' Alleyn said, 'we'll have to get him sorted out. Even if it comes to asking the President if there's a Ng'ombwanan link. He wasn't asked to the reception, of course. Oh well, press on.'

They left the CRO and returned to Alleyn's rooms, where he managed to reach Superintendent Gibson on the telephone.

'What's horrible, Fred?'

'Nothing to report,' said that colourless man. 'All quiet

inside the premises, seemingly. We've stopped the demolition. Routine precaution.'

'Demolition?'

'Clearing up after the party. The Vistas people and the electrics. It's silly really, seeing we can't go in. If nothing develops they may as well get on with it.'

'Any ingoings or outcomings of interest?'

'Post. Tradesmen. We looked over all deliveries which wasn't very popular. Callers offering condolences and leaving cards. The media of course. One incident.'

'What?'

'His Nibs, believe it or not.'

'The President?'

'That's right. Suddenly comes out by the front entrance with a dirty great dog on a leash and says he's taking it for a walk in the Park.'

Alleyn swore vigorously.

'What's that?' asked Gibson.

'Never mind. Go on.'

'My sergeant, on duty at the entrance, tries to reason with him. I'm doing a cruise round in a job car and they give me a shout and I come in and try to reason with him. He's very la-di-da, making out we're fussy. It's awkward,' said Mr Gibson drearily.

'How did you handle it, Fred?'

'I'm stuck with it, aren't I? So I say we'll keep with it and he says if it's a bodyguard I'm worried about he's got the dog and his own personal protection and with that the door opens and guess who appears?' invited Mr Gibson without animation.

'The spearsman of last night?'

'That's correct. The number one suspect in my book who we'd've borrowed last night, there and then, if we'd had a fair go. There he was, large as life.'

'You don't surprise me. What was the upshot?'

'Ask yourself. In flocks the media, telly, press, the lot. He says "no comment" and off he goes to his constitutional with the dog and the prime sus and five of my chaps in a panda doing their best in the way of protection. So they go

413

and look at Peter Pan,' said Mr Gibson bitterly, 'and nobody shoots anybody or lobs in a bomb and they come home again. Tonight it's the Palace caper.'

'That's been scaled down considerably, hasn't it?'

'Yes. Nondescript transport. Changed route. Small party.'

'At least he's not taking the spearsman with him.'

'Not according to my info. It wouldn't surprise me.'

'Poor Fred!'

'Well, it's not what you'd pick in the way of a job,' said Gibson. 'Oh yes, and there's another thing. He wants to see you. Or talk to you.'

'Why? Did you gather?'

'No. He just chucks it over his shoulder when he walks away. He's awkward.'

'The visit may be cut short.'

'Can't be too short for me,' said Gibson and they took leave of each other.

'It's a case,' Alleyn said when he'd replaced the receiver, 'of "where do we go for honey?" I dunno, Br'er Fox. Press on, press on but in what direction?'

'This Mr Sheridan,' Fox ruminated. 'He seems to have been kind of side-tracked, doesn't he? I mean from the secret society or what-have-you angle.'

'I know he does. He wasn't at the party. That's why.'

'But he is a member of whatever they are.'

'Yes. Look here, Fox. The only reason – the only tenable reason – we've got for thinking there was some hanky-panky based on this idiot-group is the evidence, if you can call it that, of Mrs C-M having loosed off a Luger with a blank charge in the ladies' loo. I'm quite convinced, if only because of their reaction – hers and the gallant Colonel's – that she's the girl who did it, though proving it will be something else again. All right. The highly suspect, the generally inadmissible word "coincidental" keeps on rearing its vacant head in these proceedings but I'll be damned if I accept any argument based on the notion that two entirely unrelated attempts at homicide occurred within the same five minutes at an Ambassadorial party.'

'You mean,' said Fox, 'the idea that Mrs C-M and this little gang had something laid on and never got beyond the first move because the spearsman hopped in and beat them to it?'

'Is that what I mean? Yes, of course it is, but blow me down flat if it sounds as silly as I expected it to.'

'It sounds pretty silly to me.'

'You can't entertain the notion?'

'It'd take a big effort.'

'Well, God knows. You may have to make it. I tell you what, Foxkin. We'll try and get a bit more on Sheridan if only for tidiness's sake. And we'll take a long shot and give ourselves the dreary task of finding out how a girl of sixteen was killed in London on the first of May, 1969. Name Glenys Chubb.'

'Car accident?'

'We don't know. I get the impression that although the word accident was used, it was not used correctly. Lurking round the fringe of my rotten memory there's something or another, and it may be so much nonsense, about the name Chubb in connection with an unsolved homicide. We weren't involved. Not on our ground.'

'Chubb,' mused Fox. '*Chubb*, now. Yes. Yes, there *was* something. Now, what was it? Wait a bit, Mr Alleyn. Hold on.'

Mr Fox went into a glazed stare at nothing in particular from whch he was roused by Alleyn bringing his palm down smartly on his desk.

'Notting Hill Gate,' Alleyn said. 'May 1969. Raped and strangled. Man seen leaving the area but never knocked off. That's it. We'll have to dig it out, of course, but I bet you that's it. Still open. He left a red scarf behind and it was identified.'

'You're dead right. The case blew out. They knew their man but they never got it tied up."

'No. Never.'

'He was coloured,' Fox said. 'A coloured chap, wasn't he?'

'Yes,' Alleyn said. 'He was. He was black. And what's more — Here! We'll get on to the Unsolved File for this one and we'll do it now, by gum.'

It didn't take long. The Unsolved Homicide file for May 1969 had a succinct account of the murder of Chubb, Glenys, aged sixteen, by a black person believed but never proved to be a native of Ng'ombwana.

Mr Sheridan's Past

When they had closed the file for unsolved homicide, subsection rape and asphyxiation, 1969, Fox remarked that if Chubb hadn't seemed to have a motive before he certainly had one now. Of a far-fetched sort, Fox allowed, but a motive nevertheless. And in a sort of fashion he argued, this went some way to showing that the society – he was pleased to call it the 'fishy society' – had as its objective the confusion, subjection and downfall of The Black.

'I begin to fancy Chubb,' said Fox.

At this point Alleyn's telephone rang. To his great surprise it was Troy who was never known to call him at the Yard. He said: 'Troy! Anything wrong?'

'Not really and I'm sorry about this,' she said rapidly, 'but I thought you'd better know at once. It's your Boomer on the blower.'

'Wanting me?'

'Strangely enough, no. Wanting me.'

'Oh?' said Alleyn with an edge in his voice. 'Well, he'll have to wait. What for? No, don't tell me. It's about his portrait.'

'He's coming. Now. Here. In full fig to be painted. He says he can give me an hour and a half. I tried to demur but he just roared roughshod over my bleating. He said time was of the essence because his visit is to be cut short. He said the conversation can be continued in a few minutes when he arrives and with that he hung up and I think I hear him arriving.'

'By God, he's a daisy. I'll be with you in half an hour or earlier.'

'You needn't. It's not that I'm in the least flustered. It's only I thought you should know.'

'You couldn't be more right. Stick him up in the studio and get cracking. I'll be there in a jiffy.'

Alleyn clapped down his receiver and said to Fox: 'Did you get the gist of that? Whistle me up a car, Fox, and see if you can get the word through to Fred Gibson. I suppose he's on to this caper, but find out. And you stay here in case anything comes through and if it does, call me at home. I'm off.'

When he arrived at the pleasant cul-de-sac where he and Troy had their house, he found the Ng'ombwanan ceremonial car, its flag flying, drawn up at the kerb. A poker-faced black chaffeur sat at the wheel. Alleyn was not surprised to see, a little way along the street on the opposite side, a 'nondescript' which is the police term for a disguised vehicle, this time a delivery van. Two men with short haircuts sat in the driver's compartment. He recognized another of Mr Gibson's stalwarts sitting at a table outside the pub. A uniformed constable was on duty outside the house. When Alleyn got out of the police car this officer, looking self-conscious, saluted him.

'How long have *you* lot been keeping obbo on my pad?' Alleyn asked.

'Half an hour, sir. Mr Gibson's inside, sir. He's only just arrived and asked me to inform you.'

'I'll bet he did,' Alleyn said and let himself in.

Gibson was in the hall.

He showed something like animation on greeting Alleyn and appeared to be embarrassed. The first thing he had heard of the President's latest caper, he said, was a radio message that the Ambassadorial Rolls with the Ng'ombwanan flag mounted, had drawn up to the front entrance of the Embassy. His sergeant had spoken to the driver who said the President had ordered it and was going out. The sergeant reached Mr Gibson on radio but before he got to the spot the President, followed by his bodyguard, came out, swept aside the wretched sergeant's attempts to detain him and shouting out the address to his driver, had been driven away. Gibson and elements of the security forces outside the Embassy had then given chase and taken up the appropriate stations where Alleyn had seen them. When they arrived the President and his *mlinzi* were already in the house.

'Where is he now?'

'Mrs Alleyn,' said Gibson, coughing slightly, 'took him to the studio. She said I was to tell you. "The Studio", she said. He was very sarcastic about me being here. Seemed to think it funny,' said Gibson resentfully.

'What about the prime suspect?'

'Outside the studio door. I'm very, very sorry but without I took positive action I couldn't remove him. Mrs Alleyn didn't make a complaint. I'd've loved to've borrowed that chap then and there,' said Gibson.

'All right, Fred. I'll see what I can do. Give yourself a drink. In the dining-room, there. Take it into the study and settle down.'

'Ta,' said Gibson wearily, 'I could do with it.'

The studio was a separate building at the back of the house and had been built for a Victorian Academician of preposterous fame. It had an absurd entrance approached by a flight of steps with a canopy supported by a brace of self-conscious plaster caryatids that Troy had thought too funny to remove. Between these, in stunning incongruity, stood the enormous *mlinzi* only slightly less impressive in a dark suit than he had been in his lionskin and bracelets. He had his right forearm inside his jacket. He completely filled the entrance.

Alleyn said: 'Good evening.'

'Good day. Sir,' said the *mlinzi*.

'I – am – going – in,' said Alleyn very distinctly. When no move was made, he repeated this announcement, tapping his chest and pointing to the door.

The *mlinzi* rolled his eyes, turned smartly, knocked on the door and entered. His huge voice was answered by another, even more resonant and by a matter-of-fact comment from Troy: 'Oh, here's Rory,' Troy said.

The *mlinzi* stood aside and Alleyn, uncertain about the degree of his own exasperation, walked in.

The model's throne was at the far end of the studio.

Hung over a screen Troy used for backgrounds was a lion's skin. In front of it, in full ceremonials, ablaze with decorations, gold lace and accoutrements, legs apart and arms akimbo, stood The Boomer.

Troy, behind a four-foot canvas, was setting her palette. On the floor lay two of her rapid exploratory charcoal drawings. A brush was clenched between her teeth. She turned her head and nodded vigorously at her husband, several times.

'Ho-ho!' shouted The Boomer. 'Excuse me, my dear Rory, that I don't descend. As you see, we are busy. Go away!' he shouted at the *mlinzi* and added something curt in their native tongue. The man went away.

'I apologize for him!' The Boomer said magnificently. 'Since last night he is nervous of my well-being. I allowed him to come.'

'He seems to be favouring his arm.'

'Yes. It turns out that his collar-bone was fractured.'

'Last night?'

'By an assailant, whoever he was.'

'Has he seen a doctor?'

'Oh, yes. The man who looks after the Embassy. A Doctor Gomba. He's quite a good man. Trained at St Luke's.'

'Did he elaborate at all on the injury?'

'A blow, probably with the edge of the hand since there is no indication of a weapon. It's not a break — only a crack.'

'What does the *mlinzi* himself say about it?'

'He has elaborated a little on his rather sparse account of last night. He says that someone struck him on the base of the neck and seized his spear. He has no idea of his assailant's identity. I must apologize,' said The Boomer affably, 'for my unheralded appearance, my dear old man. My stay in London has been curtailed. I am determined that no painter but your wife shall do the portrait and I am impatient to have it. Therefore I cut through the codswallop, as we used to say at Davidson's, and here, as you see, I am.'

Troy removed the brush from between her teeth. 'Stay if you like, darling,' she said and gave her husband one of the infrequent smiles that still afforded him such deep pleasure.

'If I'm not in the way,' he said and contrived not to sound sardonic. Troy shook her head.

'No, no, no,' said The Boomer graciously. 'We are pleased to have your company. It is permitted to converse. Provided,' he added with a bawling laugh, 'that one expects no reply. That is the situation. Am I right *maestro?*' he asked Troy, who did not reply. 'I do not know the feminine of *maestro,*' he confessed. 'One must not say *maestress.* That would be in bad taste.'

Troy made a snuffling noise.

Alleyn sat down in a veteran armchair.

'Since I am here and as long as it doesn't disrupt the proceedings – ' he began.

'Nothing,' The Boomer interposed, 'disrupts *me.*'

'Good. I wonder then if your Excellency can tell me anything about two of your last night's guests.'

'My Excellency can try. He is so ridiculous,' The Boomer parenthesized to Troy, 'with his "Excellencies".' And to Alleyn: 'I have been telling your wife about our times at Davidson's.'

'The couple I mean are a brother and sister called Sanskrit.'

The Boomer had been smiling but his lips now closed over his dazzling teeth. 'I think perhaps I have moved a little,' he said.

'No,' Troy said. 'You are splendidly still.' She began to make dark, sweeping gestures on her canvas.

'Sanskrit,' Alleyn repeated. 'They are enormously fat.'

'Ah! Yes. I know the couple you mean.'

'Is there a link with Ng'ombwana?'

'A commercial one. Yes. They were importers of fancy goods.'

'Were?'

'Were,' said The Boomer without batting an eyelid. 'They sold out.'

'Do you know them personally?'

'They have been presented,' he said.

'Did they want to leave?'

'Presumably not, since they are coming back.'

'What?'

'I believe they are coming back. Some alteration in plans. I understand they intend to return immediately. They are persons of little importance.'

'Boomer,' said Alleyn, 'have they any cause to bear you a grudge?'

'None whatever. Why?'

'It's simply a check-up. After all, it seems somebody tried to murder you at your party.'

'Well, you won't have any luck with them. If anything, they ought to feel grateful.'

'Why?'

'It is under my regime that they return. They had been rather abruptly treated by the previous government.'

'When was the decision taken? To re-instate them?'

'Let me see – a month ago, I should say. More, perhaps.'

'But when I visited you three weeks ago I actually happened to see Sanskrit on the steps outside his erstwhile premises. The name had just been painted out.'

'You're wrong there, my dear Rory. It was, I expect, in process of being painted in again.'

'I see,' said Alleyn and was silent for some seconds. 'Do you like them?' he asked. 'The Sanskrits?'

'No,' said The Boomer. 'I find them disgusting.'

'Well, then – ?'

'The man had been mistakenly expelled. He made out his case,' The Boomer said with a curious air of restraint. 'He has every reason to feel an obligation and none to feel animosity. You may dismiss him from your mind.'

'Before I do, had he any reason to entertain personal animosity against the Ambassador?'

An even longer pause. 'Reason? He? None,' said The Boomer. 'None whatever.' And then: 'I don't know what is in your mind, Rory, but I'm sure that if you think this person could have committed the murder you are – you are

422

– what is the phrase – you will get no joy from such a theory. But,' he added with a return of his jovial manner, 'we should not discuss these beastly affairs before Mrs Alleyn.'

'She hasn't heard us,' said Alleyn simply. From where he sat he could see Troy at work. It was as if her response to her subject was distilled into some sort of essence that flowed down arm, hand and brush to take possession of the canvas. He had never see her work so urgently. She was making that slight breathy noise that he used to say was her inspiration asking to be let out. And what she did was splendid: a mystery in the making. 'She hadn't heard us,' he repeated.

'Has she not?' said The Boomer and added: 'That, I understand. I understand it perfectly.'

And Alleyn experienced a swift upsurge of an emotion that he would have been hard put to it to define. 'Do you Boomer?' he said. 'I believe you do.'

'A fraction more to your left,' said Troy. 'Rory – if you could move your chair. That's done it. Thank you.'

The Boomer patiently maintained his pose and as the minutes went by he and Alleyn had little more to say to each other. There was a kind of precarious restfulness between them.

Soon after half past six Troy said she needed her sitter no more for the present. The Boomer behaved nicely. He suggested that perhaps she would prefer that he didn't see what was happening. She came out of a long stare at her canvas, put her hand in his arm and led him round to look at it, which he did in absolute silence.

'I am greatly obliged to you,' said The Boomer at last.

'And I to you,' said Troy. 'Tomorrow morning, perhaps? While the paint is still wet?'

'Tomorrow morning,' promised The Boomer. 'Everything else is cancelled and nothing is regretted,' and he took his leave.

Alleyn escorted him to the studio door. The *mlinzi* stood at the foot of the steps. In descending Alleyn stumbled and lurched against him. The man gave an indrawn gasp, instantly repressed. Alleyn made remorseful noises and The Boomer, who had gone ahead, turned round.

Alleyn said: 'I've been clumsy. I've hurt him. Do tell him I'm sorry'

'He'll survive!' said The Boomer cheerfully. He said something to the man, who walked ahead into the house. The Boomer chuckled and laid his massive arm across Alleyn's shoulders.

He said: 'He really *has* a fractured collar-bone, you know. Ask Doctor Gomba or, if you like, have a look for yourself. But don't go on concerning yourself over my *mlinzi*. Truly, it's a waste of your valuable time.'

It struck Alleyn that if it came to being concerned, Mr Whipplestone and The Boomer in their several ways were equally worried about the well-being of their dependants. He said: 'All right, all right. But it's you who are my real headache. Look, for the last time, I most earnestly beg you to stop taking risks. I promise you, I honestly believe that there was a plot to kill you last night and that there's every possibility that another attempt will be made.'

'What form will it take do you suppose? A bomb?'

'And you might be right at that. Are you sure, are you absolutely sure, there's nobody at all dubious in the Embassy staff? The servants – '

'I am sure. Not only did your tedious but worthy Gibson's people search the Embassy but my own people did, too. Very, very thoroughly. There are no bombs. And there is not a servant there who is not above suspicion.'

'*How* can you be so sure! If, for instance, a big enough bribe was offered – '

'I shall never make you understand, my dear man. You don't know what I am to my people. It would frighten them less to kill themselves than to touch me. I swear to you that if there was a plot to kill me, it was not organized or inspired by any of these people. No!' he said and his extraordinary voice sounded like a gong. 'Never! It is impossible. No!'

'All right. I'll accept that so long as you don't admit

424

unknown elements, you're safe inside the Embassy. But for God's sake don't go taking that bloody hound for walks in the Park.'

He burst out laughing. 'I am sorry,' he said, actually holding his sides like a clown, 'but I couldn't resist. It was so funny. There they were, so frightened and fussed. Dodging about, those big silly men. No! Admit! It was too funny for words.'

'I hope you find this evening's security measures equally droll.'

'Don't be stuffy,' said The Boomer.

'Would you like a drink before you go?'

'Very much, but I think I should return.'

'I'll just tell Gibson.'

'Where is he?'

'In the study. Damping down his frustration. Will you excuse me?'

Alleyn looked round the study door. Mr Gibson was at ease with a glass of beer at his elbow.

'Going,' Alleyn said.

He rose and followed Alleyn into the hall.

'Ah!' said The Boomer graciously. 'Mr Gibson. Here we go again, don't we, Mr Gibson?'

'That's right, your Excellency,' said Gibson tonelessly. 'Here we go again. Excuse me.'

He went out into the street, leaving the door open.

'I look forward to the next sitting,' said The Boomer, rubbing his hands. 'Immeasurably, I shall see you then, old boy. In the morning? Shan't I?'

'Not very likely, I'm afraid.'

'No?'

'I'm rather busy on a case,' Alleyn said politely. 'Troy will do the honours for both of us, if you'll forgive me.'

'Good, good, good!' he said genially. Alleyn escorted him to the car. The *mlinzi* opened the door with his left hand. The police car started up its engine and Gibson got into it. The Special Branch men moved. At the open end of the cul-de-sac a body of police kept back a sizeable crowd Groups of residents had collected in the little street.

A dark, pale and completely bald man, well-dressed in formal clothes, who had been reading a paper at a table outside the little pub, put on his hat and strolled away. Several people crossed the street. The policeman on duty asked them to stand back.

'What *is* all this?' asked The Boomer.

'Perhaps it has escaped your notice that the media has not been idle. There's a front page spread with banner headlines in the evening papers.'

'I would have thought they had something better to do with the space.' He slapped Alleyn on the back. 'Bless you,' he roared. He got into the car, shouted, 'I'll be back at half past nine in the morning. Do try to be at home,' and was driven off. 'Bless *you*,' Alleyn muttered to the gracious salutes The Boomer had begun to turn on for the benefit of the bystanders. 'God knows you need it.'

The police car led the way, turning off into a side exit which would bring them eventually into the main street. The Ng'ombwanan car followed it. There were frustrated manifestations from the crowd at the far end which gradually dispersed. Alleyn, full of misgivings, went back to the house. He mixed two drinks and took them to the studio, where he found Troy still in her painting smock, stretched out in an armchair scowling at her canvas. On such occasions she always made him think of a small boy. A short lock of hair overhung her forehead, her hands were painty and her expression brooding. She got up, abruptly, returned to her easel and swept down a black line behind the head that started up from its tawny surroundings. She then backed away towards him. He moved aside and she saw him.

'How about it?' she asked.

'I've never known you so quick. It's staggering.'

'Too quick to be right?'

'How can you say such a thing? It's witchcraft.'

She leant against him. 'He's wonderful,' she said. 'Like a symbol of blackness. And there's something – almost desperate. Tragic? Lonely? I don't know. I hope it happens on that thing over there.'

'It's begun to happen. So we forget the comic element?'

'Oh that! Yes, of course, he is terribly funny. Victorian music-hall, almost. But I feel it's just a kind of trimming. Not important. Is that my drink?'

'Troy, my darling, I'm going to ask you something irritating.'

She had taken her drink to the easel and was glowering over the top of her glass at the canvas. 'Are you?' she said vaguely. 'What?'

'He's sitting for you again in the morning. Between now and then I want you not to let anybody or anything you don't know come into the house. No gas-meter inspectors or window-cleaners, no parcels addressed in strange hands. No local body representatives. Nothing and nobody that you can't account for.'

Troy, still absently, said, 'All right,' and then suddenly aware: 'Are you talking about *bombs?*'

'Yes, I am.'

'Good Lord!'

'It's not a silly notion, you know. Well, is it?'

'It's a jolly boring one, though.'

'Promise.'

'All right,' Troy said, and squeezed out a dollop of cadmium red on her palette. She put down her drink and took up a brush.

Alleyn wondered how the hell one kept one's priorities straight. He watched her nervous, paint-stained hand poise the brush and then use it with the authority of a fiddler. What she's up to, he thought, and what I am supposed to be up to are a stellar journey apart and yet ours, miraculously, is a happy marriage. Why?

Troy turned round and looked at him. 'I was listening,' she said, 'I do promise.'

'Well – thank you, my love,' he said.

That evening, at about the same time as The Boomer dined royally at Buckingham Palace, Alleyn, with Fox in attendance, set out to keep observation upon Mr Sheridan in his basement flat at No. 1a, Capricorn Walk. They drove there in a 'nondescript' equipped with a multi-channel radio set. Alleyn remembered that there had been some talk of Mr Whipplestone dining with his sister who had come up to London for the night, so there was no question of attracting his attention.

They had been advised by a panda on Unit Beat that the occupant of the basement flat was at home but his window curtains must be very heavy because they completely excluded the light. Alleyn and Fox approached from Capricorn Square and parked in the shadow of the plane trees. The evening was sultry and overcast and the precincts were given over to their customary quietude. From the Sun in Splendour, further back in the Square, came the sound of voices, not very loud.

'Hold on a bit. I'm in two minds about this one, Fox.' Alleyn said. 'It's a question of whether the coterie as a whole is concerned in last night's abortive attempt if that's what it was, or whether Mrs C-M and the Colonel acted quite independently under their own alcoholic steam. Which seems unlikely. If it was a concerted affair they may very well have called a meeting to review the situation. Quite possibly to cook up another attempt.'

'Or to fall out among themselves,' said Fox.

'Indeed. Or to fall out.'

'Suppose, for instance,' Fox said in his plain way, 'Chubb did the job, thinking it was the President: they won't be best pleased with *him*. And you tell me he seems to be nervous.'

'Very nervous.'

'What's in your mind, then? For now?'

'I thought we might lurk here for a bit to see if Mr Sheridan has any callers or if, alternatively, he himself steps out to take the air.'

'Do you know what he looks like?'

'Sam Whipplestone says he's dark, bald, middle height, well-dressed and speaks with a lisp. I've never seen him to my knowledge.' A pause. 'He's peeping,' said Alleyn.

A vertical sliver of light had appeared in the basement windows of No. 1a. After a second or two it was shut off.

'I wouldn't have thought,' Fox said, 'they'd fancy those premises for a meeting. Under the circs. With Mr Whipplestone living up above and all.'

'Nor would I.'

Fox grunted comfortably and settled down in his seat. Several cars passed down Capricorn Walk towards Baronsgate, the last being a taxi which stopped at No. 1. A further half-dozen cars followed by a delivery van passed between the watchers and the taxi and were held up, presumably by a block in Baronsgate itself. It was one of those sudden and rare incursions of traffic into the quiet of the Capricorns at night. When it had cleared a figure was revealed coming through the gate at the top of the basement steps at No. 1: a man in a dark suit and scarf wearing a 'City' hat. He set off down the Walk in the direction of Baronsgate. Alleyn waited for a little and then drove forward. he turned the corner, passed No. 1 and parked three houses further along.

'He's going into the Mews,' he said. And, sure enough, Mr Sheridan crossed the street, turned right and disappeared.

'What price he's making a call on the pottery pigs?' Alleyn asked. 'Or do you fancy the gallant Colonel and his lady? Hold on, Fox.'

He left Fox in the car, crossed the street and walked rapidly past the Mews for some twenty yards. He then stopped and returned to a small house-decorator's shop on the corner where he was able to look through the double windows down the Mews past the Napoli and the opening into Capricorn Place, where the Cockburn-Montforts lived, to the pottery at the far end. Mr Sheridan kept straight on, in and out of the rather sparse lighting until he reached the pottery. Here he stopped at a side-door, looked about him and raised his hand to the bell. The door was opened on a dim interior by an unmistakable vast shape. Mr Sheridan entered and the door was shut.

Alleyn returned to the car.

'That's it,' he said. 'The piggery it is. Away we go. We've got to play this carefully. He's on the alert, is Mr S.'

At the garage where Mr Whipplestone first met Lucy Lockett there was a very dark alley leading into a yard. Alleyn backed the car into it, stopped the engine and put out the lights. He and Fox opened the doors, broke into drunken laughter, shouted indistinguishably, banged the doors and settled down in their seats.

They had not long to wait before Colonel and Mrs Cockburn-Montfort turned out of Capricorn Place and passed them on the far side of the Mews, she teetering on preposterous heels, he marching with the preternatural accuracy of the seasoned toper.

They were admitted into the same door by the same vast shape.

'One to come,' Alleyn said, 'unless he's there already.'

But he was not there already. Nobody else passed up or down the Mews for perhaps a minute. The clock in the Basilica struck nine and the last note was followed by approaching footsteps on their side of the street. Alleyn and Fox slid down in their seats. The steps, making the customary rather theatrical, rather disturbing effect of footfalls in dark streets, approached at a brisk pace and Chubb passed by on his way to the pottery.

When he had been admitted Alleyn said: 'We don't, by the way, know if there are any more members, do we? Some unknown quantity?'

'What about it?'

'Wait and see, I suppose. It's very tempting, you know, Br'er Fox, to let them warm up a bit and then make an official call and politely scare the pants off them. It would stop any further attempts from that quarter on The

Boomer unless, of course, there's a fanatic among them and I wouldn't put that past Chubb for one.'

'Do we try it, then?'

'Regretfully, we don't. We haven't got enough on any of them to make an arrest and we'd lose all chances of finally roping them in. Pity! Pity!'

'So what's the form?'

'Well, I think we wait until they break up and then, however late the hour, we might even call upon Mr Sheridan. Somebody coming,' Alleyn said.

'Your unknown quantity?'

'I wonder.'

It was a light footstep this time and approached rapidly on the far side of the Mews. There was a street lamp at the corner of Capricorn Place. The newcomer walked into its ambit and crossed the road coming straight towards them.

It was Samuel Whipplestone.

III

'Well, of course,' Alleyn thought. 'He's going for his evening constitutional, but why did he tell me he was dining with his sister?'

Fox sat quiet at his side. They waited in the dark for Mr Whipplestone to turn and continue his walk.

But he stopped and peered directly into the alleyway. For a moment Alleyn had the uncanny impression that they looked straight into each other's eyes and then Mr Whipplestone, slipping past the bonnet of the car, tapped discreetly on the driver's window.

Alleyn let it down.

'May I get in?' asked Mr Whipplestone. 'I think it may be important.'

'All right. But keep quiet if anybody comes. Don't bang the door, will you? What's up?'

Mr Whipplestone began to talk very rapidly and precisely in a breathy undertone, leaning forward so that his head was almost between the heads of his listeners.

'I came home early,' he said. 'My sister Edith had a migraine. I arrived by taxi and had just let myself in when I heard the basement door close and someone came up the steps. I dare say I've become hypersensitive to any occurrences down there. I went into the drawing-room and without turning on the lights watched Sheridan open the area gate and look about him. He was wearing a hat but for a moment or two his face was lit by the headlamps of one of some half-dozen cars that had been halted. I saw him very clearly. Very, very clearly. He was scowling. I think I mentioned to you that I've been nagged by the impression that I had seen him before, I'll return to that in a moment.'

'So,' said Alleyn.

'I was still there, at my window, when this car pulled out of the square from the shadow of the trees, turned right and parked a few doors away from me. I noticed the number.'

'Ah!' said Alleyn.

'This was just as Sheridan disappeared up the Mews. The driver got out of the car and — but I need not elaborate.'

'I was rumbled.'

'Well — yes. If you like to put it that way. I saw you station yourself at the corner and then return to this car. And I saw you drive into the Mews. Of course, I was intrigued but believe me, Alleyn, I had no thought of interfering or indulging in any — ah — ah — '

'Counter-espionage?'

'Oh, my dear fellow! Well. I turned away from my window and was about to put on the lights when I heard Chubb coming down the stairs. I heard him walk along the hall and stop by the drawing-room door. Only for a moment. I was in two minds whether to put on the lights and say, "Oh, Chubb, I'm in," or something of that sort, or to let him go. So uncomfortable has the atmosphere been that I decided on the latter course. He went out, double-

432

locked the door and walked off in the same direction as Sheridan. And you. Into the Mews.'

Mr Whipplestone paused, whether for dramatic effect or in search of the precise mode of expression, he being invisible, it was impossible to determine.

'It was then,' he said, 'that I remembered. Why, at that particular moment the penny should drop, I have no notion. But drop it did.'

'You remembered?'

'About Sheridan.'

'Ah.'

'I remembered where I had seen him. Twenty-odd years ago. In Ng'ombwana.'

Fox suddenly let out a vast sigh.

'Go on,' said Alleyn.

'It was a court of law. British law, of course, at that period. And Sheridan was in the dock.'

'Was he indeed!'

'He had another name in those days. He was reputed to come from Portuguese East and he was called Manuel Gomez. He owned extensive coffee plantations. He was found guilty of manslaughter. One of his workers – it was a revolting business – had been chained to a tree and beaten and had died of gangrene.'

Fox clicked his tongue several times.

'And that is not all. My dear Alleyn, for the prosecution there was a young Ng'ombwanan barrister who had qualified in London – the first, I believe, to do so.'

'The Boomer, by God.'

'Precisely. I seem to recollect that he pressed with great tenacity for a sentence of murder and the death penalty.'

'What *was* the sentence?'

'I don't remember – something like fifteen years, I fancy. The plantation is now in the hands of the present government, of course, but I remember Gomez was said to have salted away a fortune. In Portugal, I think. It may have been London. I am not certain of these details.'

'You *are* certain of the man?'

'Absolutely. And of the barrister. I attended the trial, I have a diary that I kept at that time and a pretty extensive scrapbook. We can verify. But I am certain. He was scowling in the light from the car. The whole thing flashed up most vividly, those one or two minutes later.'

'That's what actors call a double-take.'

'Do they?' Mr Whipplestone said absently, and then: 'He made a scene when he was sentenced. I'd never seen anything like it. It left an extraordinary impression.'

'Violent?'

'Oh yes, indeed. Screaming. Threatening. He had to be handcuffed and even then — It was like an animal,' said Mr Whipplestone.

'Fair enough,' Fox rumbled, pursuing some inward cogitation.

'You don't ask me,' Mr Whipplestone murmured, 'why I took the action I did. Following you here.'

'Why did you?'

'I felt sure *you* had followed *Sheridan* because you thought, as I did, that probably there was to be a meeting of these people. Whether at the Cockburn-Montforts' or at the Sanskrits' flat. And I felt most unhappily sure that Chubb was going to join them. I had and have no idea whether you actually intended to break in upon the assembly but I thought it might well be that this intelligence would be of importance. I saw Chubb being admitted to that place. I followed, expecting you would be somewhere in the Mews and I made out your car. So here I am, you see,' said Mr Whipplestone.

'Here you are and the man without motive is now supplied with what might even turn out to be the prime motive.'

'That,' said Mr Whipplestone, 'is what I rather thought.'

'You may say,' Fox ruminated, 'that, as far as motives go, it's now one apiece. Chubb: the daughter. The Sanskrits: losing their business. Sheridan — well, ask yourself. And the Colonel and Mrs C-M — what about them?'

434

'The Boomer tells me the Colonel was livid at getting the sack. He'd seen himself rigged out as a Field Marshal or as near as dammit. Instead of which he went into retirement and the bottle.'

'Would these motives apply,' Fox asked, 'equally to the Ambassador and the President? As victims, I mean.'

'Not in Sheridan's case, it would appear.'

'No,' Mr Whipplestone agreed. 'Not in this case.'

They were silent for a space. At last Alleyn said: 'I think this is what we do. We leave you here, Br'er Fox, keeping what I'm afraid may prove to be utterly fruitless observation. We don't know what decision they'll come to in the piggery-flat or indeed what exactly they're there to decide. Another go at The Boomer? The liquidation of the Ku-Klux-Fish or whatever it is? It's anybody's guess. But it's just possible you may pick up something. And, Sam, if you can stand up to another late night, I'd very much like to look at those records of yours.'

'Of course. Only too glad.'

'Shall we go, then?'

They had got out of the car when Alleyn put his head in at the window. 'The Sanskrits don't fit,' he said.

'No?' said Fox. 'No motive, d'you mean?'

'That's right. The Boomer told me that Sanskrit's been reinstated in his emporium in Ng'ombwana. Remember?'

'Now, that is peculiar,' said Fox. 'I'd overlooked that.'

'Something for you to brood on,' Alleyn said. 'We'll be in touch.'

He put his walkie-talkie in his pocket and he and Mr Whipplestone returned to No. 1, The Walk.

There was a card on the hall-table with the word OUT neatly printed on it. 'We leave it there to let each other know,' Mr Whipplestone explained. 'On account of the door chain.' He turned the card over to show 'IN', ushered Alleyn into the drawing-room, shut the door and turned on the lights.

'Do let's have a drink,' he said. 'Whisky and soda? I'll just get the soda. Sit down, do. I won't be a jiffy.'

He went out with something of his old sprightly air.

He had turned on the light above the picture over the fireplace. Troy had painted it quite a long time ago. It was a jubilant landscape half-way to being an abstract. Alleyn remembered it very well.

'Ah!' said Mr Whipplestone returning with a siphon in his hands and Lucy weaving in and out between his feet. 'You're looking at my treasure. I acquired it at one of the Group shows, not long after you married, I think. Look *out,* cat, for pity's sake! Now: shall we go into the dining-room where I can lay out the exhibits on the table? But first, our drinks. You begin yours while I search.'

'Steady with the scotch. I'm supposed to keep a clear head. Would you mind if I rang Troy up?'

'Do, do, do. Over there on the desk. The box I want is upstairs. It'll take a little digging out.'

Troy answered the telephone almost at once. 'Hello, where are you?' Alleyn asked.

'In the studio.'

'Broody?'

'That's right.'

'I'm at Sam Whipplestone's and will be, most probably, for the next hour or so. Have you got a pencil handy?'

'Wait a bit.'

He had a picture of her feeling about in the pocket of her painting smock.

'I've got a bit of charcoal,' she said.

'It's only to write down the number.'

'Hold on. Right.'

He gave it to her. 'In case anyone wants me,' he said. 'You, for instance.'

'Rory?'

'What?'

'Do you mind very much? About me painting The Boomer? Are you there?'

'I'm here, all right. I delight in what you're doing and I deplore the circumstances under which you're doing it.'

'Well,' said Troy, 'that's a straight answer to a straight question. Good night, darling.'

436

'Good night,' he said, 'darling.'

Mr Whipplestone was gone for some considerable time. At last he returned with a large, old-fashioned photograph album and an envelope full of press cuttings. He opened the connecting doors to the dining-room, laid his findings out on the table and displaced Lucy who affected a wayward interest in them.

'I was a great hoarder in those days,' he said. 'Everything's in order and dated. There should be no difficulty.'

There was none. Alleyn examined the album which had the faded melancholy aspect of all such collections while Mr Whipplestone looked through the cuttings. When the latter applied to items in the former, they had been carefully pasted beside the appropriate photographs. It was Alleyn who first struck oil.

'Here we are,' he said. And there, meticulously dated and annotated in Mr Whipplestone's neat hand, were three photographs and a yellowing page from the *Ng'ombwana Times* with the headline: 'Gomez trial. Verdict. Scene in Court.'

The photographs showed, respectively, a snapshot of a bewigged judge emerging from a dark interior, a crowd, mostly composed of black people, waiting outside a sun-baked court of justice, and an open car driven by a black chauffeur with two passengers in tropical kit, one of whom, a trim, decorous-looking person of about forty, was recognizable as Mr Whipplestone himself. 'Going to the Trial.' The press photographs were more explicit. There, unmistakably himself, in wig and gown, was the young Boomer. 'Mr Bartholomew Opala, Counsel for the Prosecution.' And there, already partially bald, dark, furious and snarling, a man handcuffed between two enormous black policemen and protected from a clearly menacing crowd of Ng'ombwanans. 'After the Verdict. The Prisoner,' said the caption, 'Leaving the Court.'

The letterpress carried an account of the trial with full journalistic appreciation of its dramatic highlights. There was also an editorial.

'And that,' Alleyn said, 'is the self-same Sheridan in your basement flat.'

'You would recognize him at once?'

'Yes. I thought I'd seen him for the first time – and that dimly – tonight, but it turns out that it was my second glimpse. He was sitting outside the pub this afternoon when The Boomer called on Troy.'

'No doubt,' said Mr Whipplestone drily, 'you will be seeing quite a lot more of him. I don't like this, Alleyn.'

'How do you think I enjoy it!' said Alleyn, who was reading the press cutting. 'The vows of vengeance,' he said, 'are quite Marlovian in their inventiveness, aren't they?'

'You should have heard them! And every one directed at your Boomer,' said Mr Whipplestone. He bent over the album. 'I don't suppose I've looked at this,' he said, 'for over a decade. It was stowed away in a trunk with a lot of others in my old flat. Even so, I might have remembered, one would have thought.'

'I expect he's changed. After all – twenty years!'

'He hasn't changed all that much in looks and I can't believe he's changed at all in temperament.'

'And you've no notion what became of him when he got out?'

'None. Portuguese East, perhaps. Or South America. Or a change of name. Ultimately, by fair means or foul, a British passport.'

'And finally whatever he does in the City?'

'Imports coffee perhaps,' sniffed Mr Whipplestone.

'His English is non-committal?'

'Oh, yes. No accent, unless you count a lisp which I suppose is a hangover. Let me give you a drink.'

'Not another, thank you, Sam. I must keep my wits about me, such as they are.' He hesitated for a moment and then said: 'There's one thing I think perhaps you should know. It's about the Chubbs. But before I go any further I'm going to ask you, very seriously indeed, to give an undertaking not to let what I tell you make any difference –

438

any difference at all — to your normal manner with the Chubbs. If you'd rather not make a blind commitment like this, then I'll keep my big mouth shut and no bones broken.'

Mr Whipplestone said quietly: 'Is is to their discredit?'

'No,' Alleyn said slowly, 'not directly. Not specifically. No.'

'I have been trained in discretion.'

'I know.'

'You may depend upon me.'

'I'm sure I can,' Alleyn said, and told Mr Whipplestone about the girl in the photograph. For quite a long time after Alleyn had finished he made no reply and then he took a turn about the room and said, more to himself than to Alleyn: 'That is a dreadful thing. I am very sorry. My poor Chubbs.' And after another pause. 'Of course, you see this as a motive.'

'A possible one. No more than that.'

'Yes. Thank you for telling me. It will make no difference.'

'Good. And now I mustn't keep you up any longer. It's almost midnight. I'll just give Fox a shout.'

Fox came through loud, clear and patient on the radio.

'Dead on cue, Mr Alleyn,' he said. 'Nothing till now but I think they're breaking up. A light in a staircase window. Keep with me.'

'Right you are,' said Alleyn and waited. He said to Mr Whipplestone. 'The party's over. We'll have Sheridan-Gomez and Chubb back in a minute.'

'Hullo,' said Fox.

'Yes?'

'Here they come. The Cockburn-Montforts. Far side of the street from me. Not talking. Chubb, this side, walking fast. Hold on. Wait for it, Mr Alleyn.'

'All right.'

Alleyn could hear the advancing and retreating steps.

'There he goes,' Fox said. 'He'll be with you in a minute and now, here comes Mr Sheridan, on his own. Far side of the street. The C-Ms have turned their corner. I caught a

439

bit of one remark. From her. She said, "I was a fool. I knew at the time," and he seemed to shut her up. That's all. Over and – hold on. Hold on, Mr Alleyn.'

'What?'

'The door into the Sanskrit premises. Opening a crack. No light beyond but it's opening all right. They're being watched off.'

'Keep with it, Fox. Give me a shout if there's anything more. Otherwise, I'll join you in a few minutes. Over and out.'

Alleyn waited with Mr Whipplestone for about three minutes before they heard Chubb's rapid step, followed by the sound of his key in the lock.

'Do you want to see him?' Mr Whipplestone murmured. Alleyn shook his head. They heard the chain rattle. Chubb paused for a moment in the hall and then went upstairs.

Another minute and the area gate clicked. Mr Sheridan could be heard to descend and enter.

'There he goes,' said Mr Whipplestone, 'and there he'll be, rather like a bomb in my basement. I can't say I relish the thought.'

'Nor should I, particularly. If it's any consolation I don't imagine he'll be there for long.'

'No?'

'Well, I hope not. Before I leave you I'm going to try, if I may, to get on to Gibson. We'll have a round-the-clock watch on Gomez-cum-Sheridan until further notice.'

He roused Gibson, with apologies, from his beauty sleep and told him what he'd done, what he proposed to do and what he would like Gibson to do for him.

'And now,' he said, to Mr Whipplestone, 'I'll get back to my patient old Fox. Goodnight. And thank you. Keep the scrapbook handy, if you will.'

'Of course, I'll let you out.'

He did so, being, Alleyn noticed, careful to make no noise with the chain and to shut the door softly behind him.

As he walked down Capricorn Mews, which he did firmly and openly, Alleyn saw that there were a few more

440

cars parked in it and that most of the little houses and the flats were dark now, including the flat over the pottery. When he reached the car and slipped into the passenger's seat, Fox said: 'The door was on the chink for about ten seconds and then he shut it. You could just make it out. Light catching the brass knocker. Nothing in it, I dare say. But it looked a bit funny. Do we call off the obbo, then?'

'You'd better hear this bit first.'

And he told Fox about the scrap-book and Mr Sheridan's past.

'Get away!' Fox said cosily. 'Fancy that now! So we've got a couple of right villains in the club. Him and Sanskrit. It's getting interesting, Mr Alleyn, isn't it?'

'Glad you're enjoying yourself, Br'er Fox. For my part I – ' He broke off. 'Look at this!' he whispered.

The street door of the Sanskrits' flat had opened and through it came, unmistakably, the elephantine bulk of Sanskrit himself, wearing a longish overcoat and a soft hat.

'*Now* what's he think he's doing!' breathed Mr Fox.

The door was locked, the figure turned outwards and for a moment the great bladder-like face caught the light. Then he came along the Mews, walking lightly as fat people so often do, and disappeared down Capricorn Place.

'That's where the C-Ms hang out,' said Fox.

'It's also the way to Palace Park Gardens where The Boomer hangs out. How long is it since you tailed your man, Fox?'

'Well – '

'We're off on a refresher course. Come on.'

Keeping Obbo

Fox drove slowly across the opening into Capricorn Place.

'There he goes. Not into the C-Ms, though, I'm sure,' said Alleyn. 'Their lights are out and he's walking on the opposite side in deep shadow. Stop for a moment, Fox. Yes. He's not risking going past the house. Or is he? Look at that, Fox.'

A belated taxi drove slowly towards them up Capricorn Place. The driver seemed to be looking for a number. It stopped. The huge bulk of Sanskrit, scarcely perceptible in the shadows, light as a fairy, flitted on, the taxi screening it from the house.

'On you go, Fox. He's heading for the brick wall at the far end. We go left, left again into the Square, then right, and left again. Stop before you get to Capricorn Place.'

Fox executed this flanking manoeuvre. They passed by No. 1, The Walk, where Mr Whipplestone's bedroom light glowed behind his curtains, and by the Sun in Splendour, now in eclipse. They drove along the far end of the Square, turned left, continued a little way further and parked.

'That's Capricorn Place ahead,' said Alleyn. 'It ends in a brick wall with an opening into a narrow walk. That walk goes behind the Basilica and leads by an alleyway into Palace Park Gardens. It's my bet this is where he's heading but I freely admit it's a pretty chancy shot. Here he comes.'

He crossed the intersection rather like a walking tent with his buoyant fat-man's stride. They gave him a few seconds and then left the car and followed.

There was no sign of him when they turned the corner but his light footfall could be heard on the far side of the wall. Alleyn jerked his head at the gateway. They passed through it and were just in time to see him disappear round a distant corner.

'This is it,' Alleyn said. 'Quick, Fox, and on your toes.'

They sprinted down the walk, checked, turned quietly into the alleyway and had a pretty clear view of Sanskrit at the far end of it. Beyond him, vaguely declaiming itself, was a thoroughfare and the façade of an impressive house, from the second floor balcony of which protruded a flag-pole. Two policemen stood by the entrance.

They moved into a dark doorway and watched.

'He's walking up as cool as you like!' Fox whispered.

'So he is.'

'Going to hand something in, is he?'

'He's showing something to the coppers. Gibson cooked up a pass system with the Embassy. Issued to their staff and immediate associates with the President's cachet. Quite an elaborate job. It may be, he's showing it.'

'Why would he qualify?'

'Well may you ask. Look at this, will you?'

Sanskrit had produced something that appeared to be an envelope. One of the policemen turned on his torch. It flashed from Sanskrit's face to his hands. The policeman bent his head and the light, dimmed, shone briefly up into his face. A pause. The officer nodded to his mate who rang the doorbell. It was opened by a Ng'ombwanan in livery: presumably a night-porter. Sanskrit appeared to speak briefly to the man, who listened, took the envelope, if that was what it was, stepped back and shut the door after him.

'That was quick!' Fox remarked.

'Now he's chatting to the coppers.'

They caught a faint high-pitched voice and the two policemen's 'Good night, sir.'

'Boldly does it, Br'er Fox,' said Alleyn. They set off down the alleyway.

There was a narrow footpath on their side. As the enormous tent figure, grotesque in the uncertain darkness, flounced towards them, it moved into the centre of the passage.

Alleyn said to Fox, as they passed it: 'As such affairs go I suppose it was all right. I hope you weren't too bored.'

'Oh no,' said Fox. 'I'm thinking of joining.'

'Are you? Good.'

They walked on until they came to the Embassy. Sanskrit's light footfalls died away in the distance. He had, presumably, gone back through the hole in the wall.

Alleyn and Fox went up to the two constables.

Alleyn said: 'Superintendent Alleyn, C Department.'

'Sir,' they said.

'I want as accurate and full an account of that incident as you can give me. Did you get the man's name? You?' he said to the constable who had seemed to be the more involved.

'No, sir. He carried the special pass, sir.'

'You took a good look at it?'

'Yes, sir.'

'But you didn't read the name?'

'I – I don't – I didn't quite get it, sir. It began with S and there was a K in it. "San" something, sir. It was all in order, sir, with his photograph on it, like a passport. You couldn't miss it being him. He didn't want to be admitted, sir. Only for the door to be answered. If he'd asked for admittance I'd have noted the name.'

'You should have noted it in any case.'

'Sir.'

'What precisely did he say?'

'He said he had a message to deliver, sir. It was for the First Secretary. He produced it and I examined it, sir. It was addressed to the First Secretary and had "For His Excellency The President's attention" written in the corner. It was a fairly stout manilla envelope, sir, but the contents appeared to me to be slight, sir.'

'Well?'

'I said it was an unusual sort of time to deliver it. I said he could hand it over to me and I'd attend to it, sir, but he

444

said he'd promised to deliver it personally. It was a photograph, he said, that the President had wanted developed and printed very particular and urgent and a special effort had been made to get it done and it was only processed half an hour ago. He said he'd been instructed to hand it to the night-porter for the First Secretary.'

'Yes?'

'Yes. Well, I took it and put it over my torch, sir, and that showed up the shape of some rigid object like a cardboard folder inside it. There wasn't any chance of it being one of those funny ones, sir, and he *had* got a Special Pass and so we allowed it and – well, sir, that's all, really.'

'And you,' Alleyn said to the other man, 'rang the bell?'

'Sir.'

'Anything said when the night-porter answered it?'

'I don't think he speaks English, sir. Him and the bearer had a word or two in the native language I suppose it was. And then he just took delivery and shut the door and the bearer gave us good night and left.'

Mr Fox, throughout this interview, had gazed immovably, and to their obvious discomfort, at whichever of the constables was speaking. When they had finished he said in a sepulchral voice to nobody in particular that he wouldn't be surprised if this matter wasn't Taken Further upon which their demeanour became utterly wooden.

Alleyn said: 'You should have reported this at once. You're bloody lucky Mr Gibson doesn't know about it.'

They said in unison: 'Thank you very much, sir.'

'For what?' Alleyn said.

'Will you pass it on to Fred Gibson?' Fox asked as they walked back the way they had come.

'The incident? Yes. But I won't bear down on the handling of it. I ought to. Although it was tricky, that situation. He's got the Embassy go-ahead with his special pass. The copper had been told that anybody carrying one was *persona grata*. He'd have been taking quite a chance, if

445

he'd refused.' Alleyn put his hand on Fox's arm. 'Look at that,' he said. 'Where did that come from?'

At the far end of the long alleyway, in deep shadow, someone moved away from them. Even as they glimpsed it, the figure slipped round the corner and out of sight. They could hear the soft thud of hurrying feet. They sprinted down the alley and turned the corner but there was no one to be seen.

'Could have come out of one of these houses and be chasing after a cab,' Fox said.

'They're all dark.'

'Yes.'

'And no sound of a cab. Did you get an impression?'

'No. Hat. Overcoat. Rubber soles. Trousers. I wouldn't even swear to the sex. It was too quick.'

'Damn,' Alleyn said and they walked on in silence.

'It would be nice to know what was in the envelope,' Fox said at last.

'That's the understatement of a lifetime.'

'Will you ask?'

'You bet I will.'

'The President?'

'Who else? And at the crack of dawn, I dare say, like it or lump it. Fox.' Alleyn said, 'I've been visited by a very disturbing notion.'

'Is that so, Mr Alleyn?' Fox placidly rejoined.

'And I'll be obliged if you'll just listen while I run through all the disjointed bits of information we have about this horrid fat man and see if some kind of pattern comes through in the end.'

'Be pleased to,' said Fox.

He listened with calm approval as they walked back into the now deserted Capricorns to pick up their car. When they were seated in it Alleyn said: 'There you are, Br'er Fox. Now then. By and large: what emerges?'

Fox laid his broad palm across his short moustache and then looked at it as if he expected it to have picked up an impression.

'I see what you're getting at,' he said. 'I think.'

446

'What I'm getting at,' Alleyn said, 'is — fairly simply —
this — '

II

Alleyn's threat to talk to The Boomer at the crack of dawn
was not intended to be, nor was it, taken literally. In the
event, he himself was roused by Mr Gibson wanting to
know if it really was true that the President was giving Troy
another sitting at half past nine. When Alleyn confirmed
this, Gibson's windy sighs whistled in the receiver. He said
he supposed Alleyn had seen the morning's popular press
and on Alleyn saying not yet, informed him that in each
instance the front page carried a by-lined three-column
spread with photographs of yesterday's visit by The
Boomer. Gibson in a dreary voice began to quote some of
the more offensive pieces of journalese. 'Rum Proceedings?
Handsome Super's Famous Wife and African Dictator.'
Alleyn, grinding his teeth, begged him to desist and he did
so, merely observing that all things considered he wondered
why Alleyn fancied the portrait proposition.

Alleyn felt it would be inappropriate to say that stopping
the portrait would in itself be a form of homicide. He
switched to the Sanskrit incident and learnt that it had
been reported to Gibson. Alleyn outlined his and Fox's
investigations and the conclusions he had drawn from
them.

'It seems to look,' Mr Gibson mumbled, 'as if things
might be coming to a head.'

'Keep your fingers crossed. I'm getting a search warrant.
On the off-chance.'

'Always looks "active", applying for a warrant. By the
way, the body's gone.'

'What?'

'The deceased. Just before first light. It was kept very
quiet. Back entrance. Nondescript van. Special plane. All
passed off nice and smooth. One drop of grief the less,' said
Mr Gibson.

447

'You may have to keep obbo at the airport, Fred. Outgoing planes for Ng'ombwana,'

'Any time. You name it,' he said dismally.

'From now. We'll be in touch.' Alleyn said and they rang off.

Troy was in the studio making statements on the background. He told her that yesterday's protective measures would be repeated and that if possible he himself would be back before The Boomer arrived.

'That'll be fine,' she said. 'Sit where you did before, Rory, would you, darling? He's marvellous when he focuses on you.'

'You've got the cheek of the devil. Do you know that everybody but you thinks I'm out of my senses to let you go on with this?'

'Yes, but then you're you, aren't you, and you know how things are. And truly – it is – isn't it? – going – you know? Don't say it, but – isn't it?'

He said: 'It is. Strange as it may sound, I hardly dare look. It's leapt out of the end of your brush.'

She gave him a kiss. 'I *am* grateful,' she said. 'You know, don't you?'

He went to the Yard in a pleasant if apprehensive state of mind and found a message from Mr Whipplestone asking him to ring without delay. He put through the call and was answered at once.

'I thought you should know,' Mr Whipplestone began and the phrase had become familiar. He hurried on to say that, confronted by a leaking water-pipe, he had called at his land agents, Messrs Able & Virtue, at ten past nine o'clock that morning to ask if they could recommend a plumber. He found Sanskrit already there and talking to the young man with Pre-Raphaelite hair. When he saw Mr Whipplestone, Sanskrit had stopped short and then said in a counter-tenor voice that he would leave everything to them and they were to do the best they could for him.

The young man had said there would be no difficulty as there was always a demand in the Capricorns. Sanskrit said something indistinguishable and rather hurriedly left the offices.

'I asked casually,' said Mr Whipplestone, 'if the pottery premises were by any chance to let. I said I had friends who were flat-hunting. This produced a curious awkwardness on the part of the lady attendant and the young man. The lady said something about the place not being officially on the market as yet and in any case if it did come up it would be for sale rather than to let. The present occupant, she said, didn't want it made known for the time being. This, as you may imagine, intrigued me. When I left the agents I walked down Capricorn Mews to the Piggery. It had a notice on the door. "Closed for stocktaking". There are some very ramshackle curtains drawn across the shop window but they don't quite meet. I peered in. It was very ill-lit but I got the impression of some large person moving about among packing cases.'

'Did you, by George!'

'Yes. And on my way home I called in at the Napoli for some of their pâté. While I was there the Cockburn-Montforts came in. He was, I thought, rather more than three sheets in the wind but, as usual, holding it. She looked awful.'

Mr Whipplestone paused for so long that Alleyn said: 'Are you there, Sam?'

'Yes,' he said, 'yes, I am. To be frank, I'm wondering what you're going to think of my next move. Be quiet, Lucy. I don't habitually act on impulse. Far from it.'

'Very far, I'd have thought.'

'Although lately – However, I did act impulsively on this occasion. Very. I wanted to get a reaction. I gave them good morning, of course, and then, quite casually, you know, as I took my pâté from Mrs Pirelli, I said: 'I believe you're losing some neighbours, Mrs Pirelli?' She looked nonplussed. I said: 'Yes. The people at the Pig-pottery. They're leaving, almost at once, I hear.' This was not, of course, strictly true.'

'I wouldn't be so sure.'

'No? Well, I turned and was face to face with Cockburn-Montfort. I find it difficult to describe his look, or rather his succession of looks. Shock. Incredulity. Succeeded by fury. He turned even more purple in the process. Mrs Montfort quite gasped out: "I don't believe it!" and then gave a little scream. He had her by the arm and he hurt her. And without another word he turned her about and marched her out of the shop. I saw him wheel her round in the direction of the Piggery. She pulled back and seemed to plead with him. In the upshot they turned again and went off presumably to their own house. Mrs Pirelli said something in Italian and then: "If they go I am pleased." I left. As I passed the top of Capricorn Place, I saw the C-Ms going up their steps. He still held her arm and I think she was crying. That's all.'

'And this was – what? – half an hour ago?'

'About that.'

'We'll discuss it later. Thank you, Sam.'

'Have I blundered?'

'I hope not. I think you may have precipitated something.'

'I've got to have a word with Sheridan about the plumbing – a genuine word. He's at home. Should I – ?'

'I think you might but it's odds on the C-Ms will have got in first. Try.'

'Very well.'

'And the Chubbs?' Alleyn asked.

'Yes. Oh dear. If you wish.'

'Don't elaborate. Just the news, casually, as before.'

'Yes.'

'I'll be at home in about a quarter of an hour if you want me. If I don't hear from you I'll get in touch myself as soon as I can,' Alleyn said.

He checked with the man keeping observation and learned that Sanskrit had returned to the pottery after his visit to the land agents and had not emerged. The pottery was closed and the windows still curtained.

Five minutes later Alleyn and Fox found the entrance to the cul-de-sac, as on the former visit, cordoned off by police and thronged by an even larger crowd and quite a galaxy of photographers who were pestering Superintendent Gibson with loud cries against constabular arrogance. Alleyn had a word with Gibson, entered his own house, left Fox in the study and went straight to Troy in her studio. She had done quite a lot of work on the background.

'Troy,' he said, 'when he comes. I've got to have a word with him. Alone. I don't think it will take long and I don't know how much it will upset him.'

'Damn,' said Troy.

'Well. I know. But this is where it gets difficult. I've no choice.'

'I see. OK.'

'It's hell but there it is.'

'Never mind — I know. Here *he* is. You'd better meet him.'

'I'll be back. Much more to the point, I hope he will.'

'So do I. Good luck to whatever it is.'

'Amen to that, sweet powers,' Alleyn said and arrived at the front door at the same time as The Boomer, who had his *mlinzi* in attendance, the latter carrying a great bouquet of red roses and, most unexpectedly, holding the white Afghan hound on a scarlet leash. The Boomer explained that the dog seemed to be at a loose end. 'Missing his master,' said The Boomer.

He greeted Alleyn with all his usual buoyancy and then after a quick look at him said: 'Something is wrong, I think.'

'Yes,' Alleyn said. 'We must speak together, sir.'

'Very well, Rory. Where?'

'In here, if you will.'

They went into the study. When The Boomer saw Fox who had been joined by Gibson, he fetched up short.

'We speak together,' he said, 'but not, it seems, in private?'

'It's a police matter and my colleagues are involved.'

'Indeed? Good morning, gentlemen.'

He said something to the *mlinzi*, who handed him the roses, went out with the dog and shut the door.

'Will you sit down, sir?' Alleyn said.

This time The Boomer made no protest at the formalities. He said: 'By all means,' and sat in a white hide armchair. He wore the ceremonial dress of the portrait and looked superb. The red roses lent an extraordinary surrealist touch.

'Perhaps you will put them down somewhere?' he said and Alleyn laid them on his desk. 'Are they for Troy?' he asked. 'She'll be delighted.'

'What are we to speak about?'

'About Sanskrit. Will you tell me what was in the envelope he delivered at the Embassy soon after midnight this morning? It was addressed to the First Secretary. With a note to the effect that it was for your attention.'

'Your men are zealous in their performance of their tasks, Mr Gibson,' said The Boomer without looking at him.

Gibson cleared his throat.

'The Special Pass issued under my personal cachet evidently carried no weight with these policemen,' The Boomer added.

'Without it,' Alleyn said, 'the envelope would probably have been opened. I hope you will tell us what it contained. Believe me, I wouldn't ask if I didn't think it was of great importance.'

The Boomer who, from the time he had sat down, had not removed his gaze from Alleyn, said, 'It was opened by my secretary.'

'But he told you what it was?'

'It was a request. For a favour.'

'And the favour?'

'It was in connection with this person's return to Ng'ombwana. I think I told you that he has been reinstated.'

'Was it, perhaps, that he wants to return at once and asked for an immediate clearance — visas, permits, what-

452

ever is necessary? Procedures that normally, I think, take several days to complete?'

'Yes,' said The Boomer. 'That was it.'

'Why do you suppose he told the police officers that the envelope contained a photograph, one that you had ordered urgently, for yourself?'

For a second or two he looked very angry indeed. Then he said: 'I have no idea. It was a ridiculous statement. I have ordered no photographs.'

Alleyn said: 'Mr Gibson, I wonder if you and Mr Fox will excuse us?'

They went out with a solemn preoccupied air and shut the door after them.

'Well, Rory?' said The Boomer.

'He was an informer,' Alleyn said, 'wasn't he? He was what Mr Gibson would call so unprettily but so appropriately, a Snout.'

III

The Boomer had always, in spite of all his natural exuberance, commanded a talent for unexpected silences. He now displayed it. He neither moved nor spoke during a long enough pause for the clock in the study to clear its throat and strike ten. He then clasped his white gloved hands, rested his chin on them and spoke.

'In the old days,' he said, and his inordinately resonant voice, taking on the timbre of a recitative, lent the phrase huge overtones of nostalgia, 'at Davidson's, I remember one wet evening when we talked together, as youths of that age will, of everything under the sun. We talked, finally, of government and the exercise of power and suddenly, without warning, we found ourselves on opposite sides of a great gap — a ravine. There was no bridge. We were completely cut off from each other. Do you remember?'

'I remember, yes.'

'I think we were both surprised and disturbed to find ourselves in this situation. And I remember I said something like this: that we had stumbled against a natural barrier that was as old as our separate evolutionary processes – we used big words in those days. And you said there were plenty of territories we could explore without meeting such barriers and we'd better stick to them. And so, from that rainy evening onwards we did. Until now. Until this moment.'

Alleyn said: 'I mustn't follow you along these reminiscent byways. If you think for a moment, you'll understand why. I'm a policeman on duty. One of the first things we are taught is the necessity for non-involvement. I'd have asked to be relieved of this job if I had known what shape it would take.'

'What shape has it taken? What have you – uncovered?'

'I'll tell you. I think that the night before last a group of people, some fanatical, each in his or her own degree a bit demented and each with a festering motive of sorts, planned to have you assassinated in such a way that it would appear to have been done by your spearcarrier – your *mlinzi*: it's about these people that I'd like to talk to you. First of all, Sanskrit. Am I right or wrong in my conjecture about Sanskrit? Is he an informer?'

'There, my dear Rory, I must plead privilege.'

'I thought you might. All right. The Cockburn-Montforts. His hopes of military glory under the new regime came unstuck. He is said to have been infuriated. Has he to thank you, personally, for his compulsory retirement?'

'Oh, yes,' said The Boomer coolly. 'I got rid of him. He had become an alcoholic and quite unreliable. Besides, my policy was to appoint Ng'ombwanans to the senior ranks. We have been through all this.'

'Has he threatened you?'

'Not to my face. He was abusive at a personal interview I granted. I have been told that, in his cups, he uttered threats. It was all very silly and long forgotten.'

'Not on his part, perhaps. You knew he had been invited to the reception?'

454

'At my suggestion. He did good service in the past. We gave him a medal for it.'

'I see. Do you remember the Gomez case?'

For a moment, he looked surprised. 'Of course I remember it,' he said. 'He was a very bad man. A savage. A murderer. I had the pleasure of procuring him a fifteen-years stretch. It should have been a capital charge. He – ' The Boomer pulled up short. 'What of him?' he asked.

'A bit of information your sources didn't pass on to you, it seems. Perhaps they didn't know. Gomez has changed his name to Sheridan and lives five minutes away from your Embassy. He was not at your party but he is a member of this group and from what I have heard of him he's not going to let one setback defeat him. He'll try again.'

'That I can believe,' said The Boomer. For the first time he looked disconcerted.

Alleyn said: 'He watched this house from over the way while you sat to Troy yesterday morning. It's odds on he's out there again, now. He's being very closely observed. Would you say he's capable of going it alone and lobbing a bomb into your car or through my windows?'

'If he's maintained the head of steam he worked up against me at his trial – ' The Boomer began and checked himself. He appeared to take thought and then, most unconvincingly, let out one of his great laughs. 'Whatever he does,' he said, 'if he does anything, it will be a fiasco. *Bombs!* No, really, it's too absurd!'

For an alarming second or two Alleyn felt himself to be at explosion point. With difficulty, he controlled his voice and suggested, fairly mildly, that if any attempts made upon The Boomer turned out to be fiascos it would be entirely due to the vigilance and efficiency of the despised Gibson and his men.

'Why don't you arrest this person?' The Boomer asked casually.

'Because, as you very well know, we can't make arrests

455

on what would appear to be groundless suspicion. He has done nothing to warrant an arrest.'

The Boomer scarcely seemed to listen to him, a non-reaction that didn't exactly improve his temper.

'There is one more member of this coterie,' Alleyn said. 'A servant called Chubb. Is he known to you?'

'Chubb? Chubb? Ah! Yes, by the way! I believe I *have* heard of Chubb. Isn't he Mr Samuel Whipplestone's man? He came up with drinks while I was having a word with his master who happened to mention it. You're not suggesting – !'

'That Sam Whipplestone's involved? Indeed I'm not. But we've discovered that the man is.'

The Boomer seemed scarcely to take this in. The enormous creature suddenly leapt to his feet. For all his great size he was on them, like an animal, in one co-ordinated movement.

'What am I thinking of!' he exclaimed. 'To bring myself here! To force my attention upon your wife with this silly dangerous person who, bombs or no bombs, is liable to make an exhibition of himself and kick up dirt in the street. I will take myself off at once. Perhaps I may see her for a moment to apologize and then I vanish.'

'She won't take much joy of that,' Alleyn said. 'She has gone a miraculously long way in an unbelievably short time with what promises to be the best portrait of her career. It's quite appalling to think of it remaining unfinished.'

The Boomer gazed anxiously at him and then, with great simplicity, said: 'I get everything wrong.'

He had made this observation as a solitary black schoolboy in his first desolate term and it had marked the beginning of their friendship. Alleyn stopped himself from saying, 'Don't look like that,' and, instead, picked up the great bouquet of roses, put them in his hands and said: 'Come and see her.'

'Shall I?' he said, doubtful but greatly cheered. 'Really? Good!'

He strode to the door and flung it open. 'Where

is my *mlini*?' he loudly demanded.

Fox, who was in the hall, said blandly: 'He's outside Mrs Alleyn's studio, Your Excellency. He seemed to think that was where he was wanted.'

'We may congratulate ourselves,' Alleyn said, 'that he hasn't brought his spear with him.'

IV

Alleyn had escorted The Boomer to the studio and seen him established on his throne. Troy, tingling though she was with impatience, had praised the roses and put them in a suitable pot. She had also exultantly pounced upon the Afghan hound who, with an apparent instinct for aesthetic values, had mounted the throne and posed himself with killing effect against The Boomer's left leg and was in process of being committed to canvas.

Alleyn, possessed by a medley of disconnected anxieties and attachments, quitted the unlikely scene and joined Fox in the hall.

'Is it all right?' Fox asked, jerking his head in the direction of the studio. 'All that?'

'If you can call it all right for my wife to be settled cosily in there, painting a big black dictator with a suspected murderer outside the door and the victim's dog posing for its portrait: it's fine. Fine!'

'Well, it's unusual,' Fox conceded. 'What are you doing about it?'

'I'm putting one of those coppers on my doorstep outside the studio where he can keep the *mlinzi* company. Excuse me for a moment, Fox.'

He fetched the constable, a powerful man, from the pavement and gave him his directions.

'The man doesn't speak much English, if any,' he said, 'and I don't for a moment suppose he'll do anything but squat in the sun and stare. He's not armed and normally he's harmless. You're job's to keep close obbo on him till he's back in the car with Master.'

'Very good, sir,' said the officer and proceeded massively in the required direction.

Alleyn rejoined Fox.

'Wouldn't it be simpler,' Fox ventured, 'under the circumstances, I mean, to cancel the sittings?'

'Look here, Br'er Fox,' Alleyn said. 'I've done my bloody best to keep my job out of sight of my wife and by and large I've made a hash of it. But I'll tell you what: if ever my job looks like so much as coming between one dab of her brush and the surface of her canvas, I'll chuck it and set up a prep school for detectives.'

After a considerable pause Mr Fox said judicially: 'She's lucky to have you.'

'Not she,' said Alleyn. 'It's entirely the other way round. In the meantime, what's cooking? Where's Fred?'

'Outside. He's hoping for a word with you. Just routine, far as I know.'

Mr Gibson sat in a panda a little way down the cul-de-sac and not far from the pub. Uniformed men were distributed along the street and householders looked out of upstairs windows. The crowd at the entrance had thinned considerably.

Alleyn and Fox got into the panda.

'What's horrible?' they asked each other. Gibson reported that to the best of his belief the various members of the group were closeted in their respective houses. Mrs Chubb had been out of doors shopping but had returned home. He'd left a couple of men with radio equipment to patrol the area.

He was droning on along these lines when the door of Alleyn's house opened and the large officer spoke briefly to his colleague in the street. The latter was pointing towards the panda.

'This is for me,' Alleyn said. 'I'll be back.'

It was Mr Whipplestone on the telephone, composed but great with tidings. He had paid his plumbing call on Mr Sheridan and found him in a most extraordinary state.

'White to the lips, shaking, scarcely able to pull himself

458

together and give me a civil hearing. I had the impression that he was about to leave the flat. At first I thought he wasn't going to let me in but he shot a quick look up and down the street and suddenly stepped back and motioned with his head for me to enter. We stood in the lobby. I really don't think he took in a word about the plumbers but he nodded and – not so much grinned as bared his teeth from time to time.'

'Pretty!'

'Not very delicious, I assure you. Do you know I was transported back all those years, into that court of justice in Ng'ombwana. He might have been standing in the dock again.'

'That's not an over-fanciful conceit, either. Did you say anything about the Sanskrits?'

'Yes. I did. I ventured. As I was leaving. I think I may say I was sufficiently casual. I asked him if he knew whether the pottery in the mews undertook china repairs. He looked at me as if I was mad and shook his head.'

'Has he gone out?'

'I'm afraid I don't know. You may be sure I was prepared to watch. I had settled to do so, but Mrs Chubb met me in the hall. She said Chubb was not well and would I mind if she attended to my luncheon – served it and so on. She said it was what she called a 'turn' that he's subject to and he had run out of whatever he takes for it and would like to go to the chemist's. I, of course, said I could look after myself and *she* could go to the chemist's. I said I would lunch out if it would help. In any case it was only ten o'clock. But she was distressed, poor creature, and I couldn't quite brush her aside and go into the drawing-room so I can't positively swear Sheridan – Gomez – didn't leave. It's quite possible that he did. As soon as I'd got rid of Mrs Chubb I went to the drawing-room window. The area gate was open and I'm certain I shut it.'

'I see. What about Chubb?'

'What, indeed! He *did* go out. Quite openly. I asked Mrs Chubb about it and she said he'd insisted. She said the prescription took some time to make up and he would have to wait.'

'Has he returned?'

'Not yet. Nor has Sheridan. If, in fact, he went out.'

'Will you keep watch, Sam?'

'Of course.'

'Good. I think I'll be coming your way.'

Alleyn returned to the car. He passed Mr Whipplestone's information on to Fox and Gibson and they held a brief review of the situation.

'What's important as I see it,' Alleyn said, 'is the way these conspirators are thinking and feeling. If I'm right in my guesses, they got a hell of a shock on the night of the party. Everything was set up. The shot fired. The lights went out. The expected commotion ensued. The antici-pated sounds were heard. But when the lights went on again it was the wrong body killed by the right weapon wielded by they didn't know who. Very off-putting for all concerned. How did they react? The next thing they held a meeting at the Sanskrits. They'd had time to do a bit of simple addition and the answer had to be a rat in the wainscotting.'

'Pardon?' said Gibson.

'A traitor in their ranks. A snout.'

'Oh. Ah.'

'They must at the very least have suspected it. I'd give a hell of a lot to know what happened at that meeting while you and I, Fox, sat outside in the Mews.

'Who did they suspect? Why? What did they plan? To have another go at the President? It seems unlikely that Sheridan-Gomez would have given up. Did any of them get wind of Sanskrit's visit to the Embassy last night? And who the devil was the shadow we saw sprinting round the alley-corner?'

'Come on, Mr Alleyn. What's the theory? Who, do you reckon?'

'Oh, I'll tell you *that*, Br'er Fox,' Alleyn said. And did.

'And if either of you lot,' he ended, 'so much as mumbles

the word 'conjecture' I'll put you both on dab for improper conduct.'

'It boils down to this, then,' said Fox. 'They may be contemplating a second attempt on the President or they may be setting their sights on the snout whoever they reckon him to be, or they may be split on their line of action. Or,' he added as an afterthought, 'they may have decided to call it a day, wind up the Ku-Klux-Fish and fade out in all directions.'

'How true. With which thought we, too, part company. We must be all-ways away, Br'er Fox. Some to kill cankers in the musk-rose buds — '

'What's all that about?' Gibson asked glumly.

'Quotations,' Fox said.

'Yes, Fred,' said Alleyn, 'and you can go and catch a red-hipped bumble-bee on the lip of a thistle while Fox and I war with rare mice for their leathern wings.'

'Who said all that bumph anyway?'

'Fairies. We'll keep in touch. Come on, Fox.'

They returned to their own anonymous car and were driven to the Capricorns. Here a discreet prowl brought them into touch with one of Gibson's men, a plainclothes sergeant, who had quite a lot to say for himself. The fishy brotherhood had not been idle. Over the last half-hour, the Cockburn-Montforts had been glimpsed through their drawing-room window, engaged in drinking and — or so it seemed — quarrelling in a desultory way between libations. Chubb had been followed by another plainclothes sergeant carrying artist's impedimenta, to a chemist's shop in Baronsgate where he handed in a prescription and sat down, presumably waiting for it to be made up. Seeing him settled there, the sergeant returned to Capricorn Mews where, having an aptitude in that direction, he followed a well-worn routine by sitting on a canvas stool and making a pencil sketch of the pig-pottery. He had quite a collection of sketches at home, some finished and prettily tinted with aquarelles, others of a rudimentary kind, having been cut short by an arrest or by an obligation to shift the area of investigation. For these occasions he wore jeans, a dirty

461

jacket and an excellent wig of the Little Lord Fauntleroy type. His name was Sergeant Jacks.

Mr Sheridan, the Cockburn-Montforts and the Sanskrits had not appeared.

Fox parked the car in its overnight position under the plane trees in Capricorn Square from where he could keep observation on No. 1, the Walk, and Alleyn took a stroll down the Mews. He paused behind the gifted sergeant and, in the manner of the idle snooper, watched him tinker with a tricky bit of perspective. He wondered what opulent magic Troy, at that moment, might be weaving, over in Chelsea.

'Anything done?' he asked.

'Premises shut up, sir. But there's movement. In the back of the shop. There's a bit of a gap in the curtains and you can just get a squint. Not to see anything really. Nobody been in or out of the flat entrance.'

'I'll be within range. No. 1, Capricorn Walk. Give me a shout if there's anything. You could nip into that entry to call me up.'

'Yes, sir.'

Two youths from the garage strolled along and stared.

Alleyn said: 'I wouldn't have the patience, myself. Don't put me in it,' he added. These were the bystanders; remarks that Troy said were most frequently heard. 'Is it for sale?' he asked.

'Er,' said the disconcerted sergeant.

'I might come back and have another look,' Alleyn remarked and left the two youths to gape.

He pulled his hat over his left eye, walked very quickly indeed across the end of Capricorn Place and on into The Walk. He had a word with Fox in the car under the plane trees and then crossed the street to No. 1 where Mr Whipplestone, who had seen him coming, let him in.

'Sam,' Alleyn said. 'Chubb did go to the chemist.'

'I'm certainly glad to hear it.'

'But it doesn't necessarily mean he won't call at the piggery, you know.'

'You think not?'

'If he suffers from migraine the stresses of the past forty-eight hours might well have brought it on.'

'I suppose so.'

'Is his wife in?'

'Yes,' said Mr Whipplestone, looking extremely apprehensive.

'I want to speak to her.'

'Do you? That's – that's rather disturbing.'

'I'm sorry, Sam. It can't be helped, I'm afraid.'

'Are you going to press for information about her husband?'

'Probably.'

'How very – distasteful.'

'Police work is, at times, precisely that.'

'I know. I've often wondered how you can.'

'Have you?'

'You strike me, always, as an exceptionally fastidious man.'

'I'm sorry to disenchant you.'

'And I'm sorry to have been tactless.'

'Sam,' Alleyn said gently, 'one of the differences between police work and that of other and grander services is that we do our own dirty washing instead of farming it out at two or three removes.'

Mr Whipplestone turned pink. 'I deserved that,' he said.

'No, you didn't. It was pompous and out of place.'

Lucy Lockett, who had been washing herself with the zeal of an occupational therapist, made one of her ambiguous remarks, placed her forepaws on Alleyn's knee and leapt neatly into his lap.

'Now then, baggage,' Alleyn said, scratching her head, 'that sort of stuff never got a girl anywhere.'

'You don't know,' Mr Whipplestone said, 'how flattered you ought to feel. The demonstration is unique.'

Alleyn handed his cat to him and stood up. 'I'll get it over,' he said. 'Is she upstairs, do you know?'

'I think so.'

463

'It won't take long, I hope.'

'If I – if I can help in any way – ?'

'I'll let you know,' said Alleyn.

He climbed the stairs and tapped on the door. When Mrs Chubb opened it and saw him, she reacted precisely as she had on his former visit. There she stood, speechless with her fingers on her lips. When he asked to come in she moved aside with the predictable air of terrified reluctance. He went in and there was the enlarged photograph of the fresh-faced girl. The medallion, even, was, as before, missing from its place. He wondered if Chubb was wearing it.

'Mrs Chubb,' he said, 'I'm not going to keep you long and I hope I'm not going to frighten you. Yes, please, do sit down.'

Just as she did last time, she dropped into her chair and stared at him. He drew his up and leant forward.

'Since I saw you yesterday,' he said, 'we have learnt a great deal more about the catastrophe at the Embassy and about the people closely and remotely concerned in it. I'm going to tell you what I believe to be your husband's part.'

She moved her lips as if to say: 'He never – ' but was voiceless.

'All I want you to do is listen and then tell me if I'm right, partly right or wholly mistaken. I can't force you to answer as I expect you know, but I very much hope that you will.'

He waited a moment and then said: 'Well. Here it is. I believe that your husband, being a member of the group we talked about yesterday, agreed to act with them in an attack upon the President of Ng'ombwana. I think he agreed because of his hatred of blacks and of Ng'ombwanans in particular.' Alleyn looked for a moment at the smiling photograph. 'It's a hatred born of tragedy,' he said, 'and it has rankled and deepened, I dare say, during the last five years.

'When it was known that your husband was to be one of the waiters at the pavilion, the plan was laid. He had been given detailed instructions about his duties by his employers. The group was given even more detailed information from an agent inside the Embassy. And Chubb's orders were based on this information. He had been a commando and was very well suited indeed for the work in hand. Which was this. When the lights in the pavilion and the garden went out and after a shot was fired in the house, he was to disarm and disable the spearsman who was on guard behind the President, jump on a chair and kill the President with the spear.'

She was shaking her head to and fro and making inexplicit movements with her hands.

'No?' Alleyn said. 'Is that wrong? You didn't know about it? Not beforehand? Not afterwards? But you knew something was planned, didn't you? And you were frightened? And afterwards you knew it had gone wrong? Yes?'

She whispered. 'He never. He never done it.'

'No. He was lucky. He was hoist – He got the treatment he was supposed to hand out. The other waiter put him out of action. And what happened after that was no business of Chubb's.'

'You can't hurt him. You can't touch him.'

'That's why I've come to see you, Mrs Chubb. It may well be that we could, in fact, charge your husband with conspiracy. That means, with joining in a plan to do bodily harm. But our real concern is with the murder itself. If Chubb cuts loose from this group – and they're a bad lot, Mrs Chubb, a really bad lot – and gives me a straight answer to questions based on the account I've just given you, I think the police will be less inclined to press home attempted murder or charges of conspiracy. I don't know if you'll believe this but I do beg you, very seriously indeed, if you have any influence over him, to get him to make a complete break, not to go to any more meetings, above all, not to take part in any further action against anybody – Ng'ombwanan, white or what-have-you. Tell him to cut loose, Mrs Chubb. You tell him to cut loose.

465

And at the same time not to do anything silly like making a bolt for it. That'd be about the worst thing he could do.'

He had begun to think he would get no response of any kind from her when her face wrinkled over and she broke into a passion of tears. At first it was almost impossible to catch sense of what she tried to say. She sobbed out words piecemeal, as if they escaped by haphazard compulsion. But presently phrases emerged and a sort of congruence of ideas. She said what had happened five years ago might have happened yesterday for Chubb. She repeated several times that he 'couldn't get over it', that he 'never hardly said anything, but she could tell'. They never talked about it, she said, not even on the anniversary, which was always a terrible day for both of them. She said that for herself something 'came over her at the sight of a black man', but for Chubb, Alleyn gathered, the revulsion was savage and implacable. There had been incidents. There were times when he took queer turns and acted very funny with headaches. The doctor had given him something.

'Is that the prescription he's getting made up now?'

She said it was. As for 'that lot', she added, she'd never fancied him getting in with them.

He had become secretive about the meetings, she said, and had shut her up when she tried to ask questions. She had known something was wrong. Something queer was going on.

'They was getting at him and the way he feels. On account of our Glen. I could tell that. But I never knew that.'

Alleyn gathered that after the event Chubb had been a little more communicative in that he let out he'd been 'made a monkey of'. He'd acted according to orders, he said, and what had he got for it? Him with his experience? He was very angry and his neck hurt.

'Did he tell you what really happened? Everything?'

No, she said. There was something about him 'getting in

466

with the quick one according to plan' but being 'clobbered' from behind and making 'a boss shot of it'.

Alleyn caught back an exclamation.

It hadn't made sense to Mrs Chubb. Alleyn gathered that she'd felt, in a muddled way, that because a black man had been killed Chubb ought to have been pleased but that he was angry because something had, in some fashion, been put across him. When Alleyn suggested that nothing she had told him contradicted the version he had given to her, she stared hopelessly at him out of blurred eyes and vaguely shook her head.

'I suppose not,' she said.

'From what you've told me, my suggestion that you persuade him to break with them was useless. You've tried. All the same, when he comes back from the chemist's – '

She broke in: 'He ought to be back,' she cried. 'It wouldn't take that long! He ought to've come in by now. Oh Gawd: where is he?'

'Now don't you go getting yourself into a state before there's need,' Alleyn said. 'You stay put and count your blessings. Yes, that's what I said, Mrs Chubb. Blessings. If your man had brought off what he set out to do on the night of the party you *would* have had something to cry about. If he comes back, tell him what I've said. Tell him he's being watched. Keep him indoors and in the meantime brew yourself a strong cuppa and pull yourself together, there's a good soul. Good morning to you.'

He ran downstairs and was met at the drawing-room door by Mr Whipplestone.

'Well, Sam,' he said. 'Through no fault of his own your Chubb didn't commit murder. That's not to say – '

The telephone rang. Mr Whipplestone made a little exasperated noise and answered it.

'Oh!' he said. 'Oh, yes. He is. Yes, of course. Yes.'

'It's for you,' he said. 'It's Mrs Roderick.'

As soon as she heard Alleyn's voice, Troy said:

467

'Rory. Important. Someone with a muffled voice has just rung up to say there's a bomb in the President's car.'

468

9

Climax

Alleyn said: 'Don't –' but she cut in:

'No, listen! The thing is, he's gone. Five minutes ago. In his car.'

'Where?'

'The Embassy.'

'Right. Stay put.'

'Urgent,' Alleyn said to Mr Whipplestone. 'See you later.'

He left the house as Fox got out of the car under the trees and came towards him.

'Bomb scare,' said Fox. 'On the blower.'

'I know. Come on. The Embassy.'

They got into the car. On the way to the Embassy, which was more roundabout than the way through the hole in the Wall, Fox said a disguised voice had rung the Yard. The Yard was ringing Troy and had alerted Gibson and all on duty in the area.

'The President's on his way back,' Alleyn said. 'Troy's had the muffled voice, too.'

'The escort car will have got the message.'

'I hope so.'

'A hoax, do you reckon?'

'Considering the outlandish nature of the material we're supposed to be handling, it's impossible to guess. As usual, we take it for real. But I tell you what, Br'er Fox, I've got a nasty feeling that if it is a hoax it's a hoax with a purpose. Another name for it might be red-herring. We'll see Fred and then get back to our own patch. That Royal Academician in the Mews had better be keeping his eyes open. Here we are.'

They had turned out of a main thoroughfare, with their siren blaring, into Palace Park Gardens and there, outside

469

the Embassy emerging from his police escort's car was The Boomer closely followed by his *mlinzi* and the Afghan hound. Alleyn and Fox left their car and approached him. He hailed them vigorously.

'Hullo, hullo!' shouted The Boomer, 'here are turn-ups for the books! You have heard the latest, I suppose?'

'We have,' said Alleyn. 'Where's the Embassy car?'

'Where? Where? Half-way between here and there, "there" being your own house, to be specific. The good Gibson and his henchmen are looking under the seats for bombs. Your wife required me no longer. I left a little early. Shall we go indoors?'

Alleyn excused himself and was glad to see them off. The driver of the official police car was talking into his radio. He said: 'Mr Alleyn's here now, sir. Yes, sir.'

'All right,' Alleyn said and got into the car.

It was Gibson. 'So you've heard?' he said. 'Nothing so far but we haven't finished.'

'Did *you* hear the call?'

'No. He or she rang the Yard. Info is that he probably spoke through a handkerchief.'

'He *or* she?'

'The voice was peculiar. A kind of squeaky whisper. They reckon it sounded frightened or excited or both. The exact words were: *'Is that Scotland Yard? There's a bomb in the Black Embassy car. Won't be long now.'* Call not traced. They thought the car would be outside your place and a minute or so was lost ascertaining it was on the way here. All my chaps were alerted and came on the scene pronto. Oh, and they say he seemed to speak with a lisp.'

'Like hell they do! So would they with a mouthful of handkerchief. Who's on the Capricorn ground?'

'A copper in a wig with coloured chalks.'

'I know all about him. That all?'

'Yes,' said Gibson. 'The others were ordered round here,' and added with a show of resentment, 'My job's mounting security over this big, bloody black headache and a bloody gutty show it's turned out to be.'

'All right, Fred. I know. It's a stinker. I'll get back there myself. What about you?'

'Back to the suspect car scene. Look!' said Gibson with the nearest approach to shrillness that Alleyn would have thought possible, 'it's got to such a pitch that I'd welcome a straight case of bomb disposal and no nonsense. There you are! I'd welcome it.'

Alleyn was forming what conciliatory phrases he could offer when he was again called to the radio. It was the gifted Sergeant Jacks.

'Sir,' said the sergeant in some agitation. 'I better report.'

'What?'

'This bomb scare, sir. Just before it broke the military gentleman, Colonel Whatsit, beg pardon, came walking very rigid and careful up to the pig-pottery and leant on the bell of the door into their flat. And then the scare broke, sir, Mr Gibson's chap keeping obbo in a car near the entrance to Capricorn Passage, sir, came round and told me quick, through the driving window, that it was a general alert, sir. And while he was talking, a dirty great van pulled out of the garage and obscured my view of the pottery. Well, sir, I'd got my orders from you to stay where I am. And Mr Gibson's chap drove off. Meanwhile a traffic jam had built up in the Mews, behind the van. I couldn't get a sight of the pottery but I could hear the Colonel. He'd started up yelling. Something like: 'Open the bloody door, damn you, and let me in.' And then the drivers began sounding off their horns. It was like that for at least five minutes, sir.'

'Could anybody – could two enormous people – have got out and away while this lasted?'

'I reckon not, because it sorted itself out, sir, and when it had cleared, there was the Colonel still at the piggery door and still leaning on the bell. And he's leaning on it now. And yelling a bit but kind of fading out. I reckon he's so drunk he's had it. What'll I do, sir?'

'Where are you?'

'Ducked down behind my easel. It's a bit awkward but I thought I'd risk it. Could you hold on, sir?'

An interval of street noises. Alleyn held on and the voice returned. 'I'm up the alleyway, sir. I had to duck. The gentleman from the basement of No. 1, the Walk's passed the end of the alleyway going towards the pottery.'

'Get back to your easel and watch.'

'Sir.'

'I'm on my way. Over and out. Capricorn Square,' Alleyn said to the driver. 'Quick as you can make it but no siren.'

'What was all that, then?' asked Fox. When he was informed he remarked that the painter-chap seemed to be reasonably practical and active even if he did get himself up like a right Charlie. Mr Fox had a prejudice against what he called 'fancy-dress coppers'. His own sole gesture in that line was to put on an ancient Donegal tweed ulster and an out-of-date felt hat. It was surprising how effectively these lendings disguised his personality.

When they reached the Square Alleyn said: 'We'd better separate. This is tricky. Sheridan-Gomez is the only one of the gang that doesn't know me. The others might remember *you* from your checking out activities after the party. Have you got your nighty with you?'

'If you mean my Donegal ulster, yes I have. It's in the back.'

'And the head gear?'

'Rolled up in the pocket.'

'When you've dolled yourself up in them you might stroll to the piggery by the way of the Square and Capricorn Place. I'll take the Walk and the Mews. We'll no doubt encounter each other in the vicinity of the piggery.'

Fox went off looking like a North of Ireland corn chandler on holiday and Alleyn turned into Capricorn Walk looking like himself.

Lucy Lockett, taking the sun on the steps of No. 1, rolled over at him as he passed.

No doubt, Alleyn reflected, Gibson's men patrolling the Capricorns, who had been diverted to the Embassy on the bomb alarm, would soon return to their ground. At the moment there was no sign of them.

It was the busiest time of day in the Capricorns and a pretty constant two-way stream of traffic moved along the Walk. Alleyn used it to screen his approach to the house-decorator's shop on the corner of the Mews. From here, looking sideways through the windows, he had a view down the Mews to the pottery at the far end. Inter-mittently, he had glimpses of the gifted Sergeant Jacks at his easel but commercial vehicles backing and filing outside the garage, constantly shut him off. The pottery flashed in and out of view like the fractional revelations of commercial television. Now it was Colonel Cockburn-Montfort, still at the pottery flat door, with Gomez beside him. And then, as if by sle ght-of-hand, Chubb was there with them in consultation. Now a van drove into the Mews, fetched up outside the Napoli and began to deliver cartons and crates and there was no view at all.

Between the Napoli and the garage, and next door to the flower shop there was a tiny bistro, calling itself 'The Bijou'. On fine days it put four tables out on the pavement and served coffee and pâtisseries. One of the tables was unoccupied. Alleyn walked past the van and flower shop, sat at the table, ordered coffee and lit his pipe. He had his back to the pottery but got a fair reflection of it in the flower shop window.

Gomez and Chubb were near the flat door. The Colonel still leant against it, looking dreadfully groggy. Chubb stood back a little way with his fingers to his mouth. Gomez seemed to be peering in at the curtained shop window.

He was joined there by Inspector Fox, who had arrived via Capricorn Place. He appeared to search for an address and find it in the pottery. He approached the shop door, took out his spectacles, read the notice, 'Closed for Stocktaking' and evidently spoke to Gomez, who shrugged and turned his back.

473

Fox continued down the Mews. He paused by the talented Sergeant Jacks, again assumed his spectacles and bent massively towards the drawing. Alleyn watched with relish as his colleague straightened up, tilted his head appreciatively to one side, fell back a step or two, apologized to a passer-by and continued on his way. When he reached the table he said: 'Excuse me, is that chair taken?' and Alleyn said: 'No. Please.'

Fox took it, ordered coffee and when he had been served asked Alleyn the time.

'Come off it,' Alleyn said. 'Nobody's looking at you.'

But they both kept up the show of casual conversation between strangers.

Fox said: 'It's a funny set-up back there. They act as if they don't know each other. The Colonel seems to be on the blink. If you poked a finger at him, he'd fall flat.'

'What about the premises?'

'You can't see anything in the shop. There's curtains almost closed across the window and no light inside.'

He blew on his coffee and took a sip.

'They're in a funny sort of shape,' he said. 'The Gomez man's shaking. Very pale. Gives the impression he might cut up violent. Think they've skedaddled, Mr Alleyn? The Sanskrits?'

'It would have to be after 9.10 this morning when Sanskrit was seen to go home.'

'That copper with the crayons reckons they couldn't have made it since he's been on the job.'

'He dodged up the garage alley to talk to me, he might remember. Of course that damn bomb-scare drew Fred Gibson's men off. But no, I don't think they've flitted. I don't think so. I think they're lying doggo.'

'What's the drill, then?' Fox asked his coffee.

'I've got a search-warrant. Blow me down flat, Br'er Fox, if I don't take a chance and execute it. Look,' Alleyn said drawing on his pipe and gazing contentedly at the sky. 'We may be in a bloody awkward patch. You get back to the car and whistle up support. Fred's lot ought to be available again now. We'll move in as soon as they're on tap. Call us up on the artist's buzzer. Then we close in.'

'What about Gomez and the Colonel? And Chubb?'

'We keep it nice and easy but we hold them. See you on the doorstep.'

'Fox put down his empty cup, looked about him, rose, nodded to Alleyn and strolled away in the direction of Capricorn Walk. Alleyn waited until he had disappeared round the corner, finished his coffee and, at a leisurely pace rejoined Sergeant Jacks who was touching up his architectural details.

'Pack up,' Alleyn said, 'and leave your stuff up the alley there. You'll get a shout from Mr Fox in a matter of seconds.'

'Is it a knock-off, sir?'

'It may be. If that lot, there, start to move, we hold them. Nice and quiet, though. All right. Make it quick. And when you get the office from Mr Fox, come out here again where I can see you and we'll move in. Right?'

'Right, sir.'

The delivery van from the Napoli lurched noisily down the Mews, did a complicated turn-about in front of the pottery and went back the way it had come. Alleyn moved towards the pottery.

A police-car siren, braying in Baronsgate, was coming nearer. Another, closer at hand, approached from somewhere on the outer borders of the Capricorns.

Sergeant Jacks came out of the garage alleyway. Fox and Gibson had been quick.

Gomez walked rapidly up the Mews on the opposite side to Alleyn who crossed over and stopped in front of him. The sirens, close at hand now, stopped.

'Mr Sheridan?' Alleyn said.

For a moment the living image of an infuriated middle-aged man overlaid that of the same man fifteen years younger in Mr Whipplestone's album. He had turned so white that his close-shaved beard started up, blue-black, as if it had been painted across his face.

He said: 'Yes? My name is Sheridan.'

'Yes, of course. You've been trying to call upon the Sanskrits, haven't you?'

He made a very slight movement: an adjustment of his weight, rather like Mr Whipplestone's cat preparing to spring or bolt. Fox had come up behind Alleyn. Two of Gibson's uniformed men had turned into the Mews from Capricorn Place. There were more large men converging on the pottery. Sergeant Jacks was talking to Chubb and Fred Gibson loomed over Colonel Cockburn-Montfort by the door into the flat.

Gomez stared from Alleyn to Fox. 'What is this?' he lisped. 'What do you want? Who are you?'

'We're police officers. We're about to effect an entry into the pottery and I suggest that you come with us. Better not make a scene in the street, don't you think?'

For a moment Gomez had looked as if he meant to do so but he now said between his teeth: 'I want to see those people.'

'Now's your chance,' said Alleyn.

He glowered, hesitated and then said: 'Very well,' and walked between Alleyn and Fox, towards the pottery.

Gibson and the sergeant were having no trouble. Chubb was standing bolt upright and saying nothing. Colonel Cockburn-Montfort had been detached from the bell, deftly rolled round and propped against the door-jamb by Gibson. His eyes were glazed and his mouth slightly open but, like Chubb, he actually maintained a trace of his soldierly bearing.

Four uniformed men had arrived and bystanders had begun to collect.

Alleyn rang the bell and knocked on the top of the door. He waited for half a minute and then said to one of the policemen:

'It's a Yale. Let's hope it's not double-locked. Got anything?'

The policeman fished in his breast pocket, produced a small polythene ready-reckoner of a kind used for conversion to metric quantities. Alleyn slid it past the tongue of the lock and manipulated it.

'Bob's your uncle,' the constable murmured and the door was open.

Alleyn said to Fox and Gibson, 'Would you wait a moment with these gentlemen?' He then nodded to the constables who followed him in, one remaining inside the door.

'Hullo!' Alleyn called. 'Anyone at home?'

He had a resonant voice but it sounded stifled in the airless flat. They were in a narrow lobby hung with dim native cloth of some sort and smelling of dust and the stale fumes of sandarac. A staircase rose steeply on the left from just inside the door. At the far end, on the right was a door that presumably led into the shop. Two large suitcases strapped and labelled, leant against the wall.

Alleyn turned on a switch and a pseudo-oriental lamp with red panes came to life in the ceiling. He looked at the labels on the suitcases: 'Sanskrit, Ng'ombwana.'

'Come on,' he said.

He led the way upstairs. On the landing he called out again.

Silence.

There were four doors, all shut.

Two bedrooms, small, exotically furnished, crowded and in disarray. Discarded garments flung on unmade beds. Cupboards and drawers, open and half-emptied. Two small, half-packed suitcases. An all-pervading and most unlovely smell.

A bathroom, stale and grubby, smelling of hot, wet fat. The wall-cupboard was locked.

Finally, a large, heavily furnished room with divans, deep rugs, horrid silk-shaded and beaded lamps, incense burners and a number of ostensibly African artifacts. But no Sanskrits.

They returned downstairs.

Alleyn opened the door at the end of the lobby and walked through.

He was in the piggery.

It was very dark. Only a thin sliver of light penetrated the slit between the heavy window curtains.

He stood inside the door with the two uniformed men behind him. As his eyes adjusted to the gloom, the interior began to emerge; a desk, a litter of paper and packing material, open cases and on the shelves, dimly flowering one or two pottery pigs. The end of the old stable, formed, as he remembered, a sort of alcove or cavern in which there were the kiln and a long work table. He saw a faint red glow there, now.

He was taken with a sensation of inertia that he had long ago learnt to recognize as the kind of nightmare which drains one of the power to move.

As now, when his hand was unable to grope about the dirty wall for a light switch.

The experience never lasted for more than a few seconds and now it had passed and left him with the knowledge that he was watched.

Someone at the far end of the shop, in the alcove room, sitting on the other side of the workbench, was watching him: a looming mass that he had mistaken for shadow.

It began to define itself. An enormous person, whose chin rested with a suggestion of doggy roguishness, on her arm and whose eyes were very wide open indeed.

Alleyn's hand found the switch and the room was flooded with light.

It was Miss Sanskrit who ogled him so coyly with her chin on her arm and her head all askew and her eyes wide open.

Behind the bench, with his back towards her, with his vast rump upheaved and with his head and arms and barrel submerged in a packing-case like a monstrous puppet doubled over its box, dangled her brother. They were both dead.

And between them, on the floor and the bench, were bloodied shards of pottery.

And in the packing-case lay the headless carcass of an enormous pig.

A whispered stream of obscenities had been surprised out of one of the constables but he had stopped when Alleyn walked into the alcove and had followed a short way behind.

'Stay where you are,' Alleyn said and then: 'No! One of you get that lot in off the street and lock the door. Take them to the room upstairs, keep them there and stay with them. Note anything that's said.

'The other call Homicide and give the necessary information. Ask Mr Fox and Mr Gibson to come here.'

They went out, shutting the door behind them. In a minute Alleyn heard sounds of a general entry and of people walking upstairs.

When Fox and Gibson arrived they found Alleyn standing between the Sanskrits. They moved towards him but checked when he raised his hand.

'This is nasty,' Fox said. 'What was it?'

'Come and see but walk warily.'

They moved round the bench and saw the back of Miss Sanskrit's head. It was smashed in like an egg. Beetroot-dyed hair, dark and wet, stuck in the wound. The back of her dress was saturated – there was a dark puddle on the table under her arm. She was dressed for the street. Her bloodied hat lay on the floor and her handbag was on the work table.

Alleyn turned to face the vast rump of her brother, clothed in a camel overcoat which was all that could be seen of him.

'Is it the same?' Gibson asked.

'Yes. A pottery pig. The head broke off on the first attack and the rest fell into the box after the second.'

'But – how exactly – ?' Fox said.

'Look what's on the table. Under her hand.'

It was a sheet of headed letter paper. 'The Piggie Pottery, 12 Capricorn Mews, SW3.' Written beneath this legend was: 'To Messrs Able and Virtue. Kindly . . .' And no more.

'A green ball-point,' Alleyn said. 'It's still in her right hand.'

'Fox touched the hand. 'Still warm,' he said.

'Yes.'

There was a checked cloth of sorts near the kiln. Alleyn masked the terrible head with it. 'One of the really bad ones,' he said.

'What was *he* doing?' Fox asked

'Stowing away the remaining pigs. Doubled up, and reaching down into the packing-case.'

'So you read the situation – how?'

'Like this, unless something else turns up to contradict it. She's writing. He's putting pigs from the bench into the packing-case. Someone comes between them. Someone who perhaps has offered to help. Someone, at any rate, whose presence doesn't disturb them. And this person picks up a pig, deals two mighty downward blows, left and right, quick as you please, and walks out.'

Gibson said angrily: 'Walks out! When? And when did he *walk in*? I've had these premises under close observation for twelve hours.'

'Until the bomb-scare, Fred.'

'Sergeant Jacks stayed put.'

'With a traffic jam building up between him and the pottery.'

'By God, this is a gutty job,' said Gibson.

'And the gallant Colonel was on the doorstep,' Alleyn added.

'I reckon *he* wouldn't have been any the wiser,' Fox offered, 'if the Brigade of Guards had walked in and out.'

'We'll see about that,' Alleyn said.

A silence fell between them. The room was oppressively warm and airless. Flies buzzed between the window curtains and the glass. One of them darted out and made like a bullet for the far end.

With startling unexpectedness the telephone on the desk rang. Alleyn wrapped his handkerchief round his hand and lifted the receiver.

He gave the number speaking well above his natural level. An unmistakably Ng'ombwanan voice said: 'It is the Embassy. You have not kept your appointment.'

Alleyn made an ambiguous falsetto noise.

'I said,' the voice insisted, 'you have not kept your appointment. To collect the passports. Your plane leaves at 5.30.'

Alleyn whispered: 'I was prevented. Please send them. Please.'

A long pause.

'Very well. It is not convenient but very well. They will be put into your letter-box. In a few minutes. Yes?'

He said nothing and heard a deep sound of impatience and the click of the receiver being replaced.

He hung up. 'For what it's worth,' he said, 'we now know that the envelope we saw Sanskrit deliver at the Embassy contained their passports. I'd got as much already from the President. In a few minutes they'll be dropping them in. He failed to keep his appointment to collect.'

Fox looked at the upturned remains of Sanskrit. 'He could hardly help himself,' he said. 'Could he?'

The front door bell rang. Alleyn looked through the slit in the curtains. A car had arrived with Bailey and Thompson, their driver and their gear. A smallish crowd had been moved down the Mews and into the passageway leading to Baronsgate.

The constable in the hallway admitted Bailey and Thompson. Alleyn said: 'The lot. Complete coverage. Particularly the broken pottery.'

Thompson walked carefully past the partition into the alcove and stopped short.

'Two, eh?' he said and unslipped his camera.

'Go ahead,' Alleyn said.

Bailey went to the table and looked incredulously from the enormous bodies to Alleyn, who nodded and turned his back. Bailey delicately lifted the checked cloth and said: 'Cor!'

'Not pretty,' Alleyn said.

Bailey, shocked into a unique flight of fancy, said: 'It's kind of not real. Like those blown-up affairs they run in fun shows. Giants. Gone into the horrors.'

'It's very much like that,' Alleyn said. 'Did you hear if they'd got through to Sir James?'

'Yes, Mr Alleyn. On his way.'

'Good. All right. Push on with it, you two.' He turned to Gibson and Fox. 'I suggest,' he said, 'that we let that lot upstairs have a look at this scene.'

'Shock tactics?' Gibson asked.

'Something like that. Agreed?'

'This is your ground, not mine,' said Gibson, still dully resentful. 'I'm only meant to be bloody security.'

Alleyn knew it was advisable to disregard these plaints.

He said: 'Fox, would you go upstairs? Take the copper in the hall with you. Leave him in the room and have a quiet word on the landing with the man who's been with them. If he's got anything I ought to hear, hand it on to me. Otherwise, just stick with them for a bit, would you? Don't give a clue as to what's happened. All right?'

'I think so,' said Fox placidly, and went upstairs.

Bailey's camera clicked and flashed. Miss Sanskrit's awful face started up and out in a travesty of life. Thompson collected pottery shards and laid them out on the far end of the work table. More exploratory flies darted down the room. Alleyn continued to watch through the curtains.

A Ng'ombwanan in civilian dress drove up to the door, had a word with the constable on guard and pushed something through the letter-box. Alleyn heard the flap of the clapper. The car drove away and he went into the hall and collected the package.

'What's that, then?' Gibson asked.

Alleyn opened it: two British passports elaborately stamped and endorsed and a letter on Embassy paper in Ng'ombwanan.

'Giving them the VIP treatment, I wouldn't be surprised,' Alleyn said and pocketed the lot.

Action known as 'routine' was now steadily under way. Sir James Curtis and his secretary arrived, Sir James remarking a little acidly that he would like to know this time whether he would be allowed to follow the usual procedure and hold his damned post mortems if, when and where he wanted them. On being shown the subjects he came as near to exhibiting physical repulsion as Alleyn had ever seen him and asked appallingly if they would provide him with bull-dozers.

He said that death had probably occurred within the hour, agreed with Alleyn's reading of the evidence, listened to what action he proposed to take and was about to leave when Alleyn said: 'There's a former record of drug-pushing against the man. No sign of them taking anything themselves, I suppose?'

'I'll look out for it but they don't often, do they?'

'Do we expect to find blood on the assailant?'

Sir James considered this. 'Not necessarily, I think,' he said. 'The size of the weapon might form a kind of shield in the case of the woman and the position of the head in the man.'

'Might the weapon have been dropped or hurled down on the man? They're extremely heavy, those things.'

'Very possible.'

'I see.'

'You'll send these monstrosities along then, Rory? Good day to you.'

When he'd gone Fox and the constable who had been on duty upstairs came down.

'Thought we'd better wait till Sir James had finished,' Fox said. 'I've been up there in the room with them. Chubb's very quiet but you can see he's put out.'

This, in Fox's language, could mean anything from being irritated to going berserk or suicidal. 'He breaks out every now and then,' he went on, 'asking where the Sanskrits are and why this lot's being kept. I asked him what he'd

483

wanted to see them for and he comes with it that he *didn't* want to see them. He reckons he was on his way back from the chemist's by way of Capricorn Passage and just ran into the Colonel and Mr Sheridan. The Colonel was in such a bad way, Chubb makes out, he was trying to get him to let himself be taken home but all the Colonel would do was lean on the bell.'

'What about the Colonel?'

'It doesn't really make sense. He's beyond it. He said something or another about Sanskrit being a poisonous specimen who ought to be court-martialled.'

'And Gomez-Sheridan?'

'He's taking the line of righteous indignation. Demands an explanation. Will see there's information laid in the right quarters and we haven't heard the last of it. You'd think it was all quite ordinary except for a kind of twitch under his left eye. They all keep asking where the Sanskrits are.'

'It's time they found out,' Alleyn said, and to Bailey and Thompson: 'There's a smell of burnt leather. We'll have to rake out the furnace.'

'Looking for anything in particular, Mr Alleyn?'

'No. Well – No. Just looking. For traces of anything anyone wanted to destroy. Come on.'

He and Fox went upstairs.

As he opened the door and went in he got the impression that Gomez had leapt to his feet. He stood facing Alleyn with his bald head sunk between his shoulders and his eyes like black bootbuttons in his white kid face. He might have been an actor in a bad Latin-American film.

At the far end of the room Chubb stood facing the window with the dogged, conditioned look of a soldier in detention, as if whatever he thought or felt or had done must be thrust back behind a mask of conformity.

Colonel Cockburn-Montfort lay in an armchair with his mouth open, snoring profoundly and hideously. He would have presented a less distasteful picture, Alleyn thought, if he had discarded the outward showing of an officer and –

ambiguous addition – gentleman: the conservative suit, the signet ring on the correct finger, the handmade brogues, the regimental tie, the quietly elegant socks and, lying on the floor by his chair, the hat from Jermyn Street – all so very much in order. And Colonel Cockburn-Montfort so very far astray.

Gomez began at once: 'You are the officer in charge of these extraordinary proceedings, I believe. I must ask you to inform me, at once, why I am detained here without reason, without explanation or apology.'

'Certainly,' Alleyn said. 'It is because I hope you may be able to help us in our present job.'

'Police parrot talk!' he spat out, making a great thing of the plosives. The muscle under his eye flickered.

'I hope not,' Alleyn said.

'What is this "present job"?'

'We are making enquiries about the couple living in these premises. Brother and sister. Their name is Sanskrit.'

'*Where are they*!'

'They haven't gone far.'

'Are they in trouble?' he asked showing his teeth.

'Yes.'

'I am not surprised. They are criminals. Monsters.'

The Colonel snorted and opened his eyes. 'What?' he said. 'Who are you talking 'bout? Monsters?'

Gomez made a contemptuous noise. 'Go to sleep,' he said. 'You are disgusting.'

'I take 'ception that remark, sir,' said the Colonel and sounded exactly like Major Bloodknock, long ago. He shut his eyes.

'How do you know they are criminals?' Alleyn asked.

'I have reliable information,' said Gomez.

'From where?'

'From friends in Africa.'

'In Ng'ombwana?'

'One of the so-called emergent nations. I believe that is the name.'

'You ought to know,' Alleyn remarked, 'seeing that you

485

spent so long there.' And he thought: He really is rather like an adder.

'You speak nonsense,' Gomez lisped.

'I don't think so, Mr Gomez.'

Chubb, by the window, turned and gaped at him.

'My name is Sheridan,' Gomez said loudly.

'If you prefer it.'

''Ere!' Chubb said with some violence. 'What is all this? *Names!*'

Alleyn said: 'Come over here, Chubb, and sit down. I've got something to say to all of you and for your own sakes you'd better listen to it. Sit down. That's right. Colonel Cockburn-Montfort – '

'Cert'n'ly,' said the Colonel, opening his eyes.

'Can you follow me or shall I send for a corpse-reviver?'

''Course I can follow you. F'what it's worth.'

'Very well. I'm going to put something to the three of you and it's this. You are members of a coterie which is motivated by racial hatred, more specifically, hatred of the Ng'ombwanan people in particular. On the night before last you conspired to murder the President.'

Gomez said, 'What is this idiot talk!'

'You had an informant in the Embassy: the Ambassador himself, who believed that on the death of the President and with your backing, he would achieve a *coup d'état* and assume power. In return, you, Mr Gomez, and you, Colonel Montfort, were to be reinstated in Ng'ombwana.'

The Colonel waved his hand as if these statements were too trivial to merit consideration. Gomez, his left ankle elegantly posed on his right thigh, watched Alleyn over his locked fingers. Chubb, wooden, sat bolt upright on the edge of his chair.

'The Sanskrits, brother and sister,' Alleyn went on, 'were also members of the clique. Miss Sanskrit produced your medallion in her pottery downstairs. They, however, were double agents. From the time the plan was first conceived to the moment for its execution and without the knowledge of the Ambassador, every move was being conveyed by the Sanskrits back to the Ng'ombwanan

486

authorities. I think you must have suspected something of the sort when your plan miscarried. I think that last night after your meeting here broke up, one of the group followed Sanskrit to the Embassy and from a distance saw him deliver an envelope. He had passed by your house, Colonel Montfort.'

'I don't go out at night much nowadays,' the Colonel said, rather sadly.

'Your wife perhaps? It wouldn't be the first time you'd delegated one of the fancy touches to her. Well, it's of no great matter. I think the full realization of what the Sanskrits had done really dawned this morning when you learned that they were shutting up shop and leaving.'

'Have they made it?' Chubb suddenly demanded. 'Have they cleared out? Where are they?'

'To return to the actual event. Everything seemed to go according to plan up to the moment when, after the shot was fired and the guests' attention had been deflected, you, Chubb, made your assault on the spearcarrier. You delivered the chop from behind, probably standing on a subsequently overturned chair to do so. At the crucial moment you were yourself attacked from the rear by the Ng'ombwanan servant. He was a little slow off the mark. Your blow fell: not as intended on the spearsman's arm but on his collar-bone. He was still able to use his spear and he did use it, with both hands and full knowledge of what he was doing, on the Ambassador.'

Alleyn looked at the three men. There was no change in their posture or their expressions but a dull red had crept into Chubb's face and the Colonel's (which habitually looked as if it had reached saturation point in respect of purple) seemed to darken. They said nothing.

'I see I've come near enough the mark for none of you to contradict me,' Alleyn remarked.

'On the contrary,' Gomez countered. 'Your entire story is fantasy and a libel. It is too farcical to merit a reply.'

'Well, Chubb?'

'I'm not answering the charge, sir. Except what I said before. I was clobbered.'

'Colonel?'

'What? No comment. No bloody comment.'

'Why were you all trying to get in here, half an hour ago?'

'No comment,' they said together and Chubb added his former statement that he'd had no intention of calling on the Sanskrits but had merely stopped to offer his support to the Colonel and take him home.

The Colonel said something that sounded like: 'Most irregular and unnecessary.'

'Are you sticking to that?' Alleyn said. 'Are you sure you weren't, all three of you, going to throw a farewell party for the Sanskrits and give them, or at any rate, him, something handsome to remember you by?'

They were very still. They didn't look at Alleyn or at each other but for a moment the shadow of a fugitive smile moved across their faces.

The front doorbell was pealing again, continuously. Alleyn went out to the landing.

Mrs Chubb was at the street door, demanding to be let in. The constable on duty turned, looked up the stairs and saw Alleyn.

'All right,' Alleyn said. 'Ask her to come up.'

It was a very different Mrs Chubb who came quickly up the stairs, thrusting her shoulders forward and jerking up her head to confront Alleyn on the landing.

'Where is he?' she demanded, breathing hard. 'Where's Chubb? You said keep him home and now you've got him in here. And with them others. Haven't you? I know he's here. I was in the Mews and I seen. Why? What are you doing to him? Where,' Mrs Chubb reiterated, 'is my Chubb?'

'Come in,' Alleyn said. 'He's here.'

She looked past him into the room. Her husband stood up and she went to him. 'What are you doing?' she said. 'You come back with me. You've got no call to be here.'

Chubb said: 'You don't want to be like this. You keep out of it. You're out of place here, Min.'

'I'm out of place! Standing by my own husband!'

'Look – dear – '

'Don't talk to me!' She turned on the other two men. 'You two gentlemen,' she said, 'you got no call because he works for you to get him involved, stirring it all up again. Putting ideas in his head. It won't bring her back. Leave us alone. Syd – you come home with me. Come home.'

'I can't,' he said. 'Min. I can't.'

'Why can't you?' She clapped her hand to her mouth. 'They've arrested you! They've found out – '

'*Shut up!*' he shouted. 'You silly cow. You don't know what you're saying. *Shut up!*' They stared aghast at each other. 'I'm sorry, Min,' he said. 'I never meant to speak rough. I'm not arrested. It's not like that.'

'Where are they, then? Those two?'

Gomez said: 'You! Chubb! Have you no control over your woman? Get rid of her.'

'And that'll do from you,' Chubb said, turning savagely on him.

From the depths of his armchair, Colonel Cockburn-Montfort, in an astonishingly clear and incisive tone, said: 'Chubb!'

'Sir!'

'You're forgetting yourself.'

'Sir.'

Alleyn said: 'Mrs Chubb, everything I said to you this morning was said in good faith. Circumstances have changed profoundly since then in a way that you know nothing about. You *will* know before long. In the meantime, if you please will you either stay here, quietly, in this room – '

'You better, Min,' Chubb said.

' – or,' Alleyn said, 'just go home and wait there. It won't be for long.'

'Go on, then, Min. You better.'

'I'll stay,' she said. She walked to the far end of the room and sat down.

Gomez, trembling with what seemed to be rage, shouted: 'For the last time – where are they? Where have they gone? Have they escaped? I demand an answer. Where are the Sanskrits?'

'They are downstairs,' Alleyn said.

Gomez leapt to his feet, let out an exclamation – in Portuguese, Alleyn supposed – seemed to be in two minds what to say and at last with a sort of doubtful relish said: 'Have you arrested them?'

'No.'

'I want to see them,' he said. 'I am longing to see them.'

'And so you shall,' said Alleyn.

He glanced at Fox, who went downstairs. Gomez moved towards the door.

The constable who had been on duty in the room came back and stationed himself inside the door.

'Shall we go down?' Alleyn said and led the way.

III

It was from this point that the sequence of events in the pig-pottery shop took on such a grotesque, such a macabre aspect, that Alleyn was to look back on the episode as possibly the most outlandish in his professional career. From the moment when the corpse of Miss Sanskrit received the first of her gentlemen visitors, they all three in turn became puppet-like caricatures of themselves, acting in a two-dimensional, crudely exaggerated style. In any other setting the element of black farce would have rioted. Even here, under the terrible auspices of the Sanskrits, it rose from time to time, like a bout of unseemly hysteria at the bad performance of a Jacobean tragedy.

The room downstairs had been made ready for the visit. Bailey and Thompson waited near the window, Gibson by the desk and Fox, with his notebook in hand, near the alcove. Two uniformed police stood inside the door and a third at the back of the alcove. The bodies of the Sanskrits, brother and sister, had not been moved or shrouded. The room was now dreadfully stuffy.

Alleyn joined Fox.

'Come in, Mr Gomez,' he said.

Gomez stood on the threshold, a wary animal, Alleyn thought, waiting with its ears laid back before advancing into strange territory. He looked, without moving his head, from one to another of the men in the room, seemed to hesitate, seemed to suspect and then, swaggering a little, came into the room.

He stopped dead in front of Alleyn and said: 'Well?'

Alleyn made a slight gesture. Gomez followed it, turned his head — and saw.

The noise he made was something between a retch and an exclamation. For a moment he was perfectly still and it was as if he and Miss Sanskrit actually and sensibly confronted each other. And because of the arch manner in which the lifeless head lolled on the lifeless arm and the dead eyes seemed to leer at him, it was as if Miss Sanskrit had done a Banquo and found Mr Gomez out.

He walked down the room and into the alcove. The policeman by the furnace gave a slight cough and eased his chin. Gomez inspected the bodies. He walked round the workbench and he looked into the packing-case. He might have been a visitor to a museum. There was no sound in the room other than the light fall of his feet on the wooden floor and the dry buzzing of flies.

Then he turned his back on the alcove, pointed to Alleyn and said: '*You!* What did you think to achieve by this? Make me lose my nerve? Terrify me into saying something you could twist into an admission? Oh no, my friend! I had no hand in the destruction of this vermin. Show me the man who did it and I'll kiss him on both cheeks and salute him as a brother, but I had no hand in it and you'll never prove anything else.'

He stopped. He was shaking as if with a rigor. He made to leave the room and saw that the door was guarded. And then he screamed out: 'Cover them up. They're obscene,' and went to the curtained window, turning his back on the room.

Fox, on a look from Alleyn, had gone upstairs. Thompson said under his breath, 'Could I have a second, Mr Alleyn?'

They went into the hallway. Thompson produced an envelope from his pocket and shook the contents out in his palm – two circular flattish objects about the size of an old sixpence, with concave upper surfaces. The under-surface of one had a pimple on it and on the other, a hole. They were blistered and there were tiny fragments of an indistinguishable charred substance clinging to them.

'Furnace?' Alleyn asked.

'That's right, sir.'

'Good. I'll take them.'

He restored them to their envelope, put them in his pocket and looked up the stairs to where Fox waited in the landing. 'Next,' he said, and thought: It's like a dentist's waiting-room.

The next was the Colonel. He came down in fairly good order with his shoulders squared and his chin up and feeling with the back of his heels for the stair-treads. As he turned into the shop he pressed up the corners of his moustache.

After the histrionics of Gomez, the Colonel's confrontation with the Sanskrits passed off quietly. He fetched up short, stood in absolute silence for a few seconds, and then said with an air that almost resembled dignity, 'This is disgraceful.'

'Disgraceful?' Alleyn repeated.

'They've been murdered.'

'Clearly.'

'The bodies ought to be covered. It's most irregular. And disgusting,' and he added, almost, it seemed, as an afterthought: 'It makes me feel sick.' And indeed he perceptibly changed colour.

He turned his back on the Sanskrits and joined Gomez by the window. 'I protest categorically,' he said, success-

492

fully negotiating the phrase, 'at the conduct of these proceedings. And I wish to leave the room.'

'Not just yet, I'm afraid,' Alleyn said as Gomez made a move towards the door, 'for either of you.'

'What right,' Gomez demanded, 'have you to keep me here? You have no right.'

'Well,' Alleyn said mildly, 'if you press the point we can note your objection, which I see Inspector Fox is doing in any case, and if you insist on leaving you may do so in a minute. In that case, of course, we shall ask you to come with us to the Yard. In the meantime: there's Chubb. Would you, Fox?'

In its own succinct way Chubb's reaction was a classic. He marched in almost as if Fox was a sergeant-major's escort, executed a smart left turn, saw Miss Sanskrit, halted, became rigid, asked – unbelievably – 'Who done it?' and fainted backwards like the soldier he had been.

And the Colonel, rivalling him in established behaviour, made a sharp exasperated noise and said: 'Damn bad show.'

Chubb recovered almost immediately. One of the constables brought him a drink of water. He was supported to the only chair in the room and sat in it with his back to the alcove.

'Very sorry, sir,' he mumbled, not to Alleyn but to the Colonel. His gaze alighted on Gomez.

'You done it!' he said, sweating and trembling. 'Din' you? You said you'd fix it and you did. You fixed it.'

'Do you lay a charge against Mr Gomez?' Alleyn said.

'Gomez? I don't know any Gomez.'

'Against Mr Sheridan?'

'I don't know what it means, lay a charge, and I don't know how he worked it, do I? But he said last night if it turned out they'd ratted, he'd get them. And I reckon he's kept 'is word. He's got them.'

Gomez sprang at him like a released spring, so suddenly and with such venom that it took Gibson and both the constables all their time to hold him. He let out short, disjointed phrases, presumably in Portuguese, wetting his blue chin and mouthing at Alleyn. Perhaps because the supply of invective ran out he at last fell silent and watchful and seemed the more dangerous for it.

'That was a touch of your old Ng'ombwanan form,' Alleyn said. 'You'd much better pipe down, Mr Gomez. Otherwise, you know, we shall have to lock you up.'

'Filth!' said Mr Gomez, and spat inaccurately in Chubb's direction.

'Bad show. Damn bad show,' reiterated the Colonel, who seemed to have turned himself into a sort of Chorus to The Action.

Alleyn said: 'Has one of you lost a pair of gloves?'

The scene went silent. For a second or two nobody moved and then Chubb got to his feet. Gomez, whose arms were still in custody, looked at his hands with their garnish of black hair and the Colonel thrust his into his pockets. And then, on a common impulse, it seemed they all three began accusing each other incoherently and inanely of the murder of the Sanskrits, and would no doubt have gone on doing so if the front doorbell had not pealed once more. As if the sound-track for whatever drama was being ground out had been turned back for a re-play, a woman could be heard making a commotion in the hallway.

'I want to see my husband. Stop that. Don't touch me. I'm going to see my husband.'

The Colonel whispered, 'No! For Chrissake keep her out. *Keep her out.*'

But she was already in the room with the constable on duty in the hall making an ineffectual grab after her and the two men inside the door, taken completely by surprise, looking to Alleyn for orders.

He had her by the arms. She was dishevelled and her eyes were out of focus. It would be hard to say whether she smelt stronger of gin or scent.

Alleyn turned her with her back to the alcove and her face towards her husband. He felt her sagging in his grasp.

'Hughie!' she said. 'You haven't have you? Hughie, promise you haven't. *Hughie!*'

She fought with Alleyn, trying to reach her husband.

494

'I couldn't stand it, Hughie,' she cried. 'Alone, after what you said you'd do. I had to come. I had to know.'

And as Chubb had turned on his wife, so the Colonel, in a different key, turned on her.

'Hold your tongue!' he roared out. 'You're drunk.'

She struggled violently with Alleyn and in doing so swung round in his grasp and faced the alcove.

And screamed. And screamed. And poured out such a stream of fatal words that her husband made a savage attempt to get at her and was held off by Fox and Thompson and Bailey. And then she became terrified of him, begged Alleyn not to let him get to her and finally collapsed.

There being nowhere else to put her, they half carried her upstairs and left her with Mrs Chubb, gabbling wildly about how badly he treated her and how she knew when he left the house in a blind rage he would do what he said he would do. All of which was noted down by the officer on duty in the upstairs room.

In the downstairs room Alleyn, not having a warrant for his arrest, asked Colonel Cockburn-Montfort to come to the Yard where he would be formally charged with the murder of the Sanskrits.

'And I should warn you that — '

Epilogue

'It was clear from the moment we saw the bodies,' Alleyn said, 'that Montfort was the man. The pig-pottery had been under strict surveillance from the time Sanskrit returned to it from the house-agents. The only gap came after Gibson's men had been drawn off by the bomb-scare. The traffic in the Mews piled up between Sergeant Jacks and the flat entrance where Montfort leant against the doorbell and for at least five minutes, probably longer, the façade was completely hidden by a van. During that time Montfort, who was beginning to make a scene in the street, had been admitted by one or other of the Sanskrits, with the object, one supposes, of shutting him up.

They were in a hurry. They had to get to the airport. They had planned to make their getaway within the next quarter of an hour and were packing up the last lot of pigs and writing a note for the agents. Leaving the drunken Colonel to grind to a halt, they returned to their jobs. Sanskrit put the penultimate pig in the case, his sister sat down to write the note. Montfort followed them up, found himself between the two of them, heaved up the last pig doorstop on the bench and in a drunken fury crashed it down left and right. The shock of what he'd done may have partly sobered him. His gloves were bloodied. He shoved them in the kiln, walked out and had the sense or the necessity to lean against the doorbell again. The van still blocked the view, and when it removed itself, there he still was.'

'Who raised the false alarm about the bomb?' asked Troy.

'Oh, one of the Sanskrits, don't you think? To draw Gibson's men off while the two of them did a bunk to

Ng'ombwana. They were in a blue funk over the outcome of the assassination and an even bluer one at the thought of the Ku-Klux-Fish. They realized, as they were bound to do, that they'd been rumbled.'

'It would seem,' Mr Whipplestone said drily, 'that they did not over-estimate the potential.'

'It would indeed.'

'Rory — *how* drunk was the wretched man?' Troy asked.

'Can one talk about degrees of drunkenness in an alcoholic? I suppose one can. According to his wife, and there's no reason to doubt her, he was plug-ugly drunk and breathing murder when he left the house.'

'And the whole thing, you believe, was completely unpremeditated?' Mr Whipplestone asked.

'I think so. No coherent plan when he leant on the doorbell. Nothing beyond a blind alcoholic rage to get at them. There was the pig on the work table and there were their heads. Bang, bang and he walked out again. The traffic block was just drunkard's luck. I don't for a moment suppose he was aware of it and I think he'd have behaved in exactly the same way if it hadn't occurred.'

'He had the sense to put his gloves in the kiln,' Mr Whipplestone pointed out.

'It's the only bit of hard evidence we've got. I wouldn't venture a guess as to how far the shock of what he'd done sobered him. Or as to how he may have exaggerated his condition for our benefit. He's been given a blood test and the alcoholic level was astronomical.'

'No doubt he'll plead drunkenness,' said Mr Whipplestone.

'You may depend upon it. And to some purpose, I don't mind betting.'

'What about my poor, silly Chubb?'

'Sam, in the ordinary course of things he'd face a charge of conspiracy. If it does come to that, the past history — his daughter — and the dominance of the others will tell enormously in his favour. With a first-class counsel — '

'I'll look after that. And his bail. I've told him so.'

'I'm not sure we've got a case. Apart from the *mlinzi's* collar-bone there's no hard evidence. What we would greatly prefer would be for Chubb to make a clean breast about the conspiracy in return for his own immunity.'

Mr Whipplestone and Troy looked uncomfortable.

'Yes, I know,' Alleyn said. 'But just you think for a bit about Gomez. He's the only one, apart from Montfort himself who'd be involved and believe me, if ever there was a specimen who deserved what's coming to him, it's that one. We've got him on a forged passport charge which will do to go on with, and a search of his pseudo coffee-importing premises in the City has brought to light some very dubious transactions in uncut diamonds. And in the background is his Ng'ombwanan conviction for manslaughter of a particularly revolting nature.'

'What about the Embassy angle?' Troy asked.

'What indeed? What happened within those *opéra bouffe* walls is, as we keep telling ourselves, their affair although it will figure obliquely as motive in the case against Montfort. But for the other show – the slaughter of the Ambassador by the *mlinzi* – that's over to The Boomer and I wish the old so-and-so joy of it.'

'He leaves tomorrow, I'm told.'

'Yes. At 2.30. After giving Troy a final sitting.'

'*Really!*' Mr Whipplestone exclaimed, gazing in polite awe at Troy. She burst out laughing.

'Don't look so shocked,' she said and to her own, Alleyn's and Mr Whipplestone's astonishment dropped a kiss on the top of his head. She saw the pink scalp under the neat strands of hair turn crimson and said: 'Pay no attention. I'm excited about my work.'

'Don't ruin everything!' said Mr Whipplestone with tremendous dash. 'I'd hoped it was about me.'

'By all the rules, if there were any valid ones,' Troy said at half past eleven the following morning, 'it's an unfinished portrait. But even if you could give me another sitting I don't think I'd take it.'

The Boomer stood beside her looking at her work. At no stage of the sitting had he exhibited any of the usual shyness of the sitter who doesn't want to utter banalities and at no stage had he uttered any.

'There is something African in the way you have gone about this picture,' he said. 'We have no portraitists of distinction at present but if we had they would try to do very much as you have done, I think. I find it hard to remember that the painter is not one of my people.'

'You couldn't have said anything to please me more,' said Troy.

'No? I am glad. And so I must go: Rory and I have one or two things to settle and I have to change. So it is goodbye, my dear Mrs Rory, and thank you.'

'Goodbye,' Troy said, 'my dear President Boomer, and thank you.'

She gave him her painty hand and saw him into the house where Alleyn waited for him. This time he had come without his *mlinzi* who, he said, was involved with final arrangements at the Embassy.

He and Alleyn had a drink together.

'This has been in some ways an unusual visit,' The Boomer remarked.

'A little unusual,' Alleyn agreed.

'On your part, my dear Rory, it has been characterized by the tactful avoidance of difficult corners.'

'I've done my best. With the assistance, if that's the right word, of diplomatic immunity.'

The Boomer gave him a tentative smile. Alleyn reflected that this was a rare occurrence. The Boomer's habit was to bellow with laughter, beam like a lighthouse or remain entirely solemn.

'So those unpleasant persons,' he said, 'have been murdered by Colonel Cockburn-Montfort.'

'It looks like it.'

'They *were* unpleasant,' The Boomer said thoughtfully. 'We were sorry to employ them but needs must. You find the same sort of situation in your own service, of course.'

This being perfectly true, there was little to be said in reply.

'We regretted the necessity,' The Boomer said, 'to reinstate them in Ng'ombwana.'

'In the event,' Alleyn said drily, 'you don't have to.'

'No!' he cried gaily. 'So it's an ill wind, as the saying goes. We are spared the Sanskrits. *What* a good thing.'

Alleyn gazed at him, speechless.

'Is anything the matter, old boy?' The Boomer asked.

Alleyn shook his head.

'Ah!' said The Boomer. 'I think I know. We have come within sight of that ravine, again.'

'And again we can arrange to meet elsewhere.'

'That is why you have not asked me certain questions. Such as how far was I aware of the successful counterplot against my traitor-Ambassador. Or whether I myself dealt personally with the odious Sanskrits who served us so usefully. Or whether it was I, of my own design, who led our poor Gibson so far down the Embassy garden path.'

'Not only Gibson.'

An expression of extreme distress came over the large black face. His paws gripped Alleyn's shoulders and his enormous, slightly bloodshot eyes filled with tears.

'Try to understand,' he said. 'Justice has been done in accordance with our need, our grass-roots, our absolute selves. With time we shall evolve a change and adapt and gradually such elements may die out in us. At the present, my very dear friend, you must think of us – of me, if you like, as – '

He hesitated for a moment and then with a smile and a change in his huge voice: ' – as an unfinished portrait,' said The Boomer.

Coda

On a very warm morning in mid-summer, Lucy Lockett, wearing the ornamental collar in which she seemed to fancy herself, sat on the front steps of No. 1, Capricorn Walk, contemplating the scene and keeping an ear open on proceedings in the basement flat.

Mr Whipplestone had found a suitable tenant and the Chubbs were turning out the premises. A vacuum cleaner whined, there were sundry bumps. The windows were open and voices were heard.

Mr Whipplestone had gone to the Napoli to buy his Camembert and Lucy, who never accompanied him into the Mews, awaited his return.

The cleaner was switched off. The Chubbs interchanged peaceful remarks and Lucy, suddenly moved by the legendary curiosity of her species and sex, leapt neatly into the garden and thence through the basement window.

The chattels of the late tenant had been removed but a certain amount of litter still remained. Lucy pretended to kill a crumpled sheet of newspaper and then fossicked about in odd corners. The Chubbs paid little attention to her.

When Mr Whipplestone returned he found his cat on the top step, couchante, with something between her forepaws. She gazed up at him and made one of her fetching little remarks.

'What have you got there?' he asked. He inserted his eyeglass and bent down to see.

It was a white pottery fish.

Artists in Crime

For Phyllis and John

CONTENTS

THE CHARACTERS IN THE TALE

Chief Detective-Inspector
Roderick Alleyn, C.I.D.

Miss Van Maes — *The success of the ship*

Agatha Troy, R.A. — *Of Tatler's End House, Bossicote, Bucks. Painter*

Katti Bostock — *Well-known painter of plumbers and Negro musicians*

Nigel Bathgate — *Journalist*

Lady Alleyn — *Of Danes Lodge, Bossicote, Bucks; mother of Chief Detective-Inspector Alleyn*

Cedric Malmsley — *A student with a beard*

Garcia — *A sculptor*

Sonia Gluck — *A model*

Francis Ormerin — *A student from Paris*

Phillida Lee — *A student from the Slade*

Watt Hatchett — *A student from Australia*

The Hon. Basil Pilgrim — *A student from the nobility*

Valmai Seacliff — *A student with sex-appeal*

Superintendent Blackman — *Of the Buckingham Constabulary*

Detective-Inspector Fox,
C.I.D.

Detective-Sergeant Bailey, — *A fingerprint expert*
C.I.D.

Detective-Sergeant Thompson, C.I.D.	*A photographic expert*
Dr Ampthill	*Police surgeon at Bossicote, Bucks.*
P.C. Sligo	*Of Bossicote Police Force*
A charlady	
Bobbie O'Dawne	*A lady of the Ensemble*
An estate agent	
Ted McCully	*Foreman at a car depot*
Dr Curtis	*Police surgeon, C.I.D.*
Captain Pascoe	*Of Boxover*
His servant	

Chapter 1

Prologue at Sea

Alleyn leant over the deck-rail, looking at the wet brown wharf and the upturned faces of the people. In a minute or two now they would slide away, lose significance, and become a vague memory. 'We called at Suva.' He had a sudden desire to run a mental ring round the scene beneath him, to isolate it, and make it clear, for ever in his mind. Idly at first, and then with absurd concentration, he began to memorize, starting with a detail. The tall Fijian with dyed hair. The hair was vivid magenta against the arsenic green of a pile of fresh bananas. He trapped and held the pattern of it. Then the brown face beneath, with liquid blue half-tones reflected from the water, then the oily dark torso, fore-shortened, the white loincloth, and the sharp legs. The design made by the feet on wet planks. It became a race. How much of the scene could he fix in his memory before the ship sailed? The sound, too – he must get that – the firm slap of bare feet on wet boards, the languid murmur of voices and the snatches of song drifting from a group of native girls near those clumps of fierce magenta coral. The smell must not be forgotten – frangipanni, coconut oil, and sodden wood. He widened his circle, taking in more figures – the Indian woman in the shrill pink sari, sitting by the green bananas; wet roofs on the wharf and damp roads wandering aimlessly towards mangrove swamps and darkened hills. Those hills, sharply purple at their base, lost outline behind a sulky company of clouds, to jag out, fantastically peaked, against a motionless and sombre sky. The clouds themselves were indigo at the edges, heavy with the ominous depression of unshed rain. The darkness of everything and the violence of colour – it was a pattern of wet brown, acid green, magenta and indigo. The round voices of the

509

Fijians, loud and deep, as though they spoke through resounding tubes, pierced the moist air and made it vibrant.

Everything shifted a little, stepped back a pace. The ship had parted from the wharf. Already the picture was remote, the sounds would soon fade out. Alleyn shut his eyes and found the whole impression vivid under the closed lids. When he opened them the space between vessel and land had widened. He no longer wanted to look at the wharf, and turned away.

'And am I *hart*?' the success of the ship was saying to a group of young men. 'Oh baby! I'll say I've left haff a stone back there in that one-eyed lil' burg. Hart! Phoo!'

The young men laughed adoringly.

'It's hotter than this in Honolulu!' teased one of the young men.

'Maybe. But it's not so enervating.'

'Very hot spot, Honolulu!'

'Oh boy!' chanted the success, rolling her eyes and sketching a Hawaiian movement with her hips. 'You wait a while till I show you round the lil' old home town. Gee, that label on my grips certainly looks good to me.' She saw Alleyn. 'Hello, hello, look who's here! Come right over and join the party.'

Alleyn strolled over. Ever since they sailed from Auckland he had been uneasily aware of a certain warmth in the technique of the success where he was concerned. He supposed it was rather one up to him with all these youngsters in hot pursuit. At this stage of speculation he invariably pulled a fastidious face and thought ruefully: 'Lord, Lord, the vanity of the male forties.' But she was very lonely, and the thought of her almost lent a little glamour to the possible expectation of the weary routine of a shipboard flirtation.

'Look at him!' cried the success. 'Isn't he the cutest thing! That quiet English stuff certainly makes one great big appeal with this baby. And does he flash the keep-clear signal! Boys, I'll take you right into my confidence.

510

Listen! This Mr Alleyn is my big flop. I don't mean a thing to him.'

'She really is rather awful,' thought Alleyn, and he said: 'Ah, Miss Van Maes, you don't know a coward when you see one.'

'Meaning?'

'I – I really don't know,' mumbled Alleyn hurriedly.

'Hullo, we're going through the barrier,' said one of the youths.

They all turned to the deck-rail. The sea wrapped itself sluggishly about the thin rib of the reef and fell away on either side in an enervated pother of small breakers. Over Fiji the rain still hung in ponderable clouds. The deep purple of the islands was lit by desultory patches of livid sunshine, banana-green, sultry, but without iridescence. The ship passed through the fangs of the reef.

Alleyn slipped away, walked aft, and climbed the companion-way to the boat deck. Nobody about up there, the passengers in their shoregoing clothes were still collected on the main deck. He filled his pipe meditatively, staring back towards Fiji. It was pleasant up there. Peaceful.

'Damn!' said a female voice. 'Damn, damn, damn! Oh *blast*!'

Startled, Alleyn looked up. Sitting on the canvas cover of one of the boats was a woman. She seemed to be dabbing at something. She stood up and he saw that she wore a pair of exceedingly grubby flannel trousers, and a short grey overall. In her hand was a long brush. Her face was disfigured by a smudge of green paint, and her short hair stood up in a worried shock, as though she had run her hands through it. She was very thin and dark. She scrambled to the bows of the boat and Alleyn was able to see what she had been at. A small canvas was propped up in the lid of an open paint-box. Alleyn drew in his breath sharply. It was as if his deliberately cultivated memory of the wharf at Suva had been simplified and made articulate. The sketch was an almost painfully

511

explicit statement of the feeling of that scene. It was painted very directly with crisp, nervous touches. The pattern of blue-pinks and sharp greens fell across it like the linked syllables of a perfect phrase. It was very simply done, but to Alleyn it was profoundly satisfying – an expression of an emotion, rather than a record of a visual impression.

The painter, an unlit cigarette between her lips, stared dispassionately at her work. She rummaged in her trouser pockets, found nothing but a handkerchief that had been used as a paint-rag, and ran her fingers through her hair. 'Blast!' she repeated, and took the unlit cigarette from her lips.

'Match?' said Alleyn.

She started, lost her balance, and sat down abruptly.

'How long have you been there?' she demanded ungraciously.

'Only just come. I – I haven't been spying. May I give you a match?'

'Oh – thanks. Chuck up the box, would you?' She lit her cigarette, eyeing him over the top of her long thin hands, and then turned to look again at her work.

'It is exceedingly good, isn't it?' said Alleyn.

She hunched up one shoulder as if his voice was a piercing draught in her ear, muttered something, and crawled back to her work. She picked up her palette and began mixing a streak of colour with her knife.

'You're not going to do anything more to it?' said Alleyn involuntarily.

She turned her head and stared at him.

'Why not?'

'Because it's perfect – you'll hurt it. I say, please forgive me. Frightful impertinence. I do apologize.'

'Oh, don't be ridiculous,' she said impatiently, and screwed up her eyes to peer at the canvas.

'I merely thought – ' began Alleyn.

'I had an idea,' said the painter, 'that if I worked up

512

here on this hideously uncomfortable perch, I might possibly have the place to myself for a bit.'

'You shall,' said Alleyn, and bowed to her profile. He tried to remember if he had ever before been quite so pointedly snubbed by a total stranger. Only, he reflected, by persons he was obliged to interview in the execution of his duties as an officer of Scotland Yard. On those occasions he persisted. On this an apologetic exit seemed to be clearly indicated. He walked to the top of the companion-way, and then paused.

'But if you do anything more, you'll be a criminal. The thing's perfect. Even I can see that, and I – '

' "Don't know anything about it, but I *do* know what I like," ' quoted the lady savagely.

'I was not about to produce that particular bromide,' said Alleyn mildly.

For the first time since he had spoken to her, she gave him her full attention. A rather charming grin lifted the corners of her mouth.

'All right,' she said, 'I'm being objectionable. My turn to apologize. I thought at first you were one of the "don't put me in it" sort of onlookers.'

'Heaven forbid!'

'I wasn't going to do too much,' she went on, actually as if she had turned suddenly shy. 'It's just that figure in the foreground – I left it too late. Worked for an hour before we sailed. There should be a repetition of the bluish grey there, but I can't remember – ' She paused, worried.

'But there was!' exclaimed Alleyn. 'The reflection off the water up the inside of the thighs. Don't you remember?'

'Golly – you're right,' she said. 'Here – wait a bit.'

She picked up a thin brush, broke it through the colour, held it poised for a second, and then laid a delicate touch on the canvas. 'That?'

'Yes,' cried Alleyn excitedly. 'That's done it. Now you can stop.'

'All right, all right. I didn't realize you were a painting bloke.'

'I'm not. It's simply insufferable cheek.'

She began to pack up her box.

'Well, I must say you're very observant for a layman. Good memory.'

'Not really,' said Alleyn. 'It's synthetic.'

'You mean you've trained your eye?'

'I've had to try to do so, certainly.'

'Why?'

'Part of my job. Let me take your box for you.'

'Oh – thank you. Mind the lid – it's a bit painty. Pity to spoil those lovely trousers. Will you take the sketch?'

'Do you want a hand down?' offered Alleyn.

'I can manage, thank you,' she said gruffly, and clambered down to the deck.

Alleyn had propped the canvas against the rail and now stood looking at it. She joined him, eyeing it with the disinterested stare of the painter.

'Why!' murmured Alleyn suddenly. 'Why, you must be Agatha Troy.'

'That's me.'

'Good Lord, what a self-sufficient fathead I've been.'

'Why?' said Agatha Troy. 'You were all right. Very useful.'

'Thank you,' said Alleyn humbly. 'I saw your one-man show a year ago in London.'

'Did you?' she said without interest.

'I should have guessed at once. Isn't there a sort of relationship between this painting and the "In the Stadium"?'

'Yes.' She moved her eyebrows quickly. 'That's quite true. The arrangement's much the same – radiating lines and a spotted pattern. Same feeling. Well, I'd better go down to my cabin and unpack.'

'You joined the ship at Suva?'

'Yes. I noticed this subject from the main deck. Things

514

shove themselves at you like that sometimes. I dumped my luggage, changed, and came up.'

She slung her box over her shoulder and picked up the sketch.

'Can I – ?' said Alleyn diffidently.

'No, thanks.'

She stood for a moment staring back towards Fiji. Her hands gripped the shoulder-straps of her paint-box. The light breeze whipped back her short dark hair, revealing the contour of the skull and the delicate bones of the face. The temples were slightly hollow, the cheek-bones showed, the dark-blue eyes were deep-set under the thin ridge of the brows. The sun caught the olive skin with its smudge of green paint, and gave it warmth. There was a kind of spare gallantry about her. She turned quickly before he had time to look away and their gaze met.

Alleyn was immediately conscious of a clarification of his emotions. As she stood before him, her face slowly reddening under his gaze, she seemed oddly familiar. He felt that he already knew her next movement, and the next inflexion of her clear, rather cold voice. It was a little as though he had thought of her a great deal, but never met her before. These impressions held him transfixed, for how long he never knew, while he still kept his eyes on hers. Then something clicked in his mind, and he realized that he had stared her out of countenance. The blush had mounted painfully to the roots of her hair and she had turned away.

'I'm sorry,' said Alleyn steadily. 'I'm afraid I was looking at the green smudge on your cheek.'

She scrubbed at her face with the cuff of her smock.

'I'll go down,' she said, and picked up the sketch.

He stood aside, but she had to pass close to him, and again he was vividly aware of her, still with the same odd sense of surprised familiarity. She smelt of turpentine and paint, he noticed.

'Well – good evening,' she said vaguely.

Alleyn laughed a little.

'Good evening, madam.'

She started off down the ladder, moving sideways and holding the wet sketch out over the hand-rail. He turned away and lit a cigarette. Suddenly a terrific rumpus broke out on the deck below. The hot cheap reek of frangipanni blossoms drifted up, and with it the voice of the success of the ship.

'Oh, pardon me. Come right down. Gangway, fellows. Oh say, pardon me, but have you been making a picture? Can I have a keek? I'm just crazy about sketching. Look, boys – isn't that cute? The wharf? My, my, it's a shame you haven't been able to finish it, isn't it? It would have been swell! Look, boys, it's the wharf. Maybe a snapshot would help. We'll surely have to watch our step with an artist on board. Say, let's get acquainted. We've been celebrating and we feel fine. Meet the mob. I'm Virginia Van Maes.'

'My name's Troy,' said a voice that Alleyn could scarcely recognize. A series of elaborate introductions followed.

'Well, Miss Troy, I was going to tell you how Caley Burt painted my portrait in Noo York. You've heard of Caley Burt? I guess he's one of the most exclusive portraitists in America. Well, it seems he was just crazy to take my picture – '

The anecdote was a long one. Agatha Troy remained silent throughout.

'Well, when he was through – and say, did I get tired of that dress? – it certainly was one big success. Poppa bought it, and it's in our reception-hall at Honolulu. Some of the crowd say it doesn't just flatter, but it looks good to me. I don't pretend to know a whole lot about art, Miss Troy, but I know what I like.'

'Quite,' said Agatha Troy. 'Look here, I think I'd better get down to my cabin. I haven't unpacked yet. If you'll excuse me – '

'Why, certainly. We'll be seeing you. Say, have you seen that guy Alleyn around?'

'I'm afraid I don't know – '

'He's tall and thin, and I'll say he's good looking. And is he British? Gee! I'm crazy about him. I got a little gamble with these boys, I'll have him doing figure eights trying to dope out when the petting-party gets started.'

'I've kissed goodbye to my money,' one of the youths said.

'Listen to him, will you, Miss Troy? But we certainly saw Mr Alleyn around this way a while back.'

'He went up to the boat deck,' said a youth.

'Oh,' said Miss Troy clearly. 'That man! Yes, he's up there now.'

'Atta-boy!'

'Whooppee!'

'Oh damn!' said Alleyn softly.

And the next thing that happened was Miss Van Maes showing him how she'd made a real Honolulu *lei* out of Fijian frangipanni, and asking him to come down with the crowd for a drink.

'Has this party gone cuckoo or something? We're three rounds behind the clock. C'm on!'

'Virginia,' said a youth, 'you're tight.'

'What the hell! Is it my day to be sober? You coming, Mr Alleyn?'

'Thank you so much,' said Alleyn, 'but if you'll believe it, I'm a non-drinker at the moment. Doctor's orders.'

'Aw, be funny!'

'Fact. I assure you.'

'Mr Alleyn's thinking of the lady with the picture,' said a youth.

'What – her? With her face all mussed in green paint. Mr Alleyn's not screwy yet, is he? Gee, I'll say a woman's got no self-respect to go around that way in public. Did you get a look at that smock? And the picture! Well, I had to be polite and say it was cute, but it's nobody's big sorrow she didn't finish it. The wharf at Suva! Seems I struck it lucky, but what it's meant for's just anyone's guess. C'm on, Mr Strong-Silent Sleuth, put me out of my agony and say she don't mean one thing to you.'

'Miss Van Maes,' said Alleyn, 'do you know that you make me feel very middle-aged and inexpressibly foolish? I haven't got the smallest idea what the right answer is to any single one of your questions.'

'Maybe I could teach you. Maybe I could teach you a whole lot of fun, honey.'

'You're very kind, but, do you know, I'm afraid I'm past the receptive age.'

She widened her enormous eyes. The mascaraed lashes stuck out round them like black toothpicks. Her ash-fair hair was swept back from her very lovely face into a cluster of disciplined and shining curls. She had the un-human good looks of a film star. Undoubtedly she was rather tight.

'Well,' she said, 'my bet with the boys is still good. Twenty-five'll get anybody fifty you kiss me before we hit Honolulu. And I don't mean maybe.'

'I should be very much honoured – '

'Yeah? And I don't mean the get-by-the-censor stuff, either. No, sir!'

She stared at him, and upon her normally blank and beautiful face there dawned a look of doubt.

'Say,' she said, 'you're not going to tell me you got a yen for that woman?'

'I don't know what a yen is,' Alleyn said, 'but I've got nothing at all for Miss Troy, and I can assure you she has got even less than that for me.'

Chapter 2

Five Letters

From Miss Agatha Troy to her friend, Miss Katti Bostock, the well-known painter of plumbers, miners and Negro musicians:

S. S. Niagara,
August 1st.

Dear Katti,

I am breaking this journey at Quebec, so you'll get this letter about a fortnight before I get home. I'm glad everything is fixed up for next term. It's a bore in some ways having to teach, but now I've reached the giddy heights of picking and choosing I don't find it nearly so irksome. Damn good of you to do all the arranging for me. If you can, get the servants into the house by Sept. 1st – I get back on the 3rd – they ought to have everything fixed up by the 10th, when we start classes. Your air mail reached Suva the day we sailed. Yes, book Sonia Gluck for model. The little swine's beautiful and knows how to pose as long as she behaves herself. You yourself might do a big nude for the Group Show on the 16th or thereabouts. You paint well from the nude and I think you shouldn't remain wedded to your plumbers – your stuff will get static if you don't look out. I don't think I told you who is coming next term. Here is the list!

(1) Francis Ormerin. He's painting in Paris at the moment, but says the lot at Malaquin's has come all over surrealist and he can't see it and doesn't want to. Says he's depressed about his work or something.

(2) Valmai Seacliff. That's the girl that did those dabby Rex Whistlerish posters for the Board of Trade. She says she wants to do some solid work

from the model. Quite true, she does; but I rather fancy she's on the hunt.

(3) Basil Pilgrim. If I'm not mistaken, Basil is Valmai's quarry. He's an Hon., you know, and old Lord Pilgrim is doddering to the grave. He's the 'Peer that became a Primitive Methodist' a few years ago – you remember. The papers were full of it. He comes to light with the odd spot of hell-fire on the subject of birth-control, every now and then. Basil's got six elder sisters, and Lady Pilgrim died when he was born, so we don't know what she thought about it. I hardly think Valmai Seacliff will please the old gentleman. Basil's painting nearly drove him into the Salvation Army, I fancy.

(4) Watt Hatchett. This is new blood. He's an Australian youth I found working in Suva. Very promising stuff. Simplified form and swinging lines. He's as keen as mustard, and was practically living on bananas and cheek when I ran into him. His voice is like the crashing together of old tin cans, and he can talk of nothing but his work, his enthusiasms, and his dislikes. I'm afraid he'll get on their nerves and they may put him on the defensive. Still, his work is good.

(5) Cedric Malmsley. He's got a job illustrating some *de luxe* edition of medieval romances, and wants to get down to it with a model handy. It ought to work in all right. I told him to get in touch with you. I hear he's grown a blond beard that parts in the middle and wears sandals – Cedric, not the beard.

(6) Wolf Garcia, I had a letter from Garcia. No money, but a commission to do Comedy and Tragedy in marble for the new cinema in Westminster, so will I let him stay with me and do the clay model? No stamp on the envelope and written in conte chalk on lavatory paper. He will probably turn up long before you get this letter. Let him use the studio, will you, but look out, if you've got Sonia there. Garcia's got

the use of someone's studio in London after the 20th, and hopes to have a cast ready by then, so it won't be for long. Now don't bully me, Katti. You know the creature is really – Heaven save the mark – a genius; and the others all pay me through the nose, so I can afford to carry a couple of dead-heads. Yes, you're quite right. Hatchett *is* the other.

(7) One Phillida Lee. Just left the Slade, Rich father. She sent me some of her stuff and a rather gushing little request to work under me 'because she has always longed', etc., etc. I wrote back asking the earth in fees and she snapped at it.

(8) You, bless you. I've told them all to fix up with you. Malmsley, Ormerin and Pilgrim can have the dormitory; Garcia one attic, and Hatchett the other. You have the yellow room as usual, and put Valmai Seacliff and the Lee child in the blue. The great thing is to segregate Garcia. You know what he is, and I won't have that sort of thing – it's too muddly. On second thoughts it might be better to put him in the studio and the model in the attic. I rather think they were living together in London. By the way, I'm going to do a portrait of Valmai Seacliff. It'll do for Burlington House and the Salon, drat them. She'll be good enough to paint in the slap-up grand manner.

I'm scratching this off in the writing-room on my first night out from Suva. Did a small thing looking down in the wharf before we sailed. Came off rather well. I was interrupted by a man whom I thought was a fool, and who turned out to be intelligent, so I felt the fool. There's an American ex-cinema actress running about this ship half tight. She looks like one of their magazine covers and behaves like the wrath of God. The man seems to be her property, so perhaps he is a fool, after all.

If anything amusing happens, I'll add to this. It's been an interesting holiday, and I'm glad I did it. Your letters have been grand. Splendid the work goes on so well. I look forward to seeing it. Think about a nude for the Group. You don't want to be called the Plumber's Queen.

Later. We get into Vancouver tomorrow. It's been a peaceful trip since Honolulu, where the Ship's Belle left us. Before that it was rather hellish. Unfortunately someone had the number of *The Palette* that ran a special supplement of my show. The Belle got hold of it and decided I must be a real artist after all. When she saw the reproduction of the Royal portrait she laid her ears back and settled down to a steady pursuit. Wouldn't it be just wonderful if I did a portrait of her before we got to Honolulu? Her poppa would be tickled to death. She changed her clothes six times a day and struck a new attitude whenever she caught my eye. I had to pretend I'd got neuritis in my hand, which was a curse, as I rather wanted to do a head of one of the other passengers – a very paintable subject with plenty of good bone. However, I got down to it after Honolulu. The subject is a detective and looks like a grandee. Sounds like it, too – very old-world and chivalrous and so on. Damn! that looks like a cheap sneer, and it's not meant to. I'm rather on the defensive about this sleuth – I was so filthily rude to him, and he took it like a gent and made me feel like a bounder. Very awkward. The head is fairly successful.

Well, Katti, old lady, we meet on the 3rd. I'll come straight to Tatler's End. Best love.

Yours ever,
Troy

PS. – Perhaps you'd better give Garcia a shakedown in the studio and lock him in. We'll hope he'll have gone by the 20th.

522

Katti Bostock to Agatha Troy.

Tatler's End House,
Bossicote,
Bucks.
August 14th

Dear Troy,

You are a gump to collect these bloodsuckers. Yes, I know Garcia is damn good at sculping, but he's a nasty little animal, and thinks everyone else is born to keep him. God knows how much he's got out of you already. All right, I'll shut him up in the studio, but if he's after Sonia or anyone else, he'll crawl out by the ventilator. And if you imagine you'll get rid of him before the 20th, you're wandering. And who in the name of Bacchus is this Australian blight? You're paying his fare home, of course. Well, I suppose I can't talk, as you've given me the run of your house for twelve months. It's been a godsend, and I've done my best work here. Been working on a thing of two Negro saxophonists, worm's-eye view of, with cylindrical background. Not bad, I fancy. It's finished now. I've started on a big thing, using that little devil Sonia Gluck. It's a standing pose and she's behaving abominably, blast her! However, she agreed to come next term for the usual exorbitant fee, as soon as she heard Garcia and Pilgrim were to be in the class. Malmsley arrived today. The beard is there all right, and looks like the Isle of Patmos gone decadent. He's full of the book-illustration job, and showed me some of the sketches – quite good. I've met Pilgrim several times, and like him and his work. I hear he's always to be seen with the Seacliff blight, so I suppose she's after the title. That girl's a nymphomaniac, and a successful one at that. Funny this 'It' stuff. I've never inspired a thought that wasn't respectable, and yet I get on with men all right. You're different. They'd fall for you if you'd let them, only you're so unprovocative they never know where they are, and end by taking you at your own valuation. The Seacliff and Pilgrim arrive tomorrow. I've seen Miss Phillida Lee. She's very would-be Slade. Wears hand-printed clothes with high necks, and shudders and burbles alternately. She comes on the 9th, and so does Ormerin, who writes from Paris and sounds very depressed. Nice bloke. I don't know whether it's struck you what a rum brew the class will be this term. It's impossible to keep Sonia in her place, wherever a model's place may be. Garcia, if he's here, will either be in full cry after her, which will be unpleasant, or else sick of her, which will be worse. Valmai Seacliff will naturally expect every male on the premises to be hot on her trail, and if that comes off, Sonia will get the pip. Perhaps with Basil Pilgrim on the tapis, the Seacliff will be less catholic, but I doubt it. Oh, well, you know your own business best, and I suppose will float through on the good old recipe of not noticing. You are such a bloody aristocrat. Your capacity for ignoring the unpleasant is a bit irritating to a plebeian like myself.

The servants are all right. The two Hipkins and Sadie Welsh from the village. They only tolerate me and are thrilled over your return. So am I, actually. I want your advice over the big thing of Sonia, and I'm longing to see your own stuff. You say don't forward any more letters, so I won't. Your allusions to a detective are quite incomprehensible, but if he interrupted you in your work, you had every right to bite his head off. What had you been up to, anyway? – Well, so long until the 3rd – *Katti*.

PS. – Garcia has just sent a case of clay and a lot of material – carriage forward, *of course* – so I suppose I may expect to be honoured with his company any time now. We'll probably get a bill for the clay.

PPS. – Plumber's Queen yourself.

PPPS. – The bill for Garcia's material has come.

Chief Detective-Inspector Roderick Alleyn, CID., to Mr
Nigel Bathgate, journalist.

S.S. Niagara (At Sea).
August 6th

Dear Bathgate,

How is it with Benedict, the married man? I was
extremely sorry to be away for the wedding, and
thought of you both on my mountain fastness in New
Zealand. What a perfect place that would have been
for a honeymoon. A primitive but friendly back-
country pub, a lovely lake, tall mountains and
nothing else for fifty miles. But I suppose you and
your Angela were fashionably on the Riviera or
somewhere. You're a lucky young devil, and I wish
you both all the happiness in the world, and send
you my blessing. I'm glad my offering met with Mrs
Angela's approval.

We get to Vancouver in no time now, and leave
the same day on the C.P.R. Most of the passengers
are going on. I am breaking my journey at Quebec,
a place I have always wanted to see. That will still
give me fifteen days in England before I climb back
into the saddle. My mother expects me to spend a
fortnight with her, and if I may, I'll come on to you
about the 21st?

The passengers on this ship are much like all
passengers on all ships. Sea voyages seem to act as
rather searching re-agents on character. The essential
components appear in alarming isolation. There is
the usual ship's belle, this time a perfectly terrific
American cinema lady who throws me into a fever
of diffidence and alarm, but who exhibits the closeup
type of loveliness to the nth degree of unreality.
There is the usual sprinkling of pleasant globe-
trotters, bounders, and avid women. The most
interesting person is Miss Agatha Troy, the painter.
Do you remember her one-man show? She has done

a miraculous painting of the wharf at Suva. I long to ask what the price will be, but am prevented by the circumstances of her not liking me very much. She bridles like a hedgehog (yes, they do) whenever I approach her, and as I don't believe I suffer from any of those things in the strip advertisements, I'm rather at a loss to know why. Natural antipathy, perhaps. I don't share it. Oddly enough, she suddenly asked me in a very gruff stand-offish voice if she might paint my head. I've never been took a likeness of before – it's a rum sensation when they get to the eyes; such a searching impersonal sort of glare they give you. She even comes close sometimes and peers into the pupils. Rather humiliating, it is. I try to return a stare every bit as impersonal, and find it tricky. The painting seems to me to be quite brilliant, but alarming.

Fox has written regularly. He seems to have done damn well over that arson case. I rather dread getting back into the groove, but suppose it won't be so bad when it comes. Hope I don't have to start off with anything big – if Mrs Angela thinks of putting rat's-bane in your Ovaltine, ask her to do it out of my division.

I look forward to seeing you both, my dear Bathgate, and send you my salutations the most distinguished.

Yours ever,
Roderick Alleyn

Chief Detective-Inspector Alleyn to Lady Alleyn, Danes Lodge, Bossicote, Bucks.

C.P.R.
August 15th.

My Dearest Mamma,
    Your letter found me at Vancouver. Yes, please –

I should like to come straight to you. We arrive at Liverpool on the 7th, and I'll make for Bucks as fast as may be. The garden sounds very attractive, but don't go doing too much yourself, bless you. No, darling, I did not lose my heart in the Antipodes. Would you have been delighted to welcome a strapping black Fijian lady? I might have got one to regard me with favour at Suva, perhaps, but they smell of coconut oil, which you would not have found particularly delicious. I expect if I ever do get it in the neck, she'll think me no end of a dull dog and turn icy. Talking of Suva, which I was not, do you know of a place called Tatler's End House, somewhere near Bossicote? Agatha Troy, who painted that picture we both liked so much, lives there. She joined this ship at Suva, and did a lovely thing of the wharf. Look here, Mamma, if ever a Virginia Van Maes writes and asks you to receive her, you must be away, or suffering from smallpox. She's an American beauty who looks people up in Kelly's and collects scalps. She looked me up and – Heaven knows why – she seemed inclined to collect ours. It's the title, I suppose. Talking of titles, how's the blasted Baronet? She was on to him like a shot. 'Gee, Mr Alleyn, I never knew your detective force was recruited from your aristocracy. I'm crazy to know if this Sir George Alleyn is your only brother.' You see? She threatens to come to England and has already said she's sure you must be the cutest old-world mother. She's quite capable of muscling in on the strength of being my dearest girl-friend. So you look out, darling, I've told her you're a horrid woman, but I don't think she cares. You'll be 65 on or about the day this arrives. In 30 years I shall be nearly 10 years older than you are now, and you'll still be trying to bully me. Do you remember how I found out your real age on your thirty-fifth birthday? My first really good bit of investigation, nasty little trick that I was. Well, little mum, don't flirt with the vicar, and be sure to have the red carpet out on the 7th.

Your dutiful and devoted son,

Roderick

PS. – Miss Troy has done a sketch of your son which he will purchase for your birthday if it's not too expensive.

From Lady Alleyn, Danes Lodge, Bossicote, to Chief Detective-Inspector Alleyn, Château Frontenac, Quebec.

Dear Roderick,

Your ingenuous little letter reached me on my birthday, and I was delighted to receive it. Thank you, my dear. It will be a great joy to have you for nearly a fortnight, greedily to myself. I trust I am *not* one of those avaricious mammas – clutch, clutch, clutch – which, after all, is only a form of cluck, cluck, cluck. It will be delightful to have a Troy version of you, and I hope it was not too expensive – if it was, perhaps you would let me join you, my dear. I should like to do that, but have no doubt you will ruin yourself and lie to your mother about the price. I shall call on Miss Troy, not only because you obviously wish me to do so, but because I have always liked her work, and should be pleased to meet her, as your Van Maes would say. George is with his family in Scotland. He talks of standing for Parliament, but I am afraid he will only make a fool of himself, poor dear. It's a pity he hasn't got your brains. I have brought a hand-loom and am also breeding Alsatians. I hope the bitch – Tunbridge Tessa – does not take a dislike to you. She is very sweet really. I always feel, darling, that you should not have left the Foreign Office, but at the same time, I am a great believer in everybody doing what he wants, and I *do* enjoy hearing about your cases.

528

Until the 7th, my dearest son.

Your loving
Mother

PS. – I have just discovered the whereabouts of Miss Troy's house, Tatler's End. It is only two miles out of Bossicote, and a nice old place. Apparently she takes students there. My spies tell me a Miss Bostock has been living in it during Miss Troy's absence. She returns on the 3rd. How old is she?

Chapter 3

Class Assembles

On the 10th of September at ten o'clock in the morning, Agatha Troy opened the door in the eastward wall of her house and stepped out into the garden. It was a sunny morning with a tang of autumn about it, a bland, mellow morning. Somewhere in the garden a fire had been lit, and an aromatic trace of smouldering brushwood threaded the air. There was not a breath of wind.

'Autumn!' muttered Troy. 'And back to work again. Damn! I'm getting older.' She paused for a moment to light a cigarette, and then she set off towards the studio, down on the old tennis court. Troy had built this studio when she inherited Tatler's End House from her father. It was a solid square of decent stone with top lighting, and a single window facing south on a narrow lane. It stood rather lower than the house, and about a minute's walk away from it. It was screened pleasantly with oaks and lilac bushes. Troy strode down the twisty path between the lilac bushes and pushed open the studio door. From beyond the heavy wooden screen inside the entrance she heard the voices of her class. She was out of patience with her class. 'I've been too long away,' she thought. She knew so exactly how each of them would look, how their work would take shape, how the studio would smell of oil colour, turpentine, and fixative, how Sonia, the model, would complain of the heat, the draught, the pose, the cold, and the heat again. Katti would stump backwards and forwards before her easel, probably with one shoe squeaking. Ormerin would sigh, Valmai Seacliff would attitudinize, and Garcia, wrestling with clay by the south window, would whistle between his teeth.

'Oh, well,' said Troy, and marched round the screen.

Yes, there it all was, just as she expected, the throne shoved against the left-hand wall, the easels with fresh white canvases, the roaring gas heater, and the class. They had all come down to the studio after breakfast and, with the exception of Garcia and Malmsley, waited for her to pose the model. Malmsley was already at work: the drawings were spread out on a table. He wore, she noticed with displeasure, a sea-green overall. 'To go with the beard, I suppose,' thought Troy. Garcia was in the south window, glooming at the clay sketch of Comedy and Tragedy. Sonia, the model wrapped in a white kimono, stood beside him. Katti Bostock, planted squarely in the centre of the room before a large black canvas, set her enormous palette. The rest of the class, Ormerin, Phillida Lee, Watt Hatchett, and Basil Pilgrim, were grouped round Valmai Seacliff.

Troy walked over to Malmsley's table and looked over his shoulder at the drawings.

'What's that?'

'That's the thing I was talking about,' explained Malmsley. His voice was high-pitched and rather querulous. 'It's the third tale in the series. The female has been murdered by her lover's wife. She's lying on a wooden bench, impaled on a dagger. The wife jammed the dagger through the bench from underneath, and when the lover pressed her down – you see? The knife is hidden by the drape. It seems a little far-fetched, I must say. Surely it would show. The wretched publisher man insists on having this one.'

'It needn't show if the drape is suspended a little,' said Troy. 'From the back of the bench, for instance. Then as she falls down she would carry the drape with her. Anyway, the probabilities are none of your business. You're not doing a "before and after", like a strip advertisement, are you?'

'I can't get the pose,' said Malmsley languidly. 'I want to treat it rather elaborately. Deliberately mannered.'

'Well, you can't go in for the fancy touches until you've

531

got the flesh and blood to work from. That pose will do us as well as another, I dare say. I'll try it. You'd better make a separate drawing as a study.'

'Yes, I suppose I had,' drawled Malmsley. 'Thanks most frightfully.'

'Of course,' Valmai Seacliff was saying, 'I went down rather well in Italy. The Italians go mad when they see a good blonde. They used to murmur when I passed them in the streets. "*Bella*" and "*Bellissima*". It was rather fun.'

'Is that Italian?' asked Katti morosely, of her flake-white.

'It means beautiful, darling,' answered Miss Seacliff.

'Oh hell!' said Sonia, the model.

'Well,' said Troy loudly 'I'll set the pose.'

They all turned to watch her. She stepped on the throne, which was the usual dais on wheels, and began to arrange a seat for the model. She threw a cerise cushion down, and then from a chest by the wall she got a long blue length of silk. One end of this drape she threw across the cushion and pinned, the other she gathered carefully in her hands, drew round to one side, and then pinned the folds to the floor of the dais.

'Now, Sonia,' she said. 'Something like this.'

Keeping away from the drape, Troy knelt and then slid sideways into a twisted recumbent pose on the floor. The right hip was raised, the left took the weight of the pose. The torso was turned upwards from the waist so that both shoulders touched the boards. Sonia, noticing that twist, grimaced disagreeably.

'Get into it,' said Troy, and stood up. 'Only you lie across the drape with your head on the cushions. Lie on your left side, first.'

Sonia slid out of the white kimono. She was a most beautiful little creature, long-legged, delicately formed and sharp-breasted. Her black hair was drawn tightly back from the suave forehead. The bony structure of her face was sharply defined, and suggested a Slavonic mask.

'You little devil, you've been sunbathing,' said Troy. 'Look at those patches.'

'Well they don't like nudism, at Bournemouth,' said Sonia.

She lay across the drape on her left side, her head on the cerise cushion. Troy pushed her right shoulder over until it touched the floor. The drape was pressed down by the shoulders and broke into uneven blue folds about the body.

'That's your pose, Malmsley,' said Troy. 'Try it from where you are.'

She walked round the studio, eyeing the model.

'It's pretty good from everywhere,' she said. 'Right! Get going, everybody.' She glanced at her watch. 'You can hold that for forty minutes, Sonia.'

'It's a terrible pose, Miss Troy,' grumbled Sonia. 'All twisted like this.'

'Nonsense,' said Troy briskly.

The class began to settle itself.

Since each member of Troy's little community played a part in the tragedy that followed ten days later, it may be well to look a little more closely at them.

Katti Bostock's work is known to everyone who is at all interested in modern painting. At the time of which I am writing she was painting very solidly and smoothly, using a heavy outline and a simplified method of dealing with form. She painted large figure compositions, usually with artisans as subjects. Her 'Foreman Fitter' had been the picture of the year at the Royal Academy, and had set all the diehards by the ears. Katti herself was a short, stocky, dark-haired individual with an air of having no nonsense about her. She was devoted to Troy in a grumbling sort of way, lived at Tatler's End House most of the year, but was not actually a member of the class.

Valmai Seacliff was thin, blonde, and very, very pretty. She was the type that certain modern novelists write about with an enthusiasm which they attempt to disguise as satirical detachment. Her parents were well-to-do and her work was clever. You have heard Katti describe Valmai as a nymphomaniac and will be able to draw your own conclusions about the justness of this criticism.

Phillida Lee was 18, plump, and naturally gushing. Two years of Slade austerity had not altogether damped her enthusiasms, but when she remembered to shudder, she shuddered.

Watt Hatchett, Troy's Australian protégé, was a short and extremely swarthy youth, who looked like a dago in an American talking picture. He came from one of the less reputable streets of Sydney and was astoundingly simple, cocksure, egotistical and enthusiastic. He seemed to have no aesthetic perceptions of any description, so that his undoubted talent appeared to be a sort of parasite, flowering astonishingly on an unpromising and stunted stump.

Cedric Malmsley we have noticed already. Nothing further need be said about him at this stage of the narrative.

The Hon. Basil Pilgrim, son of the incredible Primitive Methodist peer, was a pleasant-looking young man of 23, whose work was sincere, able, but still rather tentative. His father, regarding all art schools as hot-beds of vice and depravity, had only consented to Basil becoming a pupil of Troy's because her parents had been landed gentry of Lord Pilgrim's acquaintance, and because Troy herself had once painted a picture of a revivalist meeting. Her somewhat ironical treatment of this subject had not struck Lord Pilgrim, who was, in many ways, a remarkably stupid old man.

Francis Ormerin was a slight and delicate-looking Frenchman who worked in charcoal and wash. His drawings of the nude were remarkable for their beauty of line, and for a certain emphatic use of accent. He was a nervous over-sensitive creature, subject to fits of profound depression, due said Troy, to his digestion.

And lastly Garcia, whose first name – Wolf – was remembered by nobody. Garcia, who preserved on his pale jaws a static ten days' growth of dark stubble which never developed into a beard, whose clothes consisted of a pair of dirty grey trousers, a limp shirt, and an unspeakable raincoat. Garcia, with his shock of unkempt brown hair, his dark impertinent eyes, his beautiful hands, and his complete unscrupulousness. Two years ago he had presented himself one morning at the door of Troy's studio in London. He had carried there a self-portrait in clay, wrapped about with wet and dirty clothes. He walked past her into the studio and unwrapped the clay head. Troy and Garcia stood looking at it in silence. Then she asked him his name and what he wanted. He told her – 'Garcia' – and he wanted to go on modelling, but had no money. Troy talked about the head, gave him twenty pounds, and never really got rid of him. He used to turn up, sometimes inconveniently, always with something to show her. In everything but clay he was quite inarticulate. It was as if he had been allowed only one medium of expression, but that an abnormally eloquent one. He was dirty, completely devoid of ordinary scruples, interested in nothing but his work. Troy helped him, and by and by people began to talk about his modelling. He began to work in stone. He was asked to exhibit with the New Phoenix Group, was given occasional commissions. He never had any money, and to most people he was entirely without charm, but to some women he was irresistible, and of this he took full advantage.

It was to Garcia that Troy went after she had set the pose. The others shifted their easels about, skirmishing for positions. Troy looked at Garcia's sketch in clay of the 'Comedy and Tragedy' for the new cinema in Westminster. He had stood it on a high stool in the south window. It was modelled on a little wooden platform with four wheels, a substitute he had made for the usual turntable. The two figures rose from a cylindrical base. Comedy was nude, but Tragedy wore an angular robe. Above their heads they held the conventional masks. The general composition suggested flames. The form was greatly simplified. The face of Comedy, beneath the grinning mask, was grave, but upon the face of Tragedy Garcia had pressed a faint smile.

He stood scowling while Troy looked at his work.

'Well,' said Troy, 'it's all right.'

'I thought of – ' He stopped short, and with his thumb suggested dragging the drape across the feet of Comedy.

'I wouldn't,' said Troy. 'Break the line up. But I've told you I know nothing about this stuff. I'm a painter. Why did you come and plant yourself here, may I ask?'

'Thought you wouldn't mind.' His voice was muffled and faintly Cockney. 'I'll be clearing out in a fortnight. I wanted somewhere to work.'

'So you said in your extraordinary note. Are you broke?'

'Yes.'

'Where are you going in a fortnight?'

'London. I've got a room to work in.'

'Where is it?'

'Somewhere in the East End, I think. It's an old ware-house. I know a bloke who got them to let me use it. He's going to let me have the address. I'll go for a week's holiday somewhere before I begin work in London. I'll cast this thing there and then start on the sculping.'

'Who's going to pay for the stone?'

'They'll advance me enough for that.'

'I see. It's coming along very well. Now attend to me, Garcia.' Troy lowered her voice. 'While you're here you've got to behave yourself. You know what I mean?'

'No.'

'Yes, you do. No nonsense with women. You and Sonia seem to be sitting in each other's pockets. Have you been living together?'

'When you're hungry,' said Garcia, 'you eat.'

'Well, this isn't a restaurant and you'll please remember that. You understand? I noticed you making some sort of advance to Seacliff yesterday. That won't do, either. I won't have any bogus Bohemianism, or free love, or mere

536

promiscuity at Tatler's End. It shocks the servants, and it's messy. All right?'

'OK,' said Garcia with a grin.

'The pose has altered,' said Katti Bostock from the middle of the studio.

'Yeah, that's right,' said Watt Hatchett. The others looked coldly at him. His Sydney accent was so broad as to be almost comic. One wondered if he could be doing it on purpose. It was not the custom at Troy's for new people to speak until they were spoken to. Watt was quite unaware of this and Troy, who hated rows, felt uneasy about him. He was so innocently impossible. She went to Katti's easel and looked from the bold drawing in black paint to the model. Then she went up to the throne and shoved Sonia's right shoulder down.

'Keep it on the floor.'

'It's a swine of a pose, Miss Troy.'

'Well, stick it a bit longer.'

Troy began to go round the work, beginning with Ormerin on the extreme left.

'Bit tied up, isn't it?' she said after a minute's silence.

'She is never for one moment still,' complained Ormerin. 'The foot moves, the shoulders are in a fidget continually. It is impossible for me to work – impossible.'

'Start again. The pose is right now. Get it down directly. You can do it.'

'My work has been abominable since three months or more. All this surrealism at Malaquin's. I cannot feel like that and yet I cannot prevent myself from attempting it when I am there. That is why I return to you. I am in a muddle.'

'Try a little ordinary study for a bit. Don't worry about style. It'll come. Take a new stretcher and make a simple statement.' She moved to Valmai Seacliff and looked at the flowing lines so easily laid down. Seacliff moved back, contriving to touch Ormerin's shoulder. He stopped working at once and whispered in her ear.

'I can understand French, Ormerin,' said Troy casually,

still contemplating Seacliff's canvas. 'This is going quite well, Seacliff. I suppose the elongation of the legs is deliberate?'

'Yes, I see her like that. Long and slinky. They say people always paint like themselves, don't they?'

'Do they?' said Troy. 'I shouldn't let it become a habit.'

She moved on to Katti, who creaked back from her canvas. One of her shoes did squeak. Troy discussed the placing of the figure and then went on to Watt Hatchett. Hatchett had already begun to use solid paint, and was piling pure colour on his canvas.

'You don't usually start off like this, do you?'

'Naow, that's right, I don't, but I thought I'd give it a pop.'

'Was that, by any chance, because you could see Miss Bostock working in that manner?' asked Troy, not too unkindly. Hatchett grinned and shuffled his feet. 'You stick to your own ways for a bit,' advised Troy. 'You're a beginner still, you know. Don't try to acquire a manner till you've got a little more method. Is that foot too big or too small?'

'Too small.'

'Should that space there be wider or longer?'

'Longer.'

'Make it so.'

'Good oh, Miss Troy. Think that bit of colour there's all right?' asked Hatchett, regarding it complacently.

'It's perfectly good colour, but don't choke the pores of your canvas up with paint till you've got the big things settled. Correct your drawing and scrape it down.'

'Yeah, but she wriggles all the time. It's a fair nark. Look where the shoulder has shifted. See?'

'Has the pose altered?' inquired Troy at large.

'Naow!' said Sonia with vindictive mimicry.

'It's shifted a whole lot,' asserted Hatchett aggressively. 'I bet you anything you like – '

'Wait a moment,' said Troy.

'It's moved a little,' said Katti Bostock.

Troy sighed.

'Rest!' she said. 'No! Wait a minute.'

She took a stick of chalk from her overall pocket and ran it round the model wherever she touched the throne. The position of both legs, one flank, one hip, and one shoulder were thus traced on the boards. The blue drape was beneath the rest of the figure.

'Now you can get up.'

Sonia sat up with an ostentatious show of discomfort, reached out her hand for the kimono and shrugged herself into it. Troy pulled the drape out taut from the cushion to the floor.

'It'll have to go down each time with the figure,' she told the class.

'As it does in the little romance,' drawled Malmsley.

'Yes, it's quite feasible,' agreed Valmai Seacliff. 'We could try it. There's that Chinese knife in the lumber-room. May we get it, Miss Troy?'

'If you like,' said Troy.

'It doesn't really matter,' said Malmsley languidly getting to his feet.

'Where is it, Miss Seacliff?' asked Hatchett eagerly.

'On the top shelf in the lumber-room.'

Hatchett went into an enormous cupboard by the window, and after a minute or two returned with a long, thin-bladed knife. He went up to Malmsley's table and looked over his shoulder at the typescript. Malmsley moved away ostentatiously.

'Aw yeah, I get it,' said Hatchett. 'What a corker! Swell way of murdering somebody, wouldn't it be?' He licked his thumb and turned the page.

'I've taken a certain amount of trouble to keep those papers clean,' remarked Malmsley to no one in particular.

'Don't be so damned precious, Malmsley,' snapped Troy. 'Here, give me the knife, Hatchett, and don't touch other people's tools in the studio. It's not done.'

'Good oh, Miss Troy.'

Pilgrim, Ormerin, Hatchett and Valmai Seacliff began

539

a discussion about the possibility of using the knife in the manner suggested by Malmsley's illustration. Phillida Lee joined in.

'Where would the knife enter the body?' asked Seacliff.

'Just here,' said Pilgrim, putting his hand on her back and keeping it there. 'Behind your heart, Valmai.'

She turned her head and looked at him through half-closed eyes. Hatchett stared at her, Malmsley smiled curiously. Pilgrim had turned rather white.

'Can you feel it beating?' asked Seacliff softly.

'If I move my hand – here.'

'Oh, come off it,' said the model violently. She walked over to Garcia. 'I don't believe you could kill anybody like that. Do you, Garcia?'

Garcia grunted unintelligibly. He, too, was staring at Valmai Seacliff.

'How would he know where to put the dagger?' demanded Katti Bostock suddenly. She drew a streak of background colour across her canvas.

'Can't we try it out?' asked Hatchett.

'If you like,' said Troy. 'Mark the throne before you move it.'

Basil Pilgrim chalked the position of the throne on the floor, and then he and Ormerin tipped it up. The rest of the class looked on with gathering interest. By following the chalked-out line on the throne they could see the spot where the heart would come, and after a little experiment found the plot of this spot on the underneath surface of the throne.

'Now, you see,' said Ormerin, 'the jealous wife would drive the knife through from underneath.'

'Incidentally taking the edge off,' said Basil Pilgrim.

'You could force it through the crack between the boards,' said Garcia suddenly, from the window.

'How? It'd fall out when she was shoved down.'

'No, it wouldn't. Look here.'

'Don't break the knife and don't damage the throne,' said Troy.

'I get you,' said Hatchett eagerly. 'The dagger's wider at the base. The boards would press on it. You'd have to hammer it through. Look, I'll bet you it could be done. There you are, I'll betcher.'

'Not interested, I'm afraid,' said Malmsley.

'Let's try,' said Pilgrim. 'May we, Troy?'

'Oh, do let's,' cried Phillida Lee. She caught up her enthusiasm with an apologetic glance at Malmsley. 'I adore bloodshed,' she added with a painstaking nonchalance.

'The underneath of the throne's absolutely filthy,' complained Malmsley.

'Pity if you spoiled your nice green pinny,' jeered Sonia. Valmai Seacliff laughed.

'I don't propose to do so,' said Malmsley. 'Garcia can if he likes.'

'Go on,' said Hatchett. 'Give it a pop. I betcher five bob it'll work. Fair dinkum.'

'What does that mean?' asked Seacliff. 'You must teach me the language, Hatchett.'

'Too right I will,' said Hatchett with enthusiasm. 'I'll make a dinkum Aussie out of you.'

'God forbid,' said Malmsley. Sonia giggled.

'Don't you like Australians?' Hatchett asked her aggressively.

'Not particularly.'

'Well, I'll tell you one thing. Models at the school I went to in Sydney knew how to hold a pose for longer than ten minutes.'

'You don't seem to have taken advantage of it, judging by your drawing.'

'And they didn't get saucy with the students.'

'Perhaps they weren't all like you.'

'Sonia,' said Troy, 'that will do. If you boys are going to make your experiment, you'd better hurry up. We start again in five minutes.'

In the boards of the throne they found a crack that passed through the right spot. Hatchett slid the thin tip

541

of the knife into it from underneath and shoved. By tapping the hilt of the dagger with an easel ledge, he forced the widening blade upwards through the crack. Then he let the throne back on to the floor. The blade projected wickedly through the blue chalk cross that marked the plot of Sonia's heart on the throne. Basil Pilgrim took the drape, laid it across the cushion, pulled it in taut folds down to the throne, and pinned it there.

'You see, the point of the knife is lower than the top of the cushion,' he said. 'It doesn't show under the drape.'

'What did I tell you?' said Hatchett.

Garcia strolled over and joined the group.

'Go into your pose, Sonia,' he said with a grin.

Sonia shuddered.

'Don't,' she said.

'I wonder if the tip should show under the left breast,' murmuring Malmsley. 'Rather amusing to have it in the drawing. With a cast shadow and a thin trickle of blood. Keep the whole thing black and white except for the little scarlet thread. After all, it is melodrama.'

'Evidently,' grunted Garcia.

'The point of suspension for the drape would have to be higher,' said Troy. 'It must be higher than the tip of the blade. You could do it. If your story was a modern detective novel, Malmsley, you could do a drawing of the knife as it is now.'

Malmsley smiled and began to sketch on the edge of his paper. Valmai Seacliff leant over him, her hands on his shoulders. Hatchett, Ormerin and Pilgrim stood round her, Pilgrim with his arm across her shoulder. Phillida Lee hovered on the outskirts of the little group. Troy, looking vaguely round the studio, said to herself that her worst forebodings were likely to be realized. Watt Hatchett was already at loggerheads with Malmsley and the model. Valmai was at her Cleopatra game, and there was Sonia in a corner with Garcia. Something in their faces caught Troy's attention. What the devil were they up to? Garcia's eyes were on the group round Malmsley.

A curious smile lifted one corner of his mouth, and on Sonia's face, turned to him, the smile was reflected.

'You'll have to get that thing out now, Hatchett,' said Troy.

It took a lot of working and tugging to do this, but at last the knife was pulled out, the throne put back, and Sonia, with many complaints, took the pose again.

'Over more on the right shoulder,' said Katti Bostock.

Troy thrust the shoulder down. The drape fell into folds round the figure.

'Ow!' said Sonia.

'That is when the dagger goes in,' said Malmsley.

'Don't – you'll make me sick,' said Sonia.

Garcia gave a little chuckle.

'Right through the ribs and coming out under the left breast,' murmured Malmsley.

'Shut up!'

'Spitted like a little chicken.'

Sonia raised her head.

'I wouldn't be too damn funny, Mr. Malmsley,' she said. 'Where do you get your ideas from, I wonder? Books? Or pictures?'

Malmsley's brush slipped from his fingers to the paper, leaving a trace of paint. He looked fixedly at Sonia, and then began to dab his drawing with a sponge. Sonia laughed.

'For God's sake,' said Katti Bostock, 'let's get the pose.'

'Quiet,' said Troy, and was obeyed. She set the pose, referring to the canvases. 'Now get down to it, all of you. The Phoenix Group Show opens on the 16th. I suppose most of us want to go up to London for it. Very well, I'll give the servants a holiday that weekend, and we'll start work again on the Monday.'

'If this thing goes decently,' said Katti, 'I want to put it in for the Group. If it's not done, it'll do for B. House next year.'

543

'I take it,' said Troy, 'you'll all want to go up for the Group's private view?'

'I don't,' said Garcia. 'I'll be pushing off for my holiday about then.'

'What about us?' asked Valmai Seacliff of Basil Pilgrim.

'What do you think, darling?'

' "Us"?' said Troy. ' "Darling"? What's all this?'

'We may as well tell them, Basil,' said Valmai sweetly. 'Don't faint, anybody. We got engaged last night.'

Chapter 4

Case for Mr Alleyn

Lady Alleyn knelt back on her gardening-mat and looked up at her son.

'I think we have done enough weeding for today, darling. You bustle off with that barrow-load and then we'll go indoors and have a glass of sherry and a chat. We've earned it.'

Chief Detective-Inspector Alleyn obediently trundled off down the path, tipped his barrow-load on the smudge fire, mopped his brow and went indoors for a bath. Half an hour later he joined his mother in the drawing-room.

'Come up to the fire, darling. There's the sherry. It's a bottle of the very precious for our last evening.'

'Ma'am,' said Alleyn, 'you are the perfect woman.'

'No, only the perfect mamma. I flatter myself I am a *very* good parent. You look charming in a dinner jacket, Roderick. I wish your brother had some of your finish. George always looks a little too hearty.'

'I like George,' said Alleyn.

'I quite like him, too,' agreed his mother.

'This is really a superlative wine. I wish it wasn't our last night, though. Three days with the Bathgates, and then my desk, my telephone, the smell of the yard, and old Fox beaming from ear to ear, bless him. Ah well, I expect I shall quite enjoy it once I'm there.'

'Roderick,' said Lady Alleyn, 'why wouldn't you come to Tatler's End House with me?'

'For the very good reason, little mum, that I should not have been welcomed.'

'How do you know?'

'Miss Troy doesn't like me.'

'Nonsense! She's a very intelligent young woman.'

'Darling!'

'The day I called I suggested she should dine with us while you were here. She accepted.'

'And put us off when the time came.'

'My dear man, she had a perfectly good excuse.'

'Naturally,' said Alleyn. 'She is, as you say, a very intelligent young woman.'

Lady Alleyn looked at the portrait head that hung over the mantelpiece.

'She can't dislike you very much, my dear. That picture gives the lie to your theory.'

'Aesthetic appreciation of a paintable object has nothing to do with personal preferences.'

'Bosh! Don't talk pretentious nonsense about things you don't understand.'

Alleyn grinned.

'I think you are being self-conscious and silly,' continued Lady Alleyn grandly.

'It's the lady that you should be cross about, not me.'

'I'm not cross, Roderick. Give yourself another glass of sherry. No, not for me.'

'Anyway,' said Alleyn, 'I'm glad you like the portrait.'

'Did you see much of her in Quebec?'

'Very little, darling. We bowed to each other at mealtimes and had a series of stilted conversations in the lounge. On the last evening she was there I took her to the play.'

'Was that a success?'

'No. We were very polite to each other.'

'Ha!' said Lady Alleyn.

'Mamma,' said Alleyn, 'you know I *am* a detective.' He paused, smiling at her. 'You look divine when you blush,' he added.

'Well, Roderick, I shan't deny that I would like to see you married.'

'She wouldn't dream of having me, you know. Put the idea out of your head, little mum. I very much doubt if I shall ever have another stilted conversation with Miss Agatha Troy.'

The head parlourmaid came in.

'A telephone call from London for Mr Roderick, m'lady.'

'From London?' asked Alleyn. 'Oh Lord, Clibborn, why didn't you say I was dead?'

Clibborn smiled the tolerant smile of a well-trained servant, and opened the door.

'Excuse me, please, Mamma,' said Alleyn, and went to the telephone.

As he unhooked the receiver, Alleyn experienced the little prick of foreboding that so often accompanies an unexpected long-distance call. It was the smallest antici-patory thrill and was succeeded at once by the unhappy reflection that probably Scotland Yard was already on his track. He was not at all surprised when a familiar voice said:

'Mr Alleyn?'

'That's me. Is it you, Watkins?'

'Yes, sir. Very pleasant to hear your voice again. The Assistant Commissioner would like to speak to you, Mr Alleyn.'

'Right!'

'Hullo, Mr Alleyn?' said a new voice.

'Hullo, sir.'

'You can go, Watkins.' A pause, and then: 'How are you, Rory?'

'Very fit, thanks, sir.'

'Ready for work?'

'Yes. Oh, rather!'

'Well now, look here. How do you feel about slipping into the saddle three days before you're due? There's a case cropped up a few miles from where you are, and the local people have called us in. It would save time and help the department if you could take over for us.'

'Certainly, sir,' said Alleyn, with a sinking heart. 'When?'

'Now. It's a homicide case. Take the details. Address, Tatler's End House.'

'*What!* I beg your pardon, sir. Yes?'

'A woman's been stabbed. Do you know the place, by any chance?'

'Yes, sir.'

'Thrrree minutes.'

'Extend the call, please. Are you there, Rory?'

'Yes,' said Alleyn. He noticed suddenly that the receiver was clammy.

'It belongs to the artist, Miss Agatha Troy.'

'I know.'

'You'll get the information from the local super – Blackman – who's there now. The model has been killed, and it looks like murder.'

'I – can't – hear.'

'The victim is an artist's model. I'll send Fox down with the other people and your usual kit. Much obliged. Sorry to drag you back before Monday.'

'That's all right, sir.'

'Splendid. I'll expect your report. Nice to see you again. Goodbye.'

'Goodbye, sir.'

Alleyn went back to the drawing-room.

'Well?' began his mother. She looked up at him, and in a moment was at his side. 'What's the matter, old man?'

'Nothing, ma'am. It was the Yard. They want me to take a case near here. It's at Tatler's End House.'

'But what is it?'

'Murder, it seems.'

'Roderick!'

'No, no. I thought that, too, for a moment. It's the model. I'll have to go at once. May I have the car?'

'Of course, darling.' She pressed a bell-push, and when Clibborn came, said: 'Mr Roderick's overcoat at once, Clibborn, and tell French to bring the car round quickly.' When Clibborn had gone she put her hand on Alleyn's. 'Please tell Miss Troy that if she would like to come to me – '

'Yes, darling. Thank you. But I must see what it's all about first. It's a case.'

'Well, you won't include Agatha Troy among your suspects, I hope?'

'If there's a question of that,' said Alleyn, 'I'll leave the service. Good night. Don't sit up. I may be late.'

Clibborn came in with his overcoat.

'Finish your sherry,' ordered his mother. He drank it obediently. 'And, Roderick, look in at my room, however late it is.'

He bowed, kissed her lightly, and went out to the car.

It was a cold evening with a hint of frost on the air. Alleyn dismissed the chauffeur and drove himself at breakneck speed towards Tatler's End House. On the way, three vivid little pictures appeared, one after another, in his mind. The wharf at Suva. Agatha Troy, in her old smock and grey bags, staring out over the sea while the wind whipped the short hair back from her face. Agatha Troy saying goodbye at night on the edge of the St Lawrence.

The headlights shone on rhododendrons and tree-trunks, and then on a closed gate and the figure of a constable. A torch flashed on Alleyn's face.

'Excuse me, sir – '

'All right. Chief Detective-Inspector Alleyn from the Yard.'

The man saluted.

'They're expecting you, sir.'

The gate swung open, and Alleyn slipped in his clutch. It was a long winding drive, and it seemed an age before he pulled up before a lighted door. A second constable met him and showed him into a pleasant hall where a large fire burned.

'I'll tell the superintendent you've arrived, sir,' said the man, but as he spoke, a door on Alleyn's left opened and a stout man with a scarlet face came out.

'Hullo, hullo! This is very nice. Haven't seen you for ages.'

549

'Not for ages,' said Alleyn. They shook hands. Blackman had been superintendent at Bossicote for six years, and he and Alleyn were old acquaintances. 'I hope I haven't been too long.'

'You've been very quick indeed, Mr Alleyn. We only rang the Yard half an hour ago. They told us you were staying with her ladyship. Come in here, will you?'

He led the way into a charming little drawing-room with pale-grey walls and cerise-and-lemon-striped curtains.

'How much did they tell you from the Yard?'

'Only that a model had been knifed.'

'Yes. Very peculiar business. I don't mind telling you I'd have liked to tackle it myself, but we've got our hands full with a big burglary case over at Ronald's Cross, and I'm short-staffed just now. So the Chief Constable thought, all things considered, and you being so handy, it'd better be the Yard. He's just gone. Sit down, and I'll give you the story before we look at the body and so on. That suit you?'

'Admirably,' said Alleyn.

Blackman opened a fat pocketbook, settled his chins, and began.

'This property, Tatler's End House, is owned and occupied by Miss Agatha Troy, R.A., who returned here after a year's absence abroad, on September 3rd. During her absence the house was occupied by a Miss Katti Bostock, another painter. Miss Troy arranged by letter to take eight resident pupils from September to December, and all of these were already staying in the house when she arrived. There was also a Sonia Gluck, spinster aged 22, an artist's model, engaged by Miss Bostock for the coming term. The classes began officially on the 10th, but they had all been more or less working together since the 3rd. From the 10th to Friday the 16th they worked from the model every morning in the studio. On the 16th, three days ago, the class disbanded for the weekend, in order that members might attend a function in London. The servants were given Friday night off, and went to a cinema in Baxtonbridge. One student, Wolf Garcia, no permanent address, remained alone in the studio. The house was closed. Garcia is believed to have left on Saturday the 17th, the day before yesterday. Miss Troy returned on Saturday at midday and found Garcia had gone. The others came back on Sunday, yesterday, by car, and by the evening bus. This morning, September 19th, the class reassembled in the studio, which is a detached building situated about a hundred yards to the south-east of the rear eastward corner of the house. Here's the sketch plan of the house and studio,' said the superintendent in a more normal voice. 'And here's another of the studio interior.'

'Splendid,' said Alleyn, and spread them out before him on a small table. Mr Blackman coughed and took up the burden of his recital.

'At ten-thirty the class, with the exception of Garcia, who, as we have seen, had left, was ready to begin work. Miss Troy had given instructions that they were to start without her. This is her usual practice, except on the occasions when a new pose is to be set. The model lay down to resume the pose which she had been taking since September 10th. It was a recumbent position on her back. She lay half on a piece of silk material and half on the bare boards of the dais known as the model's "throne". The model was undraped. She lay first of all on her right side. One of the students, Miss Valmai Seacliff, of No. 8, Partington Mews, WC4, approached the model, placed her hands on Gluck's shoulders and thrust the left shoulder firmly over and down. This was the usual procedure. Gluck cried out "Don't!" as if in pain, but as she habitually objected to the pose, Miss Seacliff paid no attention, shifted her hands to the model's chest, and pressed down. Gluck made another sound, described by Miss Seacliff as a moan, and seemed to jerk and then relax. Miss Seacliff then said: "Oh, don't be such a fool, Sonia," and was about to rise from her stooping posture when she noticed that Gluck was in an abnormal condition. She called for the others to come. Miss Katti Bostock followed by two students, Mr Watt Hatchett, an Australian, and Mr Francis Ormerin, a Frenchman, approached the throne. Hatchett said: "She's taken a fit." Miss Bostock said: "Get out of the way." She examined the body. She states that the eyelids fluttered and the limbs jerked slightly. Miss Bostock attempted to raise Gluck. She placed her hand behind the shoulders and pulled. There was a certain amount of resistance, but after a few seconds the body came up suddenly. Miss Seacliff cried out loudly that there was blood on the blue silk drape. Mr Ormerin said: "Mong dew, the knife!" '

Mr Blackman cleared his throat and turned a page.

'It was then seen that a thin triangular blade protruded vertically through the drape. It appeared to be the blade of some sort of dagger that had been driven through a crack in the dais from underneath. It has not been moved. It seems that later on, when Miss Troy arrived, she stopped anybody from touching the dais as soon as she saw what had occurred. On examining Gluck a wound was discovered in the back somewhere about the position of the fourth rib and about three inches to the left of the spine. There was an effusion of blood. The blade was stained with blood. Miss Bostock attempted to staunch the wound with a rag. At this point Miss Troy arrived, and immediately sent Mr Basil Pilgrim, another student, to ring up the doctor. Dr Ampthill arrived ten minutes later and found life was extinct. Miss Troy states that Gluck died a few minutes after she – Miss Troy – arrived at the studio. Gluck made no statement before she died.'

Mr Blackman closed his notebook, and laid it on the table.

'That's just from notes,' he said modestly. 'I haven't got it down in a ship-shape report yet.'

'It is sufficiently clear,' said Alleyn. 'You might have been giving it to a jury.'

552

An expression of solemn complacency settled down among the superintendent's chins.

'Well,' he said, 'we haven't had a great deal of time. It's a curious business. We've taken statements from all this crowd, except, of course, the man called Garcia. He's gone, and we haven't got a line on him. That looks a bit funny on the face of it, but it seems he said he'd be leaving for a hiking trip on Saturday morning, and is due to turn up at some place in London in about a week's time. He left his luggage to be forwarded to this London address, and it had all gone when Miss Troy returned on Saturday about three o'clock. We're trying to get on to the carrier that called for it, but haven't got hold of anybody yet. It was all in the studio. It seems Garcia slept in the studio and had his gear there. I've got into touch with the police stations for fifty miles round and asked them to look out for this Garcia. Here's the description of him: Height – about five foot nine; sallow complexion, dark eyes, very thin. Thick dark hair, rather long. Usually dressed in old grey flannel trousers and a raincoat. Does not wear a hat. Probably carrying a rucksack containing painting materials. It seems he does a bit of sketching as well as sculping. We got that in the course of the statements made by the rest of this crowd. Will you look at the statements before you see anybody?'

Alleyn thought for moment.

'I'll see Miss Troy first,' he said. 'I have met her before.'

'Have you, really? I suppose with her ladyship being as you might say a neighbour – '

'The acquaintance is very slight,' said Alleyn. 'What about the doctors?'

'I said I'd let Ampthill know as soon as you came. He is the police surgeon. He heads the list in the directory, so Mr Pilgrim rang him first.'

'Very handy. Well, Mr Blackman, if you wouldn't mind getting hold of him while I see Miss Troy – '

'Right.'

'Fox and Co. ought to be here soon. We'll go and look

at the scene of action when they arrive. Where is Miss Troy?'

'In the study. I'll take you there. It's across the hall.'

'Don't bother – I'll find my way.'

'Right you are – I'll ring the doctor and join you there. I've got the rest of the class penned up in the dining-room with a PC on duty. They're a rum lot and no mistake,' said Blackman, leading the way into the hall. 'Real artistic freaks. You know. There's the library door. See you in a minute.'

Alleyn crossed the hall, tapped on the door, and walked in.

It was a long room with a fireplace at the far end. The only light there was made by the flicker of flames on the book-lined walls. Coming out of the brightly lit hall, he was at first unable to see clearly and stood for a moment inside the door.

'Yes' said a quick voice from the shadows. 'Who is it? Do you want me?'

A slim, dark shape, outlined by a wavering halo of light, rose from a chair by the fire.

'It's me,' said Alleyn. 'Roderick Alleyn.'

'You!'

'I'm sorry to come in unannounced. I thought perhaps you would rather – '

'But – yes, please come in.'

The figure moved forward a little and held out a hand. Alleyn said apologetically.

'I'm coming as fast as I can. It's rather dark.'

'Oh!' There was a moment's pause, a movement, and then a shaded lamp came to life and he saw her clearly. She wore a long plain dress of a material that absorbed the light and gave off none. She looked taller than his remembrance of her. Her face was white under the short black hair. Alleyn took her hand, held it lightly for a second, and then moved to the fire.

'It was kind of you to come,' said Troy.

'No, it wasn't. I'm here on duty.'

She stiffened at once.

'I'm sorry. That was stupid of me.'

'If I was not a policeman,' Alleyn said, 'I think I should still have come. You could have brought about a repetition of our first meeting and sent me about my business.'

'Must you always remind me of my ill manners?'

'That was not the big idea. Your manners did not seem ill to me. May we sit down, please?'

'Do.'

They sat in front of the fire.

'Well,' said Troy, 'get out your notebook.'

Alleyn felt in the inside pocket of his dinner jacket.

'It's still there,' he said. 'The last time I used it was in New Zealand. Here we are. Have you had any dinner, by the way?'

'What's that got to do with it?'

'Come, come,' said Alleyn, 'you mustn't turn into a hostile witness before there's anything to be hostile about.'

'Don't be facetious. Oh damn! Rude again. Yes, thank you, I toyed with a chunk of athletic hen.'

'Good! A glass of port wouldn't do you any harm. Don't offer me any, please: I'm not supposed to drink on duty, unless it's with a sinister purpose. I suppose this affair has shaken you up a bit?'

Troy waited for a moment and then she said: 'I'm terrified of dead people.'

'I know,' said Alleyn. 'I was, at first. Before the war. Even now they are not quite a commonplace to me.'

'She was a silly little creature. More like a beautiful animal than a reasonable human. But to see her suddenly, like that – everything emptied away. She looked fairly astonished – that was all.'

'It's so often like that. Astonished, but sort of knowing. Are there any relatives to be informed?'

'I haven't the faintest idea. She lived alone – officially.'

'We'll have to try and find out.'

'What do you want me to do now?' asked Troy.

'I want you to bring this girl to life for me. I know the circumstances surrounding her death – the immediate circumstances – and as soon as my men get here from London, I'll look at the studio. In the meantime I'd like to know if any possible explanation for this business has occurred to you. I must thank you for having kept the place untouched. Not many people think like that on these occasions.'

'I've no explanation, reasonable or fantastic, but there's one thing you ought to know at once. I told the class they were not to speak of it to the police. I knew they'd all give exaggerated accounts of it, and thought it better that the first statement should come from me.'

'I see.'

'I'll make the statement now.'

'An official statement?' asked Alleyn lightly.

'If you like. When you move the throne you will find that a dagger has been driven through the boards from underneath.'

'Shall we?'

'Yes. You don't say 'How do you know?'

'Well, I expect you're going on to that, aren't you?'

'Yes. On the 10th, the first morning when I set this pose, I arranged it to look as if the figure had been murdered in exactly this way. Cedric Malmsley, one of my students, was doing a book illustration of a similar incident.' She paused for a moment, looking into the fire. 'During the rest they began arguing about the possibilities of committing a crime in this way. Hatchett, another student, got a knife that is in the junk-room, and shoved it through from underneath. Ormerin helped him. The throne was roughly knocked up for me in the village and the boards have warped apart. The blade is much narrower at the tip than at the hilt. The tip went through easily, but he hammered at the hilt to force it right up. The boards gripped the wider end. You will see all that when you look at it.'

'Yes.' Alleyn made a note in his book and waited.

'The drape was arranged to hide the knife and it all looked quite convincing. Sonia was – she was quite – frightened. Hatchett pulled the knife out – it needed some doing – and we put everything straight again.'

'What happened to the knife?'

'Let me see. I think Hatchett put it away.'

'From a practical point of view, how could you be sure that the knife would come through at exactly the right place to do what it has done?'

'The position of the figure is chalked on the floor. When she took the pose, Sonia fitted her right hip and leg into the chalk marks, and then slid down until the whole of her right side was on the floor. One of the students would move her until she was inside the marks. Then she let the torso go over until her left shoulder touched the floor. The left hip was off the ground. I could draw it for you.'

Alleyn opened his notebook at a clean page and handed it to her with his pencil. Troy swept a dozen lines down and gave it back to him.

'Wonderful!' said Alleyn, 'to be able to do that – so easily.'

'I'm not likely to forget that pose,' said Troy dryly.

'What about the drape? Didn't that cover the chalk-marks?'

'Only in places. It fell from a suspension-point on the cushion to the floor. As she went down, she carried it with her. The accidental folds that came that way were more interesting than any laboured arrangement. When the students made their experiment they found the place where the heart would be, quite easily, inside the trace on the floor. The crack passed through this point. Hatchett put a pencil through the crack and they marked the position on the under-side of the throne.'

'Is there any possibility that they repeated this performance for some reason on Friday and forgot to withdraw the dagger?'

'I thought of that at once, naturally. I asked them. I

begged them to tell me.' Troy moved her long hands restlessly. 'Anything,' she said, 'anything rather than the thought of one of them deliberately – there's no reason. I – I can't bear to think of it. As if a beastly unclean thing was in one of their minds, behind all of us. And then, suddenly, crawled out and did this.'

He heard her draw in her breath sharply. She turned her head away.

Alleyn swore softly.

'Oh, don't pay any attention to me,' said Troy impatiently. 'I'm all right. About Friday. We had the morning class as usual from ten o'clock to twelve-thirty, with that pose. We all lunched at one. Then we went up to London. The private view of the Phoenix Group Show was on Friday night, and several of us had things in it. Valmai Seacliff and Basil Pilgrim, who were engaged to be married, left in his two-seater immediately after lunch. Neither of them was going to the private view. They were going to his people's place, to break the engagement news, I imagine. Katti Bostock and I left in my car at about half-past two. Hatchett, Phillida Lee and Ormerin caught the three o'clock bus. Malmsley wanted to do some work, so he stayed behind until six, went up in the six-fifteen bus and joined us later at the show. I believe Phillida Lee and Hatchett had a meal together and went to a show. She took him to her aunt's house in London for the weekend, I fancy.'

'And the model?'

'Caught the three o'clock bus. I don't know where she went or what she did. She came back with Malmsley, Ormerin, Hatchett and Phillida Lee by yesterday evening's bus.'

'When Friday's class broke up, did you all leave the studio together and come up to the house?'

'I – let me think for a moment. No, I can't remember; but usually we come up in dribbles. Some of them go on working, and they have to clean up their palettes and so on. Wait a second. Katti and I came up together before the others. That's all I can tell you.'

'Would the studio be locked before you went to London'

'No.' Troy turned her head and looked squarely at him.

'Why not?' asked Alleyn.

'Because of Garcia.'

'Blackman told me about Garcia. He stayed behind, didn't he?'

'Yes.'

'Alone?'

'Yes,' said Troy unhappily. 'Quite alone.'

There was a tap at the door. It opened and Blackman appeared, silhouetted against the brightly lit hall.

'The doctor's here, Mr Alleyn, and I think the car from London is just arriving.'

'Right,' said Alleyn. 'I'll come.'

Blackman moved away. Alleyn rose and looked down at Troy in her armchair.

'Perhaps I may see you again before I go?'

'I'll be here or with the others in the dining-room. It's a bit grim sitting round there under the eye of the village constable.'

'I hope it won't be for very long,' said Alleyn.

Troy suddenly held out her hand.

'I'm glad it's you,' she said.

They shook hands.

'I'll try to be as inoffensive as possible,' Alleyn told her.

'Goodbye for the moment.'

Chapter 5

Routine

When Alleyn returned to the hall he found it full of men. The Scotland Yard officials had arrived, and with their appearance the case, for the first time, seemed to take on a familiar complexion. The year he had spent away from England clicked back into the past at the sight of those familiar overcoated and bowler-hatted figures with their cases and photographic impedimenta. There, beaming at him, solid, large, the epitome of horse-sense, was old Fox.

'Very nice indeed to have you with us again, sir.'

'Fox, you old devil, how are you?'

And there, looking three degrees less morose, was Detective-Sergeant Bailey, and behind him Detective-Sergeant Thompson. A gruff chorus began:

'Very nice indeed – '

A great shaking of hands, while Superintendent Blackman looked on amicably, and then a small, clean, bald man came forward. Blackman introduced him.

'Inspector Alleyn, this is Dr Ampthill, our divisional surgeon.'

'How d'you do, Mr Alleyn? Understand you want to see me. Sorry if I've kept you waiting.'

'I've not long arrived,' said Alleyn. 'Let's have a look at the scene of action, shall we?'

Blackman led the way down the hall to a side passage at the end of which there was a door. Blackman unlocked it and ushered them through. They were in the garden. The smell of box borders came up from their feet. It was very dark.

'Shall I lead the way?' suggested Blackman.

A long pencil of light from a torch picked up a section of flagged path. They tramped along in single file. Tree-trunks started up out of the darkness, leaves brushed Alleyn's cheek. Presently a rectangle of deeper dark loomed up.

Blackman said. 'You there, Sligo?'

'Yes, sir,' said a voice close by.

There was a jangle of keys, the sound of a door opening.

'Wait till I find the light switch,' said Blackman. 'Here we are.'

The lights went up. They walked round the wooden screen inside the door, and found themselves in the studio.

Alleyn's first impression was of a reek of paint and turpentine, and of a brilliant and localized glare. Troy had installed a high-powered lamp over the throne. This lamp was half shaded, so that it cast all its light on the throne, rather as the lamp above an operating-table is concentrated on the patient. Blackman had only turned on one switch, so the rest of the studio was in darkness. The effect at the moment could scarcely have been more theatrical. The blue drape, sprawled across the throne, was so brilliant that it hurt the eyes. The folds fell sharply from the cushion into a flattened mass. In the middle, stupidly irrelevant, was a spike. It cast a thin shadow irregularly across the folds of the drape. On the margin of this picture, disappearing abruptly into shadow, was a white mound.

'The drapery and the knife haven't been touched since the victim died,' explained Blackman. 'Of course, they disarranged the stuff a bit when they hauled her up.'

'Of course,' said Alleyn. He walked over to the throne and examined the blade of the knife. It was rather like an over-sized packing-needle, sharp, three-edged, and greatly tapered towards the point. It was stained a rusty brown. At the base, where it pierced the drape, there was the same discoloration, and in one or two of the folds small puddles of blood had seeped through the material and dried. Alleyn glanced at Dr Ampthill.

561

'I suppose there would be an effusion of blood when they pulled her off the knife?'

'Oh yes, yes. The bleeding would probably continue until death. I understand that beyond lifting her away from the knife, they did not move her until she died. When I arrived the body was where it is now.'

He turned to the sheeted mound that lay half inside the circle of light.

'Shall I?'

'Yes, please,' said Alleyn.

Dr Ampthill drew away the white sheet.

Troy had folded Sonia's hands over her naked breast. The shadow cut sharply across the wrists so that the lower half of the torso was lost. The shoulders, hands and head were violently lit. The lips were parted rigidly, showing the teeth. The eyes were only half closed. The plucked brows were raised as if in astonishment.

'Rigor mortis is well established,' said the doctor. 'She was apparently a healthy woman, and this place was well heated. The gas fire was not turned off until some time after she died. She has been dead eleven hours.'

'Have you examined the wound, Dr Ampthill?'

'Superficially. The knife-blade was not absolutely vertical, evidently. It passed between the fourth and fifth ribs, and no doubt pierced the heart.'

'Let us have a look at the wound.'

Alleyn slid his long hands under the rigid body and turned it on its side. The patches of sunburn showed clearly on the back. About three inches to the left of the spine was a dark puncture. It looked very small and neat in spite of the traces of blood that surrounded it.

'Ah, yes,' said Alleyn. 'As you say. We had better have a photograph of this. Bailey, you go over the body for prints. You'd better tackle the drape, and the knife, and the top surface of the throne. Not likely to prove very useful, I'm afraid, but do your best.'

While Thompson set up his camera, Alleyn turned up

the working-lamps and browsed about the studio. Fox joined him.

'Funny sort of case, sir,' said Fox. 'Romantic.'

'Good heavens, Fox, what a macabre idea of romance you've got.'

'Well, sensational,' amended Fox. 'The papers will make a big thing of it. We'll have them all down in hordes before the night's over.'

'That reminds me – I must send a wire to the Bathgates. I'm due there tomorrow. To business, Brer Fox. Here we have the studio as it was when the class assembled this morning. Paint set out on the palettes, you see. Canvases on all the easels. We've got seven versions of the pose.'

'Very useful, I dare say,' conceded Fox. 'Or, at any rate, the ones that look like something human may come in handy. That affair over on your left looks more like a set of worms than a naked female. I suppose it *is* meant for the deceased, isn't it?'

'I think so,' said Alleyn. 'The artist is probably a surrealist or a vorticalist or something.' He inspected the canvas and the paint-table in front of it.

'Here we are. The name's on the paint-box. Phillida Lee. It is a rum bit of work, Fox, no doubt of it. This big thing next door is more in our line. Very solid and simple.'

He pointed to Katti Bostock's enormous canvas.

'Bold,' said Fox. He put on his spectacles and stared blankly at the picture.

'You get the posture of the figure very well there,' said Alleyn.

They moved to Cedric Malmsley's table.

'This, I think, must be the illustrator,' continued Alleyn. 'Yes – here's the drawing for the story.'

'Good God!' exclaimed Fox, greatly scandalized. 'He's made a picture of the girl after she was killed.'

'No, no. That was the original idea for the pose. He's merely added a dagger and the dead look. Here's the portfolio with all the drawings. H'm, very volup. and Beardsley, with a slap of modern thrown in. Hullo!'

Alleyn had turned to a delicate water-colour in which three medieval figures mowed a charming field against a background of hayricks, pollard willows, and a turreted palace. 'That's rum!' muttered Alleyn.

'What's up, Mr Alleyn?'

'It looks oddly familiar. One half of the old brain functioning a fraction ahead of the other, perhaps. Or perhaps not. No matter. Look here, Brer Fox, I think before we go any further I'd better tell you as much as I know about the case.' And Alleyn repeated the gist of Blackman's report and of his conversations with Troy. 'This, you see,' he ended, 'is the illustration for the story. It was to prove the possibility of murdering someone in this manner that they made the experiment with the dagger, ten days ago.'

'I see,' said Fox. 'Well, somebody's proved it now all right, haven't they?'

'Yes,' agreed Alleyn. 'It is proved – literally, up to the hilt.'

'Cuh!' said Fox solemnly.

'Malmsley has represented the dagger as protruding under the left breast, you see. I suppose he thought he'd add the extra touch of what *you'd* call romance, Brer Fox. The scarlet thread of gore is rather effective in a meretricious sort of way. Good Lord, this is a queer show and no mistake.'

'Here's what I call a pretty picture, now,' said Fox approvingly. He had moved in front of Valmai Seacliff's canvas. Exaggeratedly slender, the colour scheme a light sequence of blues and pinks.

'Very elegant,' said Fox.

'A little too elegant,' said Alleyn. 'Hullo! Look at this.'

Across Francis Ormerin's water-colour drawing ran an ugly streak of dirty blue, ending in a blob that had run down the paper. The drawing was ruined.

'Had an accident, seemingly.'

'Perhaps. This student's stool is overturned, you'll notice, Fox. Some of the water in his paint-pot has slopped over and one of his brushes is on the floor.'

Alleyn picked up the brush and dabbed it on the china palette. A half-dry smudge of dirty blue showed.

'I see him or her preparing to flood a little of this colour on the drawing. He receives a shock, his hand jerks sideways and the brush streaks across the paper. He jumps up, overturning his stool and jolting the table. He drops the brush on the floor. Look, Fox. There are signs of the same sort of disturbance everywhere. Notice the handful of brushes on the table in front of the big canvas – I think that must be Katti Bostock's – I remember her work. Those brushes have been put down suddenly on the palette. The handles are messed in paint. Look at this very orderly array of tubes and brushes over here. The student has dropped a tube of blue paint and then trodden on it. Here are traces leading to the throne. It's a man's shoe, don't you think? He's tramped about all over the place, leaving a blue painty trail. The modern lady – Miss Lee – has overturned a bottle of turpentine, and it's run into her paint-box. There are even signs of disturbance on the illustrator's table. He has put a wet brush down on the very clean typescript. The place is like a first lesson in detection.'

'But beyond telling us they all got a start when the affair occurred, it doesn't appear to lead us anywhere,' said Fox. 'Not on the face of it.' He turned back to Seacliff's canvas and examined it with placid approval.

'You seem very taken with Miss Seacliff's effort,' said Alleyn.

'Eh?' Fox transferred his attention sharply to Alleyn. 'Now then, sir, how do you make out the name of this artist?'

'Rather prettily, Fox. This is the only outfit that is quite in order. Very neat everything is, you'll notice. Tidy box, clean brushes laid down carefully by the palette, fresh paint-rag all ready to use. I make a long guess that it belongs to Valmai Seacliff, because Miss Seacliff was with the model when she got her quietus. There is no reason why Miss Seacliff's paraphernalia should show signs of disturbance. In a sense, Miss Seacliff killed Sonia Gluck. She pressed her naked body down on the knife. Not a very pleasant reflection for Miss Seacliff now, unless she happens to be a murderess. Yes, I think this painting is hers.'

'Very neat bit of reasoning, chief. Lor', here's a mess.' Fox bent over Watt Hatchett's open box. It overflowed with half-used tubes of oil-colour, many of them without caps. A glutinous mess, to which all sorts of odds and ends adhered, spread over the trays and brushes. Cigarette butts, matches, bits of charcoal, were mixed up with fragments of leaves and twigs and filthy scraps of rag.

'This looks like chronic muck,' said Fox.

'It does indeed.' From the sticky depths of a tin tray Alleyn picked out a fragment of a dried leaf and smelt it.

'Blue gum,' he said. 'This will be the Australian, I suppose. Funny. He must have collected that leaf sketching in the bush, half the world away. I know this youth. He joined our ship with Miss Troy at Suva. Travelled second at her expense.'

'Fancy that,' said Fox placidly. 'Then you know this Miss Troy, sir?'

'Yes. Now you see, even he appears to have put his hand down on his palette. He'd hardly do that in normal moments.'

'We've finished, sir,' said the photographic expert.

'Right.'

Alleyn went over to the throne. The body lay as it was when he first saw it. He looked at it thoughtfully, remembering what Troy had said: 'I'm always frightened of dead people.'

'She was very lovely,' said Alleyn gently. He covered the body again. 'Carry her over to that couch. It's a divan-bed, I fancy. She can be taken away now. You'll do the post-mortem tomorrow, I suppose, Dr Ampthill?'

'First thing,' said the doctor briskly. 'The mortuary car is outside in the lane now. This studio is built into the brick wall that divides the garden from the lane. I thought

566

it would save a lot of trouble and difficulty if we opened that window, backed the car up to it, and lifted the stretcher through.'

'Over there?'

Alleyn walked over to the window in the south wall. He stooped and inspected the floor.

'This is where the modelling fellow, Garcia, did his stuff. Bits of clay all over the place. His work must have stood on the tall stool here, well in the light. Wait a moment.'

He flashed his pocket-torch along the sill. It was scored by several cross-scratches.

'Someone else has had your idea, Dr Ampthill,' said Alleyn. He pulled a pair of gloves from his overcoat pocket, put them on, and opened the window. The light from the studio shone on the whole body of a mortuary van drawn up in the lane outside. The air smelt cold and dank. Alleyn shone his torch on the ground under the window-sill. He could see clearly the print of car tyres in the soft ground under the window.

'Look here, Mr Blackman.'

Blackman joined him.

'Yes,' he said. 'Someone's backed a car across the lane under the window. Miss Troy says the carrier must have called for this Mr Garcia's stuff on Saturday morning. The maids say nobody came to the house about it. Well now, suppose Garcia left instructions for them to come straight to this window? Eh? How about that? He'd help them put the stuff through the window on to the van and then push off himself to wherever he was going.'

'On his walking tour,' finished Alleyn. 'You're probably right. Look here, if you don't mind, I think we'll take the stretcher out through the door and along the path. Perhaps there's a door in the wall somewhere. Is there?'

'Well, the garage yard is not far off. We could take it through the yard into the lane, and the van could go along and meet them there.'

'I think it would be better.'

Blackman called through the window.

'Hullo there! Drive along to the back entrance and send the stretcher in from there. Keep over on the far side of the lane.'

'OK, super,' said a cheerful voice.

'Sligo, you go along and show the way.'

The constable at the door disappeared, and in a minute or two returned with two men and a stretcher. They carried Sonia's body out into the night.

'Well, I'll push off,' said Dr Ampthill.

'I'd like to get away, too, if you'll let me off, Mr Alleyn,' said Blackman. 'I'm expecting a report at the station on this other case. Two of my chaps are down with flu and I'm rushed off my feet. I needn't say we'll do everything we can. Use the station whenever you want to.'

'Thank you so much. I'll worry you as little as possible. Good night.'

The door slammed and the voices died away in the distance. Alleyn turned to Fox, Bailey and Thompson.

'The old team.'

'That's right, sir,' said Bailey. 'Suits us all right.'

'Well,' said Alleyn, 'it's always suited me. Let's get on with it. You've got your photographs and prints. Now we'll up-end the throne. Everything's marked, so we can get it back. Let me take a final look at the drape. Yes. You see, Fox, it fell taut from the cushion to the floor, above the point of the knife. Nobody would dream of disturbing it, I imagine. As soon as Miss Seacliff pressed the model over, the drape went with her, pulling away the drawing-pin that held it to the boards. That's all clear enough. Over with the throne.'

They turned the dais on its side. The light shone through the cracks in the roughly built platform. From the widest of these cracks projected the hilt of the dagger. It was a solid-looking round handle, bound with tarnished wire and protected by a crossbar guard. One side of the guard actually dug into the platform. The other just

568

cleared it. The triangular blade had bitten into the edge of the planks. The end of the hilt was shiny.

'It's been hammered home at a slight angle, so that the blade would be at right-angles to the inclined plane of the body. It's an ingenious, dirty, deliberated bit of work, this. Prints, please, Bailey, and a photograph. Go over the whole of the under-surface. You won't get anything, I'm afraid.'

While Bailey and Thompson worked, Alleyn continued his tour of the room. He pulled back the cover of the divan and saw an unmade bed beneath it. 'Bad mark for Mr Garcia.' Numbers of stretched canvases stood with their faces to the wall. Alleyn began to inspect them. He thought he recognized a large picture of a trapeze artiste in pink tights and spangles as the work of Katti Bostock. That round, high-cheeked face was the one he had seen dead a few minutes ago. The head and shoulders had been scraped down with a knife. He turned another big canvas round and exclaimed softly.

'What's up, sir?' asked Fox.

'Look.'

It was a portrait of a girl in a green velvet dress. She stood, very erect, against a white wall. The dress fell in austere folds about the feet. It was most simply done. The hands looked as though they had been put down with twelve direct touches. The form of the girl shone through the heavy dress, in great beauty. It was painted with a kind of quiet thoughtfulness.

But across the head where the paint was wet, someone had scrubbed a rag, and scratched with red paint an idiotic semblance of a face with a moustache.

'Lor',' said Fox, 'is that a modern idea, too, sir?'

'I hardly think so,' murmured Alleyn. 'Good God, Fox, what a perfectly filthy thing to do. Don't you see, somebody's wiped away the face while the paint was wet, and then daubed this abortion on top of the smudge. Look at the lines of paint – you can see a kind of violence in them. The brush has been thrust savagely at the canvas so that the tip has spread. It's as if a nasty child had done it in a fit of temper. A stupid child.'

'I wonder who painted the picture, sir. If it's a portrait of this girl Sonia Gluck, it looks as if there's been a bit of spite at work. By gum, it'd be a rum go if the murderer did it.'

'I don't think this was Sonia,' said Alleyn. 'There's a smudge of blonde hair left. Sonia Gluck was dark. As for the painter – ' He paused. 'I don't think there's much doubt about that. The painter was Agatha Troy.'

'You can pick the style, can you?'

'Yes.'

With a swift movement Alleyn turned the canvas to the wall. He lit a cigarette and squatted on his heels.

'Let us take what used to be called a "lunar" at the case. In a little while I must start interviewing people, but I'd like you fellows to get as clear an idea as possible of the case as we know it. At the moment we haven't got so much as a smell of motive. Very well. Eight students, the model, and Miss Troy have used this studio every morning from Saturday the 10th until last Friday, the 16th. On Friday they used it until twelve-thirty, came away in dribbles, lunched at the house, and then, at different intervals, all went away with the exception of Wolf Garcia, a bloke who models and sculps. He stayed behind, saying that he would be gone when they returned on Sunday. The studio was not locked at any time, unless by Garcia, who slept in it. They reopened this morning with this tragedy. Garcia and his belongings had gone. That's all. Any prints, Bailey?'

'There's a good many blue smears round the edge, sir, but it's unplaned wood underneath, and we can't do much with it. It looks a bit as if someone had mopped it up with a painty rag.'

'There's a chunk of paint-rag on the floor there. Is it dusty?'

'Yes, thick with it.'

'Possibly it was used for mopping up. Have a go at it.'

570

Alleyn began to prowl round the back of the throne.

'Hullo! More grist for the mill.' He pointed to a strip of wood lying in a corner of the studio. 'Covered with indentations. It's the ledge off an easel. That's what was used for hammering. Take it next, Bailey. Let's find an easel without a ledge. Detecting is so simple when you only know how. Mr Hatchett has no ledge on his easel – therefore Mr Hatchett is a murderer. Q.E.D. This man is clever. Oh, lawks-a-mussy me, I suppose I'd better start off on the statements. How goes it, Bailey?'

'This paint-rag's a mucky bit of stuff,' grumbled Bailey. 'It's been used for dusting all right. You can see the smudges on the platform. Same colour. I thought I might get a print off some of the smears of paint on the rag. They're still tacky in places. Yes, here's something. I'll take this rag back and have a go at it, sir.'

'Right. Now the ledge.'

Bailey used his insufflator on the strip of wood.

'No,' he said, after a minute or two. 'It's clean.'

'All right. We'll leave the studio to these two now, Fox. Try to get us as full a record of footprints as you can, Bailey. Go over the whole show. I can't tell you what to look out for. Just do your stuff. And, by the way, I want photographs of the area round the window and the tyre-prints outside. You'd better take a cast of them and look out for any other manifestations round about them. If you come across any keys, try them for prints. Lock the place up when you've done. Good sleuthing.'

Fox and Alleyn returned to the house.

'Well, Brer Fox,' said Alleyn on the way, 'how goes it with everybody?'

'The Yard's still in the same old place, sir. Pretty busy lately.'

'What a life! Fox, I think I'll see Miss Valmai Seacliff first. On the face of it she's a principal witness.'

'What about Miss Troy, sir?' asked Fox.

Alleyn's voice came quietly out of the darkness:

'I've seen her. Just before you came.'

'What sort of a lady is she?'

'I like her,' said Alleyn. 'Mind the step. Here's the side door. I suppose we can use it. Hullo! Look here, Fox.'

He paused, his hand on Fox's arm. They were close by a window. The curtains had been carelessly drawn and a wide band of light streamed through the gap. Alleyn stood a little to one side of this light and looked into the room. Fox joined him. They saw a long refectory table at which eight people sat. In the background, half in shadow, loomed the figure of a uniformed constable. Seven of the people round the table appeared to listen to the eighth, who was Agatha Troy. The lamplight was full on her face. Her lips moved rapidly and incisively; she looked from one attentive face to the other. No sound of her voice came to Alleyn and Fox, but it was easy to see that she spoke with urgency. She stopped abruptly and looked round the table as if she expected a reply. The focus of attention shifted. Seven faces were turned towards a thin, languid-looking young man with a blond beard. He seemed to utter a single sentence, and at once a stocky woman with black straight hair cut in a bang, sprang to her feet to answer him angrily. Troy spoke again. Then nobody moved. They all sat staring at the table.

'Come on,' whispered Alleyn.

He opened the side door and went along the passage to a door on the left. He tapped on this door. The policeman answered it.

'All right,' said Alleyn quietly, and walked straight in, followed by Fox and the constable. The eight faces round the table turned like automatons.

'Please forgive me for barging in like this,' said Alleyn to Troy.

'It's all right,' said Troy. 'This is the class. We were talking – about Sonia.' She looked round the table. 'This is Mr Roderick Alleyn,' she said.

'Good evening,' said Alleyn generally. 'Please don't move. If you don't mind, I think Inspector Fox and I will join you for a moment. I shall have to ask you all the

572

usual sort of things, you know, and we may as well get it over. May we bring up a couple of chairs?'

Basil Pilgrim jumped up and brought a chair to the head of the table.

'Don't worry about me, sir,' said Fox. 'I'll just sit over here, thank you.'

He settled himself in a chair by the sideboard. Alleyn sat at the head of the table, and placed his notebook before him.

'The usual thing,' he said, looking pleasantly round the table, 'is to interview people severally. I think I shall depart from routine for once and see if we can't work together. I have got your names here, but I don't know which of you is which. I'll just read them through, and if you don't mind – '

He glanced at his notes.

'Reminiscent of a roll-call, I'm afraid, but here goes. Miss Bostock?'

'Here,' said Katti Bostock.

'Thank you. Mr Hatchett?'

'That's me.'

'Miss Phillida Lee?'

Miss Lee made a plaintive murmuring sound. Malmsley said: 'Yes.' Pilgrim said: 'Here.' Valmai Seacliff merely turned her head and smiled.

'That's that,' said Alleyn. 'Now then. Before we begin I must tell you that in my opinion there is very little doubt that Miss Sonia Gluck has been deliberately done to death. Murdered.'

They seemed to go very still.

'Now, as you all must realize, she was killed by precisely the means which you discussed and worked out among yourselves ten days ago. The first question I have to put to you is this. Has any one of you discussed the experiment with the dagger outside this class? I want you to think very carefully. You have been scattered during the weekend and it is possible, indeed very likely, that you may have talked about the pose, the model, and the

573

experiment with the knife. This is extremely important, and I ask you to give me a deliberated answer.'

He waited for quite a minute.

'I take it that none of you have spoken of this matter, then,' said Alleyn.

Cedric Malmsley, leaning back in his chair, said: 'Just a moment.'

'Yes, Mr Malmsley?'

'I don't know, I'm sure, if it's of any interest,' drawled Malmsley, 'but Garcia and I talked about it on Friday afternoon.'

'After the others had gone up to London?'

'Oh, yes. I went down to the studio, you see, after lunch. I did some work there. Garcia was messing about with his stuff. He's usually rather sour when he's working, but on Friday he babbled away like the brook.'

'What about?'

'Oh,' said Malmsley vaguely, 'women and things. He's drearily keen on women, you know. Tediously over-sexed.' He turned to the others. 'Did you know he and Sonia were living together in London?'

'I always said they were,' said Valmai Seacliff.

'Well, my sweet, it seems you were right.'

'I told you, Seacliff, didn't I?' began Phillida Lee excitedly. 'You remember?'

'Yes. But I thought so long before that.'

'Did you pursue this topic?' asked Alleyn.

'Oh, no, we talked about you, Seacliff.'

'About me?'

'Yes. We discussed your engagement, and your virtue and so on.'

'Very charming of you,' said Basil Pilgrim angrily.

'Oh, we agreed that you were damned lucky and so on. Garcia turned all knowing, and said – '

'Is this necessary – ' demanded Pilgrim, of Alleyn.

'Not at the moment, I think,' said Alleyn. 'How did you come to discuss the experiment with the dagger, Mr Malmsley?'

'Oh, that was when we talked about Sonia. Garcia looked at my drawing and asked me if I'd ever felt like killing my mistress just for the horror of doing it.'

Chapter 6

Sidelight on Sonia

'And was that all?' inquired Alleyn, after a rather deadly little pause.

'Oh, yes,' said Cedric Malmsley, and lit a cigarette. 'I just thought I'd better mention it.'

'Thank you. It was just as well. Did he say anything else that could possibly have a bearing on this affair?'

'I don't think so. Oh, he did say Sonia wanted him to marry her. Then he began talking about Seacliff, you know.'

'Couple of snotty little bounders,' grunted Katti Bostock unexpectedly.

'Oh, I don't think so,' said Malmsley, with an air of sweet reasonableness. 'Seacliff likes being discussed, don't you, my angel? She knows she's simply lousy with It.'

'Don't be offensive, please, Malmsley,' said Pilgrim dangerously.

'Good heavens! Why so sour? I thought you'd like to know we appreciated her.'

'That will do, Malmsley,' said Troy very quietly.

Alleyn said: 'When do you leave the studio on Friday afternoon, Mr Malmsley?'

'At five. I kept an eye on the time because I had to bath and change and catch the six o'clock bus.'

'You left Mr Garcia still working?'

'Yes. He said he wanted to pack up the clay miniature ready to send it up to London the next morning.'

'He didn't begin to pack it while you were there?'

'Well, he got me to help him carry in a zinc-lined case from the junk-room. He said it would do quite well.'

'He would,' said Troy grimly. 'I paid fifteen shillings for that case.'

'How would it be managed?' asked Alleyn. 'Surely a clay model is a ticklish thing to transport?'

'He'd wrap masses of damp cloths round it,' explained Troy.

'How about lifting it? Wouldn't it be very heavy?'

'Oh, he'd thought all that out,' said Malmsley, yawning horribly. 'We put the case on a tall stool in the window with the open end sideways, beside the tall stool he worked on. The thing was on a platform with wheels. He just had to wheel it into the case and fill the case with packing.'

'How about getting it into the van?'

'Dear me. Isn't this all rather tedious?'

'Extremely. A concise answer would enable us to move on to a more interesting narrative.'

Troy gave an odd little snort of laughter.

'Well, Mr Malmsley?' said Alleyn.

'Garcia said the lorry would back into the window from the lane outside. The sill is only a bit higher than the stool. He said they'd be able to drag the case on to the sill and get it in the lorry.'

'Did he say anything about arranging for the lorry?'

'He asked me if there was a man in the village,' said Troy. 'I told him Burridge would do it.'

The policeman at the door gave a deprecatory cough.

'Hullo?' said Alleyn, slewing round in his chair. 'Thought of something?'

'The super asked Burridges if they done it, sir, and they says no.'

'Right. Thank you. Now, Mr Malmsley, did you get any idea when Mr Garcia proposed to put the case on board the lorry?'

'He said early next morning – Saturday.'

'I see. There was no other mention of Miss Sonia Gluck, the pose, or Mr Garcia's subsequent plans?'

'No.'

'He didn't tell you where the clay model was to be delivered?'

'No. He just said he'd got the loan of a disused warehouse in London.'

'He told me he was going on a sketching-tramp for a week before he started work,' said Valmai Seacliff.

'To me also, he said this.' Francis Ormerin leant forward, glancing nervously at Alleyn. 'He said he wished to paint landscape for a little before beginning this big work.'

'He painted?' asked Alleyn.

'Oh, yes,' said Troy. 'Sculping was his long suit, but he painted and etched a bit as well.'

'Very interesting stuff,' said Katti Bostock.

'Drearily representational though, you must own,' murmured Malmsley.

'I don't agree,' said Ormerin.

'Good God!' exclaimed Basil Pilgrim, 'we're not here to discuss aesthetics.'

'Does anyone here,' Alleyn cut in firmly, 'know who lent this warehouse to Garcia, where it was, when he proposed to go there, or in what direction he has supposedly walked away.?'

'Silence.

'He is possibly the most uncommunicative young man in England,' said Troy suddenly.

'It would seem so, indeed,' agreed Alleyn.

'There's this, though,' added Troy. 'He told me the name of the man who commissioned the 'Comedy and Tragedy'. It's Charleston and I think he's secretary to the board of the New Palace Theatre, Westminster. Is that any help?'

'It may be a lot of help.'

'Do you think Garcia murdered Sonia?' asked Malmsley vaguely. 'I must say I don't.'

'The next point is this,' said Alleyn, exactly as though Malmsley had not spoken. 'I want to arrive at the order in which you all left the studio on Friday at midday. I believe Miss Troy and Miss Bostock came away together as soon as the model got down. Any objections to that?'

578

There was none apparently.

'Well, who came next?'

'I – I think I did,' said Phillida Lee, 'and I think I ought to tell you about an *extraordinary* thing that I heard Garcia say to Sonia one day – '

'Thank you so much, Miss Lee. I'll come to that later if I may. At the moment we're talking about the order in which you left the studio on Friday at noon. You followed Miss Troy and Miss Bostock?'

'Yes,' said Miss Lee restlessly.

'Good. Are you sure of that, Miss Lee?'

'Yes. I mean I know I did because I was absolutely *exhausted*. It always takes it out of me most *frightfully* when I paint. It simply drains every *ounce* of my energy. I even forget to *breathe*.'

'That must be most uncomfortable,' said Alleyn gravely. 'You came out to breathe, perhaps?'

'Yes. I mean I felt I must get away from it. So I simply put down my brushes and walked out. Miss Troy and Bostock were just ahead of me.'

'You went straight to the house?'

'Yes, I think so. Yes, I did.'

'Yeah, that's right,' said Watt Hatchett loudly. 'You came straight up here because I was just after you, see? I saw you through the dining-room window. This window here, Mr Alleyn. That's right, Miss Lee. You went up to the sideboard and began eating something.'

'I – I don't remember that,' said Miss Lee in a high voice. She darted an unfriendly glance at Hatchett.

'Well,' said Alleyn briskly, 'that leaves Miss Seacliff, Messrs Ormerin, Pilgrim, Malmsley and Garcia, and the model. Who came next?'

'We all did – except Garcia and Sonia,' said Valmai Seacliff. 'Sonia hadn't dressed. I remember I went into the junk-room and washed my brushes under the tap. Ormerin and Malmsley and Basil followed me there.'

She spoke with a slight hesitation, the merest shadow of a stutter, and with a markedly falling inflexion. She had a trick of uttering the last words of a phrase on an indrawn breath. Everything she looked and did, Alleyn felt, was the result of a carefully concealed deliberation. She managed now to convey the impression that men followed her inevitably, wherever she went.

'They were in the way,' she went on. 'I told them to go. Then I finished washing my brushes and came up to the house.'

'Garcia was in the junk-room, too, I think,' said Ormerin.

'Oh, yes,' agreed Seacliff softly. 'He came in, as soon as you'd gone. He would, you know. Sonia was glaring through the door – furious, of course.' Her voice died away and was caught up on that small gasp. She looked through her eyelashes at Alleyn. 'I walked up to the house with the other three.'

'That is so,' agreed Ormerin.

'Leaving Mr Garcia and the model in the studio?' asked Alleyn.

'I suppose so.'

'Yes,' said Pilgrim.

'You say the model was furious, Miss Seacliff,' said Alleyn. 'Why was that?'

'Oh, because Garcia was making passes at me in the junk-room. Nothing much. He can't help himself – Garcia.'

'I see,' said Alleyn politely. 'Now, please. Did any of you revisit the studio before you went up to London?'

'I did,' said Ormerin.

'At what time?'

'Immediately after lunch. I wished to look again at my work. I was very troubled about my work. Everything was difficult. The model – ' He stopped short.

'Yes?'

'Never for a second was she still. It was impossible. Impossible! I believe that she did it deliberately.'

'She's dead now,' said Phillida Lee, on muted strings. 'Poor little Sonia.'

580

'Spare us the *nil nisi* touch, for God's sake,' begged Malmsley.

'Did you all notice the model's restlessness?'

'You bet!' said Watt Hatchett. 'She was saucy, that's what she was. Seemed to have got hold of the idea she amounted to something. She gave me a pain in the neck, dinkum, always slinging off about Aussie.'

' "Aussie," ' groaned Malmsley, ' "Aussie,", "Tassie," "a goodee," "a badee." Pray spare me those bloody abbreviations.'

'Look, Mr Malmsley, I'd sooner talk plain honest Australian than make a noise like I'd got a fish-bone stuck in me gullet. Aussie'll do me. And one other thing, too. If you walked down Bondi beach with that half-chewed mouthful of hay sprouting out of your dial, they'd phone the Zoo something was missing.'

'Hatchett,' said Troy. 'Pipe down.'

'Good oh, Miss Troy.'

'I gather,' said Alleyn mildly, 'that you didn't altogether like the model?'

'Who, me? Too right I didn't. I'm sorry the poor kid's coughed out. Gosh, I reckon it's a fair cow, but just the same she gave me a pain in the neck. I asked her one day had she got fleas or something, the way she was twitching. And did she go crook!' Hatchett uttered a raucous yelp of laughter. Malmsley shuddered.

'Thank you, Mr Hatchett,' said Alleyn firmly. 'The next point I want to raise is this. Have there been any definite quarrels with the model? Any scenes, any rows between Miss Gluck and somebody else?'

He looked round the table. Everyone seemed disconcerted. There was a sudden feeling of tension. Alleyn waited. After a silence of perhaps a minute, Katti Bostock said slowly:

'I suppose you might say there were a good many scenes.'

'You had one with her yourself, Bostock,' said Malmsley.

'I did.'

'What was that about, Miss Bostock?'

'Same thing. Wriggling. I'm doing – I was doing a big thing. I wanted to finish it in time for the Group show. It opened last Friday. She was to give me separate sittings – out of class, you know. She seemed to have the devil in her. Fidgeting, going out when I wanted her. Complaining. Drove me dotty. I didn't get the thing finished, of course.'

'Was that the trapeze artiste picture?' asked Alleyn.

Katti Bostock scowled.

'I dislike people looking at my things before they're finished.'

'I'm sorry; it is beastly, I know,' said Alleyn. 'But, you see, we've got to do our nosing around.'

'I suppose you have. Well' – she laughed shortly – 'it'll never be finished now.'

'It wouldn't have been finished anyway, though, would it?' asked Phillida Lee. 'I meant I heard you tell her you hated the sight of her, and she could go to the devil.'

'What d'you mean?' demanded Katti Bostock harshly. 'You were not there when I was working.'

'I happened to come in on Thursday afternoon. I only got inside the door, and you were having such a *frightful* row I beetled off again.'

'You'd no business to hang about and eavesdrop,' said Miss Bostock. Her broad face was full crimson; she leant forward, scowling.

'There's no need to lose your temper with *me*,' squeaked Miss Lee. 'I didn't eavesdrop. I simply walked in. You couldn't see me because of the screen inside the door, and anyway, you were in such a *seething* rage you wouldn't have noticed the Angel Gabriel himself.'

'For Heaven's sake, let's keep our sense of proportion,' said Troy. 'The poor little wretch was infuriating, and we've all lost our tempers with her again and again.' She looked at Alleyn. 'Really, you might say each of us has felt like murdering her at some time or another.'

'Yes, Miss Troy,' said Phillida Lee, still staring at Katti Bostock, 'but we haven't all said so, have we?'

'My God – '

'Katti,' said Troy. 'Please!'

'She's practically suggesting that – '

'No, no,' said Ormerin. 'Let us, as Troy says, keep our sense of proportion. If exasperation could have stabbed this girl, any one of us might be a murderer. But which-ever one of us *did* – '

'I don't see why it need be one of us,' objected Valmai Seacliff placidly.

'Nor I,' drawled Malmsley. 'The cook may have taken a dislike to her and crawled down to the studio with murder in her heart.'

'Are we meant to laugh at that?' asked Hatchett.

'It is perfectly clearly to be seen,' Ormerin said loudly, 'what is the view of the police. This gentleman, Mr Alleyn, who is so quiet and so polite, who waits in silence for us to make fools of ourselves – he knows as each of us must know in his heart that the murderer of this girl was present in the studio on the morning we made the experiment with the dagger. That declares itself. There is no big motive that sticks out like a bundle in a haystack, so Mr Alleyn sits and says nothing and hears much. And we – we talk.'

'Mr Ormerin,' said Alleyn, 'you draw up the blinds on my technique, and leave it blinking foolishly in the light of day. I see that I may be silent no longer.'

'Ah-ah-ah! It is as I have said.' Ormerin wagged his head sideways, shrugged up his shoulders and threw him-self back in his chair. 'But as for this murder – it is the *crime passionnel*, depend upon it. The girl was very highly sexed.'

'That doesn't necessarily lead to homicide,' Alleyn pointed out, with a smile.

'She was jealous,' said Ormerin; 'she was yellow with jealousy and chagrin. Every time Garcia looks at Seacliff she suffers as if she is ill. And when Pilgrim announces

583

that he is affianced with Seacliff, again Sonia feels as if a knife is twisted inside her.'

'That's absolute bosh,' said Basil Pilgrim violently. 'You don't know what you are talking about, Ormerin.'

'Do I not? She was avid for men, that little one.'

'Dear me,' murmured Malmsley, 'this all sounds very Montmartre.'

'She certainly was a hot little dame,' said Hatchett.

'It was apparent,' added Ormerin. 'And when a more compelling – more *troublante* – woman arrived, she became quite frantic. Because Seacliff – '

'Will you keep Valmai's name out of this?' shouted Pilgrim.

'Basil, darling, how divinely county you are,' said Valmai Seacliff. 'I know she was jealous of me. We all know she was. And she obviously was very attracted to you, my sweet.'

'This conversation,' said Troy, 'seems slightly demented. All this, if it was true, might mean that Sonia would feel like killing Valmai or Pilgrim or Garcia, but why should anybody kill her?'

'Closely reasoned,' murmured Alleyn. Troy threw a suspicious glance at him.

'It is true, is it not,' insisted Ormerin, 'that you suspect one of us?'

'Or Garcia,' said Katti Bostock.

'Yes, there's always the little tripe-hound,' agreed Seacliff.

'And the servants,' added Malmsley.

'Very well,' amended Ormerin, still talking to Alleyn. 'You suspect one of this party, or Garcia, or – if you will – the servants.'

'An inside job,' said Hatchett, proud of the phrase.

'Oh, yes,' said Alleyn. 'I do rather suspect one of you – or Mr Garcia – or the servants. But it's early days yet. I am capable of almost limitless suspicion. At the moment I am going to tighten up this round-table conference.' He looked at Hatchett. 'How long have you been working without a tray on your easel?'

'Eh? What d'you mean?' Hatchett sounded startled.

'It's not very difficult. How long is it since you had a ledge on your easel?'

'Haven't I got one now?'

'No.'

'Oh yeah! That's right. I took it off to hammer the dagger into the throne.'

'What!' screamed Phillida Lee. 'Oh, I see.'

'On the day of the experiment?' asked Alleyn.

'That's right.'

'And it's been kicking about on the floor ever since?'

'I suppose so. Half a tick, though – has it? Naow – it hasn't, either. I've had a ledge all right. I stuck my dipper on it. Look, I had a ledge on me easel Fridee after lunch.'

'*After* lunch,' asked Alleyn.

'Yeah, I remember now. I ran down some time after lunch to have a look at the thing I'd been painting. I met you coming away, Ormerin, didn't I?'

'Yes. I only looked at my work and felt sick and came away.'

'Yeah. Well, when I got there I thought I'd play around with the wet paint, see? Well, I'd just had a smack at it when I heard Ormerin singing out the old bus went past the corner on the main road in ten minutes. Well, I remember now; I jammed my brush into my dipper so's it wouldn't go hard, and then beat it. But the dipper was on the ledge all right.'

'And was the ledge there this morning?'

'You're right. It wasn't. And it wasn't there Sundee night either.'

'Sunday night?' said Alleyn sharply.

'That's right. After we got back, see? I ran down to the studio just after tea.'

'After tea? But I thought you didn't come back until – ' Alleyn looked at his notes. 'Until six-thirty.'

'That's correct, Mr Alleyn. We finished tea at half-past eight, about.'

'The gentleman is talking of the evening meal, Inspector,' said Malmsley. 'They dine at noon in the Antipodes, I understand.'

'Aw go and chase yourself,' invited Hatchett. 'I went down to the studio at about eight-thirty, Inspector. "After dinnah" if you've got enlarged tonsils. "After tea" if you're normal.'

'Did you get in?'

'Too right. She was locked, but the key's left on a nail, and I opened her up and had a look-see at my picture. Gosh, it looked all right, too, Miss Troy, by artificial light. Have you seen it by lamplight, Miss Troy?'

'No,' said Troy. 'Don't wander.'

'Good oh, Miss Troy.'

'Well,' said Alleyn, 'you went into the studio, and put the lights up, and looked at your work. Did you look at the throne?'

'Er – yes. Yes, I did. I was wondering, if I'd paint a bit of the drape, and I had a look, and it was all straightened out. Like it always is before she gets down into the pose. Stretched tight from the cushion to the floor. If I had a pencil I could show you – '

'Thank you, I think I follow.'

'Good oh, then. Well, I wondered if I'd try and fix it like as if the model was laying on it. I'd an idea that I might get it right if I lay down myself in the pose. Cripes!' exclaimed Hatchett, turning paper-white. 'If I'd a-done that would I have got that knife in me slats? Cripey, Mr Alleyn, do you reckon that dagger was sticking up under the drape on Sundee evening?'

'Possibly.'

'What a cow!' whispered Hatchett.

'However, you didn't arrange yourself on the drape. Why not?'

'Well, because Miss Troy won't let anybody touch the

586

throne without she says they can, and I thought she'd go crook if I did.'

'Correct?' asked Alleyn, with a smile at Troy.

'Certainly. It's the rule of the studio. Otherwise the drapes would get bundled about, and the chalked positions rubbed off.'

'Yeah, but listen, Miss Troy. Mr Alleyn, listen. I've just remembered something.'

'Come on, then,' said Alleyn.

'Gee, I reckon this is important,' continued Hatchett excitedly. 'Look, when I went down to the studio just before we all went to catch the bus on Fridee, the drape was all squashed down, just as it had been when the model got up.'

'You're sure of that?'

'I'm certain. I'll swear to it.'

'Did you notice the drape on your brief visit to the studio after lunch, Mr Ormerin?'

'Yes,' said Ormerin excitedly. 'Now you ask I remember well. I looked at my work, and then automatically I looked at the throne as though the model was still there. And I got the small tiny shock one receives at the sight of that which one does not expect. Then I looked at my treatment of the drape and back to the drape itself. It was as Hatchett describes – crumpled and creased by the weight of her body, just as when she arose at midday.'

'Here!' exclaimed Hatchett. 'See, what that means? It means – '

'It is pregnant with signification, I'm sure, Mr Hatchett,' said Alleyn. Hatchett was silent. Alleyn looked at his notes and continued: 'I understand that Miss Troy and Miss Bostock left by car. So did Miss Seacliff and Mr Pilgrim. Then came the bus party at three o'clock. Miss Lee, Mr Ormerin, Mr Hatchett, and the model. It seems,' said Alleyn very deliberately, 'that at a few minutes before three when Mr Hatchett left to catch the bus, the drape was still flat and crushed on the floor.' He paused, contemplating Cedric Malmsley. 'What did you do after the others had gone?'

Malmsley lit a cigarette and took his time over it.

'Oh,' he said at last, 'I wandered down to the studio.'

'When?'

'Immediately after lunch.'

'Did you look at the drape on the throne?'

'I believe I did.'

'How was it then?'

'Quite well, I imagine. Just like a drape on a throne.'

'Mr Malmsley,' said Alleyn, 'I advise you not to be too amusing. I am investigating a murder. Was the drape still flat?'

'Yes.'

'How long did you stay in the studio?'

'I've told you. Until five.'

'Alone with Mr Garcia?'

'I've told you. Alone with Garcia.'

'Did either of you leave the studio during the afternoon?'

'Yes.'

'Who?'

'Garcia.'

'Do you know why?'

'I imagine it was to pay a visit to the usual offices.'

'How long was he away?'

'Dear me, I don't know. Perhaps eight or ten minutes.'

'When he worked, did he face the window?'

'I believe so.'

'With his back to the room?'

'Naturally.'

'Did you look at the drape before you left?'

'I don't think so.'

'Did you touch the drape, Mr Malmsley?'

'No.'

'Who scrawled that appalling defacement on Miss Troy's painting of a girl in green?'

There was an uneasy silence, broken at last by Troy.

'You mean my portrait of Miss Seacliff. Sonia did that.'
'The model?' exclaimed Alleyn.
'I believe so. I said we have all felt like murdering her. That was my motive, Mr Alleyn.'

Chapter 7

Alibi for Troy

Alleyn lifted a hand as if in protest. He checked himself and, after a moment's pause, went on with his customary air of polite diffidence.

'The model defaced your painting. Why did she do this?'

'Because she was livid with *me*,' said Valmai Seacliff. 'You see, it was rather a marvellous painting. Troy was going to exhibit it. Sonia hated that. Besides, Basil wanted to buy it.'

'When did she commit this – outrage?' asked Alleyn.

'A week ago,' said Troy. 'Miss Seacliff gave me the final sitting last Monday morning. The class came down to the studio to see the thing. Sonia came too. She'd been in a pretty foul frame of mind for some days. It's perfectly true what they all say. She was an extraordinary little animal and, as Ormerin has told you, extremely jealous. They all talked about the portrait. She was left outside the circle. Then Pilgrim asked me if he might buy it before it went away. Perhaps I should tell you that I have also done a portrait of Sonia which has not been sold. Sonia took that as a sort of personal slight on her beauty. It's hard to believe, but she did. She seemed to think I'd painted Miss Seacliff because I was dissatisfied with her own charms as a model. Then, when they all came down and looked at the thing and liked it, and Pilgrim said he wanted it, I suppose that upset her still more. Several of these people said in front of her, they thought the thing of Miss Seacliff was the best portrait I have done.'

'It was all worms and gallwood to her,' said Ormerin.

'Well,' Troy went on, 'we came away, and I suppose she stayed behind. When I went down to the studio later

590

on that day, I found – ' she caught her breath – 'I found
– what you saw.'

'Did you tackle her?'

'Not at first. I – felt sick. You see, once in a painter's
lifetime he, or she, does something that's extra.'

'I know.'

'Something that they look at afterwards and say to
themselves: 'How did the stumbling ninny that is me, do
this?' It happened with the head in Valmai's portrait. So
when I saw – I just felt sick.'

'Bloody little swine,' said Miss Bostock.

'Oh, well,' said Troy, 'I did tackle her that evening.
She admitted she'd done it. She said all sorts of things
about Valmai and Pilgrim, and indeed everybody in the
class. She stormed and howled.'

'You didn't sack her?' asked Alleyn.

'I felt like it, of course. But I couldn't quite do that.
You see, they'd all got going on these other things, and
there was Katti's big thing, too. I think she was honestly
sorry she'd done it. She really rather liked me. She simply
went through life doing the first thing that came into her
head. This business had been done in a blind fury with
Valmai. She only thought of me afterwards. She fetched
up by having hysterics and offering to pose for nothing
for the rest of her life.' Troy smiled crookedly. 'The
stable-door idea,' she said.

'Basil and I were frightfully upset,' said Valmai Seacliff.
'Weren't we, Basil?'

Alleyn looked to see how Pilgrim would take this
remark. He thought that for a moment he saw a look of
reluctant surprise.

'Darling!' said Pilgrim, 'of course we were.' And then
in his eyes appeared the reflection of her beauty, and he
stared at her with the solemn alarm of a man very deeply
in love.

'Were there any more upheavals after this?' asked
Alleyn after a pause.

591

'Not exactly,' answered Troy. 'She was chastened a bit. The others let her see that they thought she'd – she'd – '

'I went crook at her,' announced Hatchett. 'I told her I reckoned she was – '

'Pipe down, Hatchett.'

'Good oh, Miss Troy.'

'We were all livid,' said Katti Bostock hotly. 'I could have mur – ' She stopped short. 'Well, there you are, you see,' she said doggedly. 'I could have murdered her and I didn't. She knew how I felt, and she took it out in the sittings she gave me.'

'It was sacrilege,' squeaked Phillida Lee. 'That exquisite thing. To see it with that obscene – '

'Shut up, Lee, for God's sake,' said Katti Bostock.

'Oddly enough,' murmured Malmsley, 'Garcia seemed to take it as heavily as anybody. Worse if anything. Do you know, he was actually ill, Troy? I found him in the garden, a most distressing sight.'

'How extraordinary!' said Valmai Seacliff vaguely. 'I always thought he was entirely without emotion. Oh, but of course – '

'Of course – what?' asked Alleyn.

'Well, it *was* a portrait of me, wasn't it? I attracted him *tremendously* in the physical sense. I suppose that was why he was sick.'

'Oh, bilge and bosh!' said Katti Bostock.

'Think so?' said Seacliff quite amiably.

'Can any of you tell me on what sort of footing the model and Mr Garcia were during the last week?' asked Alleyn.

'Well, I told you she'd been his mistress,' said Malmsley. 'He said that himself during Friday afternoon.'

'Not while they were here, I hope,' said Troy. 'I told him I wouldn't have anything like that.'

'He said so. He was very pained and hurt at your attitude, I gathered.'

'Well, I *know* there was something going on, anyway,' said Phillida Lee, with a triumphant squeak. 'I've been waiting to tell the superintendent this, but you were all so busy talking, I didn't get a *chance*. I know Sonia wanted him to marry her.'

'Why, Miss Lee?'

'Well, they were always whispering together, and I went to the studio one day, about a week ago, I think, and there they were having a session – I mean, they were talking – nothing else.'

'You seem to have had a good many lucky dips in the studio, Lee,' said Katti Bostock. 'What did you overhear this time?'

'You needn't be so acid. It may turn out a mercy I *did* hear them. Mayn't it, Superintendent?' She appealed to Alleyn.

'I haven't risen to superintendent heights, Miss Lee. But please do tell me what you heard.'

'As a matter of fact, it wasn't *very* much, but it was exciting. Garcia said: "All right – on Friday night, then." And Sonia said: "Yes, if it's possible." Then there was quite a long pause and she said: "I won't stand for any funny business with *her*, you know," And Garcia said: "Who?" and she said – I'm sorry, Mr Alleyn – but she said: "The Seacliff bitch, of course." ' Miss Lee turned pink. 'I *am* sorry, Mr Alleyn.'

'Miss Seacliff will understand the exigencies of a verbatim report,' said Alleyn with the faintest possible twinkle.

'Oh, I've heard all about it. She knew what he was up to, of course,' said Valmai Seacliff. She produced a lipstick and mirror and, with absorbed attention, made up her lovely mouth.

'Why didn't you tell me the swine was pestering you?' Pilgrim asked her.

'My sweet – I could manage Garcia perfectly well,' said Seacliff with a little chuckle.

'Anything more, Miss Lee?' asked Alleyn.

'Well, yes. Sonia suddenly began to cry and say Garcia ought to marry her. He said nothing. She said something

593

about Friday evening again, and she said if he let her down after that she'd go to Troy and tell her the whole story. Garcia just said – Mr Alleyn, he just sort of *grunted* it, but honestly it sounded *frightful*. Truly. And she didn't say another *thing*. I think she was *terrified* – really!'

'But you haven't told us what he did say, you know.'

'Well, he said: "If you don't shut up and leave me to get on with my work, I'll bloody well stop your mouth for keeps. Do what I tell you. Get out!" *There!*' ended Miss Lee triumphantly.

'Have you discussed this incident with anyone else?'

'I told Seacliff, in confidence.'

'I advised her to regard it as nobody's business but theirs,' said Seacliff.

'Well – I thought *somebody* ought to know.'

'I said,' added Seacliff, 'that if she still felt all repressed and congested, she could tell Troy.'

'Did you follow this excellent advice, Miss Lee?'

'No – I didn't – because – well, because I thought – I mean – '

'I have rather sharp views on gossip,' said Troy dryly. 'And even sharper views on listening-in. Possibly she realized this.' She stared coldly at Miss Lee, who turned very pink indeed.

'How did this incident terminate?' asked Alleyn.

'Well, I made a bangy sort of noise with the door to show I was there, and they stopped. And I *didn't* eavesdrop, Miss Troy, truly. I was just rooted to the ground with *horror*. It all sounded so *sinister*. And *now* see what's happened!'

Troy looked up at Alleyn. Suddenly she grinned, and Alleyn felt a sort of thump in his chest. 'Oh God,' he thought urgently, 'what am I going to do about this? I didn't *want* to lose my heart.' He looked away quickly.

'Are there any other incidents of any sort that might have some bearing on this tragedy?' he asked at large.

Nobody answered.

'Then I shall ask you all to stay in here for a little while

594

longer. I want to see each of you separately, before we close down tonight. Miss Troy, will you allow us to use a separate room as a temporary office? I am sorry to give so much trouble.'

'Certainly,' said Troy. 'I'll show you – '

She led the way to the door and went into the hall without waiting for them. Alleyn and Fox followed, leaving the local man behind. When the door had shut behind them Alleyn said to Fox:

'Get through to the Yard, Fox. We'll have to warn all stations about Garcia. If he's tramping, he can't have walked so far in three days. If he's bolted, he may be anywhere by now. I'll try and get hold of a photograph. We'd better broadcast, I think. Make sure nobody's listening when you telephone. Tell them to get in touch with the city. We must find this warehouse. Then see the maids. Ask if they know anything at all about the studio on Friday night and Saturday morning. Come along to the drawing-room when you've finished, will you?'

'Right, sir. I'll just ask this PC where the telephone hangs out.'

Fox turned back, and Alleyn moved on to the end of the hall, where Troy waited in a pool of light that came from the library.

'In here,' she said.

'Thank you.'

She was turning away as Alleyn said:

'May I keep you a moment?'

He stood aside for her to go through the door. They returned to the fire. Troy got a couple of logs from the wood basket.

'Let me do that,' Alleyn said.

'It's all right.'

She pitched the logs on the fire and dusted her hands.

'There are cigarettes on that table, Mr Alleyn. Will you have one?'

He lit her cigarette and his own and they sat down.

'What now?' asked Troy.

'I want you to tell me exactly what you did from the time you left the studio on Friday at noon until the class assembled this morning.'

'An alibi?'

'Yes.'

'Do you think for a moment,' said Troy, in a level voice, 'that I might have killed this girl?'

'Not for a moment,' answered Alleyn.

'I suppose I shouldn't have asked you that. I'm sorry. Shall I begin with the time I got up to the house?'

'Yes, please,' said Alleyn.

He thought she was very stiff with him and supposed she resented the very sight of himself and everything he stood for. It did not occur to Alleyn that his refusal to answer that friendly grin had sent up all Troy's defences. Where women were concerned he was, perhaps, unusually intelligent and intuitive, but the whole of this case is coloured by his extraordinary wrong-headedness over Troy's attitude towards himself. He afterwards told Nigel Bathgate that he was quite unable to bring Troy into focus with the case. To Troy it seemed that he treated her with an official detachment that was a direct refusal to acknowledge any former friendliness. She told herself, with a sick feeling of shame, that he had probably thought she pursued him in the ship. He had consented to sit for her, with a secret conviction that she hoped it might lead to a flirtation. 'Or,' thought Troy, deliberately jabbing at the nerve, 'he probably decided I was fishing for a sale.'

Now, on this first evening at Tatler's End House, they treated each other to displays of frigid courtesy. Troy, summoning her wits, began an account of her weekend activities.

'I came up to the house, washed, changed and lunched. After lunch, as far as I remember, Katti and I sat in here and smoked. Then we went round to the garage, got the car, and drove up to our club in London. It's the United Arts. We got there about four o'clock, had tea with some people we ran into in the club, shopped for an hour afterwards, and got back to the club about six, I should think. I bathed, changed and met Katti in the lounge. We had a cocktail and then dined with the Arthur Jayneses. It was a party of six. He's president of the Phoenix Group. From there we all went to the private view. We supped at the Hungaria with the Jayneses. I got back to the club somewhere round two o'clock. On Saturday I had my hair done at Cattcherly's in Bond Street. Katti and I had another look at the show. I lunched early at the Ritz with a man called John Bellasca. Then I picked Katti up at the club and we got back here about three.'

'Did you go down to the studio?'

'Yes. I went there to collect my sketch-box. I wanted to see what materials I had and tidy it up. I was going to work out of doors on Sunday. I brought the box in here and spent the afternoon at different tidying jobs. After that Katti and I went for a walk to look for a subject. We dined out. I asked when we got here on Saturday if Garcia had gone, and the maids told me he hadn't been in to breakfast or lunch, so I supposed he had pushed off at daybreak. They had sent his dinner down to the studio the night before – Friday night. It was easier than having it up here. He sleeps in the studio, you know.'

'Why was that?'

'It was advisable. I didn't want him in the house. You've heard what he's like with women.'

'I see. On Saturday were you long in the studio?'

'No. I simply got my sketch-box. I was painting out of doors.'

'Anyone go in with you?'

'No.'

'Did you notice the drape?'

Troy leant forward, her cropped head between two clenched fists.

'That's what I've been trying to remember ever since Hatchett said it was stretched out when he saw it on Sunday.

'Give me a moment. I went straight to my cupboard

behind the door and got out my sketching gear. I had a look in the box and found there was no turpentine in the bottle, so I took it to the junk-room and filled it up. Then I came back to the studio and – yes, yes!'

'You've remembered it?'

'Yes. I – I must tell you I hadn't screwed myself up to looking at the portrait of Seacliff again. Not since I first saw what Sonia had done to it. I just turned it face to the wall behind the throne. Well, I saw it when I came out of the junk-room, and I thought: "I can't go on cutting it dead. It can't stand there for ever, giving me queasy horrors whenever I catch sight of it." So I began to walk towards it, and I got as far as the edge of the throne, and I remember now quite clearly I walked carefully round the drape, so as not to disturb it, and I noticed, without noticing, don't you know, that the silk was in position – stretched straight from the cushion and pinned to the floor of the throne. You may have noticed that it was caught with a safety-pin to the top of the cushion. That was to prevent it slipping off when she lay down on it. It was fixed lightly to the floor with a drawing-pin that flew out when the drape took her weight. The whole idea was to get the accidental swill of the silk round the figure. It was stretched out like that when I saw it.'

'I needn't tell you the significance of this,' said Alleyn, slowly. 'You are absolutely certain the drape was in position?'

'Yes. I'd swear to it.'

'And did you look at the portrait of Miss Seacliff?'

Troy turned her face away from him.

'No,' she said gruffly, 'I funked it. Poor sort of business, wasn't it?' She laughed shortly.

Alleyn made a quick movement, stopped himself, and said: 'I don't think so. Did either of you go down to the studio at any time during yesterday, do you know?'

'I don't know. I don't think so. I didn't, and Katti had an article to do for *The Palette* and was writing in the library all day. She's got a series of articles on the Italian primitives running in *The Palette*. You'd better ask her about yesterday.'

'I will. To return to your own movements. You went out to paint in the garden?'

'Yes. At eleven o'clock. The Bossicote church bell had just stopped. I worked till about two o'clock and came in for a late lunch. After lunch I cleaned up my brushes at the house. I hadn't gone to the studio. Katti and I had a good glare at my sketch, and then she read over her article and began to type it. I sat in here, working out an idea for a decorative panel on odd bits of paper. Seacliff and Pilgrim arrived in his car for tea at five, and the others came by the six o'clock bus.'

'Sonia Gluck with them?'

'Yes.'

'Did you all spend the evening together?'

'The class has a sort of common-room at the back of the house. In my grandfather's day it was really a kind of ballroom, but when my father lost most of his money, part of the house was shut up, including this place. I had a lot of odds and ends of furniture put into it and let them use it. It's behind the dining-room, at the end of an odd little passage. They all went in there after dinner on Sunday – yesterday – evening. I looked in for a little while.'

'They were all there?'

'I think so. Pilgrim and Seacliff wandered out through the french window into the garden. I suppose they wanted to enjoy the amenities of betrothal.'

Alleyn laughed unexpectedly. He had a very pleasant laugh.

'What's the matter?' asked Troy.

' "The amenities of betrothal," ' quoted Alleyn.

'Well, what's wrong with that?'

'Such a grand little phrase!'

For a moment there was no constraint between them. They looked at each other as if they were old friends.

'Well,' said Troy, 'they came back looking very smug

and complacent and self-conscious, and all the others were rather funny about it. Except Sonia, who looked like thunder. It's quite true, what Seacliff says. Sonia, you see, was the main attraction last year, as far as the men-students were concerned. She used to hold a sort of court in the rest-times and fancied herself as a Bohemian siren, poor little idiot. Then Seacliff came and wiped her eye. She was beside herself with chagrin. You've seen what Seacliff is like. She doesn't exactly disguise the fact that she is attractive to men, does she? Katti says she's a successful nymphomaniac.'

'Pilgrim seems an honest-to-God sort of fellow.'

'He's a nice fellow, Pilgrim.'

'Do you approve of the engagement?'

'No, I don't. I think she's after his title.'

'You don't mean to say he's a son of the Methodist peer?'

'Yes, he is. And the Methodist peer may leave us for crowns and harps any moment now. The old gentleman's failing.'

'I see.'

'As a matter of fact – ' Troy hesitated.

'Yes?'

'I don't know that it matters.'

'Please, tell me anything you can think of.'

'You may attach too much importance to it.'

'We are warned against that at the Yard, you know.'

'I beg your pardon,' said Troy stiffly. 'I was merely going to say that I thought Basil Pilgrim had been worried about something since his engagement.'

'Have you any idea what it was?'

'I thought at first it might have been his father's illness, but somehow I don't think it was that.'

'Perhaps he has already regretted his choice. The trapped feeling.'

'I don't think so,' said Troy still more stiffly. 'I fancy it was something to do with Sonia.'

'With the model?'

600

'I simply meant that I thought he felt uncomfortable about Sonia. She was always uttering little jeers about engaged couples. I think they made Pilgrim feel uncomfortable.'

'Do you imagine there has ever been anything between Pilgrim and Sonia Gluck?'

'I have no idea,' said Troy.

There was a tap on the door, and Fox came in.

'I got through, sir. They'll get busy at once. The men have finished in the studio.'

'Ask them to wait. I'll see them in a minute.'

'Have you finished with me?' asked Troy, standing up.

'Yes, thank you, Miss Troy,' said Alleyn formally. 'If you wouldn't mind giving us the names and addresses of the people you met in London, I should be very grateful. You see, we are obliged to check all statements of this sort.'

'I quite understand,' answered Troy coldly.

She gave the names and addresses of her host and hostess, of the people she met in the club, and of the man who took her to lunch – John Bellasca, 44 Little Belgrave Street.

'The club porter may be useful,' she said, 'his name's Jackson. He may have noticed my goings out and comings in. I remember that I asked him the time, and got him to call taxis. The sort of things people do when they wish to establish alibis, I understand.'

'They occasionally do them at normal times, I believe,' said Alleyn. 'Thank you, Miss Troy. I won't bother you any more for the moment. Do you mind joining the others until we have finished this business.'

'Not at all,' answered Troy with extreme grandeur. 'Please use this room as much as you like. Good evening, good evening.'

'Good evening, miss,' said Fox.

Troy made an impressive exit.

Chapter 8

Sidelights on Garcia

'The lady seems a bit upset,' said Fox mildly, when Troy had gone.

'I irritate the lady,' answered Alleyn.

'*You* do, sir? I always think you've got a very pleasant way with female witnesses. Sort of informal and at the same time very polite.'

'Thank you, Fox,' said Alleyn wryly.

'Learn anything useful, sir?'

'She says the drape was in the second position on Saturday afternoon.'

'Stretched out straight?'

'Yes.'

'Well,' said Fox, 'if she's telling the truth, it looks as though the knife was fixed up between the time this Mr Malmsley walked out on Friday afternoon and the time Miss Troy looked in on Saturday. That's if Malmsley was telling the truth when he said the drape was crumpled and flat on Friday afternoon. It all points one way, chief, doesn't it.'

'It does, Brer Fox, it does.'

'The Yard's getting straight on to chasing up this Mr Garcia. I've rung all the stations round this district and asked them to make inquiries. I got a pretty fair description of him from the cook, and Bailey found a couple of photographs of the whole crowd in the studio. Here's one of them.'

He thrust a massive hand inside his pocket and produced a half-plate group of Troy and her class. It had been taken in the garden.

'There's the model, Fox. Look!'

Fox gravely put on his spectacles and contemplated the photograph.

'Yes, that's the girl,' he said. 'She looks merry, doesn't she, sir?'

'Yes,' said Alleyn slowly. 'Very merry.'

'That'll be this Garcia, then.' Fox continued. He pointed a stubby finger at a figure on the outside of the group. Alleyn took out a lens and held it over the photograph. Up leaped a thin, unshaven face, with an untidy lock of dark hair falling across the forehead. The eyes were set rather close and the brows met above the thin nose. The lips were unexpectedly full. Garcia had scowled straight into the camera. Alleyn gave Fox the lens.

'Yes,' said Fox, after a look through it, 'we'll have enlargements done at once. Bailey's got the other. He says it will enlarge very nicely.'

'He looks a pretty good specimen of a wild man,' said Alleyn.

'If Malmsley and Miss Troy are telling the truth,' said Fox, who had a way of making sure of his remarks, 'he's a murderer. Of course, the motive's not much of an affair as far as we've got.'

'Well, I don't know, Brer Fox. It looks as though the girl was badgering him to marry her. It's possible the P.M. may offer the usual explanation for that sort of thing.'

'In the family way?' Fox took off his spectacles and stared blandly at his chief. 'Yes. That's so. What did you make of that statement of Mr Malmsley's about Garcia being ill in the garden after he saw the defaced likeness? That seems a queer sort of thing to me. It wasn't as if he'd done the photo.'

'The painting, Fox,' corrected Alleyn. 'One doesn't call inspired works of art photographs, you know. Yes, that was rather a rum touch, wasn't it? You heard Miss Seacliff's theory. Garcia is infatuated with her and was all upheaved by the sight of her defeated loveliness.'

'Far-fetched,' said Fox.

'I'm inclined to agree with you. But it might be an explanation of his murdering Sonia Gluck when he realized she had done it. He might have thought to himself: "This looks like a more than usually hellish fury from the woman scorned – what am I in for?" and decided to get rid of her. There's a second possibility which will seem even more far-fetched to you, I expect. To me it seems conceivable that Garcia's aesthetic nerves were lacerated by the outrage on a lovely piece of painting. Miss Troy says the portrait of Valmai Seacliff was the best thing she has ever done.' Alleyn's voice deepened and was not quite steady. 'That means it was a really great work. I think, Fox, that if I had seen that painted head and known it for a superlatively beautiful thing, and then seen it again with that beastly defacement – I believe I might have sicked my immortal soul up into the nearest flower-bed. I also believe that I would have felt remarkably like murder.'

'Is that so, sir?' said Fox stolidly. 'But you wouldn't have done murder, though, however much you felt like it.'

'I'd have felt *damn* like it,' muttered Alleyn. He walked restlessly about the room. 'The secret of Garcia's reaction,' he said, 'lies behind this.' He wagged the photograph at Fox. 'Behind that very odd-looking head. I wish we knew more about Garcia. We'll have to go hunting for his history, Brer Fox. Records of violence and so on. I wonder if there are any. Suppose he turns up quite innocently to do his "Comedy and Tragedy" in his London warehouse?'

'That'll look as if either Malmsley or Miss Troy was a liar, sir, won't it? I must say I wouldn't put Mr Malmsley down as a very dependable sort of gentleman. A bit cheeky in an arty sort of fashion.'

Alleyn smiled.

'Fox, what a neat description of him! Admirable! No, unless Malmsley is lying, the knife was hammered through and the drape stretched out after they had all gone on Friday. And if Miss Troy found it stretched out on Saturday afternoon, then the thing was done before then.'

'If,' said Fox. And after a moment's silence Alleyn replied:
' "If" – of course.'
'You might say Miss Troy had the strongest motive, sir, as far as the portrait is concerned.'
There was a longer pause.
'Do you think it at all likely that she is a murderess?' said Alleyn from the fireplace. 'A very deliberate murderess, Fox. The outrage to the portrait was committed a week before the murder.'
'I must say I don't think so, sir. Very unlikely indeed, I'd say. This Garcia seems the likeliest proposition on the face of it. What did you make of Miss Phillida Lee's statement, now? The conversation she overheard. Looks as though Garcia and the deceased were making an assignation for Friday night, doesn't it? Suppose she came back to the studio on Friday night in order that they should resume intimacy?'
'Yes, I know.'
'He seems to have actually threatened her, if the young lady can be depended upon.'
'Miss Seacliff didn't contradict the account, and you must remember that extraordinary little party, Phillida Lee, confided the fruits of her nosy-parkering to Miss Seacliff long before the tragedy. I think we may take it that Garcia and Sonia Gluck had a pretty good dust-up on the lines indicated by the gushing Lee. You took notes in the dining-room, of course. Turn up her report of the quarrel, will you?'
Fox produced a very smug-looking notebook, put on his spectacles, and turned up a page.
'Garcia – ' he read slowly from his shorthand notes. ' "All right. On Friday night then." Sonia Gluck: "Yes, if it's possible." Then later Gluck said: "I won't stand for any funny business with her, you know." Garcia said: "Who?" and Gluck answered: "The Seacliff bitch, of course." Sonia Gluck said Garcia ought to marry her. He did not reply. She threatened to go to Miss Troy with the

whole story if he let her down. He said; "If you don't shut up and leave me to get on with my work, I'll bloody well stop your mouth for keeps." That's the conversation, sir.'

'Yes. We'll have to get hold of something about Friday night. Damn it all, the studio is built into the wall, and the window opens on the lane. Surely to Heaven someone must have passed by that evening and heard voices if Garcia had the girl in the place with him.'

'And how did he get his stuff away on Friday night or Saturday morning? They've tried all the carriers for miles around.'

'I know, Brer Fox, I know. Well, on we go. We've got to get all these people's time-tables from Friday noon till Sunday evening. What about Bailey? I'd better see him first, I suppose.'

Bailey came in with his usual air of mulish displeasure and reported that they had finished in the studio. They had gone over everything for prints, had photographed the scratched window-sill, measured and photographed the car's prints and footprints in the lane, and taken casts of them. They had found the key of the studio hanging on a nail outside the door. It was smothered in prints. Under the pillow was an empty whisky bottle. On the window-sill one set of prints occurred many times, and seemed to be superimposed on most of the others. He had found traces of clay with these prints, and with those on the bottle.

'Those will be Garcia's,' said Alleyn. 'He worked in the window.'

In the junk-room Bailey had found a mass of jars, brushes, bottles of turpentine and oil, costumes, lengths of materials, a spear, an old cutlass, and several shallow dishes that smelt of nitric acid. There was also what Bailey described as 'a sort of mangle affair with a whale of a heavy chunk of metal and a couple of rollers.'

'An etching press,' said Alleyn.

'There's a couple of stains on the floor of the junk-room,' continued Bailey. 'Look like nitric-acid stains. They're new. I can't find any nitric acid anywhere, though. I've looked in all the bottles and jars.'

'Um!' said Alleyn, and made a note of it.

'There's one other thing,' said Bailey. He opened a bag he had brought in with him, and out of it he took a small box which he handed to Alleyn.

'Hullo,' said Alleyn. 'This is the *bonne-bouche*, is it?'

He opened the little box and held it under the lamp. Inside was a flattened greenish-grey pellet.

'Clay,' said Alleyn. 'Where was it?'

'In the folds of that silk stuff that was rigged on the platform,' said Bailey, staring morosely at his boots.

'I see,' said Alleyn softly. 'Look here, Fox.'

Fox joined him. They could both see quite clearly that the flattened surface of the pellet was delicately scrolled by minute holes and swirling lines.

'A nice print,' said Fox, 'only half there, but very sharp what there is.'

'If the prints on the sill are Garcia's,' said Bailey, 'that's Garcia's too.'

There was a silence.

'Well,' said Alleyn at last, 'that's what you call a fat little treasure-trove, Bailey.'

'I reckon it must have dropped off his overall when he was stretching that stuff above the point of the knife, sir. That's what I reckon.'

'Yes. It's possible.'

'He must have used gloves for the job. There are one or two smudges about the show that look like glove-marks, and I think one of them's got a trace of the clay. We've photographed the whole outfit.'

'You've done rather well, Bailey.'

'Anything more, sir?'

'Yes, I'm afraid there is. I want you to find the deceased's room and go over it. I don't think we should let that wait any longer. One of the maids will show you

607

where it is. Come and get me if anything startling crops up.'

'Very good, Mr Alleyn.'

'And when that's done, you can push off if you want to. You've left a man on guard, I suppose?'

'Yes, sir. One of these local chaps. Getting a great kick out of it.'

'Guileless fellow. Away you go, Bailey. I'll see you later on.'

'OK, sir.'

'Nitric acid?' ruminated Fox, when Bailey had gone.

'I think it's the acid they used for etching. I must ask Miss Troy about it.'

'Looks as if all we've got to do is to find Garcia, don't it, sir?'

'It do, Fox. But for the love of Mike don't let's be too sure of ourselves.'

'That bit of clay, you know, sir – how could it have got there by rights? He'd no business up on the model's throne now, had he?'

'No.'

'And according to Malmsley's story, the drape must have been fixed when the rest of them had gone up to London.'

'Yes. We'll have to trace 'em in London just the same. Have to get on to these others now. Go and take a dip in the dining-room, Fox, and see what the fairies will send us in the way of a witness.'

Fox went off sedately and returned with Katti Bostock. She came in looking very four-square and sensible. Her short and stocky person was clad in corduroy trousers, a red shirt and a brown jacket. Her straight black hair hung round her ears in a Cromwellian cut with a determined bang across her wide forehead. She was made up in a rather slap-dash sort of manner. Her face was principally remarkable for its exceedingly heavy eyebrows.

Alleyn pushed forward a chair and she slumped herself

down on it. Fox went quietly to the desk and prepared to make a shorthand report. Alleyn sat opposite Katti.

'I'm sorry to bother you again, Miss Bostock,' he said. 'We've got a good deal of tidying up to do, as you may imagine. First of all, is nitric acid used in the studio for anything?'

'Etching,' said Katti. 'Why?'

'We've found stains in the junk-room that looked like it. Where is it kept?'

'In a bottle on the top shelf. It's marked with a red cross.'

'We couldn't find it.'

'It was filled up on Friday, and put on the top shelf. Must be there.'

'I see. Right. Now I just want to check everybody's movements from lunch-time on Friday. In your case it will be a simple matter. I believe you spent most of your time in London with Miss Troy?' He opened his note-book and put it on the arm of his chair.

'Yes,' he said. 'I see you both went to your club, changed and dined with Sir Arthur and Lady Jaynes at Eaton Square. From there you went to the private view of the Phoenix Group Show, and supped at the Hungaria. That right?'

'Yes. Quite correct.'

'You stayed at the club. What time did you get back from the Hungaria on Friday night?'

'Saturday morning,' corrected Katti. 'I left with the Jayneses at about twelve-thirty. They drove me to the club. Troy stayed on with John Bellasca and was swept out with the dust whenever they close.'

'You met again at breakfast?'

'Yes. We separated during the morning and met again at the show. I lunched with some people I ran into there – Graham Barnes and his wife – he's the water-colour bloke. Then Troy and I met at the club and came home. She lunched with John Bellasca.'

'Yes. That's all very straightforward. I'll have to ask

Sir Arthur Jaynes or someone to confirm it. The usual game, you know.'

'That's all right,' said Katti. 'You want to find out whether either of us had time to sneak back here and set a death-trap for that little fool Sonia, don't you?'

'That's the sort of idea,' agreed Alleyn with a smile. 'I know Sir Arthur slightly. Would you like me to say you've lost a pearl necklace and want to trace it, or – '

'Good Lord, no. Tell him the facts of the business. Do I look like pearls? And John will fix up Troy's alibi for her. He'll probably come down at ninety miles an hour to say he did it himself if you're not careful.' Katti chuckled and lit a cigarette.

'I see,' said Alleyn. And into his thoughts came the picture of Troy as she had sat before the fire with her cropped head between her long hands. There had been no ring on those hands.

'When you got back to the club after you left the Hungaria, did anyone see you?'

'The night porter let me in. I don't remember anyone else.'

'Was your room near Miss Troy's?'

'Next door.'

'Did you hear her return?'

'No. She says she tapped on the door, but I must have been asleep. The maid came in at seven with my tea, but I'd have had time to go out, get Troy's car and drive down here and back, between twelve-thirty and seven, you know.'

'True,' said Alleyn. 'Did you?'

'No.'

'Well – we'll have to do our best with night porters, garage attendants, and petrol consumption.'

'Wish you luck,' said Katti.

'Thank you, Miss Bostock. You got back here for lunch, I understand. How did you spend the afternoon?'

'Dishing up bilge for *The Palette*. I was in here.'

'Did you at any time go to the studio?'

'No.'

'Was Miss Troy with you on Saturday afternoon?'

'She was in and out. Let's see. She spent a good time turning out that desk over there and burning old papers. Then she tidied her sketching-kit. We had tea in here. After tea we went out to look at a place across the fields where Troy thought of doing a sketch. We dined out with some people at Bossicote – the Haworths – and got home about eleven.'

'Thank you. Sunday?'

'I was at my article for *The Palette* all day. Troy painted in the morning and came in here in the afternoon. The others were all back for dinner.'

'Did you hear the model say anything about her own movements during the weekend?'

'No. Don't think so. I fancy she said she was going to London.'

'You engaged her for this term before Miss Troy returned, didn't you?'

'Yes.'

'How did you get hold of her?'

'Through Graham Barnes. He gave me her address.'

'Have you got it?'

'Oh Lord, where was it? Somewhere in Battersea, I think. Battersea Bridge Gardens. That's it. I've got it written down somewhere. I'll try and find it for you.'

'I wish you would. It would save us one item in a loathsome itinerary of dull jobs. Now, about this business with the model and your picture. The trapeze-artiste subject, I mean. Did she pose for you again after the day when there was the trouble described by Miss Phillida Lee?'

Again that dull crimson stained the broad face. Katti's thick eyebrows came together and her lips protruded in a sort of angry pout.

'That miserable little worm Lee! I told Troy she was a fool to take her, fees or no fees. The girl's bogus. She went to the Slade and was no doubt made to feel entirely extraneous. She tries to talk "Slade" when she remembers, but the original nice-girl gush oozes out all over the place. She sweats suburbia from every pore. She deliberately sneaked in and listened to what I had to say.'

'To the model?'

'Yes. Little drip!'

'It was true, then, that you did have a difference with Sonia?'

'If I did, that doesn't mean I killed her.'

'Of course it doesn't. But I should be glad of an answer, Miss Bostock.'

'She was playing up, and I ticked her off. She knew I wanted to finish the thing for the Group Show, and she deliberately set out to make work impossible. I scraped the head down four times, and now the canvas is unworkable – the tooth has gone completely. Troy is always too easy with the models. She spoils them. I gave the little brute hell because she needed it.'

'And did she pose again for you?'

'No. I've told you the thing was dead.'

'How did she misbehave? Just fidgeting?'

Katti leant forward, her square hands on her knees. Alleyn noticed that she was shaking a little, like an angry terrier.

'I'd got the head laid in broadly – I wanted to draw it together with a dry brush and then complete it. I wanted to keep it very simple and round, the drawing of the mouth was giving me trouble. I told her not to move – she had a damnable trick of biting her lip. Every time I looked at her she gave a sort of sneering smirk. As if she knew it wasn't going well. I mixed a touch of cadmium red for the under-lip. Just as I was going to lay it down she grimaced. I cursed her. She didn't say anything. I pulled myself together to put the brush on the canvas and looked at her. She stuck her foul little tongue out.'

'And that tore it to shreds, I imagine?'

'It did. I said everything I'd been trying not to say for the past fortnight. I let go.'

'Not surprising. It must have been unspeakably maddening. Why, do you suppose, was she so set on making things impossible?'

'She deliberately baited me,' said Katti, under her breath.

'But why?'

'Why? Because I'd treated her as if she was a model. Because I expected to get some return for the excessive wages Troy was giving her. I'd engaged her, and I managed things till Troy came back. Sonia resented that. Always hinting that I wasn't her boss and so on.'

'That was all?'

'Yes.'

'I see. You say her wages were excessively generous. What was she paid?'

'Four pounds a week and her keep. She's spun Troy some tale about doctor's bills, and Troy, as usual, believed the sad story and stumped up. She's anybody's mark for sponging. It's so damned immoral to let people get away with that sort of thing. It's no good talking to Troy. Streetbeggars see her coming a mile away. She's got two dead-heads here now.'

'Really? Which two?'

'Garcia, of course. She's been shelling out money to Garcia for ages. And now there's this Australian wild-man – Hatchett. She says she makes the others pay through the nose, but Lord knows if she ever gets the money. She's hopeless,' said Katti, with an air of exasperated affection.

'Would you call this a good photograph of Mr Garcia?' asked Alleyn suddenly. He held out the group. Katti took it and glowered at it.

'Yes, it's very like him,' she said. 'That thing was taken last year during the summer classes. Yes – that's Garcia all right.'

'He was here as Miss Troy's guest then, I suppose?'

'Oh Lord, yes. Garcia never pays for anything. He's got no sort of decency where money is concerned. No conscience at all.'

'No aesthetic conscience?'

'Um!' said Katti. 'I wouldn't say that. No – his work's the only thing he is honest about, and he's passionately sincere there.'

'I wish you'd give me a clear idea of him, Miss Bostock. Will you?'

'Not much of a hand at that sort of thing,' growled Katti, 'but I'll have a shot. He's a dark, dirty, weird-looking fellow. Very paintable head. Plenty of bone. You think he murdered the model, don't you?'

'I don't know who murdered the model.'

'Well, I think he did. It's just the sort of thing he would do. He's absolutely ruthless and as cold-blooded as a flat-fish. He asked Malmsley if he ever felt like murdering his mistress, didn't he?'

'So Mr Malmsley told us.'

'I'll bet it's true. If Sonia interfered with his work and put him off his stride, and he couldn't get rid of her any other way, he'd get rid of her that way. She may have refused to give him any more money.'

'Did she give him money?'

'I think so. Ormerin says she was keeping him last year. He wouldn't have the slightest qualms about taking it. Garcia just looks upon money as something you've got to have to keep you going. He could have got a well-paid job with a monumental firm. Troy got on to it for him. When he saw the tombstones with angels and open Bibles he said something indecent and walked out. He was prac-tically starving that time,' said Katti, half to herself, and with a sort of reluctant admiration, 'but he wouldn't haul his flag down.'

'You think the model was really attached to him?'

Katti took another cigarette and Alleyn lit it for her.

'I don't know,' she said. 'I'm not up in the tender passion. I've got an idea that she'd switched over to Basil Pilgrim, but whether it was to try and make Garcia jealous or because she'd fallen for Pilgrim is another matter. She

614

was obviously livid with Seacliff. But then Garcia had begun to hang round Seacliff.'

'Dear me,' said Alleyn, 'what a labyrinth of untidy emotions.'

'You may say so,' agreed Katti. She hitched herself out of her chair. 'Have you finished with me, Mr Alleyn?'

'Yes, do you know, I think I have. We shall have a statement in longhand for you to look at and sign, if you will, later on.'

She glared at Fox. 'Is that what he's been up to?'

'Yes.'

'Pah!'

'It's only to establish your movements. Of course, if you don't want to sign it – '

'Who said I didn't? Let me wait till I see it.'

'That's the idea, miss,' said Fox, looking benignly at her over the top of his spectacles.

'Will you show Miss Bostock out, please, Fox?'

'Thank you, I know my way about this house,' said Katti with a prickly laugh. She stumped off to the door. Fox closed it gently behind her.

'Rather a tricky sort of lady, that,' he said.

'She is a bit. Never mind. She gave us some sidelights on Garcia.'

'She did that all right.'

There was a rap on the door and one of the local men looked in.

'Excuse me, sir, but there's a gentleman out here says he wants to see you very particular.'

'What's his name?'

'He just said you'd be very glad indeed to see him, sir. He never gave a name.'

'Is he a journalist?' asked Alleyn sharply. 'If he is, I shall be very glad indeed to kick him out. We're too busy for the Press just now.'

'Well, sir, he didn't say he was a reporter. He said – er – er – er – '

'What?'

'His words was, sir, that you'd scream the place down with loud cries of gladness when you clapped eyes on him.'

'That's no way to ask to see the chief,' said Fox. 'You ought to know that.'

'Go and ask him to give his name,' said Alleyn.

The policeman retired.

Fox eyed Alleyn excitedly.

'By gum, sir, you don't think it may be this Garcia? By all accounts he's eccentric enough to send in a message like that.'

'No,' said Alleyn, as the door opened. 'I rather fancy I recognize the style. I rather fancy, Fox, that an old and persistent friend of ours has got in first on the news.'

'Unerring as ever, Mr Alleyn,' said a voice from the hall, and Nigel Bathgate walked into the room.

616

Chapter 9

Phillida Lee and Watt Hatchett

'Where the devil did you spring from?' asked Alleyn.

Nigel advanced with a shameless grin.

' "Where did I come from, 'Specky dear?
The blue sky opened and I am here!'

'Hullo, Fox!'

'Good evening, Mr Bathgate,' said Fox.

'I suppose you've talked to my mamma on the telephone,' said Alleyn as they shook hands.

'There now,' returned Nigel, 'aren't you wonderful, Inspector? Yes, Lady Alleyn rang me up to say you'd been sooled on to the trail before your time, and she thought the odds were you'd forget to let us know you couldn't come and stay with us.'

'So you instantly motored twenty miles in not much more than as many minutes in order to tell me how sorry you were?'

'That's it,' said Nigel cheerfully. 'You read me like a book. Angela sends her fondest love. She'd have come too only she's not feeling quite up to long drives just now.'

He sat down in one of the largest chairs.

'Don't let me interrupt,' he said. 'You can give me the story later on. I've got enough to go on with from the local cop. I'll ring up the office presently and give them the headlines. Your mother – divine woman – has asked me to stay.'

'Has my mother gone out of her mind?' asked Alleyn of nobody in particular.

'Come, come Inspector,' reasoned Nigel, with a trace of nervousness in his eye, 'you know you're delighted to have me.'

'There's not the smallest excuse for your bluffing your way in, you know. I've a damn good mind to have you chucked out.'

'Don't do that. I'll take everything down in shorthand and nobody will see me if I turn the chair round. Fox will then be able to fix the stammering witness with a basilisk glare. All will go like clockwork. All right?'

'All right. It's quite irregular, but you occasionally have your uses. Go into the corner there.'

Nigel hurried into a shadowy corner, turned a high armchair with its back to the room and dived into it.

' "I am invisible," ' he said. ' "And I shall overhear their conference." The Bard.'

'I'll deal with you later,' said Alleyn grimly. 'Tell them to send another of these people along, Fox.'

When Fox had gone Nigel asked hoarsely from the armchair if Alleyn had enjoyed himself in New Zealand.

'Yes,' said Alleyn.

'Funny you getting a case there,' ventured Nigel. 'Rather a busman's holiday, wasn't it?'

'I enjoyed it. Nobody interfered and the reporters were very well-behaved.'

'Oh,' said Nigel.

There was a short silence broken by Nigel.

'Did you have a slap-and-tickle with the American lady on the boat deck?'

'I did not.'

'Oh! Funny coincidence about Agatha Troy. I mean she was in the same ship, wasn't she? Lady Alleyn tells me the portrait is quite miraculously like you.'

'Don't prattle,' said Alleyn. 'Have you turned into a gossip hound?'

'No. I say!'

'What!'

'Angela's started a baby.'

'So I gathered, and so no doubt Fox also gathered, from your opening remarks.'

'I'm so thrilled I could yell it in the teeth of the whole police force.'

Alleyn smiled to himself.

'Is she all right?' he asked.

'She's not sick in the mornings any more. We want you to be a godfather. Will you, Alleyn?'

'I should be charmed.'

'Alleyn!'

'What?'

'You might tell me a bit about this case. Somebody's murdered the model, haven't they?'

'Quite possibly.'

'How?'

'Stuck a knife through the throne so that when she took the pose – '

'She sat on it?'

'Don't be an ass. She lay on it and was stabbed to the heart, poor little fool!'

'Who's the prime suspect?'

'A bloke called Garcia, who has been her lover, was heard to threaten her, has possibly got tired of her, and has probably been living on her money.'

'Is he here?'

'No. He's gone on a walking tour to Lord knows where, and is expected to turn up at an unknown warehouse in London in the vaguely near future, to execute a marble statue of "Comedy and Tragedy" for a talkie house.'

'D'you think he's bolted?'

'I don't know. He seems to be one of those incredible and unpleasant people with strict aesthetic standards, and no moral ones. He appears to be a genius. Now shut up. Here comes another of his fellow-students.'

Fox came in with Phillida Lee.

Alleyn, who had only met her across the dining-room table, was rather surprised to see how small she was. She wore a dull red dress covered in a hand-painted design. It was, he realized, deliberately unfashionable and very deliberately interesting. Miss Lee's hair was parted down the centre and dragged back from her forehead with such passionate determination that the corners of her eyes had attempted to follow it. Her face, if left to itself, would have been round and eager, but the austerities of the Slade school had superimposed upon it a careful expression of detachment. When she spoke one heard a faint undercurrent of the Midlands. Alleyn asked her to sit down. She perched on the edge of a chair and stared fixedly at him.

'Well, Miss Lee,' Alleyn began in his best official manner, 'we shan't keep you very long. I just want to have an idea of your movements during the weekend.'

'How ghastly!' said Miss Lee.

'But why?'

'I don't know. It's all so terrible. I feel I'll never be quite the same again. The *shock*. Of course, I ought to try and sublimate it, I suppose, but it's so difficult.'

'I shouldn't try to do anything but be common-sensical if I were you,' said Alleyn.

'But I thought they used psycho methods in the police!'

'At all events we don't need to apply them to the matter in hand. You left Tatler's End House on Friday afternoon by the three o'clock bus?'

'Yes.'

'With Mr Ormerin and Mr Watt Hatchett?'

'Yes,' agreed Miss Lee, looking self-conscious and maidenly.

'What did you do when you got to London?'

'We all had tea at The Flat Hat in Vincent Square.'

'And then?'

'Ormerin suggested we should go to an exhibition of poster work at the Westminster. We did go, and met some people we knew.'

'Their names, please, Miss Lee.'

She gave him the names of half a dozen people and the addresses of two.

'When did you leave the Westminster Art School?'

'I don't know. About six, I should think. Ormerin had

a date somewhere. Hatchett and I had dinner together at a Lyons. He took me. Then we went to the show at the Vortex Theatre.'

'That's in Maida Vale, isn't it?'

'Yes. I'm a subscriber and I had tickets. They were doing a play by Michael Sasha. It's called *Angle of Incidence*. It's *frightfully* thrilling and absolutely new. All about three County Council labourers in a sewer. Of course,' added Miss Lee, adopting a more mature manner, 'the Vortex is purely experimental.'

'So it would seem. Did you speak to anyone while you were there?'

'Oh yes. We talked to Sasha himself, and to Lionel Shand who did the décor. I know both of them.'

'Can you give me their addresses?'

Miss Lee was vague on this point, but said that care of the Vortex would always find them. Patiently led by Alleyn she gave a full account of her weekend. She had stayed with an aunt in the Fulham Road, and had spent most of her time in this aunt's company. She had also seen a great deal of Watt Hatchett, it seemed, and had gone to a picture with him on Saturday night.

'Only I *do* hope you won't have to ask Auntie anything, Inspector Alleyn, because you see she pays my fees with Miss Troy, and if she thought the *police* were after me she'd very likely turn sour, and then I wouldn't be able to go on painting. And that,' added Miss Lee with every appearance of sincerity, 'would be the most frightful tragedy.'

'It shall be averted if possible,' said Alleyn gravely, and got the name and address of the aunt.

'Now then, Miss Lee, about those two conversations you overheard – '

'I don't want to be called as a witness,' began Miss Lee in a hurry.

'Possibly not. On the other hand you must realize that in a serious case – and this is a very serious case – personal

621

objections of this sort cannot be allowed to stand in the way of police investigation.'

'But I didn't mean you to think that because Bostock flew into a blind rage with Sonia she was capable of *murdering* her.'

'Nor do I think so. It appears that half the class flew into rages at different times, and for much the same reason.'

'I didn't! I never had a row with her. Ask the others. I got on all right with her. I was sorry for her.'

'Why?'

'Because Garcia was so beastly to her. Oh, I do think he was *foul*! If you'd *heard* him that time!'

'I wish very much that I had.'

'When he said he'd shut her mouth for keeps – I mean it's the sort of thing you might think he'd say without meaning it, but he sounded as if he did mean it. He spoke so softly in a kind of drawl. I thought he was going to do it *then*. I was *terrified*. Truly! That's why I banged the door and walked in.'

'About the scrap of conversation you overheard – did you get the impression that they planned to meet on Friday night?'

'It sounded like that. Sonia said: "If it's possible." I think that's what she meant. I think she meant to come back and bed down with Garcia for the night while no one was here.'

'To *what*, Miss Lee?'

'Well – you know – to spend the night with him.'

'What did they do when you appeared?'

'Garcia just stared at me. He's got a beastly sort of way of looking at you. As if you were an animal. I was awfully scared he'd guessed I'd overheard them, but I saw in a minute that he hadn't. I said: "Hullo, you two, what are you up to? Having a woo or something?' I don't know how I managed it, but I did. And he said: "No, just a little chat." He turned away and began working at his thing. Sonia just walked out. She looked *ghastly*, Mr Alleyn, honestly. She always made up pretty heavily

622

except when we were painting the head, but even under her make-up I could see she was absolutely *bleached*. Oh, Mr Alleyn, I do believe he did it, I do, *actually*.'

'You tell me you were on quite good terms with the model. Did she ever say anything that had any bearing on her relationship with Mr Garcia?'

Phillida Lee settled herself more comfortably in her chair. She was beginning to enjoy herself.

'Well, of course, ever since this morning, I've been thinking of everything I can remember. I didn't talk much to her until I'd been here for a bit. As a matter of fact the others were so frightfully superior that I didn't get a chance to talk to *anybody* at first.'

Her round face turned pink, and suddenly Alleyn felt a little sorry for her.

'It's always a bit difficult, settling down among new people,' he said.

'Yes, I dare say it is, but if the new people just do their best to make you feel they don't want you, it's worse than that. That was why I left the Slade, really, Mr Alleyn. The instructors just used to come round once in a blue moon and look at one's things and sigh. And the students never even seemed to see one, and if they did they looked as if one smelt. And at first this place was just as bad, though of course Miss Troy's *marvellous*. Malmsley was at the Slade, and he's *typical*. Seacliff's worse. Anyway, Seacliff never *sees* another female, much less speaks to her. And all the men just beetle round Seacliff and never give anyone else a *thought*. It was a *bit* better after she said she was engaged to Pilgrim. Sonia felt like I did about Seacliff, and we talked about her a bit – and – well, we sort of sympathized about her.' The thin voice with its faint echo of the Midlands went on and on.

Alleyn, listening, could see the two of them, Phillida Lee, sore and lonely; Sonia, God knew how angry and miserable, taking comfort in mutual abuse of Valmai Seacliff.

'So you made friends?' he asked.

623

'Sort of. Yes, we did. I'm not one to look down my nose at a girl because she's a model. I'm a communist, anyway. Sonia was furious about Seacliff. She called her awful names – all beginning with B, you know. She said somebody ought to tell Pilgrim what Seacliff really was like. She – she – said – '

Miss Lee stopped abruptly.

'Yes?'

'I don't know whether I ought to – I mean – I like Pilgrim awfully and – well, I *mean* – '

'Is it something that the model said about Miss Seacliff?' said Alleyn.

'About *her!* Ooo no! I wouldn't mind what anybody said about *her*. But I don't believe it was true about Pilgrim. I don't think he was *ever* attracted to Sonia. I think she just made it up.'

'Made what up, Miss Lee? Did she suggest there had been anything like a romance between herself and Mr Pilgrim?'

'Well, if you can call it romance. I mean she said – I mean, it was only *once* ages ago, after a party, and I mean I think men and women ought to be free to follow their sex-impulses anyway, and not repress them. But I mean I don't think Pilgrim *ever* did because he doesn't seem as if he would somehow, but anyway, I don't see why not, bcause as Garcia once said, if you're hungry – ' Miss Lee, scarlet with determination, shut her eyes and added: 'you eat.'

'Quite so,' said Alleyn, 'but you needn't guzzle, of course.'

'Oh well – no, I suppose you needn't. But I mean I should think Pilgrim never *did*.'

'The model suggested there had been a definite intimacy between herself and Pilgrim?'

'Yes. She said she could tell Seacliff a thing or two about him, and if he didn't look out she would.'

'I see.'

'But I don't think there ever was. Truly. It was because

624

she was so furious with Pilgrim for not taking any notice of her.'

'You returned in the bus yesterday evening with the model, didn't you?'

'Yes. Watt – I mean Hatchett and me and Ormerin and Malmsley.'

'Did you notice anything out of the way about her?'

'No. She was doing a bit of a woo with Ormerin to begin with, but I think she was asleep for the last part of the trip.'

'Did she mention what she had done in London?'

'I think she said she'd gone to stay with a friend or something.'

'No idea where or with whom?'

'No, Mr Alleyn.'

'Nothing about Mr Garcia?'

'No.'

'Did she ever speak much of Garcia?'

'Not much. But she seemed as if – as if in a sort of way she was *sure* of Garcia. And yet he was tired of her. She'd lost her body-urge for him, if you ask me. But she seemed *sure* of him and yet furious with him. Of course, she wasn't very well.'

'Wasn't she?'

'No. I'm sure that was why she did that *terrible* thing to Troy's portrait of Seacliff. She was ill. Only she asked me not to say anything about it, because she said it didn't do a model any good for her to get a reputation of not being able to stand up to the work. I wouldn't have known except that I found her one morning looking absolutely *green*, and I asked her if anything was the matter. She said the pose made her feel sick – it was the twist that did it, she said. She was *honestly* sick, and she felt sort of giddy.'

Alleyn looked at Miss Lee's inquisitive, rather pretty, rather commonplace face and realized that her sophistication was more synthetic than even he had supposed. 'Bless my soul,' he thought, 'the creature's a complete baby – an infant that has been taught half a dozen indecorous phrases by older children.'

'Well, Miss Lee,' he said, 'I think that's all we need worry about for the moment. I've got your aunt's address – '

'Yes, but you *will* remember, won't you? I mean – '

'I shall be the very soul of tact. I shall say we are looking for a missing heiress believed to be suffering from loss of memory, and last heard of near Bossicote, and she will think me very stupid, and I shall learn that you spent the entire weekend in her company.'

'Yes. And Watt – Hatchett, I mean.'

'He was there too, was he?'

Again Miss Lee looked self-conscious and maidenly.

'Well, I mean, not *all* the time. I mean he didn't *stay* with us, but he came to lunch and tea – and dinner on Saturday and lunch on Sunday. Of course he *is* rough, and he does speak badly, but I told Auntie he can't help that because everybody's like that in Australia. Some of the others were pretty stinking to him too, you know. They made him feel dreadfully out of it. I was sorry for him, and I thought they were such snobs. And anyway, I think his work is frightfully exciting.'

'Where did he stay?'

'At a private hotel near us, in the Fulham Road. We went to the flicks on Saturday night. Oh, I told you that, didn't I?'

'Yes, thank you. When you go back to the dining-room, will you ask Mr Hatchett to come and see me in ten minutes' time?'

'Yes, I will.'

She got up and gazed at Alleyn. He saw a sort of corpse-side expression come into her face.

'Oh, Mr Alleyn,' she said, 'isn't it all *awful*?'

'Quite frightful,' responded Alleyn cheerfully. 'Good evening, Miss Lee.'

She walked away with an air of bereavement, and shut the door softly behind her.

'Oy!' said Nigel from the armchair.

'Hullo!'

'I'm moving over to the fire till the next one comes along. It's cold in this corner.'

'All right.'

Fox, who had remained silently at the writing-desk throughout the interview with Miss Lee, joined Alleyn and Nigel at the fire.

'That was a quaint little piece of Staffordshire,' said Nigel.

'Little simpleton! All that pseudo-modern nonsense! See here, Bathgate, you're one of the young intelligentsia, aren't you?'

'What do you mean? I'm a pressman.'

'That doesn't actually preclude you from the intelligentsia, does it?'

'Of course it doesn't.'

'Very well then. Can you tell me how much of this owlishness is based on experience, and how much on handbooks and hearsay?'

'You mean their ideas on sex?'

'I do.'

'Have they been shocking you, Inspector?'

'I find their conversation bewildering, I must confess.'

'Come off it,' said Nigel.

'What do you think, Fox?' asked Alleyn.

'Well, sir, I must say I thought they spoke very free round the dining-room table. All this talk about mistresses and appetites and so forth. Very free. Not much difference between their ways and the sort of folk we used to deal with down in the black divisions if you're to believe what you hear. Only the criminal classes are just promiscuous without being able to make it sound intellectual, if you know what I mean. Though I must say,' continued Fox thoughtfully, 'I don't fancy this crowd is as free-living as they'd like us to believe. This young lady, now. She seems like a nice little girl from a good home, making out she's something fierce.'

'I know,' agreed Alleyn. 'Little donkey.'

'And all the time she was talking about deceased and body-urges and so forth, she never seemed to realize what these sick, giddy turns might mean,' concluded Fox.

'Of course the girl was going to have a child,' said Nigel complacently.

'It doesn't follow as the night the day,' murmured Alleyn. 'She may have been liverish or run-down. Nevertheless, it's odd that the little thought never entered Miss Lee's head. You go back to your corner, Bathgate, here's Mr Watt Hatchett.'

Watt Hatchett came in with his hands thrust into his trousers pockets. Alleyn watched him curiously, thinking what a perfect type he was of the smart Sydney tough about to get on in the world. He was short, with the general appearance of a bad man in a South American movie. His hair resembled a patent-leather cap, his skin was swarthy, he walked with a sort of hard-boiled slouch, and his clothes fitted him rather too sleekly. A cigarette seemed to be perpetually gummed to his under-lip which projected. He had beautiful hands.

'Want me, Inspector?' he inquired. He never opened his lips more than was absolutely necessary, and he scarcely seemed to move his tongue, so that every vowel was strangled at birth, and for preference he spoke entirely through his nose. There was, however, something engaging about him; an aliveness, a raw virility.

'Sit down, Mr Hatchett,' said Alleyn. 'I shan't keep you long.'

Hatchett slumped into an armchair. He moved with the slovenly grace of an underbred bouncer, and this in its way was also attractive.

'Good oh,' he said.

'I'm sure you realize yourself the importance of the information we have from you as regards the drape.'

'Too right. I reckon it shows that whoever did the dirty stuff with the knife did it after everyone except Garcia and Mr Highbrow Malmsley had cleared off to London.'

'Exactly. You will therefore not think it extraordinary if I ask you to repeat the gist of this information.'

Hatchett wanted nothing better. He went over the whole story again. He went down to the studio on Friday afternoon – he remembered now that it was half-past two by the hall clock when he left the house – and noticed the drape lying crumpled on the throne, as Sonia had left it when she got up at noon. It was still undisturbed when he went away to catch the bus.

'And yesterday evening it was stretched out tight. There you are.'

Alleyn said nothing about Troy's discovery of this condition on Saturday afternoon. He asked Hatchett to account for his own movements during the weekend. Hatchett described his Friday evening's entertainment with Phillida Lee and Ormerin.

'We had tea and then we went to a theatre they called the Vortex, and it was just about the lousiest show I've *ever* had to sit through. Gosh! it gave me a pain in the neck, dinkum it did. Three blokes in a sewer nagging each other for two bloody hours, and they called it a play. If that's a play give me the talkies in Aussie. They'll do me. We met the chap that runs the place. One of these die-away queens that likes to kid himself he amounts to something. You won't get me inside a theatre again.'

'Have you never seen a flesh-and-blood show before?'

'Naow, and I never will again. The talkies'll do me.'

'But I assure you the Vortex is no more like the genuine theatre than, shall we say Mr Malmsley's drawings are like Miss Troy's portraits.'

'Is that a fact?'

'Certainly. But we're straying a little from the matter in hand. You spent Friday night at the Vortex and returned with Miss Lee to the Fulham Road?'

'Yeah, that's right. I took her home and then I went to my own place close by.'

'Anyone see you come in?'

They plodded on. Hatchett could, if necessary, produce

629

the sort of alibi that might hold together or might not. Alleyn gleaned enough material to enable him to verify the youth's account of himself.

'To return to Garcia,' he said at last. 'I want you to tell me if you have ever heard Garcia say anything about this warehouse he intends to use as a studio in London.'

'I never had much to do with that bloke. I reckon he's queer. If you talk to him, half the time he never seems to listen. I did say once I'd like to have a look when he started in on the marble. I reckon that statue'll be a corker. He's clever all right. D'you know what he said? He said he'd take care nobody knew where it was because he didn't want any of this crowd pushing in when he was working. He did let out that it belonged to a bloke that's gone abroad somewhere. I heard him tell the girl Sonia that much.'

'I see. That's no go, then. Now, on your bus trip to and from London, did you sit anywhere near Sonia Gluck?'

'Naow. After the way she mucked up Miss Troy's picture, I didn't want to have anything to do with her. It's just too bad she's got hers for keeps, but all the same I reckon she was a fair nark, that girl. Always slinging off about Aussie, she was. She'd been out there once with a Vordervill show, and I tipped it was a bum show because she was always shooting off her mouth about the way the Aussies don't know a good thing when they see it. These pommies! She gave me the jitters. Just because I couldn't talk big about my home and how swell my people were, and how we cut a lot of ice in Sydney, she treated me like dirt. I said to her one time, I said: "I reckon if Miss Troy thought I was good enough to come here, even if my old pop did keep a bottle store on Circular Quay, I reckon if she thought I was OK I'm good enough for you." I went very, very crook at her after she did that to the picture. Miss Troy's been all right to me. She's been swell. Did you know she paid my way in the ship?'

'Did she?'

'Too right she did. She saw me painting in Suva. I

worked my way to Suva, you know, from Aussie, and I got a job there. It was a swell job, too, while it lasted. Travelling for Jackson's Confectionery. I bought this suit and some paints with my first cheque, and then I had a row with the boss and walked out on him. I used to paint all the time then. She saw me working and she reckoned I had talent, so she brought me home to England. The girl Sonia seemed to think I was living on charity.'

'That was a very unpleasant interpretation to put upon a gracious action.'

'Eh? Yeah! Yeah, that's what I told her.'

'Since you joined Miss Troy's classes, have you become especially friendly with any one of the other students?'

'Well, the little girl Lee's all right. She treats you as if you were human.'

'What about the men?'

'Malmsley makes me tired. He's nothing but a big sissie. The French bloke doesn't seem to know he's born, and Garcia's queer. They don't like me,' said Hatchett, with extraordinary aggression, 'and I don't like them.'

'What about Mr Pilgrim?'

'Aw, he's different. He's all right. I get on with him good oh, even if his old pot is one of these lords. Him and me's cobbers.'

'Was he on good terms with the model?'

Hatchett looked sulky and uncomfortable.

'I don't know anything about that,' he muttered.

'You have never heard either of them mention the other?'

'Naow.'

'Nor noticed them speaking to each other?'

'Naow.'

'So you can tell us nothing about the model except that you disliked her intensely?'

Hatchett's grey eyes narrowed in an extremely insolent smile.

'That doesn't exactly make me out a murderer though, does it?'

631

'Not precisely.'

'I'd be one big boob to go talking about how I couldn't stick her if I'd anything to do with it, wouldn't I?'

'Oh, I don't know. You might be sharp enough to suppose that you would convey just that impression.'

The olive face turned a little paler.

'Here! You got no call to talk that way to me. What d'you want to pick on me for? I've been straight enough with you. I've given you a square deal right enough, haven't I?'

'I sincerely hope so.'

'I reckon this country's crook. You've all got a down on the new chum. It's a blooming nark. Just because I said the girl Sonia made me tired you got to get leery and make me out a liar. I reckon the wonderful London police don't know they're alive yet. You've as good as called me a murderer.'

'My dear Mr Hatchett, may I suggest that if you go through life looking for insults, you may be comfortably assured of finding them. At no time during our conversation have I called you a murderer.'

'I gave you a square deal,' repeated Hatchett.

'I'm not absolutely assured of that. I think that a moment ago you deliberately withheld something. I mean, when I asked you if you could tell me anything about the model's relationship with Mr Pilgrim.'

Hatchett was silent. He moved his head slightly from side to side, and ostentatiously inhaled cigarette smoke.

'Very well,' said Alleyn. 'That will do, I think.'

But Hatchett did not get up.

'I don't know where you get that idea,' he said.

'Don't you? I need keep you no longer, Mr Hatchett. We shall probably check your alibi, and I shall ask you to sign a written account of our conversion. That is all at the moment.'

Hatchett rose, hunched his shoulders, and lit a fresh cigarette from the butt of the old one. He was still rather pale.

632

'I got nothing in for Pilgrim,' he said. 'I got no call to talk to dicks about my cobbers.'

'You prefer to surround them with a dubious atmosphere of uncertainty, and leave us to draw our own conclusions? You are doing Mr Pilgrim no service by these rather transparent evasions.'

'Aw, talk English, can't you!'

'Certainly. Good evening.'

'Pilgrim's a straight sort of a bloke. Him do anything like that! It's laughable.'

'Look here,' said Alleyn wearily. 'Are you going to tell me what you know, or are you going away, or am I going to remove you? Upon my word, if we have many more dark allusions to Mr Pilgrim's purity, I shall feel like clapping both of you in jug.'

'By cripey!' cried Hatchett violently. 'Aren't I telling you it was nothing at all! And to show you it was nothing at all, I'll bloody well tell you what it was. Now then.'

'Good! said Alleyn. 'Speak up!'

'It's only that the girl Sonia was going to have a kid, and Pilgrim's the father. So now what?'

Chapter 10

Weekend of an Engaged Couple

In the silence that followed Watt Hatchett's announcement Fox was heard to cough discreetly. Alleyn glanced
quickly at him, and then contemplated Hatchett. Hatchett
glared defiantly round the room rather as if he expected
an instant arrest.

'How do you know this, Mr Hatchett?' asked Alleyn.

'I've seen it in writing.'

'Where?'

'It's like this. Me and Basil Pilgrim's got the same kind
of paint-smocks, see? When I first come I saw his new
one and I thought it was a goody. It's a sort of dark khaki
stuff, made like a coat, with corking great pockets. He
told me where he got it, and I sent for one. When I got
it, I hung it up with the others in the junk-room. That
was last Tuesdee. On Wensdee morning I put it on, and
I noticed at the time that his smock wasn't there. He'd
taken it up to the house for something, I suppose. Well,
when we cleaned up at midday, I put me hand in one of
me pockets and I felt a bit of paper. I took it out and had
a look at it. Thought it might be the docket from the shop
or something, see? When I got it opened up, I see it was
a bit of a note scrawled on the back of a bill. It said, as
near as I remember: "Congrats on the engagement, but
what if I tell her she's going to have a step-child? I'll be
in the studio tonight at ten. Advise you to come." Something like that it was. I may not have got it just the same
as what it was, but that's near enough. It was signed "S".'

'What did you do with it?'

'Aw, cripey, I didn't know what to do. I didn't feel so
good about reading it. Gee, it was a fair cow, me reading
it by mistake like that. I just went into the junk-room and
I saw he'd put his smock back by then, so I shoved the

blooming paper into his pocket. That evening I could see he was feeling pretty crook himself, so I guessed he'd read it.'

'I see.'

'Look, Mr Alleyn, I'm sorry I went nasty just now. I'm like that. I go horribly crook, and the next minute I could knock me own block off for what I said. But look, you don't want to think too much about this. Honest! That girl Sonia was easy. Look, she went round asking for it, dinkum she did. Soon as I saw that note, I tipped she'd got hold of old Basil some time, and he'd just kind of thought, "Aw, what the hell" and there you were. Look, he's a decent old sport, dinkum he is. And now he's got a real corking girl like Valmai Seacliff, it'd be a nark if he got in wrong. His old pot's a wowser, too. That makes things worse. Look, Mr Alleyn, I'd hate him to think I – '

'All right, all right,' said Alleyn good-humouredly. 'We'll keep your name out of it if we can.'

'Good oh, Mr Alleyn. And, look, you won't – '

'I won't clap the handcuffs on Mr Pilgrim just yet.'

'Yeah, but – '

'You buzz off. And if you'll take a tip from an effete policeman, just think sometimes, before you label the people you meet: "No good" or "standoffish," or what is that splendid phrase? "fair cows." Have you ever heard of an inferiority complex?'

'Naow.'

'Thank the Lord for that. All the same I fancy you suffer from one. Go slow. Think a bit more. Wait for people to like you and they will. And forgive me if you can, for prosing away like a Victorian uncle. Now, off you go.'

'Good oh, Mr Alleyn.'

Hatchett walked to the door. He opened it and then swung round.

'Thanks a lot,' he said. 'Ta-ta for now.'

The door banged, and he was gone. Alleyn leant back in his chair and laughed very heartily.

'Cheeky young fellow, that,' said Fox. 'Australian. I've come across some of them. Always think you're looking down on them. Funny!'

'He's an appalling specimen,' said Nigel from the corner. 'Bumptious young larrikin. Even his beastly argot is bogus. Half-American, half-Cockney.'

'And pure Australian. The dialect is rapidly becoming Americanized.'

'A frightful youth. No wonder they sat on him. He ought to be told how revolting he is whenever he opens his mouth. Antipodean monster.'

'I don't agree with you,' said Alleyn. 'He's an awkward pup, but he might respond to reason in time. What do you make of this business of the note, Fox?'

'Hard to say,' said Fox. 'Looks like the beginnings of blackmail.'

'Very like, very like.'

'From all accounts it wouldn't be very surprising if we found Garcia had set her on to it, would it now?'

'Speculative, but attractive.'

'And then murdered her when he'd collared the money,' said Nigel.

'You're a fanciful fellow, Bathgate,' said Alleyn mildly.

'Well, isn't it possible?'

'Quite possible on what we've got.'

'Shall I get Mr Pilgrim, sir?'

'I think so, Fox. We'll see if he conforms to the Garcia theme or not.'

'I'll bet he does,' said Nigel. 'Is it the Basil Pilgrim who's the eldest son of the Methodist Peer?'

'That's the one. Do you know him?'

'No, but I know of him. I did a story for my paper on his old man. The son's rather a pleasant specimen. I fancy. Cricketer. He was a Blue and looked good enough for an M.C.C. star before he took to this painting.'

'And became a little odd?' finished Alleyn with a twinkle.

'I didn't say that, but it was rather a waste. Anyhow I

fail to visualize him as a particularly revolting type of murderer. He'll conform to the Garcia theme, you may depend upon it.'

'That's because you want things to work out that way.'

'Don't you think Garcia's your man?'

'On what we've got I do, certainly, but it's much too early to become wedded to a theory. Back to your corner.'

Fox returned with Basil Pilgrim. As Nigel had remarked, Pilgrim was a very pleasant specimen. He was tall, with a small head, square shoulders and a narrow waist. His face was rather fine-drawn. He had a curious trick while he talked of turning his head first to one member of his audience and then to another. This habit suggested a nervous restlessness. He had a wide mouth, magnificent teeth and very good manners. Alleyn got him to sit down, gave him a cigarette and began at once to establish his movements after he drove away with Valmai Seacliff from Tatler's End House on Friday afternoon. Pilgrim said that they motored to some friends of Valmai Seacliff's who lived at Boxover, twelve miles away. They dined with these friends – a Captain and Mrs Pascoe – spent the evening playing bridge and stayed the night there. The next day they motored to Ankerton Manor, the Oxfordshire seat of Lord Pilgrim, where Basil introduced his fiancée to his father. They spent Saturday night at Ankerton and returned to Tatler's End House on Sunday afternoon.

'At what time did you break up your bridge party on Friday night?' asked Alleyn.

'Fairly early, I think, sir. About elevenish. Valmai had got a snorter of a headache and could hardly see the cards. I gave her some aspirin. She took three tablets, and turned in.'

'Did the aspirin do its job?'

'Oh, rather! She said she slept like the dead.' He looked from Alleyn to Fox and back again. 'She didn't wake till they brought in tea. Her head had quite cleared up.'

'Is she subject to these headaches?'

Pilgrim looked surprised.

'Yes, she is rather. At least, she's had one or two lately. I'm a bit worried about them. I want her to see an oculist, but she doesn't like the idea of wearing glasses.'

'It may not be the eyes.'

'Oh, I think it is. Painters often strain their eyes, you know.'

'Did you sleep comfortably?'

'Me?' Pilgrim turned to Alleyn with an air of bewilderment. 'Oh, I always sleep like a log.'

'How far is Ankerton Manor from here, Mr Pilgrim?'

'Eighty-five miles by my speedometer. I took a note of it.'

'So you had a run of seventy-three miles from Boxover on Saturday?'

'That's the idea, sir.'

'Right. Now about this unfortunate girl. Can you let any light in on the subject?'

'Afraid I can't. It's a damn bad show. I feel rotten about it.'

'Why?'

'Well, wouldn't anybody? It's a foul thing to happen, isn't it?'

'Oh, yes – perfectly abominable. I meant had you any personal reason for feeling rotten about it?'

'Not more than any of the others,' said Pilgrim, after a pause.

'Is that quite true, Mr Pilgrim?'

'What do you mean?' Again he looked from Alleyn to Fox. He had gone very white.

'I mean this. Had Sonia Gluck no closer link with you than with the rest of the class?'

If Pilgrim had been restless before, he was now very still. He stared straight in front of him, his lips parted, and his brows slightly raised.

'I see I shall have to make a clean breast of it,' he said at last.

'I think you would be wise to do so.'

638

'It's got nothing to do with this business,' he said. 'Unless Garcia knew and was furious about it. My God, I don't know what put you on to this, but I'm not sure it won't be a relief to talk about it. Ever since this morning when she was killed, I've been thinking of it. I'd have told you at once if I'd thought it had any bearing on the case, but I – I didn't want Valmai to know. It happened three months ago. Before I met Valmai. I was at a studio party in Bloomsbury and she – Sonia – was there. Everyone got pretty tight. She asked me to drive her back to her room and then she asked me if I wouldn't come in for a minute. Well – I did. It was the only time. I got a damned unpleasant surprise when I found she was the model here. I didn't say anything to her and she didn't say anything to me. That's all.'

'What about the child?' asked Alleyn.

'God! Then she *did* tell somebody?'

'She told you, at all events.'

'I don't believe it's true. I don't believe the child was mine. Everybody knows what sort of girl she was. Poor little devil! I don't want to blackguard her after this has happened, but I can see what you're driving at now, and it's a serious business for me. If I'd thought the child was my affair, I'd have looked after Sonia, but everybody knows she's been Garcia's mistress for months. She was poisonously jealous of Valmai, and after our engagement was announced she threatened this as a hit at Valmai.'

'How was the matter first broached?'

'She left a note in the pocket of my painting-coat. I don't know how long it had been there. I burnt it. She said she wanted me to meet her somewhere.'

'Did you do this?'

'Yes. I met her in the studio one evening. It was pretty ghastly.'

'What happened?'

'She said she was going to have a baby. She said I was the father. I said I didn't believe it. I knew she was lying, and I told her I knew. I said I'd tell Valmai the whole

639

story myself and I said I'd go to Garcia and tell him. She seemed frightened. That's all that happened.'

'Are you sure of that?'

'Yes. What d'you mean? Of course I'm sure.'

'She didn't try blackmail? She didn't say she would go to Miss Seacliff with this story or, if that failed, she didn't threaten to appeal to your father?'

'She said all sorts of things. She was hysterical. I don't remember everything she said. She didn't know what she was talking about.'

'Surely you would remember if she threatened to go to your father?'

'I don't think she did say she'd do that. Anyway, if she had it wouldn't have made any difference. He couldn't force me to marry her. I know that sounds pretty low, but you see, I *knew* the whole thing was a bluff. It was all so foul and squalid. I was terrified someone would hear her or something. I just walked away.'

'Did she carry out any of her threats?'

'No.'

'How do you know?'

'Well, I'd have heard pretty soon if she'd said anything to my father.'

'Then she *did* threaten to tell your father?'

'God damn you, I tell you I don't remember what she threatened.'

'Did you give her any money?'

Pilgrim moved his head restlessly.

'I advise you to answer me, Mr Pilgrim.'

'I needn't answer anything. I can get a lawyer.'

'Certainly. Do you wish to do that?'

Pilgrim opened his mouth and shut it again. He frowned to himself as if he thought very deeply, and at last he seemed to come to a decision. He looked from Alleyn to Fox and suddenly he smiled.

'Look here,' he said, 'I didn't kill that girl. I couldn't have killed her. The Parkers and Valmai will tell you I spent Friday night with them. My father and everyone else at Ankerton knows I was there on Saturday. I hadn't a chance to rig the knife. I suppose there's no reason why I should shy off talking about this business with Sonia except that – well, when there's a crime like this in the air one's apt to get nervous.'

'Undoubtedly.'

'You know all about by father, I expect. He's been given a good deal of publicity. Some bounder of a journalist wrote a lot of miserable gup in one of the papers the other day. The Methodist Peer and all that. Everyone knows he's a bit fanatic on the subject of morals, and if he ever got to hear of this business there'd be a row of simply devastating magnitude. That's why I didn't want it to leak out. He'd do some tremendous heavy-father stuff at me, and have a stroke on top of it as likely as not. That's why I didn't want to say any more about it than I could possibly help. I see now that I've been a fool not to tell you the whole thing.'

'Good,' said Alleyn.

'As a matter of fact I did give Sonia a cheque for a hundred, and she promised she'd make no more scenes. In the end she practically admitted the child was not mine, but,' he smiled ruefully, 'as she pointed out, she had a perfectly good story to tell my father or Valmai if she felt inclined to do so.'

'Have you made a clean breast of this to Miss Seacliff?'

'No, I – I – couldn't do that. It seems so foul to go to her with a squalid little story when we were just engaged. You see, I happen to feel rather strongly about – well, about some things. I rather disliked myself for what had happened. Valmai's so marvellous.' His face lit up with a sudden intensity of emotion. He seemed translated. 'She's so far beyond all that kind of thing. She's terribly, terribly attractive – you only had to see how the other men here fell for her – but she remains quite aloof from her own loveliness. Just accepts it as something she can't help and then ignores it. It's amazing that she should

641

care—' He stopped short. 'I don't know that we need discuss all this.'

'I don't think we need. I shall ask you later on to sign a statement of your own movements from Friday to Sunday.'

'Will the Sonia business have to come out, sir?'

'I can promise nothing about that. If it is irrelevant it will not be used. I think it advisable that you should tell Miss Seacliff, but that, of course, is entirely a matter for your own judgment.'

'You don't understand.'

'Possibly not. There's one other question. Did you return to the studio on Friday before you left for Boxover?'

'No. I packed my suitcase after lunch. Young Hatchett came in and talked to me while I was at it. Then I called Valmai and we set off in the car.'

'I see. Thank you. I won't keep you any longer, Mr Pilgrim.'

'Very well, sir. Thank you.'

Fox showed Pilgrim out and returned to the fire. He looked dubious. Nigel reappeared and sat on the wide fender.

'Well, Fox,' said Alleyn, raising an eyebrow, 'what did you think of that?'

'His ideas on the subject of his young lady seem a bit high-flown from what we've seen of her,' said Fox.

'What's she like?' asked Nigel.

'She's extremely beautiful,' Alleyn said. 'Beautiful enough to launch a thousand crimes, perhaps. But I should not have thought the Sonia episode would have caused her to so much as bat an eyelid. She has completely wiped the floor with all the other females, and that, I imagine, is all that matters to Miss Seacliff.'

'Of course, the poor fool's besotted on her. You can see that with half an eye,' said Nigel. He glanced at his shorthand notes. 'What about his alibi?'

'If this place Boxover is only twelve miles away,'

642

grunted Fox, 'his alibi isn't of much account. Is it, Mr Alleyn? They went to bed early on Friday night. He could slip out, run over here, rig the knife and get back to Boxover almost within the hour.'

'You must remember that Garcia slept in the studio.'

'Yes, that's so. But he may not have been there on Friday night. He may have packed up by then and gone off on his tour.'

'Pilgrim must have known that, Fox, if he planned to come to the studio.'

'Yes. That's so. Mind, I still think Garcia's our man. This Mr Pilgrim doesn't strike me as the chap for a job of this sort.'

'He's a bit too obviously the clean young Englishman, though, isn't he?' said Nigel.

'Hullo,' remarked Alleyn, 'didn't Pilgrim come up to your high expectations, Bathgate?'

'Well, you were remarkably cold and snorty with him yourself.'

'Because throughout our conversation he so repeatedly shifted ground. That sort of behaviour is always exceedingly tedious. It was only because I was rough with him that we got the blackmail story at all.'

'He seemed quite an honest-to-God sort of fellow, really,' pronounced Nigel. 'I think it was that stuff about being ashamed of his affair with the model that put me off him. It sounded spurious. Anyway, it's the sort of thing one doesn't talk about to people one has just met.'

'Under rather unusual conditions,' Alleyn pointed out.

'Certainly. All the same, he talks too much.'

'The remark about bounding journalists and miserable gup was perhaps gratuitous.'

'I didn't mean that,' said Nigel in a hurry.

'I'm inclined to agree with you. Let us see Miss Valmai Seacliff, Brer Fox.'

'I wish you wouldn't make me coil up in that chair,' complained Nigel when Fox had gone. 'It's plaguily uncomfortable and right in a draught. Can't I just be here, openly? I'd like to have a look at this lovely.'

'Very well. I suppose you'll do no harm. The concealment was your own suggestion, if you remember. You may sit at the desk and make an attempt to look like the Yard.'

'You don't look much like it yourself in your smart gent's dinner jacket. Tell me, Alleyn, have you fallen in love with Miss Troy?'

'Don't be a fool, Bathgate,' said Alleyn, with such unusual warmth that Nigel's eyebrows went up.

'I'm sorry,' he said. 'Merely a pleasantry. No offence and so on.'

'I'm sorry, too. You must forgive me. I'm bothered about this case.'

'There, there,' said Nigel. 'Coom, coom, coom, it's early days yet.'

'True enough. But suppose Garcia walks in with a happy smile in answer to our broadcast? That bit of clay in the drape. Acid marks and no acid to make 'em. This legendary warehouse. Clay models of comedy and tragedy melted into the night. Damn, I've got the mumbles.'

The door was thrown open, and in came Valmai Seacliff, followed by Fox. Miss Seacliff managed to convey by her entrance that she never moved anywhere without a masculine satellite. That Inspector Fox in his double-breasted blue serge was not precisely in the right manner did nothing to unsettle her poise. She was dressed in a silk trousered garment. Her hair was swept off her forehead into a knot on the nape of her neck. Moving her hips voluptuously, she walked rather like a mannequin. When she reached the chair Alleyn had pushed forward, she turned, paused, and then sank into it with glorious certainly of a well trained show-girl. She stared languidly at Nigel, whose hand had gone automatically to his tie.

'Well, Mr Alleyn?' said Miss Seacliff.

The three men sat down. Alleyn turned a page of his

tiny notebook, appeared to deliberate, and embarked upon the familiar opening.

'Miss Seacliff, my chief concern at the moment is to get a clear account of everybody's movements during the weekend. Mr Pilgrim has told us of your motor trip with him to Boxover, and then to Ankerton Manor. I should like you to corroborate his statement if you will. Did you return to the studio before you left?'

'No, I was packing. The housemaid helped me and carried my things down to the car.'

'You arrived at Captain and Mrs Pascoe's house in Boxover on Friday afternoon?'

'Yes.'

'And spent the afternoon together?'

'Yes. The Pascoes talked about tennis but I didn't feel inclined to play. I rather loathe tennis. So we talked.'

Alleyn noticed again her curious little stutter, and the trick she had of letting her voice die and then catching it up on an intake of breath.

'How did you spend the evening?'

'We played bridge for a bit. I had a frightful headache and went to bed early. I felt quite sick with it.'

'That was bad luck. Do you often have these head-aches?'

'Never until lately. They started about a month ago. It's rather tiresome.'

'You should consult an oculist.'

'My eyes are perfectly all right. As a matter of fact a rather distinguished oculist once told me that intensely blue eyes like mine usually give no trouble. He said my eyes were the most vivid blue he had ever seen.'

'Indeed!' said Alleyn, without looking at them. 'How do you explain the headaches, then?'

'I'm perfectly certain the one on Friday night was due to champagne and port. The Pascoes had champagne at dinner to celebrate my engagement, and there was brandy afterwards. I loathe brandy, so Basil made me have a glass of port. I told him it would upset me but he went on and on. The coffee was filthy, too. Bitter and beastly. Sybil Pascoe is one of those plain women whom one expects to be good housekeepers, but I must say she doesn't appear to take the smallest trouble over the coffee. Basil says his was abominable, too.'

'When did you give up the bridge?'

'I've no idea, I'm afraid. I simply couldn't go on. Basil got me three aspirin and I went to bed. The others came up soon afterwards, I fancy. I heard Basil go into his room.'

'It was next to yours?'

'Yes.'

'Did you sleep?'

'Like the dead. I didn't wake till they brought my tea at nine o'clock.'

'And the headache had cleared up?'

'Yes, quite. I still felt a little unpleasant. It was a sort of carry-over from that damned port, I imagine.'

'Were your host and hostess anywhere near you upstairs?'

'Sybil and Ken? Not very. There was Basil and then me, and then I think two spare rooms and a bathroom. Then their room. Why?'

'It sounds rather absurd, I know,' said Alleyn, 'but you see we've got to find out as closely as possible what everyone did that night.'

'Basil didn't come into my room, if that's what you're hinting at,' said Miss Seacliff without heat. 'It wasn't that sort of party. And anyway, I'm not given to that kind of thing even when I haven't got a headache. I don't believe in it. Sooner or later you lose your glamour. Look at Sonia.'

'Quite so. Then as far as you know the household slept without stirring from Friday night to Saturday morning?'

'Yes,' said Miss Seacliff, looking at him as if he was slightly demented.

'And on Saturday you went on to Ankerton Manor. When did you start?'

646

'We had a glass of sherry at about ten, and then pushed off. Basil was in a great state lest we should be late for lunch, and wanted to get away earlier, but I saw no reason why we should go rushing about the countryside before it was necessary. We had plenty of time.'

'Why was he so anxious?'

'He kept saying that he was sure Sybil Pascoe wanted to get away. She was going up to London for a week and leaving Ken to look after himself. I pointed out that was no reason why we should bolt off. Then Basil said we mustn't be late at Ankerton. The truth was, the poor lamb wanted me to make a good impression on his extraordinary old father. I told him he needn't worry. Old men always go quite crazy about me. But Basil was absurdly nervous about the meeting and kept fidgeting me to start. We got there early as it was, and by luncheon-time the old person was talking about the family jewels. He's given me some emeralds that I'm going to have reset. They're rather spectacular.'

'You left Ankerton yesterday after luncheon, I suppose?'

'Yes. Basil was rather keen to stay on till Monday, but I'd had enough. The old person made me hack round the ancestral acres on a beastly little animal that nearly pulled my arms out. I saw you looking at my hand.'

With a slow and beautiful movement she extended her left arm, opened her hand, and held it close to Alleyn's face. It was warmly scented and the palm was rouged. At the base of the little finger were two or three scarlet marks.

'My hands are terribly soft, of course,' said Miss Seacliff, advancing it a little closer to his face.

'Yes,' said Alleyn. 'You are evidently not an experienced horsewoman.'

'What makes you say that?'

'Well, you know, these marks have not been made by a rein. I should say, Miss Seacliff, that your pony's mane had been called into service.'

She pulled her hand away and turned rather pink.

'I don't pretend to be a horsey woman, thank God! I simply loathe the brutes. I must say I got very bored with the old person. And besides, I didn't want to miss the pose this morning. I'd got a good deal to do to my thing of Sonia. I suppose I'll never get it done now.'

Fox coughed and Nigel glanced up at Valmai Seacliff in astonishment.

'I suppose not,' agreed Alleyn. 'Now, Miss Seacliff, we come to this morning's tragedy. Will you describe to us exactly what happened, please?'

'Have you got a cigarette?'

Alleyn sprang up and offered her his case.

'What are they? Oh, I see. Thank you.'

She took one and he lit it for her. She looked into his eyes deliberately but calmly, as if she followed a familiar routine. Alleyn returned her glance gravely and sat down again.

'This morning?' she said.'You mean when Sonia was killed? It was rather ghastly. I felt wretched after it was all over. Ill. I suppose it was shock. I do think it was rather cruel that I should be the one to – to do it – to set the pose. They all knew I always pushed her shoulders down.' She caught her breath, and for the first time showed some signs of genuine distress. 'I believe Garcia deliberately planned it like that. He loathed the sight of Sonia, and at the same time he wanted to revenge himself on me because I didn't fall for him. It was just like Garcia to do that. He's a spiteful little beast. It was cruel. I – I can't get rid of the remembrance. I'll never be able to get rid of it.'

'I'm sorry that I am obliged to ask you to go over it again, but I'm sure you will understand – '

'Oh, yes. And the psycho people say one shouldn't repress things of this sort. I don't want to get nervy and lose my poise. After all, I didn't do it really. I keep telling myself that.'

'When did you go down to the studio?'

'Just before class time. Basil and I walked down together. Katti Bostock was there and – let me see – yes, the appalling Hatchett youth, Lee and Ormerin and Malmsley came down afterwards, I think.'

'Together?'

'I don't remember. They were not there when I got down.'

'I see. Will you go on, Miss Seacliff?'

'Well, we all put up our easels and set our palettes and so on. Sonia came in last and Katti said we'd begin. Sonia went into the junk-room and undressed. She came out in her white kimono and hung about trying to get the men to talk to her. Katti told her to go on to the throne. She got down into the chalk-marks. She always fitted her right thigh into its trace first, with the drape behind her. I don't know if you understand?'

'Yes, I think I do.'

And indeed Alleyn suddenly had a very vivid impression of what must have taken place. He saw the model, wrapped in the thin white garment, her warm and vital beauty shining through it. He saw her speak to the men, look at them perhaps with a pathetic attempt to draw their attention to herself. Then the white wrapper would slide to the floor and the nude figure sink gingerly into a half-recumbent posture on the throne.

'She grumbled as usual about the pose and said she was sick of it. I remember now that she asked if we knew where Garcia had gone on his hiking trip. I suppose he wouldn't tell her. Then she lay down on her side. The drape was still stretched taut behind her. There is generally a sort of key position among the different canvases. When we set the pose we always look at that particular canvas to get it right. My painting was in this position so it was always left to me to push her down into the right position. She could have done it all herself but she always made such a scene. I'd got into the way of taking her shoulders and pressing them over. She wouldn't do it otherwise. So I leant over and gripped them. They felt

649

smooth and alive. She began to make a fuss. She said "Don't", and I said "Don't be such a fool". Katti said: "Oh, for Heaven's sake, Sonia!" Something like that. Sonia said: "Your hands are cold, you're hurting me". Then she let herself go and I pushed down.' Valmai Seacliff raised her hands and pressed them against her face.

'She didn't struggle but I felt her body leap under my hands and then shudder. I can't tell you exactly what it was like. Everything happened at the same moment. I saw her face. She opened her eyes very wide, and wrinkled her forehead as if she was astonished. I think she said "Don't" again but I'm not sure. I thought – you know how one's thoughts can travel – I thought how silly she looked, and at the same moment I suddenly wondered if she was going to have a baby and the pose really hurt her. I don't know why I thought that. I knew s-something had happened. I didn't know what it was. I just leant over her and looked into her face. I think I said: "Sonia's ill". I think Katti or someone said "Rot". I still touched her – leant on her. She quivered as if I tickled her and then she was still. Phillida Lee said: "She's fainted". Then the others came up. Katti put her arms behind Sonia to raise her. She said: "I can't move her – she seems stuck". Then she pulled. There was a queer little n-noise and Sonia came up suddenly. Ormerin cried out loudly: *"Mon Dieu, c'est le poignard"*. At least that's what he told us he said. And the drape stuck to my fingers. It came out of the hole in her back – the blood, I mean. Her back was wet. We moved her a little, and Katti tried to stop the blood with a piece of rag. Troy came. She sent Basil out to ring up the doctor. She looked at Sonia and said she wasn't dead. Troy put her arms round Sonia. I don't know how long it was before Sonia gave a sort of cough. She opened her eyes very wide. Troy looked up and said: "She's gone". Phillida Lee started to cry. Nobody said very much. Basil came back and Troy said n-nobody was to leave the studio. She covered Sonia with a drape. We began to talk about the knife. Lee and Hatchett said G-Garcia had

650

done it. We all thought Garcia had done it. Then the doctor came and when he had seen Sonia he sent for the p-police.'

Her voice died away. She had begun her recital calmly enough, but it was strange to see how the memory of the morning grew more vivid and more disquieting as she revived it. The slight hesitation in her speech became more noticeable. When she had finished her hands were trembling.

'I d-didn't know I was so upset,' she said. 'A doctor once told me my nerves were as sensitive as the strings of a violin.'

'It was a horrible experience for all of you,' said Alleyn. 'Tell me, Miss Seacliff, when did you yourself suspect that Garcia had laid this trap for the model?'

'I thought of Garcia at once. I remembered what Lee had told me about the conversation between Garcia and Sonia. I don't see who else could have done it, and somehow – '

'Yes?'

'Somehow it – it's the sort of thing he might do. There's something very cold-blooded about Garcia. He's quite mad about me, but I simply can't bear him to touch me. Lee says he's got masses of SA and he evidently had for Sonia – but I can't see it. I think he's rather repulsive. Women do fall for him, I'm told.'

'And the motive?'

'I imagine he was sick of her. She literally hurled herself at him. Always watching him. Men hate women to do that – ' She looked directly into Alleyn's eyes. 'Don't they, Mr Alleyn?'

'I'm afraid I don't know.'

'And of course he was livid when she defaced my portrait. She must have hated me to do that. In a way it was rather interesting, a directly sexual jealousy manifesting itself on the symbol of the hated person.'

Alleyn repressed a movement of impatience and said: 'No doubt.'

'My own idea is that she was going to have a baby and had threatened to sue him for maintenance. I suppose in a way I'm responsible.'

She looked grave enough as she made this statement, but Alleyn thought there was more than a hint of complacency in her voice.

'Surely not,' he said.

'Oh, yes. In a way. If he hàdn't been besotted on me, I dare say he might not have done it.'

'I thought,' said Alleyn, 'that you were worrying about your actual hand in the business.'

'What do you mean?'

'I mean,' Alleyn's voice was grave, 'the circumstance of it being your hands, Miss Seacliff, that thrust her down upon the knife. Tell me, please, did you notice any resistance at first? I should have thought that there might even have been a slight sound as the point entered.'

'I – don't think – '

'We are considering the actual death throes of a murdered individual,' said Alleyn mildly. 'I should like a clear picture.'

She opened her eyes wide, a look of extreme horror came into her face. She looked wildly round the room, darted a furious glance at Alleyn, and said in a strangled voice; 'Let me out. I've got to go out.'

Fox rose in consternation, but she pushed him away and ran blindly to the door.

'Never mind, Fox,' said Alleyn.

The door banged.

'Here,' said Fox, 'what's she up to?'

'She's bolted,' exclaimed Nigel. 'Look out! She's doing a bolt.'

'Only as far as the cloak-room,' said Alleyn. 'The fatal woman is going to be very sick.'

Chapter 11

Ormerin's Nerves and Sonia's Correspondence

'Well, really, Alleyn,' said Nigel, 'I consider you were hard on that girl. You deliberately upset her lovely stomach.'

'How do you know her stomach's lovely?'

'By inference. What did you do it for?'

'I was sick of that Cleopatra nonsense. She and her catgut nerves!'

'Well, but she *is* terrifically attractive. A really magnificent creature.'

'She's as hard as nails. Still,' added Alleyn with satisfaction, 'I did make her sick. She went through the whole story the first time almost without batting an eyelid. Each time we came back to it she was a little less confident, and the last time when I mentioned the words 'death throes' she turned as green as asparagus.'

'Well, wasn't it natural?'

'Quite natural. Served her jolly well right. I dislike fatal women. They reek of mass production.'

'I don't think you can say she's as hard as nails. After all, she *did* feel ill. I mean she was upset by it all.'

'Only her lovely stomach. She's not in the least sorry for that unfortunate little animal who died under her hands. All that psychological clap-trap! She's probably nosed into a *Freud Without Tears* and picked out a few choice phrases.'

'I should say she was extremely intelligent.'

'And you'd be right. She's sharp enough. What she said about Garcia rang true, I thought. What d'you say, Brer Fox?'

'You mean when she talked about Garcia's cold-bloodedness, don't you, sir?'

'I do.'

'Yes. They all seem to agree about him. I think myself that it doesn't do to ignore other people's impressions. If you find a lot of separate individuals all saying so-and-so is a cold, unscrupulous sort of person, why then,' said Fox, 'it usually turns out that he is.'

'True for you.'

'They might all be in collusion,' said Nigel.

'Why?' asked Alleyn.

'I don't know.'

'More do I.'

'Well,' said Fox, 'if this Garcia chap doesn't turn up in answer to our broadcast and ads and so on, it'll look like a true bill.'

'He's probably the type that loathes radio and never opens a paper,' said Nigel.

'Highly probable,' agreed Alleyn.

'You'll have to arrest all hikers within a three-days' tramp from Tatler's End House. What a bevy of shorts and rucksacks.'

'He'll have his painting gear if he's innocent,' said Alleyn. 'If he's innocent, he's probably snoring in a pub not twenty miles away. The police stations have all been warned. We'll get him soon enough – if he's innocent.'

'And if he's guilty?'

'Then he's thought out the neatest method of murder that I've come across for a very long time,' said Fox. 'He knew that nobody would meddle with the throne, he knew he'd got two days' start before the event came off, and he very likely thought we'd have a tough job finding anything to pin on to him.'

'Those traces of modelling clay,' murmured Alleyn.

'He didn't think of that,' said Fox. 'If Bailey's right they dropped off his overall while he fixed the knife.'

'What's all this?' asked Nigel. Alleyn told him.

'We've got to remember,' said Alleyn, 'that he'd got the offer of a good job. Marble statues of Comedy and Tragedy are not commissioned for a few pounds. It is possible, Fox, that a guilty Garcia might be so sure of

654

himself that he would turn up in his London warehouse at the end of a week or so's tramp and set to work. When we found him and hauled him up for a statement, he'd be all vague and surprised. When we asked how the traces of clay were to be accounted for, he'd say he didn't know, but that he'd often sat on the throne, or stood on it, or walked across it, and the clay might have dropped off him at any moment. We'll have to find out what sort of state his working smock was in. The bit of clay Bailey found is hardish. Modellers' clay is wettish and kept so. When faced with Phillida Lee's statement he'd say he'd had dozens of rows with Sonia, but hadn't plotted to kill her. If we find she was going to have a child he'd very likely ask what of it?'

'What about the appointment he made with her for Friday night?' asked Fox.

'Did he make an appointment with her for Friday night?'

'Well, sir, you've got it there. Miss Lee said – '

'Yes, I know, Fox. According to Miss Lee, Garcia said: "All right. On Friday night then." And Sonia answered: "Yes, if it's possible." But that may not have meant that they arranged to meet each other on Friday night. It might have meant a thousand and one things, damn it. Garcia may have talked about leaving on Friday night. Sonia may have said she'd do something for him in London on Friday night. It is true that the young Lee person got the impression that they arranged to meet here, but she may have been mistaken.'

'That's so,' said Fox heavily. 'We'll have to get on to deceased's movements from Friday afternoon till Sunday.'

'Did you get anything at all from the maids about Friday night?'

'Not a great deal, sir, and that's a fact. There's three servants living in the house, a Mr and Mrs Hipkin who do butler and cook, and a young girl called Sadie Welsh, who's housemaid. They all went to a cinema in Baxton-bridge on Friday night and returned by the front drive.

There's another girl – Ethel Jones – who comes in as a daily from Bossicote. She leaves at five o'clock in the afternoon. I'll get on to her tomorrow, but it doesn't look promising. The Hipkins seem a very decent couple. Devoted to Miss Troy. They've not got much to say in favour of this crowd. To Mrs Hipkin's way of thinking they're all out of the same box. She said she wasn't surprised at the murder and expected worse.'

'What? Wholesale slaughter did she mean?'

'I don't think she knew. She's a Presbyterian – Auld Licht – maiden name McQumpha. She says painting from the figure is no better than living in open sin, and she gave it as her opinion that Sonia Gluck was fair soused in wickedness. That kind of thing. Hipkin said he always thought Garcia had bats in the belfy, and Sadie said he once tried to assault her and she gave him a smack on the chops. She's rather a lively girl, Sadie is. They say Miss Seacliff's no lady because of the way she speaks to the servants. The only one they seemed to have much time for was the Honourable Basil Pilgrim.'

'Good old snobs. What about Garcia's evening meal on Friday?'

'Well, I did get something there, in a way. Sadie took it on a tray to the studio at seven-thirty. She tapped on the screen inside the door and Mr Garcia called out to her to leave the tray there. Sadie said she didn't know but what he had naked women exhibiting themselves on the platform, so she put it down. When she went to the studio on Saturday morning the tray was still there, untouched. She looked into the studio but didn't do anything in the way of housework. She's not allowed to touch anything on the throne and didn't notice the drape. Garcia was supposed to make his own bed. Sadie says it's her belief he just pulled the counterpane over it and that's what we found, sir, isn't it?'

'Garcia wasn't there on Saturday morning?'

'No. Sadie says he'd gone and all his stuff as far as she could make out. She said the room smelt funny, so she opened the window. She noticed a queer smell there on Friday night, too. I wondered if it was the acid Bailey found the marks of, but she said no. She's smelt the acid before, when they've been using it for etching, and it wasn't the same.'

'Look here, Fox, I think I'd like a word with your Sadie. Be a good fellow and see if she's still up.'

Fox went off and was away some minutes.

'He must have broken into the virgin fastness of Sadie's bedroom,' said Nigel.

Alleyn wandered round the room and looked at the books.

'What's the time?' he said.

'After ten. Ten-twenty-five.'

'Oh Lord! Here's Fox.'

Fox came in shepherding an extraordinary little apparition in curling-pins and red flannel.

'Miss Sadie Welsh,' explained Fox, 'was a bit uncomfortable about coming down, Mr Alleyn. She'd gone to bed.'

'I'm sorry to bring you out,' said Alleyn pleasantly. 'We shan't keep you here very long. Come over to the fire, won't you?'

He threw a couple of logs on the fire and persuaded Miss Welsh to perch on the extreme edge of a chair: with her feet on the fender. She was a girl of perhaps 22, with large brown eyes, a button nose and a mouth that looked as though she constantly said: 'Ooo.' She gazed at Alleyn as if he was a grand inquisitor.

'You're Miss Troy's housemaid, aren't you?' said Alleyn.

'Yes, sir.

'Been with her long?'

'Ooo, yes, sir. I was a under-housemaid here when the old gentleman was alive; I was sixteen then, sir. And when Miss Troy was mistress I stayed on, sir. Of course, Miss Troy's bin away a lot, sir, but when the house was opened up again this year, Miss Bostock asked me to come with Mr and Mrs Hipkin to be housemaid. I never was a real housemaid like before, sir, but Mr Hipkin he's training me now for parlourmaid. He says I'll be called Welsh then, because Sadie isn't a name for a parlourmaid, Mr Hipkins says. So I'll be "Welsh".'

'Splendid. You like your job?'

'Well, sir,' said Sadie primly, 'I like Miss Troy very much, sir.'

'Not so sure about the rest of the party?'

'No, I am not, sir, and that's a fact. I was telling Mr Fox, sir, Queer! Well, I mean to say! That Mr Garcia, sir. Ooo! Well, I dare say Mr Fox has told you. I complained to Miss Troy, sir. I asked Mrs Hipkin what would I do and she said: "Go straight to Miss Troy," she said. "I would," she said, "I'd go straight to Miss Troy." Which I did. There was no trouble after that, sir, but I must say I didn't fancy taking his dinner down on Friday.'

'As it turned out, you didn't see Mr Garcia then, did you?'

'No, sir. He calls out in a sort of drawly voice: 'Is that you, Sadistic?' which was what he had the nerve to call me, and Mr Hipkin says he didn't ought to have because Mr Hipkin is very well educated, sir.'

'Astonishingly,' murmured Alleyn.

'And then I said: "Your dinner, Mr Garcia," and he called out – excuse me, sir – he called out: "Oh Gawd, eat it yourself." I said: "Pardon?" and he said "Put it down there and shove off." So I said: "Thank *you*," I said, "Mr Garcia," I said. And I put down the tray and as I told Mrs Hipkin, sir, I said: "There's something peculiar going on down there," I said, when I got back to the hall.'

'What made you think that?'

'Well, sir, he seemed that anxious I wouldn't go in, and what with the queer perfume and one thing and another – well!'

'You noticed an odd smell?'

'Yes, I did that, sir.'

'Ever smelt anything like it before?'

'Ooo well, sir, that's funny you should think of that because I said to myself: "Well, if that isn't what Mr Marzis's room smells like of a morning sometimes." '

'Mr Malmsley?'

'Yes, sir. It's a kind of – well, a kind of a bitterish sort of smell, only sort of thick and sour.'

'Not like whisky, for instance?'

'Oh no, sir. I didn't notice the perfume of whisky till I went down next morning.'

'Hullo!' said Fox genially, 'you never told me it was whisky you smelt on Saturday morning, young lady.'

'Didn't I, Mr Fox? Well, I must of forgotten, because there was the other smell, too, mixed up with it. Anyway, Mr Fox, it wasn't the first time I've noticed whisky in the studio since Mr Garcia's been there.'

'But you'd never noticed the other smell before?' asked Alleyn.

'Not in the studio, sir. Only in Mr Marzis's room.'

'Did you make the bed on Saturday morning?'

Sadie turned pink.

'Well, no, I didn't, sir. I opened the window to air the room, and thought I'd go back later. Mr Garcia's supposed to make his own bed. It looked fairly tidy so I left it.'

'And on Saturday morning Mr Garcia's clay model and all his things were gone?'

'That queer-looking mud thing like plasticine? Ooh yes, sir, it was gone on Saturday.'

'Right. I think that's all.'

'May I go, sir?'

'Yes, off you go. I'll ask you to sign your name to a statement later on. You'll do that, won't you? It will just be what you've told us here.'

'Very good, sir.'

'Good night, Welsh,' said Alleyn smiling. 'Thank you.'

'Good night, sir. I'm sure I'm sorry to come in, such a

fright. I don't know what Mr Hipkin would say. It doesn't look very nice for "Welsh", the parlourmaid, does it, sir?'

'We think it was quite correct,' said Alleyn.

Fox, with a fatherly smile, shepherded Sadie to the door.

'Well, Fox,' said Alleyn, 'we'd better get on with it. Let's have Mr Francis Ormerin. How's the French, by the way?'

'I've mastered the radio course, and I'm on to *Hugo's Simplified* now. I shouldn't fancy an un-simplified, I must say. I can read it pretty steadily, Mr Alleyn, and Bob Thompson, the super at number three, has lent me one or two novels he picked up in Paris, on the understanding I translate the bits that would appeal to him. You know Bob.' Fox opened his eyes wide and an expression of mild naughtiness stole over his healthy countenance. 'I must say some of the passages are well up to expectation. Of course, you don't find all those words in the dictionary, do you?'

'You naughty old scoundrel,' said Alleyn. 'Go and get M. Ormerin.'

'Tout sweet,' said Fox. 'There you are.'

'And you'd better inquire after the Seacliff.' Fox went out. 'This case seems to be strewn with upheavals,' said Alleyn. 'Garcia was sick when he saw the defaced portrait. Sonia was sick in the mornings, and Miss Seacliff is heaving away merrily at this very moment, or I'm much mistaken.'

'I begin to get an idea of the case,' said Nigel, who had gone through his notes. 'You're pretty certain it's Garcia, aren't you?'

'Have I said so? All right, then, I do feel tolerably certain he laid the trap for this girl, but it's purely conjectural. I may be quite wrong. If we are to accept the statements of Miss Troy and Watt Hatchett, the knife was pushed through the boards some time after three o'clock on Friday afternoon, and before Saturday afternoon. Personally I am inclined to believe both these statements.

660

That leaves us with Garcia and Malmsley as the most likely fancies.'

'There's – '

'Well?'

'Of course if you accept her statement it doesn't arise,' said Nigel nervously.

Alleyn did not answer immediately, and for some reason Nigel found that he could not look at him. Nigel ruffled the pages of his notes and heard Alleyn's voice: 'I only said I was inclined to believe Hatchett's statement – and hers. I shall not regard them as inviolable.'

Fox returned with Francis Ormerin and once again they settled down to routine. Ormerin had attended the private view of the Phoenix Group Show on Friday night, and had spent the weekend with a French family at Hampstead. They had sat up till about two o'clock on both nights and had been together during the day-time.

'I understand that during the bus drive back from London yesterday, the model sat beside you?' said Alleyn.

'Yes. That is so. This poor girl, she must always have her flirt in attendance.'

'And you filled the rôle on this occasion?'

Ormerin pulled a significant grimace.

'Why not? She makes an invitation with every gesture. It is a long and tedious drive. She is not unattractive. After a time I fell asleep.'

'Did she say anything about her movements in London?'

'Certainly. She told me that she stayed with another girl who is in the chorus of a vaudeville show at the Chelsea Theatre. It is called *Snappy*. Sonia shared this girl's room. She went to *Snappy* on Friday evening, and on Saturday she went to a studio party in Putney where she became exceedingly drunk, and was driven home by a young man, not so drunk, to the room of this girl whose name is – *tiens!* – ah yes – Bobbie is the name of the friend. Bobbie O'Dawne. All this was told me, and for a while I was complacent, and held her hand in the bus. Then after a time I fell asleep.'

'Did she say anything at all that could possibly be of any help to us?'

'Ah! Any help? I do not think so. Except one thing, perhaps. She said that I must not be surprised if I learn soon of another engagement.'

'What engagement was that?'

'She would not tell me. She became *retenue* – *espiègle* – in English, sly-boots. Sonia was very sly-boots on the subject of this engagement. I receive the impression, however, that it would be to Garcia.'

'I see. She did not talk about Garcia's movements on Friday?'

'But I think she did!' exclaimed Ormerin, after a moment's consideration. 'Yes, it is quite true, she did speak of him. It was after I had begun to get sleepy. She said Garcia would start for his promenade through this county on Saturday morning, and return to work in London in a week's time.'

'Did she say where his work-room was in London?'

'On the contrary, she asked me if I could tell her this. She said: "I do not know what his idea is, to make such a mystery of it." Then she laughed and said: "But that is Garcia – I shall have to put up with it, I suppose." She spoke with the air of a woman who has certain rights over a man. It may, of course, have been an assumption. One cannot tell. Very often I have noticed that it is when a woman begins to lose her power with a man that she assumes these little postures of the proprietress.'

'What did you think of Sonia Gluck, M. Ormerin?'

Ormerin's sharp black eyes flashed in his sallow face and his thin mouth widened.

'Of Sonia? She was a type, Mr Alleyn. That is all one can say of her. The *gamine* that so often drifts towards studio doors, and then imperceptibly, naturally, into the protection of some painter. She had beauty, as you have seen. She was very difficult. If she had lived, she would have had little work when her beauty faded. While she was still good for our purpose we endured her temperament, her caprice, for the sake of her lovely body, which we might paint when she was well-behaved.'

'Had you so much difficulty with her?'

'It was intolerable. Never for one minute would she remain in the same position. I myself began three separate drawings of the one pose. I cannot paint in such circumstances, my nerves are lacerated and my work is valueless. I had made my resolution that I would leave the studio.'

'Really! It was as bad as that?'

'Certainly. If this had not happened, I would have told Troy I must go. I should have been very sorry to do this, because I have a great admiration for Troy. She is most stimulating to my work. In her studio one is at home. But I am very greatly at the mercy of my nerves. I would have returned when Bostock and Pilgrim had completed their large canvases, and Troy had rid herself of Sonia.'

'And now, I suppose, you will stay?'

'I do not know.' Ormerin moved restlessly in his chair. Alleyn noticed that there was a slight tic in his upper-lip, a busy little cord that flicked under the dark skin. As if aware of Alleyn's scrutiny, Ormerin put a thin crooked hand up to his lip. His fingers were deeply stained by nicotine.

'I do not know,' he repeated. 'The memory of this morning is very painful. I am *bouleversé*. I do not know what I shall do. I like them all here at Troy's – even this clumsy, shouting Australian. I am *en rapport* with them well enough, but I shall never look towards the throne without seeing there the tableau of this morning. That little unfortunate with her glance of astonishment. And then when they move her – the knife – wet and red.'

'You were the first to notice the knife, I think?'

'Yes. As soon as they moved her I saw it.' He looked uneasily at Alleyn.

'I should have thought the body would still have hidden it.'

663

'But no. I knelt on the floor. I saw it. Let us not speak of it. It is enough that I saw it.'

'Did you expect to see the blade, Mr Ormerin?'

Ormerin was on his feet in a flash, his face ashen, his lips drawn back. He looked like a startled animal.

'What do you say? Expect! How should I expect to see the knife? Do you suspect me – *me* – of complicity in this detestable affair?' His violent agitation came upon him so swiftly that Nigel was amazed, and gaped at him, his notes forgotten.

'You are too sensitive,' Alleyn said quietly, 'and have read a meaning into my words that they were not intended to convey. I wondered if the memory of your experiment with the knife came into your mind before you saw it. I wondered if you guessed that the model had been stabbed.'

'Never!' exclaimed Ormerin, with a violent gesture of repudiation. 'Never! Why should I think of anything so horrible?'

'Since you helped in the experiment, it would not be so astonishing if you should remember it,' said Alleyn. But Ormerin continued to expostulate, his English growing more uncertain as his agitation mounted. At last Alleyn succeeded in calming him a little, and he sat down again.

'I must ask you to pardon my agitation,' he said, his stained fingers at his lips. 'I am much distressed by this crime.'

'That is very natural. I shall not keep you much longer. I spoke just now of the experiment with the dagger. I understand that you and Mr Hatchett did most of the work on the day you made this experiment?'

'They were all interested to see if it could be done. Each one as much as another.'

'Quite so,' agreed Alleyn patiently. 'Nevertheless you and Mr Hatchett actually tipped up the throne and drove the dagger through the crack.'

'And if we did! Does that prove us to be – '

'It proves nothing at all, M. Ormerin. I was about to ask if Mr Garcia had any hand in the experiment?'

'Garcia?' Ormerin looked hard at Alleyn, and then an expression of great relief came upon him and he relaxed. 'No,' he said thoughtfully, 'I do not believe that he came near us. He stood in the window with Sonia and watched. But I will tell you one more thing, Mr Alleyn. When it was all over and she went back to the pose, Malmsley began to mock her, pretending the dagger was still there. And Garcia laughed a little to himself. Very quietly. But I noticed him, and I thought to myself that was a very disagreeable little laugh. That is what I thought!' ended Ormerin with an air of great significance.

'You said in the dining-room that we might be sure this was a *crime passionel*. Why are you so sure of this?'

'But it is apparent – it protrudes a mile. This girl was a type. One had only to see her. It declared itself. She was avid for men.'

'Oh dear, oh dear,' murmured Alleyn.

'*Pardon?*'

'Nothing. Please go on, M. Ormerin.'

'She was not normal. You shall find, I have no doubt, that she was *enceinte*. I have been sure of it for some time. Even at the beginning women have an appearance, you understand? Her face was a little – ' he made an expressive movement with his hand down his own thin face – 'dragged down. And always she was looking at Garcia. Mr Alleyn, I have seen him return her look, and there was that in his eyes that made one shudder. It was not at all pretty to see him watching her. He is a cold young man. He must have women, but he is quite unable to feel any tenderness for them. It is a type.'

Ormerin's distress had apparently evaporated. He had become jauntily knowing.

'In a word,' said Alleyn, 'you consider he is responsible for this tragedy?'

'One draws one's own conclusions, of necessity, Mr Alleyn. Who else can it be?'

'She was on rather uncertain terms with most of you, it appears?'

'Ah yes, yes. But one does not perform murders from exasperation. Even Malmsley – '

Ormerin hesitated, grimaced, wagged his head sideways and was silent.

'What about Mr Malmsley?' asked Alleyn lightly.

'It is nothing.'

'By saying it is nothing, you know, you leave me with an impression of extreme significance. What was there between the model and Mr Malmsley?'

'I have not been able to discover,' said Ormerin rather huffily.

'But you think there was something?'

'She was laughing at him. On the morning of our experiment when Malmsley began to tease Sonia, pretending that the knife was still there, she entreated him to leave her alone, and when he would not she said: 'I wouldn't be too damn funny. Where is it that you discover your ideas, is it in books or pictures?' He was very disconcerted and allowed his dirty brush to fall on his drawing. That is all. You see, I was right when I said it was nothing. Have you finished with me, Mr Alleyn?'

'I think so, thank you. There will be a statement later on,' said Alleyn vaguely. He looked at Ormerin, as though he wasn't there, seemed to recollect himself, and got to his feet.

'Yes, I think that's all,' he repeated.

'I shall wish you good night then, Mr Alleyn.'

'Good night,' said Alleyn, coming to himself. 'Good night, M. Ormerin.'

But when Ormerin had gone, Alleyn wandered about the room, whistled under his breath, and paid no attention at all to Fox or Nigel.

'Look here,' said Nigel at last, 'I want to use a telephone.'

'You?'

666

'Yes. Don't look at me as though I was a fabulous monster. I want to use the telephone, I say.'

'What for?'

'Ring up Angela.'

'It's eleven o'clock.'

'That's no matter. She'll be up and waiting.'

'You're burning to ring up your odious newspaper.'

'Well – I thought if I just said – '

'You may say that there has been a fatal accident at Tatler's End House, Bossicote, and that an artist's model has died as the result of this accident. You may add that the authorities are unable to trace the whereabouts of the victim's relatives and are anxious to communicate with Mr W. Garcia who is believed to be on a walking tour and may be able to give them some information about the model's family. Something on those lines.'

'And a fat lot of good – ' began Nigel angrily.

'If Garcia is not our man,' continued Alleyn to Fox, 'and sees that, he may do something about it.'

'That's so,' said Fox.

'And now we'll deal with the last of this collection, if you please, Fox. The languishing Malmsley.'

'I'll go to the telephone,' said Nigel.

'Very well. Don't exceed, now. You may tell them that there will be a further instalment tomorrow.'

'Too kind,' said Nigel haughtily.

'And Bathgate – you might ring my mamma up and say we won't be in until after midnight.'

'All right.'

Nigel and Fox collided in the doorway with Bailey, who looked cold and disgruntled.

'Hullo,' said Alleyn. 'Wait a moment, Fox. Let's hear what Bailey's been up to.'

'I've been over deceased's room,' said Bailey.

'Any good?'

'Nothing much, sir. It's an attic-room at the front of the house.'

He paused, and Alleyn waited. knowing that 'nothing

much' from Bailey might mean anything from a vacuum to a phial of cyanide.

'There's deceased's prints,' continued Bailey, 'and one that looks like this Garcia. It's inside the door where the maid's missed with the duster, and there's another print close beside it that isn't either of 'em. Broad. Man's print, I'd say. And of course there are the maid's all over the show. I've checked those. Nothing much about the clothes. Note from Garcia in a pocket. She was in the family way all right. Here it is.'

He opened his case, and from a labelled envelope drew out of a piece of paper laid between two slips of glass.

'I've printed it and taken a photo.'

Alleyn took the slips delicately in his fingers and laid them on the desk. The creases in the common paper had been smoothed out and the scribbled black pencil lines were easy to read:

Dear S. – What do you expect me to do about it? I've got two quid to last me till I get to Troy's. You asked for it, anyway. Can't you get somebody to fix things? It's not exactly likely that I should want to be saddled with a wife and a kid, is it? I've got a commission for a big thing, and for God's sake don't throw me off my stride. I'm sorry but I can't do anything. See you at Troy's. *Garcia*

'A charming fellow,' said Alleyn.

'That was in a jacket pocket. Here's a letter that was just kicking about at the back of the wardrobe. From somebody called Bobbie. Seems as if this Bobbie's a girl.'

This letter was written in an enormous hand on dreadful pink paper:

                              The Digs,
                    4 Batchelors Gardens,
                              Chelsea.
                              Monday.
Dear Sonia,

I'm sorry you're in for it dear I think it's just
frightful and I do think men are the limit but of
course I never liked the sound of that Garcia too far
upstage if you ask me but they're all alike when it
comes to a girl. The same to you with bells on and
pleased to join in the fun at the start and sorry you've
been troubled this takes me off when they know
you're growing melons. I've asked Dolores Duval for
the address she went to when she had a spot of
trouble but she says the police found out about that
lady so it's no go. Anyway I think your idea is better
and if Mr Artistic Garcia is willing OK and why not
dear you might as well get it both ways and I suppose
it's all right to be married he sounds a lovely boy but
you never know with that sort did I ever tell you
about my boy friend who was a Lord he was a scream
really but nothing ever came of it thank God. It will
be OK if you come here on Friday and I might ask
Leo Cohen for a brief but you know what manage-
ments are like these days dear they sweat the socks
off you for the basic salary and when it comes to
asking for a brief for a lady friend it's just too bad
but they've forgotten how the chorus goes in that
number. Thank you very much good morning. I
laughed till I sobbed over the story of the Seacliff
woman's picture it must have looked a scream when
you'd done with it but all the same dear your tem-
preement will land you well in the consommy one of
these days dear if you don't learn to kerb yourself
which God knows you haven't done what with one
thing and another. What a yell about Marmelade's

                              669

little bit of dirt. Well so long dear and keep smiling see you Friday. Hoping this finds you well as I am,

Cheerio. Ever so sincerely,
Your old pal,
Bobbie

PS. – You want to be sure B.P. won't turn nasty and say all right go ahead I've told her the story of my life anyhow so now what!

Chapter 12

Malmsley on Pleasure

Nigel returned while Alleyn was still chuckling over Miss O'Dawne's letter.

'What's up?' asked Nigel.

'Bailey has discovered a remarkably rich plum. Come and read it. I fancy it's the sort of thing your paper calls a human document. A gem in its own way.' Nigel read over Fox's shoulder.

'I like Dolores Duval and her spot of trouble,' he said.

'She got her pass from Leo Cohen for Sonia,' said Alleyn. 'Sonia told Ormerin she'd seen the show. Fox, what do you make of the passage where she says Sonia might as well get it both ways if Garcia is willing? Then she goes on to say she supposes it's all right to be married and he sounds a lovely boy.'

'The lovely boy seems to be the Hon. Pilgrim, judging by the next bit about her boy-friend that was a lord,' said Fox. 'Do you think Sonia Gluck had an idea she'd get Mr Pilgrim to marry her?'

'I hardly think so. No, I fancy blackmail was the idea there. Pilgrim confessed as much when he couldn't get out of it. If Mr Artistic Garcia was willing! Is she driving at the blackmail inspiration there, do you imagine? Her magnificent disregard for the convention that things that are thought of together should be spoken of together, is a bit baffling. I shall have to see Miss Bobbie O'Dawne. She may be the girl we all wait for. Anything else, Bailey?'

'Well,' said Bailey grudgingly, 'I don't know if there's anything in it but I found this.' He took out of his case a shabby blue book and handed it to Alleyn. 'It's been printed, Mr Alleyn. There's several of deceased's prints and a few of the broad one I got off the door. Some party had tried to get into the case where I found the book.'

'*The Consolations of a Critic*,' Alleyn muttered, turning the book over in his long hands. 'By C. Lewis Hind, 1911. Yes, I see. Gently select. Edwardian manner. Seems to be a mildly ecstatic excursion into aesthetics. Nice reproductions. Hullo! Hullo! Why stap me and sink me, there it is!'

He had turned the pages until he came upon a black and white reproduction of a picture in which three medieval figures mowed a charming field against a background of hayricks, pollard willows and turreted palaces.

'By gum and gosh, Bailey, you've found Mr Malmsley's secret. I knew I'd met those three nice little men before. Of course I had. Good Lord, what a fool! Yes, here it is. From *Les Très Riches Heures du Duc de Berry*, by Pol de Limbourge and his brothers. The book's in the Musée Condé at Chantilly. I had to blandish for half an hour before the librarian would let me touch it. It's the most exquisite thing. Well, I'll be jiggered, and I can't say fairer than that.'

'You can tell us what you're talking about, however,' suggested Nigel acidly.

'Fox knows,' said Alleyn. 'You remember, Fox, don't you?'

'I get you now, Mr Alleyn,' said Fox. 'That's what she meant when she sauced him on the day of the experiment.'

'Of course. This is the explanation of one of the more obscure passages in the O'Dawne's document. "What a yell about Marmelade's bit of dirt." What a yell indeed! Fetch him in, Fox – any nonsense from Master Cedric Malmsley and we have him on the hip.' He put the book on the floor beside his chair.

'You might tell me, Alleyn, why you are so maddeningly perky all of a sudden,' complained Nigel.

'Wait and see, my dear Bathgate. Bailey, you've done extremely well. Anything else for us in the room?'

'Not that I could make out, Mr Alleyn. Everything's

put back as it was, but I thought there was nothing against taking these things.'

'Certainly not. Pack them into my case, please. I want you to wait until I've seen Mr Malmsley. Here's Fox.'

Malmsley drifted in ahead of Fox. Seen across the dining-room table he had looked sufficiently remarkable with his beard divided into two. This beard was fine and straight and had the damp pallor of an infant's crest. Malmsley wore a crimson shirt, a black tie and a corduroy velvet jacket. Indeed he had the uncanny appearance of a person who had come round, full circle, to the Victorian idea of a Bohemian. He was almost an illustration for *Trilby*. 'Perhaps,' thought Alleyn, 'there is nothing but that left for them to do.' He wore jade rings on his, unfortunately, broad fingers.

'Ah, Mr Alleyn,' he said, 'you are painfully industrious.'

Alleyn smiled vaguely and invited Malmsley to sit down. Nigel returned to the desk, Bailey walked over to the door, Fox stood in massive silence by the dying fire.

'I want your movements from Friday noon to yesterday evening, if you will be so obliging, Mr Malmsley,' said Alleyn.

'I am afraid that I am not fortunate enough to have a very obliging nature, Mr Alleyn. And as for my movements, I always move as infrequently as possible, and never in the right direction.'

'London was, from your point of view, in the right direction on Friday afternoon.'

'You mean that by going to London I avoided any question of complicity in this unpleasant affair.'

'Not necessarily,' said Alleyn. Malmsley lit a cigarette. 'However,' continued Alleyn, 'you have already told us that you went to London by the six o'clock bus, at the end of an afternoon spent with Mr Garcia in the studio.'

'I am absurdly communicative. It must be because I find my own conversation less tedious, as a rule, than the conversation of other people.'

'In that,' said Alleyn, 'you are singularly fortunate.'

Malmsley raised his eyebrows.

'What did Mr Garcia tell you about Mr Pilgrim during your conversation in the studio?' asked Alleyn.

'About Pilgrim? Oh, he said that he thought Valmai would find Pilgrim a very boring companion. He was rather ridiculous and said that she would soon grow tired of Pilgrim's good looks. I told him that it was much more likely that she would tire of Pilgrim's virtue. Women dislike virtue in a husband almost as much as they enjoy infidelity.'

'Good Lord!' thought Alleyn. 'He *is* late Victorian. This is Wilde and Water.'

'And then?' he said aloud.

'And then he said that Basil Pilgrim was not as virtuous as I thought. I said that I had not thought about it at all. "The superficial observer," I told him, "is the only observer who ever lights upon a profound truth." Don't you agree with me, Mr Alleyn?'

'Being a policeman, I am afraid I don't. Did you pursue this topic?'

'No. I did not find it sufficiently entertaining. Garcia then invited me to speculate upon the chances of Seacliff's virtue saying that he could astonish me on that subject if he had a mind to. I assured him that I was unable to fall into an ecstasy of wonderment on the upshot of what was, as I believe racing enthusiasts would say, a fifty-fifty chance. I found Garcia quite, quite tedious and pedestrian on the subject of Seacliff. He is very much attracted by Seacliff, and men are always more amusing when they praise women they dislike than when they abuse the women to whom they are passionately attracted. I therefore changed the topic of conversation.'

'To Sonia Gluck?'

'That would be quite brilliant of you, Inspector, if I had not mentioned previously that we spoke of Sonia Gluck.'

'That is almost the only feature of our previous conversation that I do remember, Mr Malmsley. You told us that Garcia asked you if – ' Alleyn consulted his notebook – 'if you had ever felt like murdering your mistress just for the horror of doing it. How did you reply?'

'I replied that I had never been long enough attached to a woman for her to claim the title of my mistress. There is something dreadfully permanent in the sound of those two sibilants. However, the theme was a pleasant one and we embroidered it at our leisure. Garcia strolled across to my table and looked at my drawing. 'It wouldn't be worth it,' he said. I disagreed with him. One exquisite pang of horror! "One has not experienced the full gamut of nervous luxury," I said, "until one has taken a life." He began to laugh and returned to his work.'

'Is he at all insane, do you think?'

'Insane? My dear Inspector, who can define the borders of abnormality?'

'That is quite true,' said Alleyn patiently. 'Would you say that Mr Garcia is far from being abnormal?'

'Perhaps not.'

'Is he in the habit of taking drugs, do you know?'

Malmsley leant forward and dropped his cigarette on an ash-tray. He examined his jade rings and said:

'I really have no idea.'

'You have never noticed his eyes, for instance?' continued Alleyn, looking very fixedly into Malmsley's. 'One can usually tell, you know, by the eyes.'

'Really?'

'Yes. The pupils are contracted. Later on they occasionally become widely dilated. As you must have observed, Mr Malmsley, when you have looked in a mirror.'

'You are wonderfully learned, Mr Alleyn.'

'I ask you if, to your knowledge, Garcia has contracted this habit. I must warn you that a very thorough search will be made of all the rooms in this house. Whether I think it advisable to take further steps in following up evidence that is not relevant to this case, may depend largely upon your answer.'

Malmsley looked quickly from Fox to Nigel.

'These gentlemen are with me in this case,' said Alleyn. 'Come now, Mr Malmsley, unless you wish to indulge the – what was Mr Malmsley's remark about nervous enjoyment, Bathgate?'

Nigel looked at his notes.

'The full gamut of nervous luxury?' he said.

'That's it. Unless you feel like experiencing the full gamut of such nervous luxury as police investigations can provide, you will do well to answer my question.'

'He could not afford it,' said Malmsley. 'He is practically living on charity.'

'Have you ever treated him to – let us say – to a pipe of opium?'

'I decline to answer this question.'

'You are perfectly within your rights. I shall obtain a search warrant and examine your effects.'

Malmsley shrank a little in his chair.

'That would be singularly distasteful to me,' he said. 'I am fastidious in the matter of guests.'

'Was Garcia one of your guests?'

'And if he was? After all, why should I hesitate? Your methods are singularly transparent, Inspector. You wish to know if I have ever amused myself by exploring the pleasures of opium. I have done so. A friend has given me a very beautiful set in jade and ivory, and I have not been so churlish as to neglect its promise of enjoyment. On the other hand, I have not allowed myself to contract a habit. In point of fact, I have not used half the amount that was given to me. I am not a creature of habit.'

'Did you invite Garcia to smoke opium?'

'Yes.'

'When?'

'Last Friday afternoon.'

'At last,' said Alleyn. 'Where did you smoke your opium?'

'In the studio.'

'Where you were safe from interruption?'

'Where we were more comfortable.'

'You had the six o'clock bus to catch. Surely you felt disinclined to make the trip up to London?'

Malmsley moved restlessly.

'As a matter of fact,' he said, 'I did not smoke a full pipe. I did not wish to. I merely started one and gave it to Garcia.'

'How many pipes did you give him?'

'Only one.'

'Very well. You will now, if you please, give us an exact account of the manner in which you spent your afternoon. You went to the studio immediately after lunch. Was Garcia there?'

'Yes. He had just got there.'

'How long was it before you gave him opium?'

'My dear Inspector, how should I know? I should imagine it was round about four o'clock.'

'After your conversation about the model and so on?'

'It followed our conversation. We discussed pleasure. That led us to opium.'

'So you went to the house and fetched your jade and ivory paraphernalia?'

'Ah – yes.'

'In your first account you may remember that you told me you did not leave the studio until it was time to change and catch your bus?'

'Did I? Perhaps I did. I suppose I thought that the opium incident would over-excite you.'

'When you finally left the studio,' said Alleyn, 'what was Mr Garcia's condition?'

'He was very tranquil.'

'Did he speak after he had begun to smoke?'

'Oh, yes. A little.'

'What did he say?'

'He said he was happy.'

'Anything else?'

'He said that there was a way out of all one's difficulties

if one only had the courage to take it. That, I think, was all.'

'Did you take your opium and the pipe back to the house?'

'No.'

'Why not?'

'The housemaid had said something about changing the sheets on my bed. I didn't particularly want to encounter her.'

'Where did you put the things then?'

'In a box under Garcia's bed.'

'And collected them?'

'This morning before class.'

'Had they been disturbed?'

'I have no idea.'

'Are you sure of that?'

Malmsley moved irritably.

'They were in the box. I simply collected them and took them up to the house.'

'How much opium should there be?'

'I don't know. I think the jar must be about half full.'

'Do you think Garcia may have smoked again, after you left?'

'Again I have no idea. I should not think so. I haven't thought of it.'

Alleyn looked curiously at Malmsley.

'I wonder,' he said, 'if you realize what you may have done?'

'I am afraid I do not understand.'

'I think you do. Everything you have told me about Mr Garcia points, almost too startlingly, to one conclusion.'

Malmsley made a sudden and violent gesture of repudiation.

'That is a horrible suggestion,' he said. 'I have told you the truth – you have no right to suggest that I have – that I had any other motive, but – but – '

'I think I appreciate your motives well enough, Mr Malmsley. For instance, you realized that I should discover the opium in any case if I searched your room. You realized that if Mr Garcia makes a statement about Friday, he will probably speak of the opium you gave him. You may even have known that a plea of irresponsibility due to the effect of opium might be made in the event of criminal proceedings.'

'Do you mean – if he was tried for murder, that I – *I* might be implicated? That is monstrous. I refuse to listen to such a suggestion. You must have a very pure mind, Inspector. Only the very pure are capable of such gross conceptions.'

'And only the very foolish attitudinize in the sort of circumstances that have risen round you and what you did on Friday afternoon. Come, Mr Malmsley, forget your prose for a moment. To my aged perceptions it seems a little as if you were mixing Dorian Grey with one of the second-rate intellectuals of the moment. The result is something that – you must forgive me – does not inspire a policeman with confidence. I tell you quite seriously that you are in a predicament.'

'You suspect Garcia?'

'We suspect everyone and no one at the moment. We note what you have told us and we believe that Garcia was alone in the studio in a semi-drugged condition on Friday evening when we suppose the knife was thrust through the throne. We learn that you drugged him.'

'At his own suggestion,' cried Malmsley.

'Really? Will he agree to that? Or will he say that you persuaded him to smoke opium?'

'He was perfectly ready to do it. He wanted to try. And he only had one pipe. A small amount. He would sleep it off in a few hours. I tell you he was already half asleep when I left.'

'When do you think he would wake?'

'I don't know. How should I know? The effect varies very much the first time. It is impossible to say. He would be well enough in five hours at all events.'

'Do you think,' said Alleyn very deliberately, 'that Garcia set this terrible trap for Sonia Gluck?'

Malmsley was white to the lips.

'I don't know. I know nothing about it. I thought he must have done it. You have forced me into an intolerable position. If I say I believe he did it – but not because of the opium – I refuse to accept – '

His voice was shrill, and his lips trembled. He seemed to be near to tears.

'Very well. We shall try to establish your own movements after you left the house. You caught the six o'clock bus?'

Malmsley eagerly gave an account of his weekend. He had attended the private view, had gone to the Savoy, and to a friend's flat. They had sat up till three o'clock. He had spent the whole of Saturday with this friend, and with him had gone to a theatre in the evening, and again they had not gone to bed until very late. Alleyn took him through the whole business up to his return on Sunday. Malmsley seemed to be very much shaken.

'Excellent, so far,' said Alleyn. 'We shall, of course, verify your statements. I have looked at your illustrations, Mr Malmsley. They are charming.'

'You shake my pleasure in them,' said Malmsley, rallying a little.

'I particularly liked the picture of the three little men with scythes.'

Malmsley looked sharply at Alleyn but said nothing.

'Have you ever visited Chantilly?' asked Alleyn.

'Never.'

'Then you have not seen *Les Très Riches Heures du Duc de Berry?*'

'Never.'

'You have seen reproductions of the illustrations, perhaps?'

'I – I may have.'

Nigel, staring at Malmsley, wondered how he could ever have thought him a pale young man.

'Do you remember a book *The Consolations of a Critic?*'

'I – don't remember – I – '

'Do you own a copy of this book?'

'No – I – I – '

Alleyn picked up the little blue volume from under his chair and laid it on Malmsley's knee.

'Isn't this book your property, Mr Malmsley?'

'I – I refuse to answer. This is intolerable.'

'It has your name on the fly-leaf.'

Nigel suddenly felt desperately sorry for Malmsley. He felt as if he himself had done something shameful. He wished ardently that Alleyn would let Malmsley go. Malmsley had embarked on a sort of explanation. Elaborate phrases faltered into lame protestations. The subconscious memory of beautiful things – all art was imitative – to refuse a model was to confess yourself without imagination. On and on he went, and ended in misery.

'All this,' said Alleyn, not too unkindly, 'is quite unnecessary. I am not here to inquire into the ethics of illustrative painting. The rightness or wrongness of what you have done is between yourself, your publisher, and your conscience, if such a thing exists. All I want to know is how this book came into the possession of Sonia Gluck.'

'I don't know. She was odiously inquisitive – I must have left it somewhere – I had it in the studio one afternoon when I – when I was alone. Someone came in and I – I put it aside. I am not in the least ashamed. I consider I had a perfect right. There are many dissimilarities.'

'That is what she was driving at when she asked you, on the morning of the experiment, where you got your ideas?'

'Yes. I suppose so. Yes.'

'Did you ask her for the book?'

'Yes.'

'And she refused to give it up?'

'It was abominable. It was not that I objected to anybody knowing.'

'Did you go to her room?'

'I had every right when she refused. It was my property.'

'I see. You tried to recover it while she was away. On Friday, perhaps, before you left?'

'If you must know, yes.'

'And you couldn't find your book?'

'No.'

'Where was this book, Bailey?'

'In a locked suitcase, sir, under deceased's bed. Someone had tried to pick the lock.'

'Was that you, Mr Malmsley?'

'I was entirely justified.'

'Was it you?'

'Yes.'

'Why did you not tell Miss Troy what had happened?'

'I – Troy might not look at it – Troy is rather British in such matters. She would confess with wonderful enthusiasm that her own work is rooted in the aesthetics of the primitives, but for someone who was courageous enough to use boldly such material from the past as seemed good to him, she would have nothing but abuse. Women – English women especially – are the most marvellous hypocrites.'

'That will do,' said Alleyn. 'What was Sonia's motive in taking this book?'

'She simply wanted to be disagreeable and infuriating.'

'Did you offer her anything if she returned it?'

'She was preposterous,' muttered Malmsley, 'preposterous.'

'How much did she ask?'

'I do not admit that she asked anything.'

'All right,' said Alleyn. 'It's your mess. Stay in it if you want to.'

'What am I to understand by that?'

'Think it out. I believe I need not keep you any longer,

Mr Malmsley. I am afraid I cannot return your book just yet. I shall need a specimen of your fingerprints. We can take them from the cigarette-box you picked up when you came in, or from objects in your room which I am afraid I shall have to examine. It would help matters if you allowed Sergeant Bailey to take an official specimen now.'

Malmsley consented to this with a very ill grace, and made a great fuss over the printer's ink left on his thick white finger-tips.

'I fail to see,' he said, 'why I should have been forced to go through this disgusting performance.'

'Bailey will give you something to clean up the ink,' said Alleyn. 'Good evening, Mr Malmsley.'

'One more job for you, Bailey, I'm afraid,' said Alleyn, when Malmsley had gone. 'We'll have to look through these rooms before we let them go to bed. Are they still boxed up in the dining-room, Fox?'

'They are that,' said Fox, 'and if that young Australian talks much more, I fancy we'll have a second corpse on our hands.'

'I'll start off on Mr Malmsley's room, will I, sir?' asked Bailey.

'Yes. Then tackle the other men's. We'll be there in a jiffy. I don't expect to find much, but you never know in our game.'

'Very good, Mr Alleyn,' said Bailey. He went off with a resigned look.

'What do you make of this dope story, Mr Alleyn?' said Fox. 'We'll have to have a go at tracing the source, won't we?'

'Oh Lord, yes. I suppose so. Malmsley will say he got it from the friend who gave him the pretty little pipe and etceteras, and I don't suppose even Malmsley will give his dope merchant away. Not that I think he's far gone. I imagine he spoke the truth when he said he'd only experimented – he doesn't look like an advanced addict. I took a pot-shot on his eyes, his breath, and the colour of his beastly face. And I remembered Sadie noticing a smell. Luckily the shot went home.'

'Smoking,' ruminated Nigel. 'That's rather out of the usual in this country, isn't it?'

'Fortunately, yes,' agreed Alleyn. 'As a matter of fact it's less deadly than the other methods. Much less pernicious than injecting, of course.'

'Do you think Garcia may have done his stuff with the knife while he was still dopey?' asked Nigel.

'It would explain his careless ways,' said Fox, 'dropping clay about the place.'

'That's true, Brer Fox. I don't know,' said Alleyn, 'if, when he woke at, say, seven-thirty, when Sadie banged on the screen, he'd feel like doing the job. We'll have to have expert opinion on the carry-over from opium. I'm inclined to think he might wake feeling damned unpleasant and take a pull at his whisky bottle. Had it been handled recently, Bailey?'

'Yes, sir, I'd say it had. It's very dusty in patches, but there's some prints that were left after the dust had settled. Only a very light film over the prints. Not more than a couple of days' deposit.'

'That's fairly conclusive,' said Alleyn. 'Taken with Sadie's statement it looks as if Garcia's Friday evening dinner was a jorum of whisky.'

'What beats me,' said Fox, 'is when he got his stuff away.'

'Some time on Friday night.'

'Yes, but *how?* Not by a local carrier. They've all been asked.'

'He must have got hold of a vehicle of some sort and driven himself,' said Nigel.

'Half doped and three-quarters tight, Mr Bathgate?'

'He may not have been as tight as all that,' said Alleyn. 'On the other hand – '

'Well?' asked Nigel impatiently.

'On the other hand he may have,' said Alleyn. 'Come on, we'll see how Bailey's got on, and then we'll go home.'

Chapter 13

Upstairs

When Fox had gone upstairs and Nigel had been left to
write a very guarded story for his paper on one of Troy's
scribbling-pads, Alleyn went down the hall and into the
dining-room. He found the whole class in a state of
extreme dejection. Phillida Lee, Ormerin and Watt Hatchett were seated at the table and had the look of people
who have argued themselves to a standstill. Katti Bostock,
hunched on the fender, stared into the fire. Malmsley was
stretched out in the only armchair. Valmai Seacliff and
Basil Pilgrim sat on the floor in a dark corner with their
arms round each other. Curled up on a cushion against
the wall was Troy – fast asleep. The local constable sat
on an upright chair inside the door.

Katti looked up at Alleyn and then across to Troy.

'She's completely done up,' said Katti gruffly. 'Can't
you let her go to bed?'

'Very soon now,' said Alleyn.

He walked swiftly across the room and paused, his head
bent down, his eyes on Troy.

Her face looked thin. There were small shadows in the
hollows of her temples and under her eyes. She frowned,
her hands moved, and suddenly she was awake.

'I'm so sorry,' said Alleyn.

'Oh, it's you,' said Troy. 'Do you want me?'

'Please. Only for a moment, and then I shan't bother
you again tonight.'

Troy sat up, her hands at her hair, pushing it off her
face. She rose but lost her balance. Alleyn put his arm
out quickly. For a moment he supported her.

'My legs have gone to sleep,' said Troy. 'Damn!'

Her hand was on his shoulder. He held her firmly by
the arms and wondered if it was Troy or he who trembled.

'I'm all right now,' she said, after an hour or a second. 'Thank you.' He let her go and spoke to the others.

'I am very sorry to keep you all up for so long. We have had a good deal to do. Before you go to your rooms we should like to have a glance at them. I hope nobody objects to this.'

'Anything, if we can only go to bed,' said Katti, and nobody contradicted her.

'Very well, then. If you – ' he turned to Troy – 'wouldn't mind coming with me – '

'Yes, of course.'

When they were in the hall she said: 'Do you want to search our rooms for something? Is that it?'

'Not for anything specific. I feel we should just – ' He stopped short. 'I detest my job,' he said; 'for the first time I despise and detest it.'

'Come on,' said Troy.

They went up to a half-landing where the stairs separated into two short flights going up to their left and right.

'Before I forget,' said Alleyn, 'do you know what has happened to the bottle of nitric acid that was on the top shelf in the junk-room?'

Troy stared at him.

'The acid? It's there. It was filled up on Friday.'

'Bailey must have missed it. Don't worry – we saw the stains and felt we ought to account for them. What about these rooms?'

'All the students' rooms are up there,' said Troy, and pointed to the upper landing on the right. 'The bathrooms, and mine, are on the other side. Through here' – she pointed to a door on the half-landing – 'are the servant's quarters, the back stairs and a little stair up to the attic-room where – where Sonia slept.'

Alleyn saw that there were lights under two of the doors on the student's landing.

'Fox and Bailey are up there,' he said. 'If you don't mind – '

'You'd better do my room,' said Troy. 'Here it is.'

They went into the second room on the left-hand landing. It was a large room, very spacious and well-proportioned. The walls, the carpet, and the narrow bed, were white. He saw only one picture and very few ornaments, but on the mantelpiece sparkled a little glass Christmas tree with fabulous glass flowers growing on it. Troy struck a match and lit the fire.

'I'll leave you to your job,' she said.

Alleyn did not answer.

'Is there anything else?' asked Troy.

'Only that I should like to say that if it was possible for me to make an exception – '

'Why should you make any exceptions?' interrupted Troy. 'There is no conceivable reason for such a suggestion.'

'If you will simply think of me as a ship's steward or – or some other sexless official – '

'How else should I think of you, Mr Alleyn? I can assure you there is no need for these scruples – if they are scruples.'

'They were attempts at an apology. I shall make a third and ask you to forgive me for my impertinence. I shan't keep you long.'

Troy turned at the door.

'I didn't meant to be beastly,' she said.

'Nor were you. I see now that I made an insufferable assumption.'

' – but you can hardly expect me to be genial when you are about to hunt through my under-garments for incriminating letters. The very fact that you suspect – '

Alleyn strode to the door and looked down at her. 'You little fool,' he said, 'haven't you the common-or-garden gumption to see that I no more suspect you than the girl in the moon?'

Troy stared at him as if he had taken leave of his senses. She opened her mouth to speak, said nothing, turned on her heel and left the room.

'Blast!' said Alleyn. 'Oh, blast and hell and bloody stink!'

He stood and looked at the door which Troy had only just not slammed. Then he turned to his job. There was a bow-fronted chest of drawers full of the sorts of garments that Alleyn often before had had to turn over. His thin fastidious hands touched them delicately, laid them in neat heaps on the bed and returned them carefully to their appointed places. There was a little drawer, rather untidy, where Troy kept her oddments. One or two letters. One that began 'Troy darling' and was signed 'Your foolishly devoted, John'. 'John,' thought Alleyn, 'John Bellasca?' He glanced through the letters quickly, was about to return them to the drawer, but on second thoughts laid them in a row on the top of the chest. 'An odious trade,' he muttered to himself. 'A filthy degrading job.' Then there were the dresses in the wardrobe, the slim jackets, Troy's smart evening dresses, and her shabby old slacks. All the pockets. Such odd things she kept in her pockets – bits of charcoal, india-rubbers, a handkerchief that had been disgracefully used as a paint-rag, and a sketchbook crammed into a pocket that was too small for it. There was a Harris tweed coat – blue. Suddenly he was back on the wharf at Quebec. The lights of Troy's ship were reflected in the black mirror of the river. Silver-tongued bells rang out from all the grey churches. The tug, with its five globes of yellow light, moved outwards into the night tide of the St Lawrence, and there on the deck was Troy, her hand raised in farewell, wearing blue Harris tweed. 'Goodbye. Thank you for my nice party. Goodbye.' He slipped his hand into a pocket of the blue coat and pulled out Katti Bostock's letter. He would have to read this.

. . . You are a gump to collect these bloodsuckers . . . he's a nasty little animal . . . that little devil Sonia Gluck . . . behaving abominably . . . funny this 'It' stuff . . . you're different. They'd fall for you if you'd let

688

them, only you're so unprovocative . . . [Alleyn shook his head at Katti Bostock]. Your allusions to a detective are quite incomprehensible, but if he interrupted you in your work you had every right to bite his head off. What had you been up to anyway? Well, so long until the 3rd.
Katti

The envelope was addressed to Troy at the Château Frontenac.

'Evidently,' thought Alleyn, 'I had begun to make a nuisance of myself on board. Interrupting her work. Oh Lord!'

In a minute or two he had finished. It would have been absolutely all right if he had never asked about her room. No need for that little scene. He hung up the last garment, glanced round the room and looked for the fourth or fifth time at the photograph of a man that stood on the top of the bow-fronted chest. A good-looking man who had signed himself 'John'. Alleyn, yielding to an unworthy impulse, made a hideous grimace at this photograph, turned to leave the room and saw Troy, amazed, in the doorway. He felt his face burning like a sky sign.

'Have you finished, Mr Alleyn?'

'Quite finished, thank you.'

He knew she had seen him. There was a singular expression in her eyes.

'I have just made a face at the photograph on your tallboy,' said Alleyn.

'So I observed.'

'I have gone through your clothes, fished in your pockets and read all your letters. You may go to bed. The house will be watched, of course. Good night, Miss Troy.'

'Good morning, Mr Alleyn.'

Alleyn went to Katti Bostock's room where he found nothing of note. It was a great deal untidier than Troy's room, and took longer. He found several pairs of paint-stained slacks huddled together on the floor of the wardrobe, an evening dress in close proximity to a painting-smock, and a row of stubborn-looking shoes with no trees in them. There were odds and ends in all the pockets. He plodded through a mass of receipts, colour-men's catalogues, drawings and books. The only personal letter he found was the one Troy had written and posted at Vancouver.* This had to be read. Troy's catalogue of the students was interesting. Then he came to the passages about himself. '. . . turned out to be intelligent, so I felt the fool. . . . Looks like a grandee . . . on the defensive about this sleuth. . . . Took it like a gent and made me feel like a bounder.' As he read, Alleyn's left eyebrow climbed up his forehead. He folded the letter very carefully, smoothed it out and returned it to its place among a box of half-used oil-colours. He began to whistle under his breath, polished off Katti Bostock's effects, and went in search of Fox and Bailey. They had finished the men's bedrooms.

Fox had found Malmsley's opium-smoking impedimenta and had impounded them. The amount of opium was small. There were signs that the jar had at one time been full.

'Which does not altogether agree with Mr Malmsley's little story,' grunted Alleyn. 'Has Bailey tried the things for prints?'

'Yes. Two sets, Garcia and Malmsley's on the pipe, the lamp and the jar.'

'The jar. That's interesting. Well, let's get on with it.'

He sent Bailey into Phillida Lee's room, while he and Fox tackled Valmai Seacliff's. Miss Seacliff's walls were chiefly adorned with pictures of herself. Malmsley and Ormerin had each painted her, and Pilgrim had drawn her once and painted her twice.

'The successful nymphomaniac,' thought Alleyn, remembering Katti's letter.

A very clever pencil drawing of Pilgrim, signed 'Seacliff', stood on the bedside table. The room was

*See page 519

extremely tidy and much more obviously feminine than Troy's or Katti's. Seacliff had at least three times as many clothes, and quantities of hats and berets. Alleyn noticed that her slacks were made in Savile Row, and her dresses in Paris. He was amused to find that even the Seacliff painting-bags and smock smelt of Worth. Her weekend case had not been completely unpacked. In it he found three evening dresses, a nightdress and bath-gown, shoes, three pairs of coloured gloves, two day dresses, two berets, and an evening bag containing among other things a half-full bottle of aspirin.

'Maybe Pilgrim's,' said Alleyn, and put them in his case. 'Now for the correspondence.'

They found more than enough of that. Two of her dressing-table drawers were filled with neatly tied-up packets of letters.

'Help!' said Alleyn. 'We'll have to glance at these, Fox. There might be something. Here, you take this lot. Very special. Red ribbon. Must be Pilgrim's, I imagine. Yes, they are.'

Fox put on his spectacles and began impassively to read Basil Pilgrim's love-letters.

'Very gentlemanly,' he said, after the first three.

'You're out of luck. I've struck a most impassioned series from a young man, who compares her bitterly and obscurely to a mirage. Golly, here's a sonnet.'

For some time there was no sound but the faint crackle of notepaper. Bailey came in and said he had drawn a blank in Phillida Lee's room. Alleyn threw a bundle of letters at him.

'There's something here you might like to see,' said Fox. 'The last one from the Honourable Mr Pilgrim.'

'What's he say?'

Fox cleared his throat.

' "Darling",' he began, 'I've got the usual sort of feelings about not being anything like good enough for you. Your last letter telling me you first liked me because I seemed a bit different from other men has made me feel rather bogus. I suppose, without being an insufferable prig, I might agree that I can at any rate bear comparison with the gang we've got to know – the studio lot – like Garcia and Malmsley and Co. But that's not a hell of a compliment to myself, is it? As a matter of fact, I simply loathe seeing you in that setting. Men like Garcia have no right to be in the same room as yourself, my lovely, terrifyingly remote Valmai. I know people scream with mirth at the sound of the word 'pure'. It's gone all *déclassé* like 'genteel'. But there is a strange sort of purity about you, Valmai, truly. If I've understood you, you've seen something of – God, this sounds frightful – something of the same sort of quality in me. Oh, darling, don't see *too* much of that in me. Just because I don't get tight and talk bawdy, I'm not a blooming Galahad, you know. This letter's going all the wrong way. Bless you a thousand, thousand – " I think that's the lot, sir,' concluded Fox.

'Yes. I see. Any letters in Pilgrim's room?'

'None. He may have taken them to Ankerton Manor, chief.'

'So he may. I'd like to see the one where Miss Seacliff praised his purity. By the Lord, Fox, she has without a doubt got a wonderful technique. She's got that not undesirable party, who'll be a perfectly good peer before very long, if it's true that old Pilgrim is failing; she's got him all besotted and wondering if he's good enough.' Alleyn paused and rubbed his nose. 'Men turn peculiar when they fall in love, Brer Fox. Sometimes they turn damned peculiar, and that's a fact.'

'These letters,' said Fox, tapping them with a stubby forefinger, 'were all written before they came down here. They've evidently been engaged in a manner of speaking for about a month.'

'Very possibly.'

'Well,' said Fox, 'there's nothing in these letters of Mr Pilgrim's to contradict any ideas we may have about Garcia, is there?'

'Nothing. What about Pilgrim's clothes?'

'Nothing there. Two overcoats, five suits, two pairs of odd trousers and an odd jacket. Nothing much in the pockets. His weekend suitcase hasn't been unpacked. He took a dinner suit, a tweed suit, pyjamas, dressing-gown, and toilet things.'

'Any aspirin?'

'No.'

'I fancy I found his bottle in one of Miss Seacliff's pockets. Come on. Let's get on with it.'

They got on with it. Presently Bailey said: 'Here's one from Garcia.'

'Let me see, will you?'

Like the note to Sonia, this was written in pencil on an odd scrap of paper. It was not dated or addressed, and the envelope was missing.

Dear Valmai,

I hear you're going to Troy's this term. So am I. I'm broke. I haven't got the price of the fare down, and I want one or two things – paints mostly. I'm going to paint for a bit. I took the liberty of going into Gibson's, and getting a few things on your account. I told old Gibson it would be all right, and he'd seen me in the shop with you, so it was. Do you think Basil Pilgrim would lend me a fiver? Or would you? I'll be OK when Troy gets back, and I've got a good commission, so the money's all right. If I don't hear from you, I'll ask Pilgrim. I can't think of anyone else. Is it true you're going to hitch up with Pilgrim? You'd much better try a spot of free love with me. – G.

'Cool,' said Fox.

'Does this bloke live on women?' asked Bailey.

'He lives on anyone that will provide the needful, I'd say,' grunted Fox.

'That's about it,' said Alleyn. 'We'll keep this and any other Garcia letters we find, Fox. Well, that's all, isn't it? Either of you got any more tender missives? All right then, we'll pack up. Fox, you might tell them all they may turn in now. My compliments and so on. Miss Troy has gone to her room. The others, I suppose, will still be in the dining-room. Come on, Bathgate.'

A few minutes later they all met in the hall. Tatler's End House was quiet at last. The fires had died down in all the grates, the rooms had grown cold. Up and down the passages the silence was broken only by the secret sounds made by an old house at night, small expanding noises, furtive little creaks, and an occasional slow whisper as though the house sighed at the iniquity of living men. Alleyn had a last look round and spoke to the local man who was to remain on duty in the hall. Bailey opened the door and Fox turned out the last of the lights. Nigel, huddled in an overcoat, stowed his copy away in a pocket and lit a cigarette. Alleyn stood at the foot of the stairs, his face raised, as if he listened for something.

'Right, sir?' asked Fox.

'Coming,' said Alleyn. 'Good night.'

'Good night, sir,' said the local man.

'By the way – where's the garage?'

'Round the house to the right, sir.'

'Thank you. Good night.'

The front door slammed behind them.

'Blast that fellow!' said Alleyn. 'Why the devil must he wake the entire household?'

It was a still, cold night, with no moon. The gravel crunched loudly under their feet.

'I'm just going to have a look at the garage,' said Alleyn. 'I've got the key from a nail in the lobby. I won't be long. Give me my case, Bailey. Bathgate – you drive on.'

He switched on his torch and followed the drive round the house to an old stables-yard. The four loose-boxes had been converted into garages, and his key fitted all of them. He found an Austin, and a smart supercharged sports car – 'Pilgrim's,' thought Alleyn – and in the last garage a small motor caravan. Alleyn muttered when

694

he saw this. He examined the tyre-treads, measured the distance between the wheels and took the height from the ground to the rear doorstep. He opened the door and climbed in. He found a small lamp on a battery in the ceiling, and swtiched it on. It was not an elaborate interior, but it was well planned. There were two bunks, a folding table, a cupboard and plenty of lockers. He looked into the lockers and found painting gear and one or two canvases. He took one out. 'Troy's,' he said. He began to look very closely at the board floor. On the doorstep he found two dark indentations. They were shiny and looked as though they had been made by small wheels carrying a heavy load. The door opened outwards. Its inner surface had been recently scored across. Alleyn looked through a lens at the scratches. The paint had frilled up a little and the marks were clean. The floor itself bore traces of the shiny tracks, but here they were much fainter. He looked at the petrol gauge and found it registered only two gallons. He returned to the floor and crawled over it with his torch. At last he came upon a few traces of a greenish-grey substance. These he scraped off delicately and put in a small tin. He went into the driver's cabin, taking an insufflator with him, and tested the wheel. It showed no clear prints. On the floor of the cabin Alleyn found several Player's cigarette-butts. These he collected and examined carefully. The ray from his torch showed him a tiny white object that had dropped into the gear-change slot. He fished it out with a pair of tweezers. It was the remains of yet another cigarette and had got jammed and stuck to the inside of the slot. A fragment of red paper was mixed with the flattened wad of tobacco strands. One of Troy's, perhaps. An old one. He had returned to the door with his insufflator, when a deep voice said:

'Have they remembered your hot-water bottle, sir, and what time would you wish to be called?'

'Fox!' said Alleyn, 'I am sorry. Have I been very long?'

'Oh no, sir. Bert Bailey's in his beauty sleep in the

back of our car, and Mr Bathgate has gone off in his to her ladyship's. Mr Bathgate asked me to tell you, sir, that he proposed to make the telephone wires burn while the going was good.'

'I'd like to see him try. Fox, we'll seal up this caravan and then we really will go home. Look here, you send Bailey back to London and stay the night with us. My mother will be delighted. I'll lend you some pyjamas, and we'll snatch a few hours' sleep and start early in the morning. Do come.'

'Well, sir, that's very kind of you. I'd be very pleased.'

'Splendid!'

Alleyn sealed the caravan door with tape, and then the door of the garage. He put the key in his pocket.

'No little jaunts for them tomorrow,' he said coolly. 'Come along, Fox. Golly, it's cold.'

They saw Bailey, arranged to meet him at the Yard in the morning, and drove back to Danes Lodge.

'We'll have a drink before we turn in,' said Alleyn softly, when they were indoors. 'In here.'

Fox tiptoed after him towards Lady Alleyn's boudoir. At the door they paused and looked at each other. A low murmur of voices came from the room beyond.

'Well, I'll be damned,' said Alleyn, and walked in.

A large fire crackled in the open fireplace. Nigel sat before it cross-legged on the hearthrug. Curled up in a wing-backed chair was Lady Alleyn. She wore a blue dressing-gown and a lace cap and her feet were tucked under her.

'Ma'am!' said Alleyn.

'Hullo, darling! Mr Bathgate's been telling me all about your case. It's wonderfully interesting, and we have already solved it in three separate ways.'

She looked round the corner of her chair and saw Fox.

'This is disgraceful,' said Alleyn. 'A scene of license and depravity. May I introduce Mr Fox, and will you give him a bed?'

'Of course I will. This is perfectly delightful. How do you do, Mr Fox?'

Fox made his best bow and took the small, thin hand in his enormous fist.

'How d'you do, my lady?' he said gravely. 'It's very kind of you.'

'Roderick, bring up some chairs, darling, and get yourselves drinks. Mr Bathgate is drinking whisky, and I am drinking port. It's not a bit kind of me, Mr Fox. I have hoped so much that we might meet. Do you know, you look exactly as I have always thought you would look, and that is very flattering to me and to you. Roderick has told me so much about you. You've worked together on very many cases, haven't you?'

'A good many, my lady,' said Fox. He sat down and contemplated Lady Alleyn placidly. 'It's been a very pleasant association for me. Very pleasant. We're all glad to see Mr Alleyn back.'

'Whisky and soda, Fox?' said Alleyn. 'Mamma, what will happen to your bright eyes if you swill port at one a.m.? Bathgate?'

'I've got one, thank you. Alleyn, your mother is quite convinced that Garcia is not the murderer.'

'No,' said Lady Alleyn. 'I don't say he *isn't* the murderer, but I don't think he's the man you're after.'

'That's a bit baffling of you,' said Alleyn. 'How d'you mean?'

'I think he's been made a cat's-paw by somebody. Probably that very disagreeable young man with a beard. From what Mr Bathgate tells me – '

'I should be interested to know what Bathgate has told you.'

'Don't be acid, darling. He's given me a perfectly splendid account of the whole thing – as lucid as Lucy Lorrimer,' said Lady Alleyn.

'Who's Lucy Lorrimer?' asked Nigel.

'She's a prehistoric peep. Old Lord Banff's eldest girl she was, and never known to finish a sentence. She always

697

got lost in the thickets of secondary thoughts that sprang up round her simplest remarks, so everybody used to say "as lucid as Lucy Lorrimer." No, but really, Roderick, Mr Bathgate was as clear as glass over the whole affair. I am absolutely *au fait*, and I feel convinced that Garcia has been a cat's-paw. He sounds so unattractive, poor fellow.'

'Homicides are inclined to be unattractive, darling,' said Alleyn.

'What about Mr Smith? George Joseph? You can't say that of *him* with all those wives. The thing that makes me so cross with Mr Smith,' continued Lady Alleyn, turning to Fox, 'is his monotony. Always in the bath and always a pound of tomatoes. In and out of season, one supposes.'

'If we consider Mr Malmsley, Lady Alleyn,' said Fox with perfect gravity, 'his only motive, as far as we know, would be vanity.'

'And a very good motive, too, Mr Fox. Mr Bathgate tells me Malmsley is an extremely affected and conceited young man. No doubt this poor murdered child threatened him with exposure. No doubt she said she would make a laughing-stock of him by telling everybody that he cribbed his illustration from Pol de Limbourge. I must say, Roderick, he showed exquisite taste. It is the most charming little picture imaginable. Do you remember we saw it at Chantilly?'

'I do, but I'm ashamed to say that I didn't at first spot it when I looked at his drawing.'

'That was rather slow of you, darling. Too gay and charming for words. Well, Mr Fox, suppose this young Malmsley deliberately stayed behind on Friday, deliberately gave Garcia opium, deliberately egged him on to set the trap, and then came away, hoping that Garcia would do it. How about that?'

'You put it very neatly indeed, my lady,' said Fox, looking at Lady Alleyn with serious approval. 'May I relieve you of your glass?'

'Thank you. Well now, Roderick, what about Basil Pilgrim?'

'What about him, little mum?'

'Of course, *he* might easily be unbalanced. Robert Pilgrim is as mad as a March Hare, and I think that unfortunate wife of his was a cousin of sorts, so there you are. And she simply set to work and had baby after baby after baby – all gels, poor thing – until she had this boy Basil, and died of exhaustion. Not a very good beginning. And Robert turned into a Primitive Methodist in the middle of it all, and used to ask everybody the most ill-judged questions about their private lives. I remember quite well when this boy was born, Roderick, your father said Robert's methods had been too primitive for Alberta. Her name was Alberta. Do you think the boy could have had anything to do with this affair?'

'Has Bathgate told you all about our interview with Pilgrim?' asked Alleyn.

'He was in the middle of it when you came in. What sort of boy has he grown into? Not like Robert, I hope?'

'Not very. He's most violently in love.'

'With this Seacliff gel. What kind of gel is she, Roderick? Modern and hard? Mr Bathgate says beautiful.'

'She's very good-looking and bit of a huntress.'

'At all murderish, do you imagine?'

'Darling, I don't know. Do you realize you ought to be in bed, and that you've led Bathgate into the father and mother of a row for talking out of school?'

'Mr Bathgate knows I'm as safe as the Roman Wall, don't you, Mr Bathgate?'

'I'm so much in love with you, Lady Alleyn,' said Nigel, 'that I wouldn't care if you were the soul of indiscretion. I should still open my heart to you.'

'There now, Roderick,' said his mother, '*isn't* that charming? I think perhaps I will go to bed.'

Ten minutes later, Alleyn tapped on his mother's door. The familiar, high-pitched voiced called: 'Come in, darling,' and he found Lady Alleyn sitting bolt upright in her bed, a book in her hand, and spectacles on her nose.

'You look like a miniature owl,' said Alleyn, and sat on the bed.

'Are they tucked away comfortably?'

'They are. Both besotted with adoration of you.'

'Darling! Did I show off?'

'Shamelessly.'

'I do *like* your Mr Fox, Roderick.'

'Isn't he splendid? Mum – '

'Yes, darling?'

'This is a tricky business.'

'I suppose so. How is she?'

'Who?'

'Don't be affected, Roderick.'

'We had two minor rows and one major one. I forgot my manners.'

'You shouldn't do that. I don't know, though. Perhaps you should. Who do you think committed this horrible crime, my dear?'

'Garcia.'

'Because he was drugged?'

'I don't know. You won't say anything about – '

'Now, Roderick!'

'I know you won't.'

'Did you give her my invitation?'

'Unfortunately we were not on them terms. I'll be up betimes in the morning.'

'Give me a kiss, Rory. Bless you, dear. Good night.'

'Good night, little mum.'

Chapter 14

Evidence from a Twig

Alleyn and Fox were back at Tatler's End House at seven o'clock in the thin chilly light of dawn. A thread of smoke rose from one of the chimneys. The ground was hard and the naked trees, fast, fast asleep, stretched their lovely arms against an iron sky. The air was cold and smelt of rain. The two men went straight to the studio, where they found a local constable, wrapped in his overcoat, and very glad to see them.

'How long have you been here?' asked Alleyn.

'Since ten o'clock last night, sir. I'll be relieved fairly soon – eight o'clock with any luck.'

'You can go off now. We'll be here until then. Tell Superintendent Blackman I said it was all right.'

'Thank you very much, sir. I think I'll go straight home. Unless – '

'Yes?'

'Well, sir, if you're going to work here, I'd like to look on – if it's not a liberty, sir.'

'Stay, by all means. What's your name?'

'Sligo, sir.'

'Right. Keep your counsel about our business. No need to tell you that. Come along.'

Alleyn led them to the studio window. He released the blind and opened the window. The ledge outside was rimy with frost.

'Last night,' said Alleyn, 'we noticed certain marks on this window-sill. Look first of all at the top of the stool here. You see four marks – indentations in the surface?'

'Yes, sir.'

'We're going to measure them.'

Alleyn produced a thin steel tape and measured the

701

distance between the indentations. Fox wrote the figure in his notebook.

'Now the window-sill. You see these marks?' He pointed to two lateral marks, shiny and well defined, like shallow grooves. Alleyn measured the distance between them and found that it corresponded exactly with the previous figure. The width of the marks, the depth, and the appearance were the same as those on the stool.

'Garcia had his model on a small wheeled platform,' said Alleyn. 'Now, Malmsley told us that Garcia proposed to wheel the model into the case and then put the whole thing on board whatever vehicle called to collect it. I think he changed his mind. I think he put the empty crate in the vehicle, drew the stool up to the sill, and wheeled the model over the sill into the crate, and aboard the caravan which was backed up to the window in the lane outside.'

'The caravan, sir?' asked Sligo. 'Was it a caravan?'

'Lock this place up and come along outside. You can get over the sill, but don't touch those two marks just yet. Jump well out to the side and away from the tyre-tracks.'

In the lane Alleyn showed them the traces left by the wheels. They had been frozen hard.

'Bailey has taken casts of these, but I want you to note them carefully. You see at once that the driver of the van or whatever it was did a good deal of skirmishing about. If there were any footprints within twelve feet of the window, they've been obliterated. Farther out are traces of the mortuary van, blast it. The caravan tracks overlap, and there are four sets of them. But if you look carefully, you can pick out the last impression on top of all the others. That's when the van was finally driven away. The next set, overlaid by these, represents the final effort to get in close to the window. Damn! It's beginning to rain. This will be our last chance in the lane, so let's make the most of it. Observe the tread, Sligo. There, you see, is the clear impression of a patch. I'll measure the distance between the wheels and the width of the tyres. There a little oil has dripped on the road. The van or whatever it is has been recently greased. It was backed in and the brakes jammed on suddenly, but not quite suddenly enough. The outer edge of the window-sill has had a knock. The front wheels were turned after the vehicle had stopped. There are the marks. From them we get the approximate length of the wheel-base. Out in the middle lane they disappear under the tracks of more recent traffic. Now look at the branches of that elm. They reach across the lane almost to our side, and are very low. I wonder the county councillors have not lopped them down. Do you see that one or two twigs have been snapped off? There's been no wind, and the breaks are quite recent. See here!'

He stopped and picked up a broken twig.

'It is still sappy. There are several. One quite close to the studio wall, and there's another across the lane. If it should happen they were snapped off by the top of a vehicle, it must have moved from one side to the other. It is a fair chance, isn't it, that they were broken by our van, and, if this is so, they give an idea of its height. Right?'

'That's right, sir,' said Mr Sligo, breathing loudly through his nostrils.

'You know all this sort of stuff, of course,' said Alleyn, 'but it's a characteristic example of outside work. Now come along to the garage.'

They walked along the lane through a wide entrance into the garage yard. Alleyn unlocked the garage doors and broke the police tape. It had begun to rain steadily.

'I took some measurements here last night, but it would be as well to verify them. Suppose you have a stab at it, Sligo.'

Sligo, intensely gratified, measured the width of the tyres and the wheel-base.

'The tyres are the same, sir. Look here, sir, here's the patch on the rear tyre on the driving side. We found the trace on the left-hand as you faced the window, sir, so she was backed all right.'

'Good,' said Alleyn. 'That's the way, Sligo. Now take a look at the doorstep. Wait a moment. I'll just have a go at the handle for prints.'

He opened his bag and got out his insufflator. The grey powder showed no prints on the door or door-knob. Alleyn closely examined the three steps, which were worn and dirty.

'Don't touch these,' he said, and opened the door.

'Now then, Sligo – '

'There they are, sir, there they are. Same marks on the top step. That's the marks of them little wheels, sir, isn't it?'

'I think so. Check them to make sure. Here are the measurements of the scars on the window-sill.'

Out came Sligo's tape again.

'It's them for sure,' he said.

'Now have a look on the roof. If you climb on that bench, you'll do no harm. Go carefully, though. You never know if you won't spoil a perfectly good bit of evidence in the most unlikely spot.'

Sligo mounted the bench like a mammoth Agag, and peered over the roof of the caravan.

'Eh, there's a-plenty of scratches, sir, right enough, and Gor', Mr Alleyn, there's a bit of a twig jammed between the top roofing and the frame. Dug into the crack. Gor', that's a bit of all right, isn't it, sir?'

'It is indeed. Can you reach it?'

'Yes, sir.'

'Take these tweezers and draw it out carefully. That's right. Now you can come down. Let's have an envelope, Fox, may we? We'll put your twig in there, Sligo, and label it. How far is it from here to London?'

'Twenty miles exactly, sir, to the end of the drive from Shepherd's Bush,' answered Sligo promptly.

'Right!'

Alleyn packed his case and began with Fox and Sligo to examine the yard and the gateway into the lane.

'Here are the tracks clear enough in the lane,' said Fox. 'We've got enough here and more to show this caravan was driven into the lane, backed up to the studio window and loaded up through the window. Who does the caravan belong to?'

'Miss Troy, I think,' said Alleyn.

'Is that so?' responded Fox, without any particular emphasis.

'We'll find out presently. Seal the garage up again, will you, Fox? Blast this weather. We'd better have a look at Pilgrim's car.'

Basil Pilgrim's car was a very smart supercharged two-seater. The upholstery smelt definitely of Valmai Seacliff, and one of the side-pockets contained an elaborate set of cosmetics. 'For running repairs,' grunted Alleyn. They opened the dicky and found a man's rather shabby raincoat. Pilgrim's. 'Also for running repairs, I should think.' Alleyn examined it carefully, and sniffed at it. 'Very powerful scent that young woman uses. I fancy, Fox, that this is the pure young man's garment for changing wheels and delving in engines. Now then, Sligo, you have a look at this. It's ideal for demonstration purposes – the sort of thing Holmes and Thorndyke read like a book. Do you know Holmes and Thorndyke? You should. How about giving me a running commentary on an old raincoat?'

Sligo, breathing noisily, took the coat in his enormous hands.

'Go on,' said Alleyn; 'you're a Yard man, and I'm taking notes for you.'

'It's a man's mackintosh,' began Sligo. 'Made by Burberry. Marked "B. Pilgrim" inside collar. It's mucked up like and stained. Inside of collar a bit greasy, and it's got white marks, too, on it. Grease on one sleeve. That's car grease, I reckon, and there's marks down front. Pockets. Right-hand: A pair of old gloves used, likely, for changing

705

tyres. There's other marks, too. Reckon he's done something to battery some time.'

'Well done,' said Alleyn. 'Go on.'

Sligo turned the gloves inside out.

'Left hand inside got small dark stain on edge of palm
under base of little finger. Left-hand pocket: Piece of
greasy rag. Box of matches.' Sligo turned the coat over
and over. 'I can't see nothing more, sir, except a bit of a
hole in right-hand cuff. Burnt by cigarette, likely. That's
all, sir.'

Alleyn shut his notebook.

'That's the method,' he said. 'But – ' He glanced at his
watch. 'Good Lord, it is eight o'clock. You'd better cut
back to the studio or your relief will be giving you a bad
mark.'

'Thank you very much, sir. I'm much obliged, sir. It's
been a fair treat.'

'That's all right. Away you go.'

Sligo pounded off.

Leaving Fox at the garage, Alleyn walked round the
house and rang the front-door bell. It was answered by a
constable.

'Good morning. Do you know if Miss Troy is down
yet?'

'She's in the library, sir.'

'Ask if I may see her for a moment.'

The man came back to say Troy would receive Alleyn,
and he went into the library. By daylight it was a pleasant
room, and already a fire blazed in the open grate. Troy,
in slacks and a pullover, looked so much as she did on
that first morning at Suva that Alleyn felt for a moment
as if there had been nothing between them but the first
little shock of meeting. Then he saw that she looked as
if she had not slept.

'You are early at your job,' said Troy.

'I'm very sorry, indeed, to worry you at the crack of
dawn. I want to ask you if the caravan in the garage
belongs to you.'

706

'Yes. Why?'

'When did you last use it, please?'

'About a fortnight ago. We all went out in it to Katts-wood for a picnic and a day's sketching.'

'Do you know how much petrol there was in the tank when you got back?'

'It must have been more than half full, I should think. I got it filled up when we started, and we only went about forty miles there and back.'

'What does she do to the gallon?'

'Twenty.'

'And the tank holds – ?'

'Eight gallons.'

'Yes. It's just over a quarter full this morning.'

Troy stared at him.

'There must be a leak in the petrol tank,' she said. 'I couldn't have used more than five that day – not possibly.'

'There isn't a leak,' said Alleyn. 'I looked.'

'Look here, what is all this?'

'You're sure no one else has used the caravan?'

'Of course I am. Not with my permission.' Troy seemed puzzled and worried. Then as her eyes widened, 'Garcia!' she cried out. 'You think Garcia took it, don't you?'

'What makes you so sure of that?'

'Why, because I've puzzled my own wits half the night to think how he got his stuff away. The superintendent here told me none of the local carriers knew anything about it. Of course Garcia took it! Just like him. Trust him not to pay a carrier if he could get his stuff there free.'

'Can he drive?'

'I really don't know. I shouldn't have thought so, cer-tainly. I suppose he must be able to drive if he took the caravan.' She paused and looked steadily at Alleyn.

'I know you think he went in the caravan,' she said.

'Yes, I do.'

'He must have brought it back that night,' said Troy.

'Couldn't have been some time on Saturday before you came back?'

'He didn't know when I was coming back. He wouldn't have risked my arriving early and finding the caravan gone. Besides, anyone might have seen him.'

'That's perfectly true,' said Alleyn.

'If this warehouse place is somewhere in London, he could do the trip easily if it was late at night, couldn't he?' asked Troy.

'Yes. Dear me, I shall have to do a sum. Wait a moment. Your car does twenty to the gallon, and holds eight gallons. You went forty miles, starting with a full tank. Therefore there should be six gallons, and there are only about three. That leaves a discrepancy of sixty miles or so. How fast can she go?'

'I suppose forty to forty-five or fifty if pressed. She's elderly and not meant for Brooklands.'

'I know. I do wish he'd told one of you where this damned warehouse was.'

'But he did. At least, Seacliff said this morning she thought she remembered he said something about it being near Holloway.'

'Good Lord, why didn't she say so last night?'

'Why does she always behave in the most tiresome manner one could possibly conceive? I'm nearly as bad, not to have told you at once.'

'You're nothing like as bad. How did Miss Seacliff happen to remember Holloway?'

'It was at breakfast, which, I may tell you, was not a very sparkling event this morning. Phillida Lee would talk about every murder story she has ever read, and Hatchett was more bumptious than words can describe. At last the Lee child remarked that if a woman was convicted of murder, she was hanged at Holloway, and Seacliff suddenly exclaimed: "Holloway – that's it – that's where Garcia's warehouse is; he said something about it when he first came down." '

'Is she sure?'

'She seems to be fairly certain. Shall I send for her?'

'Would you?'

Troy rang the bell, which was answered by Hipkin, a large man with a small head and flat feet.

'Ask Miss Seacliff if she'll come and see me.'

Seacliff strolled in, dressed in black trousers and a magenta sweater. She looked very lovely.

'Good morning, Miss Seacliff,' said Alleyn cheerfully. 'Are you recovered?'

'Why, what was the matter with *you?*' Troy asked her.

Seacliff glared at Alleyn with positive hatred.

'Miss Seacliff was indisposed last night,' said Alleyn.

'What was the matter?'

'Nerves,' said Seacliff.

'Was it *you* who was sick in the downstairs bathroom?' demanded Troy with an air of sudden enlightenment. 'Sadie was furious at having to clear up. She said – '

'Need we discuss it, Troy? I'm really terribly upset.'

'You must have been,' agreed Troy, with a suspicion of a grin. 'I must say I think you might have cleared up after yourself. Sadie said she thought at least three men – '

'Troy!'

'All right. Do you want to be alone, Mr Alleyn?'

'No, no. I just wanted to ask Miss Seacliff about this Holloway business.'

'Oh,' said Seacliff. 'You mean the place where Garcia is going to sculp?'

'Yes. Did he tell you it was somewhere near Holloway?'

'Yes, he did. I'd forgotten. I suppose you are furious with me?' She smiled at Alleyn. Her glance said, very plainly: 'After all, you are rather good-looking.'

'I'd like to know exactly what he said, if you can remember the conversation.'

'I suppose I can remember a good deal of it if I try. It took place during one of his periodical attempts to make a pass or two at me. He asked me if I would come and see him while he was working. I forget what I said. Oh,

I think I said I would if it wasn't too drearily far away or something. Then he said it was near Holloway, because I remember I asked him if he thought he'd be safe. I said I knew better than to spend an afternoon with him in a deserted studio, but I might get Basil to drive me there, and, of course, that made him quite livid with rage. However, he told me how to get there and drew a sort of map. I'm afraid I've lost it. As a matter of fact, I would rather like to see that thing, wouldn't you, Troy? Still, as long as he's not arrested or something, I suppose we shall see it in its proper setting. I told Garcia I thought it was a bit of a come-down to take a commission from a flick-shop. I said they'd probably ask him to put touches of gilt on the breasts and flood it with pink lights. He turned as acid as a lemon and said the surroundings were to be appropriate. He's got absolutely no sense of humour, of course.'

'Did he tell you exactly where it was?'

'Oh, yes. He drew up the map, but I can't remember anything but Holloway.'

'Not even the name of the street?' asked Alleyn resignedly.

'I don't think so. He must have mentioned it and marked it down, but I don't suppose I'd ever remember it,' said Seacliff, with maddening complacency.

'Then I think that's all, thank you, Miss Seacliff.'

She got up, frowned, and closed her eyes for a moment.

'What's the matter?' asked Troy.

'I've got another of these filthy headaches.'

'Carry-over, perhaps.'

'No, it's not. I've been getting them lately.'

'You're looking a bit white,' said Troy, more kindly. 'Why don't you lie down? Would you like some aspirin?'

'Basil gave me his last night, thanks.' She took out her mirror and looked at herself with intense concentration.

'I look bloody,' she said, and walked out of the room.

'Is she always like that?' asked Alleyn.

'Pretty much. She's spoilt. She'd have been

710

comparatively easy to live with if she hadn't got that lovely face. She *is* beautiful, you know.'

'Oh! magnificent,' agreed Alleyn absently.

He was looking at Troy, at the delicate sparseness of her head, the straight line of her brows and the generous width between her grey-green eyes.

'Are you very tired?' he asked gently.

'Who, me? I'm all right.' She sat on the fender holding her thin hands to the fire. 'Only I can't get it out of my head.'

'Small wonder,' said Alleyn, and to himself he thought: 'She's treating me more like a friend this morning. Touch wood.'

'Oddly enough, it's not so much Sonia, poor little thing, but Garcia, that I can't get out of my head. You needn't bother to be mysterious and taciturn. I know you must suspect Garcia after what Phillida Lee and Malmsley said last night. But you see, in a way, Garcia's a sort of protégé of mine. He came to me when he was almost literally starving, and I've tried to look after him a bit. I know he's got no conscience at all in the usual sort of way. He's what they call un-moral. But he has got genius and I never use that word if I can get out of it. He couldn't *do* a shabby thing with clay. Wait a moment.'

She went out of the room for a few minutes. When she returned she carried a small bronze head, about half life-size, of an old woman. Troy put the head on a low table and pulled back the curtains. The cold light flooded the little bronze. It looked very tranquil and pure; its simple forms folded it into a great dignity. The lights shone austerely and the shadows seemed to breathe.

' "All passion spent," ' said Alleyn after a short pause.

'That's it,' agreed Troy. She touched it delicately with a long finger. 'Garcia gave me this,' she said.

'It wouldn't be too florid to say it looked as if it had been done by an inspired saint.'

'Well – it wasn't. It was done by a lecherous, thieving little guttersnipe who happens to be a superb craftsman.

711

But – ' Troy's voice wavered. 'To catch and hang the man who made it – '

'God – yes, I know – I know.' He got up and moved restlessly about the room, returning to her.

'Oh, Troy, you mustn't cry,' he said.

'What the devil's it got to do with you?'

'Nothing, nothing, nothing, and don't I know it!'

'You'd better get on with your job,' said Troy. She looked like a boy with her head turned shamefacedly away. She groped in her trousers pocket and pulled out a handkerchief disgracefully stained with paint. 'Oh blast!' she said, and pitched it into the waste-paper basket.

'Have mine.'

'Thank you.'

Alleyn turned away from her and leant his arms on the mantelpiece. Troy blew her nose violently.

'My mother's so happy about my picture,' said Alleyn to the fire. 'She says it's the best present she's ever had. She said, if you'll forgive the implication, that you must know all about the subject. I suppose that's the sort of lay remark that is rather irritating to a craftsman for whom the model must be a collection of forms rather than an individual.'

'Bosh!' said Troy down her nose and behind his handkerchief.

'Is it? I'm always terrified of being highfalutin about pictures. The sort of person, you know, who says: "The eyes follow you all round the room." It would be so remarkably rum if they didn't when the model has looked into the painter's eyes, wouldn't it? I told my mamma about the thing you did at Suva. She rather fancies her little self about pictures. I think her aesthetic taste is pretty sound. Do you know she remembered the Pol de Limbourge thing that Malmsley cribbed, for one of his illustrations.'

'What!' exclaimed Troy loudly.

'Didn't you spot it?' asked Alleyn, without turning. 'That's one up to the Alleyn family, isn't it? The drawing of the three little medieval reapers in front of the château; it's Sainte Chapelle, really, I think – do you remember?'

'Golly, I believe you're right,' said Troy. She gave a dry sob, blew her nose again, and said: 'Are there any cigarettes on the mantelpiece?'

Alleyn gave her a cigarette and lit it for her. When he saw her face, marred by tears, he wanted almost overwhelmingly to kiss it.

'Little serpent!' said Troy.

'Who – Malmsley?'

'Yes. Malmsley of all people, with his beard and his precicosity.'

'There's no such word as precicosity.'

'There may be.'

'It's preciosity if it's anything.'

'Well, don't be a scold,' said Troy. 'Did you face Malmsley with this?'

'Yes. He turned as red as a rose.'

Troy laughed.

'What a doody-flop for Cedric,' she said.

'I must get on with my odious job,' said Alleyn. 'May I use your telephone?'

'Yes, of course. There'll be an inquest, won't there?'

'Tomorrow, I think. It won't be so bad. Goodbye.'

'Goodbye.'

He turned at the doorway and said: 'Lady Alleyn's compliments to Miss Troy, and if Miss Troy would like to sample the amenities of Danes Lodge, Lady Alleyn will be very happy to offer them.'

'Your mother is very kind,' said Troy, 'but I think it would be better not. Will you thank her from me? Please say I am very grateful indeed.'

Alleyn bowed.

'I'm grateful to you too,' said Troy.

'Are you? That is rather dangerously nice of you. Goodbye.'

Chapter 15

Lady of the Ensemble

Before he left Tatler's End House Alleyn rang up Superintendent Blackman and asked if there was any news of Garcia. There was none. A discreetly-worded notice had appeared in the morning papers and the B.B.C. had instructions to send out a police message. The police, within a fifty-mile radius, had made intensive inquiries.

'It looks as if he didn't want to be found, Mr Alleyn. The weather's been fine and if he'd sketched as he said he intended to do, he wouldn't have gone far in two days. It looks to me as if the bird had flown.'

'It does a bit. Of course, he might have changed his plans and taken a train or bus. We'll have to get on to the railway stations. All that deadly game. Thanks so much, Mr Blackman. I'll let you know if there are any developments. Inquest tomorrow?'

'No, Thursday. Our gentleman's full up tomorrow. Bossicote Town Hall at eleven. He's a sensible sort of chap, our man.'

'Good. I'll call on the C.C. this morning, before I go up to London.

'Just as well. He likes to be consulted.'

'What about the post-mortem?'

'I wanted to let you know. She was going to have a child. About a month gone, the doctor says.'

'I thought as much. Look here, I think I'll get straight up to London. Make my apologies to the Chief Constable, will you? I want to catch a friend of Sonia Gluck's, and I can't risk missing her.'

'Right you are. He'll understand. So long. See you on Thursday.'

Alleyn found Fox, who had renewed his acquaintance

with the Hipkins and Sadie, and drove him back through teeming rain to Danes Lodge for breakfast.

'I've had a bit of a yarn with Ethel Jones,' said Fox.

'Ethel? Oh yes, the help from the village. What had she got to say for herself?'

'Quite a bit,' said Fox. He opened his notebook and put on his spectacles.

'You're looking very bland, Brer Fox. What have you got on to?'

'Well, sir, it seems that Ethel and her boy took a walk on Friday night down the lane. They passed by the studio window on their way home from the pictures at about eleven-thirty, perhaps a bit later. There were lights going in the studio but the blind was down. They walked straight past, but when they'd gone a piece further down the lane they stopped in the shadow of the trees to have a bit of a cuddle as you might put it. Ethel doesn't know how long it lasted. She says you're apt to lose your idea of time on these occasions, but when they got back to earth and thought about moving on, she glanced down the lane and saw someone outside the studio window.'

'Did she, by gum! Go on, Fox!'

'Well, sir, she couldn't see him very distinctly.'

'Him?'

'Yes. She says she could just see it was a man, and he seemed to be wearing a raincoat, and a cap or beret of some sort. He was standing quite close to the window, Ethel reckons, and was caught by a streak of light coming through the blind. I asked her about the face, of course, but she says it was in shadow. She remembers that there was a small patch of light on the cap.'

'There's a hole in the blind,' said Alleyn.

'Is that so, sir? That might account for it, then. Ethel says the rest of the figure was in shadow. The collar of his raincoat was turned up and she thinks his hands were in his pockets.'

'What height?'

'About medium, Ethel thought, but you know how

715

vague they are. She said to her boy: 'Look, there's some-one down the lane. They must have seen us,' and I sup-pose she gave a bit of a giggle, like a girl would.'

'You ought to know.'

'Why not, sir? Then, she says, the man turned aside and disappeared into the darker shadow and they could just hear his footfall as he walked away. Well, I went into the lane to see if I could pick up his prints, but you've been there and you know there wasn't much to be seen near the window, except the tyre-tracks where the caravan had been manoeuvred about. When you get away from the window and out into the lane there are any number of them, but there's been people and cars up and down during the weekend, and there's not much hope of picking up anything definite.'

'No.'

'I've looked carefully and I can't find anything. It's different with the car traces under the window. They're off the beaten track, but this downpour about finishes the lane as far as we're concerned.'

'I know.'

'Well, we got a description of Garcia last night, of course, but to make sure, I asked the Hipkins and Sadie and Ethel to repeat it. They gave the same story. He always wears a very old mackintosh, whether it's wet or fine, and it's their belief he hasn't got a jacket. Miss Troy gave him a grey sweater and he wears that with a pair of old flannel trousers. Mrs Hipkin says Miss Troy had given him two shirts and Mr Pilgrim gave him some under-clothes. He doesn't often wear anything on his head, but they have seen him in a black beret. Sadie says he looks as rough as bags. Ethel said straight out that she thought the figure outside the window was Garcia. She said so to her boy. She says it was the dead spit of Garcia, but then, we've got to remember it wasn't at all distinct, and she may think differently now that she knows Garcia has gone. You know how they make up all sorts of things without scarcely knowing what they're up to.'

'I do indeed. Had this figure by the window anything on its back – like a rucksack, for instance?'

'They say he hadn't, but of course, if it was Garcia, he might not have picked up his gear when they saw him.'

'No.'

'I look at it this way. He might have gone through the window to take a short cut to the garage by way of the lane, and he might have stood there, having a last look at the arrangement on the model's throne.'

'Through the hole in the blind? Rather a sinister picture, Fox. Wouldn't they have heard him open the window?'

'Um,' said Fox.

'It makes a fair amount of noise.'

'Yes. Yes, that's so.'

'Anything else?'

'No. They ambled off home. Hullo, sir, what's up?'

Alleyn had pulled up and now began to turn the car in the narrow lane.

'Sorry, Fox, but we're going back to have a look at the hole in the blind.'

And back to the studio they went. Alleyn measured the distance from the window-sill to the hole – a triangular tear, of which the flap had been turned back. He also measured the height of the lamps from the floor. He climbed on Fox's shoulders and tied a thread to the light nearest the window. He stretched the thread to the hole in the blind. Fox stood outside in the pouring rain. Alleyn threw the window up, passed the thread through the hole to Fox, who drew it tight and held it against his diaphragm.

'You see?' said Alleyn.

'Yes,' said Fox, 'I'm six foot two in my socks and it hits me somewhere – let's see – '

'About the end of the sternum.'

'That's right, sir.'

'Good enough, but we'll take a look at night. Let's go and have breakfast.'

And a few minutes later they joined Nigel Bathgate at breakfast.

'You might have told me you were going out,' complained Nigel.

'I wouldn't dream of interrupting your beauty sleep,' said Alleyn. 'Where's my mamma?'

'She finished her breakfast some minutes ago. She asked me to tell you she would be in her workshop. She's going to weave me some tweed for a shooting jacket.'

'Divine creature, isn't she? What have you written for your paper?'

'I'll show you. I've left Miss Troy's name out altogether, Alleyn. They simply appear as a group of artists in a charming old-world house in Buckinghamshire.'

'I'll try to be a good godfather,' said Alleyn gruffly.

'Good enough,' said Nigel. 'Can I publish a picture of the girl?'

'Sonia? Yes, if you can rake one up. I can give you one of Garcia. Just talk about him as a very brilliant young sculptor, mention the job for the cinema if you like, and if you can manage it, suggest that we suspect the thing to be the work of some criminal lunatic who had got wind of the way the model was posed. Far-fetched, but I understand the tallest, the most preposterous tarradiddle will be gulped down whole by your public. You may even suggest that we have fears for Garcia's safety. Do anything but cast suspicion on him. Is all this quite impossible, Bathgate?'

'I don't *think* so,' said Nigel thoughtfully. 'It can be brought out with what I have already written. There's nothing in this morning's paper. That's an almost miraculous bit of luck. Blackman and Co. must have been extraordinarily discreet.'

'The hunt will be up and the murder out, at any moment now. Show me your stuff. We're for London in twenty minutes.'

'May I come with you? I've telephoned the office. I'll make a bit of an entrance with this story.'

Alleyn vetted the story and Nigel made a great to-do at each alteration, but more as a matter of routine than anything else. He then went to the telephone to ring up his office, and his Angela. Alleyn left Fox with the morning paper and ran upstairs to his mother's workshop. This was a large, sunny room, filled with what Lady Alleyn called her insurances against old age. An enormous hand-loom stood in the centre of the room. In the window was a bench for book-binding. On one wall hung a charming piece of tapestry worked by Lady Alleyn in a bout of enthusiasm for embroidery and on another wall was an oak shrine executed during a wave of intense wood-carving. She had made the rugs on the floor, she had woven the curtains on the walls, she had created the petit-point on the backs of the chairs, and she had done all these things extremely and surprisingly well.

At the moment she was seated before her hand-loom, sorting coloured wools. She looked solemn. Turnbridge Tessa, an Alsatian bitch, lay at her feet.

'Hullo, darling,' said Lady Alleyn. 'Do you think Mr Bathgate could wear green and red? His eyes are grey, of course. Perhaps grey and purple.'

'His eyes!'

'Don't be silly, Roderick. I've promised him some tweed. Yours is finished. It's in the chest over there. Go and look at it.'

'But – your dog!'

'What about her? She's obviously taken a fancy to you.'

'Do you think so? She certainly has had her eye on me.'

Alleyn went to the hand-carved chest, closely followed by Tunbridge Tessa. He found his tweed.

'But, darling, it really is quite amazingly good,' he said. 'I'm delighted with it.'

'Are you?' asked his mother a little anxiously.

'Indeed I am.'

'Well, your eyes are so blue it was easy for me. Mr Bathgate has told me all about the baby coming. We've had a lovely talk. How did you get on at Tatler's End House, Roderick?'

'Better, thank you. We're off now, darling. I hope I'm going to spend the rest of the morning in a chorus lady's bed-sit in Chelsea.'

'Are you?' said his mother vaguely. 'Why?'

'Routine.'

'It seems to lead you into strange places. I'll come downstairs and see you off. You may take the car, Roderick.'

'I wouldn't dream of it.'

'I've already told Finch to drive you in. I've a job for him in Sloane Street.'

When they were half-way downstairs she said:

'Roderick, shall I ring her up? Would you like me to ring her up?'

'Very much,' said Alleyn.

He collected Fox and Nigel. They wrote their names in Lady Alleyn's book.

'And you will come again whenever you like?' she said.

'That will be very soon, I'm afraid,' Nigel told her.

'Not too soon. What about Mr Fox?'

'It has been very pleasant indeed, my lady,' said Fox. He straightened up, pen in hand, and gravely unhooked his spectacles. 'I shall like to think about it. It's been quite different, you see, from my usual run of things. Quite an experience, you might say, and a very enjoyable one. If I may say so, you have a wonderful way with you, my lady. I felt at home.'

Alleyn abruptly took his arm.

'You see, ma'am,' he said, 'we have courtiers at the Yard.'

'Something a little better than that. Goodbye, my dear.'

In the car Alleyn and Fox thumbed over their note-books and occasionally exchanged remarks. Nigel, next the chauffeur, spent the time in pleasurable anticipation of his reception at the office. They cut through from Shepherd's Bush to Holland Road and thence into Chelsea. Alleyn gave the man directions which finally brought them into a narrow and not very smart cul-de-sac behind Smith Street.

'This is Batchelors Gardens,' said Alleyn. 'And there's No. 4. You can put me down here. If I don't come out in five minutes take Mr Fox to the Yard and Mr Bathgate to his office, will you, French? Goodbye, Bathgate. Meet you at the Yard somewhere round noon, Fox.'

He waved his hand and crossed the street to No. 4, a set of flats that only just escaped the appearance of a lodging-house. Alleyn inspected the row of yellowing cards inside the front door. Miss Bobbie O'Dawne's room was up two flights. He passed the inevitable charwoman with her bucket of oil and soot, and her obscene grey wiper so like a drowned rat.

'Good morning,' said Alleyn, 'is Miss O'Dawne at home, can you tell me?'

'At 'ome,' said the charlady, viciously wringing the neck of the rat. ''Er! She won't be out of 'er bed!'

'Thank you,' said Alleyn and tapped at Miss O'Dawne's door. He tapped three times, closely watched by the charlady, before a submerged voice called out: 'All *right*.' There were bumping noises, followed by the sound of bare feet on thin carpet. The voice, now much nearer, asked: 'Who is it?'

'May I speak to Miss O'Dawne?' called Alleyn. 'I've an important message for her.'

'For me?' said the voice in more refined accents. 'Wait a moment, please.'

He waited while the charlady absently swilled the rat round and round in the oil and soot before slopping it over the top stair. The door opened a few inches and then widely enough to admit the passage of a mop of sulphur-coloured curls and a not unattractive face.

'Oh,' said the face, 'pardon me, I'm afraid – '

'I'm sorry to disturb you so early,' said Alleyn, 'but I would be most grateful if you could see me for a moment.'

721

'I don't want anything,' said Miss O'Dawne dangerously.

'And I'm not selling anything,' smiled Alleyn.

'Sorry, I'm sure, but you never know, these days, do you, with 'varsity boys travelling in anything from vacuums to foundation garments.'

'It's about Sonia Gluck,' said Alleyn.

'Sonia? Are you a pal of hers? Why didn't you say so at first? Half a tick, and I'll get dressed. Pardon the stage-wait, but the lonely west wing's closed on account of the ghost, and the rest of the castle's a ruin.'

'Don't hurry,' said Alleyn, 'the morning's before us.'

'I'll say! Tell yourself stories and be good!'

The door slammed. Alleyn lit a cigarette. The charlady descended three steps backwards with a toad-like posture.

'Cold morning,' she said suddenly.

'Very cold,' agreed Alleyn, noticing with a pang that her old hands were purple.

'You a theatrical?'

'No, no. Nothing so interesting, I'm afraid.'

'Not a traveller neither?'

'No – not even a traveller.'

'You look too classy now I come to look atcher. I was in service for ten years.'

'Were you?'

'Yers. In service. Lidy by the name of Wells. Then she died of dibeets and I 'adter come down to daily. It's all right in service, you know. Comferble. Meals and that. Warm.'

'It's beastly to be cold,' said Alleyn.

'That's right,' she said dimly.

Alleyn felt unhappily in his pocket and she watched him. Inside the room Miss O'Dawne began to whistle. On the next landing a door banged, and a young man in a tight fitting royal blue suit tripped lightly downstairs, singing professionally. He had a good stare at Alleyn and said: ''Morning, ma! How's tricks?'

' 'Mornin', Mr Chumley.'

722

'Look out, now, I don't want to kick the bucket just yet.' He vaulted over the wet steps and disappeared in full voice.

''E's in the choreus,' said the charlady. 'They get a lot of money in the choreus.'

She had left her dustpan on the landing. Alleyn dropped his gloves, and as he stooped he put two half-crowns under the dustpan. He did it very neatly and quickly but not neatly enough, it seemed.

'Yer dropped some money, sir,' said the charlady avidly.

'That's – that's for you,' said Alleyn, and to his relief the door opened.

'Take your place in the queue and don't rush the ushers,' said Miss O'Dawne. Alleyn walked in.

Miss O'Dawne's bed-sitting room looked a little as if it had been suddenly slapped up and bounced into a semblance of tidiness. The cupboard doors had an air of pressure from within, the drawers looked as if they had been rammed home under protest, the divan-bed hunched its shoulders under a magenta artificial-silk counterpane. Two jade green cushions cowered against the wall at the head of the bed, the corner of a suit-case peeped out furtively from underneath. Miss O'Dawne herself was surprisingly neat. Her make-up suggested that she was a quick-change artist.

'Sit down,' she said, 'and make yourself at our place. It's not Buckingham Palace with knobs on, but you can't do much on chorus work and "Hullo, girls, have you heard the news?" Seen our show?'

'Not yet,' said Alleyn.

'I've got three lines in the last act and a kiss from Mr Henry Molyneux. His breath smells of whisky, carbide and onions, but it's great to be an actress. Well, how's tricks?'

'Not so wonderful,' said Alleyn, feeling for the right language.

723

'Cheer up, you'll soon be dead. I was going to make a cup of coffee. How does that strike you?'

'It sounds delightful,' said Alleyn.

'Well, we strive to please. Service with a smile. No charge and all questions answered by return in plain envelopes.'

She lit her gas-ring and clapped a saucepan over it.

'By the way, you haven't told me who you are.'

'My name's Roderick Alleyn, I'm afraid – '

'Roderick Alleyn? Sounds pretty good. You're not in the business, are you?'

'No, I'm – '

'Well, if you'll excuse my freshness you look a bit more Eton and Oxford than most of Sonia's boyfriends. Are you an artist?'

'No. I'm a policeman.'

'And then he came to. Is this where the big laugh comes, Roddy?'

'Honestly.'

'A policeman? Where's your make-up? Pass along there, please, pass along there. Go on, you're kidding.'

'Miss O'Dawne, I'm an official of Scotland Yard.'

She looked sharply at him.

'Here, what's wrong?' she said.

'Was Miss Gluck a very close friend of yours?' asked Alleyn gently.

'*Was!* What d'you mean? Here, has anything happened to Sonia?'

'I'm afraid so.'

'What, God, she's not – !'

'Yes.'

The coffee-pot bubbled and she automatically turned down the gas. Her pert little face had gone white under the make-up.

'What had she done?' she said.

'She hadn't done anything. I think I know what you mean. She was going to have a child.'

'Yes. I know that, all right. Well – what happened?'

Alleyn told her as kindly as possible. She made the coffee as she listened to him, and her distress was so unaffected that he felt himself warm to her.

'You know, I can't sort of believe it,' she said. 'Murder. That seems kind of not real, doesn't it? Know what I mean? Why, it was only Saturday she was sitting where you are now and telling me all her bits and pieces.'

'Were you great friends?'

'Well, *you* know. We'd sort of teamed up, in a way. Mind, she's not my real pal like Maudie Lavine or Dolores Duval, but I was quite matey with her. Here's your coffee. Help yourself to shoog. God, I can't believe it. Murdered!'

She stirred her coffee and stared at Alleyn. Suddenly she made a jab at him with her spoon.

'Garcia!' she said.

Alleyn waited.

'Garcia's done it,' said Miss O'Dawne, 'you take it from me. I never liked that boy. She brought him up here once or twice and I said to her: 'You watch your business with that gentleman,' I said. 'In my opinion he's a very dirty bit of work and I don't mind who hears me.' Well, I mean to say! Letting a girl as good as keep him. And when the spot of trouble comes along it's "Thanks for the buggy ride, it was OK while it lasted." Had she tried the funny business with the kid? You know.'

'I don't think so.' Alleyn took Miss O'Dawne's letter from his pocket and handed it to her.

'We found this in her room. That's what made me come to you.'

She looked sharply at him.

'What about it?'

'You can understand that we want to collect any information that is at all likely to lead us to an arrest.'

'I can understand that all right, all right.'

'Well, Miss O'Dawne, this letter suggests that you may be able to give us this information. It suggests, at all events, that you may know more about the Sonia-Garcia situation than we do.'

'I know all there was to know. She was going to have his kid, and he'd got sick of her. Pause for laugh. Laugh over.'

'Isn't there a bit more to it than that?'

'How d'you mean?'

'I think I may as well tell you that we know she got a hundred pounds from Mr Basil Pilgrim.'

'Did he tell you?'

'Yes. Was that the plan you refer to in this letter?'

'Since you're asking, Mr Clever, it was. Pilgrim's had his fun and Sonia didn't see why he shouldn't pay for it.'

'But the child was not Pilgrim's?'

'Oh no, dear, but for all he knew – '

'Yes, I see. She said she'd go to his father if he didn't pay up. Was that it?'

'That was the big idea. Or to his girl. Sonia told me this boy Basil is a bit silly. You know – one of the purity song and dance experts. He must be a bit soft, from what she told me. Said his feeongsay thought he was as pure as her. Soft music and tears in the voice. Sonia said it was a big laugh, anyway, because the girl's not so very very ongenoo either. Anyway, Basil was all worked up and gave Sonia the cheque.'

'What did she do with his cheque?'

'Oh, she cashed it and gave the money to Garcia, dear. What do you know about that? Could you beat it? I told her she was crazy. On Saturday when she was here I said: 'Well, did it all go big?' and she said this boy Basil came in on his cue all right, but she'd handed the money to Garcia and asked him if they couldn't get married straight away. And Garcia started his funny business. He said a hundred quid wasn't enough to marry with.'

'Hadn't she got anything out of Malmsley?'

'Listen, Mr Blake, aren't you wonderful? How did you get on to the Marmalade stuff?'

Alleyn folded his arms and raised his eyebrows.

' "I have my methods," said the great sleuth.'

'Well, of course!' exclaimed Miss O'Dawne, greatly diverted. 'Aren't you a yell!'

'Please tell me,' said Alleyn. 'What happened when she offered to sell Malmsley his own book?'

'He wouldn't give more than five pounds, dear, and Sonia stuck out for twenty. Well, I mean to say, what's five pounds to a girl in her condition? So she said she'd give him the weekend to think it over. She didn't mind waiting. It wasn't as if she hadn't got – ' Miss O'Dawne stopped short, gave Alleyn another of her sharp glances, and lit a cigarette.

'Hadn't got what?' asked Alleyn.

'Look here – you're asking a lot of questions, aren't you, dear? Keep forgetting you're a booby with all this upstage-and-county manners of yours. What's wrong with a girl getting her own back like Sonia did?'

'Well, it was blackmail, you know.'

'Was it? Isn't that a pity, I don't suppose. Have some more coffee?'

'Thank you, it's extremely good.'

'That's right. I say, it's all very funny us talking away sort of cosy like this, but when I think of Sonia – honest, I *am* upset, you know. You have to keep on cracking hardy, but just the same it's a swine, isn't it? You know what I mean. Help yourself to shoog. No, reely, I *am* upset.'

'I'm quite sure you are.'

'Look, Roddy. You don't mind me calling you Roddy, do you?'

'I'm delighted,' said Alleyn.

'Well, look, if what Sonia did was blackmail, I don't want to let everybody know the dirt about her after she's gone. Don't sling off at the dead's what I've always said, because they can't come in on the cross-talk and score the laughs where they are. See? You've got on to the Garcia-Pilgrim-Malmsley tale. All right! That's your luck or your great big talent. But I'm not in on this scene. See?'

'Yes, I do see. But you don't want her murderer to get off, do you?'

'Do I look funny?'

'Very well, then. I'm afraid the blackmail is bound to come out in evidence. You can't stop that, and won't you help us? Won't you tell me anything you know that may throw a little light on the tragedy of her death? There is something more, I'm sure. Isn't there?'

'Do you mean the joke with the picture of Basil's girl?'

'No,' said Alleyn.

'Do you know about that?'

'Yes.'

'Well, then!'

'Is there anything else about the Pilgrim stunt? Did she threaten to take any further steps?'

'With Pilgrim?' Miss O'Dawne's eyes looked thoughtfully at Alleyn. 'No. She didn't. She'd done her stuff with the Hon. Bas. Mine's a Bass, I *don't* suppose.'

'Well then, had Garcia any more tricks up his sleeve?'

Miss O'Dawne twisted her fingers together. 'She's frightened about something,' thought Alleyn.

'If you know anything more about Garcia,' he said, 'I do beg of you to tell me what it is.'

'Yeah? And get a permanent shop where Sonia's gone? It's no good? It's no good, dear, I'm not in on this act.'

'I promise you that no harm – '

'No, dear, there's nothing doing. I don't know anything that you haven't found out.'

'Was Garcia off on a separate line?'

'You go for Garcia,' said Miss O'Dawne. 'That's all I'm going to say. Go for Garcia. Have you arrested him?'

'No. He's gone on a walking tour.'

'Well, that's a scream – I bloody well don't think. Pardon my refinement,' said Miss O'Dawne.

728

Chapter 16

Back to the Yard

Alleyn cursed himself secretly and heartily for that unlucky word 'Blackmail'. Miss Bobbie O'Dawne refused, point-blank, to give him any further information that might possibly come under that heading. He seemed to have come up against a tenet. If Sonia had committed blackmail and Sonia was dead, Bobbie O'Dawne wasn't going to give her away. However, she told him quite willingly how Sonia had spent the weekend, and pretty well proved that Sonia could not possibly have gone down to Tatler's End House between Friday and Monday. With this Alleyn had to be content. He thanked his hostess and promised to go and see her show.

'That's right, dear, you come along. It's a bright show. I don't have much to do, you know. I hope you don't think any the worse of me for minding my own business about Sonia?'

'No. But if it comes to – well – if it comes to the arrest of an innocent person and you know you could save them, what would you do then?'

'Garcia's not innocent, dear, not so's you'd notice it.'

'It might not be Garcia.'

'Come off it. Listen. Do you know Garcia told the poor kid that if she let on to anybody that the child was his, he'd do for her? Now! She told me that herself. She was dead scared I'd forget and let something out. She made me swear I wouldn't. She said he'd do for both of us if we talked. Isn't that good enough?'

'It's sufficiently startling,' said Alleyn. 'Well, I suppose I'd better be off. I do ask you, very seriously, Miss O'Dawne, to think over what I have said. There is more than one kind of loyalty, you know.'

'I wouldn't have said a thing about the kid if I didn't

know you'd find out. Anyway, that's the sort of thing that might happen to any girl. But I'm not going to do the dirty and have them calling her criminal names, and it's no good asking me to. Are you going, dear? Well, so long. See you some more.'

'Suppose I sent a man along from one of the evening papers, would you care to give him an interview?'

'Who, me? Well, I don't pretend a bit of publicity doesn't help you in the business,' said Miss O'Dawne honestly. 'D'you mean the "Sonia Gluck as I knew her" gag?'

'Something like that.'

'With perhaps my picture along of hers? I've got a nice picture of Sonia. You know – wound up in georgette with the light behind her. Very nice. Well, as long as they don't want the dirt about her, I wouldn't mind the ad, dear. You know. It sounds hard, but it's a hard old world.'

'I'll come again, if I may.'

'Welcome, I'm sure. Be good.'

Alleyn went thoughtfully to Scotland Yard. He saw his Assistant Commissioner and went over the case with him. Then he went to his office. He had been for a year in the south of the world and the room looked at once strange and familiar. The respectably worn leather chairs, his desk, the untidy groove where he had once let a cigarette burn itself out, the little dark print of a medieval town above the mantelpiece – there they all were, as it seemed, waiting for him after a period of suspension. He sat at his desk and began to work on the report of this case. Presently Fox came in. Alleyn realized that he had clicked right back into his socket in the vast piece of machinery that was Scotland Yard. New Zealand, the wharf at Suva, the night tide of the St Lawrence – all had receded into the past. He was back on his job.

He related to Fox the gist of his interview with Miss O'Dawne.

'What about yourself?' he asked when he had finished. 'Any news, Brer Fox?'

730

'The city's been set going on the warehouse business. It's a bit of a job and no mistake. According to Miss Troy's reckoning, we've got sixty miles to account for. That correct, sir?'

'Yes.'

'Yes. Well, supposing Garcia didn't tell lies about his warehouse, it's somewhere in London. It's twenty miles to Shepherd's Bush from the house. There and back, forty. Of course, he might not have come in by the Uxbridge Road, but it's by far the most direct route and it would be the one he was familiar with. For the sake of argument say he took it. That leaves us a radius of ten miles, roughly, from Shepherd's Bush to wherever the warehouse is. Twenty, there and back.'

'Total, sixty.'

'Yes. Of course, if this warehouse is somewhere west, north-west, or south-west, he might have branched off before he got to Shepherd's Bush, but he said Holloway to Miss Seacliff and if he went to Holloway he'd go by Shepherd's Bush. Then on by way of, say Albany Street and the Camden Road. As the crow flies, Holloway Prison is only about five miles from Shepherd's Bush, but the shortest way by road would be nearer to nine. Holloway fits in all right as far as the petrol consumption goes. Of course, it's all very loose,' added Fox, looking over his spectacles at Alleyn, 'but so's our information.'

'Very loose. Holloway's a large district.'

'Yes. Still, it squares up, more or less, with what we've got.'

'True enough.'

'Well, sir, following out your suggestion we've concentrated on Holloway and we're raking it for warehouses.'

'Yes, it's got to be done.'

'On the other hand,' continued Fox stolidly, 'as you pointed out on the trip up, it may not be in Holloway at all. Suppose Garcia lied about the position of the warehouse, having already planned the job when he spoke to Miss Seacliff. Suppose he deliberately misled her, meaning to use this warehouse as a hide-out after the job was done?'

'It doesn't look like that, Fox. She says Garcia tried to persuade her to visit him there alone. He actually gave her a sketch-map of how to get to the studio. She's lost it, of course.'

'Look here,' said Fox. 'The idea was that Pilgrim should drive her up. I wonder if there's a chance she handed the sketch-map to Pilgrim and he knows where the place is?'

'Yes. If he does know he didn't bother to mention it when I asked them all about the warehouse. Of course, that might have been bluff, but the whole warehouse story is rather tricky. Suppose Garcia planned this murder in cold blood. He would have to give up all idea of carrying out his commission for the marble group unless he meant to brazen it out, go for his walk, and turn up at the warehouse to get on with his work. If he meant to do this it would be no good to tell preliminary lies about the site, would it? Suppose, on the other hand, he meant to disappear. He wouldn't have mentioned a warehouse at all if he meant to lie doggo in it.'

'That's right enough. Well, sir, what if he planned the murder while he was still dopey after the opium?'

'That, to me, seems more probable. Malmsley left the pipe, the jar and the lamp in a box under Garcia's bed because he was afraid of your friend Sadie catching him if he returned them to his bedroom. Bailey found Garcia's as well as Malmsley's prints on the jar. There's less opium than Malmsley said there would be. It's at least possible that Garcia had another go at it after Malmsley had gone. He may have woken up, felt very dreary, and sought to recapture the bliss. He may have smoked another pipe or taken a pull at his whisky. He may have done both. He may even have laid the trap with the dagger while still under the influence of the opium and – or – whisky. This is shamefully conjectural, Fox, but it seems to me that it is not too fantastic. The macabre character of the crime is not inconsistent, I fancy, with the sort of thing one might expect from a man in Garcia's condition. So far – all right. Possible, at any rate. But would he be sensible enough to get Miss Troy's caravan, back it, however clumsily, up to the window, put the empty case on board and wheel the model through the window and into the case? And what's more, my old Foxkin, would he have the gumption to drive to this damnable warehouse, dump his stuff, return the caravan to Tatler's End House, and set out on his walking tour? Would he not rather sink into a drugged and disgusting slumber lasting well into Saturday morning? And having come to himself would he not undo his foul trap for Sonia?'

'But if he *wanted* her out of the way,' persisted Fox.

'I know, I know. But if he was going to bolt he had so much to lose. His first big commission?'

'Well, perhaps he'll turn up and brazen it out. He doesn't know he dropped the pellet of clay with his thumb-print. He doesn't know Miss Lee overheard his conversations with Sonia. He doesn't know Sonia told anyone she was going to have his child. He'll think the motive won't appear.'

'He'll know what will appear at the post-mortem. What's worrying me is the double aspect of the crime, if Garcia's the criminal. There's no reason to suppose Malmsley lied about giving Garcia the opium. It's the sort of thing he'd suppress if he could. Very well. The planning of the murder and the laying of the trap might have been done under the influence of a pipe or more of opium. The subsequent business with the caravan has every appearance of the work of a cool and clear-headed individual.'

'Someone else in it?'

'Who?'

'Gawd knows,' said Fox.

'Meanwhile Garcia does not appear.'

'Do you think he may have got out of the country?'

'I don't know. He had a hundred pounds.'

'Where d'you get that, chief?'

733

'From Miss Bobbie O'Dawne. Sonia gave him the hundred pounds she got from Basil Pilgrim.'

'I've fixed up with the people at the ports,' said Fox. 'He won't get by, now. But has he already slipped through? That's what's worrying me.'

'If he left Tatler's End House on his flat feet in the early hours of Saturday morning,' said Alleyn, 'we'll pick up his track.'

'If?'

'It's the blasted psychology of the brute that's got me down,' said Alleyn with unusual violence. 'We've got a very fair picture of Garcia from all these people. They all agree that he lives entirely for his work, that he will sacrifice himself and everyone else to his work, that his work is quite remarkably good. I can't see a man of this type deliberately committing a crime that would force him to give up the biggest job he has ever undertaken.'

'But if the opium's to blame? Not to mention the whisky?'

'If they're to blame I don't think he's responsible for the rest of the business with the caravan. He'd either sleep it off there in the studio or wander away without taking any particular pains to cover his tracks. In that case we'd have found him by now.'

'Then do you think there's any likelihood of someone else driving him up to London and hiding him in this blasted warehouse? What about the man Ethel and her boy saw in the lane? Say it wasn't Garcia, but someone else. Could he have found Garcia under the weather and offered to drive him up to London with the stuff and return the caravan?'

'Leaving the knife where it was?' said Alleyn. 'Yes, that's possible, of course. He may not have noticed the knife, this lurker in the lane. On the other hand – '

Alleyn and Fox stared thoughtfully at each other.

'As soon as I got here this morning,' said Fox at last, 'I looked up this Mr Charleson, the secretary to the board of the New Palace Theatre in Westminster. Had a bit of luck, he was on the premises and answered the telephone. He's coming in at eleven-thirty, but beyond confirming the business about this statue he can't help us. Garcia was to order the marble and start work on next Monday. They offered him two hundred pounds and they were going to pay for the marble after he'd chosen it. Mr Charleson says they'd never met anyone else at that price whose work is as good as Garcia's.'

'Bloodsucker,' grunted Alleyn.

'But he's no idea where the work was to be done.'

'Helpful fellow. Well, Fox, we'd better get a move on. We're going to spend a jolly day checking up alibis. I'll take Miss Troy's and Miss Bostock's to begin with. You start off with young Hatchett and Phillida Lee. To your lot will fall the bearded intelligentsia of the Vortex Experimental Studio theatre, the Lee aunt, and the Hatchett boarding-house keeper. To mine Sir Arthur Jaynes, Cattcherley's hairdressing establishment, Mr Graham Barnes, and the staff of the United Arts Club.'

'And this Mr John Bellasca, sir, Miss Troy's friend.'

'Yes,' said Alleyn. 'Me too.'

'And then what?'

'If we get done today we'll run down to Boxover in the morning and see the people with whom Pilgrim and Miss Seacliff stayed on Friday night.'

He opened a drawer in his desk and took out the photograph of the group at Tatler's End House.

'How tall is Garcia?' he asked. 'Five foot nine according to the statement Blackman gave us. Yes. Pilgrim looks about two and a half inches taller in this photograph, doesn't he? You get a very good idea of the comparative heights. Ormerin, Hatchett and Garcia are all within an inch of each other. Miss Bostock, Miss Seacliff and Miss Lee are much shorter. The model is a little taller than Miss Bostock, but not so tall as the others. Miss Troy is taller than the first batch, but about two inches shorter than Pilgrim. Pilgrim is the tallest of the lot. Alas, alas, Fox, how little we know about these people! We interview them under extraordinary circumstances and hope to get a normal view of their characters. We ask them alarming questions and try to draw conclusions from their answers. How can we expect to discover them when each must be secretly afraid that his most innocent remark may cast suspicion upon himself? How would you or I behave if we came within the range of conjecture in a murder case? Well, damn it, let's get on with the job.'

The desk telephone rang and he answered it.

'It's me,' said Nigel's voice winningly.

'What do you want?'

'I'd like to come and see you, Alleyn.'

'Where are you?'

'In a call-box about five minutes away.'

'Very well, come up. I've got a job for you.'

'I'll be there.'

Alleyn hung up the receiver.

'It's Bathgate. I'll send him round to get an exclusive story from Miss Bobbie O'Dawne. There's just a remote hope she may become less discreet under the influence of free publicity. I'm damn well positive she's keeping something up her sleeve about the blackmailing activities. She's rather an attractive little creature, Fox. Hard as nails and used to the seamy side of life, but a curious mixture of simplicity and astuteness. She knew we'd find out about the child and had no qualms in talking about it, but as soon as the word blackmail cropped up she doubled up like a hedgehog. I don't think it had occurred to her that Sonia's gentle art of extracting money was in any sense criminal. And I – blundering booby that I was – must needs enlighten her. She's terrified of Garcia. She's convinced he murdered Sonia and I honestly think she believes he'd go for her if she informed against him.'

He moved restlessly about the room.

'There's something missing,' he said. 'I'm positive there's something missing.'

'Garcia,' said Fox. 'He's missing all right.'

'No, blast you, not Garcia. Though Lord knows, we'll

736

have to get him. No, there was something else that the O'Dawne had on the tip of her tongue. By gum, Fox, I wonder – Look here.'

Alleyn was still talking when the telephone rang to say Nigel Bathgate had arrived.

'Send him up,' said Alleyn. And when Nigel appeared Alleyn talked about Bobbie O'Dawne and suggested that Nigel should get a special interview.

'This is extraordinarily decent of you, Alleyn,' said Nigel.

'It's nothing of the sort. You're the tool of the Yard, my boy, and don't you forget it. Now listen carefully and I'll tell you what line you're to take. You must impress upon her that you are to be trusted. If she thinks you'll publish every word she utters, she'll say nothing to the point. If you can, write the interview there and then and read it to her. Assure her that you will print nothing without her permission. Photograph the lady in every conceivable position. Then get friendly. Let her think you are becoming indiscreet. You may say that you have had instructions from the Yard to publish a story about Sonia's blackmailing activities unless we can hear, privately, exactly what they were. You may say that we think of publishing an appeal through the paper to any of her victims, asking them to come forward and tell us without prejudice what they paid her. We hope that this will lead to the arrest of Garcia. Emphasize this. It's Garcia we're after, but we can't lay it home to him without the evidence of the people Sonia blackmailed. We think Sonia refused to give him any more of the proceeds and he killed her to get them. It's a ridiculous tarradiddle, but I think if you are low and cunning she may believe you. She'll tell you about Pilgrim and Malmsley, I fancy, because she knows we have already got hold of that end of the stick. If, however, she thinks she may save Sonia's name by going a bit farther, there's just a chance she may do it. Do you understand?'

'I think so.'

'If you fail, we'll be no worse off than we were before. Off you go.'

'Very well.' Nigel hesitated, his hand in his coat pocket.

'What is it?' asked Alleyn.

'Do you remember that I made a sort of betting list on the case last time you allowed me to Watson for you?'

'I do.'

'Well – I've done it again,' said Nigel modestly.

'Let me have a look.'

Nigel took a sheet of foolscap from his pocket and laid it before Alleyn with an anxious smile.

'Away you go,' said Alleyn. 'Collect your cameraman and use your wits.'

Nigel went out and Alleyn looked at his analysis of the case.

'I'd half a mind to do something of the sort myself, Fox,' he said. 'Let us see what he makes out.'

Fox looked over his shoulder. Nigel had headed his paper: 'Murder of an Artist's Model. Possible Suspects.'

(1) Garcia

Opportunity. Was in the studio on Friday after all the others had gone. Knew the throne would not be touched (rule of studio).

Motive. Sonia was going to have a baby. Probably his. He had tired of her and was after Valmai Seacliff (V.S.'s statement). They had quarrelled (Phillida Lee's statement), and he had said he'd kill her if she pestered him. Possibly she threatened to sue him for maintenance. He may have egged her on to blackmail Pilgrim and taken the money. If so, she may have threatened to give him away to Troy. He had taken opium at about four o'clock in the afternoon. How long would he take to get sufficiently over the effect to drive a car to London and back?

(2) Agatha Troy

Opportunity. Could have done it on Saturday after she returned from London, or on Sunday. We have only her word for it that the drape was already arranged when she visited the studio on Saturday afternoon.

Motive. Sonia had hopelessly defaced the portrait of Valmai Seacliff – on Troy's own admission the best picture she had painted.

(3) Katti Bostock

Same opportunities as Troy.

Motive. Sonia had driven her to breaking-point over the sittings for her large picture.

(4) Valmai Seacliff

Opportunity. Doubtful, but possibly she could have returned from Boxover after they had all gone to bed. The headache might have been an excuse.

Motive. Unless you count Sonia's defacement of her portrait by Troy, there is no motive. If she had heard of Pilgrim's affair with Sonia, she might be furious, but hardly murderous. Anyway, she had cut Sonia out.

(5) Basil Pilgrim

Opportunity. Same as Seacliff. Perhaps more favourable. If she had taken aspirin, she would sleep soundly, and the others were nowhere near his room. He would have slipped out after they had all gone to bed, taken his car, gone to the studio and fixed the knife.

Motive. Sonia had blackmailed him, threatening to tell Seacliff and Lord Pilgrim that the child was Basil's. He seems to have a kink about purity and Seacliff. On the whole, plenty of motive.

N.B. If Seacliff or Pilgrim did it, either Garcia was not at the studio or else he is a confederate. If he was not at the studio, who took the caravan and removed his stuff? Could he have done this before Pilgrim arrived, leaving the coast clear?

(6) Cedric Malmsley

Opportunity. He could have fixed the knife after he had knocked Garcia out with opium.

Motive. Sonia was blackmailing him about his illustration. He is the type that would detest an exposure of this sort.

(7) Francis Ormerin

Opportunity. If Hatchett and Malmsley are correct in saying the drape was still crumpled on Friday afternoon after Ormerin had left, and if Troy is correct in saying it was stretched out on Saturday before he returned, there seems to be no opportunity.

Motive. Only the model's persistent refusal to keep still (v unlikely).

(8) Phillida Lee

Opportunity. Accepting above statements – none.
Motive. None.

(9) Watt Hatchett

Opportunity. On Malmsley's and Troy's statements – none.

Motive. Appears to have disliked her intensely and quarrelled over the pose. Sonia gibed about Australia (poor motive).

Remarks. It seems to me there is little doubt that Garcia did it. Probably gingered up by his pipe of opium. If he fails to answer advertisements, it will look still more suspicious.

Suggestion. Find warehouse.

Alleyn pointed a long finger at Nigel's final sentence.

'Mr Bathgate's bright idea for the day,' he said.

'Yes,' said Fox. 'It looks nice and simple just jotted down like that.'

'The thing's quite neat in its way, Fox.'

'Yes, sir. And I think he's got the right idea, you know.'

'Garcia?'

'Yes. Don't you?'

'Oh Lord, Fox, you've heard my trouble. I don't see how we can be too sure.'

'There's that bit of clay with his print on it,' said Fox. 'On the drape, where it had no business.'

'Suppose it was planted? There'd be any number of bits like that lying on the floor by the window. We found some. Let's get Bailey's further report on the prints, shall we?'

Alleyn rang through to Bailey's department and found that Bailey had finished his work and was ready to make a report. In a minute or two he appeared with a quantity of photographs.

'Anything fresh?' asked Alleyn.

'Yes, sir, in a sort of way there is,' said Bailey, with the air of making a reluctant admission.

'Let's have it.'

Bailey laid a set of photographs on Alleyn's desk.

'These are from the empty whisky bottle under Garcia's bed. We got them again from different parts of the bed-frame, the box underneath and the stool he used for his work. Some of them cropped up on the window-sill and there's a good thumb and forefinger off the light switch above his bed. These – ' he pointed to a second group – 'come from bits of clay that were lying about the floor. Some of them were no good, but there's a couple of clear ones. They're made by the same fingers as the first lot. I've marked them "Garcia".'

'I think we may take it they are his,' said Alleyn.

'Yes. Well then, sir, here's the ones off the opium-box and the pipe. Four of those I've identified as Mr Malmsley's. The others are Garcia's. Here's a photo of the clay pellet I found in the drape. Garcia again. This set's off the edge of the throne. There were lots of prints there, some of them Mr Hatchett's, some of Mr Pilgrim's and some the French bloke's – this Mr Ormerin. They seem to have had blue paint on their fingers, which was

741

useful. But this set is Garcia's again and I found it on top of the others. There were traces of clay in this lot, which helped us a bit.'

Alleyn and Fox examined the prints without comment. Bailey produced another photograph and laid it on the desk.

'I got that from the drape. Took a bit of doing. Here's the enlargement.'

'Garcia,' said Alleyn and Fox together.

'I reckon it is,' said Bailey. 'We'd never have got it if it hadn't been for the clay. It looks to me, Mr Alleyn, as if he'd only half done the job. There's no prints on the knife, so I suppose he held that with a cloth or wiped it after he'd finished. It must have been a paint-rag, because there's a smudge of blue on the knife. You may remember there were the same blue smudges on the throne and the easel-ledge that was used to hammer in the dagger. Now, this print we got from the bit of paint-rag that you suggested was used to wipe off the prints. Some of the paint on the rag was only half dry, and took a good impression. It matches the paint smudges on the knife. Blue.'

'Garcia's?'

'That's correct, sir.'

'This about settles it, Mr Alleyn,' said Fox.

'That Garcia laid the trap? I agree with you.'

'We'll have to ask for more men. It's going to be a job getting him, sir. He had such a big start. How about letting these alibis wait for today, Mr Alleyn?'

'I think we'd better get through them, but I tell you what, Fox. I'll ask for another man and leave the alibi game to the pair of you. I'm not pulling out the plums for myself, Foxkin.'

'I've never known you do that, Mr Alleyn, don't you worry. We'll get through these alibis,' said Fox. 'I'd like to see what our chaps are doing round the Holloway district.'

'And I,' said Alleyn, 'think of going down to Brixton.'

742

'Is that a joke?' asked Fox suspiciously, after a blank pause.

'No, Fox.'

'Brixton? Why Brixton?'

'Sit down for a minute,' said Alleyn, 'and I'll tell you.'

Chapter 17

The Man at the Table

At four o'clock on the following afternoon, Wednesday, September 21st, Alleyn turned wearily into the last land and estate agents' office in Brixton. A blond young man advanced upon him.

'Yes, sir? What can I have the pleasure of doing for you?'

'It's not much of a pleasure, I'm afraid. If you will, *and* if you can, tell me of any vacant warehouses in this district, or of any warehouses that have let part of themselves to artists, or of any artists who, having rented such premises, have taken themselves off to foreign parts and lent the premises to a young man who sculps. As you will probably have guessed, I am an officer of Scotland Yard. Here's my card. Do you mind awfully if I sit down?'

'Er – yes. Of course not. Do,' said the young man in some surprise.

'It's a weary world,' said Alleyn. 'The room would be well lit. I'd better show you my list of all the places I have already inspected.'

The list was a long one. Alleyn had continued his search at eleven o'clock that morning.

The blond young man ran through it, muttering to himself. Occasionally he cast a glance at his immaculately-dressed visitor.

'I suppose,' he said at last, with an avid look towards an evening paper on the corner of his desk, 'I suppose this wouldn't happen to have any connection with the missing gentleman from Bucks?'

'It would,' said Alleyn.

'By the name of Garcia?'

'Yes. We believe him to be ill and suffering from loss

of memory. It is thought he may have wandered in this direction, poor fellow.'

'What an extraordinary thing!' exclaimed the young man.

'Too odd for words,' murmured Alleyn. 'He's a little bit ga-ga, we understood. Clever, but dottyish. Do you think you can help us?'

'Well now, let me see. This list is pretty comprehensive. I don't know if – '

He bit his finger and opened a large book. Alleyn closed his eyes.

'What an extraordinary thing!' exclaimed the young man. 'I mean to say, any of the warehouses round here might have a room to let and we'd never hear of it. See what I mean?'

'Alas, yes,' said Alleyn.

'Now there's Solly and Perkins. Big place. Business not too good, they tell me. And there's Anderson's shirt factory, and Lacker and Lampton's used-car depot. That's in Gulper Row, off Cornwall Street. Just by the water-works. Opposite the prison. Quite in your line, Inspector.'

He laughed shrilly.

'Damn funny,' agreed Alleyn.

'Lacker and Lampton's foreman was in here the other day. He's taken a house from us. Now, he did say something about there being a lot of room round at their place. He said something about being able to store his furniture there if they went into furnished rooms. Yes. Now, I wonder. How about Lacker and Lampton's?'

'I'll try it. Could you give me the foreman's name?'

'McCully's the name. Ted McCully. He's quite a pal of mine. Tell him I sent you. James is my name. Look here, I'll come round with you, if you like.'

'I wouldn't dream of troubling you,' said Alleyn firmly. 'Thank you very much indeed. Goodbye.'

He departed hurriedly, before Mr James could press his offer home. A fine drizzle had set in, the sky was leaden, and already the light had begun to fade. Alleyn turned up the collar of his raincoat, pulled down the brim of his hat and strode off in the direction of Brixton Prison. Cornwall Street ran along one side of the waterworks and Gulper Row was a grim and deadly little alley off Cornwall Street. Lacker and Lampton's was at the far end. It was a barn of a place and evidently combined wrecking activities with the trade in used cars. The ground floor was half full of spare parts, chassis without wheels, engines without chassis, and bodies without either.

Alleyn asked for Mr Ted McCully, and in a minute or two a giant in oil-soaked dungarees came out of a smaller workshop, wiping his hands on a piece of waste.

'Yes, sir?' he asked cheerfully.

'I'm looking for an empty room with a good light to use as a painting-studio,' Alleyn began. 'I called in at the estate agents, behind the prison, and Mr James there said he thought you might have something.'

'Bert James?' said Mr McCully with a wide grin. 'What's he know about it? Looking for a commission as per usual, I'll bet.'

'Have a cigarette. Will that thing stand my weight?'

'Thank you, sir. I wouldn't sit there; it's a bit greasy. Take the box.'

Alleyn sat on a packing-case.

'Have you any vacant rooms that would do to paint in?'

'Not here, we haven't, but it's a funny thing you should ask.'

'Why's that?'

'Well, it's a bit of a coincidence,' said Mr McCully maddeningly.

'Oh?'

'Yes. The world's a small place, you know, sir. Isn't it, now?'

'No bigger than a button,' agreed Alleyn.

'That's right. Look at this little coincidence, now. I dare say you've had quite a ramble looking for this room you want?'

'I have rambled since eleven o'clock this morning.'

'Is that a fact? And then you look in on Bert James and he sends you round here. And I'll swear Bert knows nothing about it, either. Which makes it all the more of a coincidence.'

'Makes what, though?' asked Alleyn, breathing through his nostrils.

'I was just going to tell you,' said Mr McCully. 'You see, although we haven't got the sort of thing you'd be wanting, on the premises, there's a bit of a storehouse round the corner that would do you down to the ground. Skylight. Paraffin heater. Electric light. Plenty of room. Just the thing.'

'May I –'

'Ah! Wait a bit, though. It's taken. It's in use in a sort of way.'

'What sort of way?'

'That's the funny thing. It was taken by an artist like yourself.'

Alleyn flicked the ash off his cigarette.

'Really?' he said.

'Yes. Gentleman by the name of Gregory. He used to look in here pretty often. He once took a picture of this show. What a thing to want to take a photo of, I said, but he seemed to enjoy it. I wouldn't have the patience myself.'

'Is he in his studio this afternoon?'

'Hasn't been there for three months. He's in Hong Kong.'

'Indeed,' murmured Alleyn, and he thought: 'Easy now. Don't flutter the brute.'

'Yes. In Hong Kong taking pictures of the Chinks.'

'Would he sublet, do you know?'

'I don't know whether he *would* but he *can't*.'

'Why not?'

'Because he promised the loan of it to someone else.'

'I see. Then somebody else is using it?'

'That's where the funny part comes in. He isn't. Never turned up.'

'Gosh!' thought Alleyn.

'Never turned up,' repeated Mr McCully. 'As a matter of fact I asked the boss only yesterday if I might store some bits of furniture there during Christmas because the wife and I are moving and it's a bit awkward what with this and that and the other thing – '

He rambled on. Alleyn listened with an air of sympathetic attention.

'. . . so the boss said it would be all right if this other chap didn't turn up, but all Mr Gregory said was that he'd offered the room to this other chap and given him the key, and he'd just come in when he wanted it. So that's how it stands.'

'What was this other man's name, do you know?'

'Have I heard it now?' ruminated Mr McCully, absently accepting another of Alleyn's cigarettes. 'Wait a bit now. It was a funny sort of name. Reminded me of something. What was it? By crikey, I remember. It reminded me of the rubbish van – you know – the chaps that come round for the garbage tins.'

'Garbage?'

'Garbage – that's the name. Or nearly.'

'Something like Garcia, perhaps.' And Alleyn thought: 'Has he read the evening paper or hasn't he?'

'That's it! Garcia! Well, fancy you getting it. Garcia! That's the chap. Garcia.' Mr McCully laughed delightedly.

Alleyn stood up.

'Look here,' he said, 'I wish you'd just let me have a look at this place, will you? In case there is a chance of my getting it.'

'Well, I suppose there's nothing against that. The boss is away just now, but I don't see how he could object. Not that there's anything to see. We don't go near it from one week to another. I'll just get our key and take you along. Fred!'

'Hooray?' said a voice in the workshop.

'I'm going round to the shed. Back before knock-off.'

'Right-oh.'

Mr McCully got a key from behind a door, hooked an old tarpaulin over his shoulders and, talking incessantly, led the way out of the garage by a side door into a narrow alley.

It was now raining heavily. The alley smelt of soot, grease, and stagnant drainage. Water streamed down from defective gutters and splashed about their feet. The deadliness and squalor of the place seemed to close about them. Their footsteps echoed at the far end of the alley.

'Nasty weather,' said Mr McCully. 'It's only a step.'

They turned to the left into a wider lane that led back towards Cornwall Street, McCully stopped in front of a pair of rickety double-doors fastened with a padlock and chain.

'Here we are, sir. Just half a tick and I'll have her opened. She's a bit stiff.'

While he fitted the key in the padlock Alleyn looked up the lane. He thought how like this was to a scene in a modern talking-picture of the realistic school. The sound of the rain, the grime streaked with running trickles, the distant mutter of traffic, and their own figures, black against grey – it was almost a Dostoievsky setting. The key grated in the lock, the chain rattled and McCully dragged the reluctant doors back in their grooves.

'Darkish,' he said. I'll turn up the light.'

It was very dark inside the place they had come to. A greyness filtered through dirty skylights. The open doors left a patch of light on a wooden floor, but the far end was quite lost in shadow. McCully's boots clumped over the boards.

'I don't just remember where the switch is,' he said, and his voice echoed away into the shadows. Alleyn stood like a figure of stone in the entrance, waiting for the light. McCully's hand fumbled along the wall. There was a click and a dull yellow globe, thick with dust, came to life just inside the door.

'There we are, sir.'

Alleyn walked in.

The place at first looked almost empty. A few canvases stood at intervals with their faces to the wall. Half-way down there was a large studio easel, and beyond it, far away from the light, stood a packing-case with a few odd chairs and some shadowy bundles. Beyond that again, deep in shadow, Alleyn could distinguish the corner of a table. An acrid smell hung on the air. McCully walked on towards the dark.

'Kind of lonesome, isn't it?' he said. 'Not much comfort about it. Bit of a smell, too. There was some storage batteries in here. Wonder if he broke one of them.'

'Wait a moment,' said Alleyn, but McCully did not hear him.

'There's another light at this end. I'll find the switch in a minute,' he said. 'It's very dark, isn't it? Cripes, what a stink. You'd think he'd – '

His voice stopped as if someone had gagged him. He stood still. The place was filled with the sound of rain and with an appalling stench.

'What's the matter?' asked Alleyn sharply.

There was no answer.

'McCully! Don't move.'

'Who's that!' said McCully violently.

'Where? Where are you?'

'Here – who – *Christ*!'

Alleyn strode swiftly down the room.

'Stay where you are,' he said.

'There's someone sitting at the table,' McCully whispered.

Alleyn came up with him and caught him by the arm. McCully was trembling like a dog.

'Look! Look there!'

In the shadow cast by the packing-case Alleyn saw the table. The man who sat at it leant across the top and stared at them. His chin seemed to be on the surface of the table. His arms were stretched so far that his hands reached the opposite edge. It was an uncouth posture, the attitude of a scarecrow. They could see the lighter disc that was his face and the faint glint of his eyeballs. Alleyn had a torch in his pocket. He groped for it with one hand and held McCully's arm with the other. McCully swore endlessly in a whisper.

The sharp beam of light ran from the torch to the table. It ended in the man's face. It was the face of a gargoyle. The eyeballs started from their sockets, the protruding tongue was sulphur yellow. The face was yellow and blue. McCully wrenched his arm from Alleyn's grasp and flung it across his eyes.

Alleyn walked slowly towards the table. The area of light widened to take in an overturned cup and a bottle. There was a silence of a minute broken by McCully.

'Oh, God!' said McCully. 'Oh, God, help me! Oh, God!'

'Go back to your office,' said Alleyn. 'Telephone Scotland Yard. Give this address. Say the message is from Inspector Alleyn. Ask them to send Fox, Bailey, and the divisional surgeon. Here!'

He turned McCully round, marched him towards the door and propped him against the wall.

'I'll write it down.' He took out his notebook, wrote rapidly and then looked at McCully. The large common face was sheet-white and the lips were trembling.

'Can you pull yourself together?' asked Alleyn. 'Or had I better come with you? It would help if you could do it. I'm a C.I.D. officer. We're looking for this man. Come now, can you help me?'

McCully drew the back of his hand across his mouth.

'He's dead,' he said.

'Bless my soul, of course he is. Will you take this message? I don't want to bully you. I just want you to tell me if you can do it.'

'Give us a moment, will you?'

751

'Of course.'

Alleyn looked up and down the alley.

'Wait here a minute,' he said.

He ran through the pelting rain to the top of the alley and looked into Cornwall Street. About two hundred yards away he saw a constable, walking along the pavement towards him. Alleyn waited for him, made himself known, and sent the man off to the nearest telephone. Then he returned to McCully.

'It's all right, McCully, I've found a PC. Sit down on this box. Here.' He pulled a flask from his pocket and made McCully drink. 'Sorry I let you in for this,' he said. 'Now wait here and don't admit anyone. When I've turned up the light at the back of this place, close the doors. You needn't look round.'

'If it's all the same to you, sir, I'll wait outside.'

'All right. Don't speak to anyone unless they say they're from the Yard.'

Using his torch, Alleyn went back to the far end of the room. He found the light switch, turned it on, and heard McCully drag the doors together.

The lamp at this end of the room was much more brilliant. By its light Alleyn examined the man at the table. The body was flaccid. Alleyn touched it, once. The man was dressed in an old mackintosh and a pair of shabby grey trousers. The hands were relaxed, but their position suggested that they had clutched the edge of the table. They were long, the square finger-tips were lightly crusted with dry clay and the right thumb and forefinger were streaked with blue. On the backs of the hands Alleyn saw sulphur-coloured patches. Not without an effort he examined the terrible face. There were yellow spots on the jaw amongst the half-grown beard. The mouth was torn, and a glance at the finger-nails showed by what means. On the chin, the table and the floor Alleyn found further ghastly evidence of what had happened before the man died.

Alleyn dropped his silk handkerchief over the head.

He looked at the overturned bottle and cup. The bottle was marked clearly with a label bearing a scarlet cross. It was almost empty and from its neck a corroded patch spread over the table. The same marks appeared on the table round the cup. The table had been heavily coated with dust when the man sat at it. His arms had swept violently across the surface. The floor was littered with broken china and with curiously shaped wooden tools, rather like enormous orange-sticks. Alleyn looked at the feet. The shoes, though shabby and unpolished, had no mud on them. One foot was twisted round the chair-leg, the other had been jammed against the leg of the table. The whole posture suggested unspeakable torture.

Alleyn turned to the packing-case. It was five feet square and well made. One side was hinged and fastened with a bolt. It was not locked. He pulled on his gloves and, touching it very delicately, drew the bolt. The door opened smoothly. Inside the case, on a wheeled platform, was an irregularly shaped object that seemed to be swathed in cloths. Alleyn touched it. The cloths were still damp. 'Comedy and Tragedy,' he murmured. He began to go over the floor. McCully's and his own wet prints were clear enough, but as far as he could see, with the exception of the area round the table, the wooden boards held no other evidence. He turned his torch on the border where the floor met the wall. There he found a thick deposit of dust down the entire length of the room. In a corner there was a large soft broom. Alleyn looked at this closely, shook the dust from the bristles on to a sheet of paper and then emptied it into an envelope. He returned to the area of floor round the table and inspected every inch of it. He did not disturb the pieces of broken china there, nor the wooden tools, but he found at last one or two strands of dark-brown hair and these he put in an envelope. Then he looked again at the head of the dead man.

Voices sounded, the doors rattled open. Outside in the pouring rain was a police car and a mortuary van. Fox and Bailey stood in the doorway with McCully. Alleyn walked quickly towards them.

'Hullo, Fox.'

'Hullo, sir. What's up?'

'Come in. Is Curtis there?'

'Yes. Ready, doctor?'

Dr Curtis, Alleyn's divisional surgeon, dived out of the car into shelter.

'What the devil have you found, Alleyn?'

'Garcia,' said Alleyn.

'Here!' ejaculated Fox.

'Dead?' asked Curtis.

'Very.' Alleyn laid his hand on Fox's arm. 'Wait a moment. McCully, you can sit in the police car if you like. We shan't be long.'

McCully, who still looked very shaken, got into the car. A constable and the man off the local beat joined the group in the doorway.

'I think,' said Alleyn, 'that before you see the body I had better warn you that it is not a pleasant sight.'

'Us?' asked Fox, surprised. 'Warn us?'

'Yes, I know. We're pretty well seasoned, aren't we? I've never seen anything quite so beastly as this – not even in Flanders. I think he's taken nitric acid.'

'Good God!' said Curtis.

'Come along,' said Alleyn.

He led them to the far end of the room, where the man at the table still sat with a coloured handkerchief over his face. Fox, Bailey and Curtis stood and looked at the body.

'What's the stench?' asked Fox. 'It's bad, isn't it?'

'Nitric acid?' suggested Bailey.

'And other vomited matter,' said Curtis.

'You may smoke, all of you,' said Alleyn, and they lit cigarettes.

'Well,' said Curtis, 'I'd better look at him.'

He put out his well-kept doctor's hand and drew away the handkerchief from the face.

754

'Christ!' said Bailey.

'Get on with it,' said Alleyn harshly. 'Bailey, I want you to take his prints first. It's Garcia all right. Then compare them with anything you can get from the bottle and cup. Before you touch the bottle we'll take a photograph. Where's Thompson?'

Thompson came in from the car with his camera and flashlight. The usual routine began. Alleyn, looking on, was filled with a violent loathing of the whole scene. Thompson took six photographs of the body and then they covered it. Alleyn began to talk.

'You'd better hear what I make of all this on the face of the information we've already got. Bailey, you carry on while I'm talking. Go over every inch of the table and surrounding area. You've got my case? Good. We'll want specimens of this unspeakable muck on the floor. I'll do that.'

'Let me fix it, sir,' said Fox. 'I'm out of a job, and we'd like to hear your reconstruction of this business.'

'You'd better rig something over your nose and mouth. Nitric acid fumes are no more wholesome than they are pleasant, are they, Curtis?'

'Not too good,' grunted Curtis. 'May as well be careful.'

The doors at the end opened to admit the PC whom Alleyn had left on guard.

'What is it?' asked Alleyn.

'Gentleman to see you, sir.'

'Is his name Bathgate?'

'Yes, sir.'

'Miserable young perisher,' muttered Alleyn. 'Tell him to wait. No. Half a minute. Send him in.'

When Nigel appeared Alleyn asked fiercely: 'How did you get wind of this?'

'I was down at the Yard. They'd told me you were out. I saw Fox and the old gang tootle away in a car, then the mortuary van popped out. I followed in a taxi. What's up? There's a hell of a stink in here.'

'The only reason I've let you in is to stop you pitching

some cock-and-bull story to your filthy paper. Sit down in a far corner and be silent.'

'All right, all right.'

Alleyn turned to the others.

'We'll get on. Don't move the body just yet, Curtis.'

'Very good,' said Dr Curtis, who was cleaning his hands with ether. 'Speak up, Alleyn. Are you going to tell us this fellow's swallowed nitric acid?'

'I think so.'

'Bloody loathsome way of committing suicide.'

'He didn't know it was nitric acid.'

'Accident?'

'No. Murder.'

Chapter 18

One of Five

'I think,' said Alleyn, 'that we'll start off with the packing case.'

He walked over to it and flashed his torch on the swathed shape inside.

'That, I believe, is Garcia's clay model of the Comedy and Tragedy for the cinemas at Westminster. We'll have a look at it when Bailey has dealt with the case and the wet clothes. The point with which I think we should concern ourselves now is this. How did it get here?'

He lit a cigarette from the stump of his old one.

'In the caravan we looked at this morning?' suggested Fox from behind a white handkerchief he had tied across the lower half of his face. He was doing hideous things on the floor with a small trowel and a glass bottle.

'It would seem so, Brer Fox. We found pretty sound evidence that the caravan had been backed up to the window. Twig on the roof, tyre-tracks under the sill, traces of the little wheeled platform on the ledge and the step and floor of the caravan. The discrepancy in the petrol fits in with this place quite comfortably, I think. Very well. That was all fine and dandy as long as Garcia was supposed to have driven himself and his gear up to London, and himself back to Tatler's End House. Now we've got a different story. Someone returned the caravan to Tatler's End House, and that person has kept quiet about it.'

'Is it possible,' asked Fox, 'that Garcia drove the car back and returned here by some other means?'

'Hardly, Fox, I think. On Friday night Garcia was recovering from a pipe or more of opium, and possibly a jorum of whisky. He was in no condition to get his stuff aboard a caravan, drive it thirty miles, open this place up, manoeuvre the caravan inside, unload it, drive it back, and then start off again to tramp back to London or catch a train or bus. But suppose somebody arrived at the studio on Friday night and found Garcia in a state of semi-recovery. Suppose this person offered to drive Garcia up to London and return the caravan. Does that quarrel with anything we have found? I don't think it does. Can we find anything here to support such a theory? I think we can. The front part of the floor has been swept. Why the devil should Garcia sweep the floor of this place at midnight while he was in the condition we suppose him to have been in? Bailey, have you dealt with the bottle on the table?'

'Yes, sir. We've got a fairly good impression of the deceased's left thumb, forefinger and second finger.'

'Very good. Will you all look now at the hands?'

Alleyn turned to the shrouded figure. The arms projected from under the sheets. The hands at the far edge of the table were uncovered.

'Rigor mortis,' said Alleyn, 'has disappeared. The body is flaccid. But notice the difference between the right hand and the left. The fingers of the right are still curved slightly. If I flash this light on the under-surface of the table, you can see the prints left by the fingers when they clutched it. Bailey had brought them up with powder. You took a shot of these, Thompson, didn't you? Good. As rigor wore off, you see, the fingers slackened. Now look at the left hand. It is completely relaxed and the fingers are straight. On the under-surface of the table-edge, about three inches to the right of the left hand, are four marks made by the fingers. They are blurred, but the impression was originally a strong one, made with considerably pressure. Notice that the blurs do not seem to have been caused by any relaxation of the fingers. It looks rather as if the pressure had not been relaxed at all, but the fingers dragged up the edge while they still clutched it. Notice that the present position of the hand bears no sort of relation to the points – it is three inches away from them. Did you find any left-hand prints on the top of the table, Bailey?'

'No, sir.'

'No. Now, taking into consideration the nature and direction of the blurs and all the rest of it, in my opinion there is a strong assumption that this hand was forcibly dragged from the edge of the table, possibly while in a condition of cadaveric spasm. At all events, there is nothing here to contradict such an assumption. Now have a look at this cup. It contains dregs of what we believe to be nitric acid and is standing in a stain made, presumably, by nitric acid. It is on the extreme right hand of the body. You've tried it for prints, Thompson, and found – ?'

'Four left-hand fingerprints and the thumb.'

'Yes, by Jove!' Alleyn bent over the cup. 'There's a good impression of the left hand. Now see here. You notice these marks across the table. It was thickly covered in dust when this man sat down at it. Dust on the under-surface of his sleeves – lots of it. If we measure these areas where the dust has been removed and compare it with the length of the sleeve, we find pretty good evidence that he must have swept his arms across the surface of the table. Something like this.'

Alleyn took the dead arms and moved them across the table. 'You see, they follow the marks exactly. Here on the floor are the things he knocked off. Modeller's tools. A plate – smashed in four pieces. Two dishes that were probably intended for use as etching baths. There's almost as much dust under them as there is on the rest of the floor, so they haven't been there more than a day or two. They themselves are not very dusty – he brushed them with his sleeves. Agreed that there's a strong likelihood he swept them off?'

'Certainly,' said Fox.

'All right. Now look again at the table. This bottle which held the nitric acid and this cup into which it was poured – these two objects we find bang in the middle of the area he swept with his arms in the violent spasm that followed the moment when he drank. Why were they not hurled to the floor with the plate and the modeller's tools?'

'By God, because they were put there afterwards,' said Curtis.

'Yes, and why was that cup which he held with his left hand put down on the right of the table with the print on the far side? To put the cup down where we found it he must have stood where I am now – or here – or perhaps here. Well, say he drank the stuff while he was in such a position. After taking it he put the cup at this end of the table and the bottle, which has a left-hand print, beside it. He then moved to the chair, swept away the other stuff in his death throes, but replaced the bottle and the cup.'

'Which is absurd,' said Thompson solemnly.

'Ugh,' said Bailey.

'I think it is,' said Alleyn. He glanced at Curtis. 'What would happen when he drank nitric acid?'

'Undiluted?'

'I think so.'

'Very quick and remarkably horrible.' Curtis gave a rapid description of what would happen. 'He wouldn't perform any intelligent action. The initial shock would be terrific, and intense spasms would follow immediately. It's quite beyond the bounds of possibility that he would replace the cup, seat himself, or do anything but make some uncontrolled and violent movement such as you've described in reference to the arms. But I cannot believe, Alleyn, that anybody in his senses could ever take nitric acid without knowing what he was doing.'

'If he was not in his senses, but half doped with opium, and very thirsty? If he asked for a drink and it was put beside him?'

'That's more likely, certainly, but still – '

'If he was asleep in his chair with his mouth open, and it was poured into his mouth,' said Alleyn. 'What about that?'

'Well then – of course' – Curtis shrugged – 'that would explain everything.'

'It may be the explanation,' said Alleyn. 'The stuff had spilled over the face very freely. I want you now to look at the back of the head.' With his long, fastidious fingers he uncovered the hair, leaving the face veiled.

'He wore his hair long, you see. Now look here. Look. Do you see these tufts of hair that are shorter? They seem to have been broken, don't they? And see this. Hold your torch down and use a lens. The scalp is slightly torn as though a strand of hair has actually been wrenched away. On the floor behind this chair I found several hairs, and some of them have little flakes of scalp on the ends. Notice how the hair round the torn scalp is tangled. What's the explanation? Doesn't it suggest that a hand has been twisted in his hair? Now see the back of the chair. I think we shall find that these stains were made by nitric acid, and the floor beneath is stained in the same way. These are nitric stains – I'm afraid I'll have to uncover the face – yes – you see, running from the corners of the mouth down the line of the jaw to the ears and the neck. Notice the direction. It's important. It suggests strongly that the head was leaning back, far back, when the stuff was taken. Now if we lean him back in the chair – God, this is a filthy business! All right, Bathgate, damn you, get out. Now, Curtis, and you, Fox. Look how the hair fits between the acid stains on the back of the chair, and how the stains carry on from the jaw to the chair as if the stuff had run down. Would a man ever drink in this attitude with his face to the ceiling? Don't you get a picture of someone standing behind him and pouring something into his mouth? He gasps and makes a violent spasmodic movement. A hand is wound in his hair and holds back his head. And still nitric acid is poured between his lips. God! Cover it up again. Now, let's go to the door.'

They walked in silence down the place, opened the door, and were joined by a very green Nigel. Alleyn filled his pipe and lit it. 'To sum up,' he said, 'and for Heaven's sake, all of you, check me if I go too far – we have difficulty in fitting the evidence of the hands, the table, the position of the body, the cup and the bottle, with any theory of suicide. On the other hand, we find nothing to contradict the suggestion that this man sat at this table, was given a dose of nitric acid, made a series of violent and convulsive movements, vomited, clutched the edge of the table and died. We find nothing to contradict the theory that his murderer dragged the left hand away from the ledge of the table and used it to print the bottle and the cup, and then left them on the table. I don't for a moment suggest there is a good case for us here, but at least there is a better case for murder than for suicide.' He looked from one dubious face to another.

'I know it's tricky,' he said. 'Curtis – how long would he take to die?'

'Difficult to say. Fourteen hours. Might be more, might be less.'

'Fourteen hours! Damn and blast! That blows the whole thing sky-high.'

'Wait a moment, Alleyn. Have we any idea how much of the stuff he took?'

'The bottle was full. Miss Troy and Miss Bostock said it was full on Friday morning. Allowing for the amount that splashed over, it might have been quite a cupful.'

'This is the most shocking affair,' said little Curtis. 'I – never in the whole course of my experience have I – however. My dear chap, if a stream of the stuff was poured into his mouth while his head was held back, he may have died in a few minutes of a particularly unspeakable form of asphixiation. Actually, we may find he got some of it down his larynx, in which case death would be essentially from obstruction to breathing and would take place very quickly unless relieved by tracheotomy. You notice that the portions of the face that are not dicoloured by acid are bluish. That bears out this theory. If you are right, I suppose that's what we shall find. We'd better clear up here and get the body away. We'll have the autopsy as soon as possible.'

It was almost dark when they got back to the Yard. Alleyn went straight to his room, followed by Fox and by a completely silent Nigel. Alleyn dropped into an armchair. Fox switched on the light.

'You want a drink, sir,' he said, with a look at Alleyn.

'We all do. Bathgate, I don't know what the hell you're doing here, but if you are going to be ill, you can get out. We've had enough of that sort of thing.'

'I'm all right now,' said Nigel. 'What shall I do about this? The late edition – '

'A hideous curse on the late edition! All right. Tell them we've found him and where, and suggest suicide. That's all. Go away, there's a good chap.'

Nigel went.

'For pity's sake, Fox,' said Alleyn violently, 'why do you stand there staring at me like a benevolent bullock? Is my face dirty?'

'No, sir, but it's a bit white. Now, you have that drink, Mr Alleyn, before we go any further. I've got my emergency flask here.'

'I poured most of mine down McCully's gullet,' said Alleyn. 'Very well, Fox. Thank you. Have one yourself and let's be little devils together. Now then, where do we stand? You were very silent in that place of horror. Do you agree with my theory?'

'Yes, sir, I do. I've been turning it over in my mind and I don't see how any other theory will fit all the facts, more especially the tuft of hair torn from the scalp and found, as you might say, for the greater part on the floor.'

Fox briefly sucked in his short moustache and wiped his hand across his mouth.

'He must have jerked about very considerably,' he said, 'and have been held on to very determinedly.'

'Very.'

'Yes. Now sir, as we know only too well, it's one thing to have a lot of circumstantial evidence and another to tie somebody up in it. As far as times go, we're all over the shop here, aren't we? Some time late Friday night or early Saturday morning's the nearest we can get to when Garcia left Tatler's End House. All we can say about the time the caravan was returned is that it was probably before it was light on Saturday morning. Now, which of this crowd could have got away for at least two hours?'

'At the very least.'

'Yes. Two hours between seven-thirty on Friday evening, when Sadie Welsh heard Garcia speak, and before anybody was about – say, five o'clock – on Saturday morning. Do you reckon any of the lot that were up in London may have met him here?'

'Murdered him, taken the caravan to Tatler's End House and returned here – how?'

'That's true.'

'And I repeat, Fox, that I cannot believe a man in Garcia's condition could have gone through all the game with the caravan and the transport. We don't even know if he could drive and I should not be at all surprised if we find he couldn't. It would take a tolerably good driver to do all this. If it was one of the London lot, he went to Tatler's End House by means unknown, brought Garcia here and murdered him, returned the caravan and came back here, again by means unknown. You've seen the alibis. Pretty hopeless to fit anything on to any single one of them, isn't it?'

'I suppose so.'

'Except, perhaps, Malmsley. Could Malmsley have stayed behind and not caught the six o'clock bus? Where's the stuff about Malmsley?'

Fox got a file from the desk and thumbed it over.

'Here we are, sir. I saw the conductor of the six o'clock this morning. He says four people got on at Bossicote corner on Friday evening. One woman and three men. He's a dull sort of chap. I asked him if any of the men had beards and he said he couldn't rightly remember, but he thinks one had a very wide-brimmed hat and wore a muffler, so he might have had a beard. Silly sort of chap. We did see a wide-brimmed affair in Malmsley's wardrobe, too, but we'll have to try and get closer to it than that.'

'Yes. If Malmsley did it, what about his dinner at the Savoy and his late night with his friend? I suppose he could have driven the caravan, killed Garcia and left the body here at about seven to eight-thirty, come back after he'd seen his friend to bed, and done all the rest of it. But how the devil did he get back from the studio to London after returning the caravan?'

'That's right.' Fox licked his thumb and turned a page. 'Now, here's Miss Troy and Miss Bostock. Their alibis are the only ones we seem to have a chance of breaking among the London push. They've been checked up all right and were both seen by the club night porter when they came in, Miss Bostock at about one o'clock and Miss Troy at two-twenty. I've seen Miss Troy's friend, Mr Bellasca, and he says he took her back to the club at two-twenty, or thereabouts. So that fits.'

'Is he a reliable sort of fellow?'

'I think so, sir. He's very concerned on Miss Troy's behalf. He's been ringing her up, but apparently she didn't exactly encourage him to go down there. He's a very open sort of young gentleman and said she always treated him as if he was a schoolboy. However, the time at the club's all right. The porter says definitely he let Miss Troy in at two-twenty. She exclaimed at the time, he says, so he remembered that. He says neither she nor Miss Bostock came out again, but he sits in a little cubby-hole by the lift, and may have dozed off. The garage is open all night. Their car was by the door. The chap there admits he slipped out to the coffee stall at about three o'clock.' Fox glanced up from the notes, looked fixedly at Alleyn's white face, and then cleared his throat. 'Not that I'm suggesting there's anything in that,' he said.

'Go on,' said Alleyn.

'Well, sir, we may still admit there's a possibility in the cases of these two ladies and Malmsley. On the evidence in this file I'd say all the others are wash-outs. That leaves us with what you might call a narrowed field. The Hon. Basil Pilgrim, Miss Seacliff, Miss Troy, Miss Bostock, and Mr Malmsley.'

'Yes. Oh Lord, Fox, I forgot to ask Bathgate if he had any success with Miss Bobbie O'Dawne. I must be sinking into a detective's dotage. I'd better go along and tell the AC about this afternoon. Then I'll write up my report and I think this evening we'd better go broody on the case.'

Alleyn had a long interview with his Assistant Commissioner, a dry man with whom he got on very well. He then wrote up his report and took Fox off to dine at his own flat in a cul-de-sac off Coventry Street. After dinner they settled down over the fire to a systematic review of the whole case.

At eleven o'clock, while they were still at it, Nigel turned up.

'Hullo,' said Alleyn, 'I rather wanted to see you.'

'I guessed as much,' said Nigel complacently.

'Get yourself a drink. How did you hit it off with Bobbie O'Dawne? I see your extraordinary paper has come out strong with a simpering portrait.'

'Good, isn't it? She liked me awfully. We clicked.'

'Anything to the purpose?'

'Ah, ah, ah! *Wouldn't* you like to know!'

'We are not in the mood,' said Alleyn, 'for comedy.'

'All right. As a matter of fact, I'm afraid from your point of view the visit was not a howling success. She said she wouldn't have Sonia's name blackened in print and gave me a lot of stuff about how Sonia was the greatest little pal and a real sport. I took her out to lunch and gave her champagne, for which I expect the Yard to reimburse me. She got fairly chatty, but nothing much to the purpose. I told her I knew all about Sonia's little blackmailing games with Pilgrim and Malmsley, and she said that was just a bit of fun. I asked her if Sonia had the same kind of fun with anyone else, and she told me, with a jolly laugh, to mind my own business. I filled up her glass and she did get a bit unreserved. She said Garcia found out Sonia had told her about the Pilgrim game. Garcia was absolutely livid and said he'd do Sonia in if she couldn't hold her tongue. Of course, Sonia told Bobbie all this and made her swear on a Bible and a rosary that she wouldn't split to anyone. It was at this stage, Alleyn, that Bobbie took another pull at her champagne and then said – I memorized her actual words – 'So you see, dear, with an oath like that on my conscience I couldn't say anything about Friday night, could I?' I said: 'How d'you mean?' and she said: 'Never mind, dear. She oughn't to have told me. Now I'm scared. If he knows she told me, as sure as God's above he'll do for me, too.' And then, as there was no more champagne, the party broke up.'

'Well – I'll pay for the champagne,' said Alleyn. 'Damn this girl, Fox, she's tiresome. Sink me if I don't believe she knows who had the date with Garcia on Friday night. She's proved that it wasn't Sonia. Sonia spent the week-end with her. Well – who was it?'

The telephone rang. Alleyn picked up the receiver. 'Hullo. Yes, Bailey? I see. He's sure of that? Yes. Yes, I see. Thank you.'

He put down the receiver and looked at Fox.

'The hole on the cuff of Pilgrim's coat was made by an acid. Probably nitric acid.'

'Is that so?' said Fox. He rose slowly to his feet.

'There's your answer!' cried Nigel. 'I don't see how you can get away from it, Alleyn. You've got motive and opportunity. You've got evidence of a man who stood in the lane and looked in at the studio window. It might just have been Malmsley, but by God, I think it was Pilgrim.'

'In that case,' said Alleyn, 'we'll call on Captain and Mrs Pascoe at Boxover, where Pilgrim and Miss Seacliff spent the night. Run along, Bathgate. I want to talk to Inspector Fox. I'm most grateful for your work with Bobbie O'Dawne and I won't tell your wife you spend your days with ladies of the chorus. Good evening.'

Chapter 19

Alleyn makes a Pilgrimage

The inquest on the body of Sonia Gluck was held at Bossicote on the morning of Thursday, September 22nd. The court, as might have been expected, was jammed to the doors; otherwise the proceedings were as colourless as the coroner, a gentleman with an air of irritated incredulity, could make them. He dealt roundly with the witnesses and with the evidence, reducing everything by a sort of sleight-of-hand to a dead norm. One would have thought that models impaled on the points of poignards were a commonplace of police investigation. Only once did he appear to be at all startled and that was when Cedric Malmsley gave evidence. The coroner eyed Malmsley's beard as if he thought it must be detachable, abruptly changed his own glasses, and never removed his outraged gaze from the witness throughout his evidence. The barest outline of the tragedy was brought out. Alleyn gave formal evidence on the finding of Garcia's body, and the court was fraught with an unspoken inference that it was a case of murder and suicide. Alleyn asked for an adjournment, and the whole thing was over by eleven o'clock.

In the corridor Alleyn caught Fox by the arm.

'Come on, Brer Fox. We're for Boxover. The first stop in the pilgrimage. I've got my mother's car – looks less official. It's over there – wait for me, will you?'

He watched Fox walk away and then turned quickly into a side lane where Troy sat in her three-seater. Alleyn came up to her from behind, and she did not see him. She was staring straight in front of her. He stood there with his hat in his hands, waiting for her to turn her head. When at last she woke from her meditation and saw him, her eyes widened. She looked at him gravely and then smiled.

'Hullo. It's you,' said Troy, 'I'm waiting for Katti.'

'I have to say a word to you,' said Alleyn.

'What is it?'

'I don't know. Any word. Are you all right?'

'Yes, thank you.'

'I'm afraid it's difficult for you,' said Alleyn, 'having all these people still in the house. This second case made it necessary. We can't let them go.'

'It's all right. We're doing some work out of doors when it's fine, and I've moved everything round in the studio and got a man from the village to sit. Katti's doing a life-size thing of the policeman at the front gate. It's a bit – difficult – at times, but they seem to have made up their minds Garcia did it.'

'This last thing – about Garcia. It's been a pretty bad shock to you.'

'In a way – yes,' said Troy. 'It was kind of you to send me a telegram.'

'Kind! Oh, well, if it broke the news a bit, that's something. You had no particular feeling about him, had you? It was his work, wasn't it?'

'True enough. His work. That clay group was really good, you know. I think it would have been the best thing he ever did. Somebody will do the marble from the model, I suppose.' She looked directly in Alleyn's eyes. 'I'm – I'm horrified,' she whispered.

'I know.'

'Nitric acid! It's so beyond the bounds of one's imagination that anyone could possibly – Please tell me – they seemed to suggest that Garcia himself – I *must* know. Did he kill her and then himself? I can't believe he did. He would never do that. The first – all that business with the knife – I *can* imagine his suddenly deciding to kill Sonia like that. In a ghastly sort of way it might appeal to his imagination, but it's just because his imagination was so vivid that I am sure he wouldn't kill himself so horribly.

770

Why – why, Ormerin once spilt acid from that bottle on his hand – Garcia was there. He knew. He saw the burn.'

'He was drugged at the time he died. He'd been smoking opium.'

'Garcia! But – All right. It's not fair to ask you questions.'

'I'm so sorry. I think we're nearly at an end. Tomorrow, perhaps, we shall know.'

'Don't look so – worried,' said Troy suddenly.

'I wonder if it has ever entered your head,' said Alleyn, 'that it is only by wrenching my thoughts round with a remarkable effort that I can keep them on my job and not on you.'

She looked at him without speaking.

'Well,' he said. 'What have you got to say to that, Troy?'

'Nothing. I'm sorry. I'd better go.'

'A woman never actually objects to a man getting into this state of mind about her, does she? I mean – as long as he behaves himself?'

'No. I don't think she does.'

'Unless she happens to associate him with something particularly unpleasant. As you must me. Good God, I'm a pretty sort of fellow to shove my damned attentions on a lady in the middle of a job like this.'

'You're saying too much,' said Troy. 'You must stop. Please.'

'I'm extremely sorry. You're perfectly right – it was unpardonable. Goodbye.'

He stood back. Troy made a swift movement with her hands and leant towards him.

'Don't be so "pukka sahib",' she said. 'It is quite true – a woman doesn't mind.'

'Troy!'

'Now I'm saying too much. It's her vanity. Even mixed up with horrors like these she rather likes it.'

'We seem to be an odd pair,' said Alleyn. 'I haven't the smallest idea of what you think of me. No, truly,

771

not the smallest idea. But even in the middle of police investigations we appear to finish our thoughts. Troy, have you ever thought of me when you were alone?'

'Naturally.'

'Do you dislike me?'

'No.'

'That will do to go on with,' said Alleyn. 'Good morning.'

With his hat still in his hand he turned and walked away quickly to his mother's car.

'Off we go, Fox,' he said. 'Alley houp. The day is ours.'

He slipped in the clutch and in a very few minutes they were travelling down a fortunately deserted road at fifty miles an hour. Fox cleared his throat.

'What's that, Brer Fox?' asked Alleyn cheerfully.

'I didn't speak, Mr Alleyn. Are we in a hurry?'

'Not particularly. I have a disposition of speed come upon me.'

'I see,' said Fox dryly.

Alleyn began to sing.

> 'Au clair de la lune
> Mon ami, Pierrot.'

Trees and hedges flew past in a grey blur. From the back of the car a muffled voice suddenly chanted:

> 'I thought I saw Inspector Alleyn hunting for a clue.
> I looked again and saw it was an inmate at the Zoo.
> "Good God," I said, "It's very hard to judge between these two." '

Alleyn took his foot off the accelerator. Fox slewed round and stared into the back of the car. From an upheaval of rugs Nigel's head emerged.

'I thought,' he continued, 'I saw Gargantua in fancy worsted socks.

> I looked again and saw it was a mammoth picking locks.
> "Good God," I said, "it might have been my friend Inspector Fox." '

'Rude is never funny,' said Alleyn. 'When did you hide in my mother's car?'

'Immediately after the old gentleman pronounced the word "adjournment." Where are we bound for?'

'I shan't tell you. Alley houp! Away we go again.'

'Mr Fox,' said Nigel, 'what has overtaken your chief? Is he mad, drunk, or in love?'

'Don't answer the fellow, Brer Fox,' said Alleyn. 'Let him burst in ignorance. Sit down, behind, there.'

They arrived at Boxover and drew up outside a rather charming Georgian house on the outskirts of the village.

'Twenty minutes,' said Alleyn, looking from his watch to the speedometer. 'Twenty minutes from Bossicote and twelve miles. It's two miles from the studio to Bossicote. Fourteen miles and a straightish road. We slowed down once on Bathgate's account and once to ask the way. At night you could do the whole trip in a quarter of an hour or less. Now then. A certain amount and yet not too much finesse is indicated. Come on, Fox.'

'May I come?' asked Nigel.

'You? You have got the most colossal, the most incredible, the most appalling cheek. Your hide! Your effrontery! Well, well, well. Come along. You are a Yard typist. Wait by the car until I give you a leery nod, both of you.'

He rang the front door bell and whistled very sweetly and shrilly.

'What *is* the matter with him, Fox?' asked Nigel.

'Search me, Mr Bathgate. He's been that worried over this case ever since we found Garcia, you'd think he'd never crack a joke again, and then he comes out from this inquest, crosses the road to have a word with Miss Troy and comes back, as you might say, with bells on.'

'Oh ho!' said Nigel. 'Say you so, Fox. By gum, Fox, do you suppose – '

The door was opened by a manservant. Alleyn spoke to him and gave him a card. The man stood back and Alleyn with a grimace at them over his shoulder, stepped inside, leaving the door open.

'Come on, Mr Bathgate,' said Fox. 'That means us.'

They joined Alleyn in a little hall that was rather overwhelmed with the horns, masks, and hides of dead animals.

'Mrs Pascoe is away,' whispered Alleyn, 'but the gallant captain is within. Here he comes.'

Captain Pascoe was short, plump and vague-looking. He had prominent light blue eyes and a red face. He smelt of whisky. He looked doubtfully from Alleyn to Fox.

'I'm sorry to bother you, Captain Pascoe,' said Alleyn.

'That's all right. You're from Scotland Yard, aren't you? This business over at Bossicote, what?'

'That's it. We're checking up everybody's movements on the night in question – you'll understand it has to be done.'

'Oh quite. Routine, what?'

'Exactly. Inspector Fox and Mr Bathgate are with me.'

'Oh ya',' said Captain Pascoe. 'H' are y'. H' are y'. Have a drink.'

'Thank you so much, but I think we'll get on with the job.'

'Oh. Right-ho. I suppose it's about Valmai – Miss Seacliff – and Pilgrim, isn't it? I've been followin' the case. Damn funny, isn't it? They're all right. Spent Friday here with us. Slept here and went on to old Pilgrim's place next day.'

'So they told us. I'm just going to ask you to check up the times. It won't take a moment.'

'Oh, quite. Right-ho. Sit down.'

Alleyn led him through the weekend from the moment when Valmai Seacliff and Pilgrim arrived, up to the time they all sat down to dinner. Captain Pascoe said nothing to contradict the information given by the other two. Alleyn complimented him on his memory and on the crispness of his recital, which was anything but crisp. The little man expanded gratefully.

'And now,' said Alleyn, 'we come to the important

period between ten o'clock on Friday night and five the following morning. You are a soldier, sir, and you understand the difficulties of this sort of thing. One has to be very discreet – ' Alleyn waved his hands and looked respectfully at Captain Pascoe.

'By Jove, ya'. I 'member there was feller in my reg'-ment' – the anecdote wound itself up into an impenetrable tangle – 'and, by Jove, we nearly had a court martial over it.'

'Exactly. Just the sort of thing we want to avoid. So you see, if we can account, now, for every second of their time during Friday evening they will be saved a lot of unpleasantness later on. You know yourself, sir – '

'Oh, quite. All for it. Damned unpleasant. Always flatter myself I've got the faculty of observing detail.'

'Yes. Now I understand that during dinner Miss Seacliff complained of a headache?'

'No, no. Not till after dinner. Minor point, but we may's well be accurate, Inspector.'

'Certainly, sir. Stupid of me. Was it about the time you had coffee that she first spoke of it?'

'No. Wait a bit, though. Tell you what – just to show you – what I was saying about my faculty for tabulatin' detail – '

'Yes.'

'I 'member Valmai made a face over her coffee. Took a swig at it and then did a sort of shudder and m'wife said: "What's up?" or words to the same effect, and Val said the coffee was bitter, and then Pilgrim looked a bit sheepish and I said: "Was yours bitter?" and he said: "Matter of fact it was!" Funny – mine was all right. But my idea is that Val was feeling a bit off colour then, and he just agreed the coffee was bitter to keep her in countenance. In my opinion the girl had a liver. Pilgrim persuaded her to have a glass of port after champagne, and she said at the time it would upset her. Damn bad show. She's a lovely thing. Damn good rider to hounds. Lovely hands. Goes as straight and as well as the best of 'em. Look at that.' He fumbled in a drawer of his writing-desk and produced a press photograph of Valmai Seacliff looking magnificent on a hunter. Captain Pascoe gloated over it, handed it to Alleyn, and flung himself back in his chair. He appeared to collect his thoughts. 'But to show you how one notices little things,' he resumed. 'Not till after dinner that she talked about feeling under the weather. Matter of fact, it was when I took her empty cup. Precise moment. There you are.' And he laughed triumphantly.

'Splendid, sir. I wish everyone was as clear-minded. I remember a case where the whole thing hinged on just such an incident. It was a question of who put sugar in a cup of tea, and do you think we could get anyone who remembered? Not a bit of it. It's only one witness in a hundred who can give us that sort of thing.'

'Really? Well, I'll lay you a tenner, Inspector, I can tell you about the coffee on Friday night. Just for the sake of argument.'

'I'm not betting, sir.'

'Ha, ha, ha. Now then. M'wife poured out our coffee at that table over there. Pilgrim handed it round for her. He put Val's down beside her with his own, told her he'd put sugar in it, and went back to the table for mine. There you are, Inspector. Val complained her coffee was bitter. She asked Pilgrim if his tasted funny and he said it did, and – ' He stopped short and his eyes bulged. 'Look here,' he said, 'way I'm talking anybody might think this was a case of hanky-panky with the coffee. Good Lord, Inspector. Here! I say, I hope you don't – '

'Don't let that bother you, sir. We're only taking a sample case and I congratulate you. We don't get our information as lucidly as that very often, do we, Fox?'

'Very nice, indeed, sir,' agreed Fox, wagging his head.

'And then,' said Alleyn. 'I believe you played bridge?'

'Yes. That's right. But by that time Val was looking very seedy and said her head was splitting, so after two or three hands we chucked it up and m'wife took Val up to her room.'

'Gave her some aspirin perhaps?'

'No. Pilgrim rushed off and got some aspirin for her. Anxious about her as an old man. Engaged couples, what? Ha! She took the bottle up with her. M'wife tucked her up and went to her own room. Pilgrim said he was sleepy – I must say he's a dreary young blighter. Not nearly good enough for Val. Said he felt like bed and a long sleep. Dull chap. So we had a whisky and soda and turned in. That was at half-past ten. I wound up the clocks, and we went and had a look at Val and found she was in bed. Very attractive creature, Val. Naughty little thing hadn't taken the aspirin. Said it made her sick trying to swallow. So Pilgrim dissolved three in water and she promised she'd take 'em. M'wife looked in later and found her sound alseep. We were all tucked up and snoozing by eleven, I should think. And now let's see. Following morning – '

Captain Pascoe described the following morning with a wealth of detail to which Alleyn listened with every sign of respect and appreciation. Drinks were again suggested. 'Well, if you won't, I will,' said Captain Pascoe, and did, twice. Alleyn asked to see the bedrooms. Captain Pascoe mixed himself a third drink, and somewhat noisily escorted them over the house. The guest-rooms were at the top of the stairs.

'Val had this one, and that fellow was next door. What! Felt like a good long sleep! My God.' Here the captain laughed uproariously and pulled himself together. 'Not that Val'd stand any nonsense. Thoroughly nice girl. Looks very cometoish, but b'lieve me – na poo. I know. Too much other way 'fanything. I mean, give you 'ninstance. Following morning took her round rose garden. Looking lovely. Little purple cap and little purple gloves. Lovely. Just in friendly spirit I said, ''ffected little thing, wearing little purple gloves,' and gave little left-hand purple glove little squeeze. Just like that. Purely platonalistic. Jumped as if I'd bitten her and snatched away. Pooff!'

Captain Pascoe sat on the edge of Valmai's bed and finished his drink. He glared round the room, sucking his upper lip.

'Tchah!' he said suddenly. 'Look 't that. Disgraceful. Staff work in this house is 'bominable. M'wife's away. Maid's away. Only that feller to look after me. Meals at club. Nothing to do, and look at that.'

He pointed unsteadily to the mantelpiece.

' 'Bominable. Never been touched. Look at this!'

He turned his eye on the bedside table. Upon it stood a row of books. A dirty table-napkin lay on top of the books. Captain Pascoe snatched it up. Underneath it was a tumbler holding three fingers of murky fluid.

'D'yer know what that is? That's been there since Friday night. I mean!' He lurched again towards the bedside table. Alleyn slipped in front of him.

'Maddening that sort of thing. I wonder if we might see Mr Pilgrim's room, sir.'

'By George, we'll see every room in this house,' shouted Captain Pascoe. 'By God, we'll catch them red-handed.'

With this remarkable pronouncement he turned about and made for the door. Alleyn followed him, looked over his shoulder at Fox, raised his left eyebrow, and disappeared.

To Nigel's surprise, Fox said: 'Wait here, Mr Bathgate, please,' darted out of the room and reappeared in about a minute.

'Stand by that door if you please, Mr Bathgate,' whispered Fox. 'Keep the room clear.'

Nigel stood by the door and Fox, with surprising dexterity and speed, whipped a small wide-necked bottle from his pocket, poured the contents of the tumbler into it, corked it, and wrapped the tumbler up in his handkerchief.

'Now, sir. If you'll take those down to the car and put

them in the chief's case – thank you very much. Quickly does it.'

When Nigel got back he found that Captain Pascoe, accompanied by Alleyn, had returned to the hall and was yelling for his servant. The servant arrived and was damned to heaps. Fox came down. Captain Pascoe suddenly collapsed into an armchair, showed signs of drowsiness, and appeared to lose all interest in his visitors. Alleyn spoke to the servant.

'We are police officers and are making a few inquiries about the affair at Bossicote. Will you show us the garage, please?'

'Very good, sir,' said the man stolidly.

'It's nothing whatever to do with your employer, personally, by the way.'

Captain Pascoe's servant bestowed a disappointed glance upon his master and led his visitors out by the front door.

'The garage is a step or two down the lane, sir. The house, being old and what they call restored, hasn't many conveniences.'

'Do you keep early hours here? What time do you get up in the mornings?'

'Breakfast is not till ten, sir. The maids are supposed to get up at seven. It's more like half-past. The Captain and Mrs Pascoe breakfast in their rooms, you see, and so do most guests.'

'Did Mr Pilgrim and Miss Seacliff breakfast in their rooms?'

'Oh yes, sir. There's the garage, sir.'

He showed them a double garage about 200 yards down the lane. Captain Pascoe's Morris Cowley occupied less than half the floor space.

'Ah yes,' said Alleyn. 'Plenty of room here. I suppose, now, that Mr Pilgrim's car fitted in very comfortably?'

'Oh yes, sir.'

'Nice car, isn't it?'

'Very nice job, sir. Tiger on petrol, sir.'

'Really? What makes you think that?'

'Well, sir, I asked the gentleman on Saturday morning was she all right for petrol – I'm butler-chauffeur, sir – and he said yes, she was filled up as full as she'd go in Bossicote. Well, sir, I looked at the gauge and she'd eaten up two gallons coming over here. Twelve miles, sir, no more. I looked to see if she was leaking but she wasn't. Something wrong there, sir, isn't there?'

'I agree with you,' said Alleyn. 'Thank you very much, I think that's all.'

'Thank you very much indeed, sir,' said the butler-chauffeur, closing his hand gratefully.

Alleyn, Fox and Nigel returned to their car and drove away.

'Get that tumbler, Fox?' asked Alleyn.

'Yes, sir. And the liquid. Had to go down to the car for a bottle.'

'Good enough. What a bit of luck, Fox! You remember the Seacliff told us Mrs Pascoe was leaving on Saturday and giving the maids a holiday? My golly, *what* a bit of luck.'

'Do you think the stuff was the melted aspirin Pilgrim doled out for her on Friday night?' asked Nigel.

'That's my clever little man,' said Alleyn. 'I do think so. And if the tumbler has Pilgrim's prints, and only his, we'll know.'

'Are you going to have the stuff analyzed?'

'Yes. Damn quick about it, too, if possible.'

'And what then?'

'Why then,' said Alleyn, 'we'll be within sight of an arrest.'

Chapter 20

Arrest

The analyst's report on the contents of the tumbler came through at nine-thirty that evening. The fluid contained a solution of Bayer's Aspirin – approximately three tablets. The glass bore a clear imprint of Basil Pilgrim's fingers and thumb. When Alleyn had read the analyst's report he rang up his Assistant Commissioner, had a long talk with him, and then sent for Fox.

'There's one thing we must make sure of,' he said wearily, 'and that's the position of the light on the figure outside the studio window. Our game with the string wasn't good enough. We'll have to get something a bit more positive, Brer Fox.'

'Meaning, sir?'

'Meaning, alas, a trip to Tatler's End.'

'Now?'

'I'm afraid so. We'll have a Yard car. It'll be needed in the morning. Come on.'

So for the last time Alleyn and Fox drove through the night to Tatler's End House. The Bossicote church clock struck midnight as Fox took up his old position outside the studio window. A fine drizzle was falling, and the lane smelt of leaf-mould and wet grass. The studio lights were on and the blind was drawn down.

'I shall now retire to the shady spot where Ethel and her boy lost themselves in an interlude of modified rapture,' said Alleyn.

He walked down the lane and returned in a few minutes.

'Fox,' he said, 'the ray of light that comes through the hole in the blind alights upon your bosom. I think we are on the right track.'

'Looks like it,' Fox agreed. 'What do we do now?'

'We spend the rest of the night with my mamma. I'll
ring up the Yard and get the official party to pick us up
at Danes Lodge in the morning. Come on.'

'Very good, Mr Alleyn. Er – '

'What's the matter?'

'Well, sir. I was thinking of Miss Troy. It's going to be
a bit unpleasant for her, isn't it? I was wondering if we
couldn't do something to make it a bit easier.'

'Yes, Fox. That's rather my idea, too. I think – damn
it all, it's too late to bother her now. Or is it? I'll ring up
from Danes Lodge. Come on.'

They got to Danes Lodge at twelve-thirty, and found
Lady Alleyn reading D. H. Lawrence before a roaring
fire in her little sitting-room.

'Good evening,' said Lady Alleyn. 'I got your message,
Roderick. How nice to see you again, Mr Fox. Come and
sit down.'

'I'm just going to telephone,' said Alleyn. 'Won't be
long.'

'All right, darling. Mr Fox, help yourself to a drink and
come and tell me if you have read any of this unhappy
fellow's books.'

Fox put on his spectacles and gravely inspected the
outside of *The Letters of D. H. Lawrence*.

'I can't say I have, my lady,' he said, 'but I seem
to remember we cleaned up an exhibition of this Mr
Lawrence's pictures a year or two ago. Very fashionable
show it was.'

'Ah yes. Those pictures. What did you think of them?'

'I don't exactly know,' said Fox. 'They seemed well
within the meaning of the act, I must say, but the colours
were pretty. You wouldn't have cared for the subjects,
my lady.'

'Shouldn't I? He seems never to have found his own
centre of gravity, poor fellow. Some of these letters are
wise and some are charming, and some are really rather
tedious. All these negroid deities growling in his interior!
One feels sorry for his wife, but she seems to have had

782

the right touch with him. Have you got your drink? That's right. Are you pleased with your progress in this case?'

'Yes, thank you. It's coming on nicely.'

'And so you are going to arrest somebody tomorrow morning? I thought as much. One can always tell by my son's manner when he is going to make an arrest. He gets a pinched look.'

'So does his prisoner, my lady,' said Fox, and was so enraptured with his own pun that he shook from head to foot with amazed chuckles.

'Roderick!' cried Lady Alleyn as her son came in, 'Mr Fox is making nonsense of your mother.'

'He's a wise old bird if he can do that,' said Alleyn. 'Mamma, I've asked Miss Agatha Troy if she will lunch here with you tomorrow. She says she will. Do you mind? I shan't be here.'

'But I'm delighted, darling. She will be charming company for me and for Mr Bathgate.'

'What the devil – !'

'Mr Bathgate is motoring down tomorrow to their cottage to see his wife. He asked if he might call in.'

'It's forty miles off his course, the little tripe-hound.'

'Is it, darling? When I told him you would be here he said he'd arrive soon after breakfast.'

'Really, Mum! Oh well, I suppose it's all right. He's well trained. But I'm afraid he's diddled you.'

'He thinks he has, at all events,' said Lady Alleyn. 'And now, darling, as you are going to make an arrest in the morning, don't you think you ought to get a good night's sleep?'

'Fox?'

'Mr Fox has been fabulously discreet, Roderick.'

'Then how did you know we were going to arrest anybody?'

'You have just told me, my poor baby. Now run along to bed.'

At ten o'clock the next morning two police cars drove up

to Tatler's End House. They were followed by Nigel in a baby Austin. He noted, with unworthy satisfaction, that one or two young men in flannel trousers and tweed coats hung about the gate and had evidently been refused admittance by the constable on duty. Nigel himself had been given a card by Alleyn on the strict understanding that he behaved himself and brought no camera with him. He was not allowed to enter the house. He had, he considered, only a minor advantage over his brother journalists.

The three cars drew up in the drive. Alleyn, Fox, and two plain-clothes men went up the steps to the front door. Nigel manoeuvred his baby Austin into a position of vantage. Alleyn glanced down at him and then turned away as Troy's butler opened the front door.

'Will you come in, please?' said the butler nervously. He showed them into Troy's library. A fire had been lit and the room would now have seemed pleasantly familiar to Alleyn if he had been there on any other errand.

'Will you tell Miss Troy of our arrival, please?'

The butler went out.

'I think, Fox, if you don't mind – ' said Alleyn.

'Certainly, sir. We'll wait in the hall.'

Troy came in.

'Good morning,' said Alleyn, and his smile contradicted the formality of his words. 'I thought you might prefer to see us before we go any further.'

'Yes.'

'You've realized from what I said last night on the telephone that as far as the police are concerned the first stage of this business may come to an end this morning?'

'Yes. You are going to make an arrest, aren't you?'

'I think we shall probably do so. It depends a little on the interview we hope to have in a minute or two. This has been an abominable week for you. I'm sorry I had to keep all these people together here and station bluebottles at your doors and before your gates and so on. It was partly in your own interest. You would have been overrun with pressmen.'

'I know.'

'Do you want me to tell you – ?'

'I think I know.'

'You *know*?'

'I think I do. Last night I said to myself: "Which of these people do I feel in my own bones is capable of this crime?" There was only one – only one of whom it did not seem quite preposterous to think: "It might – it just *might* be you!" I don't know why – there seems to be no motive, but I believe I am right. I suppose woman's instinct is the sort of phrase you particularly abominate.'

'That depends a little on the woman,' said Alleyn gravely.

'I suppose it does,' said Troy and flushed unexpectedly.

'I'll tell you who it is,' he said after a moment. And he told her. 'I can see that this time the woman's instinct was not at fault.'

'It's – so awful,' whispered Troy.

'I'm glad you decided to lunch with my mother,' said Alleyn. 'It will be easier for you to get right away from everything. She asked me to say that she would be delighted if you would come early. I suggest that you drive over there now.'

Troy's chin went up.

'Thank you,' she said, 'but I'm not going to rat.'

'There's no question of ratting – '

'After all, this is *my* ship.'

'Of course it is. But it's not sinking and, unfortunately, you can't do anything about this miserable business. It may be rather particularly unpleasant. I should take a trip ashore.'

'It's very kind of you to think of me, but, however illogically, I would feel as if I was funking something if I went away before – before you did. I've got my students to think of. You must see that. And even – even Pilgrim – '

'You can do nothing about him – '

785

'Very well,' said Troy angrily, 'I shall stay and do nothing.'

'Don't, please, be furious with me. Stay, then, but stay with your students.'

'I shan't make a nuisance of myself.'

'You know perfectly well that ever since I met you, you have made a nuisance of yourself. You've made my job one hundred per cent more difficult, because you've taken possession of my thoughts as well as my heart. And now, you go off to your students and think that over. I want to speak to Pilgrim, if you please.'

Troy gazed bleakly at him. Then she bit her lips and Alleyn saw that her eyes were full of tears.

'Oh, hell and damnation, darling,' he said.

'It's all right. I'm going. Shut up,' mumbled Troy, and went.

Fox came in.

'All right,' said Alleyn. 'Tell them to get Pilgrim, and come in.'

Fox spoke to someone outside and joined Alleyn at the fire.

'We'll have to go warily, Fox. He may give a bit of trouble.'

'That's so, sir.'

They waited in silence until Basil Pilgrim came in with one of the Yard men. The second man walked in after them and stood inside the door.

'Good morning,' said Pilgrim.

'Good morning, Mr Pilgrim. We would like to clear up one or two points relating to your former statement and to our subsequent investigations.'

'Certainly.'

Alleyn consulted his notebook.

'What does your car do to the gallon?' he asked.

'Sixteen.'

'Sure of that?'

'Yes. She may do a bit more on long runs.'

'Right. Now, if you please, we'll go back to Friday

786

evening during your visit to Captain and Mrs Pascoe. Do you remember the procedure when coffee was brought in?'

'I suppose so. It was in the hall.'

He looked, with that curiously restless turn of his head, from Alleyn to Fox and back again.

'Can you tell us who poured out and who handed round the coffee?'

'I suppose so. Though what it can have to do with Sonia – or Garcia – Do you mean about Val's coffee being bitter? Mine was bitter, too. Beastly.'

'We should like to know who poured the coffee out.'

'Mrs Pascoe.'

'And who handed it round?'

'Well – I did.'

'Splendid. Can you remember the order in which you took it round?'

'I'm not sure. Yes, I think so. I took mine over with Val's to where she was sitting, and then I saw Pascoe hadn't got his, and I got it for him. Mrs Pascoe had poured out her own. Then I went back and sat with Val and I had my coffee.'

'You both took black coffee?'

'Yes.'

'And sugar?'

'And sugar.'

'Who put the sugar in the coffee?'

'Good Lord! I don't know. I believe I did.'

'You didn't say anything about your coffee being bitter?'

'I didn't like to. I gave Val a look and made a face and she nodded. She said: "Sybil, darling, your coffee is perfectly frightful." Mrs Pascoe was – ' he laughed – 'well, she was a bit huffy, I think. Val is always terribly direct. They both appealed to me and I – well, I just said I thought the coffee wasn't quite what one usually expects of coffee, or something. It was dashed awkward.'

'It must have been. Later on, when Miss Seacliff complained of feeling unwell, you gave her some aspirin, didn't you?'

'Yes. Why?' asked Pilgrim, looking surprised.

'Was the bottle of aspirins in your pocket?'

'What do you mean? I went upstairs and got it out of my suitcase. Look here, what are you driving at?'

'Please, Mr Pilgrim, let us get this tidied up. When did you actually give Miss Seacliff the aspirins?'

'When she went to bed. I tell you I got them from my suitcase and took them downstairs and gave her three.'

'Did she take them?'

'Not then. We looked in after she was in bed and she said she could never swallow aspirins, and so I dissolved three in water and left the tumbler by her bedside.'

'Did you see her drink this solution?'

'No. I think I said, Inspector, that I left it at her bed-side.'

'Yes,' said Alleyn, 'I've got that. Where's the bottle?'

'What bottle? Oh, the aspirin. I don't know. I suppose it's in my room upstairs.'

'After you left Miss Seacliff's room on Friday night where did you go?'

'I had a drink with Pascoe and went to bed.'

'Did you get up at all during the night?'

'No.'

'You slept straight through the night?'

'Like the dead,' said Pilgrim. He was no longer restless. He looked steadily at Alleyn and he was extremely pale.

'It is strange you should have slept so soundly. There was a very severe thunderstorm that night,' lied Alleyn. 'Lightning. Doors banging. Maids bustling about. Didn't you hear it?'

'As a matter of fact,' said Pilgrim, after a pause, 'it's a funny thing, but I slept extraordinarily soundly that night. I'm always pretty good, but that night I seemed to be fathoms deep. I suppose I'd had a bit too much of Pascoe's 1875 Courvoisier.'

'I see. Now, Mr Pilgrim, I want you to look at this, if you please.'

He nodded to one of his men, who came forward with a brown-paper parcel. He opened it and took out a most disreputable garment.

'Why,' said Pilgrim, 'that's my old car coat.'

'Yes.'

'What on earth do you want with that, Mr Alleyn?'

'I want you to tell me when you burnt this little hole in the cuff. There, do you see.'

'I don't know. How the devil should I know! I've had the thing for donkey's years. It never comes out of the car. I've crawled under the car in it. It's obviously a cigarette burn.'

'It's an acid burn.'

'Acid? Rot! I mean, how could it be acid?'

'That is what we would like you to tell us.'

'Well, I'm afraid I can't tell you. Considering the use the thing's had, I suppose it might have come in contact with acid some time or another.'

'This is a recent stain.'

'Is it? Well then, it is. So what?'

'Might it be nitric acid?'

'Why?'

'Do you do any etching, Mr Pilgrim?'

'Yes. But not in my garage coat. Look here, Mr Alleyn – '

'Will you feel in the pockets?'

Pilgrim thrust a hand into one of the pockets and pulled out a pair of gloves.

'If you look on the back of the right-hand glove,' said Alleyn, 'you will see among all the greasy stains and worn patches another very small mark. Look at it, please. There. It is exceedingly small, but it, too, was made by an acid. Can you account for it?'

'Quite frankly, I can't. The gloves are always left in the pocket. Anything might happen to them.'

'I see. Have you ever lent this coat to anyone else? Has anyone else ever worn the gloves?'

'I don't know. They may have.' He looked up quickly and his eyes were suddenly bright with terror. 'I think it's quite likely I've lent it,' he said. 'Or a garage hand might have put it on some time – easily. It may be acid from a battery.'

'Have you ever lent it to Miss Seacliff, for instance?'

'Never.'

'It's an old riding Burberry, isn't it?'

'Yes.'

'You didn't lend it to her to hack in at your father's house – Ankerton – during the weekend?'

'Good Lord, no! Valmai has got very smart riding clothes of her own.'

'Not even the gloves?'

Pilgrim achieved a laugh. 'Those gloves! I had just given Valmai six pairs of coloured gloves which she tells me are fashionable. She was so thrilled she even lunched in purple gloves and dined in scarlet ones.'

'I mean to ride in?'

'She had her own hunting gloves. What *is* all this?'

'She goes well to hounds, doesn't she?'

'Straight as the best.'

'Yes. What sort of horse did you mount her on?'

'A hunter – one of mine.'

'Clubbed mane and tail?'

'Yes.'

'Look inside the right-hand glove – at the base of the little finger. Do you see that bloodstain?'

'I see a small stain.'

'It has been analysed. It is a bloodstain. Do you remember recently cutting or scratching the base of your little finger?'

'I – yes – I think I do.'

'How did it happen?'

'I forget. I think it was at Ankerton – on a bramble or something.'

790

'And you had these gloves with you at the time?'

'I suppose so. Yes.'

'I thought you said the gloves and coat always lived in the car?'

'It is rather absurd to go on with this,' Pilgrim said. 'I'm afraid I must refuse to answer any more questions.'

'You are perfectly within your rights. Fox, ask Miss Seacliff if she will be good enough to come in. Thank you, Mr Pilgrim; will you wait outside?'

'No,' said Pilgrim. 'I'm going to hear what you say to her.'

Alleyn hesitated.

'Very well,' he said at last. He dropped the coat and gloves behind the desk.

Valmai Seacliff arrived in her black slacks and magenta pullover. She made, as usual, a good entrance, shutting the door behind her and leaning against it for a moment to survey the men.

'Hallo,' she said. 'More investigations? What's the matter with you, Basil, you look as if you'd murdered somebody?'

Pilgrim didn't answer.

Alleyn said: 'I have sent for you, Miss Seacliff, to know if you can help us.'

'But I should adore to help you, Mr Alleyn.'

'Did you drink the solution of aspirin that Mr Pilgrim prepared for you on Friday night?'

'Not all of it. It was too bitter.'

'But you said, before, that you drank it.'

'Well, I did have a sip. I slept all right without it.'

'How is your cut hand?'

'My – ? Oh, it's quite recovered.'

'May I see it, please?'

She held it out with the same gesture that she had used on Monday night, but this time the fingers trembled. Below the base of the little finger there was still a very thin reddish scar.

'What's this?' said Pilgrim violently. 'Valmai – don't answer any of his questions. Don't answer!'

'But, why not, Basil!'

'You told me that you cut your hand on your horse's mane,' said Alleyn.

'No. You told me that, Mr Alleyn.'

'You accepted the explanation.'

'Did I?'

'How do you say, now, that you cut your hand?'

'I did it on the reins.'

'Mr Pilgrim, did you see this cut on Saturday evening? It must have been quite sore then. A sharp, thin cut.'

'I didn't see her hand. She wore gloves.'

'All through dinner?'

'Scarlet gloves. They looked lovely,' she said, 'didn't they, Basil?'

'Do you remember that on Monday night you told me you had no pretensions to being a good horsewoman?'

'Modesty, Mr Alleyn.'

Alleyn turned aside. He moved behind the desk, stooped, and in a second the old raincoat and the gloves were lying on the top of the desk.

'Have you ever seen those before?' asked Alleyn.

'I – don't know. Oh yes. It's Basil's, isn't it?'

'Come and look at it.'

She walked slowly across to the desk and looked at the coat and gloves. Alleyn picked up the sleeve and without speaking pointed a long forefinger to the acid hole in the cuff. He lifted the collar, and turned it back, and pointed to a whitish stain. He dropped the coat, took up the left-hand glove and turned it inside out. He pointed to a small stain under the base of the little finger. And still he did not speak. It was Basil Pilgrim who broke the silence.

'I don't know what he's driving at, Val, but you've never worn the things. I know you haven't. I've told him so. I'll swear it – I'll swear you've never worn them. I *know* you haven't.'

'You bloody fool,' she screamed. 'You bloody fool!'

792

'Valmai Seacliff,' began Alleyn, 'I arrest you for the murder of Wolf Garcia on – '

Chapter 21

Epilogue in a Garden

Troy sat on a rug in the central grass plot of Lady Alleyn's rose garden. Alleyn stood and looked down at her.

'You see,' he said, 'it was a very clumsy, messy, and ill-planned murder. It seemed the most awful muddle, but it boils down to a fairly simple narrative. We hadn't much doubt after Monday night that Garcia had set the trap for Sonia. He left his prints on the opium jar and, as Malmsley had prepared the first pipe, Garcia evidently gave himself another. He must have been in a state of partial recovery with a sort of exalted carry-over, when he got the idea of jamming the knife through the floor of the throne. Motive – Sonia had been badgering him to marry her. She was going to have his child and wouldn't let him alone. He had exhausted her charms and her possibilities as a blackmailing off-sider, and he was nauseated by her persistence. She came between him and his work. She probably threatened to sue him for maintenance, to make a full-sized scandal, to raise hell with a big stick in a bucket. The opium suggested a beautifully simple and macabre way out of it all. I saw Sonia's friend in the chorus – Miss O'Dawne – again this morning after the arrest. I got a rather fuller account of the blackmailing game. Sonia and Garcia were both in it. Sonia had tackled Pilgrim and threatened to tell the Methodist peer that Basil was the father of her child. He wasn't, but that made no odds. Basil stumped up and Sonia handed the cash to Garcia. We found a note from Garcia to Valmai Seacliff in which he coolly said he'd bought painting-materials at her shop and put them down to her. The wording of the letter suggested that he had some sort of upper hand over her, and when I first saw Bobbie O'Dawne she obviously had information up her sleeve

794

and admitted as much. She told Bathgate that Sonia had said Garcia would kill both of them if they babbled. When Sonia died Bobbie O'Dawne was certain Garcia had done it, and that she'd be the next victim if she didn't keep quiet. Now he's dead, and we've got Valmai Seacliff, Miss O'Dawne is all for a bit of front-page publicity, and told me this morning that Sonia had kept her *au fait* with the whole story. Garcia blackmailed Valmai Seacliff. He said he'd tell Basil Pilgrim that she'd been his – Garcia's – mistress. He said he'd go to the Methodist peer with a story of studio parties that would throw the old boy into a righteous fury, and completely cook Seacliff's goose. Garcia worked the whole thing out with Sonia. She was to tackle Pilgrim while he went for Valmai Seacliff. Garcia had started to work with Seacliff, who at first wouldn't rise. But he'd done some drawings of Seacliff in the nude which he said he'd sent to old Pilgrim with a suitable letter, and he told her that Sonia was also prepared to do her bit of blackmail as well. At last, Valmai Seacliff – terrified of losing Pilgrim – said she'd meet Garcia on Friday night in the studio, when they were all safely away, and discuss payment. All this Garcia told Sonia, and Sonia told Bobbie O'Dawne, swearing her to secrecy. O'Dawne was too frightened of Garcia to tell me the Seacliff side, and I also think she honestly felt she couldn't break her word. She's got a sort of code, that funny hard little baggage, and she's stuck to it. But, of course, without her evidence we'd got no motive as far as Seacliff was concerned.'

'When did you suspect Valmai?'

'I wasn't very certain until I saw that the person who murdered Garcia had held his head back by the hair, and that he had struggled so hard that – well, that he had struggled. I then remembered the cut on Seacliff's hand, and how she had showed it to me only when she saw me looking at it, and how she had said it had been made by her horse's reins, when it had obviously been made by some thing much finer. I remembered how, when I suggested it was not the reins, but the horse's mane, she had agreed. But to go back a bit. From the moment we learned that it was Seacliff who posed the model I felt that we must watch her pretty closely.'

'I don't understand that. You say Garcia set the trap with the knife.'

'Yes, but I believe Seacliff watched him through a hole in the studio window-blind.'

'Seacliff!'

'Yes. She had put three aspirins in Pilgrim's coffee to ensure his sleeping soundly. When she realized he had noticed the coffee tasted odd – he made a face at her – she quickly raised an outcry about her own. She pretended to have a headache in order to get them all to bed early. She slipped out to the garage, wearing slacks and a sweater, put on Pilgrim's old coat and gloves, and drove back to the studio, getting there about midnight, with the intention of arguing about blackmail with Garcia. This was the meeting Miss Phillida Lee overheard Sonia discussing with Garcia. Sonia told Miss Bobbie O'Dawne all about it, and Miss O'Dawne told me, this morning. But you should remember that until this morning Miss O'Dawne had only elaborated what we already knew – the Pilgrim-Sonia side. However, I give you the whole thing as completely as I can. Valmai Seacliff arrived at the studio in a desperate attempt to placate Garcia. She must have left the car somewhere in the lane and walked down, meaning to come in at the side gate. Your maid Ethel and her boy, returning from the flicks, saw the figure of a shortish man standing outside the studio window, apparently looking through the hole in the blind. He wore a mackintosh with the collar turned up. The ray of light caught his beret, which was pulled down on one side, hiding his face. Both Garcia and Pilgrim were too tall for the light to get them anywhere above the chest. So was Malmsley. Seacliff seemed to be the only one about the right height. When we saw Pilgrim's old coat in his car we noticed whitish marks on the collar that suggested face- or neck-powder, and they smelt of Sea-cliff. It was so dirty it didn't seem likely she would let him embrace her while he was wearing it. When we looked inside the left-hand glove we noticed a bloodstain that corresponded with the cut on her hand. That, of course, came into the picture after the Garcia affair. I believe that she actually watched Garcia set his trap for Sonia and decided to say nothing about it. I believe she went in, probably got him to drink a good deal more whisky, and offered to drive him up to London. You told me he did a little etching.'

'Yes. He'd prepared a plate a few days before he went.'

'Then perhaps he said he'd take the acid to bite it. Is that the right word? Anyway, she got out your caravan and backed it up to the window. There's a slope down from the garage – enough to free-wheel into the lane and start on compression. The servants wouldn't think anything odd if they heard a car in the lane. Malmsley had helped Garcia get everything ready. All she had to do was open the window, wheel the clay model over the sill into the caravan, get Garcia aboard and start off. The packing-case had already been addressed by Garcia. So she knew the address, even if he was incapable of direct-ing her. I think myself that he had told her exactly where the warehouse was when he asked her to go there to see him, and she has admitted that he gave her a sketch-map. Probably his idea was that she should pay blackmail to him while he was there. She made another rather interest-ing slip over that. Do you remember how she said she was reminded of the warehouse address by a remark someone made at breakfast about Holloway? She told me – and, I think, you – that as soon as she heard the word Holloway she remembered that Garcia had said his warehouse was near the prison, and she had told him to be careful he didn't get locked up. Holloway is a woman's prison. Her very feeble joke would have been a little less feeble if he was blackmailing her, and the place of assignation was not Holloway, but Brixton. By giving us Holloway as the district, she was sending us off in exactly the opposite direction to the right one. We might have hunted round Holloway for weeks. I wondered if she had been the victim of a sort of word-association and I decided to go for Brixton. Luckily enough, as it turned out. As a matter of fact, she had twice fallen into the trap of substituting for the truth something that is linked with it in her mind. The first time was over the cut on her hand. It had been made when she was standing above Garcia with her hand wound in his hair. She saw me looking at the scar, decided to speak of it before I did, was perhaps, reminded subconsciously of horses' hair, a mane gripped in the hand, rejected the idea of hair altogether and substituted reins. Have you had enough of this, Troy?'

'No. I want to know all about it.'

'There's not much more. She drove Garcia to his warehouse. He'd got the keys. She murdered him there, because she was hell-bent on marrying Pilgrim, and becoming a very rich peeress, and because it was in Garcia's power to stop her. She's an egomaniac. She drove the caravan back to your garage and drove herself back to the Pascoes' house in Pilgrim's car. The distance to the warehouse is thirty miles. At that time of night she'd do it easily in an hour and a half. She must have been back at the studio by three and probably got to the Pascoes' by half-past. Even supposing she lost her way – and I don't think she would, because there's a good map in the caravan – she'd a margin of two hours before there was a chance of the servants being about.'

'Why didn't you think it was Pilgrim?'

'I wondered if it was Pilgrim, of course. After we had checked all the alibis, it seemed to me that Pilgrim and Valmai Seacliff were by far the most likely. I even wondered if Pilgrim had drugged Seacliff with aspirin instead of Seacliff drugging Pilgrim – until she lied about her cut hand, her horsemanship and the address of the warehouse. On top of that there was the glove and the smell of the raincoat. She said she had taken the aspirins Pilgrim gave her. We found that she hadn't. We found that she had aspirins of her own in the evening bag she had taken to Boxover. Why should she pretend she had none? And why, after all, should Pilgrim kill Garcia? He had paid Sonia off, but as far as we know, Garcia had kept out of the picture where Pilgrim was concerned. Garcia was tackling Valmai Seacliff, not Pilgrim. No, the weight of evidence was against her. She lied where an innocent woman would not have lied. And – I'm finishing up where I began – I think that an innocent person would not have pressed Sonia down upon the point of that knife after she had cried out. She would not have disregarded that first convulsive start. She murdered Sonia, knowing the knife was there, as deliberately as she murdered Garcia.'

'Will they find her guilty?'

'I don't know, Troy. Her behaviour when we arrested her was pretty damning. She turned on Pilgrim like a wild cat because he kept saying he'd swear she'd never worn the coat. If he'd said she had often worn it, half our case would have gone up in smoke.'

Alleyn was silent for a moment, and then knelt down on the rug beside Troy.

'Has this all made a great difference to you?' he said. 'Is it going to take you a long time to put it behind you?'

'I don't know. It's been a bit of a shock for all of us.'

'For Pilgrim – yes. The others will be dining out on it in no time. Not you.'

'I think I'm sort of stunned. It's not that I liked any of them much. It's just the feeling of all the vindictiveness in the house. It's so disquieting to remember what Seacliff's thoughts must have been during the last week. I almost feel I ought to have a priest in with bell and book to purify the house. And now – the thought of the trial is unspeakably shocking. I don't know where – I am – '

She turned helplessly towards Alleyn and in a moment she was in his arms.

'No, no,' said Troy. 'I mustn't. You mustn't think – '

'I know.' Alleyn held her strongly. He could feel her

heart beating secretly against his own. Everything about him, the trees, the ground beneath him, and the clouds in the still autumn sky, rose like bright images in his mind and vanished in a wave of exultation. He was alone in the world with her. And with that moment of supremacy before him came the full assurance that he must not take it. He knew quite certainly that he must not take it. He knew quite certainly that he must let his moment go by. He heard Troy's voice and bent his head down.

' – you mustn't think because I turn to you – '

'It's all right,' said Alleyn. 'I love you, and I know. Don't worry.'

They were both silent for a little while.

'Shall I tell you,' said Alleyn at last, 'what I think? I think that if we had met again in a different way you might have loved me. But because of all that has happened your thoughts of me are spoiled. There's an association of cold and rather horrible officiousness. Well, perhaps it's not quite as bad as all that, but my job has come between us. You know, at first I thought you disliked me very much. You were so prickly. Then I began to hope a little. Don't cry, dear Troy. It's a great moment for me, this. Don't think I misunderstand. You so nearly love me, don't you?' For the first time his voice shook.

'So nearly.'

'Then,' said Alleyn, 'I shall still allow myself to hope a little.'